D1559545

BY PAUL HORGAN

NOVELS

The Fault of Angels · The Habit of Empire · No Quarter Given
The Common Heart · Main Line West · Give Me Possession
A Lamp on the Plains · Memories of the Future · A Distant Trumpet
Far from Cibola · Whitewater
Mountain Standard Time
(containing *Main Line West, Far from Cibola,* and *The Common Heart*)
Mexico Bay

THE RICHARD TRILOGY

Things As They Are · Everything to Live For · The Thin Mountain Air

OTHER FICTION

The Return of the Weed · The Saintmaker's Christmas Eve
Figures in a Landscape · Humble Powers · The Devil in the Desert
Toby and the Nighttime (juvenile) · One Red Rose for Christmas
The Peach Stone: *Stories from Four Decades*

HISTORY AND OTHER NONFICTION

Men of Arms (*juvenile*) · From the Royal City
New Mexico's Own Chronicle (*with Maurice Garland Fulton*)
Great River: The Rio Grande in North American History
The Centuries of Santa Fe · Rome Eternal · Citizen of New Salem
Conquistadors in North American History
Peter Hurd: *A Portrait Sketch from Life* · Songs After Lincoln
The Heroic Triad: *Essays in the Social Energies of
Three Southwestern Cultures* · Maurice Baring Restored
Encounters with Stravinsky: *A Personal Record* · Approaches to Writing
Lamy of Santa Fe: *His Life and Times*
Josiah Gregg and His Vision of the Early West
Of America East and West: *Selections from the Writings of Paul Horgan*
The Clerihews of Paul Horgan, *Drawings by Joseph Reed*
Under the Sangre de Cristo · A Writer's Eye: *Watercolors and Drawings*
A Certain Climate: *Essays in History, Arts, and Letters*

The Richard Trilogy

THE
RICHARD
TRILOGY

THINGS AS THEY ARE

EVERYTHING TO LIVE FOR

THE THIN MOUNTAIN AIR

PAUL HORGAN

FOREWORD BY ROBERT COLES

AFTERWORD BY WALKER PERCY

WESLEYAN UNIVERSITY PRESS

PUBLISHED BY

UNIVERSITY PRESS OF NEW ENGLAND

HANOVER AND LONDON

The University Press of New England is a consortium of universities in New England dedicated to publishing scholarly and trade works by authors from member campuses and elsewhere. The New England imprint signifies uniform standards for publication excellence maintained without exception by the consortium members. A joint imprint of University Press of New England and a sponsoring member acknowledges the publishing mission of that university and its support for the dissemination of scholarship throughout the world. Cited by the American Council of Learned Societies as a model to be followed, University Press of New England publishes books under its own imprint and the imprints of Brandeis University, Brown University, Clark University, University of Connecticut, Dartmouth College, University of New Hampshire, University of Rhode Island, Tufts University, University of Vermont, and Wesleyan University.

Printed in the United States of America
∞

Library of Congress Cataloging-in-Publication Data
Horgan, Paul, 1903–
The Richard trilogy / by Paul Horgan ; foreword by Robert Coles ; afterword by Walker Percy.
Contents: Things as they are — Everything to live for — The thin mountain air.
ISBN 0-8195-5234-8 — ISBN 0-8195-6234-3 (pbk.)
I. Title.
PS3515.06583R5   1990   813'.52—dc20   89-24872
Rev

First Edition, 1990
Wesleyan Paperback, 1990

5   4   3   2   1

Contents

Foreword

WHEN I WAS A MEDICAL STUDENT I earnestly wanted to be a pediatrician
and, especially, do work in what was then called "adolescent medicine." I took several electives with Rustin McIntosh, who ran Babies
Hospital in New York City and who had a lively interest in the way
young people grow up psychologically as well as physically. I thought
he knew everything and wondered if I'd ever feel even remotely as
learned and adequate with respect to pediatrics as he, every day,
showed himself to be. One day, we were together going on rounds,
this time on a ward filled with "older" pediatric patients—above
twelve and below sixteen or seventeen. Dr. McIntosh moved from
bed to bed—a question here, a comment there, and always his stethoscope held to the chest and heart, his neurological hammer applied to
elicit one or another reflex, his otoscope and ophthalmoscope summoned to penetrate the hidden mysteries of the ear, the eye. When we
were through, and though we were late, he suggested we sit down for
a cup of coffee and a moment to catch our breath, stop and think about
the worsening patients as well as those who seemed to be improving.

All these years later I remember that moment between us. I had
been pressing hard about the medical prospects of a particular boy
who had a cerebral aneurysm (a congenitally malformed blood vessel)
that had "leaked"—causing a mild left-sided paralysis. But, of course,
the vessel might leak some more; indeed, the lad might, all of a sud-

den, die. He was such a decent youth—sensitive, bright, thoughtful, anything but self-centered, no easy feat for someone seriously ill. I wanted to know what to expect, "the worse-case scenario," as we medical students and young house-officers were wont to say. Suddenly, a tired Dr. McIntosh, who also had taken a liking to this patient, stopped me in the middle of a question with an uncharacteristically sharp comment that seemed to come out of nowhere and lead me nowhere: "He has lived. He will die. Meanwhile, he is learning about life."— a pause, while I tried to catch my bearings. And then this: "It is more painful to learn about life than to be born or to die." I had "rotated" through obstetrics, and so had some idea of the pain that goes with birth (for mother and child both), and I had by then witnessed a substantial number of painful deaths. I had never, though, thought to compare such moments with the everyday effort "to learn about life"; nor could I fail to notice, then, as I *did* ponder such a comparison, the look on Dr. McIntosh's face, one of wry, even melancholy resignation.

I kept thinking of that moment in my life as I read, yet again, in 1989, Paul Horgan's *Richard Trilogy*. I had first read two of the three novels that follow in the early 1970's, when my wife, Jane, and I and our three sons were living in New Mexico. We were trying to learn how Indian and Spanish-speaking young people in that state grow up, and I was also trying to learn what I could about the social and cultural history of the Southwest. We turned with pleasure to the Paul Horgan of *Great River* and *The Centuries of Santa Fe*, and soon we were reading, also, his novels and stories, his essays—this extraordinarily gifted writer of such broad and deep sensibility. He taught us a lot about a particular region's history, of course, but he offered us much more—a wise and thoughtful look at "life," its ups and downs, its complexities, ironies, ambiguities, contradictions, inconsistencies: such a refreshing and edifying contrast with all the social science texts coming at us from all directions.

I read *Things As They Are* and *Everything to Live For* with pleasure—a break from the work I was doing with Pueblo youths north of Albuquerque, or so I thought, originally. Yet, as I talked with Pueblo youths and children or high schoolers who lived in the old Hispano-American communities north of Santa Fe (Truchas, Madrid), I often thought of Richard, the hero of *Things As They Are* (he is also, of course, the main character in the two later *Richard* novels in this extraordinary trilogy). Horgan's first novel in that series especially came to mind because, so often, the young New Mexicans I was getting to know were struggling hard to figure out what this life meant, where (if any place) they were headed, and, very important, how they ought to get along with the world their parents had handed to them. Here, for instance, is Mark, in certain respects no Richard (who came from a well-to-do Catholic family of German ancestry) but very much kin to Richard, I would often think, as I listened to him: "I guess, being a Pueblo, I should feel different [from others in the town north of Albuquerque where he lived], but I don't. I will be shaving, and it's still new to me, and I get lost trying to do a good job, and not cut myself. Once in a while, though, I nick myself, and the blood comes, and for a second I'll just look at it, and it's funny: I'll say, 'That's me, my blood, and no one else's, and I've got this life, and I never asked for it, but it's here, it's me, and now what do I do.' I mean, should I stay here and try to be a Pueblo Indian, or should I go into the service, maybe, and never come back here—settle someplace where I'm really free to be myself?"

A pause, a smile addressed to himself, a shrug, as if he had answered an unspoken question—and then a return to that question, now put to himself out loud, in the presence of another person: "I don't know what I'll do. I have these wishes—hopes: I'd like to be a doctor or a lawyer, maybe. But I don't know if I can pull it off. I like to read. I'm pretty good in school. But I [day] dream a lot; I sit [in school] and stare out the window. I wonder what will become of me, and my friends. I try to like people—trust them. But you grow older, and you meet people who aren't good; they just aren't. I used to think the world is good, mostly. Now I know better. It's only the last year or so that I've begun to realize that it's trouble out there—I mean, with people: they'll cross you, even someone you know pretty well, and he's your friend. I'm not becoming too suspicious. My mom, she's taught us to love the world. She does—she's got a Pueblo heart. Dad says: she won't even kick the dirt! She'll see birds, and she rushes to feed them. She'll see a dead branch, and she'll take it down, and we'll hear about 'life and death,' and all that happens in between! She's 'wise,' our grandpa says—she was born that way, he remembers. She had a big smile [when a baby], but sometimes 'a shadow came over her,' that's how her dad says it! I know those shadows! They come over me! I'll be thinking of people I know, and what's ahead, and I'll be confident, you know, and looking ahead, but then I remember all the troubles our people [Pueblos] have had, and the way you can be tricked and trapped, and suddenly, I'm not so sure about anything. I'll be sitting, I'll be standing, and I'll look up there to the sky, and I'll talk to it: 'Hey, what's in store for me, and who's to be trusted, and what's the right thing to do?' I've got my life ahead, and I should be glad. But you have to figure out what the situation is. Sure, it's no big city here; you can be a little slower here, but even so, even if we're way up near the mountains, and we're closer to God, maybe, even so, you've got to stop and take stock of yourself, before you just go leaping into life, or else, life comes and grabs you, and you haven't prepared your-self [for it], and that can mean real trouble ahead."

I am not really comparing the Richard of Paul Horgan's trilogy to the Mark I knew rather well in New Mexico, though Mark, too, lived in "thin mountain air," and, of course, very much feared leaving it for the urban smog that gets called "progress." Mark, too, tried hard during those adolescent years of his (when I met with him weekly) to figure out the nature of reality, its psychological and social and cultural and regional and historical and national aspects—the sum of so much that impinges on us, gives shape to our hopes and worries, our desires and fears, our ambitions and our moments of doubt and inertia: "things as they are" for us, as well as for others, different from us in one way, another way. Moreover, Mark, too, could decide, at least on certain days, that he had "everything to live for," yet, in a sudden reconsideration of "things as they are," wonder loud and strong whether, indeed, that New Mexico mountain air wasn't too thin by far: the stifling side of life as it deprives us of psychological and spiritual breath.

In this second half of the twentieth century—another millenium only a decade off—we in America tend to look at our children, our youths as they ready themselves for life, through psychological and sociological lenses: the endless generalizations of the social sciences, with their theories, their "stages" and "phases," their formulations if not reifications, their paradigms which seem so fetching to a secular bourgeois world. I suppose we are in debt to that modernity, the gift of some information for which we can be grateful, but at a cost—the smugness and bloated self-importance, and worst of all, the dreary banality of so much that passes for "new" knowledge. In contrast, there is a tradition to which these three novels of Paul Horgan's belong—the lives of young people regarded carefully, shrewdly, with great wisdom, tact, suggestiveness: Agee's *A Death in the Family*, Elizabeth Bowen's *Death of the Heart*, Henry James's "What Maisie Knew," Tolstoy's *Boyhood* and *Youth*, J. D. Salinger's *The Catcher in the Rye*, Ralph Ellison's *Invisible Man*, and not least, William Carlos Williams's Strecher trilogy, also about an American family's effort—through the eyes, predominantly, of a girl, Flossie, rather than the boy Richard—to become fully a part of this great and complex nation and, in so doing, to learn what one might do, what one might want to do, what one ought to do with a life (and the three are not always the same).

So many of us, these days, are hungry for certainties, and more adrift morally than we may care to know—in great need, therefore, of what these novels offer in such abundance: a wise and visionary storyteller's subtlety, his rendering of the elusive, the inevitably contingent and mysterious side of life. I only hope, for the sake of all of us, that an abundance of readers awaits these three novels, which provide, still, a thoughtful, knowing examination of what we have become in today's America, and by implication, what we need to do, if our moments of expectation and anticipation are not to founder, again and again, on all sorts of disappointments and betrayals. I only hope, too, that those readers, many of them young, will hand one another along, so to speak—acknowledge Paul Horgan's way of seeing things as the moral treasure it is, to be passed from person to person, a gesture of our commitment each to the other.

ROBERT COLES

Author's Note

THESE THREE NOVELS were originally published years apart—*Things As They Are* in 1964, *Everything to Live For* in 1968, and *The Thin Mountain Air* in 1977. In my own view they have always belonged together, but their serial connection was not widely considered in those years. My plan is now to be seen in this volume, for which I am grateful to the publishers.

In sequence, the novels reflect three phases of life—childhood, adolescence, and early maturity. Accordingly, the narrative tone reflects the differences in those stages of change and growth. In the first volume we meet an air of pure simplicity, as of life seen at the plane surface of a mirror—the child's vision; in the second, the adolescent's mode of lyric irony amid the confusions of social values and discovered love; in the third, the young man's sense of dawning realism as experience turns the self outward.

The point of view throughout is that of a mature narrator sifting the foundations of a newly imagined life of which he is both subject and observer.

P.H.

Every man is not only himselfe; there have been many Diogenes, *and as many* Timons, *though but few of that name; men are lived over againe, the world is now as it was in ages past, there was none then, but there hath been some one since that parallels him, and is as it were his revived selfe.*

SIR THOMAS BROWNE,
Religio Medici, 1643.

Book One

THINGS AS THEY ARE

FOR D.B.

CHAPTER I

❦

Original Sin

"RICHARD, RICHARD," they said to me in my childhood, "when will you begin to see things as they are?"

But they forgot that children are artists who see and enact through simplicity what their elders have lost through experience. The loss of innocence is a lifelong process—the wages of original sin. Guilt is the first knowledge.

"Richard," they said, "are you terribly sorry?"

"Oh, yes."

❦

Coming home from the country, I remembered everything, though I did not want to.

My grandfather was interested in a farm about fifty miles from home in up-state New York. He knew the farmer well and used to go out for a week or two in the hot summer weather to stay at the farmhouse. I heard long afterward that he owned a mortgage on the farm. In that particular summer—it must have been in 1908 or 1909—he took me along.

[1]

I did not particularly want to go, for my grandfather—my mother's father—was sometimes formidable when his mood changed. I did not care for anything to be different from one time to another, and I could never be sure when he would be stern or remote, lost in some lofty inner criticism of life—his life in particular, with its circumstances of old age, loneliness since the death of my grandmother, and the loss of his many children to their many worlds. I was a very small boy in that summer—four or five years old—and young enough to be homesick, especially at night, when it was time for me to be put to bed.

They put me in a narrow wooden bed in a small room under the eaves, where the ceiling leaned over me at a sharp angle. The farmer's wife, Mrs Klopstock, was a kind woman, all the color of dough, hair and skin, and made as lumpishly. But she declared that she knew all about children through her own, who were now gone away, and she always gave me a few extra moments at night, when the only sounds in the humid dark outside came from crickets and nightbirds, and the only ones from inside came from the rumbling talk downstairs between my grandfather and Mr Klopstock.

On the first night I was muted with longing for home and the touch of my mother, and when Mrs Klopstock tried to have me speak, I could think of nothing to say but that I wanted to go home, which I could not bring myself to say.

On the second night I asked her,

"Do you know how to hug?"

Her eyes grew larger with ready tears and she threw herself down to her wide knees by my bed and took me in her arms and hugged me till my ribs ached.

"There!" she said, "was that a hug?"

"Oh, yes. Thank you."

"Now will you be able to sleep?"

[2]

"Yes."

"Good night, Richard."

"Good night, Mrs Klopstock."

She went downstairs. Falling asleep I had a vision of the meadowy world in which I had spent the day and which would await me in the morning.

ꞅ

I was there a giant among grasses that rose to my waist. Long wide slopes lay up behind the white farmhouse and showed waves of white stars and snowflakes bent into shadow by the breezes—daisies, milkweed, Queen Anne's lace, poppies, with here and there goldenrod and wild cosmos in every color. When I slashed my way through this meadow with important strides, the soft stems of the wild flowers gave up a tickling fragrance, and the long grasses stung my bare legs with their wiry whips. I had to watch out for bees, and if I fell down I had to look along the tiny forest aisles of the plants and grasses at my very eyes to see if a garter snake might be watching me there on the damp brown earth which smelled like a cellar. Getting up, I went on to a real woods. It stood where the meadow became a low hill which dipped down to meet another hill making a wandering cleft where flowed a steep and narrow little creek.

They told me at the house not to go out of sight, but I did not know whether they could see me at the creek, and I did not think about it. It was the best place to play. I could walk up into the little copse, and though I wished hard for someone to be there to play along the creek with me, I still managed to have a splendid time. I took off my shoes and stockings and walked in the creek

[3]

bed, knowing how the chill of the water and the sharp stones and the slipperiness would hurt and feel full of chance. The sunlight broke in little darts and coins and pools through the woods. The creek was swift, full of miniature rapids along the small stones yielded to it by the slopes. It took several turns, winding against the cheeks of the low hills, until it came free in the meadow, when it ran deep and open across the farm, and then under the road in front, and then out of sight in distant green country which I never explored.

When they wanted me at the farmhouse they would ring a heavy dinner bell out on the back stoop, and I would dry off my feet and go to dinner, which they had at midday, or supper, which they had at five o'clock.

On some days my grandfather took me all through the barns and pens to see the cattle, the horses, the pigs and the chickens. He touched them with his cane and when the cows turned slowly to look at him, he gave his wheezy, low laugh. The rank smells of the animals, as strong as ammonia, and their frank beings, with their wettings and their droppings, their dripping mouths, the heavy hang and sway of their sex or their udders, made me thoughtful and dimly self-aware. Sometimes my grandfather had me walk in the meadow with him, saying nothing much, but pleased to have someone for whom he was responsible. Now and then,

"Be careful, my boy," he would say, pointing to a great flat animal dropping which lay buzzing with jewelled flies in the grass, "don't step in the cow pie."

A meadow was for boys. He looked sad to me in the pathless grasses, among bees that set blossoms to nodding on their long stems. He wore a wide-brimmed panama hat which according to word in my family cost him one hundred dollars, and a gray alpaca suit with cutaway frock, and shiny black leather boots with elastic inserts at the sides. They said I looked like him, but how could I,

[4]

when I had no white beard and mustache, or tiny, gold-rimmed eyeglasses, or heavy pink cheeks, or such a wide front that extended far out and looked as hard as wood? At that age I valued him chiefly because he was familiar. He served in no way to relieve my lonesomeness in the country. I finally found relief otherwise, but in the end, when it was time for me to be taken home to Dorchester again, I tried to forget how my lonesomeness was lifted for a while and then restored worse than ever. But in spite of myself, I remembered.

❦

We went home on the train. I was allowed to sit next to the window, which was open. The fields we ran through were like the ones we had just left, and I was glad to know what "the country" was, after hearing about it for so long. Engine smoke spangled with hot cinders flew in the train windows, and several times my grandfather had to use the corner of his handkerchief to take a cinder out of my eye, which he did with much suppressed wheezing, and with joy at having something to do for someone other than to shout orders when he was furious in his own house, which at best was a lonely pleasure, and which left him with a dyspeptic upset. I was not certain of how to manage it, but I said to myself that I would never be an old man. I did not mean that I would not live a long life—I intended to live forever, but certainly not as an old man.

Glad as I was to leave the country, I wished, the nearer we came to Dorchester, that I was back with Mrs Klopstock and the creek and the meadow, even in spite of what happened there. What if my mother and my father should see in my face the secret I must never tell?

[5]

I went silent in the train and my grandfather said, in his grand German accent (he was born in Bavaria),

"Richard? You do not feel well?"

"Yes, Grosspa."

"Your stomach?"

"No, Grosspa."

"Come. We must have smiles for Mother."

"Will she be at the station?"

"No. We will go in a cab to your house. Then I will go to my house."

A weight of love and guilt lay about my heart at the prospect of seeing my mother again.

Over an exciting triangular system of switches and tracks the train backed into the station at Dorchester so it would be headed right for its return trip. The station was built of brick long begrimed with engine smoke. It had high round vaults overhead in the waiting room which gave me the feeling I had in church—lost and small in familiar surroundings.

We went rapidly through the station to the cab rank where my grandfather summoned a cab with an imperious lift of his gold-headed cane. The cab-horse was a bony creature who seemed to be asleep. The driver had to cluck him up several times before he moved. My grandfather put me into the dark blue padded interior which smelled of wet straw, and then stepped in himself, making the lightly-sprung brougham tip under his weight. Pushing back against the cushions I tried to have the cab go more slowly; but now that he was stirring, the old horse went off at a bright trot, while we rocked and jogged gallantly along over cobblestones and streetcar tracks, and came at last to our street, where my mother would be waiting for me.

Under elms meeting overhead, it was a shady street. The houses were set back fairly deep. Our house had a wooden-railed porch

[6]

with a round bay at one end, tracing the shape of a round alcove in our living room. A little shingled turret rose above this at the top of the house three stories up. It was all of wood, painted brown, with white trimwork. With all my heart I wished we had lightning rods; I would pray at night that before lightning could strike us and burn us to the ground, as a house up the street had burned recently after midnight amidst shouts and gongs and falls of fire and spark, God would send us lightning rods. Watching the fire, and listening to it, and recalling the lightning, my heart beat until it hurt.

It did this now as we drew up at our house, yet I knew I must show nothing of the trouble which inhabited me as if my very body were designed to be its shape.

My grandfather stepped to our cement carriage block and then with comic ceremony turned and held the door for me. I hopped forth and immediately saw that loved and dreaded face in the window of the round sitting room upstairs, at the turret end of the house. My mother was holding the curtains aside, smiling and waving; and then the curtains fell together and I knew she was hurrying down to meet me.

On any other return I would have run to her as fast as my legs would carry me, like a very small boy in a story, but now I made a great affair of lingering to watch my grandfather pay the cab driver, who lifted his scuffed and dented top hat as he received his tip and then drove off above the humping old bones of his horse. There was nothing more to detain me. We went up to the porch. The front door opened and I was in my mother's embrace.

"Oh, Richard, Richard, my darling, how good to have you home again. How we have missed you. Every day I unrolled your napkin and then rolled it up again and put it back in its ring. Let me look at you."

It was the moment I sorrowed for.

Holding me away she looked dearly into my eyes and touched

a cinder smudge on my cheek and then pulled me close again, and said,

"Did you miss us? The country agreed with you, darling, you look so sunburned and well-fed and sweet."

I buried my face in her breast and my heart went whirring on. How astounding that I could look just as usual, with nothing to notice in my appearance of what lay buried in my soul.

"Was he a good boy?" asked my mother of her father and he replied,

"He was a very good boy, ate everything on his plate, said his prayers every night, so Mrs Klopstock told me, and played alone all day, quite happily. If we did not hold long philosophical conversations the fault must be more with me than with him."

"Oh, Papa," she said, "you mustn't tease him in front of me. Come. I will ask Anna to bring us some tea."

She held her arm about my shoulder and took us to the round bay in the living room and disposed us for tea and cakes, which our lifelong friend and servant brought. When Anna came in, lumbering heavily with the tray, I thought perhaps I could run away with her to the kitchen and escape my trouble; but she gave me a little nod of mock elegance, set the tray down, and retreated with an air which indicated that she knew when to leave the family alone to theirself. The effect was a reproach to me, as though Anna, with her pale, deep-set eyes in her wide, gray face, could see through me, and must hold herself above what she saw.

"Now tell me what you did in the country," commanded my mother playfully, and I was face to face with my dreadful test. In my fear of revelation, I thought she must already know what I would never tell, and was asking me to do so explicitly. But her smile was so lovely, her love so calm, that in another breath I knew she knew nothing, and my guilt turned to guile, and I made a cheeky face, quite as though I were acting the role of a small boy, which small boys deliberately do at times, in order to discover what they themselves are really like, and I said,

"Why, Mother, you never saw such a wonderful place. We had a creek out in the meadow, and I played there all day long. I made some tiny boats with little sticks and leaves and things—you know how—and I had them do all kinds of things."

"Did you swim?"

"Oh, no, it wasn't deep enough for a boy to swim."

"Oh? How deep was it?"—idle inquiry, dangerously close to my hidden subject.

"Oh, about so"—holding my hands apart to show. "But I went wading all the time."

"I went too, you know," announced my grandfather.

I stared at him. When?

"Yes," he said, "one afternoon while you were having your nap, I took off my shoes and stockings and went wading."

"Why Papa!" exclaimed my mother.

What was it? There seemed a curious shame in the fact that my old grandfather should have bared his feet and rolled up his gray alpaca city trousers and gone wading like a child. A part of him was naked which otherwise was always clothed—this was shocking in one I knew so well.

"Yes," he added, "it cooled me off."

"Did you have anyone to play with?" asked my mother, brushing my hair lightly down across my brow with her exquisite hand which was so clever at so many charming skills.

"No," I said.

"Ah, but yes," said my grandfather. "He had a cat."

"A cat? Darling, did you have a cat?"

"A kitty," I said, nodding brightly over a sense of doom.

"How sweet. What color?"

"Black and white."

[9]

"How sweet. Did it have little white boots?"

"Yes." I felt hollow with apprehension. How did my mother know so well that particular cat?

"Where did you find it?"

"It came to the farm one day. Mrs Klopstock gave it some milk on the back stoop. She said I could have it if I would take care of it."

"And did you?"

It was a frightful question to answer. I said,

"I fed it."

"Did it sleep on your bed?"

My mother, through half-closed eyes, and with her head a little on one side, studied how I looked with my hair brushed forward over my brow, and changed her mind. She brushed it back off my forehead and said,

"I love to see your whole forehead. Like your Daddy's. So wide. Those little shadows you can hardly see. So young."

"It did sometimes," I replied.

"Ach, Papa," she cried, turning to her father, "do you remember the *times* we used to have at home with cats? Oh! how furious you used to be when"—speaking of her sisters and brothers—"we would smuggle a new kitten upstairs and keep it for days without letting anyone know. And then the time the Right Reverend Bishop came to dinner, and the cat got away, and ran downstairs, and Fritz chased him, trying to catch him, and chased him right through the living room before dinner, and almost knocked the Bishop over without even seeing him! Oh! What a licking he got for that! But Mama told us afterward the Bishop laughed so hard she thought he was going to choke to death. —What was your kitty's name?" she asked, turning to me again.

"I just called him Kitty."

"What a perfect name for a cat. Tell me, what did you do with him when you left?"

My grandfather spared me an answer.

"The cat disappeared one day," he said.

"Disappeared?"

"Simply vanished. Richard went calling, 'Here, kitty, kitty, kitty,' and Mrs Klopstock put out some chicken wings for it, and we looked everywhere, a cat just doesn't disappear like that on a farm with only one house for a mile or two, but no, there was no answer, and we never saw it again. Richard was miserable."

"Of course, darling," said my mother. "It is awful to lose a pet." She looked at me. "But no, my darling, it is over, and you must not cry for it any more. Here. Have another little cake. Chocolate, that one, with the little silver pill on top."

For there were tears in my eyes, and she thought she knew why. I took the cake and ate it with my jaws moving ruefully, while fear and guilt tasted of chocolate crumbs and crushed silver sugar, and I wished I were alone.

"Well," said my grandfather, standing up, "I think I must be going along now."

"Did you send your cab away?"

"Yes. I will take the street car."

"But you will have far to walk to get it, and then when you get off."

"Very well, I will have far to walk," he said testily, rejecting her concern for his age, weight and dignity. But she was no longer his child, she belonged to my father, who would soon be home from his office, and with a little lift of her head, she let my grandfather know that his days of tyranny over her were no more. It was my mother's gift that she could show independence and love to the same person. My grandfather now gave a heavy sigh at the betrayals which any man knew if he lived long enough, and went heavily to the door, and took his way home.

[11]

"Oh, Richard, how glad Daddy will be to see you. We have missed you frantically. Come here."

She hugged me and gave me a kiss. Something in my rigid body was so unfamiliar that she set me off to look at me and asked,

"What a strange boy you are. Aren't you glad to be home again?"

"Oh, yes, yes."

"Do you feel all right?"

"Yes, Mother."

"Is something wrong?"

"No."

"Did anything happen in the country that upset you? Weren't they kind to you, those Klopstocks, I never could see what Grosspa saw in them, they are so common, he is quite fond of them, they weren't mean to you?"

"Oh, no."

With a little tremor of exasperation which threaded through her whole body, she suddenly grew formal with me.

"Well, perhaps after you've been home a little while you may find that you like it after all."

I wanted to throw myself into her arms in a passion of longing to be forgiven for everything in the world, but this would have led to loving questions, and then to revelations. She took up the tea tray instead of ringing for Anna, and went to the pantry. I went upstairs to the nursery, which was what they still called my room, and wondered what I could do until my father got home, and what would happen about everything then.

※

Leafing through some of my favorite books, I read little, for my senses were all attuned to the latening of the day. The later the hour, the sooner would my father return. Daylight began to show gradual but ominous change out in the treetops above the street. Autumn was pressing against the trees. Twilight fell below them sooner than it did above. I was sorry that night was not already here, with all in darkness, and myself in bed, asleep, safe from the calm and loving gaze of my father.

His eyes were blue, like all of ours in the family, and they were as clear as water, and his open, wide brow showed the frontal bone of his skull without wrinkles to hide it. His forehead seemed like the abode of honor. How could I face it? His smile was complete, using all his features and even changing the sound of his voice when he spoke. He had several voices—one for my mother, which often made her catch her breath a trifle and expel it in a little gust of pleasure, as if to say, "What am I going to do—I love him so." Another voice was for the world, a half-mocking but friendly sound. And one was for me, which sounded confidential, a little husky, as if to put secrets between us even in the presence of other people. He had a trick of grinding his jaws together gently and sticking out his chin when he talked to me or when he worked with me on some project, and now and then he adopted some of my early mispronunciations to give our exchanges a more intimate feeling—*insteresting* for *interesting, vomick* for *vomit, sippise* for *surprise.* When he uttered my variations, they seemed to mean far more than the originals. It was a private language and it bound us together. When he came home every night and I heard the welcome signal of the heavy front door closing after him, I always went flying down the stairs into his hug. We made a great commotion, which moved my mother to pretended crossness—"Oh, you two!" she would exclaim—but she usually joined our embrace, after which she took his hat and coat and put them neatly in the hall closet, and with him home again, I fell into the richest contentment, for all was in order, and my evening was the happiest time of the day, even if all too soon I had to go to bed and leave the components of my joy for another long night.

The sky was turning yellow as the sun declined, and on that evening I listened without joy for the front door to rumble shut after my father. Hearing it at last, I pretended that I had not. I stayed in my room, resembling a boy lost in a book. It was so that he found me when, with my mother right after him, he came into the nursery bearing a large package. Ordinarily my expert guess what a present might be, judging by its size, shape and wrapping, would have combined with my greed to hurl me upon it.

But now I looked up, as if startled, and when he called out in his "my" voice, "Hello, Doc!" I merely replied, "Hello, Daddy."

My mother gave him a glance as if to say, *You see how he is acting, I told you.* He shook his head slightly to put her off, set the package on the floor, and came to me and took me in his arms. He chinned my cheek once or twice with a rough rub, and said, with happy excitement,

"Guess what."

"What."

"I'm glad to see you."

I longed to say the same to him, and I tried, but could not. He set me down and indicating the package said,

"See that?"

"Yes."

"It's a sippise."

"For me?"

Being funny, he looked around and said,

"I don't see anybody else here. Yes. It's for you, Richard. Don't you want to see what it is?"

"Yes."

My mother said in a cold, unfamiliar voice,

"He may not touch it until he thanks his Daddy for thinking of him and bringing it to him."

"Let Richard open it first," said my father, "then he can thank me. —That is, if he likes it—," and he grinned with perfect confidence that I would be overcome with happiness at what he had brought.

I knelt down by the package and tore at the wrappings so wastefully that my mother exclaimed at the loss of so much good parcel paper. There on my floor I exposed a toy fire engine—the kind they used to call a steamer—with three horses in harness, and all its nickel brightly polished, and all its red paint glaring in splendor. A toy fireman made of cast iron sat on the box and drove the forever plunging horses, and another stood behind the boiler on the rear step of the steamer. Both wore firemen's hats with white front plates bearing the legend "Engine Company Number 9" and both wore firemen's water-coats. I was appalled at the sacrifice I faced—for of course in my unworthiness I could not receive the present. I said nothing.

"How about it, Doc?" said my father, coming down to the floor next to me. "It's your homecoming present. Do you like it?"

The love and the trust of my father and mother were all mixed up with the glorious toy they had brought to welcome me home, and I did not deserve them or their fire engine. I broke into a sob and hid my face in my arm.

"Why Doc!" exclaimed my father. My mother had another response. She leaned down to feel my forehead to discover if I had a temperature.

"Come on, Doc, what's the matter?"—and my father took me up and put his knuckle under my chin to raise my face and make me look at him.

I shook my head.

"I'll call Doctor Grauer," said my mother.

"No," said my father. "He's not sick. It's something else. —Come on, Doc. Come on up here and tell me about it."

He went to a chair and took me with him and hauled me on to his knees. His gentleness anguished me. I was eaten within by my first knowledge of evil and I longed to confess it. Like all men, I was the victim of original sin, whose forms in daily life are as many as there are beings. The fact that the evil I mourned was my own was the most dreadful part of my trouble.

"Poor old Doc. It's all right. It's all right."

"Something happened in the country," said my mother. "I told you."

"Let him wait. It's all right, Doc."

Finding a thread of voice, I said,

"It was the kitty."

"The what?"

"Yes," said my mother, "he had a kitten at the farm. Grosspa told me."

"What about the kitty, Richard?" asked my father. "Is there something about the kitty you are worried about?"

"I hurt it," I said.

"You did? How."

"I put it in the creek."

"You mean you drowned it?"

"The water went by some stones and there was a deep little place and I grabbed the kitty and threw him in the rough part of the water. He tried to get out."

"What did you do then?"

"I grabbed him again."

"Didn't you feel it try to get away?"

"Yes."

"Did it scratch you?"

[16]

"Yes."

I pulled up my sleeve and showed the long scaly tracks of the claws.

"Oh, Richard," murmured my mother, "it didn't want to be hurt!"

"I know it. I know it. I hurt it."

※

I could remember the hot thin supple body of the kitten under its wet fur, and the pitifully small tube of its neck, and the large clever space between its ears at the back, where all its thoughts seemed to come from, and the perfectly blank look on its wide-eyed face as it strove to escape me and the hurt I was possessed of, the hurt I must do the little animal who had been my cunning companion for days, and whom I loved. Even as I clutched it with strength I did not know I had in my fingers and forearms, I felt sorry for the kitten. My belly was knotted with excitement, sorrow, and zest. The fever of a game arose in me and as the kitten fought me I was determined to win my victory over it. I fell down beside the creek and threw myself half into it, holding the kitten in my arms with the embrace of dear love, and the smaller and feebler it began to feel in my grasp, the more I loved it, and sorrowed for it, and the more expertly I pressed its doom. The current rushed down to us from between the rocks, making a roar next to my ear, but even so I could hear the kitten's tiny gasps mixed with water.

※

My father looked at me for a long quiet moment. His wide brow was lumpy with an inquiring frown, as though he were trying to

[17]

look past me to the creek where I had become a criminal. Finally he said softly,

"What else, Doc? What finally happened?"

"I don't know. I let the kitty go and the water took him away to the deep part."

"Did he climb out and run away?"

"I don't know."

"Did you ever see him again?"

"No."

Without using the word, he was trying to discover if the kitten was dead.

"It didn't come back to the farmhouse?"

"No."

"What did you do afterward?"

"I played in the meadow till my shirt was dry. Then they rang the dinner bell and I went back to the house."

"How did you feel?"

I burst into tears again.

My mother felt the contagion of my remorse and also began to cry.

"To think that my boy Richard—" she said, but my father said her name once, strongly and mildly, and she halted her expression of adopted shame. He then shook me by the shoulders, and said,

"Doc, what you did was horribly wrong. Do you know that?"

"Yes."

"And are you terribly sorry for doing it?"

"Oh, yes."

"Then you must ask God to forgive you and help you to be kind all the rest of your life to poor little things whom you can hurt if you want to. Do you understand?

"Yes, Father."

"Now stop your blubbering and think of this. Perhaps the kitty got away. How many lives has a cat?"—this playfully said, to restore a livable world.

"Nine."

"Well, you had a young kitty, and he probably had eight to go. He's probably hiding right now in the meadow, wondering if you are coming back to play with him."

"Do you think so?"

"It could be."

"But I'm not there."

"But if you were, would you be good to the kitty?"

"Oh, yes, yes, I would."

"I think you would. Oh, my little boy"; he said solemnly, talking past my ear, as though counting the sum of his own life, "I hope you can be good even when it is hard to be, the rest of your life.—Now do you feel better?" he asked, setting me off. He searched my eyes to see if there was anything more I must expel before I could be his son again, but finding nothing, he energetically went down to the floor and the fire engine, and hauled me down beside him, and cried, "But you have not seen what goes on in here!" indicating the shiny toy boiler of the steamer of Engine Company Number 9. I knelt down beside him and watched him create a marvel.

He took a little brown paper envelope, tore open its corner, and poured a half spoonful of some brown powder into the fire door of the steamer, and then struck a match and lighted the powder. At once, white and black smoke began to pour out of the chimney of the boiler. And then he drew the horses ahead on the rug, and as he did so, a toy gong hidden under the carriage rang out with every revolution of the high red rear wheels, and he called out in an assumed voice full of urgency and magic,

"Look out, look out, here comes Engine Company Number 9, where's the fire, where's the fire!"

And in my imagination I rode the rear step of the steamer, and I became the master of fire, even fire that may once have frightened me, and we played intently until it was time for my supper. This, as a concession, I was allowed to have downstairs while my parents sat with me and watched my meal. The fire engine was on the floor beside me at the table.

"He must promise," said my mother, "never to light the powder when he is alone."

"Yes. Do you promise?" asked my father.

"I promise."

It was an evening of promises. The final ones were made to God in my night prayers. I promised not to sin again, and I meant it, but the burden of self-knowledge was upon me now, and as I fell asleep, I felt again the kitten's tiny, striving will to live, and I knew yet another hidden thrill at the memory of the struggle by the creek, and since all I knew about anything was only what had happened to me in my life so far, I wondered and wondered over the sinner's eternal question about his resolve to be good, which was—how could I be sure?

CHAPTER II

꽃

The Dawn of Hate

But if I had made promises to God, He let me go to sleep in His promise to me. Even then I knew it was a stronger promise than mine. In this knowledge there was the beginning of the end of innocence. Another stage of this loss presently came along.

One day I built a boat out of a board with twigs for masts and string for railings. I took it to show Anna in the kitchen.

"Can't we go and sail it?" I asked.

"I'm busy," she said in her sing-song, dreamy voice. Anna, our old cook and laundress, lived a visionary life which she pursued above the task in hand. Dreaming awake, she would sing monotonously to herself of love (her husband had disappeared years ago), or of God (she went to Mass every morning), or of nothing at all; and when she had time she tended me as nurse. A friend to us all, she could bridle with privilege and mourn her estate in the same instant. Now and then she would seize me in her large, lumbering grasp in which she hugged fugitively the graces of a time when she was young and venturesome long ago, before living in other people's kitchens, or spending long mornings in their basement laundries whiling away the acrid steamy hours with hooted song and muffled memory. Her ardent nature expressed itself in one way through her pores, which exuded a fume of oniony sweat that for a reason I cannot quite capture always gave me the feeling of, "Poor Anna!"

"Well," I said, blurring my eyes to see my boat as great and real, "I will go and sail it by myself, then."

"You-will-not."

"Why not?"

"You know you're too young to go out alone."

"I'm five."

"And I'm a hundred and five, and I'm busy, and I'm tired."

She leaned aside, looking upward, a martyr, with her lonely life, her sense of sin, and this boy nagging at her.

"Please, Anna, don't you love my boat?"

"Oh, Lord, it's glorious!" she shouted, but she began to take off her apron and joyfully I knew we were going to Yates Circle, at the end of our street, where in the center an immense round bowl of polished granite enclosed a pool from which rose a forest of water spouts. It was the finest fountain in Dorchester, and it made music in air and sunshine all day long. All the children of the neighborhood, and some from across town, came there to sail their boats.

"Come on, Richard," sighed Anna, "bring your old boat."

"It's my new boat."

"Your new boat, then, God give me strength."

This was on a golden afternoon in October. My mother was upstairs sewing in the bay window of her bedroom, where thin white curtains blurred the sunlight all about her, until she seemed to me a creature of light herself.

Anna called up from the foot of the stairs that she was taking me to the Circle.

"Put on his light overcoat," replied my mother in a lifted, happy voice. "It's chilly even in the sun. Come straight home. Do you want me to watch anything in the kitchen?"

"No," said Anna, "we'll be back to start things for dinner."

While I held my boat first with one hand and then the other, she roughly hauled my overcoat on to my arms and buttoned me up.

"That boat," she said scornfully. But her voice and acts were full of love, and I was content, for I loved her as she loved me. I never thought of her grey, pock-marked, wide face, and her loose, colorless hair, and her dark tight clothes that strained across the full shapes of her old womanly arms and bosom and belly. She was to me neither young nor old, beautiful nor ugly. She belonged to me, and was therefore worthy. All persons seemed to commit their acts for my benefit, and all events were interesting only as they pleased me or met my needs.

"Come on," she said rudely, and we went out the front door.

※

Leaves were whispering down through the yellow air. The street was empty, or so we thought. Far ahead I could see the white crests of the water at the fountain.

"Come on, Anna, you are so slow."

"Wait till your feet kill you some day."

"Well, I know, but come *on*."

She began to sing gently one of her hooting tunes. She was holding one of my hands while with the other I cradled my ship. It was meant to be an ocean greyhound. I could not wait to learn whether it would float on an even keel.

We were not even half-way to the Circle when Anna stopped and halted me.

"What's the matter?" I asked.

"Never mind."

She was peering up the street at a figure which came idling into

[23]

view along the sidewalk on our side of the street. It was a man. He moved slowly, with little steps that hardly advanced his progress. His body was oddly in motion, almost as if he were dancing in his shoes with tiny movements. From a distance I could see that he was dressed in old grey clothes, very shabby, which were too large for him.

"Is it a tramp?" I asked, with a leap of interest and fright—for the word tramp was one to strike terror in the women of our household, who took great precautions against tramps when my father was not at home.

"I think so. Come," said Anna, "we will cross the street and go on the other walk."

She led me abruptly across and quickened her pace. Looking proud and unafraid in case the man really was a tramp, she lifted her head and began to exhibit her idea of what a grand lady was like, striding daintily yet hugely, and making angry little tosses of her head. She picked up with thumb and one finger a fold of her dress and held it athwart her hip. She seemed to say, I'll show him, that tramp, I'll dare him to ask me for a nickel for a glass of beer, he wouldn't dare try anything, me with my boy along here with me, going to sail a boat in Yates Circle, where there's often *a policeman* around to see that the children don't fall in the water and drownd theirself!

I lagged, staring at the tramp with fascination as we approached to pass each other on opposite sides of the street. Anna refused even to see him, but kept up her lofty plan to pass him by as if he did not exist.

Now I could see him clearly and intimately. He had a wide grin on his unshaven grey face with red cheeks and nose and bleached-looking places about the eyes. He blinked at us and bowed in a friendly way. Shabby, drifting, uncertain, he seemed to be reaching for us—for me, I was sure, since all life was directed toward me. There was an ingratiating gaiety about him, and when he left his sidewalk to come toward us, in his shambling little dance, I saw something else which puzzled me.

He nodded and smiled, and I thought he nodded and smiled at me. When he was halfway across the street toward us, keeping pace now with Anna's angry, ladylike advance—her eyes forward and her head up—I tugged at her and asked,

"Anna, what's he doing?"

At the sound of my voice the tramp laughed weakly in a beery little cough, and ducked his head, and smiled and smiled, hungry for response. I then saw how his clothes were disarrayed in what was later called indecent exposure.

"Anna!" I insisted.

"Never mind, come along," she said with a toss of her head as though she wore plumes.

"But he wants to show me something," I protested.

At this, she glanced aside at the tramp, who presented himself and his antic lewdness hilariously at her.

It took her only that glance to understand.

"Holy God in heaven!" she cried, and turned and in a single sweep of her heavy arm swung me all but through the air toward home, causing me to drop my boat. At a half-run she dragged me along the walk toward our house.

"My boat! My boat!" I kept crying, but she paid no heed, only muttering and groaning the names of saints, giving forth holy ejaculations. We came breathless to the house, where she slammed and locked the front door behind us, and ran through to the kitchen door and locked that too. Hearing this, and the sound of my angry sobs at the loss of my new ship, my mother came downstairs laughing, and saying,

"Slam, slam, cry, cry—what on earth is happening? Why are you home so soon?"

"My boat!" I stormed, running against her and angrily hugging

[25]

her hips and butting my head against her waist. "She made me lose it! We didn't even sail it once!"

"Anna?" called my mother through the hall.

Anna loomed in the pantry door and beckoned to my mother.

"Don't bring him," Anna said, raising her chin at me. "I must tell you."

The manly voice which Anna now used as she caught her breath conveyed to my mother an air of something ominous.

"Then, Richard," said my mother, "take your coat off and put it away, and go upstairs and wash your face. You are a fright. Wait for me in your room."

Unwillingly I took the stairs one step at a time, and as the pantry door closed after my mother, I heard in Anna's voice the words "tramp" and "crazy drunk," and then a grand, long, running line of narrative blurred away from detail by the shut door, punctuated by little screams of shock and horror from my mother.

❦

My room was at the front of the house next to the bedroom of my father and mother. I sat in the window seat looking out, mourning for my ship, which lay broken and worthless up the street, and then I saw the tramp, of whom I still thought as my funny new friend, come idling into view along the sidewalk. Now restored to modesty, he was eating with a sad air a crust-end of a sandwich. He leaned against a tree and rubbed his back against the bark like an old dog. He nodded right and left at the afternoon in general. He was a small man, I now saw, and he seemed sleepy and lonesome. In another moment, he slid gently against the tree trunk to the ground, and fastidiously searched in his loose pockets for something, and brought it forth—it was a pint bottle, empty. He raised it to his mouth. Nothing to drink ran forth, and with a little heave, he threw the empty bottle up on the lawn of the house next door, and then he fell sideways into a deep sleep on the ground, resembling a bundle of old clothes ready for the poor.

The voices downstairs went on, now heavy and baleful, now light and firm. I heard my mother use the telephone—she was calling my father at his office. Then a long silence fell in the house, while I wondered. In a quarter of an hour I heard a thrilling sound of clanging gongs come down the street, mixed with the rattle of hooves on the pavement. I leaned to see, and sure enough, it was a police patrol wagon, all shiny black with big gold lettering on the sides of the van.

The driver slowed down before our house to let two policemen, in their long-coated blue uniforms and domed grey helmets, and carrying their gleaming clubs, jump down from the rear door. I greatly admired the police for their uniforms, their horses, and their power. Anna had threatened me with their authority many times when I misbehaved. I watched now with abstracted excitement as they went to the tree where the tramp lay asleep. They took him up and shook him awake.

With an air of courtesy, he awoke and smiled his dusty, weak-necked smile at the two policemen.

For being smiled at by a degenerate, one of the policemen struck him in the face with his immense open hand.

A look of bewilderment came into the tramp's face.

The other policeman gave an order to hold the tramp, and then ran up to our front door and jabbed at the bell. In a moment Anna was taken forth to confront the man whom she had reported as a committer of public outrage. I saw her nod when the police pointed at the tramp. She identified him, though in her agitated modesty she could only look at him over her crooked elbow.

But this was enough for the police. They told her to go, she returned to the porch, and I heard her heavy steps running for the door and then the door slam behind her.

At the street curbing, while I knelt up on the window seat to see, one policeman knocked the tramp to the ground with his club and the other kicked him in the belly to make him stand up again. He tried to become a ball like a bear asleep in the zoo against the cold of winter, but they pulled his arms away from his head and between their hands they punched his head back and forth. They knocked his knees down from protecting his loins and kicked him there until he screamed silently. Suddenly he went to the ground of his own weight. The policemen looked at each other and in silent, expert accord took him up between them and carried him to the patrol wagon, threw him in the door, climbed in after him, and the wagon got up and away from a starting trot. I watched until they were all gone. My thoughts were slow, separate, and innocent.

Why did they beat him so?

Did they arrest him just because he was a tramp?

Or because he didn't look like everybody else?

Or because he was a "crazy-drunk?"

Or for sleeping under somebody else's tree?

Or for how he had presented himself to me and Anna?

Why didn't they want him to do what he had done up the street?

Didn't they know it hurt when they kicked and beat someone else?

In any case, it was an immense event, full of excitement and mystery, and I fell asleep on the window seat from the sheer emotion of it. When I awoke it was to find the barricade of our house lifted, and my mother, pretending that nothing whatever had happened, standing by me to say that it was time for me to get ready for supper.

[28]

"Daddy will be home soon, and he will come and see you when you have your tray."

❦

But he did not.

I heard him come in, and then I heard the famous sounds of private, grown-up discussion in the living room, with the sliding doors closed. Anna was summoned to give all over again her account of what had happened, while my father listened in silence, and my mother made little supplementary exclamations.

The mystery grew for me as all such attention was paid to it, and it became complete when my father ran upstairs at last to put me to bed. There was something stern and righteous in his air. I understood that we had all survived a dreadful danger, though of what nature I was not sure.

"Well, Doc," he said, "it was quite a day. Sit down here on my knee and listen to me for a minute."

He pretended to knock me out with a fisted blow to my chin, and he smiled and scowled at the same moment. In his dark blue eyes there was a light like that of retained tears, as he mourned for the presence of evil in the world and the tender vulnerability of innocence. Trying his best to resolve for us all the event of the afternoon, he said,

"Doc?"

"Yes, Daddy."

"Promise me something."

"Yes, Daddy."

"Promise me to forget absolutely everything that happened this afternoon, with that tramp. Will you?"

[29]

"Yes."

"We must never keep thoughts about those things"—(what things?)—"in our heads. God does not want us to. When we see something terrible that happens near us we must get away and forget it as fast as we can. Do you understand?"

"Yes."

"Good."

"You mean," I asked, "what the policeman did to the man?"

"No, no, I mean what the man did. He was crazy and he was drunk and nobody else acts that way. Don't think other men are like that. They don't go around in public that way."

"Was he a bad man?"

"Oh, yes. A very bad man. But forget him. Promise?"

"Yes."

"He can't scare you again if you forget him, you see."

"He didn't scare me. He scared Anna."

"Well, then, Doc, it is because you didn't understand." He set me down and stood up. "All right, now? We won't have a thing to do again about it?"

"No."

"Good. Then up comes the young giant and the old giant will take him to his castle for the night!"

And he swung me to his shoulders and walking hunchily and with great heavy spread steps the way giants walked he took me to my bed across the room and undressed me and put my pajamas on me and laid me down and kissed my forehead and said, "We'll leave just a crack," and went to the door and left it open just a crack so the upstairs hall light would stand like a golden lance of safety all night long between me and the dark, and went downstairs to dine with my mother. Their voices grew easier as the minutes passed and faded into sleep.

[30]

But the very first thing I thought of when I awoke was the tramp, and the more I said to myself that I had promised to forget him and all of it, the more I remembered. During the morning, when Anna was in the basement laundry, I went down to see her.

"Anna, why was the tramp a bad man?"

"You are not to talk about it."

"But he didn't do anything!"

"Oh, God," she said, reviving her sense of shock with hushed pleasure.

"He was trying to make friends with me. He was doing something funny, but—".

"Don't you know," she asked in a hoarse whisper, "what he was doing?"

"No, I don't."

She pointed to my groin.

"There, and all like that," she moaned, "and it was a terrible sin he committed, doing that, and doing it to a lady and a little boy, and Hell don't have fires enough to punish him for what he did!"

"It doesn't?"

"Not fires enough!"

I stared at her. Her tired, sad, grey bulk was alive with some glory of rage, some fullness of life, and suddenly I knew for the first time in my years what it was she and all the others in the house had been talking about. From I could not know where, the knowledge of new sins, and their power, dawned within me, and they seemed to reside just there where Anna had pointed.

I began to jig up and down.

"Anna!" I cried, "He was a bad man, my father said he was! He was bad!"

"Well," she said with the massive placidity of vested virtue, "why do you suppose I dragged you away from seeing such a thing, and why do you suppose your Máma called your Pápa, and he called the police station, and they sent a patrol wagon for the man? Well, I know, and you know, now."

"The police beat him!" I cried exultantly.

"I saw," she said. "Nothing they could do to him would be too much."

How could I ever have liked the tramp, or have felt sorry for him?

"Bash!" I exclaimed, imitating the blows of the police, "Blong!"

"Run along now, and don't think any more about it, it is all over."

But my interest was at a high pitch since I knew how to think about the affair, and I ran next door to see my friend Tom Deterson, who was my age, and with whom I exchanged secrets.

※

"Did you hear about the tramp?" I asked out of breath.

"No," said Tom. "What tramp?"

I had the rich opportunity, then, to tell him everything—all that I had seen and heard and was supposed to forget. Tom and I were in the old carriage house at the foot of his yard. Nothing was kept there but the discards of the Deterson household. It made a fine playhouse, for it was removed, musty, dim, and private. As I told him what I knew, we sat on an old ruined sofa whose springs sagged into view below. Its cushions were awry and stained.

Tom's eyes were huge in his flushed, thin little face. He had curly hair and jangling nerves. He was never at rest. He was like a hot-nosed, insistent puppy climbing against all objects and persons and mysteries with an assumption of universal good will. At that time he was my best friend.

When I reached the most dreadful part of my story, I showed in pantomime what the tramp kept doing. Tom stared and jiggled as if he saw the actuality instead of a mockery of the scandal.

"What for?" he asked.

"I don't know. But he was crazy-drunk. They all do it. You know what?"

"No. What."

"He was a bad man."

"He was?"

"Yes, he was. My father said so, and Anna said so, and the police took him away."

"What did they do?"

"I'll show you what they did."

I seized an old split cushion from the sofa and threw it on the floor of the carriage house and I began to kick it.

"This is what they did!" I cried in heightening excitement. I picked up the cushion and punched it and threw it to Tom. He caught it and punched it and his eyes fired with power and purpose, and he threw the cushion down and he kicked it, and I kicked it again, and then we found some old thin brass curtain rods on the floor and we took these up and with them whipped the cushion.

"I'll tell you what I would do to that tramp!" I shouted. "I would beat him and push him until all his stuffing came out, and I would hit him"—and I did—"and I would kick him"—and I did—"and I would burn him in hell with all the fire that all the fire engines can't put out!"

"I have some matches!" cried Tom.

"Get them!"

[33]

He dug them from under the upholstery at the arm of the sofa and he lit a match and touched it to the split cushion where its dismal cotton stuffing showed through. It took on a feeble flame, making heavy white smoke. Exalted, we danced about the victim, telling each other to kick him, to whip him, to burn him. Suddenly the cushion made a spurt of fire and scared us. We had more fire than we expected.

"Say!" shouted Tom in a changed voice.

"Yes, yes, put it out!" I called.

He began to stamp with his flat sandalled feet at the burning corner of the cushion, but without much effect.

"Danged old tramp!" he said, "doing that!"

The cotton stuffing made little explosions with flying sparks.

"I know what," I said, "we can put out the fire—let's both of us—" and seeing what I did, Tom did the same, and with a sense of high glee, triumph, and even carnal fulfillment, we made our water together over the cushion and quelled the flame. The fire in the cushion guttered down into little worms of crinkling coal which finally expired yielding up a few last threads of noisome smoke.

"There!" said Tom.

"Yes!" I said.

We made ourselves proper again as passion gave way to shame. We kicked the cushion against the brick wall behind the sofa and went out into the unknowing, cool, golden October morning.

This loss of innocence was not in seeing what I saw, but in hearing what I was told about it—for we are subject to what we are taught to hate.

CHAPTER III

Muzza

How do we manage to love at all when there is so much hatred masquerading in love's name? I saw, if I did not understand, how this could be when I lost forever a friend whom I tried to rescue from peril. But a larger peril claimed him.

His name was John Burley. Nobody ever loved him enough to give him a natural nickname. Instead, he was the subject of a mocking refrain.

"John, John, the dog-faced one," sang the other boys our age when they saw John and me playing together in our neighborhood. He was my next-door neighbor, and I didn't know there was anything really different about him until I saw him abused by other children.

Before we were old enough to go to school we owned the whole world all day long except for nap time after lunch. We played in the open grassy yards behind and between our houses, and when John was busy and dreaming with play, he was a good friend to have, and never made trouble. But when people noticed him, he became someone else, and now I know that his parents, and mine, too, out of sympathy, wondered and wondered how things would be for him when the time came for him to go off to school like any other boy and make a place for himself among small strangers who might find his oddness a source of fun and power for themselves.

In the last summer before schooltime, 1909, everyone heard the cry of "John, John, the dog-faced one," and even I, his friend, saw him newly. I would look at him with a blank face, until he would notice this, and then he would say crossly, with one of his impulsive, self-clutching movements,

"What's the matter, Richard, what's the matter, why are you looking crazy?"

"I'm not looking crazy. You are the one that's crazy."

For children pointed at him and sang, "Crazy, lazy, John's a daisy," and ran away.

Under their abuse, and my increasing wonderment, John showed a kind of daft good manners which should have induced pity and grace in his tormentors, but did not. He would pretend to be intensely preoccupied by delights and secrets from which the rest of us were excluded. He would count his fingers, nodding at the wrong total, and then put his thumbs against his thick lips and buzz against them with his furry voice, and look up at the sky, smacking his tongue, while other boys hooted and danced at him.

They were pitiably accurate when they called him the dog-faced one. He did look more like a dog than a boy. His pale hair was shaggy and could not be combed. His forehead was low, with a bony scowl that could not be changed. His nose was blunt, with its nostrils showing frontward. Hardly contained by his thick, shapeless lips, his teeth were long, white, and jumbled together. Of stocky build, he seemed always to be wearing a clever made-up costume to put on a monkey or a dog, instead of clothes like anybody else's. His parents bought him the best things to wear, but in a few minutes they were either torn or rubbed with dirt or scattered about somewhere.

[36]

"The poor dears," I heard my mother murmur over the Burley family.

"Yes," said my father, not thinking I might hear beyond what they were saying, "we are lucky. I can imagine no greater cross to bear."

"How do you suppose—" began my mother, but suddenly feeling my intent stare, he interrupted, with a glance my way, saying,

"Nobody ever knows how these cases happen. Watching them grow must be the hardest part."

What he meant was that it was sorrowful to see an abnormal child grow physically older but no older mentally.

❊

But Mr and Mrs Burley—Gail and Howard, as my parents called them—refused to admit to anyone else that their son John was in any way different from other boys. As the summer was spent, and the time to start school for the first time came around, their problem grew deeply troubling. Their friends wished they could help with advice, mostly in terms of advising that John be spared the ordeal of entering the rigid convention of a school where he would immediately be seen by all as a changeling, like some poor swineherd in a fairy story who once may have been a prince, but who would never be released from his spell.

The school—a private school run by an order of Catholic ladies founded in France—stood a few blocks away from our street. The principal, who like each of her sisters wore a white shirt-waist with a high collar and starched cuffs and a long dark blue skirt, requested particularly that new pupils should come the first day without their parents. Everyone would be well-looked-after. The pupils

[37]

would be put to tasks which would drive diffidence and homesickness out the window. My mother said to me as she made me lift my chin so that she could tie my windsor tie properly over the stiff slopes of my Buster Brown collar, while I looked into her deep, clear, blue eyes, and wondered how to say that I would not go to school that day or any other,

"Richard, John's mother thinks it would be so nice if you and he walked to school together."

"I don't want to."

I did not mean that I did not want to walk with John, I meant that I did not want to go to school.

"That's not very kind. He's your friend."

"I know it."

"I have told his mother you would go with him."

Childhood was a prison whose bars were decisions made by others. Numbed into submission, I took my mother's goodbye kiss staring at nothing, eaten within by fears of the unknown which awaited us all that day.

"Now skip," said my mother, winking both her eyes rapidly, to disguise the start of tears at losing me to another stage of life. She wore a small gold fleur-de-lys pin on her breast from which depended a tiny enamelled watch. I gazed at this and nodded solemnly but did not move. With wonderful executive tact she felt that I was about to make a fatally rebellious declaration, and so she touched the watch, turning its face around, and said, as though I must be concerned only with promptness,

"Yes, yes, Richard, you are right, we must think of the time, you mustn't be late your first day."

I was propelled then to the Burleys' house next door, where John and his mother were waiting for me in their front hall, which was always filled with magic light from the cut glass panes in bright colors flanking their front door.

[38]

Mrs Burley held me by the shoulders for a moment, trying to tell me something without saying it.

"Richard," she said, and then paused.

She looked deep into my eyes until I dropped my gaze. I looked at the rest of her face, and then at her bosom, wondering what was down there in that shadow where two rounded places of flesh rolled frankly together. Something about her personality led people to use her full name when they referred to her even idly—"Gail Burley"—and even I felt power within her.

Her husband had nothing like her strength. He was a small grey man with thin hair combed flat across his almost bald skull. The way his pince-nez pulled at the skin between his eyes gave him a look of permanent headache. Always hurried and impatient, he seemed to have no notice for children like me, or his own son, and all I ever heard about him was that he "gave Gail Burley anything she asked for," and "worked his fingers to the bone" doing so, as president of a marine engine company with a factory on the lakefront of our city of Dorchester in up-state New York.

Gail Burley—and I cannot say how much of her attitude rose from her sense of disaster in the kind of child she had borne—seemed to exist in a state of general exasperation. A reddish blonde, with skin so pale that it glowed like pearl, she was referred to as a great beauty. Across the bridge of her nose and about her eyelids and just under her eyes there were scatterings of little gold freckles which oddly yet powerfully reinforced her air of being irked by everything.

She often exhaled slowly and with compression, and said "Gosh," a slang word which was just coming in in her circle, which she pronounced "Garsh." Depending on her mood, she could make it into the expression of ultimate disgust or mild amusement. The white skin under her eyes went whiter when she was cross or angry, and then a dry hot light came into her hazel eyes. She seemed a large woman to me, but I don't suppose she was—merely slow, challenging and annoyed in the way she moved, with a flowing governed grace which was like a comment on all that was intolerable. At any moment she would exhale in audible distaste for the circumstances of her world. Compressing her lips, which she never rouged, she would ray her pale glance upward, across, aside, to express her search for the smallest mitigation, the simplest endurable fact or object, of life. The result of these airs and tones of her habit was that in those rare moments when she was pleased, her expression of happiness came through like one of pain.

"Richard," she said, holding me by the shoulders, and looking into my face to discover what her son John was about to confront in the world of small school children.

"Yes, Mrs Burley."

She looked at John who was waiting to go.

He had his red and black plaid japanned collapsible tin lunch box all nicely secured with a web strap and he made his buzzing noise of pleasure at the idea of doing something so new as going to school. Because he showed no apprehension over what would seem like an ordeal to another boy, she let forth one of her breaths of disgust. She had dressed him in a starched collar like mine which extended over the smart lapels of his beautiful blue suit, with its Norfolk jacket. His socks were well pulled up and his shoes were shined. She looked at me again, trying to say what she could not. Her white face with its flecks of fixed displeasure slowly took on a pleading smile. She squeezed my shoulders a little, hoping I would understand, even at my age, how John would need someone to look out for him, protect him, suffer him, since he was a child of such condition as she could not bring herself to admit. Her plea was resolved into a miniature of the principle of bribery by which her life was governed—even, I now think, to the terms on which Howard Burley obtained even her smallest favors.

[40]

"Richard," she said, "when you and John come home after school"—and she pressed those words to show that I must bring him home— "I will have a nice surprise waiting for you both."

John became agitated at this, jumping about, and demanding, "What is it, Muzza, what is it?"

She gave one of her breaths.

"John, John, be quiet. Garsh. I can't even say anything without getting you all excited."

For my benefit she smiled, but the gold flecks under her eyes showed as angry dark spots, and the restrained power of her dislike of John was so great that he was cowed. He put his hands to his groin to comfort himself, and said, using his word for what he always found there, "Peanut."

At this his mother became openly furious at him.

"John! Stop that! How many times have I told you that isn't nice. Richard doesn't do it. Doctor Grauer has told you what will happen if you keep doing it. Stop it!"

She bent over to slap at his hands and he lunged back. Losing his balance, he fell, and I heard his head go crack on the hardwood floor of the hall where the morning light made pools of jewel colors through the glass panels. He began to cry in a long, burry, high wail. His mother picked him up and he hung like a rag doll in her outraged grasp. The day was already in ruins, and he had not even gone off to school. The scene was one of hundreds like it which made up the life of that mother and that son. I was swept by shame at seeing it.

"Now stop that ridiculous caterwauling," she said. "Richard is waiting to take you to school. Do you want him to think you are a cry baby?"

John occasionally made startling remarks, which brought a leap of hope that his understanding might not be so deficient as everyone believed.

[41]

"I *am* a cry baby," he said, burying his misery-mottled face in the crook of his arm.

A sudden lift of pity in his mother made her kneel down and gently enfold him in her arms. With her eyes shut, she gave her love to the imaginary son, handsome and healthy, whom she longed for, even as she held the real John. It was enough to console him. He flung his arms around her and hugged her like a bear cub, all fur and clumsiness and creature longing.

"Muzza, Muzza," he said against her cheek.

She set him off.

"*Now* can you go to school?" she asked in a playfully reasonable voice.

John's states of feeling were swift in their changes. He began to smack his lips, softly indicating that he was in a state of pleasure.

"Then go along, both of you," said his mother.

She saw us out the door and down the walk. Curiously enough, the self-sorrowing lump in my throat went away as I watched the scene between John and his mother. Things seemed so much worse with the Burleys than with me and my start in school.

❊

I led John off at a smart pace, running sometimes, and sometimes walking importantly with short busy steps. We paused only once, and that was to look in the window at a little candy and news shop a block from the school, where with warm, damp pennies it was possible to buy sticky rolls of chocolate candy, or—even better—stamp-sized films which when exposed to light darkened in shades of red to reveal such subjects as the battleship *New York,* or the Woolworth Building, or the Washington Monument.

[42]

John always had more money than I.

"Let's get some," he proposed.

"No. After school," I replied. "We will be late if we stop and we will catch the dickens."

"Catch the dickens," he said, and began to run away ahead of me. I overtook him and we entered the main door of the school—it was a red brick building with a portico of white pillars veiled in vines—and once in the dark corridors with their wood-ribbed walls, we seemed to lose ourselves to become small pieces of drifting material that were carried along to our classrooms by a tide of children. Boys went separate from girls. John and I were finally directed to a room containing twenty boys in the first grade, presided over by Miss Mendtzy.

She met us at the door and without speaking but sustaining a kindly smile, sent us with a strong thin finger on our shoulders along the aisles where we would find our desks. We gave her wary glances to see what she was like. She had a narrow little face above a bird's body. Her hair was like short grey feathers. Before her large, steady, pale eyes she wore a pair of nose glasses that trembled in response to her quivering nerves and sent a rippling line of light along the gold chain that attached her glasses to a small gold spring spool pinned to her shirtwaist.

John and I were at desks side by side. When all the room was filled, Miss Mendtzy closed the door, and our hearts sank. There we were, in jail. She moved trimly to her platform. Her slim feet in black, high-buttoned shoes, looked like feet in a newspaper advertisement, because she stood them at such polite angles to each other. On her desk she had placed a vase of flowers with a great silk bow to give a festive air to the opening day. Touching the blossoms with a flourish of artistic delicacy, she launched into a pleasant little speech. Everyone sat quietly out of strangeness while she said,

"Now I want all of my new first-graders to come up here one by one, beginning with this aisle on my left"—she showed where in a gesture of bloodless grace—"and shake hands with me, and tell me their names, for we are going to be working together for months and years, as I will be your home room teacher until the sixth grade. Think of it! Quite like a family! And so we are going to become great friends, and we must know each other well. Miss Mendtzy is ready to love each and every one of you, and she hopes each and every one of you will learn to love her. We are going to get along splendidly together, if everybody is polite, and works hard, and remembers that he is not the only boy in this world, or in this school, or in this room, but that he is a boy among other boys, to whom he must show respect, even while playing. Now, shall we start here, with this boy, at the front of the first row?"

One by one we went to her platform, stepped up on it, shook hands, spoke our names, received a bright, lens-quivered smile and a deep look into our eyes, and then were sent on across her little stage and down the other side and back to our seats. Some among us swaggered, others went rapidly and shyly, hiding from such a public world, one or two winked on the final trip up the aisles, and all felt some thumping at the heart of dread followed by pride as we went and returned.

❋

There was no incident until John's turn came. When it did, he would not rise and go forward.

"Come?" said Miss Mendtzy, beckoning over her desk and twinkling with her chained glasses. "We are waiting for the next boy?"

I leaned over to John and whispered,

"It's your turn, John. Go on. Go on."

[44]

He went lower in his seat and began to buzz his lips against his thumbs, terrified of rising before a crowd of small strangers, who were now beginning to nudge each other and whisper excitedly at the diversion. I heard someone whisper "John, John, the dog-faced one," and I could not tell whether John heard it. But, a professional, Miss Mendtzy heard it. She smartly whacked her ruler on the flat of her desk. It was like a nice pistol shot. Silence fell. She put on her face a look which we all knew well at home— that look of aloof, pained regret at unseemly behavior.

"I must say I am surprised," she said quietly and deadlily, "that some of us are not polite enough to sit silently when we see someone in a fit of shyness. Some of the finest people I know are shy at times. I have been told that our Bishop, that humble, great man, is shy himself when he has to meet people personally. Now I am going down from my platform and down the aisle and"—she glanced at her seating plan of the classroom—"I am going to bring John Burley up here myself as my guest, and help him over his shyness, and the only way to do that is by helping him to do the same things everybody else has done. So."

She went to John and took his hand and led him to the platform and stood him where each of us had stood, facing her, in profile to the rest of the room. Speaking as though he had just come there by his own will, she said,

"Good morning, John. I am Miss Mendtzy. We are pleased that you are with us," first giving us a sidelong glare to command our agreement, and then like a lady holding forth her hand to John, with a slightly arched wrist and drooping fingers.

John put his hands behind him and buzzed his lips and looked out the window.

"John?"

"John, John, the dog-faced one," again said an unplaceable voice in the rear of the classroom, softly but distinctly.

[45]

"Who said that!" demanded Miss Mendtzy, going pink, and trembling until her lenses shimmered. The very first day of school, she seemed to say, and already there was an unfortunate incident. "I simply will not have bad manners in my room, and I simply will not have one of my boys treated like this. Whoever said that is to stand up and apologize instantly. I think I know who it was"—but clearly she did not—"and if he apologizes now, and promises never, never to do such a rude thing again, we shall all be friends again as we want to be. Well? I am waiting?"

The silence and the tension grew and grew.

John stood with head hanging. I saw his hands twitching behind his back. He was trying not to clasp them over himself in front.

"One more minute?" declared Miss Mendtzy, "and then I will do something you will all be very sorry for?"

Silence, but for a clock ticking on the wall above her blackboard.

John could not bear it. Moving as fast as a cat, he threw himself forward to Miss Mendtzy's desk and swept her vase of flowers to the floor where it shattered and spilled.

All the boys broke into hoots and pounded their hinged desk tops upon their desks, making such a clamor that in a moment the door was majestically opened and the Principal, always called Madame de St. Étienne, who came from nobility in France, heavily entered the room. Even as she arrived, someone in the rear of the room, carried on by the momentum of events, called out, "Crazy, lazy, John's a daisy."

The Principal was a monument of authority. Above her heavy pink face with its ice-blue eyes rose a silvery pompadour like a wave breaking back from a headland. Her bosom was immense in her starched shirtwaist. Over it she wore a long gold chain which fell like a maiden waterfall into space below her bust and ended in a loop at her waist where she tucked a large gold watch. Her dark skirt went straight down in front, for she had to lean continuously forward, we thought, if the vast weight and size behind her were not to topple her over backward.

She now glared at Miss Mendtzy with frigid reproach at the breach of discipline in her classroom loud enough to be heard down the hall, and then faced us all, saying in a voice like pieces of broken glass scraped together at the edges,

"Children, you will rise when the Principal enters the classroom." She clapped her hands once and we rose, scared and ashamed.

"Now who is this?" she demanded, turning to the tableau at the teacher's platform.

"This is John Burley, Madame," replied Miss Mendtzy, and got no further, for John, seeing the open door, bolted for the hall and freedom.

Madame de St. Étienne gave another queenly, destructive look at Miss Mendtzy, and said,

"Pray continue with the exercises, Miss Mendtzy."

She then left the room, moving as though on silent casters, for her skirt swept the floor all about her short, light steps, amazing in a woman so heavy and so enraged.

Burning with mortification, Miss Mendtzy began our first lesson, which was an exercise in neatness—the care of our pencil boxes and schoolbooks. There was a happy material interest in this, for the pencils were all new, and smelled of cedar, and we went in turn to sharpen them at the teacher's desk. Our erasers—promises of foreordained smudges of error—showed a tiny diamondlike glisten if we held them in a certain way to the light of the window. If we chewed upon them, little gritty particles deliciously repelled our teeth. Our schoolbooks cracked sweetly when we opened them, and the large, clear, black type on the pages held mystery and invitation. We became absorbed in toys which were suddenly now something more than toys, and our cheeks grew hot, and we were

[47]

happy, and we forgot to want to go to the bathroom, and I was hardly aware of it when the door opened again before Madame de St. Étienne. Late, but earnestly, we scrambled to our feet, as she said,

"Which is Richard—?" giving my full name.

I put my hand up.

"Pray come with me, Richard," she ordered, ignoring Miss Mendtzy entirely. "Bring your boxes and books."

A stutter of conjecture went along the aisles at this, which Madame de St. Étienne, gliding on her way to the door, suppressed by pausing and staring above the heads of everyone as though she could not believe her ears. Quiet fell, and in quiet, with my heart beating, I followed her out to the hallway. She shut the door and turned me with a finger to walk ahead of her to her office at the entrance way inside the pillared portico. I wanted to ask what I had done to be singled out for her notice which could only, I thought, lead to punishment.

But it appeared that she had enlisted me as an assistant. In her office, John was waiting, under guard of the Principal's secretary. He was sitting on a cane chair holding a glass of water, half full.

"Finish it, John," commanded Madame.

"I don't like it," he said.

"Hot water to drink is the best thing for anyone who is upset," she answered. "It is the remedy we always give. Finish it."

Raising a humble wail, he drank the rest of the hot water, spilling much of it down on his chin, his windsor tie, his starched collar.

"You are John's friend?" she asked me.

"Yes."

"Who are his other friends?"

"I don't know."

"Has he none, then?"

"I don't think so."

John watched my face, then the Principal's, turning his head with jerky interest and rubbing his furry hair with his knuckles in pleasure at being the subject of interest.

"You brought him to school?"

"Yes."

"Yes, *Madame*."

"Yes, Madame."

"And you will take him home?"

"Yes, Madame. After school."

"I have spoken on the telephone with his mother, to arrange for him to go home. She prefers not to have him come home until the end of school after lunch. Until then, I will ask you to stay here in my office with him. You will both eat your lunches here and I will see that you are not disturbed. Tomorrow you will be able to return to your classroom."

"With John?"

"No. John will not be with us after today."

John nodded brightly at this. Evidently the Principal had given an ultimatum to Mrs Burley over the telephone. I can imagine the terms of it—careful avoidance of the words abnormal, special case, impossible to measure up to the progress of others boys his age, and such. With arctic, polite finality, Madame de St. Étienne would have read John out of the human society where his years put him but where his retarded mind and disordered nerves, so clearly announced by his rough, doglike appearance, must exclude him. Gail Burley's despair can be felt. How could she ever again pretend even to herself that her child, if only thrown into life, would make his way like anyone else? How could she love anything in the world if she could not love the son who was mismade in her womb? What a bitter affront it was to her famous good looks of face and body, her hard brightness of mind, her firm ability to govern everything else that made up her life, if she must be responsible for such a creature as John. How to face a lifetime of exasperated pity for him? How to disguise forever the humiliation which she must feel? The daily effort of disguising it would cost her all her confident beauty in the end.

"Why don't we go home now?" I asked.

"John's mother thinks it would look better if he simply came home like the other children when school is dismissed this afternoon."

Yes, for if they saw him come earlier, people would say once again what she knew they were always saying about John. I knew well enough the kind of thing, from hearing my own father and mother talk kindly and sadly about my playmate.

Let him come home after school, like everyone else, and tomorrow, why, then, tomorrow, Gail Burley could simply say with a shrug and a speckled smile, that she and Howard didn't think it was really just the school for John. There was something about those teachers, neither quite nuns, nor quite ordinary women, which was unsettling. The Burleys would look around, and meantime, John could be tutored at home, as Gail herself had been one winter when she had gone as a little girl with her parents to White Sulphur Springs. Leaving the school could be made, with a little languid ingenuity, to seem like a repudiation by her, for reasons she would be too polite to elaborate upon for parents of other children still attending it.

❧

The day passed slowly in the Principal's office. At eleven o'clock there was a fire drill, set off by a great alarm gong which banged slowly and loudly in the hall just above the office door. The door was kept closed upon us, but we could hear the rumble and slide of the classes as they took their appointed ways out of the building to the shaded playgrounds outside.

"I want to go, I want to go!" cried John at the window. "Everybody is there!"

"No," said Madame de St. Étienne, turning like an engine in her swivel chair, "we will remain here. They will presently return."

John began to cry.

The Principal looked to me to manage him and calmly turned back to the work on her desk, placing a pince-nez upon the high bridge of her thin nose with a sweep of her arm which was forced to travel a grand arc to bypass her bosom.

❦

But at last, when the clock in the office showed twenty-five minutes past two, she said,

"Now, John, and now, Richard, you may take your things and go home. School is dismissed at half-past two. Perhaps it would be prudent for you to leave a little before the other boys. You will go straight home."

"Yes, Madame."

She gave us each her hand. To John she said,

"May God bless you, my poor little one."

Her words and her manner sent a chill down my belly

But in a moment we were in the open air of the autumn day, where a cold wind off the lake was spinning leaves from the trees along the street. John capered happily along and when we reached the candy store, he remembered how we would stop there. I wondered if stopping there would violate our orders to go "straight home," but the store was on the way, and we went in.

John enjoyed shopping. He put his stubby finger with its quick-bitten nail on the glass of the candy counter, pointing to first one then another confection, and every time he made up his mind he changed it, until the proprietor, an old man with a bent back in a dirty grey cardigan, sighed and looked over his shoulder at his wife, who sat in the doorway to their back room. His glance and her return of it plainly spoke of John's idiocy.

"There!" said John finally, aiming his finger and his hunger at a candy slice of banana, cut the long way, and tasting, I knew, of cotton mixed with gun oil. The candy banana was white in the center with edges stained orange and yellow.

I moved on to the counter where you could buy the magic photographic plates which showed nothing until you exposed them to the light. I wanted to buy one but I had no money. John came beside me and said,

"Richard, I'll get you one."

"Oh, no."

"Oh, yes. I'll get you two."

He put down four pennies to pay for two prints and the storekeeper gave me the box to choose my prints. On the edge of each little plate was the name of its subject. I chose the liner *Mauretania* and Buckingham Palace.

"Here," I said to John, offering him one of them. "You keep one."

He put his hands behind his back and blew his tongue at me between his thick lips.

"All right, then, thanks, we have to go home now. Come on, John," I said.

Eating his banana John was compliant. We came out of the store and went on to the corner where we turned into our street. Our houses were a block and a half away. We could just see them. Under the billowing trees and the cool autumn light they looked asleep. They called to me. I wanted suddenly to be home.

"Let's run, John," I said.

We began to run, but we got no further than a large hedge which ran up the driveway of the second house from the corner.

※

It was a great house, with a large garage in back, and a deep lawn. I knew the brothers who lived there. Their name was Grandville. They were a year or two older and very self-important because of their family automobiles, and their electric train system which occupied the whole top floor of their house.

They now jumped out from behind the hedge. With them were three other boys. They had all just come home from school. While we had idled in the candy store, they had gone by to wait for us.

"John, John, the dog-faced one!" they called, and took John, and dragged him up the driveway toward the garage in the windy, empty neighborhood. "Crazy, lazy, John's a daisy," they chanted, and I ran along yelling,

"Let us go, let us go!"

"Shut up, or we'll get you too," cried one of the brothers.

"Richie!" moaned John, "Richie!"

The terror in his blurry voice was like that in a nightmare when you must scream and cannot make a sound. His face was belly-white and his eyes were staring at me. I was his protector. I would save him.

"Richie! Richie!"

But I could do nothing against the mob of five, but only run along calling to them to "let go of us"—for I felt just as much captive as

John whom they dragged by arms and legs. He went heavy and limp. They hauled him through the chauffeur's door—a narrow one beside the big car doors, which were closed—and shut the door after us all. The center of the garage was empty for the big Pierce-Arrow limousine was out, bearing Mrs Grandville somewhere on a chauffeur-driven errand.

"Put him there!" yelled one of the brothers.

Four boys held John on the cement floor by the drain grille while the other brother went to the wall, uncoiled a hose and turned the spigot. The hose leaped alive with a thrust of water.

"Now let go and get back or you'll all get wet," called the Grandville boy. As the others scampered back he turned the powerful blow of the hose water on John. It knocked him down. He shut his eyes and turned his blind face to the roof. His shapeless mouth fell open in a silent cry. Still clutching his candy banana he brought it to his mouth in delayed memory of what it was for, and what had been a delight was now a sorrowful and profitless hunger for comfort in misery.

"Get up, dogface," yelled one of the boys.

Obediently John got up, keeping his eyes closed, suffering all that must come to him. The hose column toppled him over again. Striking his face, blows of water knocked his head about until it seemed it must fly apart.

"I know!" cried an excited and joyful young voice, "let's get his clo'es off!"

There was general glee at this idea. The hose was put away for the moment, and everyone seized John and tore at his clothes. He made his soundless wail with open mouth and I thought he shaped my name again.

When he was naked they ordered him to stand again, and he did so, trying to protect his modesty with his thick hands. They hit him with the hose again and buffeted him like a puppet. The hose water made him spin and slide on the oily floor. The noise was doubled by echoes from the peaked high roof of the garage.

❊

Nobody thought of me.

I backed to the door and opened it and ran away. On the concrete driveway was a tricycle belonging to the younger Grandville. I mounted it and rode off as fast as I could. My chest was ready to break open under my hard breathing. My knees rose and fell like pistons. My face was streaming with tears of rage at John's ordeal and the disgrace of my helplessness before it. I rode to John's house and threw myself up the front steps but before I could attack the door it was opened to me. Gail Burley was watching for us and when she saw me alone in gasping disorder, she cried,

"Why, Richard! What's the matter! Where's John!"

At first I could only point, so I took her hand and tugged at her to come with me. It was proof of the passion and power I felt at the moment that without more questioning she came. I remounted the tricycle and led her up the street to the Grandvilles'. In a little while as I went I was able to tell her what was happening.

When she understood, she increased her stride. She became magnificent in outrage. Her hazel eyes darkened to deep topaz and her reddish golden hair seemed to spring forward into the wind. She was like a famous ship, dividing the elements as she went.

"Oh! Those horrid, cruel, little beasts!" she exclaimed. "Oh! What I would do to them—and Richard, you are an absolute *darrling* to get away and come for me. Oh! That poor John!"

[55]

We hurried up the driveway. The game was still going on. We could hear cries and the hiss of the hose. Gail Burley strode to the door and threw it open. She saw her son pinned against the far brick wall by the long pole of the spray. He tried to turn his face from side to side to avoid its impact. It swept down his white soft body and he continually tried to cover himself with his hands. Nonresistant, he accepted all that came to him. His eyes were still closed and his mouth was still open.

Stepping with baleful elegance across the puddles of the floor, Gail Burley threw aside the boys who were dancing at the spectacle, and came to the Grandville brother with the hose. She astounded him. In his ecstatic possession, he had heard no one arrive. She seized the hose and with a gesture commanded him to turn off the water, which he did. She dropped the hose and went to John and took him dripping and blue with cold into her arms. He fell inert against her letting his hands dangle as she hugged him. But he made a word at last.

"Muzza," he said thickly, "Oh, Muzza, Muzza."

"John-John," she said, holding his wet head against the hollow of her lovely neck and shoulder, "It's all right. It's all right. Muzza is here. Poor John-John."

The boys were now frightened. The oldest said,

"We were only trying to have some fun, Mrs Burley."

"Go to the house," she commanded in the flattest tone which held promises of punishment for all as soon as she could inform their parents, "and bring a big towel and a blanket.—Richard, you might throw together John's things and bring them along."

She was obeyed soberly and quickly. In a few minutes she and I were taking John home. He was huddled inside a doubled blanket. He was shivering. His teeth chattered.

"Where's my banana?" he managed to say

"Oh, never mind," said his mother. "We can get you another banana. What were you doing with a banana anyway?"

"It was a candy one," I explained.

"I see."

Her thoughts were falling into order after the disturbance of her feelings by the cruelty she had come to halt.

※

My perceptions of what followed were at the time necessarily shallow, but they were, I am sure, essentially correct.

"Those wretches!" exclaimed Gail Burley, leading John by the hand while I trotted alongside. "What would we ever have done without Richard? You are a true friend, Richard!—Oh!" she said, at the memory of what she had seen. And then, as John stumbled because she was walking so fast and his blanket folds were so awkward to hold about himself, she jerked his hand and said, "Stop dragging your feet, John! Why can't you walk like anybody else! Here! Pull up and keep up with me!"

At her suddenly cold voice, he went limp and would have fallen softly, like a dropped teddy bear, to the sidewalk. But she dragged him up, and said with her teeth almost closed,

"John Burley, do you hear me? Get up and come with me. If you do not, your father will give you the whaling of your life when he comes home tonight!"

"No, Muzza, no, Muzza," muttered John at the memories which this threat called alive. He got to his feet and began half-running along beside her, dragging his borrowed blanket which looked like the robe of a pygmy king in flight.

I was chilled by the change in Mrs Burley. Her loving rage was gone and in its place was a fury of exasperation. She blinked away angry tears. With no thought of how fast John could run along with her, she pulled and jerked at him all the way home, while her face told us after all that she was bitterly ashamed of him.

For at last she took the world's view of her son. Represented by his own kind, other children, the world had repudiated him. Much as she hated the cruelty of the Grandvilles and their friends, sore as her heart was at what her son had suffered through them, she knew they were society, even if it was shown at its most savage. It was the determining attitude of the others which mattered. She had seen it clearly. Her heart broke in half. One half was charged with love and pity as it defied the mocking world which allowed no published lapse from its notion of a finally unrealizable norm. The other half was pierced by fragments of her pride. How could it happen to *her* that *her* child could be made sport of as a little animal monster? Gail Burley was to be treated better than that.

"John?" she sang out in warning as John stumbled again, "you heard what I said?"

Her cheeks usually pale were now flushed darkly. I was afraid of her. She seemed ready to treat John just as the boys had treated him. Was she on the side of his tormentors? Their judgements persuaded her even as she rescued her child. She longed for him both to live—and to die. Cold desire rose up in her. If only she knew some way to save this poor child in the future from the abuse and the uselessness which were all that life seemed to offer him. How could she spare John and herself long lifetimes of baffled sorrow? She made him dance along faster than he could, for being such a creature that others mocked and tortured him, at the expense of her pride.

When we reached her house, she said,

"Richard, you are an angel. Please drop John's wet things in the butler's pantry. I am going to take him upstairs to bed. He is having a chill. I'll never be able to thank you enough. Your after-school surprise is on the hall table, an almond chocolate bar. Come over and see John later."

※

But that evening just before my nursery supper when I went to show John the developed prints of the *Mauretania* and Buckingham Palace, his father met me in the living room and said that John was ill—his chill had gone worse. His mother was upstairs with him, and I must not go up.

"Well, Richard," said Howard Burley, "God only knows what they would have done to John if you hadn't come to get his mother. They will catch it, never fear. I have talked to their fathers."

I had been feeling all afternoon a mixture of guilt and fright for having snitched on the boys. Now I was sure they would avenge themselves on me. Something of this must have shown in my face.

"Never fear," said Mr Burley. "Their fathers will see to it that nothing happens to you. Come over and see John tomorrow."

But the next day they said that John was really ill with grippe.

"Did they send for Doctor Grauer?" asked my mother.

"I don't know," I said.

He was our doctor, too, and we would have known his car if he had come to attend to John. But all day nobody came, and the next day, John was worse, and my mother said to my father, with glances that recalled my presence to him which must require elliptical conversation,

"Grippe sometimes goes into pneumonia, you know."

"Yes, I know," replied my father. "But they know how to treat these things."

[59]

"Yes, I know, but sometimes something is needed beyond just home remedies."

"Then Grauer has not yet—?"

"No, not today, either."

"That is odd. Perhaps he isn't so sick as we think."

"Oh, I think so. I talked to Gail today. She is frantic."

"Well."

"But she says she knows what to do. They are doing everything, she says. Everything possible."

"I am sure they are.—Sometimes I can't help thinking that it might be better all around if—"

"Yes, I have too," said my mother hastily, indicating me again. "But of course it must only be God's will."

My father sighed.

I knew exactly what they were talking about, though they thought I didn't.

※

On the third day, John Burley died. My mother told me the news when I reached home after school. She winked both eyes at me as she always did in extremes of feeling. She knelt down and enfolded me. Her lovely heart-shaped face was an image of pity. She knew I knew nothing of death, but some feeling of death came through to me from the intensity of color in her blue eyes. The power of her feeling upset me, and I swallowed as if I were sick when she said,

"Richard, my darling, our dear, poor, little John died this morning. His chill grew worse and worse and finally turned into pneumonia.

They have already taken him away. His mother wanted me to tell you. She loves you for what you tried to do for him."

"Then he's gone?"

"Yes, my dearie, you will never be able to see him again. That is what death means."

I was sobered by these remarks, but I did not weep. I was consumed with wonder, though I was not sure what I wondered about.

There was no funeral. Burial, as they said, was private. I missed John, but I was busy at school, where I was cautious with the Grandvilles and the others until enough days passed after the punishments they had received to assure me that I was safe from their reprisals. Perhaps they wanted to forget that they had given away death in heedless play. Howard Burley went to the office quite as usual. His wife stayed home and saw no one for a while.

"I cannot help wondering," said my mother, "why she never called Doctor Grauer."

"Hush," said my father. "Don't dwell on such things."

But I dwelled on them now and then. They were part of my knowledge on the day when Gail Burley asked my mother to send me to see her after school.

"Mrs Burley has some things of John's that she wants to give you. You were his best friend."

I knew all his toys. Some of them were glorious. I saw them all in mind again. I went gladly to see his mother.

The housemaid let me in and sent me upstairs to Mrs Burley's sitting room. She was reclining against many lacy pillows on a *chaise longue* in the bay window. She was paler than ever, and perhaps thinner, and there was a new note in her voice which made her seem like a stranger—a huskiness which reflected lowered vitality. She embraced me and said,

"Do you miss John?"

"Yes."

"Poor little John."

Her hazel eyes were blurred for a moment and she looked away out the window into the rustling treetops of autumn, as though to conceal both emotion and knowledge from me. "Oh, my God," I heard her say softly. Then she let forth one of her controlled breaths, annoyed at her own weakness as it lay embedded in the general condition of the world, and said with revived strength,

"Well, Richard, let's be sensible. Come and pick out the toys you want in John's nursery. What you don't take I am going to send to Father Raker's Orphanage."

She led me along the upstairs hall to John's room. His toys were laid out in rows, some on the window seat, the rest on the floor.

"I suppose I could say that you should just take them all," she said with one of her unwilling smiles, "but I think that would be selfish of us both. Go ahead and pick."

With the swift judgement of the expert, I chose a beautiful set of Pullman cars for my electric train which had the same track as John's, and a power boat with mahogany cabin and real glass portholes draped in green velvet curtains, and a battalion of lead soldiers with red coats and black busbys and white cross belts tumbled together in their box who could be set smartly on parade, and a set of water color paints, and a blackboard on its own easel with a box of colored chalks. These, and so much else in the room, spoke of attempts to reward John for what he was not—and, for what they were not, the parents, too. I looked up at his mother. She was watching me as if never to let me go.

"Your cheeks are so flushed," she said, "and it is adorable the way the light makes a gold ring on your hair when you bend down. Richard, come here."

She took me in her hungry arms. I felt how she trembled. There was much to make her tremble.

"Do you want anything else?" she asked, again becoming sensible, as she would have said. Her concealed intensity made me lose mine.

"No, thank you, Mrs Burley."

"Well, you can take your new toys home whenever you like. You can't carry them all at once."

"I'll take the boat now," I said.

"All right. Garsh, it's big, isn't it. John loved to sail it when we went to Narragansett."

She took me downstairs to the door. There she lingered. She wanted to say something. She could have said it to an adult. How could she say it to me? Yet most grown people spoke to me as if I were far older than my years. Leaning her back against the door, with her hands behind her on the doorknob, and with her face turned upward, so that I saw her classical white throat and the curve of her cheek until it was lost in the golden shadows of her eye, she said,

"Richard, I wonder if you would ever understand—you knew, didn't you, surely, that our poor little John was not like other children?"

"Sometimes, yes."

"His father and I suffered for him, seeing how hard it was for him with other children; and then we thought of how it would have to be when he grew up—do you know?"

I nodded, though I did not know, really.

"We are heartbroken to lose him, you must know that. He was all we had. But do you know, we sometimes wonder if it is better that God took him, even if we had to lose him. Do you know?"

She looked down at me as if to complete her thought through her golden piercing gaze. When she saw the look of horror on my face, she caught her breath. Conventional, like all children, I was amazed that anyone should be glad of death, if that meant not seeing someone ever again

[63]

"Oh, Richard, don't judge us yet for feeling that way. When you grow up and see more of what life does to those who cannot meet it, you will understand." She was obsessed. Without naming it, she must speak of the weight on her heart, even if only to me, a first-grader in school. In my ignorance, perhaps I might be the only safe one in whom to confide. "Garsh, when you see cripples trying to get along, and sick people who can never get well, you wonder why they can't be spared, and just die."

The appalling truth was gathering in me. I stared at her, while she continued,

"John was always frail, and when those horrid boys turned on him, and he caught that chill, and it went into pneumonia, his father and I did everything to save him, but it was not enough. We had to see him go."

Clutching John's beautiful power boat in both arms, I cowered a little away from her and said,

"You never sent for a doctor, though."

A sharp silence cut its way between us. She put one hand on her breast and held herself. At last she said in a dry, bitter voice,

"Is that what is being said, then?"

"Doctor Grauer always comes when I am sick."

She put her hand to her mouth. Her eyes were afire like those of a trapped cat.

"Richard?" she whispered against her fingers, "what are you thinking? Don't you believe we loved John?"

I said, inevitably,

"Did you have him die?"

At this she flew into a golden, speckled fury. She reached for me to chastise me, but I eluded her. I was excited by her and also frightened. Her eyes blazed with shafted light. I managed to dance away beyond her reach, but I was encumbered by the beautiful power cruiser in my arms. I let it crash to the floor. I heard its glass break.

Escape and safety meant more to me just then than possession of the wonderful boat. I knew the house. I ran down the hall to the kitchen and out the back door to my own yard, and home, out of breath, frightened by what I had exposed.

𝖲

The Burleys never again spoke to my parents or to me. My parents wondered why, and even asked, but received no explanation. All of John's toys went to Father Raker's. In a few weeks the Burleys put up their house for sale, in a few months Howard retired from business, and they went to live in Florida for the rest of their lives.

✻

CHAPTER IV

Far Kingdoms

I did not then recognize what I had so heedlessly exposed—the power of truth, which if it can create can also destroy.

But all growth is discovery of power—or powers. Language is one of these. The first time I ever heard anyone use the expression, "How dare you!" I thought I had never heard anything so splendid. Language became an instrument of power; style entered into character; and I learned how I might be someone else just by sounding different or special. From creating someone else for who I was, it was not much of a step to creating all sorts of other beings who could be believed in, if someone might only know of them. The artist must first create, and then communicate. But who would listen? Who would see?

✻

One day my mother and I were on a streetcar coming home from the Catholic Union Library where we went for books every week or two—children's books for me at seven years old; Mrs Humphrey Ward, Edith Wharton, H. G. Wells, Monsignor Robert Hugh Benson for my parents.

It was a winter afternoon with brown slush on the streets and wan daylight failing into gaslight in the streetlamps with their mantles. People were hurrying home for the night.

The car was crowded. My mother held me on her lap to make room for someone else who came to sit next to us—a small, grey man with meek-looking eyeglasses and grey cloth gloves. His eyes watered from the cold—it was a heavy winter in Dorchester that year—and he kept making apologetic little sounds deep in his head behind his nose as he tried to clear congested air passages. He stared straight ahead and held himself stiffly. Just in front of us sat two small children who were taking care of each other as they were riding the car alone. Holding on to each other like waifs in a fairy tale, they occupied the space for one adult.

After one of its clanging stops, the car admitted a stout woman who came down the aisle like a blind force of nature, perhaps like a flow of congealing lava, making bulbous entries with her round hard shapes through apertures of the passenger crowd, to their murmured discomfort.

She came toiling toward us and when she saw the two children seated in front of us, she leaned down and with her huge red naked hand, which was packed with hard fat under shining, cracked skin, she pushed the children off the seat and squeezed past them to take their place, giving forth a loud, tired sigh. The children began to cry, standing together in an embrace. The small proper man next to us instantly stood up and leaned over the fat woman and said,

"Madam, how dare you do a thing like that!"

His eyeglasses now blazed with strong light which must have come from his little eyes, and his grey silk hands, now made into claws, trembled in the air beside his suddenly pink face. Transformed, he was a champion. He created opinion. People stirred in approval of his rebuke. I stared at him with awe.

The woman, now swollen further with added ill temper which

seemed to roil within her to find a way to emerge, as through a pustule which had not yet been formed, began to mutter, scowling straight ahead,

"I'll slap him to bits; see if I don't, the nasty little dandy!"

"Come, Richard," said my mother, who hated to witness any loss of grace, "we must start for the door. We must get off next. Hold tight to your books."

It would mean walking an extra block or two. Keeping over my shoulder with my gaze as much of the drama as I could until we left the car, I never knew what happened next. But enough had been discovered for me to know that I, like the mouse-grey man on the streetcar, could be anybody I wanted to be. Some of the consequences came to pass later in the winter when my Uncle Frederick appeared in Dorchester for a week.

芃

His work—his need—in life was to create transports of excitement for others. It was a dangerous magic, as at moments he seemed to know, yet he exercised it fully, with charm.

In evening, in winter, when the lamps were turned on, and the newel post in the downstairs hall upheld a lighted moon below me, just before bedtime I stood on the upper landing, gazing down, but not gazing, really—pouring myself, rather, through my eyes which must have looked huge and dark blue, and not standing, really, but almost dancing in eagerness and excitement within my dark red velours bathrobe and white flannel pajamas, while the joy of waiting was equalled by its anxiety.

For who was it who was arriving outside, in a carriage with horses, and who came in from the snow, was received and divested while snowflakes fell like little stars to the floor, and who then turned slowly, looked up, saw me, extended both hands upward and exclaimed, in a rich voice trained to convey loving expectation, among other emotions, including fulfilled joy,

"Ri-chard!"

How he said it gave my very name a new value which I would never forget. In that instant I became more Richard than ever, and to be Richard in just that way, called alive by that persuasive, grown-up voice, was to be the most desirable being in the world, and thus the most fortunate.

My Uncle Frederick came laughing up to me taking the stairs two at a time, and embraced my hot, striving person which was now suffused with a sense of its own dearness and worth. Then letting me go,

"Ha! my king!" he cried in his crackling, dark voice, falling to one knee and sweeping his right arm awide as he made a fast, courtly bow, "I have high and glorious matters for your ear. Full many a day have I hasted hither to give you news of your far kingdom, and it now me rejoices to pay Your Majesty my homage and my love."

"Fritz?" called my mother from the real world downstairs in a laughing irritation at his nonsense, for she knew its every possibility as his older sister, "do let him go to bed and come down and wash your hands and have your cocktail. Dan will be home any minute."

Uncle Fritz closed his eyes in comic patience, and then looked at me again, with a wink, to make us conspirators, and said,

"Let them run their world, Richard, my lord, and we will make our own.—I'll come upstairs again to tuck you in after I have been polite below."

I doubt if he ever left anybody without a promise of some sort, and it is known only in heaven—or hell—how many he ever kept. He was an actor, and his play was on tour, and he would be in Dorchester for two weeks, playing at the Shubert Theatre. I had been promised a matinee performance so that I could see him on the stage. My mother was more interested in seeing the once-great, and still famous, actress who had chosen him as her leading man in her present play, which was a period piece laid in Tudor England.

Uncle Fritz was like my mother in many ways, but the ways were exaggerated. His charm was like hers, darting and impulsive, but raised at times to invite rather than bestow admiration. His ruddy face had the same heart-shape as my mother's, though wider and longer. Under the heavy, dark eyebrows of the family, his eyes were blue, and could blaze like prisms with diamond-blue fire in the spotlight. Trimly made, he was very vain of his fine shoulders and legs. He moved swiftly, unless for dazzling effect he made long, grave gestures intended to be sombrely meaningful—though what about, did not always seem clear. His lips were full and his jaw was somewhat heavy, with chin thrust forward habitually. When he looked solemn, the world darkened for those with him, and when he smiled, his smile was repeated—sometimes reluctantly—on every face that saw him. Like all actors he was everybody and he was nobody. Who he was the first time I saw him I remember still. It was at the house of my grandmother—his mother.

She was still living, though she could not leave her bed, or speak, or move any part of her person except her eyelids. For twelve years she had lain in her bed in the front drawing room of my grandfather's house. One day long before I was born her carriage horse had run away, she had been thrown out and dragged, and paralysis resulted. Her patience was saintly—so much that it sometimes irritated those of her children who took care of her, for their inability to equal it. I was taken to see her once a week, and when I was four, I played on the flowered carpeting of her room, making public buildings out of a set of dusty red, blue and yellow stone blocks which included turret shapes, and pinnacles, and arches, as well as ordinary squares and oblongs.

From the front drawing room you could look down the whole depth of the house through a series of doors to other rooms—a sitting room, a parlor, a little library—until you saw the dining room at the far end. It was a perspective in miniature of the Kaiser's palace in Berlin, which my grandfather had visited one time to receive an imperial decoration for being a proper specimen of German culture in the United States. He brought home postcard views of the palace and used to show them to me as I sat on his slippery alpaca lap. If I held the cards close to my face until they blurred slightly, I could imagine that the receding doors in perspective were those of my grandfather's house in Dorchester. The farthest room seemed immeasurably far to me at four, and what might show there, if it was at all unusual, could be startling, and perhaps terrifying.

※

One Sunday morning I was building a railroad station on my grandmother's rug when I looked up idly and glanced along the long view through the tunnel of doors. What I saw made the blocks fall from my fingers.

In the dining room, infinitely far away, loomed an irregular

[71]

pillar of black which soon took the aspect of a giant. It was robed all in black and it wore a black hat with odd flaring planes that stood upright on top. Smoke clouded its head and face. It posed for a moment in the farthest doorway and then began to move in gliding elegant strides down the rooms toward me. As it came by windows in the third room, then the second, it passed through zones of light, and then after each doorway it entered relative darkness, with changing effect and aspect. I fell back and my throat closed in dry terror so that I could not free the scream that filled me. Still the black column wreathed in smoke moved toward me, making long human steps. As it reached the door of the front room, I was thrown into action at last.

"Grossma, Grossma," I cried so forcefully that my voice split into two notes, "save me, save me, it is the Devil!"

I threw myself upon my grandmother's immense bed and burrowed into her vast, pitiably inert shape, sobbing. She made the only sound she could make—a dove-like mourning note that fell and fell each time, by which she meant to comfort me. My shrieks continued and I dared not look up or around until my mother, in answer to my fright, came and took me up. She was laughing till the tears ran down her cheeks as she soothed me, while I kept up my cry of,

"It is the Devil, the Devil!"

"Nonsense, Richard, my darling, it is your Uncle Fritz, home from the seminary for the weekend. Now come and see him and give him a kiss and be friends.—Fritz, now do be sweet to him. He is really frightened."

"It is a new experience," said my Uncle Fritz, "to be mistaken for the Devil himself while studying for the priesthood and wearing its habit."

For his career had started with a determination to become a priest, a great philosopher, and eventually a bishop. His father told him he must absolutely become a bishop, and this was a command to be obeyed. I had never seen him before. Other priests who had come to our house were dressed in black suits, never in black cassocks and birettas like my uncle. I looked at him now with subsiding grief. But if resentment was mixed with the drying salt of my tears, wonder grew as I was exposed to his comic charm.

"Yet I suppose," he said, "with my black skirts and the cigar smoke around my head, he might be excused for his conclusion. And what if he were right, after all? Out of the mouths of babes." He seemed to look inward for a moment, escaping us all, while he murmured, "*Ora pro nobis, nunc et in hora.*" When his features lost their animation, they sagged. But he brightened resolutely, and cried, "Come on, my cherub," taking me from my mother, "let us get acquainted. Did you ever see smoke come out of anyone's eyes? Then I will show you."

He sat down and put me facing him on his knees and took a mouthful of cigar smoke and held it behind shut lips, and then brought his face slowly to mine and when we were eyelash to lash he released a wisp of smoke which drifted upward and truly seemed to come right out of his eyes.

"Did you see?" he asked.

"Yes."

"Now watch my ear—this one, the right one."

And he made me see smoke come out of his right ear, just because he said it would.

"Now watch me build a cathedral," he said, and began to twine his fingers so that the two middle ones remained upright together making a spire.

"Now see the front doors," he said, and showed how he could open his bent thumbs apart to make an entrance.

"Now look inside and see the bishop," and he wriggled a finger

[73]

which hung downward in the little pink darkness of his cupped palms.

I began to smile grudgingly.

"Why don't you try it?" he asked, and I began to fumble a cathedral into existence with my fingers, while Uncle Fritz corrected me and helped me until I too had a steeple, and church doors, and a bishop jigging upside down within.

By afternoon we were intensely friends, and later in the day one of his classmates came to visit, and the two talked Latin conversationally in front of all the family, until grown-up sisters and brothers looked at each other in marvelling pride which they did not try to conceal from the gratified seminarians. But I remember thinking, as I heard their florid rumbling Latin which sounded like nothing I had ever heard, "They are just making it all up."

Before supper, while the household gathered behind him on their knees, Uncle Fritz knelt by my grandmother's bed and led us in the recitation of the rosary. His voice rose and rang and fell in such power and style that everyone was more certain than ever that he must become the youngest bishop in the land.

But within a year he was no longer even a seminarian, for what reason nobody was told at home. But my grandfather must have known in patriarchal anger, for he never again spoke to that son, who in some way mortal to sanctity had betrayed the family vocation for the lordly office of bishop. Presently Uncle Fritz found his next vocation, which was for the theatre.

He went on the stage, as they used to say, and more rapidly than most young actors he attained to leading roles. The fact was, even in the seminary days, he had always been an actor. His devil-magic kept up, and on his return to Dorchester as leading man in *The Tudor Rose* he had his opportunity to achieve his masterpiece for me. For magic to succeed, there must be one who reveals and one who believes. I believed every word and every act he revealed to me.

On his arrival at our house that winter evening he had made me a king. How did he know that in my time of childhood my only proper companions were kings and queens, who lived in castles, went hunting, presided at tournaments, gave orders, and wore their crowns all day long? The make-believe was more plausible than the real, and it was so precious that I revealed bits of it only accidentally to my parents and to Anna. But Uncle Fritz needed to be told nothing about me. He knew who I really was.

"Are you about ready to go to sleep?" he asked when he came upstairs after waiting to greet my father.

"No."

"They will be furious with me if I keep you awake. You must go to sleep."

"You said a far kingdom."

"I did?"

"Yes, when you came. You said my far kingdom. But you didn't tell me what."

"Yes, of course." To invent was as easy for him as to be. "They are waiting for Your Majesty. The people go on long pilgrimages from castle to castle, hoping to find Your Majesty in each one, but they never do. I have heard them pray for your return. The Cardinal sings a Te Deum in the Cathedral every evening for you. The poor hold up their arms and beg in your name. The rich nobles laugh at them and say that as long as they have anything to say, Your Majesty will never return to the kingdom."

"Why?"

He gave a velvety, sardonic laugh.

"Because so long as you are the Young Lost King, they will be able to have all the jewels and the gold and the castles for themselves, and they do not care what happens to your poor people."

"They don't?"

I stirred under my covers with love of my poor people and my heart felt hot at the injustices visited upon them which I would redress.

"No. It is a beautiful kingdom and the wicked nobles have stolen it."

"Where is it?"

"Beyond the Sapphire Mountains and at the edge of the Emerald Sea. If you shut your eyes tight you might be able to see it, far away, far away, so that everything is tiny, but perfectly clear. The people will look five inches tall, and their castles will be no higher than a chair, and their hunting horns will sound like mosquitoes outside your ear. But they are all as real as real, like everybody and everything, only small, because they are far away. I think you will be able to see them if you become perfectly still and perhaps fall asleep."

"When?"

"Oh, we never know when these things will happen. We only know they will happen. We must be patient. The Young Lost King is always patient, and in the end, he always enters into his kingdom."

"He does?"

"But certainly."

"I see."

"And now before they make me go downstairs again, I must tell you about seeing a real king and queen."

I felt real, in my kingship, of course, but I knew, too, that we had been acting, and if he had seen a living king and queen I must hear about it.

"I have been in London, you know, playing at the Haymarket Theatre. I had a splendid part, and the critics were kind. We had a great success "

"What is a haymarket theatre?"

"Oh, you are not to think of cows and horses and barns, Richard. It is just an old name for a very old playhouse in London. Well, one day the company had word that the King and Queen of England were supposed to come to see our play, and sit in the royal box, and receive us afterward to say good evening."

"Did they come?"

"They came. The orchestra played *God Save the King* and everybody stood and faced the royal box and in they came, bowing right and left. I looked out through a peep-hole in the curtain. They were magnificent. When the curtain went up and the play began we all played better than we knew how to. I gave the performance of my life."

"What is that?"

"I acted my best."

"I see."

"All during the play we did not look directly at the King and Queen in the royal box, but just the same we kept seeing them, you know how you can do, out of the side of your eye? And when I was off the stage I could look from the wings. They loved us."

"They did?"

"Yes, and when the play was done, three or four of us were sent for to be congratulated, and of course I was one of them. The King shook hands and the Queen bowed. See this hand? It has shaken the hand of the King of England. Don't you want to shake it? Your Majesty is also a king. I am collecting quite a number of kings."

We shook hands seriously. I said,

"What did they look like?"

"Oh, like a real king and queen. He has a brown beard, and blue eyes, and he wore medals and stars, he looks like his cousin the Czar of Russia, and she has golden hair, dressed up high, and she glittered and sparkled with jewels like water in the sun. Her face is rosy pink. I am taller than both of them."

"Did they wear their crowns?"

"Not all the time. Sometimes they took them off and gave them to someone behind their chairs to hold for them. Crowns are very heavy, you know."

"Why?"

"Did you ever weigh a diamond?"

What a master he was—asking me this as though it would be the most natural thing on earth for me to weigh diamonds.

"No," I said, stirring with satisfaction.

"Open your hand," he commanded, and drew from his finger a large amethyst surrounded by small diamonds set in a gold ring. He dropped the ring from a little height into my palm where it struck with weight and force the most part of which I endowed it with. "You see how heavy this one amethyst and these eleven small diamonds are? Well: imagine one hundred and eighty-seven diamonds, and dozens of pearls, rubies, sapphires and emeralds all clustered together on a crown. Very heavy indeed."

"What did you do then?"

"Then? Oh, I simply bowed very deeply, and murmured something like this—*Your Majesties do us immense honor,* which made them glance at each other. I think they will remember me."

"Did they have a royal coach?"

"Of course. All glass and gold. It was waiting outside all that time."

"Did you watch them drive away?"

"Oh, no. I simply let them go. But it was a charming moment. And now, Sire, if I may have your permission to withdraw, it must be time for your royal slumbers?"

He bowed by my bed.

"Is that how you bowed to them?" I asked.

"Yes. Like this"—and he repeated his courtly grace. "Good night. You will have the royal box at my Wednesday matinee. Everything is arranged."

"Good night, Uncle Fritz."

"No, no, you should call me Prime Minister."

"Good night, Prime Minister."

"That's better. Good night, Your Majesty."

I was so drugged with golden visions and intimations of royal power and privilege that I could not stay awake for my father's usual bedtime visit.

❦

In the morning I heard remarks at breakfast. It seemed that Uncle Fritz had stayed very late and had left for his hotel in a condition of extreme intoxication. They didn't see how he would ever be able to open his play tonight.

"I wonder when this started," said my mother.

"I saw it several years ago," said my father. "About the time he had that trouble with your father. He was drinking heavily then but he tried to hide it. Now he doesn't seem to care who knows."

"Do you suppose that was why the seminary had to—?"

"It could be. Anyhow, we don't know, and we won't find out by wondering, and furthermore, it is not our affair."

"Did you know he tried to see Papa this time?"

"No. What happened?"

"Papa refused to see him. Fritz then sent him tickets to the play. Papa returned them."

"It does seem rather hard, doesn't it."

"Oh, yes. But when Papa makes up his—"

"It isn't his mind. It is something else. Not his mind."

She sighed.

Much of what you hear means nothing until afterward, when events make it significant. Uncle Fritz remained for me the Prime Minister who alone in the world knew me for my true person and position—the Young Lost King, who would one day return to my people, and be acclaimed with bells, fireworks, prayers and fountains, ending with my marriage in the cathedral to the beautiful princess from the neighboring kingdom who need sorrow no more for my return.

※

On Wednesday morning when I awoke the day was lost in a blizzard. I ran to the window to see the wonder of it—wind made visible by long whistling veils of snow, and ice cunningly fixed upon every branch and twig of my bedroom window tree, and a gray light beating with the wind upon everything. And then I had a second thought which was anguished—what if we could not go to the matinee in weather like that?

And in fact, this was already the decision when I went down to breakfast.

"Unless the storm breaks," declared my father.

"Oh, no, this is going to last all day," said Anna, dreamily putting our plates before us. "I know the signs. You catch your death going out in this."

"Then will you stay home?" I asked my father with a pang of hope—for if he stayed home we could play together all day.

"Oh, no. I'll have to be at the office regardless. I'll get to the corner and see if a streetcar is running."

[80]

All morning I watched with desire for the storm to stop. About noon the light turned from silver to gold, and presently the phone rang. It was my father calling to say that if the livery stable could send a carriage for us, and wait all afternoon to bring us home, we could go to the Shubert Theatre.

It was still snowing, but gently, when we set out, and the day was now wet and raw where before it had been lashed with wind from the lake. At the theatre we were expected. A man in a cutaway coat led us to the right stage box.

"The royal box," he announced with a smile. "We were particularly told to have it ready for a certain young gentleman."

"Thank you," said my mother a little sharply. She was suspicious of Uncle Fritz's games with me; she was uneasy at the intensity of my imagined state.

We were alone in the box, whose high, red velvet drapings, caught up in thick loops of gold rope with heavy tassels, and golden armchairs cushioned in red velvet, and red velvet footstools, and a chandelier of crystals hanging directly above us, all seemed to me so fine that they made an excellent place to live, day and night, particularly for a king. In those days theatres imitated the airs of palaces, which had been their ancestors in society.

When the house went dark and the curtain rose releasing a bath of light from another world over all who watched and listened, I was lost even to my kingship. The play was full of great halls with leaded, mullioned windows, and ruffs and farthingales, and rapiers and daggers and small jewelled caskets of secret papers, and a traitorous cardinal, and a noble royal lady—played by the cat-nosed old actress who was the star—and a reckless hotblood of a young nobleman—my Uncle Fritz—who threw himself into risk of the king's wrath to serve her, if "he might but gain her lily hand to kiss."

I leaned on the red velvet rail of the box and poured myself to the stage. It was my first play. It gave me another life again. My uncle was my uncle, that was clear; but he was also that raking young lord with his trimmed small mustaches and beard, just put on for the play, who could cross the floor of the great hall in four grand strides, and spring his rapier from its leather baldric while he tensed himself against the tapestry of the wall until he heard who came, and when who came was only a page boy dressed in white hose and white silk doublet bringing a letter heavy with red wax seals, a sudden new air of lovely ease came over all, and when they on the stage took a deep breath of gallant relief, so, obediently, did I.

The page fell to one knee and bent his head, showering his pale gold long hair forward by his cheeks, and surrendered his letter to my lord. I then and there became that page boy, for he must have been my age, and yet there he was, in white light and white court dress, nimbly using the stage with his slim elegantly covered legs, speaking in a clear light voice, inhabiting a Tudor palace, and taking all eyes to himself for the moments while he was before us. I was riven with stabs of love for the circumstance of such a life. I mourned that I was not a page boy exactly like that other one, and I thought that I must run away and become an actor. My mother felt my forehead. It was hot. She made a little breathy sigh, wondering if she should take me home.

At the curtain call after the first act, my uncle, with tender gallantry mixed with teasing comedy, led the star forward to the footlights; and when the applause swelled over them, he bowed not to the audience but exclusively to her, which drove the applause fuller and louder, so that when he came at last alone to bow, he was acclaimed as a great gentleman as well as a dashing actor. But he was not yet done with his people, for when they called him back again, he walked straight to the apron of the stage below the royal box and bowed to me the way he had bowed to the King of England.

"Oh! that monkey!" exclaimed my mother, who disliked for us to be conspicuous in any way not playfully devised by herself.

The audience clapped harder when they saw this, not knowing why they must do so. Some genius of the occasion filled me. I rose and bowed back to my uncle, and I was restored, in that gesture, in public, to my royal if secret estate. The curtain fell to a buzz of speculation. I went limp against the cushions of my chair.

"What is it, darling?" asked my mother.

"Nothing." I wanted only to be alone with my dreams.

"I think you're catching cold."

She felt my face.

"Why, Richard, you're burning up! Come, my dearie, we must go."

"Oh, no."

We had not seen all—the curtain promised to rise again, this time upon a forest glade by moonlight, for the program said so, and the golden page would return, and with him, whom I loved as myself, or who made me love myself as him, would return more of that power to create which stirred within me ever since the scene on the streetcar, a power which my Uncle Fritz—my Prime Minister—drove so strongly into action for me.

"I am afraid we must," said my mother. "You are coming down with something."

At this moment an usher of the theatre brought a folded note with a superscription written in a florid hand. It read, "To His Majesty." The usher handed the note to me but my mother took it from me and read it before I could try.

"Thank you," she said to the usher, "please say that we shall be unable to come backstage after the play as my little boy is ill and I must take him home."

"But I want to stay," I pleaded. "I want to meet the boy in the white clothes and ask him about things."

My mother smiled and dismissed the usher with a firm little nod.

Hurrying me to our carriage, she behaved as though she were rescuing me from evil.

By the time we reached home my fever was like a storm continuously breaking over my perception and wiping it out. I was put to bed, Doctor Grauer was summoned, and when my father reached home late in the evening through delayed traffic in the snow, there was even talk of sending for a nurse to stay by all night. But finally my parents took turns sitting by me in a deep armchair, dozing and listening all night while a little blue glass votive lamp with its candle cast a wavering light over the Holy Mother of God who was present in a delicate blue and gold statue on the wall opposite my bed.

※

That night was the first of many nights of high, clear, loving fantasy, when I felt weightless and insubstantial.

In the mornings I was exhausted but sane for a little while as the fever dropped with daylight. They would take me up soaking wet and bathe me with alcohol and change my pajamas and put me down again, and I would lie gazing at the complicated construction which stood on a low table beside my bed.

It was something I had made weeks earlier—a castle of cardboard overlaid with a thick coating of rock-grey plasticene. The walls and turrets, the battlements, great keep, deep court, and moat showed carefully marked lines of masonry, for with an orange stick given to me by my mother I had incised in the plasticene the shape of every stone in the castle. Painted banners hung from the towers and one wall could be swung aside to reveal the great hall where on a dais stood thrones for a king and queen.

Could the fever—could Uncle Fritz alone—wholly account for the vision of life which now rose so abundantly in me? They could only reveal what I had already created. For a whole week of my illness I could not say where the familiar truth of life ended or where the other world of my creative fever began.

For I was the host of a vision that persisted, and I knew that what I saw and what lived with me were my own creations—the children and the wards of my own fathering. I believed in them so hungrily that I dared to speak of them to my father and mother, certain that they must see as I saw.

"There, in the castle," I said. "Do you see them?"

"Who? What?" they asked fondly.

"The people," I said. "They are just the right size to live in the castle. They are there all the time. They talk to me and I talk to them. They go about doing things and I watch them. Don't you hear them? Don't you see them?"

They comforted me and gave me a drink of cool water and told me to be quiet and go to sleep, now, sleep now, Richard, Richard.

It made my head hurt with bewilderment that they refused to understand how what I told them of was actual, and dear beyond saying. My people. The castle was inhabited by a population of tiny creatures, all exquisitely lovely, all perfectly made in miniature as human beings, and all alive. I thought of them as elves, and in the dazzling and aching logic of my fever, I said to myself that I had read of elfland in many stories, all of which stated that elves lived long ago and did delightful deeds; and if they lived long ago, what was to prevent their living again right now? Imagined into being by myself, they populated the castle as king and queen, and courtiers, and men at arms, and ladies in tall cone-like headpieces from which long veils swept to the stone floor of the great hall, and pages in white who stood by the throne when the king and queen were seated there, and who otherwise played games and pranks up and down the stone stairways which led to the battlements within the walls.

I had only to turn my head on my pillow to see the life of the castle in all its intent glistening activity.

One night in the blue wavering light of Our Lady some of my exquisite little ones brought a long and narrow plank with which they made a bridge from the castle to my bed. They then marched across it to visit me. The king and queen came, and the ladies of the court, and spearmen and bannermen, and the pages with their tiny greyhounds as if they were going out to hunt, and a huntsman in green on a dancing grey horse who raised his horn and wound a call through the night. They spoke to me and I answered, they gave me love and I returned love, the love that had begot them. They told me to sleep peacefully and to get well, and I promised to. The king asked if I would sleep sooner and better if he ordered his knights to make a jousting play for me on my bedspread, and I nodded. In a twinkling the bed became a plain and the court took their places at one side under the shelter of my long legs. The knights entered the lists and in exquisite animation charged each other with lances forward. The clash when they met was like the distant breaking of thin glass, a music of elfland, and they charged and charged. Presently the meadow of the bedspread darkened until it seemed that a storm was coming and would break. At a gesture from the king, the company withdrew in brave display to the castle. The bridge was withdrawn; the castle wall closed after them; a few torches showed in the archers' deep lancet windows and then went out and the storm passed and moonlight like the lamp of Our Lady broke over the silent towers and when my people were all asleep and safe, it was safe for me then to go to sleep myself, feeling my mother's cool hand on my brow, and hearing her tell my father,

"The dream is gone. He is quiet again."

[86]

"It seemed like a happy dream."

"Yes. But exhausting, just the same."

But I knew that the world I made was not merely a dream that could be dismissed with a thankful word from relieved parents.

※

Toward the end of last week Uncle Fritz was allowed to come to see me for a few minutes. Evidently he had been cautioned not to excite my imagination with too much powerful suggestion of his own world. Even so I was still the Young Lost King, and sitting down beside me he nodded gravely over my castle, and said,

"That, of course, is where Your Majesty lives for the moment?"

"It is mine."

"You have many men at arms, and archers, and huntsmen?"

How did he know?

"Can you see them?" I asked eagerly. "They come to see me mostly at night. In the daytime the castle is closed."

"Very properly. Tell me, what are they like?"

I told him how high they stood—the king was the tallest, five inches high. They were all perfectly made, just like anyone big, but tiny, and perfectly dressed in the proper clothes for each. When they spoke to me they had to come close to my ear, but I could hear them clearly, and they told me of the treasure deep in the castle dungeons, which they promised to bring out and show me one night. They all wished to serve me, and begged me to say what I would have them do, but I had asked nothing of them but their loyalty, until now. But now I would tell them something very great which they must do for me.

If my father and mother refused to believe in them, I would ask them to prove they were real by showing themselves to someone else—to my Uncle Fritz.

"Open the castle," I said.

"But it is only afternoon," he protested.

"Yes, but, yes, but I want you to see the people."

"Won't they hide if they see me?"

"I will tell them not to."

"Has anybody else seen them?"

"My father and mother didn't see them. They don't believe they are there at all."

Uncle Fritz sighed fastidiously. His breath carried a sharp, sweet smell of whiskey across my bed.

"No," he said like one of the few in the world who understood the laws of creation, "how could they unless they saw them? And of course they wouldn't be able to see them unless they believed the tiny people were really there."

"But you do, don't you, Uncle Fritz?"

"But of course, if you tell me you have seen them. —Come, let us see."

Following my finger where I pointed, he leaned down to the castle and opened the wall. I saw my people, as usual.

"Do you see them?" I asked.

"But of course. —I must speak to the king."

He bent close to the great hall, making his stage face of excited interest, with his huge blue eyes wide open under a delighted scowl. He thinned his voice until it was just a thread of sound, quite suitable for conversing with elfin royalty, and said,

"I am immensely honored to be received by Your Majesties"—he turned to whisper swiftly to me that the queen was there too—"and I am deeply grateful for all you have done for my lord, the Young Lost King. He is not well at the moment, but when he is completely recovered, surely Your Majesties and your people will help him to find his kingdom again."

Such was his power that I watched him, instead of the king and queen in the castle, to whom he spoke. He turned his ear to hear their reply, and when he had it, he repeated it for me, saying,

"They say they will of course place all their treasure at your disposal, and all their warriors, to help Your Majesty come into his own kingdom. They say that until then you are welcome to live in the castle with them, where you will be treated with royal honors."

"Don't they think I am too big?"

"But if you went to live in the castle, you would be just as small as they are, while you were there."

"Oh," I cried, "let me go right now."

Burning with delight, I began to climb from my bed.

"Oh, no," he said, "I wouldn't do that just yet—the king meant that after you got well, you could decide to—"

"Right now!" I said loudly, and began to struggle against him as he held me in my bed.

"No, Richard, please—"

Our small commotion brought my mother.

"Oh, Fritz, what have you done to him! I told you not to excite him!—Here, darling," she said, taking me against her breast as she knelt by the bed, "be quiet and rest now. Uncle Fritz has been here long enough. He must go now and you must lie down and be quiet for Doctor Grauer when he comes."

"He told me I could go to live in the castle!" I insisted, weakly breaking into tears.

My mother gave her brother a look of worried annoyance and with a little imperious lift of her head, commanded him to leave the room.

"Yes, then," he said. "Goodbye, my lord," and made his bow, throwing his arm away and bending deep. "We are leaving town after the play tonight; but before I go I shall write to the King and Queen of England about you. You will hear from them."

"I will?"

"They will write to you."

"When?"

"Fritz—?" said my mother.

"Yes, I am hasted away," he said, with a glaring smile under a meaningless frown, "adieu, my lord. *Do not believe what they will say of me when I am gone!*"

He went to the door, turned, bowed again with his hand up like a statue's—and then even while I watched under his spell, he vanished. I did not see him so much as take a step or turn into the hall past the doorway—he was there one moment, and the next he was gone. My mother murmured,

"Lie down, my dearie, that was just what he used to call his vanishing trick when we were children at home. He practiced it for days on end. It was a terribly quick sidestep which was so fast you hardly saw him move. Now be easy and dear and do not think of magic any more, or things like that."

"When will the King and Queen of England write to me?"

She made a furious little sigh at the mischief her brother must plant in any mind he met, and said,

"How can I possibly say? Now sleep."

"But I want to know!"

"Hush."

※

I awoke during the night. I felt cool and tired but substantial. The fever was gone. I would soon be ready to enter the castle, assuming the proper size in which to live with my creatures who loved me and whom I loved.

I turned to the castle and opened the wall, eager to tell my people of my good fortune and theirs. There was no one there. The castle was empty. Everyone had gone. All the rest of the night I lay awake, begging them to return. Where were they? Who had taken them away? In the morning my motner found me sitting up, quite restored to the world, but unhappy beyond telling.

"Oh, you are better—so much better!" she exclaimed. "But what is the matter?"

"They are all gone."

"Who?"

I motioned toward the castle which I could not bear to look at now.

"Ah, Richard, Richard, it was the fever, it was a dream. Never mind, darling. You will not miss them in a day or two."

"But they were mine!"

"Of course. —Now let us see about some lovely cold orange juice and breakfast. Doctor Grauer will be so pleased."

And so I continued all day to recover in my sorrow. It was Sunday, and my father was home. He said that we would all have a picnic lunch in my room. I ate very little, and soon felt drowsy, and lay down, and dozed, while my parents finished their lunch slowly, drinking Rhine wine with seltzer and talking gently. They were sitting in the bay window, which made a little sounding shell for their voices. They could not know how much I might hear.

I was alerted from my disconsolate nap when my father said impatiently,

"I am glad he has gone. He is a bad influence on Richard. It is one thing when a child makes up people and places, but to have some grown man dazzle him with deliberate nonsense and unreality—this is dangerous."

"We always saw it in him at home," said my mother.

"And what's more, he drinks far too much."

"Yes, he told me that coming home to Dorchester always upset him. Mama's accident and her death. Papa's hardness. So much to forget. So much he couldn't forget."

"He ought to stop drinking," declared my father with an air of irritable virtue, "and get married, and settle down. If he doesn't, then I tell you, he's headed for no good end."

"Poor darling," sighed my mother. "He is so talented. Really, underneath it all, so sweet. He always was the one to do for everybody else. He wants so terribly to be loved."

"Well, the way to get me to love him is by not telling my son that elves are real, and that he will have the King and Queen of England write to him. —I must tell Richard not to expect anything from them." Bitterly he added, "Fritz has never been in England. Why did he lie to him?"

"Oh—oh, don't," said my mother in a pleading whisper. "Nothing will come, of course, and he will just forget about it, but please, dearie, don't spoil another dream for him just now. He isn't strong yet. Please."

"Oh, all right. I suppose I forget that seven years old is not entirely ready for the truth, the whole truth, and nothing but the truth, about everything. Perhaps you can start too soon with it. But I don't know. I keep feeling that Fritz—Fritz is some kind of a devil, who has to be fought against."

"Oh, no, no. There may be some of the imp in him—Mama used to shake her head sadly over him and say just that. But he is not the devil, himself. Please don't say that."

"Very well, I won't. We'll just let Richard gradually forget him and his imaginary kings and queens."

[92]

"Dearie:" said my mother gratefully.

The telephone bell rang downstairs in the front hall and my father went to answer it. I was falling really asleep when—it seemed a long afternoon while afterward—he returned and took my mother's hand and led her out of the room.

"What is it?" she asked, in a gust of fear at his serious air.

"I'll tell you downstairs, dearie. It is pretty terrible."

They went downstairs and I heard him speak against her cheek, and then I heard her lift a desolate cry and say in a storm of feeling to deny the impossible,

"No, oh, no, he couldn't have! Oh, what could we have done for him!"

My father comforted her for the dreadful news he had repeated from the telephone, the main fact of which was kept from me for a long while, until I was completely well; and which in its entirety I heard only many years later, and which told of the death of my Uncle Fritz.

※

The road company of *The Tudor Rose* closed its engagement at the Dorchester Shubert Theatre on Saturday night and with baggage and scenery was to leave by train in the small hours of Sunday morning. It was a snowy night. Everyone was tired, and if anyone looked out for anyone else, they paid attention only to the old star, whom they loved, and who was exhausted.

It was not until the train pulled into Cleveland the next afternoon that anyone noticed that my Uncle Fritz was not on board. The company manager telephoned his hotel in Dorchester. He had not checked out. The hotel desk called his room. There was no answer.

After a considered interval, the hotel detective broke open the door of his room and found him there.

He was dead. In habiliments out of the stock of a theatrical costumer, Uncle Fritz was lying in state on his hotel bed, wearing a bishop's mitre, and a scarlet chasuble over alb and cassock, and a pair of gold-embroidered scarlet gloves. His hands were folded upon his breast and on his right ring-finger his large amethyst edged with diamonds had now become a bishop's ring. Over his face was a faint smile, even though his brows were drawn upward in shadowy sorrow. *So young,* they would say when they found him, *so young to be a lord of the Church, and so handsome, even in death! Such a saintly man!* There was no evidence that anybody else had been in the room with him. Many empty whiskey bottles were neatly arranged on the desk. They soon found a pill box on the floor under the bed. The prescription label revealed that it had contained a sleeping drug to be taken sparingly. In his final act, Uncle Fritz had swallowed all of its contents. The coroner took charge, the verdict was suicide, and he was buried in Dorchester, though not in the family plot in the Catholic cemetery. My grandfather refused to attend the funeral but went at the funeral hour to his own parish church to pray for the repose of the soul of the son he had condemned.

When the news came which I was not immediately told, I felt that everything was different at home; but my mother winked back her tears and touched my face as if to praise life, and all the necessary observances of the funeral were carried out without my knowing anything of them until long afterward.

But Uncle Fritz was not yet quite gone. There was one more gesture from him. On Monday in the mail I received a picture postcard such as were then sold at newsstands showing King George V and Queen Mary of England standing side by side, he in full uniform as Admiral of the Fleet, wearing all his decorations and resting his hands upon a dress sword, and she in a prow-like crown of diamonds and many other jewels and a long gown shining with scabs of light. Addressed to me, the card bore this message on the back in flourished handwriting:

"To our Dear and Respected Cousin, fond wishes for early recovery and restoration to Your Majesty's Throne. George RI—Mary RI."

"You see!" I cried when this was delivered to me, "he was right! He was in England, and he does know them, and he did tell them to write to me!"

I reckoned nothing of the time of mails between England and America. My legacy from my Uncle Fritz was a reality to me until that time long later when I understood the circumstances of his end, and then it was clear that he must have bought the card and mailed it to me shortly before his fatal last scene.

But while it lasted, the illusion he willed to me was powerful, and one day when Anna, in a grumpy mood, serving my lunch in the kitchen, set my dish of cereal down noisily and rudely, I said to her,

"You must not do it that way. I am the Young Lost King!"

"Aah—" she growled, "you just think you are!"

Her scorn, not her words, offended me. After all, how did you know what was true except what you thought?

"How dare you!" I exclaimed.

Anna turned her grey, plate-like old face to the ceiling and shouted,

"Oh, my good God and Jesus!—Go on," she then grumbled, speaking for the real world in the weighty voice that she used in anger, "eat your farina or I'll *how-dare-you* myself!"

The powers which she represented must dethrone me in the end. I ate my farina.

CHAPTER V

✻

Magic

Yet illusion—with its consolations and empowerments—never really dies in us all our lives long, for we have to keep it alive to conceal our true selves from us. If we seem to be less subject to it as we age, this is only a trick of the personality.

But as childhood is a pursuit of a self, illusion is first of all needed to find the powers of which the self is capable. When I lost my kingdom, I was for a time diffident about my own abilities in the simple tests of boyhood, especially those performed in public. I never expected to know someone worse off than I, from whom to learn how to return safely to the imagination, and thus find harmony with the common world.

✻

"We go that way to the fort," said the boy in the lead, pointing ahead through the moldy woods.

We had just learned that his name was Jock and that as an older boy he had been told off to take the other boy and me to the fort on the mountain by ourselves because we were late in arriving at summer camp. All the others had already been to the fort and back.

"We always show the new fellows the fort on their first afternoon in camp," said Jock. "It gives everybody a lot of spirit. The camp is called Camp St. George and the fort is called Fort St. George. Only, the fort came first, you see, in the Revolutionary War."

He moved along the path like a forest animal. All of us were in the camp uniform which consisted only of sneakers and khaki shorts. We went in single file, and soon we lost far behind us the voices of boys back in camp. Gold light fell through the thick trees and touched to the leafy floor in silence. In my eighth summer it was the silence that I was most aware of as I met it among all the mysteries of the woods.

Jock striding ahead made almost no noise. The boy who followed me kept falling behind and then running to catch up. Jock wore a hunting knife in a leather sheath behind his right hip. Presently he reached for it, stopped us with his left hand, and threw the knife, which landed with a fine thick sound in the scarred trunk of a birch tree and stayed there like a ray of light.

"I always do that," he said, turning to smile at us, "to make people remember this place." He pointed to a fork of the trail. "That way, to the right, goes down to the lake, to Moccasin Cove. This way, to the left, goes on up the mountain to the fort. We'll rest a minute."

"Thank you," said the boy next to me with his forefinger diffidently on his mouth, as if to excuse the manners he had remembered to invoke.

Jock nodded to him kindly, then told me my name in order to be sure of it.

"You are Richard."

I nodded.

"I didn't get yours," he said to the other one.

"Yes," said the other boy, and then went miserably silent at who he was. We looked at him. He was a little taller than I, but the same age. He was thin and ivory white. His hair was silver yellow,

[98]

cut short. He hugged his visible ribs trying to conceal himself, smiling with his mouth but not with his large grey eyes. If I was lost in hidden bewilderment at where I found myself on this first day among competent young strangers, and conspicuous as a late arrival, he seemed worse off than I. I betrayed him in his misery by turning to Jock with a superior and knowing look. Jock saw me but did not acknowledge my unkind appeal to make a league with him against another. My spirits fell, for he was right and I was wrong.

"Suppose you just tell me and Richard, then," he said gently, "what to call you."

"Yes, well," came the shivering reply as though he had been chilled through by a long cold swim, "my name is Bayard."

"Where are you from, Bayard?" asked Jock to pass easily to other matters from such an odd name.

"New York."

"Very good. —And you, Richard?"

"Dorchester."

"Very good.—All right, let's go, men, if we want to have some daylight on the way back."

The woods at once seemed darker at his words. The heavy sweet rot of humus hung in the air. Slender aisles of light strode away from us in every direction. The sky was white above the pierced treetops. Jock recovered his knife and led us up the mountain. We saw great boulders and tiny meadows of moss hugging them to the ground. The trail rose more sharply. Bayard and I began to pant. Jock glanced around, but judged that we would do without another pause.

At last the ferns by the path stood in brighter green, and more sky showed ahead, and the trees thinned, and we saw a rocky mound up against clouds, and we broke out of the woods on a grassy crest where brown walls of huge blocks of stone outlined the ruined fort.

Jock began to run crossing the slope and climbed a tumble of fallen stones to reach the crown of an old battlement He turned to beckon us on, like one who had breached the walls. He was master of the mountain top, and the whole wooded side that stretched down to the long blue lake, where the forest war of wooden gunboats against scarlet-coated soldiers and painted Indians had won upper New York State for the colonies so long ago.

※

We joined him on the rim, and he gave us each a poke to commend us for taking the fort with him. He showed us the old overgrown gun-ports, and the dim rocky outline in the grass of where the powder magazine had been, and the clever placing of the casemates to command a sweep up and down the lake. We could just see scattered in and out of the blue woods of the far shore the little white buildings of the village called Old Foundry, New York, with its sky-blue steeple, and a drift of smoke from its sawmill. That was where the roads ended, and train stopped, and the mail came. We had crossed from it earlier in the afternoon by the camp launch. Everything lay far away beyond it—all certainties now lost, the cities we came from, the families who had consigned us to our four weeks of wilderness in July and August.

"Look at this," said Jock, leaping down from the heights. We followed. Half-buried, an old iron howitzer with a crown cast in relief above its touch-hole lay like a lichened rock in a bay of the battlements pointing toward the lake. "How do you like this? They used to call it 'The Old Sow.'"

We stroked it, peered into its mouth where leaves and spider webs softened all edges, and in high spirits Jock like a boy younger than we drove his fist as an iron cannonball through the air and made a soft cavernous "Voom!" with his voice, and we imagined a blast of

[100]

flame and a white puff of smoke and a plumy splash dying away over the lake. How much he knew.

"And look here," he cried, scrambling up a steep pile of huge blocks at one corner of the fort, "this is where they had the flagpole, and where we ran up our flag when we captured the fort from the British."

We went to follow him. I got to the top beside him and we both looked back for Bayard who was loyally reaching for block after block to join us. He was nearly there when he missed his footing and fell belly-down against the sharp edges of the blocks, slipped across several, and then ended at the bottom in a fall. We went to him.

He couldn't move or speak. His mouth was open like someone shocked into laughter but making no sound. His hands were hovering stiffly above his right leg. The whole shin was bared to the white bone and seeping blood. The pain he felt took his breath away. He was pale blue in his flesh. Jock bent down to him. Bayard looked up at him, and shook his head and shrugged his shoulders. It was a grown-up gesture that apologized for being a nuisance, and it made Jock laugh with pride in someone so brave in such agony.

"Can you straighten it out, Bayard?" he asked.

Bayard tried. His mouth was still open and we could hear his breath now. Jock examined him for fractures. There were none.

"Can you stand?"

He could not, so we lifted him taking an arm each around our necks.

"Hang on, and we'll get you back to camp."

Tears began to run down Bayard's cheeks. He tried to stop them with sharp shakes of his head. They were tears of pain, and had nothing to do with crying. He hoped we knew that. Using his left leg and holding up the other, he hopped along between us as we entered the trail going down from Fort St. George. It was already evening in the woods. The air was almost cold. We were in a misty blue tunnel. Though we had a sense of haste, we seemed to be barely advancing. When we paused to rest now and then we heard silences outside silences and they roared in our ears. I felt guilty because I was only eight, instead of fourteen, like Jock, and pallid instead of Indian brown like him, and because I was in the presence of such great pain, and because I waited to be told what to do in life instead of thinking of it by myself. It was easier for me to make a decision about an imagined problem than about a real one. I remember thinking that if Jock fell dead, and a bear came, I could take the hunting knife and defend Bayard who could not move.

❧

It was nearly dark when we heard the music of games calling aloud from the clearing before the camp. Soon afterward we came out of the woods down by the lake. The infirmary was in a log-built lodge across the clearing from the half-moon of tents that followed the line of woods leading in from the shore.

Jock took us straight to the doctor, who was just done with his annual opening-day checkup on conditions at camp St. George. He was closing his bag to return across the lake to Old Foundry where he lived. He was an old man with hair like a dog, and something of a dog's friendly desire, yet inability, to express himself fully to mankind. After helping to lay Bayard down, he just gazed for a second at the white bone and seemed absolutely to see its wild emanations of pain. Then he touched Bayard with his old paw and said,

"Hurts pretty bad, 'm?"

Bayard shook his head but tears came back not only for pain but the idea of it.

"We're going to have to clean it out," said the doctor, now putting

on a waggish old voice, "bits of leaf mold in it, and lichen, and this
and that. —Want me to whiff you some chloroform?—Iodine'll sting
like blazes, most likely, I'll have to pour it right out of the bottle."
   Bayard looked at Jock, and then at me, and said in indrawn breath
making a long word out of it, "No," and then added on the last gulp
of air, "—thank you."
   "Very well, sir, damn it," said the doctor, and spent no more time
on anything but what needed doing. "You," he commanded Jock,
"go find Mr Mac and tell him I want to see him here." Jock ran out.
"You," he said to me, "hold on to my fine fellow here." And while
the doctor worked adding pain to pain, the mystery of inexpressible
friendship, born of these events that had befallen young strangers,
sprang alive between Bayard and me.
   When he was done, the doctor said,
   "That's a young man without fear, isn't it?" and cuddled one of
his old hands on Bayard's head.

※

   And I thought so too, for quite some days, as the camp activities
became habitual, and every day brought challenge. If they only knew,
I thought, how different I am at home; how much I am loved there;
how many times I am able to do splendid things in my own place
and make everyone look across the top of my head to trade glances
about me. Here, at camp, I could not make my own terms, but had
to observe those already powerful and inexorable among the boys.
   There were some boys younger than I, some older, and a few
veterans, like Jock, who had been coming to camp every summer for
four years or more. Jock was the lord of all. Mr Mac, the blue-eyed,
white-haired director of the camp, puffing on his pipe, lurching a

[103]

little like an elderly boy, was often seen walking thoughtfully with Jock, getting his advice on how to handle a difficult case among the "Tadpoles," as the littlest campers were called. And Jock always had something to tell him, with confident respect and yet an air of magnificent indifference, as if it meant nothing to him whether Mr Mac, or any of the councilors, took his advice. Even the boys soon understood that it was wise of Mr Mac to have Jock on his side. Jock had influence. All the boys wanted to be like him, and, such was the mercy that played over them at their stringy stage of life, many thought they were. He was tall, but not yet as tall as he was going to be. His skin was tanned light brown, his eyes were dark brown. His round face was always friendly, which was reassuring, in view of his admired bunches of muscle, and the intuitions of savage power they aroused in so many of us.

Bayard could not leave his cot for many days. He lived in the last tent, farthest from the lake, and nearest the mountain. There were six boys to a tent. His mates brought him his food, and Mr Mac, beaming upon him for recovering without complications, came and saw him every day, or if he could not come, sent Jock. I went whenever I was not obliged to attend "Activities." Alone with me, Bayard was easily communicative. I believed that he had special talk because he was a New York boy. Actually, he was only using expressions he had grown up hearing at home, which were special since he came from a special family, as we presently learned.

"What are they doing today?" he would ask, and I would tell him of the world outside his tent.

"I talked to Jock for quite a while."

"You did? Yes. Let me imagine what you talked about."

"You never will."

"Why? What rubbish. What was it."

"You."

"Me? Oh, what rubbishy rubbish."

"No, the day you got hurt, he said Mr Mac came running, and all Mr Mac could say over and over was, Why did it have to be *that* boy? Oh-my-God, why did it have to be *that* family? And baa-baa-baa, and Why did it have to be on the first day of camp? Baa-baa-baa."

When I told him this, Bayard sat up sharply and cried in a sort of over-bred horror,

"He didn't send for them, in heaven's name!"

"I don't know. But Jock said he was certainly scared about your family."

That was how it got around that Bayard came from one of the two or three richest families in America—so rich that they were public, and so helplessly public that their youngest son was what he was.

It was known that Mr Mac went across the lake to Old Foundry every day to make a long distance call about Bayard. The flaps on Bayard's tent were rolled up all day, and he would lie on his cot and stare at the path that came from the dock, dreading to see his father or his mother arriving to publish not only how frantic they were about him, but also how special he was, and how silly it was for him to hope that he might hide anywhere, which, in his lively intelligence, was most of all what he thought of in any situation.

But no family appeared, and he worked to prepare himself for the day when he must leave his cot and return to the lake-side world where everyone now knew who he was.

"What are they doing now?" he would ask.

"Activities," I would answer.

"In heaven's name, what kind?"

My heart sank as I told him, for, feeling my own doubts more than his, I lived over again all my shortcomings. But I tried loyally to sound enthusiastic.

"They climb the rope."

"Does everybody watch?"

"Oh, sure."

"How gash-ghastly." He tried to smile. "What else?"

"We have archery matches."

"I can do that."

"And we play baseball. They choose up different sides all the time."

He twisted on his cot, and said,

"They'll never choose me, and I don't care a tinker's damn.—Do they choose you?"

"Sometimes. Not always."

"What do you do if they don't?"

"I watch and yell for my side."

"I see.—What else?"

"And then they blow the whistle and everybody has to run lickety-split down to the lake, and then it is time for water games."

"I suppose it couldn't be more tiresome.—How do they do it?"

I told him, and remembering how I despised myself for being so awkward, so ill at ease in the water where everyone, where Jock especially, was so spectacular and brilliant, I became defensive and I boasted of the fun. When the whistle sounded, everybody stopped what they were doing no matter what, and ran for the shore. There in furious haste everyone tore off his sneakers and shorts and plunged into the lake "to get wet all over." Jock usually trotted out to the end of the dock to show off a few dives. Unlike all the rest of us, he wore trunks, to identify him with Mr Mac and the senior councilors, who also wore them.

After Jock's expert diving demonstration, two canoes were pushed out into the water. A boy stood in each, while another paddled, and a fight ensued between the canoes. The weapons were long poles padded at the ends with which the standing boys thrust at each other.

"Who does that?" asked Bayard.

"Everybody. You have to take turns."

"You mean with everybody else watching?"

Yes, everybody watched. And then there was follow-the-leader, when everybody lined up and came in turn to the end of the dock and had to do what Jock did first—various dives, jumps, and tricks.

"What do they do when they watch?"

"Haven't you ever been around a bunch of kids, Bayard?"

"No, no, I haven't, how should I know?"

"Well, they yell and whistle if you're good, and they splash and say pee-yu if you're not."

"No," he said, "my family sent me here to learn how to be with people. How absurd.—Does anybody tell you how to do it if you don't know how?"

"Yes. Jock helps everybody."

"I suppose he can do them all, the wretch?"

How treasonable, to call Jock a wretch—and how distinguished!

"Oh, yes."

We both saw him intensely in imagination for a moment.

"Look, Richard," said Bayard, "do you do all the things?"

"Y-yes," I lied. "Of course I do."

I denied him the companionship in failure which he had hoped for. He felt of his leg which was healing rapidly, and which would soon be well enough for him to join the outer life again. He licked his lips. He gulped.

"Oh, dear God," he said.

Full of what was the matter with me, I never wondered if the same thing was the matter with him.

The day finally came when Bayard was let out on crutches, and then the day when he could do without them. Mr Mac put his arm around Bayard's shoulders and said he was proud to see him ready now to take his place in the "wholesome, well-rounded activities which every boy enjoyed at Camp St. George."

"Can you swim, Bayard?"

Bayard nodded and swallowed.

"Fine. Fine."

The whistle blew, everyone raced to the shore. The water broke in diamond sprays about young thundering bodies. Echoing off the lake our voices rose into the woods, up to the rim of our mountain cup, as we broke the calm of the elements. Bayard was lost in the flashing turmoil when Jock dove off the pier and swam over to me.

"You take number one boat," he ordered, and in a friendly way ducked me under the water. The canoes were being swum out as I came up. I was hauled into one and given the pole. The bathers made a wide ring about the two canoes which now approached each other. Partisan cries arose. I saw the other pole searching toward me in the high sunshine. Holding my pole with a tortured grip I leaned forward in a grinding resolve to distinguish myself. The pole was long and trembled heavily because I held it too close to the near end. To keep in balance I had to lean back again and I leaned too far. The canoe skidded aside under me, I threw away the pole, and fell into the water in defeat. My boat lost even before it had engaged the enemy.

I felt my heart and my ears ready to burst under the water. I stayed under as long as I could, wavering dimly among the broken skeins of sunlight, the fronds of green that grew from the clear lake-floor, and a little troop of fish that I saw swim toward me and then all looking sideways flip away together in a darting glide.

I broke into air at last. My place was already filled in my canoe. A new battle was making. I was forgotten, when all I now wanted was another chance. If I got it, how I would—and I comforted myself with a cloudy picture of winning a naval engagement in a wooden frigate coming under the guns of Fort St. George with a glory of flame, smoke and thunder, to take the whole wooded mountain where fame had passed me by.

"Follow-the-leader!" yelled Jock in a little while. He harried the boys out of the water and up the dock, making them get in line. Among them he found Bayard. With brilliant happiness he dragged him past dozens of others and thrust him into the line near its head. It was a gesture that told everyone that Bayard had his esteem, and that he was glad to welcome him after his long and painful absence, and that he must have a preferred place at his first follow-the-leader. Then Jock went to the edge of the dock where the springboard was and made a perfect swan dive. The next boy, and the next followed him, doing as well as they could. Bayard was then at the springboard, and all eyes and voices turned on him.

With his arms hugged about his ribs he stood looking down, trying to vanish.

Yells arose to make him dive.

He stood lost. He was paralyzed. Those near enough could see him shivering.

Catcalls and jeers.

The ones waiting in line danced with impatience. He was exposed as the center of furious attention.

Finally he moved. He took a deep breath, he shrugged in his familiar way, and turned and walked away from the springboard, and down the line to the shore. Silence fell in amazement. At the edge of the wood he found his shorts and sneakers and put them on. Without glancing around at us, he went toward the tents.

Presently I followed him. Jock caught up with me. We both saw Bayard stumble to his knees. He vomited like a sick cat and at once rose and went on to his tent, where he threw himself on his cot. When he heard us come in, he turned and said, "I'm sorry," rapidly, in a grown-up, social way, and his teeth chattered.

Jock sat down next to him like a family doctor and looked at him in a long silence. Then he smiled, to remember that the world was fair, and all good things would come to pass, and not a man lived who would not in the end perceive the right.

"Never mind, Bayard," he said, "you'll do all right tomorrow."

Bayard rolled his head on his hard unpillowed cot.

"Oh, no, I won't," he said, deathly-white, "I want to, I want to, but I can't, I can't."

And he couldn't. He went each day to lose himself in the throng, but each time when he was thrust out before them all, his agony of shyness turned him rigid and he could not move. He was pushed off the dock by those who told him he was crazy. Promptly agreeing with them, he fell, he recovered himself, and ran away.

One day I followed him. He took the forest trail up the mountain, and at the fork, turned right, and ended up at Moccasin Cove. He did not hear or see me. Nobody ever went there alone. A water moccasin had been seen there years before, and in the imagination of the camp, much developed by speculation and joyful horror, it was now a fearsome place. Bayard, alone, climbed a rock in the cove, and there by himself performed the dives he could not do in public. Whatever he was afraid of, it was not physical.

It was necessary with a smile of professional understanding for Mr Mac, and even Jock, to conclude that Bayard was "a special case." Jock, already guardian of order and sanity in the affairs of life around him, had a quiet talk with Mr Mac. If the doctor might say that Bayard, in order not to risk infection in his recent wound, which though healed might rip open again some day, must not quite yet undertake violent exercise, then even if it came a little late, there would be a proper explanation of so much that bothered everyone. Bayard could thus be ordered not to do what he refused to do, which would restore health to authority. The other boys would hear a logical excuse for special arrangements accorded one of their number, and would thus have no grounds for resentment. Bayard himself might benefit by an official removal of pressure.

The whole plan was very much Jock, and Mr Mac, crinkling his face with thanks for manliness renewed once again in life through Jock, acted. An appointment was made for Bayard to cross the lake in the launch one afternoon to see the doctor at Old Foundry. I wanted to go with him, but was feverish from a thick map-like outbreak of poison oak all over me, and was supposed to lie in my tent covered with sugar of lead, that smelled of the sting it made when applied. Bayard stopped to see me on his way down to the dock.

"Is there anything you want from the village?"

"No. I wisht I was going along."

"So do I, by all means. Thank whatever gods there be they are not sending anyone with me, in charge of me, I mean.—I plan to do a little shopping."

"What are you going to get?"

"I haven't the faintest idea. Just look around, I expect, as soon as I've done with the absurd old leech."

I looked at him with an idea that came in a flash.

"You aren't going to run away, are you?" I asked.

"What rubbish. Of course not—" but I saw how the idea was not new to him. A look of hungry abashment came into his face, as though his innermost longings had been exposed. He nodded and went rapidly off to the dock. I got a lump in my throat at the idea of the freedom that lay beyond Old Foundry, New York, and Bayard gone into it forever.

I took a nap and on awakening saw that something odd was going on in Bayard's tent, the last one in the line of which mine was in the middle. The tents made a half-circle backed up by the woods. With flaps up, day and night, unless it rained, the tents were open to the forest breath. Now I could see Jock and Mr Mac and one of the councilors going through the lockers in the distant tent. There were no boys about. Soon the lockers in the next tent were inspected, and the next, until they came to my tent.

"It's all right, Richard," said Jock, "this is a routine check-up," but he winked his off-eye as if to say he had more to tell me, and would do so when the ancient adults were not about. If he was now enacting with them a role in the law, he was still nearer to boy than to man, and to me than to them. Later when Mr Mac and the other councilor were already entering the next tent, Jock lingered a second to whisper to me that some money had been stolen from Bayard's locker, and they were looking for what they could find. I was not to mention this to anyone for fear of alerting the thief. But with my poison oak, and all, he just thought it would make me feel better to know what was going on. Dazed with admiration for his leadership—a quality much discussed at Camp St. George—I thanked him in a mumble which he accepted with expert apprecia tion of its concealed worth.

"Jock—" I added, ready to show him my gratitude and also to make a sensation by telling him that Bayard had run away; but when he paused to hear me, I felt a stronger loyalty to Bayard, and I said, "Oh, nothing."

Jock made a gesture of comic obscenity at me and joined the others. I watched the inspection reach the other end of the row, and if it turned up any discoveries, there was no sign.

❧

The lake was white with late afternoon light when the launch appeared from Old Foundry. It cut a fine, long, black curve in the surface of the still water, coming to the dock with exactly enough momentum to reach the soft wet timbers with a velvety nudge. I was astonished to see Bayard spring from it before it stopped moving. He went off toward Mr Mac's office in the lodge, and then in a few minutes headed for me. He carried three brown paper bags.

"What did you buy?" I asked.

"Oh, nothing.—Here," and he handed me one of the packages, "I got you something."

I tore open the bag, to reveal a violently colored photograph of Fort St. George at sunset, framed in mother of pearl with small gilded pine-cones tacked to the corners, and lettered in black across the bottom of the frame, "Souvenir of Old Foundry, New York."

"Do you like it?" he asked, looking at me with a puzzled air.

"Oh, yes, by all means," I replied, meaning to sound like him. "Thank you very much. It's a peach."

"But I thought you'd laugh," he said. "It's so gash-ghastly it's wonderful. I mean at home, we always try to find each other the most awful thing we can buy."

[113]

Embarrassed at missing the point, I said stubbornly, "No, it's beautiful. I really like it." He shrugged. "What's in the other ones?" I asked.

He put one, a flat package, between his knees and opened the other, a large one bulging with interesting lumps, to reveal a dozen long fat cannon firecrackers.

"Don't tell anybody," he said. "We are not supposed to have any. I bought all they had, left over from the Fourth of July. We can use them sometime."

"What's in that one?" I demanded, pointing to the thin bag.

"Oh, that." He took it and waved it idly. "Nothing much. Just something I got."

But his efforts at sounding off-hand were not convincing. His teeth chattered once or twice till he clamped them together. Charged with excitement, he refused to show it. He changed the subject.

"I saw the absurd leech. He gave me a letter to take to Mr Mac. He says my leg won't let me do activities. He's crazy. My leg's all right. He was just overcome with his own importance."

The twilight was coming. Boys were drifting back to the tents to get ready for supper. Bayard went to his own. That evening after supper, while Mr Mac was reading aloud by the council fire out in the open, Jock drew aside some of the boys a couple at a time, and told them that everybody had a chance to show real leadership now, and help Bayard along, and not make fun of him because he wasn't allowed to do the things other people could do, because of his leg, for the doctor had said so, and nobody wanted anybody to come down with a terrible infection, like blood poisoning, and have a leg chopped off, or anything, did they? None questioned his right and power to create opinion, and all fell in with his program of mercy for Bayard, who would never again be asked to disgrace himself before all eyes. With this preparation, what happened next day at water games was all the more astounding.

[114]

My poison oak was better, and I was returned to activities. The canoe fights were over, and follow-the-leader was well along, when from the woods at the shore broke a running figure of a boy, stripped for swimming. It was nobody we recognized, for its face was covered by a large, stiff, rubberized mask with huge ears that stuck out on each side of a wide painted grin. It was the face, though wildly exaggerated, of someone I had seen somewhere long before—the face of a comic tramp. Its eyes bulged with white under heavy black eyebrows arched in indignant surprise. Its cheeks were shiny red. Its nose was like a tomato. Its jaws were painted in the heavy ash color of a tramp's unshaven beard. From one corner of its mouth protruded a brown cigar stub fixed in place. The zany head looked much too large for the young thin body which it crowned with wild hilarity.

Racing down the dock past the line of everybody who waited to follow the leader, the figure roughly pushed aside the next boy up, ran out on the springboard without pausing, and in an airy sprawl of complete abandon, threw itself off the board and fell into the water with an immense splash.

After a clap of amazed silence, a collective shout went up.

The tramp reappeared from the lake, climbed the ladder to the dock, took the board again, and with his outrageous grin lifted to the sky, performed a perfect swan dive.

We watched spellbound to see him come up, but he did not break the water where he had disappeared. How could anyone stay down that long? Yelling began. Jock dived off the dock to look for him, and came up without him. The excitement was furious, until we heard a muffled cry from another direction, and turned to see the

[115]

tramp waving grotesquely from the other side of the dock, to which he had gone under water, and where having climbed up he now cawed like a crow for attention. As soon as he had it from everyone, he ran splay-legged along the dock and off into space as if he didn't know where the dock ended, and signalling mock-anguish in midair, hit with a resounding belly-flop and sank. With the most careless splendor, he could do anything.

Staring and yelling, we believed the mask, not the body. In brilliant sunshine, our familiar surroundings only made the visitor seem more wonderful and strange. A power beyond doubting was among us and we were dazzled even while our bellies ached with laughter. If I suspected in one box of my mind who it was who found magic release behind the mask, in another I was under the spell of a mystery as old as myth. When the tramp came up for air again, and this time was captured and dragged to the shore and thrown down on the sand, I was among those who crowded close to see who it was as Jock, choking with laughter, pulled off the mask to reveal Bayard's serious, excited face.

When the commotion was over and Bayard was let go, I walked back to his tent with him and saw him toss the mask carelessly into the locker at the foot of his cot.

"Was that the other thing you bought yesterday?" I asked.

"Yes, in the same store where I got that vile affair for you."

"Do they have any more?"

"No. This was the only one."

I was saddened by the news, and with many inner qualms came to my decision as the night fell and the camp gathered about the council fire. I completed my plans and when the camp was asleep in its tents with the flaps rolled open to the aromatic night, I carefully left my cot, stooped my way out of the rear of my tent into the edge of the woods, and went on the soft, loamy ground to the last tent in the line. I entered stilly, opened Bayard's locker, and stole his mask. I did not ask myself how, after the expensive gift he had given me, I could rob my friend. With his mask, I could go to Moccasin Cove alone, and wearing it I could find the power to perform in glory, amidst future acclaim, those feats at which I tried and failed before my fellows every day.

Retreating to the woods with the treasure which was still damp in my grasp, I was taken by hands and revealed by a flashlight.

"We've got him," whispered Mr Mac.

They took me away to the lodge, a thief.

"Where is the money?" they asked. "We knew whoever had stolen once would try it again. It was just a matter of watching for him. Where is it?"

But in the end, they believed me, and wondered why anybody would take such risks just to steal a mask. They kept the mask to return it to Bayard in the morning. Jock took me to my tent. On the way he made me promise many times never again to take anything that was not mine, and when he left me, he said that so long as I kept my promise, he—and he meant the wide, good world—would forget the whole thing.

❧

But with morning I knew great remorse, and went by myself up to Fort St. George to consider how I could make it up to Bayard for what I had done to him. Suppose I had never been caught, and Bayard's mask were gone? Without it, how could he again repeat his triumphs? So in just the stage of civilization to do so, I respected wholly the magic in the mask.

The morning was pungent all about the old fort. The silvery dampness of the night hung in rock shadows. Far up the lake lingered morning mist. All was quiet until I heard someone coming to the mouth of the trail. I dropped behind fallen stones to hide.

It was Bayard, carrying one of his paper bags. He looked all about. I heard him say, "I could have sworn on a Gutenberg Bible that he came up here," and he seemed perplexed and friendly. I stood up and called across the grassy cup of the fort.

"There you are," he said. "It's high time. Come here."

We met in the middle of the fort. He reached into the bag and hauled out the mask and held it toward me.

"Here," he said. "I won't need it any more."

"Oh, no," I said.

He had been brought up in the anguished enlightenment of his family to give away anything he had that someone else wanted. Possessions were not owned, but only held in trust.

"I can't," I said, and because in shame I could not then accept the mask, I felt the need of it for some years thereafter.

He shrugged, stuck it back in the bag, and said,

"They told me all about it. Nobody cares. What I did was much worse."

"What."

"I lied when I told them my money was stolen. Nobody stole any. I just said so, so they wouldn't think I had twenty-five dollars that I could run away on."

I regarded him gravely. An inkling of pity long later to be understood struggled to reach between us. What desperate plots lay dearly alive just under so many faces, and what relentless confessions fell in idle courage from the same lips that could smile and lie.

"So I told old Mr Mac this morning, and *he: was: furious.*"

"Then what happened?"

"Then," he said, dismissing all nuisances along with our separate crimes, "I went to the mess hall, and snagged a handful of matches, and look here."

He dumped the fat bag out on the stones, making a scarlet mound of cannon crackers. Taking one, he went to the half-buried howitzer called the "Old Sow." He put the cracker into its maw, lighted its fuse with a match, and we both flopped down behind the cannon which with gestures we pretended to aim out over the lake.

There was a breathless moment beaded with the sputter of the fuse, and then in a deep, hollow roar, the "Old Sow" spoke. Cannonading sounded again from Fort St. George in ruins on the mountain.

We loaded and fired again and again, making sport with our history that was all about us in the bright air. We shook the mountain and dominated the lake, capturing the future with heroic attitudes out of the past. We imagined gunboats under sail riding heavily below us, and blue tail-coats that showed white facings, and heavy fringed gold epaulettes falling across shoulders twisting in action, and the flash of cutlasses, and the hoot of commands; and on both shores of the lake, the long points of wooded land faded one beyond another paler and paler blue till in the distance all—lake, land, and sky—merged in airy white like a page that we would write on with our lives.

CHAPTER VI

✻

Black Snowflakes

So, it seemed, I most often learned from one thing what another was.

It was this way when we all went from Dorchester to New York to see my grandfather off for Europe, a year or two before the first World War broke out. His thoughts and longings returned more and more to his homeland as the years in America brought him loss and sorrow and ailings. His wife was gone, his youngest son, whom he had dedicated to glory, was dead in scandal, unforgiven, and desire itself must have seemed to turn toward an order in design which a sense of time wasting made urgent.

As I grew through boyhood, I was increasingly fearful of him, for I no longer took him for granted as in infancy. Large, splendidly formal in his dress, and majestic in manner, he yet led me to wonder about him with something like love, for he made me know in ways I cannot describe that he believed me someone worthwhile. At nine years old, I could now imagine being like him myself, with glossy white hair swept back from a broad pale brow, and white eyebrows above china-blue eyes, and rosy cheeks, a fine sweeping mustache and a full but well-trimmed beard which came to a point. Except for his smaller beard, he looked something like Johannes Brahms in his last phase. He sometimes wore eyeglasses with thin gold rims and I practiced in secret how to put these on and take them off. I suppose I had no real idea of what he was like, for I never imagined that my elders had feelings.

※

There was something in the air about going to New York to see him off that troubled me. I did not want to go.

"Why not, my darling?" asked my mother the night before we were to leave. Before going down to dinner, she busily came in to see me, to kiss me goodnight, to turn down the night-light, to glance about my room with her air of giving charm to all that she saw, and to whisper a prayer with me, looking toward Our Lady, that God would keep us.

"I don't want to leave Anna."

"What a silly boy. Anna will be here when we return, doing the laundry in the basement or making Apfelkuchen just as she always does. And while we are gone, she will have a little vacation. Won't that be nice for her? You must not be selfish."

"I don't want to leave Mr Schmitt and Ted."

My mother made a little breath of comic exasperation, looking upward for a second.

"You really are killing," she said in the racy slang of the time, "why should you mind leaving the iceman and his old horse Ted for a few days? They only come down our street twice a week. What is so precious about Mr Schmitt and Ted?"

"They are friends of mine."

"Ah. Then I understand. We all hate to leave our friends. Well, they too will be here when we return. Don't you want to see Grosspa take the great ship, you can even go on board the liner to say goodbye, you have no idea how huge those ships are, and how fine? This one"—she let a comic effect come into her voice as she often did when pronouncing German words—"is called the *Doppelschrauben Schnelldampfer Kronprinzessin Cecilie.*"

"Why can't I go the next time he sails for Germany?"

At this my mother's eyes began to shine with a sudden new light, and I thought she might be about to cry, but that did not seem possible, for she was also smiling. She leaned down to hug me and said,

"This is one time we must all go, Richard. If we love him, we must go. Now you must not keep me. People are coming for dinner. Your father is waiting for me downstairs. You know how he looks up the stairs to see me come down. Now sleep. You will love the train as you always do. And yes: in New York you may buy a little present for each one of your friends and bring them back to them."

It was a lustrous thought to leave with me as she went, making a silky rustle with her long dinner dress that dragged on the floor after her. I lay awake thinking of my friends and planning my gifts.

※

Anna came to us four days a week from the Lithuanian quarter of town and I spent much time in her kitchen or basement laundry listening to her rambling stories of life on the "East Side." I remember wondering if everybody on the "East Side" had deep pock marks like those in her coarse face, and one day, with inoffensive candor, I asked her about them, and she replied with the dread word, "Smallpox."

"They thought I was going to die. They thought I was dead."

"But you weren't?"

"Oh, no," quite as serious as I, "I fooled them all. But look at me. There was a time when I thought I would have been better off dead."

"Why, Anna?"

"Who wants a girl looking like this?"

"Did they care?"

"Oh, my man came along, and I forgot about it."

"What is it like to be dead, Anna?"

"Oh, dear saints, who can tell that who is alive?"

It was all I could find out, but the question was often with me. Sometimes in late still afternoons, when I was supposed to be taking my nap, I would think about it, and I would hear Anna singing, way below in the laundry, and her voice was like something hooting far away up the chimney. It always seemed the same song that she sang, and I think now that she simply made up a tune long ago, and was satisfied with it, and so hooted it over and over, with words I never understood. Drowsily I wondered if the song were about dying. What should I buy for Anna in New York?

And for Mr Schmitt, the iceman. He was a heavy-waisted German-American with a face wider at the bottom than at the top, and when he walked he had to lumber his huge belly from side to side to make room for his great jellying thighs as he stepped. He had a big, hard voice, and we could hear him coming blocks away, as he called out the word "Ice!' in a long cry. Other icemen used a bell, but not Mr Schmitt. I waited for him when he came, and we always exchanged words, while he stabbed at the high cakes of ice in his hooded wagon, chopping off the pieces we always took—two chunks of fifty pounds each. His skill with his tongs was magnificent, and he would swing his cake up on his shoulder, over which he wore a sort of rubber chasuble, and wag his way in heavy grace, hanging his free hand out in the air to balance his burdened progress up the

[123]

walk along the side of our house to the kitchen porch. He made two trips, one for each cake of ice, and he blew his breath with extra effort to interest me.

"Do you want to ride today?" he would ask, meaning that I was welcome to ride to the end of the block on the seat towering above Ted's rump, where the shiny, rubbed reins lay in a loose knot, because Ted needed no guidance, but could be trusted to stop at all the right houses and start up again when he felt Mr Schmitt's heavy vaulting rise to the seat. I often rode to the end of the block, and Ted, in his moments of pause, would look around at me, first from one side, and then the other, and stamp a leg, and shudder his rattling harness against flies, and in general treat me as one of the ice company, for which I was grateful.

What to buy for Ted? Perhaps in New York they had horse stores. My father would give me what money I would need, when I told him what I wanted to buy, and for whom. I resolved to ask him, provided I could stay awake until the dinner party was over, and everybody had gone, when my father would come in on his way to bed to see if all was well in the nursery. At such times I might hear him and awaken and answer him still dreaming. He called me "Doc" because he believed that I would one day study medicine and carry a narrow black bag full of delicious colored pills like coarse sand in little phials, like the ones in the toy doctor's kit which I owned. How much love there was all about me, and how greedy I was for even more of it.

※

Having no voice in the decision, I was with everyone else the next day when we assembled at the station to take the Empire State Express. It was a heavy, grey, cold day, and everybody wore fur but me and my great-aunt Barbara—Tante Bep, as she was called. She was returning to Germany with my grandfather, her brother.

This was an amazing thing in itself, for first of all, he always went everywhere alone, and second, Tante Bep was so different from her magnificent brother that she was generally kept out of sight. She lived across town on the East Side in a convent of German nuns who received money for her board and room from Grosspa. I always thought she resembled an ornamental cork which my grandfather often used to stopper a wine bottle opened but not yet emptied. Carved out of crisp soft wood and painted in bright colors, the cap of the cork represented a Bavarian peasant woman with a blue shawl over her flat-painted grey hair. The eyes were tiny dots of bright blue lost in deep wooden wrinkles, and the nose was a heavy wooden lump hanging over a toothless mouth sunk deep in an old woman's poor smile. Despite the smile the carved face showed anxiety. The same was true of Tante Bep. Left alone in Germany many years ago, she might have starved, if her splendid brother, who had become prosperous in America, had not saved her. He sent for her and gave her what American life she knew with the German nuns who reassuringly kept the ways of the old country. Her gratitude was anguish to behold. Now, wearing her jet-spangled black bonnet with chin-ribbons, and her black shawl and heavy skirts which smelled rather like dog hair, she was returning to Germany with her brother, and I did not know why.

But her going was part of the strangeness which I felt in all the circumstances of our journey. In the Empire State Express my grandfather retired at once to a drawing room at the end of our car. My mother went with him. Tante Bep and I occupied swivelled arm chairs in the open part of the parlor car, and my father came and went between us and the private room up ahead.

"Ach Gott!" exclaimed Tante Bep many times that day, looking out the window at the passing snowy landscape, and then at me, moving her tongue inside her sunken mouth, as she smiled to console me and blinked both eyes to encourage me—for what? Tante Bep prayed her rosary, trying to hide her beads in the voluminous folds of her skirt. But I could see the rosewood beads and the worn, heavy crucifix now and then as she progressed by Hail Marys, using her work-toughened old thumbs to advance the stages of her chain of mercy.

In the afternoon I fell asleep after the splendors of lunch in the dining car. Grosspa's lunch went into his room on a tray, and my mother shared it with him. I hardly saw her all day, but when we drew into New York, she came to awaken me, saying,

"Now, Richard, all the lovely exciting things begin! Tonight the hotel, tomorrow the ship! Come, let me wash your face and comb your hair."

"And the shopping?" I said.

"Shopping?"

"For my presents."

"What presents?"

"Mother, Mother, you have forgotten."

"I'm afraid I have, but we can speak of it later."

It was true that people did forget at times, and I knew how they tried then to render unimportant what they should have remembered. Would this happen to my plans for Anna, and Mr Schmitt, and Ted? My concern was great—but just as my mother had told, there were excitements waiting, and even I forgot, for the while, what it had seemed treacherous of her to forget.

We drove from the station in two limousine taxis, like high glass cages on wheels. I worked all the straps and handles in our cab. My father rode with me and Tante Bep. He pointed out famous sights as we went. It was snowing lightly, and the street lamps were rubbed out of shape by the snow, as if I had painted them with my water colors at home. We went to the Waldorf-Astoria Hotel on

Fifth Avenue. Soon after I had been put into my room, which I was to share with Tante Bep, my father came with an announcement.

"Well, Doc," he said, lifting me up under my arms until my face was level with his and his beautifully brushed hair which shone under the chandelier, and letting his voice sound the way his smile looked, "we are going to have a dinner party downstairs in the main dining room."

I did not know what a main dining room was, but it sounded superb, and I looked pathetic at the news, for I knew enough of dinner parties at home to know that they always occurred after my nightly banishment.

"It won't be like at home, will it," I said, "it will be too far away for me to listen."

"Listen? You are coming with us. What did you think?"

"Well, I thought—."

"No. And do you know why you are coming with us?"

"Why?"

"Grosspa specially wants you there."

"Ach Gott," murmured Tante Bep in the shadows, and my father gave her a frowning look to warn her not to show so much feeling.

❧

A few minutes later we went downstairs. I was in a daze of happiness at the grand room of the hotel, the thick textures, the velvety lights, the distances of golden air, and most of all at the sound of music coming and coming from somewhere. In a corner of the famous main dining room there was a round table sparkling with light on silver, ice, glass, china and flowers, and in a high armchair sat my grandfather—rosy face, blue eyes and white beard. He inclined himself forward to greet us and seated us about him. My mother was at his right, in one of her prettiest gowns, with jewels. I was on his left.

"Hup-hup!" said my grandfather, clapping his hands to summon waiters now that we were assembled. "Tonight nothing but a happy family party, and Richard shall drink wine with me, for I want him to remember that his first glass of wine was poured for him by his *alter Münchner Freund, der Grossvater.*"

At this a wet sound began with Tante Bep, but a look from my father quelled it, and my mother, blinking both eyes rapidly, which made them look prettier than ever when she stopped, put her hand on her father's and leaned and kissed his cheek above the crystal edge of his beard.

"Listen to the music!" commanded Grosspa, "and be quiet, if every word I say is to be a signal for emotion!"

It was a command in the style of his household terror, and everybody straightened up and looked consciously pleasant, except me. For me it was no effort. The music came from within a bower of gold lattice screens and potted palms—two violins, a 'cello, and a harp. I could see the players clearly, for they were in the corner just across from us. The leading violinist stood, the others sat. He was alive with his music, bending to it, marking the beat with his glossy head on which his sparse hair was combed flat. The restaurant was full of people whose talk made a thick hum, and to rise over this, and to stimulate it further, the orchestra had to work with extra effort.

The rosy lamp shades on the tables, the silver vases full of flowers, the slowly sparkling movements of the ladies and gentlemen, and the swallow-like dartings of the waiters transported me. I felt a lump of excitement where I swallowed. My eyes kept returning to

[128]

the orchestra leader, who conducted with side-jerks of his nearly bald head, for what he played and what he did seemed to me to command the meaning of the astonishing fact that I was at a dinner party in public with my family.

"What music are they playing?" I asked.

"It is called *Il Bacio,*" answered Grosspa.

"What does that mean?"

"It means *The Kiss.*"

What an odd name for a piece of music, I thought, as I watched the musicians who went at their work with a kind of sloping ardor. All through dinner—which did not last as long as it might have—I inquired about pieces played by the quartet, and in addition to the Arditi waltz, I remember one called *Simple Aveu* and the Boccherini *Minuet.* The violins had a sweetish mosquito-like sound, and the harp sounded breathless, and the 'cello mooed like a distant cow, and it was all entrancing. Watching the orchestra, I ate absently, with my head turned away from my fork until my father, time and again, had to turn me to face my plate. And then a waiter came with a silver tub on legs which he put at my grandfather's left, and showed him the wine bottle which he took from its nest of sparkling ice. The label was approved, a sip was poured for my grandfather to taste, he held it to the light and twirled his glass slowly, he sniffed it, and then he tasted it.

"Yes," he declared, "it will do."

My mother watched him in this ritual, and over her lovely heart-shaped face, with its silky crown of rolled tresses, I saw memories pass like shadows, as she thought of all the times she had attended the business of ordering and serving wine with her father. Blinking both eyes rapidly, she opened a little jewelled lorgnon she wore on a fine chain and bent forward to read the menu which stood in a little silver frame beside her plate. But I could see that she was not

[129]

reading, and again I wondered what was the matter with everybody.

"For my grandson," said Grosspa, taking a wineglass and filling it half full with water, and then pouring it full with wine. The yellow pour turned pale in my glass. There was too much ceremony about it for me not to be impressed. I took the glass he handed me, and when he raised his, I raised mine, and while all the others watched, we drank together. And then he recited a proverb in German which meant something like,

> *When comrades drink red wine or white*
> *They stand as one for what is right,*

and an effect of intimate applause went around the table at this stage of my growing up.

I was suddenly embarrassed, for the music stopped, and I thought all the other diners were looking at me; and, in fact, many were, and I had a picture-like impression of how all smiled at a boy of nine, ruddy with excitement and confusion, drinking a solemn pledge of some sort with a pink and white old gentleman.

Mercifully the music began again and we were released from our poses, as it were, and my grandfather drew out of one vest pocket his great gold watch with its hunting case, and unhooked from a vest button the fob which held the heavy gold chain in place across his splendid middle. Repeating an old game we had played when I was still a baby, he held the watch toward my lips, and I knew what was expected of me. I blew upon it, and—though long ago I had penetrated the secret of the magic—the gold lid of the watch flew open. My grandfather laughed softly in a deep wheezing breath, and then shut the watch with a lovely cushioned click, saying,

"Do children ever know that what we do to please them pleases us more than it does them?"

"Ach Gott," whispered Tante Bep, and nobody reproved her, and then he said,

"Richard, I give you this watch and chain to keep all your life, and by it you will remember me."

"Oh, no!" exclaimed my mother in an uncontrollable waft of feeling.

He looked gravely at her and said,

"Yes, now, rather than later," and put the heavy wonderful golden objects into my hand.

I regarded them in silence. Mine! I could hear the wiry ticking of the watch, and I knew that now and forever I myself could press my thumb on the winding stem and myself make the gold lid fly open. The chain slid like a small weighty serpent across my fingers.

"Well," urged my father gently, "Richard, what do you say?"

"Yes, thank you, Grosspa, thank you."

I leaned up out of my chair and put my arm around his great head and kissed his cheek. Up close, I could see tiny blue and scarlet veins like something woven under his skin.

"That will do, my boy," he said. Then he took the watch from me and handed it to my father. "I hand it to your father to keep for you until you are twenty-one. But remember that it is yours and you must ask to see it any time you wish."

Disappointment spread heavily through my entrails, but I knew how sensible it was for the treasure to be held for me instead of given into my care.

"Any time you wish. You wish. Any time," repeated my grandfather, but in a changed voice, a hollow, windy sound that was terrible to hear. He was gripping the arm of his chair and now he shut his eyes behind his gold-framed lenses, and sweat broke out on his forehead which was suddenly dead white. "Any time," he tried to say again through his suffering, to preserve a social air. But stricken with pain too merciless to hide, he lost his pretenses and staggered to his feet. My mother quickly supported him, and my father left my side and hurried to him. Together they helped him from the table, while other diners watched, staring with neither curiosity nor pity. I thought the musicians played harder all of a sudden to distract the people from the sight of an old man in trouble being led out of the main dining room of the Waldorf-Astoria.

"What is the matter?" I asked Tante Bep, who had been ordered with a glance to remain behind with me.

"Ach, Grosspa is not feeling well."

"Should we go with him?"

"But your ice cream."

"Yes, the ice cream."

Though we waited, my family did not return from upstairs. Finally, hot with wine and excitement, I was in my turn led to the elevator and to my room where Tante Bep saw me to bed. Nobody else came to see me, or if anyone did, long later, I did not know it.

❦

During the night more snow fell. When I woke up and ran to my hotel window the world was covered and the air was thick with snow still falling. Word was sent to me to dress quickly, for we were to go to the ship almost at once. I was now eager to see the great ship that would cross the ocean.

Again we went in two taxicabs, I with my father. The others had gone ahead of us. My father pulled me to him to look out the cab window at the spiralling snow-fall. We went through narrow dark streets to the west side of Manhattan, where we boarded the ferry-boat that would take us across the North River to Hoboken. The cab rumbled its way to the deck and into the cold damp interior of the ferry.

"Let's get out and stand out on the deck," said my father.

We went forward into the clear space at the bow just as the boat moved into the blowing curtains of snow. All I could see was the dark green water where we sailed, a little sideways, across to the Jersey shore. The city disappeared. We might have been at sea, as Grosspa would soon be. I felt something like loneliness, to be closed away by the storm from sight of what I knew. Yet I noticed how the ferryboat seemed like a great duck, and the trundling action of her power under water seemed like the engine-work of huge webbed feet. At a moment I could not exactly fix, the other shore began to show through the snow, and we docked with wet, grudging blows against the old timbers of the slip.

When we returned to the cab to disembark, my father said, "We are going to the piers of the North German Lloyd."

"What is that?"

"The steamship company where Grosspa's ship is docked. The *Kronprinzessen Cecilie.*"

"Can I go inside her?"

"Certainly. Grosspa wants to see you in his cabin."

"Is he there?"

"Yes, by now. The doctor wanted him to go right to bed."

"Is he sick?"

"Yes."

"Did he eat something?—" a family explanation often used to account for my various illnesses at their onset.

"Not exactly. It is something else."

"Will he get well soon?"

"We hope so."

He looked away as he said this. I thought, He does not sound like my father.

The cab was running along the Hoboken docks now. Above the snowy sheds rose in silent grandeur the funnels and masts of ocean ships, and now I could see how huge they were. They made me ache with a bowel-changing longing. The streets were furious with noise —horses, cars, porters calling and running, and suddenly a white tower of steam that rose from the front of one of the funnels, to be followed in a second by a deep roaring hoot.

"There she is," said my father. "That's her first signal for sailing."

It was our ship. I stared up at her three masts with pennons pulled about by the blowing snow, and her four tall ochre funnels, spaced separately in pairs.

As we went from the taxi into the freezing air of the long pier, all I could see of the *Kronprinzessen Cecilie* were glimpses through the pier shed of white cabins, rows of portholes, regiments of rivet heads on the black hull, and an occasional door of polished mahogany. A hollow roar of confused sound filled the long shed. We went up a canvas covered gangway and then we were on board, and I felt immediately the invisible but real lift and slide and settle of a ship tied to a dock. There was an elegant creaking from the shining wood work. I felt that a ship was built for boys, because the ceilings were so low, and made me feel so tall.

Holding my hand to keep me by him in the thronged decks, my father led me up a stairway whose curve was like the gesture of a sweeping arm. At the top we came to an open lobby with a skylight whose panes were colored—pale yellow, pale blue, pale green, orange—in a fancy design. From there we entered a narrow corridor that seemed to reach toward infinity. Its walls were of dark shining wood, glowing under weak yellow lights overhead. Its floor sloped down and then up again far away, telling of the ship's construction. Cabin doors opened on each side. There was a curious odor in the air—something like soda crackers dipped in milk, and distantly, or was it right here, in every inch of the ship around us, a soft throbbing sound kept up. It seemed impossible that anything so immense as this ship would presently detach itself from the land and go away.

"Here we are," said my father at a cabin door half-open.

We entered my grandfather's room, which was not like a room in a house, for none of its lines squared with the others, but met only to reflect the curvature of the ship's form.

At the wall across the stateroom, under two portholes whose silk curtains were closed, lay my grandfather in a narrow brass bed. He lay at a slight slope, with his arms outside the covers, and evidently he wore a voluminous white nightgown. I had never before seen him in anything but his formal day or evening clothes. He looked white—there was hardly a change in color between his beard and his cheeks and his brow. Seeing us, he did not turn his head, only his eyes. He seemed all of a sudden dreadfully small, and he gave the effect of being cautious in the world where before he had magnificently gone his way ignoring whatever might threaten him with inconvenience, rudeness, or disadvantage. My mother stood by his side and Tante Bep was at the foot of the bed in her black crocheted shawl and full peasant skirts.

"Yes, come, Richard," said Grosspa in a faint wheezy voice, searching for me with his eyes anxiously turned.

I went to his side and he put his hand an inch or two toward me —not enough to risk effort which would revive such a pain as had thrown him down the night before, but enough to call for my response. I set my hand in his and he lightly tightened his fingers over mine.

"Will you come to see me?" he asked in gallant playfulness.

"Where?" I asked in a loud clear tone which made my parents look at each other, as if to inquire how in the world the chasms which divided age from youth, and pain from health, and sorrow from innocence, could ever be bridged?

[135]

"In Germany," he whispered. He shut his eyes and held my hand and I had a vision of Germany which may have been sweetly near to his own; for what I saw in mind were the pieces of cardboard scenery, lithographed in dusty color, which belonged to the toy theatre he had brought to me from Germany on one of his returns from his journeys abroad—the Rhine in printed blue haziness with a castle high on a wooded crag; a deep green forest with an open glade in the far distance where gold lithographed light played through the leaves; a medieval street with half-timbered houses; a throne room with a deep perspective of white and gold pillars, a golden throne on a dais under a dark red canopy.

"Yes," I replied, "Grosspa, in Germany."

"Yes," he whispered, opening his eyes and making the sign of the Cross on my hand with his thumb. Then he looked at my mother. She understood him at once.

"You go now with Daddy," she said, "and wait for me on deck. We must leave the ship soon. Yes, Richard, *schnell,* now, skip!"

My father took me along the corridor and down the grand stairway. The ship's orchestra was playing somewhere—it sounded like the Waldorf. We went out to the deck just as the ship's siren let go again, and now it shook us gloriously and terribly. I covered my ears but still I was in the power of that immense deep voice. When it stopped, the ordinary sounds around us did not come close again for a moment. I leaned over the top of the railing and looked down at the narrow gap of water between us and the dock, where the spill and filth, the snake-like glide of small eddies, so far down below, gave me a chill of desire and fear. Snow was still falling—heavy, slow, thick flakes, each like several flakes stuck together, the way they used to stick in my eyelashes when I went out to play in winter.

A cabin boy came along beating a brass cymbal, calling out for all visitors to leave the ship.

I began to wonder if my mother would be taken away to sea while

[136]

my father and I were forced to go ashore. Looking carefully, I saw her at last. She came toward us with a rapid, light step, and saying nothing, she turned us to the gangway and we went down. She held my father's arm when we reached the pier. She was wearing a spotted veil, and with one hand she now lifted this up just under her eyes and put her handkerchief to her mouth. She was weeping. I was abashed by her grief.

We hurried to the dock street, and there we lingered to watch the sailing of the *Kronprinzessen Cecilie*.

We did not talk. It was bitter cold. Wind came strongly from the North, and then, after a third shaking blast from her voice, the ship slowly began to change—she moved like water itself, leaving the dock, guided by three tugboats which made heavy black smoke in the thick air. Everything went by in a trance-like slowness, but at last I could see the ship, all of her, at one time.

I was amazed how tall and narrow she was as she stood out to the river at a long angle, stern first. Her four funnels seemed to rise like a city against the blowy sky. I could squint at her and know just how I would make a model of her when I got home. In midstream she slowly turned to face the lower bay. Her masts were like lines I drew with my pencils. Her smoke began to blow forward. She looked gaunt and proud and topheavy. At a moment which no one could fix she ceased backing and turning and began to steam clear and straight down the river and away.

"Oh, Dan!" cried my mother in a caught sob, and put her face against my father's shoulder. He folded his arm around her. Their faces were stretched with sorrow.

[137]

Just then a break in the sky across the river let light open on the snowy day and I stared in wonder at the change. I was the only one who saw it, for my father, watching after the departed liner in his thoughts, said to my mother,

"Like some old wounded lion crawling home to die."

"Oh, Dan," she sobbed, "don't, don't!"

I could not imagine what they were talking about. In my own interest and wonder, I tugged at my mother's arm and said with excitement, pointing to the thick flakes everywhere about us, and against the light beyond,

"Look, look, the snowflakes are all black!"

My mother suddenly could bear no more. My witless excitement released all her feelings. She leaned down and shook me and said in a voice now strong with anger,

"Richard, why do you say black! What nonsense. Stop it. Snow-flakes are white, Richard. White! White! When will you ever see things as they are! Oh!"

Her grief gave birth to her rage.

"Come, everybody," said my father. "I have the car waiting."

"But they *are* black!" I cried.

"Quiet!" commanded my father

We rode to the hotel in silence.

❧

We were to return to Dorchester on the night train. All day I was too proud to mention what I alone seemed to remember, but after my nap, during which on principle I refused to sleep, my mother came to me, and said,

"You think I have forgotten. Well, I remember. We will go and arrange your presents."

My world was full of joy again. The first two presents were easy to find—there was a little shop full of novelties a block from the hotel, and there I bought for Anna a folding package of views of New York, and for Mr Schmitt a cast iron model of the Statue of Liberty. It was more difficult to think of something Ted would like. My mother let me consider by myself many possibilities among the variety available in the novelty shop, but the one thing I thought of for Ted I did not see. Finally, with an inquiring look at my mother to gain courage, I asked the shopkeeper,

"Do you have any straw hats for horses?"

"*What?*"

"Straw hats for horses, with holes for their ears to come through. They wear them in summer."

"Oh. I know what you mean. No, we don't."

My mother took charge.

"Then, Richard, I don't think this gentleman has what we need for Ted. Let us go back to the hotel. I think we may find it there."

"What will it be?"

"You'll see."

When tea was served in her room, she poured a cup for each of us, and asked,

"What do horses love?"

"Hay. Oats."

"Yes. What else."

Her eyes sparkled playfully across the tea table. I followed her glance.

"I know! Sugar!"

"Exactly"—and she made a little packet of sugar cubes in an envelope of Waldorf stationery from the desk in the corner, and my main concern in the trip to New York was satisfied. My father returned with all the tickets and arrangements to go home.

At home, in the next few days, I could not wait to present my gifts.

[139]

Would they like them? In two cases I never really knew. Anna accepted her folder of views and opened it up to let the pleated pages fall in one sweep, and remarked,

"When we came to New York from the old country, I was a baby, and I do not remember one thing about it."

Mr Schmitt took his Statue of Liberty in hand, turned it over carefully, and said,

"Well—."

But Ted—Ted clearly loved my gift, for he nibbled the sugar cubes off my outstretched palm until there was not one left, and then bumped me with his hard itchy head making me laugh and hurt at the same time.

"He likes sugar," I said to Mr Schmitt.

"*Ja.* Do you want to ride?"

❦

Life, then, was much as before until the day a few weeks later when we received a cablegram telling that my grandfather was dead in Munich. My father came home from the office to comfort my mother. They told me the news with solemnity in our long living room where the curtains were now closed against the light of the world. I listened, and I had a lump of pity in my throat for the look on my mother's face, but I did not feel anything else.

"He dearly loved you," they said.

"May I go now?" I asked.

They were shocked. What an unfeeling child. Did he have no heart? How could the loss of so great and dear a figure in the family not move him?

But I had never seen death, I had no idea of what death was like.

Grosspa had gone away before now and I had soon ceased to miss him, what if they did say now that I could never see him again, as I had never again seen John Burley next door in all these years? I could show nothing. They shook their heads and let me go.

Anna was more offhand than my parents about the whole matter. "You know," she said, letting me watch her at her deep zinc laundry tubs in the dark, steamy, confidential basement, "that your Grosspa went home to Germany to die, you know that, don't you?"

"Is that why he went?"

"That's why."

"Did he know it?"

"Oh, yes, sure he knew it."

"Why couldn't he die right here?"

"Well, when our time comes, maybe we all want to go back where we came from."

Her voice, speaking of death, contained a doleful pleasure. The greatest mystery in the world was still closed to me. When I left her she raised her old tune under the furnace pipes and I wished I were as happy and full of knowledge as she.

My time soon came.

On the following Saturday I was watching for Mr Schmitt and Ted when I heard heavy footsteps running up the front porch and someone shaking the door knob forgetting to ring the bell. I went to see. It was Mr Schmitt. He was panting and he looked wild. When I opened the door he ran past me into the front hall calling out,

"Telephone! Let me have the telephone!"

I pointed to it in the bend of the hall where it stood on a gilded wicker taboret. He picked up the receiver and began frantically to click the receiver hook. I was amazed to see tears roll from his eyes and down on his cheeks which looked ready to burst with redness and fullness.

"What's the matter, Mr Schmitt?" I asked.

I heard my mother coming along the hallway upstairs from her sitting room.

Mr Schmitt suddenly put down the phone and pulled off his hat and shook his head.

"What's the use," he said. "I know it is too late already. I was calling the ice plant to send someone to help."

"Good morning, Mr Schmitt," said my mother coming downstairs. "What on earth is the matter?"

"My poor old Ted," he said, waving his hat toward the street. "He fell down and just died in front of the Weiners' house."

"Oh—" and my mother spoke words of sympathy.

I ran out of the house and up the sidewalk to the Weiners' house, and sure enough, there was the ice wagon, and in the shafts, lying heavy and gone on his fat side, was Ted. There lay death on the asphalt paving. I confronted the mystery at last.

Ted's one eye that I could see was open. A fly walked across it and there was no blink. His teeth gaped apart letting his long tongue lie out on the street. His body seemed twice as big and heavy as before. Without even trying to lift it I knew how mortally heavy it was. His front legs were crossed, and the great horn cup of the upper hoof was slightly tipped, the way he used to rest it at ease, bent over the pavement. From under his belly flooded a pool of pale yellow fluid—his urine—and from beneath his tail flowed the last of his excrement, in which I could see oats. In his fall he had twisted the shafts which he had pulled for so many years. His harness was awry. Melting ice dripped at the back of the hooded wagon. Its wheels looked as if they had never turned. What would ever turn them?

"Never," I said, half aloud. I knew the meaning of this word now.

In another moment my mother came and took me back to our house, and Mr Schmitt settled down on the curbstone to wait for people and services to arrive and take away the leavings of his changed world.

I went and told Anna what I knew. She listened with her head on the side, her eyes half-closed, and she nodded at my news and sighed.

"Poor old Ted," she said, "he couldn't even crawl home to die."

This made my mouth fall open, for it reminded me of something I had heard before, somewhere, and all day I was subdued and private, quite unlike myself, as I heard later, and late that night, I awoke in a storm of grief so noisy in its gusts that my parents came to me asking what was the trouble?

I could not speak at first, for their tender, warm, bed-sweet presences doubled my emotion, and I sobbed against them as together they held me. But at last when they said again,

"What's this all about, Richard, Richard?" I was able to say,

"It's all about Ted."

This was true, if not all the truth, for I was thinking also of Grosspa now, crawling home to die, and I knew what that meant, and what death was like. I imagined Grosspa's heavy death, with his open eye, and his loss of his fluids, and his sameness and his difference all mingled, and I wept for him at last, and for myself if I should die, and for my ardent mother and my sovereign father, and for the iceman's old horse, and for everyone.

"Hush, dear, hush, Richard," they said, and it was all they could say, for who could soften or change the fact of death?

A pain in my head began to throb remotely as my outburst diminished, and another thought entered with rueful persistence, and I said in bitterness,

[143]

"But they were black! Really they were!"

They looked at each other and then at me, but I was too spent to continue, and I fell to my pillow, and even if they might insist that snowflakes were white, I knew that when seen against the light, falling out of the sky into the sliding water all about the *Kronprinzessen Cecilie,* they were black. To children—as to artists—all life is metaphor. Black snowflakes against the sky. Why could they not see that? Black.

CHAPTER VII

※

Center of Interest

Summer was the time when the world seemed to open itself distance upon distance ahead. Some things that happened in growing summers were stranger and stranger afterward, as though created afar by distance itself, and never to be seen close to.

On our first evening at the United States Hotel in Saratoga in the following summer, I heard a man and a woman talking behind a lattice twined with vines and electric lights that divided one section of the long piazza from another.

I was already washed and dressed for dinner after the whole day's drive from Dorchester. We were on our way to a vacation in the Adirondack Mountains on a little island which my father had leased. Saratoga was magical to my eyes. The evening was warm, and shadows were falling in the groves of the deep park behind the hotel. Colored lights were everywhere, even in the fountain of the courtyard, where they changed the hues of the ever-arching waters as I watched. The vast corridors with their moon-like lamps and the endless piazzas with their platoons of rocking chairs and the deep carpeting inside and the gallantry of guests all dressed up for evening held great appeal for me at ten years of age. They said a band was going to play in the court during dinner and afterward.

I was so full of curiosity about this place where we planned to rest for two or three days on our motor trip to the mountains that when I came downstairs before my parents were ready, I left behind me in my room my new toy sailboat which I had carried in my hands all the way from home. She was bound for her launching in the mountain lake where our island—Thunder Island—awaited us.

After exploring the main floor and the grounds of the United States Hotel, I settled into a rocking chair by the lattice to watch the fountain where the water was playing with sounds like whispers of laughter repeated over and over. Against this I heard from beyond the vines the conversation whose meaning I reconstruct here.

"He was with them when they arrived," said a man's voice. "I was in the lobby at the time."

"Yes," said the woman, "I saw him. They make a nice little family. She is a pretty thing."

"I hardly noticed. I could hardly take my eyes off him."

"Who—the father?"

"No—the boy."

"Oh. Oh, yes. I see." Her voice flattened. "Of course. He is a sweet looking little fellow."

"Sweet looking?" The man laughed in a muted horn-like tone. "Marjorie, you never really see what you look at, you know."

"Oh, I don't know. Sometimes I don't want to."

"Ah. Thank you. Though perhaps you don't mean what it sounded like."

"No, really. I meant nothing."

"No, I hoped not. But his eyes are so deeply blue, and he has all that dark gold hair brushed so thickly, it falls over his forehead on one side. And his cheeks are ruddy without being hot-looking— really, I wish I knew them so they would let me paint him. I would paint a wonderful thing. He stands beautifully, too. How old do you suppose he is?"

"Oh, perhaps eleven or so."

"It is the last of the age of innocence, isn't it. You can say what you like as a school teacher, Miss Marjorie, but true beauty disappears when knowledge arrives."

The woman laughed scoffingly, and with affection.

"Oh, Hubert, you're no good at philosophy. Every time we meet for our summer holiday together I wonder what your new tack is going to be."

"Always trust a New England female friend to be handy with the disagreeable truth," said the man with a comic sigh.

I held my rocking chair still so I could hear this exchange. Their voices interested me. They did not sound like anything in Dorchester. Marjorie's was dry, her words were clipped, and her accent, I know now, suggested Boston. Hubert sounded like a New Yorker, perhaps a grown-up Bayard, though his tone was richer and more mellow than you heard generally in New York. He had a mocking sort of elegance in the way he said things. What did they look like?

※

Leaving my chair so carefully that it did not even creak, I went to the lattice and peered through the vines. By the bright fountain light I saw that Marjorie looked old enough to be Hubert's mother—grey-haired, thin-faced, and wearing a black lace shawl over her grey silk evening dress. Hubert sat facing me. He was perhaps my father's age, very slim, with black eyes that had a hard gaze in his thin face. His nose was odd—once broken, it was still bent, like a parrot's bill, I thought, and when he spoke, his voice sounded bent. Revealed by a constant, downward smile, his teeth were irregular in shape and color. A tired, if humorous, look of perpetual disappointment and hope came out of all these elements. Since most people dressed for

[147]

dinner at the United States Hotel, he was in a dinner jacket. He held his narrow shoulders stiff and high.

"How would you paint him, then?" asked Marjorie.

"As I first saw him, I think. He was wearing a blue serge jacket with brass buttons and white ducks and he was holding a toy sailboat and he was looking at the boat with his head a little to one side, and dreaming the boat into life. You know?"

"Oh, yes, yes, I see it."

I held my breath. They were talking about me.

I felt an obscure thrust of pleasure and love—self-love, I suppose. It was an exalting feeling. I longed to hear more, but just then I recognized sharp little footsteps behind me on the bare wood between the carpeting inside and the raffia runners on the planking of the piazza, and my mother called, generally toward the fountain,

"Hoo-hoo, Richard! Here we are!"

She didn't see me until I turned and went to her. She looked particularly lovely in her evening dress with her bits of jewellery. Her color was high. She was in love with my father and with me. It was a comfortable state for our family at that time. My father, feeling as charming as he looked in his dinner jacket, took my right hand formally and said,

"Good evening, Doctor. I believe we are to enjoy your company at dinner?"

My mother bridled at his comedy, as she always did, in case anybody might be about who would not understand our jokes.

"Oh, you two," she said. "Do come. I'm starving. I adore this place. I must never leave it."

My father put his arm around my shoulders and said,

"Doc, how about trying the boat in the fountain tomorrow? Do you think she'd work?"

"I don't know. There's a lot of spray. She might get her sails wet."

"And then she would tip over, I believe," he said.

[148]

"Yes."

"Well, if your mother wants to stay here in Saratoga, she can simply stay, and you and I will go on to the lake, and sail that pretty boat all day long."

"Very well," she said gaily, "I'll stay. You two can go on at any time. I won't be bored. I never saw so many attractive men anywhere."

"Well, of course," declared my father, putting on a stern look which fooled nobody, "that settles it. We'll all leave in the morning."

My mother decided to be fooled.

"Why Dan, how can you talk like that. We promised ourselves two or three days here. We wanted to find another couple and play bridge in the evenings. I've already asked the lady from Elmira. Really. Your jealousy is such a bore."

She began to use the word that summer.

"Oh, so I am a bore?" said my father.

"I didn't say that. I said—."

"I know what you said. We're scaring Doc, now. Let's forget it and go to dinner and have two cocktails each."

And in truth, I was uneasy about their mock quarrel, for who could ever be sure when grown-up people meant what they said or not? Laughing together, they put me between them and we went to the vast dining room which even then just before the first World War looked old-fashioned enough to be interesting.

※

During dinner the band began to sound from the fountain court. The lights, the water and the music all made me sleepy and cloudy in mind. I felt everything in a mist of formless pleasure, as though once again all had been devised for my own particular enjoyment.

[149]

When we left the table, it was time for me to go to bed, but as a special observance of the first evening of our family holiday, we all strolled together in the fountain court and out through an arch of tall trees into the park where flowering bushes and little groves grew darker and more mysterious and inviting the farther we walked from the music and the lights.

"What a place for a honeymoon," said my father huskily.

There was an occasional ornamental iron lamp among the leaves to guide lovers along the paths, but these served only to make little coves of darkness and summery sweetness where bushes or trees grew like enclosing walls.

We soon turned around and went back to the court and up the steps to the piazza. There I saw Hubert with Marjorie. As we passed him, I heard him say to her, for his voice followed me as his eyes did,

"I know it's your bedtime, Marjie, so I'll just look around for a table of bridge. Let's meet late for breakfast."

She nodded and went indoors.

After a few steps, my father said,

"Why don't I go ask him if he will join us, and make a fourth?"

"Yes, do," replied my mother. "I'll take Richard upstairs and pop him into beddy-bye, and be right down. Where will I find you?"

"There's a big red card room off the sun porch. Look for me there."

He gave me a punching sort of hug and sent me off with her. I watched as long as I could to see him go to speak to Hubert, and the last I saw was a delighted, astonished look on Hubert's face, and a rapid nod of agreement to join a table of bridge.

At breakfast, they talked about him with me.

"Well, Doc," said my father, "how would you like to be famous?"

"Oh, Dan, don't spoil him so," murmured my mother.

"How?" I asked.

"We met a man last night," said my father, "who is famous. His name is Hubert Monckton. He is a famous portrait painter. Even I have heard of him."

I already knew more than my parents about all this but I kept silent. My father continued,

"We played bridge with him and the lady from Elmira, and what do you think. He wants to paint your picture."

I looked at my mother to find out how I should think about this.

"Yes, he really does," she said. "Of course, I told Daddy it was all nonsense. But Mr Monckton did rave about you."

"He says you are like a Sir Thomas Lawrence. Eighteenth century. English."

"I still think," mused my mother idly, "that it is most odd that he would try to interest perfect strangers in letting him paint their child."

"He wasn't angling for a commission," replied my father with maddening reasonableness, "he doesn't have to do that. He said—you heard him say—that wherever he found a fine subject he always tried to establish some connection so that he could work it up into a sketch, and maybe a painting."

"Well, we'll only be here a little while longer," said my mother, "and he would never get a picture done in that time."

"He asked me where we were going. When I told him Thunder Island, he said he had friends up at our lake and might come there."

"Well," said my mother, "I am sure it is all very flattering and exciting and I can think of nothing that would bore Richard more horribly than posing for his portrait. You ought to see how he acts when I take him to the photographer's! Pity he didn't ask me to pose for him."

It was a strange, disturbing feeling to be the center of such unexpected interest, and I wished that my parents regarded Hubert Monckton's request as more than a breakfast joke.

"Well, anyway," said my father, "he plays a splendid game of bridge and I look forward to this evening again."

"Oh, yes, he really played brilliantly, didn't he," answered my mother. "He's really the most charming man I've met in years. Isn't it odd. He's not good looking. But he has great charm. I suppose it is the way he has of looking at somebody as if he never saw anyone as charming as they are."

"No," said my father, "it's more than that. He talks well. He seems to know everything about everybody and more than enough about everything else. So, when he says *anything,* he draws on so much that *whatever* he says it is interesting. I hope I make myself clear?"

"Who was that old lady with him?" I asked.

"Why? Did you see her?"

"Yes"—but I did not explain where I first saw her.

"She's his mother's best friend," explained my mother. "Miss Hobson. She teaches at a ladies' college in Boston. His mother is dead, but they used to have their vacations together all three, and now the two of them keep it up, in memory of his mother. He says he wouldn't know what to do without Miss Hobson.—Richard, you have not eaten a thing. Sit up now and come to the party."

My cereal spoon began to travel its appointed course in an abstracted sort of way. I felt powers and mysteries behind all that my parents discussed so lightly, and I tried to think what could be the

[152]

meaning of what I had overheard the evening before. But there were limiting blurs at the edge of my thought, and it made my head ache slightly to try to pierce beyond them, and I was happy and relieved when my father said at the end of breakfast,

"Come on, Doc, let's try the boat in the fountain."

❦

Action in sunlight and spray was a joy. We sailed my sloop along the edge of the fountain basin, keeping the sails dry, and if you put your cheek down on the cold wet stone of the basin and half closed your eyes and watched the sloop from that unaccustomed angle of vision, you could have her at sea, tipping before the breeze, and you could make her little darting turns slow down and become grand long tacks of a full-sized vessel with yourself on board at the wheel.

"Good morning," said a voice I knew.

"Oh, hello, Monckton," said my father. "We're trying out a new sailboat."

"She's a beauty," said Hubert.

"Richard," said my father, "get up and speak to Mr Monckton."

Hubert and I shook hands. He looked as though he couldn't stop smiling if he tried.

"Well, I'm glad to know all the family now," he said to me. "Your father and mother and I became great friends last night over the bridge table. I hope you and I will be too."

Again I had the feeling of knowing more than any of them, though I couldn't say what about.

My father answered for me.

"Richard makes friends easily wherever he goes. We're very

[153]

glad of it, since he is an only child.—Look, look, Doc!" he exclaimed, turning me around to the fountain, "she's getting away from us!"

I went back to my sailing. After a few more words with my father, Hubert strolled away.

※

I did not see him again until early evening. Then he came idling along the gravel walk and found me sitting on the grass in the lighted fountain court, writing postcards to my friends at home. He was, I thought, dressed up like a society artist on a resort holiday. His hat was a straw sailor. He wore a white silk shirt with a loosely knotted tie, and a blue and black striped blazer. Tapering with his slender legs, his trousers were of white flannel, and he wore white buckskin shoes, and he carried a light, whiplike cane of bamboo.

"I'm out for a little walk," he said. "Would you like to join me?"

I wanted to finish what I thought of as my correspondence, but invitations from adults were really commands, and I scrambled to my feet and put my postcards into my jacket pocket.

We walked into the park. It was already dark under the trees and the lanterns were glowing. The damp ground gave off a musty fragrance that made your breath feel heavy. Crickets sounded in the bushes. From very far away, it seemed, the hushed laughter of the fountain water came and went behind us on the wafts of air. We saw nobody else in the park—people were indoors changing for dinner.

"Richard," asked Hubert as we walked driftingly into the deepest part of the gardens, "how old are you?"

"Ten."

"No! I would have thought a year or two older. You seem such a grown-up boy in many ways."

"I wish I was."

He laughed.

"The irony of it. All too soon you will be wishing you were a boy again."

"No, I won't."

"You will see.—Would you mind if I smoked?"

"No."—Why would he ask me that? I had heard men ask women the same question, but why ask me?

He lighted a cigarette from a gold case. His hands trembled slightly as he managed the matches.

"Richard," he asked then, "do you have a happy life?"

"I guess so."

"You have such charming parents. So beautiful, both of them."

My mother was beautiful, but how could he say that of my father, or any man?

"I am sure," he added, "that they are very good to you."

"Oh, yes. They are."

"And do you make them happy?"

"I don't know.—They know I love them."

"Do you tell them everything?"

"What do you mean, everything?"

"Oh, you know—everything you do. Or do you keep some things to yourself?"

"I guess I tell them everything I remember. But sometimes I have so many things that I forget some."

"How delightful. How delightfully you put it.—Tell me, what is it like, at home, in Dorchester?"

Under his brief, prodding questions, I told him of our house, and Anna, who had gloomily helped me to grow up, and of our leafy neighborhood, and of my school, and of our church.

"Then, you go to Mass regularly, all of you?"

"Yes."

"Do you like it?"

Who ever thought of that before? I neither liked it nor disliked it. It was beauty and it was faith and it was like the day or the night, enclosing all. Lamely I replied,

"I like to see the candles all lighted and the colors of the vestments and hear the music."

"Yes, I know. I know exactly what you mean.—Tell me, Richard, have you everything you want?"

"I suppose so."

"No, I mean, is there some particular thing you don't have that you'd love to have, that somebody could give you?"

He induced a luxurious greed in my thought, and I began to think hotly of a real motor boat, not a toy, and a live pony, and a full-sized cavalry sabre. But a great part of love was secrecy, and I could not speak of these objects of my desire—the only sort of desire my years could reveal to me.

"No," I said.

"What a wonderful, strange boy.—I hope you don't mind—I've been looking at you from a distance all day." His voice was full of extra breath. He spoke near to me. "Let's sit down here—there's a little bench in the bushes."

We sat side by side and I let my legs swing.

"What will you be when you grow up, Richard?"

"My father calls me Doc. I am going to be a surgeon."

"How fine. To save lives. I am sure you will make a wonderful surgeon. Let me see your hands." He threw away his cigarette and took my hands and turned them over. "Yes. They are the hands of an artist or a surgeon. Long fingers. Sensitive fingers." He pressed my hands damply and then released them. "Imagine how it will be when you have your own office, and those wonderful little pinpoint lamps to use for examining people, and all the clean, bright instruments, and everybody coming because they need you."

I said,

"My father says there are great discoveries that have to be made. He says medicine has the greatest things to find out for people. I think I will try to find out all sorts of things and tell all the other doctors so they can use them too. I will never ask poor people for a single dollar, but I will take care of them free, and I will make them get well. My father says a man should always love his work, and he says I will love my work as a doctor, but he says that a doctor loves his work, yes, but more than that, he has to love *people, all* people, he says, and has to work for them, because he has to relieve suffering! That is what I am going to do! I am going to do it, when I grow up!"

My thoughts, suddenly opening into this pour of words, gave me a feeling of power. Imagination made the future immediate and real for me. I was already a great surgeon. I spoke with commanding certainty. I was physically alive with passion. My face felt hot with passion. My body quivered with passion. It destroyed Hubert.

"Ah, Richard," he said with a sound like a swallowed sigh. Then, with movement so slow that he seemed to watch his gesture as if helplessly betrayed by it, even as he gazed at himself, he succumbed. Subject to the rustling night, with the far band music beginning its evening waltzes, and against a distant shimmer of fountain light reflected on the topmost and farthest trees, and enclosed by shadows like substance in the grove, and under the night scent, and pierced by the prickling song of the crickets in the bushes, he closed his arms about me and his lips searched for me in a moaning intensity which carried with it the breath of his recent cigarette. I had no idea of what he meant as he grasped me with a sinewy nervousness against

[157]

which I struggled on principle like a young cat who refuses to be held.

As the cat always does, I gained my freedom, and I burst into a loud mocking laugh.

Fear, pleasure, shock, disgust—he might have anticipated these and perhaps could have met them out of experience. But hilarity? It was the last response he expected. Stricken away from his embrace, he asked in an urgent whisper,

"What are you laughing at?"

"You!"

"What for? It may have been a lot of other things, but it wasn't funny!"

"Oh, yes it was!"

"Why was it?" He sounded full of anguish and hope.

"Because only girls kiss!"

The hearty conventionality of this ended his hope and started his panic.

"Richard!" he said, standing up suddenly to impress me the more, "please, please forget what happened, and please, please, don't tell anybody about it. Will you promise? You said there are some things you forget to tell. Oh, forget this, will you? You don't know how important it is, Richard? I didn't mean anything!"

Only then did I become frightened of what had happened and of him.

"No," I said heartlessly, "I'll tell anybody I want to!"

"Oh, anything—if you will promise, and keep your promise, I will get you anything you want!"

Without answering I ran away down the path. I heard him running after me. He must have been in terror. He called my name in soft gasps, pleading with me to wait and listen before we should be overhead. But I ran and he dared not overtake me as I reached the fountain court where the light was so full and the music so loud. He remained in the shadows, surely in anguish.

My father and mother were on the piazza steps.

"Where on earth have you been?" asked my mother.

"What have you been doing, Doc?" asked my father.

Something in their faces made a secret of what I could have told them. How little do parents really know of the lives they have given to the world. Panting from my run, I said,

"Nothing. I was in the woods, and I thought it must be time for dinner, and I ran."

"Well, it is indeed, we have been looking everywhere for you. Go up and wash your paws and come down as soon as you can. We're going to play bridge again and we're already a little late to start the evening."

❦

We were just finishing dinner when Miss Hobson came to our table and my father and I rose to greet her.

"The strangest thing," she said. "My friend Hubert Monckton, you know? He has been most unexpectedly called away. He has already packed and gone. He asked me to make his excuses to you for not making a fourth at bridge with you this evening."

"Oh, what a shame," said my father. "I hope he did not hear some bad news?"

"I cannot say. He was much agitated, and only spoke to me briefly. My holiday is quite ruined. But I am sure he had good reason—he is a most conscientious man."

"Oh, we liked him so much," said my mother.

"He took quite a shine to our boy," said my father with a proud, innocent smile.

[159]

"Yes, I know. He spoke of wanting to paint him."

I stood under all this with bowed head and private knowledge. I resolved never to tell anyone what I knew and I never have.

After Miss Hobson made her way upstairs, my mother sighed prettily and said,

"What a bore. Now we must find another fourth."

CHAPTER VIII

❧

The Spoiled Priest

With what wonderful ease a boy could live in two worlds at the same moment—the world of whatever books he might be reading, and that other world believed in by the people about him.

❧

The snow hardly stopped falling on Paris in the winter of 1451. It clung to all the roofs and towers like great featherbeds. In the narrow, crazy, medieval streets, snow lodged against doorways and piled sloping banks against one side of the passageways between houses. By night the wind staggered the snow off roofs in a stinging shower and if you happened to be passing that way you felt it on your cheeks and against your eyes, especially if you went before dawn, when all was so dark. The cold breathed inside your clothes and against your prickled skin. You pressed your lips tight because a draught of air made your teeth ache. There were few lights to be seen. The sky was only just lighter than the city. People were dying of plague in certain houses and children who went to sleep a few hours ago might never awaken, but would forever be like waxen angels with their eyelids closed over blue chicken-eye shadows. The poor were starving and the rich—even the king and queen and the royal princes in their stone towers above the freezing river—had little enough to eat and drink. They all prayed to the Blessed Infant of Prague for food and safety. If you had to be out at night hurrying on some adventure or act of duty you heard sounds that froze the blood in your veins. The wind tore itself around chimney tops and towers, now crying like a child, again shrieking like an evil spirit. You hurried to be indoors, not daring to pause until you came where you must be. If you stopped you heard the most terrible sound of all hurrying after you along the driving air. It was the howling of wolves on the very outskirts of Paris. Some said they even ventured into the town, for they too were starving, and would be glad enough to come upon someone, especially a boy, who went alone before daylight through the streets of Paris until he could reach the narrow sacristy door set under its deep pointed arch in the grey stone of the cathedral. When you came at last to the cathedral close and in spite of the whipping snow saw the door dimly dark against the wintry walls, you hurried still faster out of relief, and also out of final respect for the wolves who lived on snow and wind and who called out their angry hunger as if they knew you were there to be taken and who if they stood upright would be as tall as your father. Sometimes there was a sweet crack of light showing under the door but sometimes all was yet dark. In any case you must throw yourself against the heavy iron ring of the door hoping that the sexton had already come to unlock it from within. Then you could let yourself in, stamping the snow off your feet and saying a prayer of thanks that once again you had come safely past the night and the wolves of Paris to serve the early Mass at Holy Angels Cathedral where the curate, Father Coach, in his languid and muscular way, would be the celebrant at the high altar. Only then, safely indoors, did you know with the other part of your mind that the winter darkness and the sharp cold before daylight and the empty streets were those of Dorchester, New York, in the year 1915.

※

And then I was of course safely in the world of everybody else, and the streets had held no wolves, but only distant streetcars which made occasional flashes of blue electric light as their trolleys jumped gaps in the power lines overhead. I always remembered the grinding song of their wheels on the ice-cold rails when they turned a corner. I had to walk seven blocks from my house to the cathedral, which was our parish church. I must have come to the sacristy with my vision of medieval Paris still in my eyes, for Father Coach said when he saw me,

"Richard, what are you so excited about?"

"Nothing, Father."

"You look as if you had seen a ghost or a tiger."

It was a temptation to say, "No, Father, a wolf," but I knew enough not to expect anybody that much older to see what I saw, even though Father Coach was only in his early thirties, and seemed more like a boy than most men I knew.

"Never mind," he said, "you have one minute and sixteen seconds to get into your cassock and surplice. I have already lighted the candles myself. I would like some day to be able to count on a boy not to be late to whom I have cheerfully given my whole and entire trust."

"Yes, Father. My clock almost didn't go off at all."

"I think with one or two simple questions I could demolish that statement.—Are you ready?"

He put on his biretta, took up his veiled chalice and the tabernacle key with its golden chain and real gold tassel, dipped his hand in the holy water font and gave me his wet fingertips to take a few drops for myself, we crossed ourselves, and went forth to the almost empty church to celebrate together the Holy Sacrifice.

As I did each time, I felt a hollow, carved-out sensation at my stomach, wondering if I would make any mistakes this morning, and whether if I did so, God, and Father Coach, would forgive me. My worst usual mistake was to move too fast, whipping the skirts of my cassock with my legs, and audibly bumping the carpeted floor and steps of the altar with my knee as I genuflected. True reverence, I remembered, was never hasty. On the other hand, it was worse to be lazy or dull. But who could exactly match that wonderful combination of ease and intensity which Father Coach showed in all he did? Move like an athlete who need never hurry because he knew exactly how to do all? Stroll with the effect of marching, and turn like a sail in the wind? He was my model and my despair, both of which he intended to be, for the good of my soul and for the purpose which he had sought within me.

❧

Who that was there could forget the day when he came to our classroom to look us over and assure us that he had no hope at all of finding the sort of boy among us whom he searched for?

Without warning the classroom door opened and there he stood, glaring and smiling at our teacher, Miss Mendtzy, and nodding his head as if to say "I thought so" about nothing.

Miss Mendtzy all but genuflected as though he were the Blessèd Sacrament or a bishop, and cried,

[164]

"Oh! Father! We are so honored! Pray come in!"

Still nodding silently he lounged through the door ignoring us who all rose as we had been trained to do when a priest entered the room. He took off his biretta and unbuttoned the long black coat he wore over his cassock and finally said,

"What grade are these boys in, Miss Mendtzy?"

"Fifth grade, Father," she answered, motioning us to be seated.

"A pretty ragged crew, I suppose?"

"Oh, no—they are bright, splendid, hard-working boys, Father. Just ask them questions. You will see."

We dreaded "questions." Everything we ever knew flew out of our heads like sparrows when a visitor asked a question.

"No. No questions," said Father Coach. "I know without asking that I won't find what I want in here. God knows where I will find it if I ever do. When I think," he said slowly, nodding sorrowfully and yet with courage at Miss Mendtzy, "when I think how Our Lord is patiently waiting, and how hard it is to find anybody to come and serve Him, and how if you think you have found someone they almost always let you down, and what is worse, let *Him* down, why, then, I almost give up."

"Oh, no, Father!"

"Yes, Miss Mendtzy. But of course we have to go on, we both know that. But honestly, now, Miss Mendtzy, can you stand there and tell me that you really and truly think there are boys, there's even two boys, no, wait, even *one* boy, in this room who could ever do what Our Lord has to ask him to do to serve Mass?"

"Oh, Father."

"No, I know it is hard for you to say. But when you think of what it takes, you just have to wonder."

"Yes, yes," murmured Miss Mendtzy, hypnotised by his fervor and his strong, slow speech, "to be neat and prompt!"—the prime virtues she stressed for us in the classroom.

"Ho. If that were all." He seemed almost to menace her with his keen gaze as he addressed her for our benefit. "Do you know, Miss Mendtzy, what it is to hear the alarm go off in pitch darkness, *yangggg!*",—we jumped in our seats at the sudden violence of this —"and how cold it is in winter, and then to get up shivering and strip off your nice warm pajamas and go like a man to take your cold shower"—she cast her glance away in modesty at the idea of male nakedness in the shower "—and then without breakfast to pull on your earmuffs and your mittens and your mackinaw and set out through the empty dark streets where who knows what danger may be lurking? And do you know that if you are in a state of sin how Our Lord grieves at seeing you come to serve Him with a black mark on your soul? Do you know that if you have a headache, or ate something the night before that don't set so well this morning, you still have to get up and go before anybody else is awake and stirring? Our Lord never sleeps. Is it so much to ask if someone will get up after a good night's sleep to be with Him?"

"Oh, I know, yes, Father, my gracious."

He still did not look at us but he gave one hand in a slow, wide gesture indicating us all.

"*You* know, Miss Mendtzy, and *I* know, but do *they!*"

Respectful of him, she was also loyal to us. She loved us. We teased her sometimes, but we loved her, too.

"Oh, yes, Father, I believe they know." She turned to us. "Don't you, boys?"

"Yes, Miss Mendtzy." We sang out our dictated answer instantly in unison, in the pattern of our schoolroom manners.

Only now did Father Coach face toward us. He scowled. His wide pink young face went darker. His pale eyes burned with light. His short-cropped blond hair seemed to stand up more stiffly. He positively threw his spirit at us, and we thought, "Coach!", for his ideal for the priesthood was to make it take on the manner of the athletic coach, and in fact he insisted that his name be pronounced as if it were spelled Father Coach, though actually it was Koch.

"All right!" he cried loudly, with a whirl of his arms, "I don't think any of you have got what it takes. I think you're all yellow! I think you would rather lie in bed and keep snug and think about breakfast and pretend to be still asleep and take naps like a cat until your mother comes and says—" he imitated a woman's voice inexpertly—" 'Come on, now, Willie, time to get up out of your bedsy-wedsy!' "

We writhed with shame. How did he know exactly how we felt in bed?

"You!" he shouted at the boy in front of me. "If you had the stomach-ache and absolutely knew you couldn't get out of bed that day, would you have the guts to ignore how you felt, and get up, and get dressed, and go out in the snow, and hurry to the cathedral in time to serve six o'clock Mass for me?"

"I don't know, Father," said the boy out of honest confusion.

Father Coach threw his hands and let them fall against his long thighs and said,

"What did I tell you? Is there *anyone* here with the heart of a soldier and the will of an athlete who thinks he *could* serve Our Lord however hard it might be?"

We threw ourselves forward against our desks and reached our hands toward him, snapping our fingers in the air to be noticed individually, aching to be chosen.

"Me, Father," "Yes, Father, here, here," "Me, me, Father!"

He let us snap and pant for a long moment in the agony of our desire to prove him wrong about us. Then slowly he began to nod. He murmured aloud as though to himself, and we heard Greatness musing.

"Well, who knows. Perhaps I am wrong. Perhaps there *is* a boy here who would literally rather lie down and die than miss his duty at six o'clock every morning, rain or shine, winter or summer. Where is he?" He roved our faces with his stern, light-lashed gaze to make us die for him if he would ask. Suddenly he pointed at me and I had a strike of certainty that he had meant to pick me all along. "You. Who are you?"

I rose and told him.

"All right, Richard. How far is it from your house to Holy Angels?"

"Seven blocks, Father."

"Does the street car run by that way?"

"No, Father, it runs downtown instead."

"So you'd have to walk, is that it?"

" 'S, Father."

"Are you a good walker—Is he a pretty good walker, class?" he asked, turning to us all, now radiantly genial, so that if we loved Father Coach when he was furious at us, we must worship him when he liked us.

"Yes, Father—" but somebody hidden in back made a tongue and lip noise of derision. A sacred silence fell. Then Father Coach said in deep quiet,

"Whoever did that will tell about it when he goes to Confession on Saturday. I feel sorry for him. He is full of envy because he was not chosen. He is in the grip of one of the Seven Deadly Sins. I will ask Richard to pray for him at the foot of the altar. Richard: you: are: chosen. Report to me today and every day after school for instruction. I will telephone your mother to congratulate her on the great honor you have won today. Thank you, Miss Mendtzy. Please do not punish the individual who made that disgusting noise. His punishment will come from Somewhere Else."

Resuming his biretta with a lazy bend of his head sideways, and squaring his shoulders, he left the room with an exhibition of physical power under control which made us desire to be exactly like him in every way.

And yet I was now cast down by my new eminence. How could I ever measure up to Father Coach's standards? Matters were not helped for me with my classmates when Miss Mendtzy, sparkling with happiness behind her pince-nez, declared,

"Class, I am sure we are all very pleased for Richard, and very proud that this great honor has fallen on one of our own boys. To be almost a preesst! To think of the good of it for his soul!"

An atmosphere of gloom settled over the rows of desks and with a heavy heart I prepared to enter the service I had striven for. I wondered if my soul had begun to feel different.

❦

For a long time in my childhood I thought my soul—and therefore every soul—was a small, flattish lump of wax lodged obscurely in the spinal column. It was there, but nobody could see or touch it. My image of it was derived from the holy object called the Agnus Dei, which was a small square or oval packet of velvet or fine baize or silk, edged with fancy tatting by nuns, and showing a colored picture of the Lamb of God on its front. It was slightly padded, and the padding was a piece of blessed bees' wax which could not be seen but whose thickness could be felt. The Agnus Dei was pinned to the underside of a boy's lapel or to some hidden fold of a girl's dress. The blessing it carried was a protection against the world. Mine—I wore one for a little while in the third grade—almost made me rich.

For one day while I was playing with a friend at his house in our neighborhood his grandmother came to smile upon us. She was a thin, tall woman with a face, I thought, like that of a chipmunk who gazed through frail golden eyeglasses. From the wrists of her black silk dress lace cuffs fell over her hands, which she carried crossed at her waist. Finding my jacket where I had thrown it carelessly, she picked it up to fold and smooth it and set it away more properly, and she saw my Agnus Dei under my lapel.

"Richard, what is this?" she called.

"It is my Agnus Dei."

"What is it for?"

"It was blessed by the priest and so you wear it to be protected."

Her cheek pouches seemed to fill and quiver with horror. I had never thought about it, but my friends in that house were not Catholics. Now the grandmother put down my jacket with a shudder. She was thinking about something. In a moment she called,

"Richard, do you believe all those things that the priest tells you? And the sisters?"

"Yes."

"Do you believe in God?"

"Certainly."

"But you do not read the Bible, do you?"

"No. They read it to us in church."

"But how can you know God if you don't read the Bible? It is the only way to know Him. All the rest that they do to you has nothing to do with God. It is just for the sake of the Church and themselves. Don't you know that?"

"I don't believe you."

She smiled with bitter patience.

"You are too young to know, Richard.—Would you like to have a dollar?"

"Yes."

"I will give you a dollar every week if you will do something for me. For yourself."

"What is that?"

"If you will read the Bible every day for five minutes I will give you a dollar every Saturday, after you tell me what you have read. Here. Wait." She hurried to her room and returned with a small black limp Bible with edges stained red. "Take this with you and oh, my poor boy, be faithful! How I wish I could save you!"

Save me? I who had a guardian angel who was beside me at that moment though nobody could see him? I smiled and took the Bible.

"All right," I said.

"Dear, good Richard. Here is a dollar in advance. I just know you will earn it between now and Saturday and then we will talk and I will explain what you did not understand in the Bible and then you will have another dollar."

"Well, gosh, Grandma," said my friend, complaining because he had no such swift rise to fortune. She silenced him with a colorless glance of unexpected force.

❊

That evening my father came to say goodnight in my room.

"How's the Doctor?" he asked.

"Fine."

"What did you do today?"

"I played after school at Dodie's."

"What did you play?"

"We played soldiers. He has a thousand hundred of them."

"Did you have a battle?"

"Yes."

"Who won?"

"He did."

[171]

"Why."

"It was his house."

"I see. Was anybody else there?"

"His grandma."

"Oh, Lord. Yes, I suppose so. Poor old soul."

"Why is she poor old soul?"

"Why, you know, they're Presbyterians. They never have any fun out of life."

"They don't?"

"No."

"Why not?"

"It's too hard to explain."

"But she's very, very nice."

"Of course. They're all nice.—Why is she very, very nice?"

"She gave me a dollar. I put it in my bank."

"Why did she give you a dollar?"

He was getting that keen, whitened look he got when finding out something. His eyes darkened and his mouth went thin sideways a little. I began to be sorry I had mentioned the dollar. He didn't seem to like the idea.

"She gave it to me to read something."

"You mean if you promised to read something she would give you a dollar?"

"Yes. A dollar every week."

"*What?*" He stood up from my bed. "And what is it you are supposed to read to earn a dollar every week at your age?"

"The Bible. She gave me one. She said it was the only way to know God, and to save me."

He took a step backward. His mouth fell open. On his brow came a frown like that of God the Father. His eyes rayed blue fire. I never saw him so angry. He made a fist of his right hand which trembled at the punishment he would inflict upon the meddling old woman who sought to corrupt his son away from his Faith.

"And for *money!*" he shouted hoarsely, completing his thought. "To take an innocent child and tempt him with what no child could resist!—Where is that Bible?" he demanded.

"On the dresser."

He went and took it up.

"And where is that bank?"

"Behind my Book of Knowledge."

He went to my bookshelf and threw down several volumes of the Book of Knowledge until he found the bank which was made of cast iron in the shape of a spaniel one of whose ears lifted up to receive deposits of money. He threw the bank to the floor with force. It broke. A folded green dollar bill lay among small coins.

"Is this her dollar?" he asked.

"Yes."

"Say goodbye to it. And don't you ever, ever accept money from her, or anybody else, unless you come and ask me first whether you may do so. Is that clear?"

"Yes, Father."

"Do you know what she tried to do to you?"

"No."

"She tried to take you away from our Holy Mother Church. Would you want that?"

"No."

"I should hope not." He sickened a little as his anger subsided from its first power. "My poor old Doc. First he got rich and then he got poor. Never mind, boysie, your father will take care of you. I'll get you a new bank. Now you ask God to forgive you if you had any idea of what you were doing, and ask Him to keep you, and say a prayer of thanks to your guardian angel for how this turned out, and go to sleep."

"What are you going to do?"

[173]

"I am going to return her Bible and her dollar and tell her that you will not be allowed to go to their house again."

"Can't I ever play with Dodie again?"

"Yes. Over here. Not at his house so long as that old buttinsky is there."

"Well, gosh."

"I know. But I don't want you near her. She will go to Hell for this."

"She will?"

It was an awesome thought made the more so because he delivered it with shocked regret.

"Yes," he said, "and so would you, if she had her way. I'm going right over there."

A few minutes later I heard the front door thunder and tremble gently with its great oval pane of plate glass. As I went to sleep I spoke to my guardian angel as usual, who answered me, not in words, for he never used words, but in thoughts or ideas which came in return for my prayers to him. It was a momentous exchange that night, for as clear and lovely as light on water the idea came to me that in return for my escape from Hell I would do well to give my life to God by becoming a priest. Wonder and greatness, all in explicit detail, enfolded me as I went to sleep an ordained priest that night.

In the morning when I awoke my idea was still with me, and it remained with me in secret all that year, and when Dodie's grandmother died one night, I sorrowed for where she had gone. Presently I drew nearer to my vocation when Father Coach chose me as server for his six o'clock. In my own eyes, I was a miniature priest, already close to the Divine Mysteries, and I was impatient to come closer still.

One morning after Mass I lingered alone in the sacristy. It would be half an hour before the rector of the Cathedral, our pastor, old Monsignor Tremaine, came to vest himself for his own Mass at seven. His vestments were all laid out for him on a wide deep counter above ranks of tray-like drawers. His black biretta was there too, with its silky pom-pom of red violet.

How would I look if I were a priest and wore it? And that maniple and stole of white heavy watered silk with hard thick gold embroidery over which the light zipped when you turned to give a blessing? The chasuble had a heavy, rich design of rose vines in gold, tracing the shape of the cross. It was too large for me to wear, and I fingered it hungrily; but I could manage the other things. I put the stole around my neck and slipped the maniple over my left arm. The counter was about the height of an altar. It became my altar.

I put the biretta on my head. It was only slightly too large. I put it on and off several times as though observing the sacred name during the *Gloria* or the *Credo,* and then I set it down on the counter and bent over and kissed the altar and then raising my arms to God I recited, "Benedicat vos omnipotens Deus," preparing to turn and bless the people, "Pater et Filius et Spiritus Sanctus," and I turned, and there watching me stood Monsignor Tremaine in the doorway of the sacristy.

My blessing died away in midair.

He came forward slowly, looking at me with keen and serious brown eyes in his creamy pink face. He usually smiled and hummed a continuous tune, but now he came silently and gravely to me.

"Richard, what is the meaning of this?"

[175]

"Nothing, M'nsígnor," I said.

"Have you forgotten your instructions that servers are never, never to handle the vestments except to assist Father?"

"No, M'nsígnor."

"Then why did you dress yourself up in them? Don't you know they are holy objects, with sacred meaning? They have been blessed. Don't you know that?"

"Yes, M'nsígnor."

He took the stole and maniple from me and laid them on the counter and picked up his biretta and put it on. He wore it toward the back of his head. It gave him at once a look of Old Testament strangeness and authority.

"Did you mean to desecrate these things?"

"No, M'nsígnor."

"What were you *doing,* then. Playacting?"

"No, M'nsígnor."

Usually patient and kind, he now grew exasperated.

"Don't be such a dunce. What *were* you doing, then?"

"I was trying to feel how it would feel to be a priest, and say Mass."

"You weren't making fun of it?"

"Oh, no, M'nsígnor."

"I see. Well. Richard. Let me see."

He became solemn and gentle. He leaned down and put his hand on my shoulder. He let it rest there heavily as to impress me with the seriousness of what I might say.

"Why did you want to feel that, Richard?"

"I don't know."

"I think you do. Tell me truly, now. Do you think you want to become a priest?"

It must be, I thought, that there are simply no secrets which children can keep from their elders.

[176]

"Yes, M'nsígnor."

"Then this makes a great difference. Come with me."

He led me to the sanctuary and he knelt down on the lowest step of the high altar and had me kneel beside him and he said,

"Let us ask Our Lord to help us to know if this a true vocation you have or not. If it is, you shall have all the help we can give you. It is the greatest thing I could hope for you. *Our Father Who art in Heaven,*" he prayed, and *"Hail Mary full of grace,"* and *"Glory be to the Father,"* and I prayed with him, giving the responses aloud to each prayer.

Then it was time for him to vest himself for his Mass, and he sent me off to breakfast and school, for the world went on and he must go with it, and so must I.

※

The next morning after Mass Father Coach said to me,

"So there's some sort of idea running around in that empty head of yours."

"I don't know, Father."

"Yes, you do. Monsígnor told me. He has put me in charge of your vocation. How old are you?"

I told him.

"Ten years more, and five or six years on top of that. Do you think you can last that long?"

"I don't know, Father."

"Do you want to know something?"

"What, Father?"

"It gets harder all the way. Do you know that?"

"Yes, Father."

[177]

"No, you don't. You don't know the first thing about it. Well, I'll try to give you some idea. If you can take the first hurdles maybe you can last the race. We'll see. Beginning tomorrow morning, I'm going to say a Mass at five-thirty, and you're going to serve it, and we'll see just how much you mean all this wearing of vestments and saying 'Dominus vobiscum.' "

"Yes, Father."

"After that we'll think of other ways for you to prove yourself. Nobody ever claimed the way was easy. It wasn't for me. Well, I made it. We're going to find out if you're man enough."

" 'S, Father."

"Skiddoo."

How he would have loved to have his own son whom he could train as an athlete from the first hour of life, in the image of one who had no thought but to serve God. He believed he had the most solemnly great reason in the world for putting me through an ordeal which would have been difficult for a man. He became a tyrant as he tested me in all ways he could imagine. He taunted me with mockery and weakened me with harsh criticism. Nothing I did could ever satisfy him. When I faltered at serving Mass, or left without saying the extra prayers of thanksgiving after Mass which he had set me as exercises proper to one who thought he was a priest, or had a cold and could not swallow my sneezes, or missed Communion on a weekday because of sins I could not confess until Saturday, he rose over me with lazy contempt, slowly nodding at how much of a fool he had been to give his time and trust to someone so faithless. He began to make me twist and flee him in my dreams, so that I awoke exhausted, and audibly yawned at Mass, for which I would again know his scorn.

I decided that he hated me, but—a master of the change of pace, like any good coach—every now and then he would suddenly ease up in my training, and take me with him to get books at the Catholic Union Library, or do some extra shopping for the rectory table; and then he would be easy and confidential with me, letting me have bits of gossip or even a sarcastic comment or two on the life of the rectory, quite as though I already belonged to his sacred brotherhood whose members, being human, had opinions and sometimes vented them.

"Monsignor, you know?" he would say, raising an eyebrow at me, "God bless him, Monsignor thinks of himself as a musician. Can you beat it? Thinks he can play the piano. Gave up a concert career to be a priest."

"Well, can he play?"

"All thumbs. They say the Bishop calls him Maestro. They were classmates."

Or,

"If you want cookies and milk after Mass, you'll have to get in good with the housekeeper at the rectory. But I advise against it."

"Why, Father?"

"The price is too great."

"Well, what is it?"

"You know that gasping, smelly old dog of hers, the one she calls Scruffy?"

"'S, Father."

"Offer to give Scruffy a bath, or walk him around the block. She'll give you the moon. But if you start it, you'll have to keep it up. Lay off, is my advice. She's—" and he made a finger go round and round like a little wheel at his temple. "The only reason His Nibs keeps her on is that she can bake the best mince pie in Upstate New York. And I'll tell you another thing, if you ever come around me smelling of Scruffy, *we're through*. Get me?"

Threatening to end our league, he handsomely established its existence for me, and I kindled warmly to his fondness. At such moments I would think my troubles were over.

[179]

But they never were. One morning he said,

"I suppose you think you believe in God?"

"Oh, yes, Father."

"Who is your favorite in the Holy Family?"

"Jesus."

"Which statue do you pray before?"

"The Infant of Prague."

"Why?"

"He is a boy."

"He is a King."

"I know. He has a crown."

"And an orb, which means the world, which He holds in His very own hand, and He blesses the world with His other hand. Well, this King, then. Do you pray to Him about your vocation?"

I had honestly to admit that I had never done so.

"And yet," he scoffed, "you say you believe in Him."

"But I do."

"No, you don't. If you did, you'd ask Him every day and every night to tell you to be true to Him and go all the way to become one of His priests."

"How could He tell me?"

"How could He tell you? Don't you ever get the feeling that your prayers are being heard and answered?"

"I don't know, Father."

He scratched his head in knuckly despair at such a boy.

"I suppose," he said with almost a lisping drawl of sarcasm, "you won't be satisfied until He appears to you in a vision and says, 'Hello, Richard, how's the boy! Great news I hear about you. Keep up the old fight!' Go on. Get out of here. Don't be late in the morning."

They noticed at home how restless I was, and unable to eat. I looked thin and felt thinner. Nobody knew what I was suffering and why. If only I could be sure that I must suffer, then I believed I could suffer all that might have to come to me. But how could I know?

I woke up one night remembering Father Coach's taunt about expecting a vision. My heart jumped against my bony chest to mark the moment of a great discovery. Why should I not ask for a miracle? If I could make the Infant of Prague hear me and believe how I loved Him and wished to serve Him, then I could make Him appear to me and give me the answer I needed. Once again I slept at peace, for I knew what I must do, however dangerous and difficult it might be to arrange.

Since Dodie's grandmother had died, I was allowed to go to his house again. Sometimes I went to stay all night with him.

I now got him to ask me to spend the night and then I reported this to my mother. She gave permission. I went to Dodie's for supper and then told his family I suddenly had to go home. They protested, and for a moment Dodie's mother meant to telephone my mother to ask if I might not stay? But quickly I said she must not do this, as I had not brought my plaid bag full of homework, which was true, and they let me go.

I was free for the night and my great purpose lay before me.

❊

I went to the Cathedral of the Holy Angels and entered by one of the four side doors. It was about half-past seven. The doors would be locked at eight. As I knew, all the doors—even the sacristy door— had bolts which were secured from within by heavy keys which the sexton would carry away with him on their iron ring.

Three or four people—women and a man—were kneeling far

[181]

apart from each other in the cavernous twilight of the church. The only illumination came from two immense bronze lanterns high in the transepts.

All was so still that now and then when a little draught stirred the wick of a votive lamp this became a large event. The soaring vaults of the ceiling seemed as far away as the sky. Like cloth woven of darkness itself, long rows of shadows hung as pillars from the arches of the aisles.

The smallest sound—a creak of a bench under one of the praying people, a door opening or closing far off in the sacristy, the beady click of a rosary against a pew—set up echoes in the high vaults with the sound of a whispered voice saying, "H-o-w-w-w?" in a long sigh that seemed to take forever to die away.

The sanctuary lamp threw no light but only hung in the air like a red star, how near or far who could say? The altars were dark. Before some of the statues burned little wicks in colored glass. One of these was my goal—the Infant of Prague, whose crown, orb and blessing I could barely discern from the rear pew where I crouched.

I kept my eyes upon Him because I must come to Him later; and also because if my eyes roamed, they might be drawn to certain objects which even in broad daylight always gave me a heavy fear in my soul—that flat wax lump caged within me—and which in this sighing darkness made my mouth dry up at the thought of them.

These were the tombs of the two previous bishops of Dorchester which stood against the rear wall of the sanctuary, one on each side of the high altar. Marble sarcophagi which rose high as a man, they were carved and indented with miniature Gothic colonnades on all sides. Carved marble mitres and heraldic devices rested on the massive lids. Bishops, I knew, were buried in their vestments. It was sorrowful and terrifying to think of them as richly robed they lay there in those great boxes of marble, unlike all the other dead who were part of the earth in green cemeteries.

[182]

The presence of the dead bishops almost made me give up my resolve to stay the whole night in the locked cathedral, kneeling before the image of my patron the Infant of Prague, Who before daylight came and the doors were unbolted must appear to me in a vision. If He would do this, no doubt would remain about my vocation, and perhaps I would be left in peace by Father Coach.

At a few minutes before eight the sexton came around and told the people it was time for them to leave. They all seemed to be old people who rose heavily to their feet and one by one made their aching way down the aisle and out the main door, while I cowered in the dark under my pew. I was in a panic to run out after them, but already it was too late for escape. The sexton had already secured the side doors, and now after the last visitors of the night had left God to go down the outside steps, he rang home the heavy bolts in the bronze main door. Going up the center aisle to the sanctuary where he paused to look around for a last duty that night, the sexton, himself an old man, genuflected in a rapid little cringe and went on to the sacristy. In a moment, out of sight, he turned off the two lanterns in the vaults of the transepts. Leaving the sacristy for the rectory where he would hang up his key-ring in the kitchen, he left me alone behind him. Only the distant, pure points of flame in the votive lights in their ranks of blue, red and yellow glass, and a few other candle lamps before certain statues, remained to define the darkness.

"H-o-w-w-w . . ." sighed the vaults so far above me. The church was cold. In the darkness where I could not see I felt huge for a moment, and then small—smaller than I was.

Perhaps he had forgotten to lock one of the doors. I went to each of the side doors, and even to the main doors, but all were securely locked. My footsteps sounded like those of someone else following me. I looked to see who it might be and could not see who was there. Far at the end of a side aisle was the shrine of the Infant of

[183]

Prague. I hurried there and knelt down in the first pew before it. A candle lamp with red glass burned at His feet. The light flowing upward over Him made His eyes look empty in cups of shadow above His plump young cheeks. I said,

"Blessèd Infant of Prague, have mercy on me,

"Blessèd Infant of Prague, have mercy on me,

"Blessèd Infant of Prague, have mercy on me," and I felt myself losing command of my imagination, as happened in times of intense feeling.

※

You could see in the red glass how the fires of Hell always looked, except that this glass was only one little pool of fiery light, and those fires were everywhere all about you. You could not count the bodies of the damned. In their legions, they were thrown upon each other, fixed in writhen positions upon red-hot rocks, and they were naked, men and women alike, as you had seen in your grandfather's copy of Dante's *Inferno* with plates by Gustave Doré. Their mouths were open and silent. Their eyes were gazing and empty.

You had seen fires burn—wood, leaves, refuse; and it was the law of fire that after a little while in the flames nothing was left of any-thing except ash. But in Hell nothing ever burned away, it simply kept on existing in the fire, and it would do so forever and ever. You thought that if fire would only burn those condemned bodies up once and for all this would have been terrible but it could be accepted as an idea: short, frightful suffering, and then the end of feeling. But you forgot when you thought in that way how the very law of Hell was to provide suffering that had no end. And so you saw those quadrillions of men and women burning forever and yet never consumed.

[184]

In a moment you saw someone you knew. She tried to cover her-self from your wondering gaze. She said nothing, her mouth hung open, and her hollow eyes looked and looked at you, and she bowed her head slowly and sadly at you, and you recognized Dodie's grand-mother. She made you feel responsible for sending her there. Would she have gone if you had not told about her? It was something you would never know. Not knowing was another kind of punishment if it was something you absolutely had to know.

Did you know anybody else in Hell? Your grandfather had died in Germany. Was he in the fires or was he in Heaven? He must be in Heaven.

The bishops in their marble boxes—how was it with them, and their golden croziers and their jewelled rings and crosses and the zipping light over all the silks and embroideries of their vestments? When the cathedral vaulting whispered "H-o-w-w-w . . ." it might have been their voices that you heard, for they were to lie there forever, and there was no way for you to get out either. You would rather be a martyr in an open place in ancient Rome than die here and be enclosed forever in white marble darkened by night.

The catacombs must be like a whole train of tombs. You knew how their corridors wound along underground like the burrowed tracks of great worms. There the early Christians had found safety with their single candles and their hidden Masses. You thought probably they too had been afraid but they went on praying under the ground as if they lived and would die in their own graves. You knew how courageous they were, and what great examples, but you did not want to live in your own grave until you died and had to use it forever. Who knew? Perhaps, you thought, they too may have wanted to live in the open air?

Pity for the longings which lay buried with all the dead of the world rose within you and made your throat thicken and your eyes smart. You knew about rising from the dead. Why was it so terrifying? Because it was contrary to nature. It would be something happening that simply could not happen. But if enough wishing took place, perhaps by all the dead of the world, then they might rise again, even if this was contrary to nature?

Now because your eyes were used to the darkness you could see most faintly the shapes of familiar objects in the cathedral. You could see the tombs of the two bishops. If the marble lids, which weighed tons, began to open slowly, perhaps twisting sidewise smoothly and silently as if oiled, you would be able to see this happen.

The lids opened, it seemed, during a passage of hours, but at last in either sarcophagus there was enough open space in the shape of a wedge of pitch darkness to allow the dead to rise into view. You could see rising first the coiled and jewelled head of the golden crozier which was buried alongside the bishop; and then his hand, wearing scarlet gloves, embroidered in gold, with his episcopal ring on the outside of his glove, grasping the marble edge of the box, and then the white pod-shaped crown of his mitre lifting up. And then he would come into the air of the church he had loved, where he had sat on his throne so many times amidst incense and candle-light and air mightily shaken by the voices of organ and choir, and if he turned and looked at you without eyes and spoke to you, you would have to answer in proper singsong, "Yes, Right Reverend Bishop." What if he looked like Uncle Fritz who died to become a bishop? You would love to see Uncle Fritz again—but alive, not dead. And then what if—as you had read somewhere—the bishop's body might in an instant fall down in dust on its encounter with the air of the living world after so long a time in the breathless dark of the tomb?

And yes: if that could happen, then the statues in the locked cathedral might also move on their altars, and you would be surrounded by others risen from the dead, for the saints were all once alive.

[186]

"Blessèd Infant of Prague," you prayed, suddenly remembering Him, "let them stay dead!"

You shook as if you were freezing. Your teeth clattered in your skull. In the dark it was difficult for your hands to find each other in order to join in prayer. Terror exhausted you so that you thought you might fall asleep at any minute, as if you could not endure any more of the night of the dead.

And just then you could hardly believe what began to happen. You watched it with your eyes wide open.

❁

The statue of the Infant of Prague began to glow with light. The light came from all around it and inside it and in front of it. It was a kind of light that did not light up anything else around. It lighted only the statue in still radiance. Kneeling before the light, you put your arms wide back with your hands opened to it as if to receive it. You were no longer frightened; only too amazed to say anything.

The Infant of Prague opened His arms aside as if to say, "Yes, it is true, Richard, this is a vision, I am appearing to you," and then brought them back to their usual position holding His right hand up in blessing, carrying the orb in His left. His face was like a real child's, alive with joy.

For a long time nobody said anything, but just exchanged their gaze. Then the little painted plaster mouth of the Infant of Prague, moving like the mouth of a real child, said, clearly,

"Never fear, Richard. They will stay dead."

Though He was only a child, He spoke like someone grown to all knowledge.

[187]

"They will?" you asked in wonderful relief.

"Yes. Now was there anything else?"

But if you had something else to ask Him, you did not remember what it was. Happiness and safety put such peace over you that you began to fall asleep not out of fear now but out of ease. The last thing you recalled was how the Infant of Prague, who always held His right hand with His fingers fixed to make a blessing, now actually moved His hand again and blessed you. His light then vanished. The statue was dark again above its red lamp.

※

When I felt a rough grasp on my shoulder I awoke throwing myself hard against the back of the pew. Father Coach was there. At the windows faint light was announcing the day.

"Get up," commanded Father Coach. "Come with me."

His voice was level and hard. I rubbed myself awake and found out where I was.

"Get going," he added. There was no comfort to be had from his sound. I went rapidly ahead of him to the sacristy where we could talk out loud without disrespect to the Blessèd Sacrament.

"Now explain yourself," he said.

I looked down tongue-tied.

"How long have you been in the cathedral?"

"All night."

"I see. I am not ready to explain your presence all night as an act of piety. How do *you* account for it? What leads me, when I arise before five o'clock to come here and perform my usual early morning devotions, to find a delinquent intruder? Do your parents know you are here?"

"No, Father."

"So you had no thought of how they must be frantic with worry?"

"No, Father. I mean, yes, Father. They thought I went to stay all night at Dodie's."

"But instead, you stayed here. Is that it?"

"Yes, Father."

"So you are a liar as well as a trespasser."

"No, Father."

"You aren't?"

"Yes, Father."

"And I had the stupid belief that here was a boy who would some day be a man, and that man a priest. How do you like that."

"Yes, Father, that's why I came."

"Why you came?"

"Yes, Father. You said the Infant of Prague would have to appear to me and tell me about being a priest."

"I never did. Watch your tongue, young man."

"Yes, Father. But you did. So I came and stayed before Him all night."

"And I suppose He took the trouble to come down from Heaven and appear to you? What makes you think you would be worthy of such a thing?"

"I'm not, Father. But He did."

"Did what:"

"He did appear to me."

"Now just you look out, young fellow, I won't take much of this. I don't have to stand here and listen to blasphemy!"

"But He did. I saw Him. He talked to me. He was as bright as an electric light."

"And what, if I may make so bold as to ask, did He say to you?"

I saw then that my case was about to be lost, for in truth, the Infant of Prague said nothing to me about becoming a priest, which was what I was supposed to discuss with Him. Miracles, I saw for the first time, were not always clear in their meaning.

"Richard?" prompted Father Coach with an edge of threat in his voice. I knew how flat it must sound when I had to reply,

"He told me not to be afraid."

"Afraid? Of what:"

"He said all the dead people would stay dead."

Father Coach folded his arms and set his head to one side and looked at me with his eyes drowsily half-closed as if to see me for the first time. Then he began to nod slowly like a man who has had to accept an unwelcome fact.

"All right, Richard," he said with ominous patience, "you get along home. I'll telephone your parents you are on your way. I'll report what you have told me. They will know best how to deal with it. I'm just sorry that all my faith in you, and my confidence, the hours I have given over to your training, the thought I put in day after day on how to toughen you up for your future, I'm just sorry all this has been for nothing."

"But Father, I have to serve your five-thirty."

"Not any more, you don't. Not after all this record of breaking every rule in the cathedral, and lying to your parents, and trumping up this crazy vision you had, and thinking I would accept all this."

"I never meant anybody to know. I just wanted to know myself."

"Well, you know now, and what's more important, so do I. I hate to tell Monsígnor all about this. It will merely break his heart, that's all. Go on, get going."

When I came home the sun was not yet up. All the lights in our house were on. After Father Coach's call, my father was on the porch waiting for me. In silence he grasped me by the arm, hurried me upstairs to my mother's room where she lay with witch-hazel on a handkerchief cooling her throbbing brow while tears welled out of her eyes. When she saw me she reached for me and pulled me to her breast.

"All night long!" she murmured against my cheek. "We have been frantic. The police are looking for you! Your father has been driving around through the streets all night long, looking and looking, between here and Dodie's. How could you do this to us!"

"Is that my son?" asked my father coldly. "To act out a lie to his parents? Only by accident did I find out. I saw your plaid homework bag under the hall bench and I drove over with it to Dodie's so you could do your homework, and they said you had gone home." He turned to my mother. "That will do. Let him go. It is time he came with me."

"Oh, no, Dan," she said. "Don't."

"Let him go. He has to learn. Come with me, Richard. And all that talk about a vision of the Infant of Prague. You simply fell asleep and had a dream. Come on."

This was what Father Coach meant by having my parents deal with me. My father whipped me with his mahogany-colored razor strop and then sent me to bed. In an effort to resolve one kind of trouble I had thrown myself into another kind. Was that how life went? Once again I took refuge in sleep and slept all day until late afternoon. Then I was awakened by a delegation.

My father came bringing Monsignor Tremaine. I shrank in my bed toward the wall.

"No, my boy," said Monsignor Tremaine, "I have not come to scold you. Sit up."

My father put a chair for him and he sat down, leaning toward me. He sparkled with freshness—his white starched collar, his trim black suit, the thread of red-violet showing above his high-buttoned vest, his pink and white head.

"You are feeling rested, now, Richard?" he asked gently. His kindness made me want to cry for the first time that day.

"Yes, M'nsígnor."

"Well, you have given us all more to talk about than we've had for years. Some people want to punish you. Others think you are perhaps a little over-sensitive to some things, and perhaps you need a little while of getting more sleep and eating well and putting some flesh on your bones. I don't really know why you did what you did. I think maybe you don't know why, yourself, really." (But I did.) "But now that it's over, no real harm has been done, and I came to see you and tell you not to worry. It may be too soon for many things, Richard. I myself, you know, I didn't know until I was in college that I was meant to be a priest. And even then it took me a mighty long time, and not a happy time, altogether, I can tell you, until I knew."

"Yes, M'nsígnor."

I did not understand at the time what he was trying to tell me; I felt only his warm humanity, and the forgiveness it was made of. He turned to my father and said, as though I had ears but would hear not,

"You know, Daniel, the whole thing looks like boyish nonsense, somewhat overwrought and feather-headed, and of course, it may be just that. But never forget the chance in a thousand that there may be real holiness somewhere in it. Only God knows which it might be. But what if He meant it the way Richard received it? See what I mean?"

My father looked at the floor like a young man and nodded silently. Monsignor Tremaine turned back to me and said, as he arose,

"Get yourself rested and healthy again, my boy, and your imagination won't give you as much trouble. But if it does, don't be sorry for yourself. God gave us all our faculties, including that one. It may lead you to Him to serve Him for life, or it may lead you to bring something to your fellow-men as an artist of some sort. For the present, try to be just a boy. God bless you."

CHAPTER IX

⚜

A Discharge of Electricity

A summer later, a bond of fear was broken for me in honor of another bondage—perhaps one more tyrannical.

⚜

"Do you think—?" asked my mother, looking at the sky above the darkening mountains across the mottling lake.

"It may," said my father. "What do you say, Miles?" he asked Miles O'Connor who with his wife Nell and their son Billy—a boy in my class at school—had come to spend the weekend with us at our cottage on Thunder Island in the small Adirondack lake where we were again spending the summer.

"What if it does?" replied Miles in his loud voice which always gave what he said a furious sound, despite what he may have felt. "We would only get wet."

We were on the rustic porch of the cottage where the air was already chilled by the rain that began to sweep toward us across the lake. Our picnic was all packed in hampers, we had extra cushions waiting in a heap, and Miles O'Connor had his banjo by the throat, ready to bring it along so that after we had eaten and the embers were renewed with under-scrub from the woods where we were going in a cove on the mainland he could sing for us to his own accompaniment. There was an unexpected sweetness in his voice when he sang, a hint of a self the world never otherwise knew. But all secrets ask to be heard, and my mother once said that next to making money, Miles O'Connor would rather sing than anything.

The wind reached us and as it did the sky opened in a sustained rip of white lightning. There was a short horrifying pause as if all breath were cut off and then the thunder cracked over us and the rain came down like a waterfall repeated endlessly in a sky-wide mirror. In one moment we could see our white launch, the *Arrow*, sliding and rocking at our dock below the cottage, and in another she was erased by the rain. It suddenly seemed hours ago instead of minutes that we had been ready to board her gaily to ride across the lake for our Friday evening picnic.

"This won't last," shouted Miles to my father.

❊

I heard no more, for I ran into the house and down the damp hallway whose raw wooden walls released the smell of pitch-pine, and into my room where Billy was to sleep with me. I slammed the door and went to my clothes closet and shut myself in and sat on the floor with my hands over my ears. My heart shook me with a slow pounding stab at every beat. I prayed for my life, as the air cracked like mountains about our island in the storm.

"My Jesus, mercy!" I thought at every bolt. "Hail Mary full of grace," I said in between times, and "Oh, my God, I am heartily sorry for having offended Thee"—for I knew from nuns, and from

Anna, and from the bravely concealed winces of my mother every time it lightninged and thundered how I might be struck dead by God's rage, which was surely what sounded out of the sky.

I felt rather than heard a banging on my closet door. I uncovered my ears to hear.

"Come out of there!" called my father, pulling at the closet door. I tried to hold it fast. He sounded disgusted but full of control.

"Please: Dan:" said my mother. "There is no use making him even more afraid." She talked across his shoulder.

"In front of those people," said my father. How could his son so fully have humiliated him before his business partner, whose boy Billy was never afraid of anything? "It's time he had this nonsense whaled out of him once and for all."

"I know," said my mother. "But just please, dear, leave this to me."

The storm struck again and I hid my senses in the frail darkness of the closet. When again I listened my father had gone back to the O'Connors on the porch, where they stood silently staring at the storm which though lessened in force still held on and slashed them with rain, which they endured because Miles refused to budge.

The door of my closet opened when my mother gently pulled at its rusty iron latch.

"Richard:" she said. "Don't you think you might decide to live, and come out, now?"

I regarded her in silence.

"The storm is going away," she said.

As though to contradict her, a bolt struck a tree at the tip of our island and the crack of it seemed to set all things in the world an inch or two aside. My mother shrugged in exasperation.

"Oh, I don't like it either," she scolded, "I hate it. But really: my dear: we have guests: we *must*—"

Her social spirit was stronger than her own nervousness (I had often seen her cross herself secretly during thunder and lightning) and she now tried to make me into the son of her braver self by adding,

"When this clears, it may still be light enough to see, and we will go in the *Arrow,* and you can bring your new airplane kite that Daddy brought you from town, and you can show Billy how to fly it."

"I don't want to show Billy how to fly it. It's mine."

"Then don't, don't, oh, my God, why am I given such a boy!" But she knelt down and embraced me, and said, "What geese we all are, *everybody* is afraid of *something,* only they don't show it."

"My father isn't," I said resentfully.

"Oh! If you knew! But he is brave. Don't you want to be brave?"

"I don't care."

"Oh, yes you do. Every man does."

"I never cry any more."

"I know you don't, my darling. You are very brave."

"My father said a man does not cry."

"He did? Of course he did. Well, then, you must believe him."

But her voice seemed to carry some sad knowledge otherwise. She sighed and pulled me to stand, saying,

"Come, Richard, we simply must go back to the others."

"I don't want to"—for now I was ashamed of myself. She knew why. She said,

"Yes, one of the things about behaving badly in front of others is that the time always comes when we must be with them again. The only way is to go back immediately. So come. Miles is furious at having his picnic spoiled by the storm. We mustn't spoil it even more."

We returned to the porch.

The thunder was now hiding behind the mountains and the rain was hanging in open curtains instead of in solid falls. Outspoken like his father, Billy O'Connor said to me,

"What's the matter with you?"

"Now Billy," said Nell O'Connor, with a smile of complicit understanding at my mother, "don't be rude. Richard has come back to us, and we're all going to have a scrumptious time."

I know from old photographs how pretty she was, and how much at that time her son looked like her. He had her high, round, flushed cheeks, and her blue-grey eyes, and her petal mouth, always smiling over nothing. She made a great point of being sensible. She seemed not to want to change anything in the conditions about her in the world. She hardly ever stopped talking, which may have explained why when they said anything her husband and her son shouted.

Looking at me, Miles O'Connor said to my father,

"If he were my boy I'd never let him get away with anything like that."

"He isn't your boy," replied my father with his widest smile, and yet with a wrinkle of warning in his brow.

"Now Miles," chaffed Nell, "everybody is trying to calm things down, don't you stir them up again."

"Lightning," declared Billy, with his stocky little chest stuck out, "is only a discharge of electricity."

"That's right," said his father with approval. "You'd better teach Richard a few lessons."

"Quit it, will you, please, Miles?" said my father.

"Oh, all right, what the hell," muttered Miles causing my mother to wince at the ugly word. "We might as well give up the whole show. It's getting dark. If we went, we might see a little heat lightning, and then we'd have another scene."

He kicked his way into the house and put his banjo back into its black case which was lined in blue plush.

"It's really better this way," said Nell to my father. "You and Miles have a lot of business to talk over this weekend, he told me so, you can get started tonight, and get it out of the way, we can have supper right here, everything is ready anyway, we brought the most delicious piccalilli, my cook makes it, and I said to her, They will die when they taste it, it's so good, just that pinch of red pepper makes all the difference, and I said, it's so good, we must take them a couple of jars, I said, and we. . . ."

Her voice trailed after her as she and my mother went inside to unpack the hampers and get supper ready at home.

To show whose side he was on, my father pulled me over against him with his strong thin arm. He squeezed my shoulder silently a few times, trying to tell me he was sorry for scolding me when I was frightened by something I could not yet control. He was all refuge for me then. He was honor and forgiveness. He was a man who would never say *that word* in front of women and children.

"Well, what sh'we do?" asked Billy, impatiently jigging his members by the porch railing.

"The rain is stopping," said my father. "Do you boys want to take a lantern and go down to the end of the island and see if a tree got struck? You might see one of the beavers, too. Sometimes they come out at twilight."

"Come on, Richard," said Billy.

In a few minutes, carrying the coal oil lantern my father had lighted for me, I led Billy toward the other end of the island, which was only about six hundred yards away. The ground was covered with wet pine needles. The smell of cold wet cedar was in the air. Within the woods that rose from the middle of the island, darkness was already immense and foreign. The lake was quiet after the storm. We could hear lappets of shallow waves whispering up the narrow edge of white sand where the island sloped into the water. There was no other cottage but ours on the island. The only way to reach the other side of the lake, at the village of Aetna, was by boat, either in the *Arrow,* or by the mail boat, the *Mollie,* which touched at the private docks all about the lake every day during the vacation season. Removed from everywhere, the island seemed my kingdom. It was now doubly fine because I had a friend there with whom to share it.

"Let me carry the lantern," demanded Billy. "I know how."

"So do I."

"But I can do it better."

"Why can you?"

"Because my father says I can."

"When did he say you could?"

"Never mind. Give it to me."

"You won't know where to go. You'll get lost. I know the way."

We were slipping along the hidden path inside the woods.

"Anybody can see where to go. Give it to me."

I gave it to him and he took the lead. The path turned suddenly to avoid a moss-covered boulder higher than either of us. Billy missed the path and struck the boulder. He dropped the lantern, which tipped over. Its dim yellow flame was smothered out. We were in complete darkness. The house at the other end of the island was concealed by the woods.

"Well, why didn't you tell me?" asked Billy.

"Tell you what?"

"Not to run into that rock."

"You could see it."

"I couldn't either."

"You wanted the lantern."

"Well, anyway, it's out. Have you got a match?"

"No."

"We better go back."

I reached around on the ground for the lantern, felt its dying heat, and took up its wire handle.

"Can you see?" I asked

"No. Can you?"

"No."

"Which way do we go?"

"I don't know."

"Well, *which?*" he asked, angrily. After all, it was my island and I must know. We stood and listened. The trees dripped. The lake came and came up to the sand with a sound like a sleeper's breath. Suddenly there was a slow clatter somewhere under branches on the woods floor.

"What was that!" asked Billy in a hush.

"I don't know."

"You don't know. You don't know. What *do* you know? This is your island!"

His voice carried into the trees. With a clap like boards struck flatly together, a great bird left the topmost tree near us and went heavily into the air.

"What was that!" cried Billy in a tight whisper.

[201]

"It was the owl."

"What owl?"

"There is an old owl who lives at this end of the island. You scared him away."

"I did not."

"Yes, you did. He scared you, too."

"He did not."

"He did too."

"Come on," said Billy, "let's get back to the house."

We started out. Billy held on to my shirt because he could not see to follow.

※

You felt your way tree by tree, but in the dripping nightfall you did not know where you were. If seconds were days, and days years, and the woods a forest, and the island a continent, and the hour an unending midnight, in your anxiety and hunger you knew the doubtfulness of men lost in wilderness. The overland march from the interior of Thunder Island to find the lights of civilization after the torrential rain was without time and measure. You slid and fell on the wet pine needle carpet of the forest and you bruised your arms and knees and brow against unseen rocks and trees. All sounds were compounded by the drumming of blood in your ears. The whole history of courage as you knew it was focussed into a few minutes. The explorer's instinct came alive in you as leader of the expedition, and you believed that if you struck out for the coast you would come to the shoreline which would lead you by a longer and possibly more arduous but sure route to the settlements. But in the hemispheric darkness there was no way to know with any certainty which way to turn. Man could only persist against the unknown by making the movements it was his habit to make.

"Let's yell," said Billy.

"Why?"

"They might hear us."

"I don't want to."

"Why?"

"I'm not scared yet."

This was not true. It was only that I did not want so soon again to show myself afraid before him.

"Who's scared?" he said. "I'm hungry."

"So'm I."

"What's that!"

We heard the faraway engine whistle of the short freight train which drew into Aetna every night. Its sound, so familiar and so homely, called us home. We hurried again blindly. Then we stood each other still with a grasp and listened again. There came a sound. It was nearer than seemed possible without our having heard it before.

". . . And really, my dear, if I ever saw anyone look completely ridiculous," it said, "the way she wore it, and the hat itself, and besides, when you consider how old she. . . ."

It was Nell O'Connor. In another second we saw a flashlight ray wandering about just as her mind wandered, and I heard my mother murmur, "I know, I know," and then they came upon us.

"Where have you been? Supper is waiting and waiting. Come, darling," said my mother. She and Nell, wearing yellow sou'wester raincoats, had come for a little stroll along the wet path to find us.

When we came back to the cottage our fathers were seated at right angles to each other at the far end of the table, beneath a Coleman lantern. They were arguing.

"Oh, you crazy things," scoffed Nell. "Wrangle, wrangle. Still at it. It's time to eat."

The fathers drew in their elbows and we all sat down, but not to a meal in the social sense. The discussion kept up at the end of the table. Its energy became disagreeable. It had to do with details of a new enterprise they had incorporated outside of their general partnership in the insurance business. Who would get what percentage of the profits?—for Miles had thought of the idea behind the new business and believed he should have the greater share; but it was my father who had the most energy and imagination to bring to its operation, and all he asked was an equal share.

"All right," yelled Miles, drowning out everything we tried to say to each other at our end of the table, "just answer me this. If it weren't for my idea, just how much added income of any sort would you get?"

"Not a cent, of course," replied my father, speaking slowly in a calm rage, "but that is not the issue. The issue is whether you'd make a dime out of your idea if someone didn't come along and run it for you."

"Oh, it is, eh. I see. I may have a lot of brainy ideas but when it comes to carrying them out, I am an incompetent, is that what you're getting at?"

"Now Miles. For God's sake be reasonable."

My father was suddenly pleading through a sort of sickened gentleness in his voice. How could matters go so perversely wrong between him and his best friend and partner?

[204]

"Reasonable! Now I'm unreasonable!" shouted Miles. "I'm sick and tired of being in the wrong, day in and day out. I came up here to have a nice, quiet talk with you, and get affairs in order, and I run into this. Well, let me tell you something. I'm just about through!"

"Oh, Miles," said Nell, looking at my mother to register shock and good sense for all concerned, "you don't mean that."

"Try me and see!" snapped Miles.

My father leaned back and gazed at him for a long while, and then said,

"You know something? I think you came up here with your mind all made up to have a row. What for, I can't imagine. But from the minute we began to talk—."

Miles jumped up and slammed his hands flat on the table. He flushed a dark Irish purple. I remember now how the truth must have hurt worse than an empty insult. He could not bear it, for he knew it would one day be known that already, and in secret, he had made an arrangement with another businessman to take over my father's interest in the new company. Threatened with failure in accomplishing the separation which was the private object of his visit, he responded with all his might. He looked very young and as handsome as a fine animal in danger. We all saw him with fear and admiration. Billy watched his father with eyes like blue-burning steel—bright reflectors of energy and personality. Nell shivered as if remembering an instant of Miles's love-making. He could hardly speak through his fury.

"I don't have to sit here and listen to this! Come on, Nell. Billy. Get your things! We're leaving."

My father stood up and reached his hand to Miles's shoulder. Miles flung it off.

"Miles," said my father. "For the love of God. We're only trying to talk business. You can't leave. There's no train till tomorrow. There's no place to stay in the village. Let's forget all this and get together with cooler heads in the morning. Good Lord, don't you remember? *We're partners!*"

The white-hot core of Miles's anger began to cool to red and then dulled itself further. But something had been burned out forever, it seemed, in his guilty heart. Coldly, now, he said,

"I've been thinking for a long time that there might be a more sensible thing for us to be than partners."

"Oh, Miles!" exclaimed my mother. She knew how much the business association with Miles O'Connor meant to my father in personal as well as financial terms. "Don't say things, my dear, that will be hard to think of and take back tomorrow!"

"Are you coming, Nell?" he said. "I'm going to bed. We'll leave tomorrow. What time is the train?" he suddenly asked me, as though he would rather not have any exchanges with my parents.

"At noon," I said, "if it leaves on time."

He turned and went to the bedroom prepared for him and Nell. My father walked alone out to the porch and down to the shore. I could hear his long, trudging steps. Billy and I were forgotten for the moment.

"Really," said Nell, "aren't they ridiculous! They really, you know, love each other like brothers. That's probably just the trouble."

"Yes," said my mother, "in some ways they're too much alike."

"Why, they couldn't *do* without each other. If Miles has said it once he's said it a thousand times, that he wouldn't know what to *do* if anything ever happened to Dan, he leans on him so much, why, they're ideal partners, think of how well they're doing, I know *I* never expected to be living so well so early in our married life. . . ."

"Nell, I'm frightened."

"Oh, now, don't, after all, it's just a flare-up."

"I don't know." My mother suddenly saw me listening. "Whiii —off to bed with you boys. Trot along now. Come give me a hug, both of you."

I did and Billy did and we went to my room and because the evening was now late and the air cold off the lake our teeth chattered as we undressed and got into our pajamas and climbed into bed where the sheets were heavy with cold and damp.

Through the thin board partition we could hear Miles O'Connor still fighting as he heaved and turned himself in the bed next to my room trying to get to sleep but unable to deny himself the consoling and bitter joy of remembering what had been said all through the quarrel.

Where was my father? Outside, alone, doing the same thing, down by the narrow shore of Thunder Island. I see now how comely they both were as men and fathers, as husbands and friends and doers in the world, and how frightening they became in their sudden bad blood. If men could go that way who loved each other, how then could it be with families, and playmates, nations, and all mankind? I learned more about all this the next morning.

※

The O'Connors slept late, or pretended to.

Billy and I were up soon after sunrise.

"Let's go down to the lake," I said during the morning. "I know a place."

"What for?"

"We can build something."

"What?"

"A harbor."

"Like Dorchester?"

"Yes. We can put the docks and the freight boats and the cranes. I've already got a little tugboat I made that floats, and a freighter, too."

[207]

"I'll build the breakwater."

"There are lots of little stones to put for it."

We worked without much talk for over an hour, quite as though nothing serious had happened the night before. Our model of Dorchester harbor took form in a miniature cove a few yards from the house. The sun crowned us with golden nap on our heads. We were half in, half out of the water, wearing our swimming trunks. Billy was a stocky little reproduction of Miles, with a high, challenging lift to his chest and an aggressive thickness about his shoulders. He was adroit with his hands and built his breakwater with swift, light touches. The water was clear as air, and almost as warm. Those little breathing waves broke at us and washed the sugary sand off our toasting skin. The pines on the island gave out the waft of their scent. Across the lake we could see Aetna as clear as if it were a carved model of a village made inside a glass shadow-box by an old sailor. I erected a grain elevator beside a dock where my long freight boat, assembled from a length of two-by-four and little square blocks of wood for the deck houses fore and aft, was tied up. My tug-boat lay at her bow. In the wetted sand of the shoreline I traced with a stick a set of lines like railroad tracks and I ran to the house to get my toy engine to set along the dock. Freight from all over the United States came to the dock by the railroad, and was transferred to the freighter, which when loaded would turn slowly away from the dock and head out beyond the breakwater built of sparkling pebbles, and sail across the lake to Europe.

My mother was on the porch having coffee with Nell. She waved to me as I ran by to fetch my train.

"What are you boys doing?" she called idly.

"Playing," I yelled over my shoulder, impatient at the idiotic questions of parents. My father and Miles O'Connor were nowhere to be seen.

When I returned to the harbor, I found that Billy had turned the freight boat around end for end.

"What did you do that for?" I demanded.

"It's better that way."

"It isn't the right way. I had it the right way." I began to turn it back the other way. He watched me with scowling eyes.

"No," he said, "you see, the way you have it, she can't go out past my breakwater unless she turns all the way around. My way is better."

"No. My way. Besides, I saw real ships do it the way I have it."

"Oh, hell. Who cares."

Last night's bad feeling began to show through. It had never been dissipated.

"You needn't swear," I said.

"I'll swear if I want to. Hell, hell, hell!" he added, as if dared. Then, wondering if he had gone too far, he said in a hurry to restore our mood of play, "It's a fine harbor. I wish I could take it home."

"Well," I said, "you can't. It's mine."

"I know I can't. But not because it's yours. But because you can't move a lake and take it home with you. But the harbor is not yours. It is ours. We both made it."

"But it is here, on my lake, so it's mine."

"We'll see whose it is," he said, and waded with a heavy splash into the harbor and kicked it apart, destroying the breakwater, and the dock, and the railroad lines along the edge, and lofting the freighter with his bare foot into the air and up to the needly edge of the woods, where it crashed to pieces. "There's your old harbor!"

Because our fathers fought, we fought. I threw myself upon him in the shallow water, shouting,

"Your father is wrong, my father says so."

"He is not."

[209]

"He is too."

"You damn thing you," gasped Billy, rolling in the water where I held on to him.

"Don't you swear at me."

"I will too."

"You're a rotten old b.m.," I cried, in an access of daring, while I tore and beat at Billy in a passion to invade and despoil his body. I was slighter than he, and he began to pound me against the wet sand till my head made sounds of cracking and I saw odd lights. Kicking and clawing, we rolled up the shore to be pierced by pine needles and choked with leafy mud. Our noise brought our mothers running, but not until we knew blood, and nose-run, and tears mixed with sand, and mouths full of stinging bits of earth, and rubbed bones that would ache all day and night. Panting, we were drawn apart amidst dim impulses of unspoken insults much better than those we had given.

"What on earth got into you two?" asked Nell O'Connor. "Why, Billy, you're a sight!"

"He wrecked my harbor," I said.

"It was our harbor," said Billy. "Not just his."

"Richard," said my mother, "apologise to Billy. He is your guest. You must give way to him if you have to."

"I don't have to."

"Ah, but you do."

"I don't want his old damn apologise," said Billy.

His mother shook him dutifully in punishment, at the same time saying to my mother,

"Just like their fathers. *Men! Oh!*"

She took her son away to clean him up and get him dressed. My mother said gravely,

"I am ashamed of you."

"He was wrong."

[210]

"Who knows?" she sighed. "All I know is, we cannot let them all go away feeling like this. They are to take the mail boat when she comes by at eleven-thirty and go home on the noon train. Sometimes I wonder why I even try. . . ."

But try what, she did not, or could not, say.

"Well, where's my father?" I asked

"In our room. He tried to talk to Miles but Miles wouldn't talk to him, so he wrote a note and put it under Miles's door an hour ago. It's still there, you can see it sticking out a little, he won't touch it. I feel dreadful about it all. There must be some way to keep them here until everybody feels better. Then they can go if they have to. But not this way. Not this way. It would do something awful to Daddy."

Her distress made her seem young and pretty and very close to me. I longed to help. I said,

"Well, why don't I go and get Billy, and say we will fly my airplane kite, and once she's in the air we can run with the string down to the dock and tie it there and watch it above the lake?"

Her eyes filled a little at all the feelings of the past hours.

"Thank you, my darling. Perhaps they would stay. Yes. Ask him."

"And another thing," I said. "If he likes it, I will *give* the kite to Billy."

"Oh, would you give it up?"

"I would, if you want me to."

"Then try! Your Daddy would feel so good about it if Miles would let them stay!"

I had a fine surge of feeling that we were acting as a family, and that I had as great a part as anyone else in making our world. I ran off to get my kite and then to find Billy and show it to him as the great peace offering I meant it to be. The kite had not yet even been assembled out of its long flat box. I knocked at the door of the O'Connor bedroom, calling,

"Well, say, Billy?"

I was not aware of voices within until they went silent as I waited. My father's folded note was gone from under the door. Nell must have picked it up when she went to wash Billy with water from the blue and white pitcher and basin on the corner washstand of the guest room.

"Don't answer him," said Miles O'Connor within.

"Billy?" I said, "come on out and we can assemble my new airplane kite and we can go down to the dock and fly it. You can have it for keeps if you like it."

"Billy?" said his father in warning.

I knew of no weapon then, and know of none now, against silence. I waited until I felt small and idiotic, and then I returned to the porch where my father and mother were both waiting for me.

"Well?" asked my father. His face was drawn and sick-looking.

"I did, but they won't," I said.

He shrugged at my mother and she touched his arm consolingly.

"There comes the *Mollie*," I said. The mail boat was rounding across to us in a long shining path on the water. Every morning I ran down to the dock to meet her. Unless she was to bring or take passengers, she merely slowed down, passing the end of the dock in a movement expertly steered by Dick Burlington, the postmaster's twenty-year-old son from Aetna. To me he was the captain of an ocean liner and a brave man of noble parts including wisdom, who threw the canvas mail bag to the dock as he went by with a wide, lazy wave of his hand. I pretended that I resembled him, who— though I did not know it—was only like any just-grown incurious country boy with a ripe body.

"Run down to the dock," said my father, "and tell Dick to stop for passengers."

"Oh, Dan," said my mother, "then you really will let them go?"

"Let them? What can I do about it?"

"Oh, no," she said against her fingers. "Oh, no."

❦

I ran down and waited for Dick. I began to wave before he could hear me call. He understood my signal and brought the *Mollie* sweetly against the dock with hardly an inch or two of headway. As he docked he gave two short toots on her pressure whistle.

"Hi, Richard," he called from the awning shadow over his cockpit where he moved in his summery competence amidst dials and gauges and his boat's wheel.

I nodded. He threw me the mail bag. It was light. I threw back our empty which he would use on the next round.

"Well, there they are," he said, nodding past my shoulder up the little slope of the island. I turned to see.

The O'Connors were coming along in single file, Miles in the lead carrying two suitcases. Nell followed and then Billy. None of them looked at any of us. My father and mother walked slowly after them in silence. Dick expertly kept the *Mollie* bumped against the dock by the use of his engine. He put up his hand to help Nell and Billy over to the deck. Miles jumped in after them. The atmosphere of rage and dignity reached Dick and he raised his fuzzy eyebrows at me.

"All right, come on, come on, let's go, let's go," snapped Miles at Dick Burlington. Nell looked then searchingly at each of us as the *Mollie,* with a silky ruffle of her exhaust, drew away from us into the blinding sparkle of the morning sun on the blue water.

Turning his back on my mother and me, my father made a huge choking sob. He sounded just like me when I used to cry. To see his

[213]

father cry who had said men don't cry! What son who had given up crying would not know fear at this? My father drew back his right arm and then smashed his fist against the tall piling at the end of the dock.

"God damn him!" he wept, "God damn him to hell!" while he smashed his hand again and again on the old piling.

"Dan! Don't!" cried my mother, coming to him to restrain his driven arm. She lifted his hand. It was bleeding and torn. His hand was broken. The physical pain of it now began to reach him through the pain of losing his trusted friend and partner. He let his head down to my mother's shoulder and with her arm around him she took him to the house.

※

In a few minutes she called to me.

"You know how to start up the *Arrow,* don't you, Richard?"

"Oh, yes!"—but I was not sure without trying.

"We must get Daddy to the doctor. He has hurt himself badly. Go get some clothes on and go down and get the boat started. We'll be right down."

Soon I was on board the *Arrow.* If Dick Burlington had his ship, I had mine. Fiercely I remembered how my father always started the engine by setting the spark, putting the gears in neutral, and whirling the heavy flywheel. The *Arrow* was a white launch with a canopy over all her length and red plush seat cushions on her side benches. Her engine was exposed amidships. The pilot sat in the stern and steered by the wheel which was set in the planking at his side. We had a flag at the bow and another at the stern. With my father by, I had often steered her in the open lake, but I had never taken her out. Now I was in command.

After several heaves I got the engine to run. I reset the spark. I cast off the bow line and held us to the dock by boat hook. Soon my parents came to board us. My father, cradling his hurt hand with the other, looked at me in pallid abashment and said,

"Can you take her out, Doc?"

I nodded and threw off the stern line and I said to myself, "Now let me see," thinking about what to do next. But before I could do much thinking, I had the *Arrow* on her way across the lake to Aetna.

From halfway across we saw the last gesture that spoke of the O'Connors. We saw the noon train couple her engine and in a few minutes start off Down State. We heard her steam whistle and her bell and saw her rich blooms of black smoke go blowing upward against the bright air as the O'Connors once more left us with our trouble.

Coming to the dock at Aetna was the great test. My father came to sit beside me as we neared shore.

"Cut her now," he said. "Take a long curve to come in. Better to lose too much power and start up again than keep too much and have to crash or go by."

I begged silently that he would not take the wheel with his good hand at the last minute. He seemed to hear me, for he made no move. I docked the *Arrow* for the first time by myself. We made a hard bump and then a long scrape, but we caught the pilings and we tied up and my heart rose. In my selfish joy of achievement, I tried,

"Everything's going to be all right, now!"

"God help us," groaned my father hardly audible.

"You wait here, Richard," said my mother. "We'll be back as soon as the doctor can take care of Daddy. You did beautifully. Come, dear," she said lightly to my father, as if taking him to a party to which he did not particularly want to go.

"Yes," he said, "yes, it hurts like the devil, thanks to nobody but myself."

"Hush. Come."

They went up the dock to the village and I worked on the *Arrow*, as I had seen Dick Burlington do on the *Mollie* in port, putting her to rights. In an hour or so we all returned to Thunder Island. My father's hand was in a plaster cast.

❦

Then began for him a period of long chastening, of sorrowful self-judgement, of mourning for his friend. In about a week a letter came from a lawyer at home in Dorchester to institute proceedings to dissolve the partnership between Miles O'Connor and my father. In the same mail came a letter from another friend in town who said he had heard how Miles O'Connor and somebody or other were getting together on a scheme they had been working on for several months: was this the same scheme my father and Miles had long talked of? So my father learned of his betrayal. White about the jaws and mouth, he dictated to my mother whatever was needed in written form to do his part in the dissolution. With that he began to lose some quality of his health forever.

My mother said to me in a private moment,

"Richard, don't ever get so involved."

"In what?"

She shrugged and sighed. Anything. Everything.

❦

The summer was almost over and I was glad, for my holiday happiness was ruined anyway, since this must depend on whether or not my father and mother were happy. But before we went home for the start of school and the changes to be made in my father's office, I once again was crowded toward darkness by fear, though this time with new results.

During lunch one day a particularly violent thunderstorm broke over us almost without warning.

I made a move.

My father said sternly,

"Richard!"

Thunder and lightning seemed to spring at us from the very trees at our door.

Fear drove me from the table in spite of the commands of my father. I ran to hide with my heart beating out the ejaculatory prayers of safety. "My Jesus, mercy!" said my bones at every house-cracking crash.

In a few moments the door of my closet was pulled open. My mother was there, wearing her heavy stiff yellow raincoat and holding my smaller one.

"Richard? Come?"

"No!"

"Come with me, my darling. *Schnell?* Come?"

Her voice was sharp and commanding. She reached for my arm and pulled me from the closet and held out my sou'wester. "Put this on! Quick!"

The storm was making the house cry in its wooden ribs.

"No! No!"

She slapped me hard on the cheek, which she had never done before. Appalled by shock, I put on my raincoat. She took my arm and led me to the porch.

"Where are we going?"

"We are going to meet the storm, not run away from it."

"No!"

She took me down the steps, down the island slope, down to the dock, down to the far end of the dock where there was no refuge —where there was much actual danger from lightning bolts. We were soaked through in a second, for the wind tore at our raincoats. The lake danced wildly with waves. The far shore was lost except when the lightning flashed over there and here above us and everywhere. Calling to me above the wind, my mother said,

"Richard, look!" She shook me and pointed to the wild sky, the sweeps of rain on the lake, and then at the tearing strikes of lightning amidst the clouds. "Richard! Look! Why be afraid? *It is so beautiful!*"

She put her arm about my shoulders and when the lightning struck I could feel how she too trembled before the power of God. But how new was her idea that this power was beautiful! I stared at the new idea as I stared at a world I had never been able to see before. I met an entirely fresh way to regard the thing that had terrorized my childhood. About to be convinced, I shouted,

"But it's dangerous!"

"Of course it's dangerous," she replied. The wind tried to hollow out her words and sweep them away, but I heard her meaning even so. "There is something dangerous about all beauty, and it is still beautiful! I don't know what it is, but—."

We stood there and the thunder and lightning broke over us, here, and afar, and my vision cleared, and I knew that what she said was true. After the great gift of life itself, it was the finest gift she made me, this means of losing fear. In immediate terms, then, and afterward, any storm was charged, for me, as much with beauty as with danger.

We stayed on the dock until the worst of it had passed over us, and the thunder went tumbling farther and farther away behind the mountains on the other shore. The light came changing in a calm of gold while an aromatic breeze was left behind by the spent ozone of the retreating storm. The moving air took my thoughts aloft.

"My kite!" I cried.

"Yes, but first go dry off and change your clothes," said my mother, sending me safely to my own affairs.

At the far end of Thunder Island was a miniature meadow edged by tall trees. There I took my airplane kite and assembled it and ran with it across the meadow until it caught the breeze and went aloft, pulling at the string which played burningly through my fingers. The kite was fashioned like a biplane aircraft. It had a wooden propeller at the nose and fine Japanese rice paper over its wing structures and tail fin. Up, up, it went, taking the very sky and giving it to me.

When the string played out as far as it could go, I tied the end to a stump and sat down leaning my back against the stump and I looked up, and all that existed turned into the ever-lasting present.

Above me is my ship in the sky. It takes me with it, I travel in the wind, the propeller is I, I cunningly use the air, I see all from there, and my vision is that of God. And yet I am of course sitting here below, looking upward, upward, feeling the mossy damp beneath my rump bones, and breathing the island earth, and I discover somewhere within me how I am, like everyone, a creature of bone and breath, of rock and air, of earth and heaven, of sorrow and joy, of body and soul.

CHAPTER X

❧

Parma Violets

When children love, they do not give, they only receive. It is a love that creates only a self. The aching desire to give, to create life beyond the self, calls boy into man. Gratified, this love creates an analogue of heaven on earth. Denied or betrayed, it sets forth the terms of hell in the very stuff of life, unless it can be resolved by sanctity.

During the first World War, imprisoned as I was in the last year of childhood, I knew intuitions of what people meant when they spoke of love.

At that time, the most frequent and beloved visitor at our house in Dorchester was a lady I called Aunt Bunch. I had given her this name because so very often she wore a bunch of Parma violets, now pinned to her grey fur coat, now to an ermine muff she carried, or again at her waist in the style of the period. She was not a real aunt. The title was merely a possessive courtesy.

I loved her with tyranny and excitement. I believed her to exist for me alone, and I behaved accordingly. When she came to see us, I rudely interposed myself between her and all other persons and relationships, until general laughter resulted, and I was returned to the childhood which I was ready to lose—which, in fact, I had forgotten.

There lay the key to my worship. She treated me not like a youngster in black ribbed cotton stockings, itchy knee breeches, a jacket whose sleeves never seemed long enough, and a starched collar, but like a young man to whom she could send silent messages confident that they would be received and understood, no matter what the world might hear her say or see her do in ostensible propriety.

She was I now think in her early thirties. Her hair was so blonde as to seem silvery. She wore it loosely in a maddening way—I wanted to put my hands into it and make it all fall down, heavily sliding like gold and silver treasure whose surrender would mean everything that I could not precisely imagine. Her eyes were violet-blue, which must have accounted for her bunches of violets, and the effect she knew they made. Dark lashes shadowed her gaze in which great liquid purities shone forth right into your heart. Her mouth fascinated me. The lips were full, yet ever so delicate in their scrolling, and when she smiled, they flattened slightly against her white teeth. Her cheeks always looked warm, but felt cool, as I knew.

I knew, because our ardent relationship included embraces. She would come in from a winter day with snowflakes on her furs, her violets, her lashes, her veil, and let me climb against her until we both hurt. She would kiss me, put her cheek on mine, press me in her arms a few times, and I smelt snow, and violets, and felt the exquisite tickle of melting snowflakes between our faces. Her face was always softly glowing as though in the light of a rose-shaded lamp. If she ever looked archly and humorously just over my head at other adults I never saw her do it.

She belonged to me. How could I doubt it? She always called me "My dear," as she might call a man, and in that winter we became acknowledged as a cunning joke, "lovers," with quotation marks, and many an eyebrow went up, and voice went down, and pang went deep, at the spectacle we made, and the living reference we were to all that was meant by love, and suffered, and revered, in its name.

※

My own part in this passion explains itself if enough years are allowed to ensue. But for her part—why did she come to take me out driving in the afternoons, after school, in her electric car? The cushions were grey, there were always violets in the little crystal vases flanking the curved plate glass of the front window, and we were alone together as the batteries hummed us along, and the elegant bell rang at street crossings. We rode for the most part in ecstatic silence through the park, watching for swans on the lake, and if we saw one, our excitement made us hold one another. Sometimes she let me steer the electric. To do so, I had to crowd near to her, and lean upon her lap, the better to manage the long black bar which made the wheels point this way or that. I would steer, she would control the speed by a shorter bar above the other, and we would spin on our way with joy.

"Poor dear, she has no children, and he is like a son to her"—this was one explanation I overheard. It meant nothing to me. What did it matter why, so long as she would put her head down to mine, and leave it there in dreaming silence and contentment? Or hold my hand and play with my fingers, one after another, slowly and broodingly, while flooding me with the daytime moonlight of her eyes? I believed that she never looked at anyone else that way. How could she, what could it possibly mean to anyone else, when she was mine entirely?

Sometimes on our drives she would take me to Huyler's for a

chocolate soda, or again to her house in the park for cocoa with whipped cream. If we were early enough, I preferred her house, where we could be so intimate and private about nothing, but if we were late, I was unwilling to go there because we might then encounter her husband, "Uncle" Dylan.

My reluctance to meet him there had nothing to do with guilt over my love for his wife. I simply preferred to meet him at my house because as a visitor there he always brought me some sort of present. For this I despised him even as I greedily reached for his pockets. He was a rich man, much older than Aunt Bunch, and doubtfully he demanded all that his money could get him. His small, pale eyes always looked dry, in his sandy face, behind his pince-nez glasses. I once heard my father remark that it was somehow easy to see how Dylan would look dead. It was a strange and powerful statement, and I saw what he meant. I'd seen dead birds. Their inert plumage and milked-over eyeballs did suggest Uncle Dylan. He was tormented by the very gifts he made, though everyone always said he was generous. Still, what joy was there in giving if he could never be sure that what he gave was lovingly received because it brought him with it? And so,

"Now, Richard," he would say to me, one greedy creature virtuously reproving another, "let us not be so sure we have a present today. Why should we have? What have we done to earn it? Do we think others are made of money? Presents cost something, my boy. Do you ever think of your poor old Uncle Dylan except when he has something for you?"

Such an attitude made me shudder for him, as he looked over to his wife to see if she smiled upon his humor, blinking both his dry scratchy eyes at her, and as he then besought my parents to witness his openness of heart, forcing them to deprecate his latest gift, and to swear that I would not be allowed to accept another single thing after this time. Then, confirmed and strengthened in his poor power

[223]

over us all, he would sigh, and say, "Try the left-hand pocket," and I would plunge my hand in and find nothing. But by then I was impervious to alarm for I knew that he could not afford to fail me, and when with a feeble start of surprise like that of a vaudeville magician, he would say, "Try the right-hand one, then," I knew the sorry game was about to be over to my advantage.

Even as I bled him unmercifully every chance I had, and knew him for a dullard, I never considered him an odd choice as a husband for Aunt Bunch. He simply *was* her husband, and that ended the matter. As such, he belonged to my world, as she belonged, and I could not possibly imagine any disturbance of its order. So long as they remained fixed, any relationships were accepted. If a new one should appear, the quicker it were absorbed and fixed, the better. Only, let it be added to what existed, without changing anything.

꙰

In that season of so much love, when the heavy winter brought snow that would stay for weeks, and the warmth and light of our house made a twilight joy after the steely cold out of doors during the day, a familiar friend returned to us as somebody new. He was my father's business associate who had come into his office after the treason of Miles O'Connor. Many months ago he had joined the Army, and was now a captain of artillery on leave before receiving new orders, which everybody knew meant going overseas to France to fight the Hun in World War I.

Now he came to see us in his uniform, with its high collar and stiff stock; its Sam Browne belt, pegged breeches and officer's boots and spurs. Captain Jarvis McNeill seemed like an entirely new individual, with no relation to the occasional visitor of the same name before the war. He was unmarried and so appeared at parties mostly as a stray, to fill in. Now home on leave, he took to coming to our house late in the day, when the curtains were drawn, a fire was rippling in the fireplace, and other friends dropped in and out without announcement. Sometimes such little gatherings would turn into supper parties, people would stay, and the animation and conviviality of my parents would have happy expression. Almost always, late in such an evening, the piano would sound, and then Captain Jarvis McNeill would sing in a crackling baritone voice distinguished by volume and purity both. Rather like Miles O'Connor before him, he had an Irish instinct for facile sentiment that wanted most of all to be communicated, and when he sang, I was moved in formless sorrow for what people knew, and were, and did, beyond the boundaries of my certain knowledge.

I always knew when Captain Jarvis McNeill arrived. I would know it by the sound of his boots in the entrance hall. They made a tubey sort of noise when he stamped off the snow. He was a big fellow, and his movements and gestures were necessarily large, though not awkward. In his ruddy face there was a comic appeal that he be understood and forgiven for anything he might do—with a broad hint, in his raised brows, his blue eyes, his dark shaved cheeks, his crescent smile, that he might indeed do anything.

When I heard him below, I held my breath the better to overhear messages from life beyond me. His speaking voice had heavy grain and carried through the rooms. I listened to hear if it grew louder in my direction. Then I would hear the heavy trot of his big body coming up the stairs. He was coming to see me in my room—a real captain, a soldier who fired cannons, who had a sword, and wore boots and spurs, and would himself hang the Kaiser, and was a hero.

One of the qualities of heroes may be their instinct for true worship amid all the false. Captain Jarvis McNeill repaid mine with serious and simple appreciation, which took the form of getting down on the floor of my room where my imaginative possessions were marshalled, and playing there, as I played, so long as the company downstairs would let him. He filled the room with his presence in every way, including the way he brought the spicy, sharp aromas of a barbershop with him—the clean, adventurous smell of a man who has been combed, spanked and shined to his most presentable state, for private and urgent purposes. His cheeks got hotter like mine as he bent down to the miniature tasks of imagination with my large relief model of battlefields in France, set with leaden soldiery and wooden artillery. His collar choked him, his big legs were in the way but splendid with boots and spurs, and he made the double magic of seeing with my eyes and making me see with his.

"Do you have a sword?" I asked.

"Yes. Would you like me to bring it?"

"Yes."

※

He brought it next time, and let me have it for several days. It lay by me in bed, sheathed and shining. My belly hung heavy in me at the glories that leaped out of the scabbard with that blade. Only in secret did I strap the big sword to my belt, for I was now old enough to know that it would look ridiculous to anyone else. I gave it up with a scowl of indifference that fooled nobody when Captain Jarvis McNeill said to me on our floor one evening that he had to pack a lot of stuff to be shipped, and he supposed his officer's sword had better go too.

"But when I come back you can have it again," he said, and put his big hand like a heavy helmet on my head and roughed me once or twice. That promise was enough for me. To whom else was he

[226]

offering his beautiful acid-etched sword with its gold sabre-knot and its tinkling scabbard? He was a great captain, a hero, and my friend, and he came to my house almost daily to see me, to crawl with much humorous breathing and difficulty of scale among the delicate litter of my parapets and trenches, my tanks and ambulances and field hospitals. To see me. He was mine to love and to own, through whom I could extend myself into a heroic life as a soldier.

He would stay so long in my playroom that almost invariably others would come upstairs to inquire: and standing in the doorway they would smile and chatter at the sight of the handsome young officer and the hot-faced boy both intent upon war games. At such moments I realized that the grown-up world was about to win all over again. Aunt Bunch usually was one of those who came to see. The sight of her, waiting for me to admit to bedtime, changed, dropped, my spirits, I knew not why. Dimly I did not want her and Captain Jarvis McNeill with me together. I wanted them with me each separately. More, I wanted them never to be together at all, lest each might forget me. How complicated that fidelity, and that betrayal.

At last with comfortable sighs of change, the Captain would rise and put himself in order for his return downstairs with the company. Aunt Bunch would let him go, as she lingered to assuage the endless disappointments of day's end. Invisibly the tendrils of scent from Parma violets sought me out and wrapped me round; and when she left me to go below where unimaginably trivial events were gathering purpose for the adults, I was proved again in love, and the terms I imagined for it were unquestioned, and I felt choked with well-being, rich emotion, and a swelling conviction that nothing would ever change that I loved.

For a boy at the shore of boyhood's farewell, those were passionate loves—Aunt Bunch and Captain Jarvis McNeill; and that was a passionate if scornful loyalty—Uncle Dylan. The issue was not

whether I was a small monster of sensibility, but whether the power
of love is ever really contained within conventions, no matter how
desperately appearances may be preserved.

※

We take our parents for granted till we have lost them.

"Richard, Richard," they would say, fondly shaking their heads at
each other over my infatuations, recognizing how fixed was my
view of life, and how innocent it was of any other values but my
fierce, joyful, tyrannical ones which seemed to me eternal, and to
them dangerous. They saw everything, even to what must be coming, though not in what event it might come. They tried to rob me
painfully but healthily of the possessions of my heart.

"You must not make yourself a nuisance when Jarvis comes,
Richard, after all, there are others who want to see him."

"He comes to see me."

"Ah, my darling boy."

"Well, he does too, he told me so."

"Yes, of course, of course," in hurried agreement, as though to
conceal from me after all a truth best left with my elders. Or again,

"You will be a young man before long, and you will look for a
pretty girl your own age to love."

"I love Aunt Bunch."

"Now, yes. But she is already married. And her age!"

"I thought you loved her too."

"We do, we do, my boy."

"And I thought you loved me."

"Ah, Richard, as if you did not know."

And I hated my father and mother for their good sense which
then seemed to me so evil and so hard.

[228]

Our household liked to combine music and society. There was a dinner party before a concert to be given by an illustrious American singer who came to Dorchester as part of the excited Liberty Bond campaign. Uncle Dylan had taken a box for the concert at a price which made a happy outrage upon his patriotism and briefly fed his longing for esteem. The party was to consist of my father and mother, Uncle Dylan and Aunt Bunch, Captain Jarvis McNeill and Monsignor Tremaine, who was very musical and had no prejudice against good company outside the rectory. Largely because of his presence extra effort was made before the dinner party. Special glass and silver and wines were brought out. To help Anna, a caterer was engaged who would lighten the kitchen load, especially after dinner, so she would not have to be "up all night with the dishes," which, sometimes, she felt she could throw one after the other down the cellar stairs to hear them break on the cement floor one by one, and if anyone should scold her, she would tell them to go chase theirself.

It was snowing when the guests arrived. I looked out the window and saw their cars—Uncle Dylan's big limousine with its cabin lighted and his chauffeur standing by the door; Monsignor Tremaine's old touring car with its cracked side curtains up. I counted. Someone was missing. Captain Jarvis McNeill had not arrived with the others. By prearrangement I was permitted to stay downstairs until I had toured the party to say good evening and display my dancing school manners—jerked handshake, ducked bow.

"My. How we have grown, all of a sudden. And are we still a very good young fellow?"

"Yes, M'nsígnor."

A pair of shining, hard, old brown eyes like horse-chestnuts polished in spring seemed to knock at my heart, sounding its formless guilt. *What have we here: a boy who is already feeling certain things? Does he know their true and holy purpose? Does he have to think too much about them? Does he have to lose them in troubling dreams? Ah: how hard it is to inherit feeling before there is knowledge. Ah: does knowledge really help? Let us trust in the mercy of God. God bless you, Richard.* Then the beloved old pastor laughed genially over his power to enter into the secrets of man, and let me go on to Uncle Dylan.

"Well, Richard? And why do you look at me like that? As if I had something for you tonight! Well, sir, let me tell you, you have another think coming."

How disgusting, this arch attempt to torture me, and draw the attention of all to the act of material generosity about to appear, as inevitable, hoped-for and boring as the magician's dry silk flag out of the glass of water.

"All right, Uncle Dylan, excuse me, then,"—and I made as if to pass on.

"He what? Look at him. I never knew such a boy, so impatient, can't he take a little joke from an old man?—All right, try the left-hand pocket."

My father revealed the shame and irritation of us all, though he kept smiling and silent above his tall evening collar and wide white bow tie.

"—No?" exclaimed Uncle Dylan blinking his sandy eyes, "not there? Nothing? How peculiar. Then try the other side!"

So I found a small leather case ("Well, go on, go on, Richard, open it, let us all see what it is, I've even forgotten since I bought it for you") containing a shiny brass telescope, so beautiful it shamed me for all my sins of opinion. I wanted so much to own it that I handed it back to Uncle Dylan.

"What? The ungrateful. No, really, it is for you."

Unable to resolve my feelings, I stood looking at the floor with my hands behind my back. Aunt Bunch saved me. She came forward and knelt down to me as if we were quite alone. By doing this she made me taller than herself. She put her white arms around me and drew my face down to hers. We both shut our eyes: audible smiles once again in the room at the spectacle of the "lovers." Her hair shone like waves under sunset light. She wore a heavy shining dress of some pale color that showed much of her bosom and back and all her arms bare. Violets were held to her breast by a great spray of diamonds in a pin. In a moment she gave me a pat, and said, "There!", and made me release her as she lightly took the telescope from Uncle Dylan and gave it back to me. I kept it. Was there anyone else in the world for whom she had so much love, which she would show so proudly? She had put a spell over everyone by her scene with me, and now it broke, and my father said to her that she had never looked so beautiful in her life, and that—he laughed delightedly—he supposed she couldn't help it.

"Oh, Dan," she replied, but with such a buried passion of hopelessness and hope that without understanding her at all, I was startled and stared at her.

"And now," said my mother, also moved by the extraordinary without grasping its meaning, "you may say good night, Richard, and go up to your tray, and to bed."

"But I want to wait and see the Captain."

"He will not be here for quite some time," she said. "He telephoned. He is delayed. If you are not sleeping when he comes, he may run up to see you for a moment. Now good night, darling."

"Delayed?" said Uncle Dylan. "How delayed? I have not been informed about this. I have his ticket for a box seat right here in my pocket. I might have been told."

"But we just learned," said my mother.

"Dylan, it does not matter," said Aunt Bunch. "If he comes, well and good. If not, everybody will have a seat anyway."

"But in a box," he murmured, drilling for appreciation.

"You are most generous," said Monsignor Tremaine kindly.

"Not at all, the Liberty Bond drive, you know," answered Uncle Dylan, but with the tone of one assuaged for the moment.

A look from my father, fierce in the eye, sweet in the mouth, drove me finally from the room. As I left, I heard them discussing the concert that was to come. The singer was Geraldine Farrar, so gifted, so beautiful, so romantic. My mother, who sang prettily, and was a graceful and animated mimic, began laughingly to sing, "Vissi d'arte, vissi d'amore," with enough exaggeration to excuse the impersonation, so that everyone laughed with her, and said, "Farrar!", and (as I learned later) it was Monsignor Tremaine who moved to the piano, and picked up the accompaniment and went with the aria until the charming joke lost its point and ended in general exclamations and the arrival of cocktails.

⚜

Anna came achingly up the back stairs with my supper tray and watched me eat for a few minutes, and told of Uncle Dylan's chauffeur sitting in the kitchen, having his dinner before anyone else at all. She said he was a self-satisfied piece, but company was company, and who was she to judge? Soon her mind was elsewhere. Her heart was cocked toward the lives and joys of others.

"Listen!" she said, setting her attitude toward the gaiety downstairs, "How they love it, what dear souls they are. . . ." Smash their dishes? Never in your life.

She made me hear, and in her grey, pocked, Anna-like old face, I saw the glowing room, the fire in the grate, the silky colors and the flowers, the rosy lamps and the dressed-up people, the sparkle of highlight and the rubbed gloss of velvet, as though they belonged not in our house, where I had so recently left them myself, but else-where, away, wonderful and desirable. And then, as though having done a duty in transferring her hungry and idle vision to me, she lumbered to her feet and groaning abstractedly, "Oh, well, God have mercy," she went back to the kitchen refreshed and ready for the responsible moments that were coming to her with dinner.

※

I hurried through my supper tray, changed to my pajamas, carried the tray to the head of the back stairs as was the custom, and then on my belly went to the head of the carpeted front stairs to watch and to listen. I saw them all downstairs when they crossed the hall to the dining room to sit down under the many shaded candles above the table. I strained to hear every car out in the street making its grinding song on snow with tire chains, thinking every car would bring Captain Jarvis McNeill. When the company was through dinner and returning to the drawing room for coffee, I picked out one then another with my new telescope from the distance of the flight of stairs. There, glowing in midair, rimmed faintly with pale blue and yellow optical magic, were those familiar faces, brought near and separate in a new kind of ownership.

A brief halt between dining room and drawing room took place for an important question.

"But what shall I do if he does not come?" asked Uncle Dylan, taking out his wallet and carefully spreading his six box seat tickets like a hand of cards. "I have all the tickets."

"I cannot understand," said my mother. "He did not think he would be this late."

"He must have a thousand things to do," said Aunt Bunch, "getting ready for his orders, and of course he cannot talk about them. —There is no reason," she added with persuasive sweetness, "for anybody who does not have to to miss the concert. Here," she said, leaning forward with grace and swiftly taking the tickets from Uncle Dylan, "leave me two, and since we are the hosts at the box party, I will wait for Jarvis here a little while, and bring him if he comes; and if he does not come soon, I will follow alone. There!" she finished, giving four tickets back to Uncle Dylan, and shutting two into her bag of solid gold mesh, as Uncle Dylan always called it.

"Oh, why, no," said Uncle Dylan, "never," then leaving his mouth open as he looked from face to face for strength; but found none. Nobody confessed to what Uncle Dylan dared not carry further in the presence of others. "But how, what car?" he asked Aunt Bunch in a surge of renewal—a last move to assert authority and save what was already lost.

"You can leave me ours," she said easily, "and Dan can take all of you in his."

"Of course," agreed my father.

"I shall go in my own," said the Monsignor, "for I must hurry home right afterward."

The current had swept once again strongly past and beyond Uncle Dylan. They all vanished into the other room for coffee.

Soon my mother came to say goodnight. I was discovered virtuously in bed. She wore what was called an opera cloak and, to protect her against the snow, a pair of opera boots of blue silk and ermine. She kissed me, idly told me to be good and go right to sleep, and then asked me if I did not love my new telescope.

"Yes," I replied.

"Yes, Richard, then love what you have, *and can have,* and not what you do not have. Good night, my darling," she said in a whisper, leaving me baffled and somehow reduced in spirit.

I listened intently until the sounds of departure were all done.

[234]

From the kitchen dimly came the after-dinner work, and unaccustomed rumbles of conversation as Aunt Bunch's chauffeur talked with Anna and the caterer, who would soon be done with his work, and would head for the streetcar tracks two blocks away leading downtown. I listened for sounds from the drawing room where Aunt Bunch must be. I heard nothing. Planning to go down and see, I fell asleep.

※

How much later I didn't know, but it felt much later, I awoke to the icy sizzle and clank of tire chains slowing down and stopping in the caked snow out in the street. Then I heard boots on the porch, and the door open and shut as someone let Captain Jarvis McNeill in, and then the stamp in the vestibule to loosen the snow from his spur chains.

He was here at last and my pulse began to rip along. I leaped from my bed, turned on my light, and went over my toys rapidly. The regular ones were ready. In a moment he would come up to see me, to settle down on the floor, as usual, to create and enter in the world where he and I, and only we, were heroes. Leaving the light on for encouragement, I went to my door to wait for him.

But he did not come.

I listened.

Where was he? I heard nothing from below, not even the soft but penetrating diapason of his heavy Irish voice that could enter the fabric of our house and make it vibrate in response.

I turned to my toys that waited with me. Was it possible that he had forgotten my old castle with its real drawbridge, and rows of leaden archers on the battlements, and in the great hall a double throne with a king and queen under a canopy? I had outgrown these things, but surely he had not, who had known them for only a few months! And in the corner, the tracks of a train winding in and out of sized muslin mountains and along a painted river? And in my own country of France that battery of wooden cannons, modeled in perfect detail, that could shoot pellets with a spring? And what else? My grandfather's toy theatre from Germany with its red curtain rolled up on a baton, and its woods scenery in place behind its stiff actors who entered upright in grooves? And even my old fire engine, long broken, but never discarded? Not to speak of the new telescope which he had not even seen?

The silence took on so great a strangeness that a hint of panic came with it.

I could not wait any longer. I took my telescope and went swiftly down the carpeted stairs. He was there, somewhere, for I had heard him come in. And then everything became clear to me. I'd been a fool. It was plain that Captain Jarvis McNeill was enjoying a game with me. He was hiding somewhere in the big front room, waiting for me, even as I had waited for him. The happy hunter came alive in me. I went down to my belly and crawled silently from the hall into the drawing room with my telescope ready. Coming around the forest-like obstruction of a green velvet chair with heavy wooden arms and legs (moss and rock), I carefully put my glass to my eye and slowly swept the softly-lighted far end of the room to find him.

Familiar details came into view—a picture on the wall, flowers on a table, books, a lamp—as I ranged from left to right, toward the great sofa that stood across the last corner of the room. Everything was colored softly and as though by a brush, and as still as the dead.

As still as the dead until into my telescope glided life and motion, and I saw the gloss of dark hair turning and turning and ruddy cheeks above pale cheeks and the heavy massed treasure of golden waves of hair, and pure piercing bolts of light from pale violet eyes that opened and closed, gazed away, and again near, away, and near, with such intensity of expression that it could have meant the extreme of suffering or of joy, or of both, and there came the restricted but mortal leverage of arms holding and closing and enclosing, and all in stillness that with such vision was not quite silence, for little sounds of breath, and lips, and thrust weight traveled to me and told the same that the telescope told, and at the same time, and with the same shattering power.

My world fell.

I knew sharply and deeply that what was mine was no longer mine. Aunt Bunch was mine in just my way no more. Captain Jarvis McNeill was lost to me in the arms of love. Even Uncle Dylan suffered breaking change in the discovery, for he was Aunt Bunch's, and thus mine, though with scorn, in the old order of the world which was now broken.

But he came to see me, Captain Jarvis McNeill? And yes—I knew now that every time Aunt Bunch was there too, as it "happened." I was torn with rage and betrayal.

And this evening? When he was late, who arranged everything, to wait for him, in her great beauty so enhanced by hope and hopelessness? What were the warnings of my parents, and how general were they, and how particular?

I understood nothing, really, except that I was overwhelmingly robbed, and of what, even, I was not then very sure. But the two lost people in my round lens were alone and far away. I must make them crash with me, or I must vanish into thin air.

"No!" I cried out, and lurched to my feet, and threw my telescope at the wall where it broke some picture glass. I turned over the big chair where I had played my hunter's game of hide and seek. So I declared myself.

The more-than-kiss broke apart and the real lovers stared at me with vacant faces.

"Oh—dear," said Aunt Bunch softly and slowly, with solemn sweetness and pity that made a thickness come to my throat until I began to fear the emotions I had made between us all.

Captain Jarvis McNeill roughly pulled himself together and then made for me with his hands outstretched as though to choke me.

"—Than a sneak," he whispered loudly, having said in his mind that there was nothing worse.

"Hush, Jarvis," said Aunt Bunch quietly, knowing what I felt. She was settling her hair, her gown.

"Yes, I'm sorry," he said, and knelt down before me to be reasonable and winning, and tried to take me kindly; but I kicked and flailed at him, shocked by the scared look in his face, a look I was mature enough to know since fear of exposure was childhood's one explicit emotion. In a gesture he tried to recover me, but I pushed at him and ran upstairs to my room, turned off the light and, trampling my battlefield in France which had lost its point, forever, went into my bed with my hands over my ears and my mouth open. I was full of chagrin at the fall of man.

꩜

Presently in the ringing darkness of my misery with my ears covered and my eyes squeezed shut, I inhaled a waft of that cool, moist fragrance that always meant Aunt Bunch. The scent of Parma violets would always seem to me the odor of purity itself, and yet just as intimately and powerfully, and at the very same time, that of profane love.

She knelt by my bed and put her quiet hand on my hot neck. She said nothing but waited for me to speak if I must. Soon I was trying to rebuild my follies.

[238]

"You will stay here with me, alone?" I whispered urgently.

But she refused to be false to what we all now knew.

"Nonsense, my dear," she said gently, "you are going to sleep, and we are going to the concert."

"But—but—" but I could not think of what crowded in me to want. I clung to her and like any betrayed lover begged for lies with my touches. She would not tell them, even with caresses, any more. She held me and I began to die into sleep, suffering for the last time from the confusion called childhood.

The last I remember as I fell asleep, bitter with spent woe under her touch, was the sound of her voice. It returns to me a lifetime later whenever I meet the fragrance of her little flowers, saying the only thing to say in pity and certainty that made me ache even as it promised of life all I did not yet know, "Some day . . . some day. . . ."

Book Two

EVERYTHING

TO LIVE FOR

FOR ERNST BACON

AT THAT TIME OF LIFE and for a little while in that summer of 1921, my cousin Max was everything I wished I were. When they said I must visit his family I was polite about it, not wanting particularly to go. But they all said he was handsome, so original, as they put it, and would one day be so preposterously rich, with all the girls drawn to him, and with every boy, even younger than I, sure to learn much from a few days in his atmosphere, that I saw I must agree to go, if only to please my parents.

My invitation to a house party for the Fourth of July came from my mother's first cousin, who was married to the senior member of the Chittenden family, a ranking partner in the great fortune known by their name. Maximilian was the only son of that branch. As such he was the principal heir of the six generations of manufacturing money which reached back to the time of the Revolution, when the family wealth began to gather in all its self-reproductive weight as a result of Chittenden-built ships needed by General Washington and the Colonies.

"Their place is so beautiful—so immense," I was told. "There will be parties, and swimming and dances, and the famous fireworks concert, and imagine that great stable of motorcars of every kind. Cousin Alexander even has one of the great private libraries in the country, and you can browse there if all the rest doesn't interest you."

"Does Max read?" I asked.

"How do I know? But he goes to Harvard."

"If they live in the country, how can they have enough people for dances? Girls, I mean?"

"It is the kind of country where every hill has a great house filled with relatives and friends and they all know each other. They ride together—everyone keeps horses, and they play tennis and polo *at home,* and swim. Why don't you want to go?"

"They'll all be so full of themselves and they don't know me at all."

"If it is your hay fever you're worried about, don't worry. The summer nights in Eastern Pennsylvania are cool, especially in the Chittenden Hills, and our nights are so warm here, you'll be happy to be away. And you love to travel. Yes, to go visiting people so rich is like traveling in a foreign country. And everyone says Maximilian is so charming—so like his mother. She was the bright star of our generation. —You'll go?"

"I suppose so," I said.

"Oh, darling Richard, who can pull a longer face over something nice!" exclaimed my mother, and my father said,

"I believe it is considered proper never to be impressed, when you are seventeen?"

They both looked at me with fond appraisal, and I saw that they were working to keep heart at the spectacle of anyone young as he came to the threshold of any test—especially one for whom they held every hope. Life, they knew and as I did not yet know, was a series of barriers to meet and cross until the very last and most mysterious one of all. They had fondly brought me to pass so many already, some small, some great.

"But I still hate summer," I said, needing to lose my position with at least one small personal flourish.

"Hate summer! When everybody else can't wait for it!"

I had recently learned to make a mysterious smile and I used it now, with fine effect.

❊ ❊ ❊

It was true that for many years summer gave me a vague, hollowed feeling of dread such as I knew in no other season of the year. For a long time I didn't really know this, but as I grew older, I began to recognize how summer in its rankness of growth was like my own body as it reached new dimensions and pricked me with new sensations, mysterious, inviting, but also bewildering. I had something in my mind akin to the sudden rains of summer—showers of thought that came as from behind hills which obscured their origin; and like summer rains such storms brought heat instead of coolness, and grasses seemed to swarm and tendrils to climb and cling within my desires as powerfully as they did in the woods and fields. Certain wild flowers had such power that they made my breath close in my breast when hot damp nights persisted. Summer demanded my distrust, for how could you be sure which leaf would or would not poison you, or thorn produce swellings which sent their allergens through the blood and caused running tears and blurred sight? What were equally disheartening about summer were

[3]

its beauties, so that I thought of misery and delight as inseparable; and I always went out when we were in the country and walked or rode a pony in the meadows where blue air seemed to part for me as I went, and far away amongst hills the blue was so dense that I knew just the pan of water color which would copy it. My heart sank at the impossibility of saving on paper what I loved across the fields. Passing through the wild flowers and whiplike grasses which opened before and closed after me, I was accompanied by a garment of color and sound, a little flying tapestry of insects—bees, gnats, dragonflies, heavy wasps— with whom I seemed to have a mysterious pact of immunity so long as I paid them no attention. Even if the pony stumbled and I had to make a sudden motion of recovery they let me alone, only intensifying their singing drone as they flew in new space to keep their adjustment to my sweating bulk. On the days when hazes hung over the meadows, and nothing seemed to breathe or move, my suspended feeling of expectation and dread grew heavier. I learned what it meant when the barometer fell; and I wondered if my heart fell within me accordingly. What was going to happen? I had the sense that something was coming. If only I knew what, I could be ready, and summer would lose its steamy, enfolding menace. But nothing told me, and so I went around with a false air of confidence, and in shame rehearsed *how to be* in front of the long mirror inside my bedroom door. I never liked what I saw there, and I think now that if I were to make an account of my unseen life as it was in that summer long ago I would entitle it "Apology for My Body." Once overhearing people talking about me with my parents I heard the phrase, "the awkward age," and I grew hot with anger, not because it said so much but so little. "Awkward" came nowhere near describing my outer state and its inmost desperations, the most powerful of which was a desire to be somebody—anybody—else. But how to escape? We are prisoners of our very selves, and the prison could be seen, touched, caressed, pleased, wounded, in its substantial being, while always abided the conviction that the outlook for deliverance was hopeless. But if you would believe what you heard, perhaps love would deliver me? But I fell in love with somebody different every day, and nobody ever knew it. It was an exhausting profusion of passions, and I concluded that nobody else in the world, behind all their smiling or preoccupied or sorrowing faces, knew as much as I did about what life was actually like; for if they did know, how could they present their unalarming aspects to the world?

"Richard is such an even-tempered fellow," I heard. "So clean, always, so well-groomed, it must be wonderful to be so nice-looking and be so contented. So many young people throw themselves about so. . . ."

Yes, nobody knew anything, and all you could do was be what they expected and hope for escape into the cool of autumn, and the cold of winter, when you could always take comfort in the suppression of summer, when all acts of life seemed exaggerated, too close, too powerful; for how could you escape heat that lay over the whole world and made everything swell and climb and burst, in blind fulfillment of appointed nature? In winter, at least, it was possible to come in from the snow and approach the fire and control the light and make the world for yourself.

Late in the morning of July 3rd Max came to meet me himself as my train made its brief stop between Philadelphia and Baltimore. They had telegraphed that I would be met, but I did not expect him. I had never seen him but I knew him at once. He was strolling amiably along looking with frank and charming curiosity at everyone, as though to ask their needs, which he would take steps to fulfill. The day was hot, moist and bright, the station platform and the stairs down to the pavement shone with grime, and everyone else looked weary and useless. It was impossible not to identify him. He was like someone moving in his own light.

"*That's* my cousin Richard!" he exclaimed as I approached, wondering how to risk addressing him.

"Yes."

"Let me have your bag."

Not awaiting, not expecting, an answer, he took it from me and in his hand it looked shabbier than ever, and my ship and hotel labels from Europe a summer ago seemed like schoolboy souvenirs.

"You have saved my life," he said, taking me down to the street where his car—an Isotta-Fraschini with its top strapped back, its long hood shining in fire-engine red, and its engine negligently running since it was a nuisance to start it each time by turning a key—stood exactly in front of a sign which read *No Parking*.

"How?" I asked.

"Nobody else is coming, they've all regretted at the last minute, and it wouldn't be a party with just us at Newstead. You make it one."

It was a responsibility, and he laughed at my expression.

"Jump in. —But don't be alarmed. My girl Marietta who lives here will be with us a lot, and we'll find things to do."

Things to do usually sounded ominous to me, but Max made the prospect seem unchallenging and bright.

We drove off through the city and into the rolling country-side at high speed made elegant by the way he drove and the rich drone of the car. In populated areas I thought various strangers recognized him, but he took no notice. He conveyed me with the air of one who often did kind and simple things for others, even though, as the wage earners on the sidewalks might say, "he didn't have to."

"What is Newstead?" I asked.

"My father's place. My grandfather built it. He was a collector. He was gone on Lord Byron. If you like that sort of thing you can see the manuscripts and editions in the library. He named the house after Byron's."

"Yes, I wondered. I remember pictures of it."

"Ours isn't a copy, just a sentiment. It is hideous, as you will see, and huge, I suppose. In a couple of minutes you can see it on top of the hill. I'm never going to live there."

He meant when he inherited his great share of the Chittenden resources, including his father's house.

"Who is Marietta?"

"I told you. She is my *friend*. Marietta Osborne. She lives on the *next* hill. She is coming with us tonight and we three are going out dancing. She will like you. I can tell that now. And if she likes you, you will like her. It is always that way with Marietta. If it is the other way, there is no hope ever. I am the only one she likes whom she began by not liking, but then we were children, and I always knew it would change,

[7]

and it has. I think her name made you smile. Does it sound too much *débutante* to you?"

"No, it didn't. I like it."

"Then you just smile a lot, is that it?"

"I don't know. I didn't know it."

"Well, anyway, let's make it a good house party, no matter what. My Ma can't wait to meet you. She says your mother was always the bright star of their generation."

I laughed at him for his light spirits and said,

"No, that's what my mother told me about yours."

"Women. They probably hate each other and go around being sweet to cover it up. —Look, there's the house. From here, it always looks like a state hospital, don't you think?"

He turned the car into a narrow country road which ran up and down over hills. Off to our left was a high hill, put farther by the blue haze of the day. On its crest was a heat-grayed fieldstone house. It had many wide chimneys rising from a great central temple which threw out long wings leading to lesser temples at each end. There was an impression of white columns and three browlike pediments at middle and ends. Woods broke up against the crest of the hill like great waves, leaving the top clear, except for formal planting.

"They've put you in rooms near mine, so we can at least talk without shouting," said Max.

At this he turned sideways to look at me. His eyes were swimming with fun in their shining gray light. He was dusky with tan over high color. His hair was bleached on top from the sun, but at the sides was a glossy light brown. He had a classic short nose and carved lips and a strong round chin. His profile belonged on a Roman medallion. You would have to say, implying no softness, that he had

[8]

extraordinary beauty, both of face and body, and that the flickering humor which played all through his very use of his features and gestures mocked his appearance and his state of being. He was three years older than I and in all that he indicated between us he elevated me to his own age. It was a princely grace for a senior at Harvard to bestow upon a second cousin in his last year of school.

❧ ❧ ❧

Max devoted all of that first day to me. We made a fine spiral up the hill to the garages—it was necessary to use the plural—between the house and the stables. Max climbed out over the side of the car rather than open the door as I did and we walked away toward the semicircular conservatory at the rear of the house which overlooked the back entrance.

"Max," I said, "shouldn't the motor be turned off?"

"They'll do it," he said, opening the conservatory door for me. We entered into an indoor summer, where tropical plants hung in a sweaty stillness of regulated temperature. "This is Ma's department"—indicating the hot-house—"but it needn't bother us except that she loves to talk about it."

"Will I see her?"

"Not today, they say. She is resting." He did not say why. "And Pa is in town for something directorial. We'll lunch alone and then I'll show you around."

"I would like to see the library."

"Somehow, I thought so. Do you want a swim before lunch?"

[9]

"Do you?"

"Not particularly."

How like him, to propose or offer, and then show indifference.

"I think not, thanks."

Hoisting my bag to his shoulder with comic ease, he led me upstairs and far down a white paneled corridor to rooms at the far end of the wing. The door was open. He preceded me within and put the bag on a rack and said,

"Here you are. I'm just across the hall. If you want to wash up now, I'll meet you in my sitting room for a cocktail. It's great you're here. You'll have to tell me everything about yourself."

He left me in my high, large, square rooms—a sitting room with a fireplace and bookcases, a bedroom, and a bath with a huge marble tub long enough for the "petrified giant" I had seen in a traveling carnival sideshow years ago. It seemed insufficient merely to wash my hands in such surroundings, but in effect I had been commanded to do so, and I did, wondering why the grand scale and rich materials of such a house had an odor unlike that of any house I knew. There seemed also to be a special stillness about the place. Was it because Maximilian's mother—Cousin Alicia, or Lissy, as she was always spoken of—was resting? But surely where she rested was far enough away and sufficiently insulated by doors and fabrics to protect her. I suddenly realized how expensive it was to obtain perfect quiet.

I returned to my sitting room and tried out all the armchairs, and then looked out my windows. I could see a meadow below the rolling hill, where a paddock was prettily marked off by white rail fences to make an outdoor riding hall. The striped goal posts of a polo field showed beyond. A white dairy barn, with a dark roof like the lid of a chest, and fancy lightning rods, stood at the end of another meadow, where black and white cows grazed and seemed never to move. Where the hills rose opposite again, I saw a long rambling white house dappled with trees on the next hilltop, and I said, "Marietta Osborne." Between the two windows of the sitting room a French desk stood at right angles to the wall. A trim small armchair enclosed in varnished caning stood waiting before it. I sat down in it and reached for writing paper which bore the name, mail and telegraph addresses, telephone number, and rail junction of the house, with appropriate symbols, and began a letter.

"Dear Mother, Dear Father, I have just arrived and all is big, beautiful, and silent as the tomb. I am as it turns out the only guest. Max met me at the train himself, I thought they'd send a chauffeur. He is like a crown prince and I think he—"

Just then without a knock the door opened and he came in. "What's keeping you? —Oh: writing letters."

Smiling splendidly he walked over to me and picked up my letter and read it as if he were expected to approve it before it could be sent. His air was so friendly and wholesome that a flicker of resentment died down in my breast. What in anyone else would have been an intrusion upon privacy seemed with him to be consuming interest, aroused by affection. He laughed and put my letter down and said,

"Yes, isn't it dreadful, all of it, most of all the crown prince business. I have been accused of it before. What were you going to say about me in the letter just as I walked in?"

I was going to write, "I think he likes me," but all I said to Max was, "I've forgotten."

[11]

"Well, you'll tell me later, in some way or other. Cocktail?"

I had never had one, only a little wine on occasions of ceremony at home.

I followed him across the hall to his study, as he called it. It was the same size and shape as my sitting room, but where mine was neat and arid in its luxury, his looked like a junkshop in which everything was particularly valuable. There were only two chairs free of litter. Window seats, sofas, chairs, the corners, the tops of bookcases, were cluttered beyond confusion—all merged into a thick random texture of books, papers, sporting equipment, sweaters, riding boots, a piece or two of bronze sculpture, beer mugs, and whatever. His desk supported a typewriter and four or five drinking glasses and bottles and a pile of papers of all sizes and conditions. It would have been more worldly if I had ignored the clutter, but he saw my astonishment, and he said with a laugh,

"Don't mind it. This is the one place I have told them they may not touch. I know where everything is, and feel at home here, like an old dog with a blanket nest full of ratholes. Every time I go away to college they try to straighten it up, but it doesn't take long for it to be made comfortable again. —I'll admit it isn't much like the rest of the house. I hope you don't mind."

Mind! I thought it distinguished beyond words to live in a mess, if that's what you wanted to do in the midst of riches.

"Of course not."

"Are you neat?"

"I suppose so."

"It doesn't matter if it doesn't bother you. —You know

[12]

something? Almost all my clothes are things I have bought secondhand. Really."

I looked at him, so splendid in his country tweeds and checks. He was stirring a drink at the desk.

"Yes," he said, "all these, and it doesn't mean I want anything that wouldn't do. I just like the old feel of somebody else's things."

Out of my self-knowledge, I said,

"Maybe you want to feel like somebody else, too."

"Richie, good shot!" he exclaimed with great high spirits. "I've wondered about that. I really don't know. My parents can't understand it. My Ma sometimes looks at me as if I had fleas. —Here's your drink."

We tipped our glasses to each other and had a drink. It was strong and bitter.

"Was that Marietta Osborne's house I saw through my window?" I asked.

"Yes. She rides over almost every day. We're going to pick her up tonight at seven-thirty. Do you like to dance?"

"I went to dancing school."

"That's no answer, though perhaps it is. But when you dance with her, it isn't really dancing. It is an ambulant conversation. If I try to get her to pay attention to the dance band, she puts her lips together and shoots her breath out through her nose and shakes her head and tells me I am impossible, who ever went to a dance in order to *dance!*, she means. Her father's a physician, besides being on our board of directors. —Do you manage with girls?"

His question muted me by its suddenness. He added,

"No, I mean, plenty of men in my class at college are still all confused about it, and usually all wrong. I just meant—"

He blinked both eyes at me like a kindly elder, and to close the subject comfortably for me, while giving me the benefit of every doubt, he said,

"The only way to manage is to take them for granted. Let's go down for lunch. We'll have it on trays in the library, since we're alone, and you like libraries. I believe they're ready for us."

With a rough slap on my shoulder blade he turned me to the door in his easy sense of command and trust.

❦ ❦ ❦

A great hall or gallery ran the whole length of the central unit of the house. The illusion of beds of flowers was created by banks of potted plants set in bays paved with loose chips of white marble along the pale rose marble walls. Hitherto I had seen houses like this only in luxurious early movies and there all the grandeur was painted on canvas with occasional wrinkles in it.

We went along and then entered a great room which took all the first floor of the far wing. It was the library. Shelves, spaced between unstained walnut paneling where portraits hung, extended behind gilded grilles to the coffered ceiling. Two fireplaces faced each other at opposite ends of the room. Now in summer both were filled with tubs of flowering plants. A pair of immensely long refectory tables stood in the center of the room. They supported lamps, Renaissance bronzes, and folio volumes. Long deep velvet sofas were backed up to the tables. We walked to a corner of the room lighted by a standing lamp. Two easy chairs with low tables in front of them stood in a circle of light. We heard a small noise across the room in the opposite corner and Max called out,

"Oh, Andy, excuse us, we just came in to have lunch on a tray."

"Yes, of course," said Andy, coming up from his desk as though discharged by concussion. "I was just going out for mine. Excuse me."

"Thank you," said Max, and as the small young man left rapidly, we watched after him. He walked in a rocking gait somehow appropriate to his general appearance, which, with his pale fuzz-clipped haircut, suggested an Easter chick wearing heavy horn-rimmed glasses. Max added, "Andrew Dana, our librarian. Pa saved him from a college job. He really does know a lot about Byron and all that. And of course he orders in all the new books of any interest. The latest ones are always on that table over there. Take your pick whenever. Let's sit down."

As we did so he pressed an electric button in the paneling, and presently two footmen in day jackets came in bearing our trays which they set down before us. Max thanked them and indicated that we would need nothing more and they withdrew. Like Mr Dana, they might have been, for Max, performing dogs in appropriate costumes.

"So many flowers everywhere," I said. "All down the long gallery, and here in the fireplaces."

"My Ma. It is all she thinks of since her difficulty began." I wanted to know what this was but he went right on. "Aren't you an only child?"

"Yes." (I came late to my parents.)

"I almost am. I have a sister but she's much older and lives abroad. I had a younger brother who died at birth. So you see I'm the only one also."

"Have you minded?"

"That means you have."

"Yes, sometimes."

"Not really," he said. "The chief bother is in having to make up your mind whom to love, instead of loving them before you know it, just by living with them. You know?"

"I haven't thought about it."

"But you think quite deliberately much of the time, don't you, Richie? Does anyone else call you Richie? If they do, I'll think of something else."

"No, they don't. I wish I really could think. Sometimes I think I have nothing up here to do it with."

He laughed while chewing. He ate in big bites and frank appetite.

"I had a time like that. Or rather, everything I made up my mind about immediately suggested the very opposite, and I would switch over to believing *that*."

"How did you settle it?"

"It cleared up by itself when I began to drink and sleep with girls." But he gave me a keen look to see if I believed this.

"Oh."

"Not that we're going to talk about that"—for he had seen in his quick pale glance that it was what I most wanted to hear about, and he never made his gifts in response to what was actually wanted. "I think you might plan to come in here tomorrow morning and look around. Either Mr Dana or my father can show you things. A nice way to have a quiet Fourth of July."

"Will you be busy?"

"I never know. Anyway, I don't know much about all this." This remark was an affectation, as I knew later.

We finished our trays more or less in silence and great speed, Max setting the pace. With a nod he led me out of the library and out of the house. The Isotta was waiting at the front door. The engine was running. His negligences, then, were rules, and he had the power to impose them.

"Do you want to drive?" he asked.

"Thanks, no. I've never driven anything like this, and I didn't bring my license."

"Nonsense. Get in. I'll tell you what to do."

I obeyed and under his coaching the superb car moved off down the hill toward the meadows. I drove carefully. Those were fairly early days of motoring, and the first great cars had wonder built into them. I felt a faintly choked emotion as I handled the big polished steering wheel of striated wood. Manhood spoke to me in my belly and groin with the kind of joy that dreams could bring. Max leaned around to look directly at me. If I had been aching to drive, he would not have been so willing; but seeing my delight, after my hesitancy, he felt like someone who has created something new, out of the most immalleable of elements, which were those of human desire.

"How about it, Richie?" he asked in a soft, intense sound that carried shivers of indefinable intimacy with it. "How about it, boy? Eh?" He ground his admirable teeth together gently, moving his jaw as if in recollection of ultimate pleasure. "Give her the gun, we've got a good straight stretch just over this hill. I'll tell you when to slow down. Gun it, Cousin! You're doing fine!"

The humid air flew past us. He rode leaning forward. His eyes were half closed by a suspended smile. His hands were

[17]

knotted between his thighs. Tensely he gave himself to sensation. I remember thinking how interesting and strange it was for anyone to find sensual pleasure in speeding by motorcar, for that is just what his fine face and head, with bronze hair modeled by the wind, seemed to show. It was not long until I knew that he met every physical sensation in the same spirit.

❧ ❧ ❧

He showed me the way around the entire Chittenden barony—his father's own place, and the estates of his uncles and cousins. Either on hilltops or sweepingly revealed at the far end of a fold of hills, the family houses presided over the landscape. We returned to Newstead by a back road. About two miles from the house we came alongside a glass structure like a municipal palace of horticulture. This was what it was—"Ma's greenhouse," Max said. It was clearly more than that, for it had broad terraces on its long side facing the valley, where tables and chairs and other furniture, including a fountain set slightly lower on the slope, proposed social events. I could see tall tropical trees inside the towering glass vault of the building.

"We used to have parties there, and concerts," said Max. "All that we do now is the Fourth of July fireworks party every year. You'll see it tomorrow night. We ask a hundred people who come and sit there"—the terrace—"and all the country people from miles around come and sprawl all over the hills where they can see just as well. We're having a dance with it this year, presumably because Marietta and I would like it."

"Won't you?"

"Would you?"

"Why not?"

"Complete with peasants and operatic villagers in the respectful middle distance?"

"But I thought you didn't mind servants and—and—"

"And being rich? I don't, up close. But it's when you back off and look that it seems idiotic. Are your people rich?"

"Not like this. Not anything like it. We have only a cook and one car and we go away in the summer. You can *stay home* every summer."

He laughed at my statement of terms.

"Well, nobody is supposed to talk about it, so I won't. We're supposed to look satisfied and pretend that everybody else lives exactly the way we do, even our poor relations."

"Is that what I am?" I asked, somewhat irritably.

"Would you rather be me?" he asked suddenly without his bantering indifference.

Yes, I said to myself, I would, and at that time it was still true, but before I would say so, I would cut my tongue out. I didn't answer. He leaned and gazed at me. We were still driving and he put a hand on the wheel as if to change my aim. He said,

"Would you? Why can't you tell me. I want to know."

It was like being asked if I loved him. I had no idea about that, but his urgency, the blaze in his eyes, his swift descent into intimacy, paralyzed my thought and word, and I drove on past my Cousin Alicia's botanical garden in silence.

In a moment Max slumped back in his seat and said,

"Well, good for you, Richie. You took a risk and it came out all right. I can respect that."

Risk? I wondered. But now I know what it was and why he admired my silence.

❀ ❀ ❀

Below the last hill near the house we saw the tennis house and courts. Just beyond was a swimming pool with a colonnaded bathhouse.

"How about a couple of sets of singles?" asked Max. "But you didn't bring a racquet."

"No. I did not suppose anyone here played seriously."

He blurted a laugh and said,

"You're picking up our style fast, to say a thing like that. —How do you know I don't play tennis seriously? I suppose you do?"

"Yes. It is the only sport I'm any good at."

"Let's stop. I can lend you everything."

We played. It was mid-afternoon. I was soon running with sweat. He played hard and well but I took the first set six-three. As we changed courts Max paused at the net and gave me a droll smile shining with the golden light of his sweat. There was a kindly glow of approval in it, and also an edge of disbelief that I had beat him so far. He ran his tongue along his upper lip in a calculating taste of the joy it would be to take the next two sets and leave me in my proper place. But I was on a good streak of control and I knew it, and his bantering, threatening amusement did not

[20]

worry me. My father was a fine player and taught me from early years how to make every stroke a completed act of form. Accuracy and power came later, and by the time I was finishing school tennis was the only sport I loved. My best reassurances came from playing. My doubts vanished, my body obeyed me well, the spring and flight of the ball after a beautiful impact in the exact center of the racquet gave me, at that age, one of the examples, perhaps the only one, of perfect satisfaction in a personal action. All of me went into each stroke, and each seemed for its own sake absolutely worth-while at the instant. What did it matter that afterwards I remembered that it was only a game, and the outcome could not possibly be of any importance? I was fulfilled and delivered whenever I played as well as I knew how to. My pleasure never lasted long; I wished I knew how to gain the same feeling and confirmation from something in life that mattered.

"I'll be God damned," said Max at the end of the second quick set which I took six-love. He stood with his hands on his hips, one leg negligently thrust forward while he examined me from a distance of ten feet as though I were a new species. "Where did you ever learn to play like that? Do you know something? I haven't been beaten for two years. I'd never believe it, looking at you." If now he admired me his candor made it plain that he had not really admired me earlier.

"My father and I have played since I was eight. It doesn't mean anything."

"Anything! Why should it depress you to be so good at tennis?"

"Because even if I am good at it, it doesn't matter at all."

"Oh, yes, by God, it does. You've got to be wonderful at

everything." He shrugged. "At least, that is the law I grew up under, because otherwise my so-called advantages might count for too much." And now he looked at me as if he wished he were I—or so I thought for a moment. The ambiguities in the half-glimpsed awarenesses of young people: what longings struggled to find easement in release, and what poverties of expression stood in the way. Max, not yet quite believing he had been defeated, and on his own court at that, Max, full of some mystified marveling and want, called up such a strong feeling of affinity in me that I suddenly blushed and put my towel up to my streaming face. His tact was equal to the moment.

"Very well," he said, "we need a swim, now, in this heat, after all that."

He led me to the pool. In the little pillared temple at one end we found dressing rooms and showers.

In the water he was like a dolphin streaked with light. In that element he excelled me and was glad of it. He led me in dives which I executed awkwardly. He raced me two lengths and won by half a length. We cooled off and dried and dressed.

"I would think if you can play such good tennis you also might be a good swimmer," he murmured as we sat down on canvas-cushioned long chairs in the shade of the porch.

"I know, it is odd, but I have always been a little uneasy in the water, ever since I can remember."

"That explains it. I suppose someone threw you in when you were too young, leaving you to fight your way to survival, which you did. But ever since, you have thought of swimming as dangerous, which it isn't, really."

I was astonished.

"That is exactly what happened and what it did," I said.

[22]

"My father had me taken to the Dorchester Club on Saturday mornings to learn to swim in the pool. The instructor, an old man named Mr Mac, felt how timid I was right away, and saying he would keep an eye on me, he threw me up in the air and into the water. I nearly drowned. An older boy pulled me out. Mr Mac was dismissed. I didn't go back to the water for two years. Even now when I open my eyes under water I feel a little panic."

"You have not yet taken complete command of your whole environment," said Max.

This struck me as a magisterial statement. How could three years of age make so great a difference in the possession of wisdom? For I never considered that there might be more than a difference of age to explain his power and glory. We are told the young learn best through emulation. I intended to return to Dorchester in complete command of my whole environment as a new Maximilian. They would not know me, at home. They would look at me in wonder and think about it before addressing me.

"How do you get command of your whole environment?" I asked.

"The minute you decide it is true, it will be," he replied. "Most people never stop to think of it. —Let's go on up. It is going to rain. You can finish your letter. I am going to go to sleep for a while. I'll come get you when it's time to go for Marietta."

She was thin and small, but she hung heavy like inert matter in my touch as we danced. One flat white arm lay on my shoulder. With the other she dragged my hand down. In her continuing touch I felt an unceasing tremulous energy, a force over which she seemed to have no control. Her color was ghostly, so insubstantial did she look, while her power was frankly physical in how she moved and spoke. Her pale hair was long and loose, cut in a bang across her forehead. Under this her eyes were set in a permanent scowl which seemed to be the prediction of an unsuppressible smile. Trapped light came out in her gaze, which was deep in the shadow of her brow, and heavy shadows smudged the white under her eyes. She wore no make-up but lipstick, in a pale rose color. Her knee-length flat evening frock, in the period style with glass beads scattered over it, hung on her inertly and added its weight to her air of exhaustion. We rocked and stepped against the music of the college-boy dance band, as it was her will to counter her surroundings even in trivial ways. She pressed her lips together as though to deny them the smile which they were made for. Shaking invisibly in my grasp, she made me feel responsible for her, and turning her head away when I said something so that she would be able to control an impulse to laugh hysterically, she delighted me. Her fragrance was heavy, something like the air outside, which since nightfall had been hanging densely in a threat of warm rain. As we moved past the tall open doors of the Glenmere Hunt Club, where we were dining and dancing, I could see fireflies weaving their texture of tiny lights all across the broad meadow below. Max had danced with her once and then given her to me and disappeared.

"He makes me feel married," she said.

"How?"

"Handing me over and going off like that. Husbands hate to look responsible."

"He said you grew up together."

"We did. I nearly killed him once."

"How."

"How, how, how. It is your best word, isn't it?"

"How?" I said.

"You see?"

I had made a poor joke, but she was right, and all my sense was in one or another way given to the question "How?" as I reached to understand anything at all in that year of my life. Childhood had been so sure. She felt that she had reached one of my private vulnerabilities, and her secret little engine shook her until I felt it, and then she said,

"There's so much I could tell you."

"I hope you will."

"No, I mean, it would take a long time. —Come back next summer, will you?"

"I haven't even gone yet."

She made a breathy little groan, and said,

"NGod, I never say the thing I think I'm going to. You don't know how awful it is."

"You said you almost killed Max."

"That. I mean I tried to. It wasn't even an accident. He was seven and I was five, and I got furious because he said I could not be the queen. He was the king and he said if he needed to have a queen he would let me know but so far he did not need one. It was in my playroom on a rainy day and there was a fire in the fireplace. Max was wearing a long royal robe of red crêpe paper. I took a long match from the

[25]

hearth and I lit it in the fire and I set fire to his cape. He watched me do all this, refusing to be bothered or to make me stop, which made me wild. The match caught, and in a second, the king's robe was all flame. It reached up and burned the hair off the back of his head and set fire to his gold paper crown. It went so fast it burned itself out as fast, and didn't light his real clothes. If it had he would have burned up. I ran away crying. He didn't mind my trying to burn him to death, but he told me later I should never run away crying. They had the doctor for him who said he was all right. After he heard that, Max acted frightened for the first time, thinking about what might have happened."

"Were you punished?"

"Nobody ever knew that I did it."

"He didn't tell?"

"No. I did, but nobody believed me, and when they asked him, he said no. I wanted a scandal, but he wouldn't give it to me. Isn't he dreadful?"

"But you became friends again."

"I said I would never forgive him, but he said I would sooner or later. I don't think I ever have, but then."

She lifted and then slumped in my grasp, and gave me one of her sudden direct glances, and through her general air of suppressions, I saw glee and mischief, as well as some suggestion of extraordinary strength, contained within her exhausted air and her little shaking indirectness.

"But then what?" I asked.

"But then we are engaged, though not publicly. A few people are supposed to be told about it tomorrow night at Newstead. A ball. Fireworks. Promise to dance with me. He won't, and nobody else will."

We moved along in silence for a few vaguely walked

steps, and then I said, feeling I had been accepted within her world,

"Yes, I want to. Thank you."

"NGod, how polite all you people from places like Dorchester are."

In a word she put me outside again, after I had been forgetfully comfortable.

"—Oh, I didn't mean it that way," she said, for her little throbbing bones told her what I felt. "I only mean—oh, it's so awful, never to be like what you want to be, I mean, we are all so ghastly around here, we are rude and we say anything we think of no matter what, and I mean, I loved it when you said thank you. I mean Dorchester must be divine, if they are all like you. You know. Like that. Richard," she ended, making somewhere behind her nose a comic groan out of my name, "if you want to stop dancing with me this minute we can go and sit down and stare at our empty plates till Max comes back."

"Will he come back?"

"Oh, yes. He always does." She gave a breath of a laugh through her nostrils and said, "I suppose it is the best I can ever hope for."

"No, let's dance till the music stops."

It stopped just then on an unresolved chord.

"There he is," she said.

She pointed. Max was at the orchestra platform, talking to the youth who led the band from his piano bench. In another moment, Max was coming toward us.

"Do you begin to see Max?" she asked. "Who else would stop the band just to make us stop dancing?"

"Did he? Is that why?"

"Oh, yes, he did, it is."

Max came to us and stepped between us. He took us each by an arm and led us away.

"We have all had enough of this dreariness, don't you think?" he asked.

"But we were going to dance until I wore holes in my fine slippers," said Marietta.

"I know. But I am ready to go."

"You've been drinking," she said.

"Yes. Do you want a drink?"

"We all do."

"I have a bottle in the car"—the Prohibition style.

"It is beginning to rain."

"Yes. We'll get wet."

"Oh, lovely."

We found Marietta's little evening coat of flimsy gold India silk and we all went out into the rain. She put her coat up over her head and ran with us to the car.

"Are you going to put up the top?" asked Marietta.

"No," replied Max, opening the car door for her. The deep leather seat was slick with rain. We sat together and drank from a bottle of Canadian rye whiskey which Max brought out and then he started the car and turned on the great headlamps. Raindrops fell like pellets of gold in the long shafts of light we threw ahead. We rode soaking wet along the hilly roads, drinking as often as Max felt like it, and shivering in the air which we stirred by our speed, while the warm rain fell heavily. We were mostly silent. Once or twice Max looked past Marietta at me to see how I regarded the mournfully perverse episode, and something told me to show no feeling. I gazed back at him blankly, and then turned away. I was seized by baffled admiration, and I was also aware of a resentment which I knew to be unworthy of my membership in the league of those who rode around for hours in pouring rain with no protection; a resentment which I could not suppress; for I was wearing the only clothes I had brought in which to dress up in the evening, and they were now ruined. My cousin could find himself other things to wear, but I could not. The gallantry of the adventure was for me mixed with the misery of a country cousin who can never hope to meet the affluent and grand on their own terms. But—so anguished and proud are the young—it was impossible for me to show my honest concern over such a matter, and the Canadian whiskey kept me from recognizing the pathos of the drenched merry-making into which Max took us in darkness, torrent, and puddle, with nowhere really to go.

❃ ❃ ❃

"My dear Richard," said the note in the smallest hand-writing I have ever seen, "they tell me you are here. Welcome. We are always curious to see the next generation. Maximilian has a notion that you would like to look about the library. Unless he has mysterious and complicated plans for you, would you care to join me at ten o'clock in the library and let me show you a few pieces in the collection? Mr Dana is coming to work with me at ten-forty-five, but until then I shall be pleased to see you. I am afraid that may be our only chance, as the day will be busy, and you are to leave us, I'm afraid, on the sixth, and I alas must be in Philadelphia on the fifth.

Alexander Chittenden."

It was addressed to me with "Esqre." after my name—the first time I had ever been given the title. The envelope was on my breakfast tray which was brought to my sitting room. My first response to the note was to think that an extremely small man must have written it—someone to match the scale of the minute script. But as I discovered later, I was wrong. My Cousin Alexander was very tall and lean, with a small protuberant belly under his unaccented black suit. I had never seen a photograph of him, but when I actually met him, he made me think of a photograph, for all his colors were in values of gray and white and black. His eyes were black, set, like his son's, under dark porches, but their light had been long extinguished by I knew not what. Over them he wore large, perfectly round spectacles, in frames of the thinnest gold. His face was narrow and pale, with deep downward lines about the mouth. His hands were long, white, and moist; they held to each other much of the time. When he moved it was with a strange, angular animation, almost like gaiety, with wide swings of his narrow shoulders and stylish strides of his long legs. He was almost bald, with a few streaks of still dark hair brushed flat across his head. A long-linked gold watch chain across his waistcoat made an accent of light in his general dark. In no way, except perhaps in the trait of character or habit of command which led him to limit the terms of our meeting and my visit, did he remind me of Max. I thought his note a trifle unnecessarily cautious about when I must leave him and I did not think it wonderfully polite that he reminded me of the day I was expected to depart. I daydreamed for a moment of the luxury it would be to send another note back—"Dear Cousin Alexander, how good of you to suggest a visit to the library, but actually, I have other plans for the morning, and in fact, it may be that I will have to leave a day earlier than I had planned. Perhaps another time. If you are ever in Dorchester, do call us. I am sure my parents would be pleased to see you, even if I should happen to be engaged. With regrets and thanks for my visit to Newstead, which I find a very pleasant place, I am Yours faithfully"—but the bridling, precocious rudeness of this was soon lost like any dream, and when the valet came to take away my tray, I was dressing for ten o'clock.

"Is my Cousin Max done with his breakfast?" I asked.

"No, sir. He is sleeping. We are not to call him before twelve."

"Oh. I see. Oh—my suit got soaked through last night—I wonder if there is any way you could help with—"

"I have it now, sir. It is still damp, but we're drying it out and it will be pressed and ready for you before this evening."

I thanked him, wondering if I should ask him whether it had shrunk. He nodded cheerfully at me, almost with a wink, which could mean either that he was a young pink-faced Irishman naturally agreeable, or that he saw through my unaccustomed air of ease to my real concern as a young man with only one suit on a visit to another world.

"Yes, sir. It will be very grand this evening, with the music and the fireworks. You didn't bring a dinner jacket, sir?"

"Oh, no. Will they wear them tonight?"

"Oh, yes, sir. The invited people will all dress."

The possibility had never occurred to any of us in Dorchester, for youths my age did not possess evening clothes, even though my father and mother put on their special finery several times a week during the winters.

"But I'm sure your blue suit will do very well, sir."

"It will have to," I said bitterly, full of regret that I had come.

"Unless you could use one of Mr Max's, sir? You're a trifle taller, but we could let down the braces and 'twould never be noticed."

How to decide which would be the distinguished thing to do—to borrow a dinner jacket carelessly, or smile with forgiveness upon those who thought it mattered how one dressed for a formal dinner dance followed by a fireworks concert in Chittenden Hills? A phrase came to my rescue from the tone of family councils at home when a decision of some importance was hovering over us unresolved.

"Thank you," I said, "we'll see."

"Of course, sir. Thank you, sir."

He took away my tray from which at the last instant I rescued the note. I felt deeply unhappy; and I thought I had felt so ever since my arrival. I could not say why, in particular, but the general feeling of the whole place, the persons and the events in whose midst I found myself, seemed to me so alien that I had a gulping wave of homesickness, though I refused to give it that name even in my thoughts, for if I had made conscious the word, I would have had to admit that what I was homesick for was my childhood, when I was the center of all events and concerns, and when it was I who made the laws within certain conventions which were acceptable as they were devised for my welfare, and when my view of the world was lovely to those who saw it with me.

[32]

The library doors were open on a deep avenue of rich shadow where symmetrical pools of golden light shone down the room. As I appeared in the doorway,

"Yes, do come in, how nice," said Alexander Chittenden in a voice of high register which seemed to issue through a whole crosshatching of scratches until it sounded like an old Victrola record.

He walked from the farthest golden pool to meet me, swaying through long strides with a sort of prim elegance. He took my hand without grasping it. His touch was cold. He looked at his watch to see whether I had come precisely at ten, and since I had, he put it back into his waistcoat pocket saying,

"Oh, good." His pronunciation was sandily precise, with little special effects which I thought of as belonging to his caste—that of the few millionaires in the country whose wealth had come down through several generations of severe education and ingrown style. I won't try to sustain a phonetic rendering of this, but an occasional example or two might bring him more sharply to mind. He said "wirld" for "world," and he lengthened certain vowels fastidiously. When he meant "girl" he said "geel," and "pearl" came out "pirl," and "first" was "feest." Now he said, "Well, feest, Richard, as I shall call you, and as we are remote cousins by mahrriage, I do think it abseed if we say Mister to me, don't you: and yet Cousin Alexander seems odd, too, don't we think? At owah difference in age and the rest? I have thought we would settle on Uncle Alec for me, and Ahnt Lissy for my wife. You do think so?"

My father had said with comic awe that Alexander Chittenden was supposed to be worth upwards of four hundred million dollars, and he had added, "Poor fellow." "Poor fellow?" said my mother with charming scorn, "I could bear it if you were as poor as that. I cannot find it necessary to pity Lissy and Alec." "Yes," said my father, "think of having to work hard to be like other people." I had been mystified by this at the time, but now I remembered it, and I saw that Uncle Alec did work hard to be friendly and easy, like other people, but I saw too that he failed, since his idea of what other people were like, as it showed in him, was like nothing I had ever known. If he was rather a caricature, he seemed to make people he encountered into caricatures also.

"How kind of you to come to be with my son," he said. "There is no one to amuse him here. I am shaw you chaps are going to have a bully time togethah. I do hope you'll come agane."

Brightly scratched forth, this remark like his note carried hints of dismissal but now it was clear that he was anticipating my departure with regret and so must hasten to absorb it as an accepted fact.

"Thank you. Perhaps I can."

"But do let's get to wirk," he said, "as the librarian will soon be here with some new catalogues. —Do you care for Lord Byron and his period?"

"I don't know much about it."

"How very good. Then I can tell you the little I know—" and satisfaction leaked through the scratches of his throat, and he took me to the grilled and locked shelves and began what was a set-piece which he always enjoyed giving for visitors, whether scholars or schoolboys.

We began with a complete flight, as he called it, of feest

editions of all the known wirks of Byron. As he told me about them, he took down an occasional volume. Thinking he meant to hand it to me, I reached for it, but he didn't notice, but kept hold of the book, turning a few pages delicately with his long middle finger, and lingering over the paper with the lightest of touches. He was able to point out which volumes had been gathered by his father and which by himself, for it appeared that he had taken the collection much farther toward uniqueness and completeness than the founder of it. He said the delight in collecting was to reconstruct a whole life through the scattered items brought together in such a place as this. From complete first editions we moved on to special editions and then to single volumes of interest. I remember his pleasure in showing me but not handing to me several volumes of Byron which bore Shelley's autograph in the flyleaves. Others had belonged to Leigh Hunt. There was one rather smudged volume signed "Claire" on the title page, and in margins of later pages it bore exclamation points, question marks, dots, and wavy lines alongside various passages which for reasons never to be known had arrested the attention, and possibly the pathetic feelings, of Byron's discharged mistress. As he showed me these Uncle Alec's long dry cheeks glowed faintly with a little color, and he said to me with careful restraint, most becoming to an elder who speaks of risky matters to a youth,

"They were lovers, as you know. She bore his child—a daughter. He treated her badly—" and at this, restraint gave way to withdrawal of his lips in what was surely a smile of relish which could not be suppressed. But a sudden dry, cracking sound from somewhere in the great room made him look up and about with a drawn frown. "What on eeth was that!"

"I don't know—it sounded like a piece of wood breaking."

"It couldn't have been. How disagreeable. —I cannot *stand* unexplained noises," he said irritably, yet with a hint of shame at his distress. He put up a finger to hold silence until we should hear the noise again. It did not come. Presently he aroused himself, snapped poor Claire Claire- mont's book shut and replaced it, and with it, put out of sight and mind the excitement that had begun to show in him at the idea of treating a mistress badly. He unlocked a case of deep sliding trays containing manuscripts. These were poems by Byron; those were by Shelley; here was a sheaf of letters by Trelawney —"uttah cad, yet somehow fascinating"; some essays by Godwin in brown ink on blue paper, tied with yellowed muslin tape; and here—"a most precious piece, for I found it myself, in of all places Brighton, in a peefectly commonplace tourist antique shop, and I had it out of there in five minutes for one pound seven shillings, and dealers have since made me preposterous offers for it, but one of them had overlooked it a week before, for he told me so!" Uncle Alec was wanly alight with the renewed joy of his bargain and the fruits of his own expertness in which no dealer had served him. The item was a letter written by Edward Bulwer-Lytton from Brocket, where as a youthful beau who reminded some people of Lord Byron himself when young, he was staying with Lady Caroline Lamb in her sequestration and dotty misery. You see, explained Uncle Alec, she had had that wild affair with Byron, it ended in hatred and bitterness, and yet she could not uproot him from her heart, and she used to send for young Bulwer- Lytton to come and play the organ for her and she would stare at him remembering Byron. His cheeks began to flush again with a hectic grayish orange stain below the skin. Ah me, he murmured more to himself than to me, returning the letter to its case, if one looked long enough, in the right places, with the right questions, one could find almost all there was to know about any lives of long ago. He touched a first edition of *Glenarvon* by Caroline Lamb saying that it was a positive beehive of the bitterest honey in the account it gave of her affair with Byron.

"Where to stop?" he suddenly asked with a widened smile of proprietary pleasure. "Yes, for example, this d'licious item."

He took down a blue morocco case, opened its elegantly fitted little door, and from an inner folder drew out a thick pile of pages which crackled under his touch.

"Have you the faintest idea what this is?" he asked.

I shook my head.

"For ever so long it was believed lost and destroyed. Byron mentions it to his little friend Miss Pigot in a letter he wrote from Trinity, at Cambridge. I remember the exact words. 'I have written 214 pages of a novel,' he wrote. Every young man writes a novel, I daresay you have done so yourself, Richard? —Ha. I thought so. —Yes. Well. But this is Byron's. We found it through the most killing coincidences which I have promised not to tell. Scholars long to publish it; but again I have promised not to let them. Meantime, think of it: I have read it, quite idiotic and fascinating, you know, ruins by moonlight, mad heiresses, that sort of thing, you know, doomed heroes, though nobody knows why the doom. But how *readable*: his supreme gift. The letters: Max loves the letters, too. He pores over them, copies out bits of them. I recommend them as a book to travel with."

He replaced the manuscript and we went on.

The collection took in Byron, all his friends, all his places, all his available memorabilia—"if you like locks of hair, we have one"—and of course the requirement was to possess only manuscripts, first editions, association editions with clear evidence either attached or inscribed, and objects authenticated by certified credentials. Take the Thorwaldsen bust on the pedestal, there: it was one of two, the other being in the Murray collection. This one was a secret copy. It was a rather vulgar thing, no life in it, but it had to be had, once you knew it was available. Authentic duplicates, if you could call them that, were peefectly legitimate. Here was another —in a narrow glass case on thin table legs, on a blue velvet bed, and lighted from within the glass, was a long saber in its scabbard, wearing a tarnished gold bullion loop and knot on the elaborately chased gold hilt, which Byron had kept at Missolonghi. With other effects it had been brought home to England by Fletcher.

Uncle Alec took a glance at his watch. There was time for only one more item.

"A great treasure of the collection," he said, and moved me to a paneled space between bookshelves where a blue velvet curtain covered the wall. He touched a button, a light came on, he touched another, and the curtains parted to reveal a heavily framed and glassed notebook pencil sketch of a man in profile. His forehead was bald far beyond an expected hairline. His hair was wavy but looked thin against his skull. His face was fleshy about the jowl, which was partially concealed by a black silk neckcloth. The eye was dotted in lightly so that it looked pale. The eyebrow was gallant and firm. Straight and long, the nose was unremarkable above the scrolled lips which held a pout of appetite or doubt. The body, with narrow shoulders, was clothed in a ruffled shirt, waistcoat, and lounging coat. A jeweled stud held the shirt together in front. It was, said my cousin, a drawing of Lord Byron by Count Alfred D'Orsay which had been done at Genoa in 1823. There was another in London which Uncle Alec had seen, but he thought this one, obviously done at the same sitting, much finer. Nobody knew of its existence, permission had never been given to reproduce it, and of all the likenesses of Byron—and they were all here in one form or another—this had always struck Uncle Alec as the one nearest to life, though it had so little real skill.

"Don't you think?"

"But I don't know," I said. "I always thought Lord Byron was handsome."

"So we are told. But everything changes, and of course, he lived recklessly, and did not care how he looked after he left England, and for too long, in any case, he looked like a superb boy. Sometimes I wonder what Maximilian will look like when he is my age?"

Uncle Alec gazed at me soberly through his large circles of clear lens. I think he was looking through my youth at his own before life had drained away his color and sent his passions to sleep. I had a stir of pity for a moment, and then a little chill of dislike, though whether for him or for what life must do to everyone, I did not know. He closed the curtain and shut off the light.

"What," he asked, in the dry manner of a teacher administering the Regents' Examination, "what words of Byron's do you think you will never forget?"

"Oh, I think *There was a sound of revelry by night,*" I replied.

"Yes, most people would I think give that. But the one phrase I think has all of him in it is this one, also from

Childe Harold." He paused, and then in a much reduced voice so that the scratches almost drowned out the words, he said, *"The late remorse of love."*

He gave me a bleak look, somewhat like that of an animal pet in a moment of shamed regret for some pathetic transgression. On that morning that phrase of Byron held no such meaning for me as that which muted Uncle Alec; but now I know that "the late remorse of love" needs a lifetime for its resonance to echo in the heart.

The spill of morning light from the main gallery was cut and shafted by the small alert entrance of the librarian, exactly on time at a quarter before eleven.

His employer greeted him with relief, I was introduced, and Uncle Alec said,

"Do browse when you have a moment, Richard. There are many books of interest which are not kept locked. The lib'ry is usually unoccupied between two and four. Mr Dana will be happy to help you."

Mr Dana cringed agreeably in silence to support this offer of his services.

"Now what did you bring for me?" asked Uncle Alec, and without further ceremony, he and Mr Dana escorted the acquisitive instinct to the librarian's corner at the far end of the room.

᭡ ᭡ ᭡

Air, I said to myself without using the word, and I went to the great front door of Newstead and let myself out. The driveway with its sickle curve of white marble chips looked hot in the hazy morning. I walked down the avenue of hemlocks that attached the hilltop to the valley below. I felt that too much from a dead life had been laid upon me too quickly. I felt cross at Max for not being awake and about, so I could talk to him or play tennis. The hum of summer sounded above the rolling meadows—or else in my inmost ear. I heard another sound—the busy, cupping clops of a horse walking, and around a curve between the hemlocks came Marietta riding a tall and shining mare the color of a violin. When she saw me she broke into a trot and posted up to me, halted, and sat smiling at the ground beyond me. She wore jodhpurs and short boots, a silk blouse, and a starched stock with a gold safety pin thrust through it.

"Did you ever dry out?" she asked.

"I'm as dusty as a mummy," I answered.

"You've been in the library."

"Just now."

"Where shall we go?"

"Do you want to go somewhere?"

"I thought we would."

"But you're riding."

She dismounted and took the bridle over the head to lead her horse.

"There's a gate just there. We'll go in the meadow. I know a little brook. My tall friend here can have a nice graze."

"Max is asleep."

"I know. I telephoned to ask you both to ride with me. They told me he was not to be called and that you were with Alexander."

"Do you call him that?" I asked.

"No. Just to myself. God knows what I'll call him when I'm married. —What do you call him?"

[41]

"He told me to call him Uncle Alec, though really we are cousins."

She made one of her painfully suppressed smiles as if her amusement at everything, or fondness for me, were simply too intense to be allowed out, and said,

"I adore people who tell other people what to call them. It's like making them use a flattering nickname for you which you made up for yourself, because what other people might make up would be awful. —We can stretch out here."

There was a small sky-rippling brook between tall grasses and wild flowers. An immense old oak tree stood a little away but its shadow was so commodious that it took us in. Marietta was pale, her eyes were hooded by shadows beneath the delicate skin. I saw her little wrists and arms. She appeared more fragile in the summer daylight than she had the night before. She suddenly looked at me directly, as she so rarely did.

"I know how you feel," she said.

"You do?"—wondering myself really how I felt.

"Yes," and she told me.

※ ※ ※

So alien, she said. She had grown up here and yet there were days when even she felt unreal with the Chittendens, or, in self-preservation, had to conclude that they were unreal.

"Oh, dear," she said. "Other people must be simple in lots of things. Why can't we be? Can you help me? Or all of us? Or any of us?"

"Lord. I don't know."

But she gazed at me again, as if I were a doctor or a priest; and then at my perplexity she laughed and reached out and took my near hand and turned it palm upward, pushed my cuff back to expose my inner wrist, and began lightly, with the touch of a butterfly, to stroke the skin where my blue veins showed through and my pulse made its tiny vital lump every second.

"Doesn't it feel lovely?" she asked.

"Oh, yes."

"Do mine."

She gave me her wrist and I stroked it in the same way.

"Oh, why can't everything be as easy and lovely as this feels, all the time. You are a darling and I love your being bothered all the time. Nobody I know is bothered by anything, except something that never shows, whatever it is. Do you want to kiss me?"

"Yes."

But if she was engaged to my cousin Max perhaps I shouldn't. Before I could decide, she said, drawing a little away,

"No, you are right. I am just lonely."

"That is a good reason to be kissed."

"I think you are lonely too."

"Sometimes."

"Why?"

"I don't know."

"No, but I know why I am," she said. She picked a few wild flowers that grew between us where we reclined on the damp earth which still smelled of last night's rain. She began to twine the stems together making a small wreath. It became a bracelet which she slipped over her white narrow hand to her wrist.

"But you ought not to be lonely if you are in love with Max."

"Oh, you sweet Richard, that is just why. —What do you think of him?"

"Oh, he is—" and I remembered how I went on to describe him in my letter to my parents, and more. I saw his ample air, his fine looks, his sudden absences even while he was right with you, his unconscious sense of privilege, his ability to laugh at himself, and his preference for disorder over the dead calm order of the domestic life all about him. I had to admit that I was surprised that he slept the morning away.

"Does he always sleep all morning?" I asked.

"He wakes up early and he telephones me and we talk. We talked half an hour about you this morning. Then he often goes back to sleep. But he doesn't really sleep. He reads, or thinks lying down, or simply exists, as he says. He says he has a great desire for privacy."

This seemed striking in a youth, and I recognized something of myself in him, or of my daydreams about myself, and not for the first time since the day before.

"He asked me if I minded being an only child. He said he felt like one, though actually he isn't."

"No. His sister. She lives in Venice. She married an Italian and made a scandal."

"Really? A scandal?"

"Yes. She became a Catholic."

"Oh. Is that a scandal here?"

"Oh, yes."

"I am a Catholic."

"We know that."

"But it doesn't matter, outside, you mean?"

"Something like that. —Don't be troubled. It only matters to Alexander and Alicia. Not to me or Max. —What do you think matters to Max?"

"Let me see. I think what matters to him," I said carefully, feeling worldly and penetrating, as I rarely did, "is to have everybody think he is the most fortunate and happy man in the world, and most people do, but sometimes he forgets how to have them think so, and then something else matters, but I don't know what."

She leaned and swiftly and lightly kissed my cheek and then sat away and looked down the long meadow toward the pretty barriers of the paddock and said,

"When he is sure of anyone, he doesn't try any further. It doesn't mean he doesn't want them, just the same. Do you know what first made us stop thinking of each other as children—playmates?"

"No?"

"It was the day I saw him suffer for the first time. I think perhaps my heart—probably anyone's—is made of something like a wishbone in a bird. Because that day when I saw him I felt something go crack right here exactly like a wishbone when we pulled it in the nursery"—her hand at her breast—"and it was for him."

"What happened to make something break like that?"

When Maximilian was seventeen, four years ago: my own age in the summer in the meadow with Marietta—he was stricken with a responsibility of the heart which was like a watershed in the inner landscape of his life. In fact, it was so great that his father Alexander could not meet it. Someone of the family had to do it and Max was the only one they thought of.

His mother was then, everyone said, still wonderfully beautiful. Max was very close to her. He was supposed to look like her. Nobody ever saw any trace of his father in him. Everyone decided this with hidden relief, for Alexander Chittenden, aside from his fortune, for years had had little about him which interested other people, and it seemed to them that he was quite satisfied that this be so. The one person he cared for—his daughter—had gone away long ago. He settled a great dowry upon her, forgave her formally for her desertion, and for her marrying an Italian of title, and for her conversion. With the boyhood of his other child he had little connection thereafter. His wife was absorbed in Maximilian's life, though she kept their love for each other in place with a playful etiquette of miniature formalities. Amidst the magnificence and profusion into which she had married, quite unlike the terms of her own early life, she held herself like a reigning consort. Her enthusiasms were real though controlled, and she worked devotedly for every good cause in the countryside and the large cities beyond. She loved flowers, and had developed a charming talent for painting them in still life. All year she worked at her pictures and by Christmas her gift problem was plentifully solved; for, as everyone knew, she could buy anything at all to give away, and therefore a purchased gift seemed meaningless, so the best possible evidence of her fondness was to give something she herself had spent loving hours upon. In the evenings, friends would see with pleasure and amusement that a faint stain of pigment in the fingers of her right hand might remain after the morning's work in her studio, and they would ask what she was working on, and she would answer, "Oh, one of my eighteenth-century floral excesses, I am quite out of fashion, you know."

She tried to get Max to draw, but he had no talent. He did better at writing, and his letters from school and college were careless, irregular in their sequence, and often wickedly outspoken; but they had him there right on the page, and she read and reread and kept them all.

"We all did. I did," said Marietta. "His very voice is on the paper. He was the most high-spirited—nobody could really describe what he was like. His mother and I used to trade his letters and then meet to talk about them. She adored him more than he ever knew. —Oh, the *thingness* of everything!"

"Everything?"

"You'll see. —Now he looks at everyone as if he would find in their faces something he has to know."

Then in his last year at school, as I was now, he was suddenly summoned home. Marietta was staying at home that year working with a tutor. Her father, the physician, was in charge at Newstead, and it was he who had asked for Max to return. Having called in surgeons in consultation, he had grave news for Max about both his mother and his father. Marietta remembered all of it, in detail.

Mrs Chittenden had felt a throbbing inflammation in a

finger of her right hand, but not believing in self-indulgence she ignored it for several days. Only when holding a brush became awkward and painful did she ring up her neighbor Doctor Osborne to ask him what to do for an infection surrounding a fingernail. (There was a name for it which Marietta could not remember.) The doctor declared that he should see it. He recognized what it was, said it must be lanced, drained, and watched rather closely to be sure it did not persist, as those things often did. He looked further to discover whether the inflammation might have spread through the blood vessels of the hand and forearm.

Marietta took my arm again, but not this time for tender play, but to show what she knew of the doctor's next discovery.

"There," she said, pressing a spot above my wrist on the inner surface of my arm. "There was a strange sort of lump or swelling in her arm. He asked her how long she had had it, and she said that she had noticed it, but had thought nothing of it. She asked if it had anything to do with the finger."

Doctor Osborne thought not. Had she bruised her arm in any way? She could not remember. He treated the finger, bandaged it, and asked her if she would go into Philadelphia the next day to see a certain surgeon, and if advised to do so, whether she would consent to have x-rays taken of the arm swelling.

Mrs Chittenden asked him what he was thinking of, and he told her. It was by no means a certainty, but under any such possibility as this swelling suggested, it was sensible to take every precaution without delay. She had a certain look, said Marietta, which she used when there was any occasion for understanding beyond words. Doctor Osborne received that look now. They were old friends. He nodded.

Some days later he had the report from Philadelphia. The x-rays revealed nothing definitive. However, Doctor de Kranowitz, the Philadelphia surgeon, recognized certain suggestive symptoms, and advised an immediate surgical exploration. Doctor Osborne examined Mrs Chittenden again, and found changes in the arm. He talked the case over with Doctor de Kranowitz by telephone. They agreed that no time should be lost, even though the tumor should prove to be benign, for the risk of the opposite condition was equally present, and in that event they came to conclusions about what would have to be done.

Alexander Chittenden was in Washington, where he served on a committee on war supplies convened by Secretary Newton D. Baker. Doctor Osborne spoke to him on the telephone, advising him to return home at once, before the committee adjourned, and when he reached home, described to him the strange, and possibly grave, condition which had been discovered in his wife.

"Alexander asked what it meant," said Marietta, "and my father had to tell him."

"Tell what."

"Tell that if it was the worst, they would have to amputate. They wouldn't know until they actually began the operation."

On hearing this, Alexander Chittenden nearly fainted. He was obliged to sit down and lean over, with Doctor Osborne's large, competent hand on the back of his neck.

"What did they do?" I asked.

"They sent for Max."

Max came home within twelve hours. His mother had already been taken to the hospital in Philadelphia. Her husband was of no help to her. Doctor Osborne saw him collapse into the state of querulous terror and inaction which accompanied what was then called "nervous prostration." As head of the family, he had had to be given the technical facts about his wife's forbidding illness. If formal sanction had to be given for the surgeons to proceed in the event of amputation this would be asked of the patient, still, it was of the utmost importance for her psychological state and proper strength of will that she have the loving support of someone close to her. She would have to face a dreadful ordeal, if the worst should come true. Her husband, managing fortunes every year in his office, or giving his dry intelligence and rather low vitality to the wartime disposal of huge resources governing millions of statistical human destinies, met tasks which were within his capacity, for they remained abstractions; it was for such things, said Marietta, that he lived. The possible necessity of maiming a living individual who belonged to him, even though for years only nominally, was an act too concrete for him to face. Doctor Osborne ordered him to bed rest, sent for nurses, and waited for Max.

When Max heard the story he asked, Why hadn't they gone ahead? The doctor replied that in cases of this kind, they would not know how far they must go until they had taken tissue and examined it actually during the operation; and if it should prove to be necessary, then the surgeons would feel easier if they had authorization. Max wanted to know who gave the authorization. Usually, said Doctor Osborne, if the patient was in sound mind, it was the patient. In case the patient was under anesthesia, then he or she would have given someone close by—not a minor—the authority to act. And my mother? asked Max. Does she know? Yes, she knew, and she suggested that her husband be at hand to make the decision if it should be necessary. Well, would he? asked Max. Doctor Osborne hoped so.

Well: what was to be done?

Well: they would try to help Alexander to pull himself together and go to the hospital this afternoon, but it seemed clear that Max must be there to help him to speak for the family if he had to. If the first stage of the operation supported the worst suspicions, the doctors would expect approval in going ahead.

And if this were not given?

Doctor Osborne explained the eventually mortal alternative. He put his hand on Maximilian's shoulder and braced him with affectionate strength. He had delivered Max at birth, and had always been close to him without seeming to be. The touch of sympathy released Max's youthful rage at shocking circumstance. He burst angrily into tears and pounded Doctor Osborne's chest with his forehead. Something terrible might be asked of him. Between his gulping sobs, he muttered bitterly about his father, saying things he had said at various times to Marietta. "My father: he should: he has never: for years he has acted as if he had no blood in his veins: none of us have been quite human in his eyes."

No, no, murmured the doctor, trying to disagree with Maximilian, but without conviction. It was Alicia whom everybody loved, Max most of all, and the doctor told Marietta later that he could quite feel the warmth of Max's love for his mother as they drove through the country and into Philadelphia to the hospital. In the end, Alexander Chittenden was unable to face the endurance awaiting them all at the hospital—Max went alone with Doctor Osborne.

How did it all happen? Max wanted to know.

[51]

The doctor said they could not be sure. The more serious difficulty was discovered quite by accident.

Max wanted to know what could have caused that.

"Your mother doesn't remember, but a bruise, a contusion which took its effect quite some time later, may have begun the tumor. We all bump ourselves now and then and do not pay much attention to the hurt, which is usually temporary. Now and then, quite rarely, actually, one of these things develops into something more serious."

Max scowled. A small nudge of memory was working to remind him of something. His face went cold and he glanced sidewise at the doctor, who was driving. A bruise? he said. Yes, some blow on the tender, inner forearm.

Would it matter how long ago this may have happened?

Oh, surely, replied Doctor Osborne. Anything dating from a year or so ago would by now have meant nothing, if symptoms had not appeared earlier. A few months—two to four—would probably show the effect if any were to develop.

"I see," said Max.

"Why?" asked the doctor. Max looked flushed now and at the same time haggard.

"I just remembered."

The doctor nodded and Max told him about something which had happened at the start of the Thanksgiving vacation thirteen weeks ago. Somehow it was easier to tell about it sitting beside the doctor than if they had been facing each other in a room.

One evening there was a rustic party at Newstead, with costumes and country dances, for Max and all his young friends who were home from school for the holiday. Parents attended, loyally dressed up as rubes and hoboes, dairymaids and pioneer women. There was straw on the floor of

[52]

the big dairy barn down in the meadow. The family servants were also present. Once a year Alexander Chittenden made it a point to dance with the cook. The climax of the evening was a square dance. Max went as a scarecrow, holding a rusty, broken rake in his torn cotton gloves which had straw sticking out of the finger holes. He kept his rake in the dance and used it grandly to thump the floor in accent with the hired music, which came from a fiddle, an earthenware jug, a bowed saw, a tub (bottom end up), and a set of dented sleighbells on a length of harness strap. The party was animated, for a great vat of hard cider was open to those who felt thirst. In one of the dance figures, the men and women wove in and out of each other's ranks in braided lines. When dancers came to the end of their row, they whirled sharply and dropped hands and with their other hands reached for new partners. It was a pretty gesture which men made with waggery, ladies with comically exaggerated grace. Max dropped the hand of Frazier's wife, whirled energetically holding his rake handle gallantly out, and reached for his new partner. In the same second he saw that it was his mother and that as she reached for him with her right arm her gesture collided with the oaken staff he brandished so recklessly. She exclaimed. He threw away his rake and took her arm to see if he had hurt her. She pressed her lips with pain but shook her head, and then recovering herself, she seized his hand and danced him along after the couple ahead while he stammered his apologies. He suddenly stopped feeling like a joyous scarecrow. She felt the change and shook him gaily, reminding him by her tugging at him that they must always set the spirit of any event of which they were part. Their guests must now not be allowed to notice any mishap or its brief consequences. The fiddle squeaked, the jug pooped, the saw sang, the tub thumped, the sleigh-bells wrangled, and the dance went on. Max never picked up his rake again. He could feel too well the jar and ache of the blow he had given his mother.

He looked aside at Doctor Osborne with inquiry.

"Possibly," mused the doctor. "It is always mysterious."

"Oh, no," said Max, covering his eyes with his hand.

"You mustn't think about it," said the doctor. "There may have been any number of other abrasions—"

There was a silence, and then Max asked,

Will I see her?

Yes, for her sake certainly. For his, too.

Yes, surely, yes—Max looked wild, experiencing in imagi-nation what lay behind and what might lie ahead.

"How do you mean?" I asked.

Marietta crumpled herself together with the effect of shak-ing off sense and silently asking how it was that you came to know truths which lay beyond words. Then she said,

"He didn't know enough about it to be scientific about it, like my father. But he knew enough about the ghastly idea of it to feel it in his very own bone and flesh. —He always feels everything, all over, on himself, everything he hears about what happens to anyone else. When that thing was coming toward them all, about his mother, he wished it could happen to him instead. But it couldn't. But still there was a ray of hope, and that's what he had to keep thinking in front of all the other feelings—especially the one about the rake at the square dance. But."

Marietta pressed a desperate breath out of her little chest as she remembered more of what she had been told.

At the hospital they went up in an elevator and down a long echoing corridor. Max went alone to his mother. The nurses said she was drowsy but awake. Doctor Osborne waited outside. Max returned to him after ten minutes. He was still wearing the schoolboy smile with which he had greeted his mother, but his face was white as milk, and for a moment he did not want to speak.

Presently he told Doctor Osborne that he had embraced his mother, wanting her to exult in the surprise of his return from school for a few days. She murmured a word of concern that he should miss classes, and he said it did not matter, as his marks were so good he could afford it. He intended to stay around to keep her amused until she was better. She asked where his father was, and he lied enthusiastically, not protecting his father as he was but his wish for the father as he wanted him to be, saying that he was at home, unable to leave, because of long-distance calls from Washington on war business.

Max said she touched his face with her free hand and looked calmly and deeply into his eyes. Did she remember what he had just now revived so vividly during the ride from Newstead to the hospital? He could not imagine asking her. He realized that she knew everything, but he thought she wasn't sure whether he knew everything as well; and to spare him, in case he did not know, she smiled and nodded, he said, and when he saw her do her best to spare him, he had to leave. He bent over and kissed her and came out feeling angry and alone in his guilt. The surgical orderlies passed him on their way to bring his mother to the operating room.

"Do you know?" he said to Marietta afterward, and she never forgot it, "the worst of it was, was the way I felt about it all. I said to myself, *It is all disgusting*. Disgusting: that I thought this really frightened me. I went there feeling sick with love and sorrow at what they might have to do to her;

but when the time came I said it was simply *disgusting*. What happened to me?"

But Marietta said to him not to think that way—he was just so full of worry and horror that all his ideas and feelings were upside down. Sometimes things happened that were too much to bear, and when they did, why, you just made them into something else, in order to bear them.

He didn't know. He could hardly feel. When he thought of his father, his heart turned to ice. He did not dare to think of his mother and when they wheeled her past him to the double doors leading into the operating area he looked away.

There were a few metal armchairs in the bay of the hallway opposite the operating-room entrance. Max went to lean upon a window looking up a featureless avenue gray in the winter afternoon.

He closed his eyes to the impersonal life of the street below and away. He stood because he could not sit quietly, waiting for the surgeon's report. He nodded his head, saying in the consuming silence, Yes, yes, please, hurry, hurry.

֍ ֍ ֍

"I used to spend hours with her before," said Marietta. She compressed her lips and shook her head against her feeling. She stroked her hair back from her brow and resettled the black ribbon which held it away so that it fell in a dark golden shower to her shoulders. "Alicia was the most of everything I wished I could be," she added.

"How?"

She had to give me a downward smile at my famous word, but she did it fondly, and said,

"Her loveliness, and, what: yes: her *capability*."

We both laughed at the flat moderation of the word, but as Marietta said it, it held more than reckless praise could have. She meant that Aunt Lissy was so clever with her hands—her paintings were really charming, unpretentious, but very skillful, and with an exquisite sense of the damp, fugitive life of flowers. She sewed beautifully, too, and played the piano always at half-voice but with style. She was sensitive to everything that went on in the whole of Chittenden Hills, and without being a busybody, she seemed often to come at just the right moment to be of help to anyone in difficulty. She gave her time and her mind when these could be the best of gifts; and as for the other kind of gift, she was openhanded and unshrewd to the point of provoking the dry protest of her husband who felt that vast wealth imposed an obligation to account for every penny, a business over which she never lingered. She knew that her philanthropies of wealth were at times as useful as those of her spirit, and just as she never measured these, so she never kept a ledger of the others. It was the same when she gave parties. She was like a queen who indicated general wishes, and then with a happy air of surprise and fulfillment enjoyed them when they came true through the imaginative skill of those who served her. The great corridors, rooms, terraces, and vistas of Newstead used to know a magnificence which made even Uncle Alec proud, for the delight of his guests belonged safely to him, as well as to his wife. Her joy was full when her son was old enough to dine with guests, and she saw him through the golden lights and the thronged flowers of her rooms with amusement as dear as her love. He was infinitely charming, he kept up an imposture of diffidence which excused his splendor of face and being, and his mother knew how much of his delightful effectiveness to take credit for, and how much was actually unaccountable. Even then, she had always granted him in her thoughts the freedom to be like nobody but himself, for whom he alone must be responsible. It was a pity he could not draw, but he had every other grace, and she smiled when she thought how his father expected him to become another in the long ancestral chain of Chittendens who actively dealt with the family financial interests first as employees and of course finally in control. Maximilian, she laughingly predicted, would never sit in a paneled office either as a clerk or as an officer. She had no idea what he wanted to do, for neither had he. In the hours when they read aloud to each other, they would pause to talk about his future. His vision of this changed with every year as he grew older, and she followed him asking only that in whatever he did he must think of others as well as himself. With idealism, he promised. Because she was so faithful to him when he needed her in his childhood illnesses, or his disappointments, or his rushes of love for a populous succession of friends, boys and girls, he made his claims on her with confidence. She would never fail him, nor he her, just as neither would ever hurt the other knowingly. He used to laugh at her incessant activity. She kept a secretary busy all day over her appointments and the notes which must precede and follow them. She remained his ideal of the uses of living. She had given him breath, and on his later birthdays he used to write her notes to put under her sitting-room door in which he would thank her for the gift of life. She showed these to Marietta, who was like a daughter to her, and they would say they had never heard of any other son who used his birthday just so. When he did wrong, she did not spare him, but flashed out at him with her wit until he felt ashamed of himself. His childish cruelties were like other children's, but, said Marietta, somehow even at his most wicked he seemed angelic, and his mother had admitted to her that many a time when she was whipping him verbally she could hardly keep from bursting into laughter, and always did so as soon as he had been removed to the nursery to cultivate remorse.

"They were really so like each other, you know, Richard," said Marietta, "without exactly looking alike. It was mostly the way they instantly understood each other about everything. They were quicker than cats at leaping at the same idea. A thousand times I have seen them look at each other when somebody said something, and then start to answer it in exactly the same way, in words, or by laughing out, or, you know, anything. One time he was terribly mean to me and when he came to apologize I refused to answer him. I would *never* forgive him. I was frozen, like a princess whose disfavor means death. He said, 'Oh, look, dear child, save your acting for something worth getting.' It was Alicia's kind of remark, and he even had her amused tone of voice which always put an end to anything pretentious. For a second I was more of a princess than ever, and then the strain was simply too awful and I crumpled, and fell to my knees, and put my hands over my face and laughed. 'That's better,' he said, and simply went home with this work done, with the air of someone with more work to do elsewhere— just like her. As for the apology, it somehow got lost."

I was still young enough to feel much of this within the reference of my own mother and my closeness to her—

though the dimensions were grander here, and we didn't have as much reference to style about our manner of communicating at home. Still, the chaffing love shown by my father, and the sighing gaiety with which my mother gave animation to her duties and concerns, gave me much with which to think of Max and the life he knew and the ordeal which he had come home to.

"He must have thought about all such things," I said, "while he was waiting at the hospital."

Marietta nodded sharply. A glare of lighted coals deep in her eyes made her face look whiter than ever. She had the kind of beauty which proclaims the bone beneath the skin, and raises the image of the skull into mortal loveliness, bringing a pang even while it asks for desire.

❦ ❦ ❦

He must have been waiting for about forty minutes, now standing with his forehead against the cold windowpane—this all took place in ebb-winter—and again tiptoeing to the door to listen, though there was nothing to hear, for two sets of double swinging doors separated him from the operating room. He thought he could hear a remote sound of escaping steam, and there were various antiseptic aromas afloat in the heated air. Now and then an electric bell would make an insistent chiming somewhere far away, and he was reminded of school corridors, where other moments of dread had given him—for reasons long forgotten—a thick, heavy fall of something hollow just where he supposed his stomach would be. Now the fall had turned into something lasting and he wondered if it would ever go away. Suddenly the sound of hissing steam grew briefly louder, and he saw that both sets of double doors had opened and closed allowing the head surgeon to come toward him. The man was all but invisible within his antiseptic wrappings—rumpled, flax-colored muslins, rubber gloves, a mask across his face exposing only deep-lensed, rimless eyeglasses. The doctor's voice was slightly muffled but his remarks were audible. Behind him stood Doctor Osborne, also in operating gown and mask, but subordinate as an observer and family practitioner.

"Max," he said, "this is Doctor de Kranowitz."

"Yes," said the surgeon. "We have the result of the test. It is necessary now to go further. Your mother gave us permission a little while ago, depending on what we found."

It was not really a long hesitation which followed, but long enough for Max to feel as though the weight of the earth were pulling him down. Ever afterward he must behave as though he had no connection with this event. Something enabled him to do so now.

"Do you have to do very much?" he asked.

Doctor de Kranowitz indicated with a finger on his own forearm about where he would make the section.

"We perhaps should take more," he said. "But it is a fairly safe risk to stop here, for we have found this in an early stage."

"Take the risk," said Max impassively. "Save what you can."

"Yes."

"How long will it take?"

"Perhaps two hours."

"Shall I stay? —Yes."

The surgeon nodded and returned at once to the double doors, the escaping steam of the sterilizers, and the task awaiting him. Doctor Osborne said,

"Max."

"Yes?"

"Max," and turned and followed his colleague.

Long later I thought of how it was the living necessity of wounds to heal themselves. When they did, scar tissue was always stronger than the tissue that had been cut or torn. On that day waiting in the hospital Max may have started to heal his inner wound by sealing it off. Perhaps he said to himself out of final necessity that he had not done anything—it was the scarecrow who had done it, and the scarecrow's rake had been thrown down and punished. Otherwise he could not have borne the truth. Let it be forgotten, or if that was not possible, let it be thrust behind legend. He did not consider, just then, the daily reminder in the evidence which his mother could not help exhibiting, however loving her sufferance, and modesty. Did she remember the square dance and the riotous blow? If so, there was never any sign of it. Love knew how to forget as well as remember.

❦ ❦ ❦

"You know?" said Marietta, "lifetimes can happen in two hours. I saw him later that day. It was the day he began to hate. He decided without really knowing it that nobody could ever love him again."

[62]

"But hate?"

"Yes. Hate. I told him long afterwards that this was true, and he said it was nonsense. So I never argued. But I saw everything, though we never discussed it, but simply kept on laughing expensively at things to show how really simple and unpretentious we really were."

"I never know just what you mean."

"I know. They all say I talk at right angles."

She gave me a direct, self-deriding smile, and I wished I were one year older than she, instead of two years younger.

"You know what?"

I inquired with a lift of my head, while my eyes pulled at her lips. She said,

"Oh! If we only knew what things keep punishing people inside their heads!" She paused. I waited. She remembered more.

Doctor Osborne brought Max away from the hospital. Presently he said to him in an offhand way,

"Everything was done successfully. De Kranowitz is one of the best. —One thing you must remember, Max," he went on, coming to the heart of his purpose, "is this: there is no certainty of any direct connection between this operation and the incident you told me of, the thing at the barn dance."

He told Marietta later that by the way Max looked at him it was all the boy had been thinking about. "Get it out of your head," added Doctor Osborne roughly, as if scorn would erase another's dangerous thoughts.

Max nodded. They drove up to the Osbornes' house, where Max was to be sheltered that night.

The doctor found his daughter alone for a moment. In a storm of sympathy for Alicia, for her father, for Max, she hugged her father feeling like a child, and rubbed her petal-smooth cheek against his tired, grainy jaw. Hurriedly he told her of the day, and asked if she remembered the Thanksgiving barn dance at Newstead. Yes, she did. Had she seen anything odd that may have happened? She couldn't remember. He told her Max's story about the rake, then said,

"He must not keep thinking about it now. You must help him to forget it if you can. But don't ever, ever mention it to him, because if you do he will think everybody else is thinking about it all the time. Promise, Mari!" She promised. "But if he brings it up himself," said her father, "make him drop the idea."

Oh, she said, nothing she could ever do would make Max do anything. But she would try.

The doctor kissed her troubled forehead and heavily went to ready himself for what must be a bleak dinner.

"And did Max ever mention it?" I asked.

"No," said Marietta.

"Did you?"

"No. —But I almost did several times. —I don't know. He has a secret chamber inside where no one can go. Nobody knows what's in it. I think he doesn't know. If anyone could find it, how happy it might be for us all!"

"Us all?"

"All of us who love him. —Because we do love him, you know."

I remember saying, like a sage, "But I do know. *Somebody* always loves *somebody*."

My manner could have made her shriek with laughter and point at me, but my meaning made her nod with solemnity.

If Aunt Lissy remembered anything about the barn dance, nobody ever knew it, least of all Max; for if he had known that she did, nothing could have kept him from talking with Marietta about it, of this she was sure.

"But didn't your father think the rake thing was really the cause?" I asked.

Marietta put her hands to her mouth as if to pray silence. In the dappled shade from the great oak tree by the creek, she shook her head, saying silently, like the child who is fearful of breaking a spell, *Never ask that!*

The memory of that evening after the operation was again strongly alive for her. She seemed to want me to know all she could tell me, however painful for her to revive it.

"When they came to tell him it was over, do you know what he thought of? He told me that night, back at home, I mean at my house, where my father brought him."

They tried to make a meal at dinner, but managed poorly at it. Later, the Osborne parents left Marietta and Maximilian alone. They huddled in the dark in front of a library wood fire. They let the fire go out. Max said little at first, and that was spaced out until the ashes were cold. They lay locked in each other's arms on the hearth rug, passionless, united, hungry, and somber in thought. Pressing no claims on each other, they implicitly gave each other the ultimate claim, and thereafter took it for granted that they were given to each other, and one day would prove it in the flesh. She thought he slept at moments, but just when his breathing seemed to go easy and mindless, he would say something, and she shivered at holding in her arms the nursery king whom she had tried to burn to death, the cruel playmate who owed her a thousand apologies and had never given one, and she heard him as clearly as though he had not said a word. She read in her mind a coherent recital which she made of his private allusions and long silent gaps between them, rather as though she were deciphering a poem of the post World War I style.

There was, at the end of the work in the surgery, a quick current of activity—doors swinging, persons departing for other rooms, others entering to clean the premises, orderlies taking orders, nurses processing alongside doctors, and rubber-tired wheels bearing away an inert figure classically folded in sweeps of white cloth. Max waited but no one came for him for a long time. He had no idea of where to go. He looked out the cold window. Evening and snow were falling together. Electric vistas in the hushed streets were now indescribably lovely. He saw them even as he thought of something else.

One time when he was a small child, running and playing out of doors, one of his shoelaces came untied. He trod on it and fell and bumped his head on the edge of the flagstone terrace on the south side of Newstead. His mother was sitting in a pool of light and shade under a great maple tree. She was working at needlepoint. She put down her frame and went rapidly but without excitement to him, took him up, kissed the hot lump that was rising on his wide, clear forehead to make it well, and hushed him with her concern, though surely he would have liked her to show a little more indignation at his unjust fate. She took him to her tree and murmuring coolly to him, held him on her lap and took up his small inert foot and addressed a droll scolding to the wicked shoelace which had brought on the mishap. She then tied the lace in good, tight loops, and he remembered his staring fascination at how she did it—the flashing cleverness of her hands, the shuttling skill of her lovely, capable fingers at their little task. Who else ever tied a shoelace with that swift neatness, and made such pleasant sounds so close to the ear that he could feel cool lips on his hot, outraged cheeks? Thick-handed nursemaids until then. How quickly all was mended now.

If memory would only mend as firmly at it revived. Doctor Osborne finally came to take him home. There was nothing more to do here. Maximilian had done all he was supposed to do; and it was more than he knew how to do. He could not remember whether his mother had ever finished that piece of needlepoint that day under the tree by the terrace.

In the meadow, in the long grass dappled by the old oak, alongside the pale little brook, I presently said,

"I wonder when I will see Max's mother."

"Today. We are all lunching together," said Marietta, "at Newstead."

"Are you coming too?"

"Yes."

"I am glad."

"I may help."

"Help?"

"Oh—to dilute it all by one more part."

"Everything is so still in the huge house," I said.

"The house has never recovered."

I heard how Alicia, my Cousin Lissy, my Aunt Lissy, slowly won her way back to a sense of life. It took years. The general commiseration was hardest to bear of all her trials, and she wondered when she might ever confront people at large again. She thought of going abroad, which the doctors approved; but one day she told Doctor Osborne that if she went, she might never return, for her victory would have to be won here, at home, in the most painfully familiar surroundings, or it might never be won at all. Merriman Osborne, after a moment's reflection, agreed with her. She was determined to stare down her difficulties every day without the aid of fleeting distractions. If she ran away from them, and later returned, perhaps in high spirits, and met them again, her whole life might collapse as her husband's had done. His illness was one of her great trials. The other was a stony change in her son's feeling for her—in his very behavior as he struggled to leave adolescence and enter early manhood. Neither of these burdens ever entered into her conversation with even intimate friends. But they saw how the weight of both held back her own recovery, and cost her the serene beauty of her own countenance. They had always said that she never seemed aware of her beauty—until it was gone. Not that she spoke of it; but a veil of delicate shame seemed to hang before her face. When people told her, now, how lovely she was, she knew they were saying it to conceal the opposite from her—as if they could. I would soon see for myself how all this was.

As for Uncle Alec, his nervous prostration kept him upstairs for a year. Having failed, at love and duty, he collapsed; and then, having to admit his failure, the knowledge of it extended his state of shock. He was another year in getting back to his office for an hour or two each day. Everyone said that it was Lord Byron who saved him. Doctor Osborne dated the beginning of his slow recovery, which would never actually be complete, from the time when Uncle Alec thought of his father's genteel hobby and decided to make it the best private collection in the world on the subject. He resigned as chairman of the Chittenden board, reverting to the position of a simple member, who now voted, where previously he had disposed. His active life had been built upon a talent for abstractions—the upper configurations of finance. Now he gave himself to another —the itemization of a life once prodigal in its hot lusts, but now merely subject to record.

Between these two maimed parents, my Cousin Max grew from schoolboy into college man with an air of solicitous affability which served for the most part to conceal another impulse entirely—a desire to find feeling in himself by whatever means.

❦ ❦ ❦

"Come on," said Max at two minutes before one o'clock, leaning into my room. "We must be punctual. I hate it, but in the end it is simpler."

I was ready. We went along the second-floor corridor to the great central court where the stairway divided above the high door to the drawing room. As we came to the stairs, a door opened beyond, and in a blur of reflected light, Maximilian's mother came into the hall. We halted as she approached.

"Mummy, this is Richard," said Max. He pointed a finger at me as if I were a comic specimen whom he had never seen before. He was suddenly constrained.

"My dear Richard": said Mrs Chittenden. She held her left hand to me. She wore pale gray silk gloves on both hands. Habitually, she supported the right with the left, for it seemed heavy and immovable, a carved, useless representation of a hand with fingers delicately, and permanently, arched.

[69]

"My dear cousin's boy. How like her you are." I had always thought I resembled my father. She turned to Max. "Shall we go down?" He nodded, expecting his duty. He came to her left side. She took his arm and slowly we descended the marble stairs which were made comfortable by a lane of dark crimson velvet. I followed by a step or two. Waiting below were Uncle Alec and Marietta.

"Good morning, Lissy, my dear," said Uncle Alec with his laryngeal scratch. He smiled at her sideways. She nodded pleasantly at him, and spoke to Marietta, who replied,

"Aunt Lissy, may I come this way?"—indicating her riding clothes. A kind smile was her answer and we proceeded through the great drawing room to the rotunda of marble columns and glass, with trellises of greens, where luncheon was set at a small round glass table. Max ceremonially seated his mother. Uncle Alec took a chair facing her. I was at her right, between them. Max and Marietta were opposite me. From behind a tall screen of many folds painted to show an Italian landscape, two serving maids in black with white caps, aprons and gloves, immediately began to serve lunch. As Aunt Lissy turned to take a morsel I was able to gaze at her forgetful of being watched.

※ ※ ※

She was like a season's end, with a premonition of further change to come, and in her, beauty was the season. She was my mother's age, I knew, and yet I could not keep her there, for she seemed a generation older. I thought she looked like a ghost that yet waited to go. She gave an effect of silver pointed up with touches of black. Her eyes were black, surrounded by lashes so thick and black they made me think—without prejudice—of spiders' legs. Her brows were also dark, and when she chose, she could make her eyes sparkle, or seem to, by deliberately contracting all the blacks and smiling, so that light was trapped for an instant before it was reflected in a flash. Not quite a double blink, it must have been a facial gesture developed for the reassurance of others during her long convalescence, when it would have been a great effort to say much or move bodily. Her face was narrow and surprisingly smooth, but age, too soon, pressed its contours downward. She was always heavily powdered and wore no other cosmetic. In her upper lip a few small wrinkles converged toward the center like those of rueful monkeys I had seen in the zoo, and the faintest fur was made visible there by the powder that lodged in it and in the convergent lines. Her lips were unrouged. Their outline was blurred, as though eroded by years of compression toward a center of denied expression of violent or anguished feeling. She wore much the same costume every daytime that I saw her—a plain dress of fine gray or pale blue or champagne-colored silk, with high collar, full sleeves, and skirts so long that they caught in carpets. When she moved it was with composed grace, and when she spoke her voice was cool, clear, and faint, as if distantly overheard. Always she held her fixed, artificial right hand and forearm with her live left hand, both always gloved alike. Her hair was silvery, done in dove wings that swept past her ears, showing them and the earrings of small, single, gray pearls which she always wore. A fine veil of black threads held her hair in place and came down over her brow and eyes and added a degree of shadowed charm to her glance. When she made her eyes sparkle, the veil was like delicate foliage behind which lights moved briefly.

"Tell her," my mother had said, "that I always try to imitate her expression when I want someone to give me something. Tell her I never do it properly. There was nobody else at school whom we all tried to be like. Ask her if she remembers the picnic at Lilydale, and how dreadfully I behaved. Tell her she must forgive me even now. Tell her."

But Aunt Lissy was one of those who outlive their shared moments of the past, which the others of the time never forget, but tug at her in their memories, as if she might save for them what was already gone.

❈ ❈ ❈

The laws of occasion ruled at Newstead when people gathered. True to breeding and class, my cousins—except for Maximilian—enacted the proper imposture of mutual interest and response. When one spoke, another half-smiling, as if in marveling regard across the table, gave visible and, at suitable moments, audible support. Uncle Alec made the first play. Turning his pale head aside, and lifting his pinched profile with its curving nose so that he seemed to take energy from the air through his long, thin nostrils, he said with muted waggery,

"Lissy, I think we have another recruit for the growing aamy of Lord Byron's loyal followers. Our visiting cousin positively devoured me all morning in the libr'y. —D'you know my word for it, Richard?"

[72]

Aunt Lissy forced her furry twinkle at me to share her husband's wit with me in advance, and when it came, she gave her eyes to him to tell everyone how clever he was.

"I mean," he continued, "what my father called a *hobby,* I always call *h-obsession.*"

As Max's spirits visibly fell at this statement, Marietta loyally showed animation. She put her hands on Uncle Alec's near arm and let him feel her inner temblor for a moment. "Oh, Alexander Chittenden—" she said, and stopped, as if choked with admiration. I laughed dutifully. He bowed slightly.

"How delicious, Alec," said his wife, as if she had not heard his pun a hundred times. I knew later that they never exchanged a word except in company.

"People have probably told you you ought to send that in," said Marietta. "I adore it when they say things like that. Send it in *where?* Where is *in?*"

"Oh: oh: the *Sat'day Evening Post,* of course," said Uncle Alec. "Wherever else?"

"We are all loyal Philadelphians," murmured Max.

"Ceetainly, my dear," said his father, making affirmative the disagreeable cast of Max's remark. Max was not to be sold out so cheaply.

"Will that take care of Lord Byron for the moment?" he asked, with a spectacular smile of false innocence which made Marietta see him with a starved look.

"No, I have a question," said his mother, to protect her husband from his son's unkindness.

"Oh, bully," cried Uncle Alec.

"What did you find in Mr Dana's catalogues this morning?"

"You knew? That he brought some? How on eeth?"

[73]

Mr Dana always brought some, so the question was a safe one, but Aunt Lissy chose to give a mysterious little shrug as if to say she had her ways of knowing.

"Well, actually," continued Uncle Alec, "there *is* an item sure to turn up at Sotheby's if we don't get there feest. A quite wonderful one. A copy of Lady Blessington with marginalia in Moore's handwriting."

"Oh, Alec. Surely you have already—"

"We cabled before lunch."

"Oh, how splendid."

And now, with Byron carried far enough to obliterate Max's rudeness, Aunt Lissy was ready to drop him in her turn. She turned to me and found me staring at her false hand as it rested on her closed left hand. I looked away before I could look at her face, and when I did, I found her eyes waiting for mine in the kindest forgiveness. She blinked them both, as if to say that many people of greater experience than mine had been unable to ignore the fascination of her visible disadvantage, and that she had long grown used to being an object of natural curiosity. As I read something like this into her smile, I blushed deeply.

"Mummy," said Max, inexorably, "stop punishing Richard. You've made him blush for something he couldn't help."

She did not turn away from me to him and so I saw the pain that came and went swiftly in her face. She said to me,

"Well, you may as well know it, Richard, I have my own h-obsession, also."

Uncle Alec swayed in his chair with pleasure at the quotation.

"Do tell us, Lissy," he said, unnecessarily, with a birdlike turn of his narrow head.

"Well, you know, Richard, once upon a time, a long time ago, I used to amuse myself and burden my friends by painting flowers and giving them away. Now I've gone one step farther. I have become a horticulturist."

"Max showed me the great greenhouse," I said. "It looks like the botanical gardens at home in Dorchester."

"Max called it the Crystal Palace when we built it. He saw a picture in an old *Illustrated London News* in the library which made him think of it. —Darling," she said, turning to him, "would you be a lamb and drive me down there after lunch? There is something wonderfully exciting going on. Mr Standish telephoned me this morning about it. —Mr Standish is our head gardener," she explained to me. She waited, facing me, fearful of what Max would say.

"If you like," he said, "though perhaps Frazier or somebody could follow in another car and let me go on from there."

He meant that with three chauffeurs and a dozen motor-cars available, it did seem regrettable that she should make him drive her the two and a quarter miles to the greenhouse when he might well have other things to do with his afternoon.

"We'll take Richard and Marietta with us," said his mother, "I really am quite excited about what is happening."

"Oh, what: what, Lissy," demanded Uncle Alec with dim animation.

"My night-blooming cereus," she said. "Mr Standish says it will surely open either tonight or tomorrow night. He has been watching it night and day."

"D'you mean," asked Uncle Alec for my benefit, so that I would be properly instructed in the nature of the marvel, "that it blooms only in the nighttime?"

"Yes," said Max before his mother could answer, "as its name implies, or rather, affirms."

"It is the only one in this whole part of the country," said Aunt Lissy. "Unimaginably lovely. This one has never opened before. We must all watch it."

Her eagerness was depressing, for no one else really shared it. She turned to her son.

"I know," she said.

"You know what, Mummy?"

"About you and flowers."

"I do have other interests."

"Yes, but flowers bore you. —My flowers, mostly, I suppose," and she made a slow, coquettish smile for him, which sought to grant him the freedom he had already seized. "Never mind. We won't be long—I just want to run down and see it at this stage, and of course we cannot expect anything to happen by day."

"Oh, no, never, never," exclaimed Marietta nervously. She wanted to turn on Max and claw him for his unkindness and then kiss him. Aunt Lissy caught this and said,

"Please: Mari darling: let him alone. He has learned at Harvard that one must not love one's mother." She gave Max another pulling smile, to suggest to the world that their devotion was secure under all this rude banter. He shrugged away her invisible reach. He knew how by many small claims upon him—a drive to the Crystal Palace and back— she tried to recover the large central claim that was gone. She turned to me. "You will still be here?"

"I believe he leaves day after tomorrow," said Uncle Alec.

"We must have it for you."

"I hope so," I said, "I have never seen one."

"I do so hope it will open while you are here," she said.

She dared to show her real excitement over the night-blooming cereus when she talked to me about it, and I am sure my face took on the look of open wonder that showed on hers. Her animation seemed almost to exhaust her even as it gave off light and heat.

"All this commotion," said Max, "over a stage in the life cycle of a vegetable obscenity. Really."

"Max, really," murmured his father.

"Oh, is it? Is it?" asked Marietta with relief to have a real scandal to turn to.

"I am sure no one knows what he means," said Aunt Lissy.

"I know precisely. The typical stalk of the affair is unmistakably phallic. That it will be crowned by some sort of emitted blossom is merely a flourish of metaphor."

Aunt Lissy was equal to the attack. She leaned forward, cradling her lost hand, and said with velvety control,

"But how fascinating, dear. One would never have thought of it in that way, but any dimension of reference is of interest, and an occasional one is astonishing. I find your remark astonishing."

"It was meant to be," he said, and smiled upon his mother with his brows drawn together, so that the resemblance between mother and son was striking for a moment. She closed her mouth so firmly over what she was tempted to say next that a tiny fall of powder left her upper lip. If her son was young, articulate, and reckless, he would find his mother restrained in her answer to him while she lived. The strength of suffering and loss, futility acknowledged, and unpierced solitude belonged to her. I gave her a secret look, hunting for the girl within her whom my mother remembered with such long devotion. I saw nothing but the care-

[77]

laden presence of a semi-invalid who, as everyone knew, tired easily, but bravely.

Yet how could anyone's fortitude be so crushing? Because —the knowledge is now mine—it was fashioned of the very reasons which always ask too much of love.

Our silence lasted too long for Uncle Alec.

"Lissy," he called like a proud husband, "tell us about your plans for this evening!"

"Everything is done. We finished the seating this morning. Miss Magruder is leaving a copy of the diagram on your desk."

"Are we to have music?"

"Oh, yes."

"And the young things will dance. —What time do we have the fireworks concert?"

"At half-past ten, between supper and the dancing."

"You mustn't do too much this afternoon, Lissy," he said, suddenly reviving his executive manner, "we want you to sparkle tonight. Hang every bauble from your jewel box on yourself wherever you can."

"Oh," she cried, "not for a fireworks party, do you think?"

For some reason this set Marietta to laughing. Aunt Lissy was grateful. She caught the contagion of relief in Marietta's laughter, and began to laugh with her, until great lateral tears appeared between her thick lashes and swam with light. The muscular effort of the laugh brought a spasm of some sort to her right arm and she lifted it and lowered it to ease pain. Laughing, she wore the look of someone weeping. How could I ever remember all this to tell at home?

"Lissy, may we have coffee in the lib'ry?" —Uncle Alec clearly felt it was time to adjourn such a luncheon party. She nodded and readied to rise. I sprang to pull her chair for her.

"Thank you, Richard," she said fondly, and while Maximilian glared, she took my arm and walked with me to the library, where a manservant was just entering with a coffee tray.

"Yes. Peefectly. Yes," mused Uncle Alec, as he saw his household functioning well.

※ ※ ※

Half an hour later we stood—Aunt Lissy, Max, Marietta, and myself—in a far aisle of the Crystal Palace listening to Mr Standish make his report. He spoke slowly in a smoky voice and with the emphasis of someone who knew and loved his job.

"I have kept it in normal conditions," he said, "without forcing in any way. Just the natural light and temperature of this wing of the house. I noticed the buds changing color four days ago—"

"Growing paler?" asked Aunt Lissy.

"Yes, ma'am, and somewhat waxy-looking, though nothing t'what they'll be later when open."

"You have seen a cereus in bloom elsewhere?"

"Yes, ma'am. —And then I checked about every hour to see the rate of change; and I am confi-dent that we can't be kept waiting much more than twenty-four hours."

"Whatever shall we do if it should decide to open tonight!" she exclaimed. Mr Standish, ruddy, stocky, and even-minded, remained silent but his question was visible on his face. "I mean," she added, "we are having this unnerving party in the greenhouse tonight and out on the terrace, and I wouldn't want not to be able to come and stay with the flower when it begins. —You *will* notify me, Mr Standish? Wherever and whenever?"

"Oh, yes, ma'am. I don't guarantee, for when they start they sometimes move fast—"

"One can actually see the petals unfold?" asked Marietta.

"Yes, ma'am." He pursed the stubby fingers of his right hand to make a closed bud, and then opened them very slowly. "You can see it happen as easy as this. Slower, but moving."

Aunt Lissy looked at me with radiance.

"Richard, isn't it going to be wonderful?"

On the waist-high bench holding carefully raked damp earth the night-blooming cereus stood alone. It was in a wooden tub which rested on a square flagstone. The plant had five thick dark green stalks, each reaching generally upward in a different radius. Each was finely defended by a mist of pale needles. A closed bud stood on a short stem at the tip of each stalk. We had heard so much of the living movement of the flowers that they now seemed to be sleeping, and we stood waiting to be told when they would awaken. Beyond the plant which was the object of so much energy, planning, care, and expense, receded the perspective of the Crystal Palace in moist air that grew bluer the farther the eye reached within the glass walls. Mr Standish kept his candid countryman's gaze upon his ma'am. His concern for the plant was as real as hers, but perhaps his had an even closer intimacy with it, for he was responsible in a way she did not share. He was the guardian; she merely the owner.

"Oh—how intense!" exclaimed Marietta, somehow enacting the word itself in her posture. She looked at Max for approval, but he maintained his calm.

"Yes," said Aunt Lissy with a hint of apology and sadness, "I suppose it is. And yet, why not?" She turned to me and the longing in her face brought a remote thump to my breast. She seemed to say that if I might think she was merely displaying a pleasing interest in an expensive plaything, I was wrong. It must be clear that here was her earnest and loving absorption—the life of this flower to which she gave time and thought. What else in life just now was there to demand her interest? to help her forget pain? to keep her from going mad? to hold her from dying? Look around me, she implored silently, and say who makes claim upon my existence? For the love of God, believe in my flowers with me, and don't nod kindly at a whimsical preoccupation which helps to fill my days. My excitement is real. Let it remain so. Help me. Exclaim in wonder at the marvel I offer you—all I have to offer.

❧ ❧ ❧

Was I confronting another of those barriers, as I called them earlier, or perhaps I could call them tests, by the passing of which we mark stages of growth? I remember the way my parents, trying to conceal their vigilance but failing, would watch how I met my encounters with new experience and knowledge. They knew in that summer how I was coming to the stage of life when I would begin to see the lives of other families in relation to my own, and they could only wonder how I would judge not only the new, but

[81]

the old. They had pressed me to come to Newstead, and they surely waited to discover what I would bring home. I don't know how explicitly I told them later, but they must have seen that for the first time I was aware of the possibility that the lives all about us consisted of two aspects—the outer one shown to the world and maintained as long as dignity or desperation made this possible; and the inner one which in the end could never be wholly concealed. There was much pathos in the realization that it was just the most imperatively kept secrets which in the end revealed themselves through the mere being of their possessors. In my country the rich could never be wrong about anything—so we grew up believing. Could we blame them for fostering this convention themselves? Looking homeward from the Crystal Palace I was suffused by a wave of homesickness; for I longed to be at ease in the Chittenden Hills, but the Chittendens, in their various self-centered needs, made this impossible.

"Marietta," I thought, realizing that when I was away from her, I felt unlike myself. I now sought refuge in her. For the first time I was in love for more than a few hours.

🦋 🦋 🦋

She left us at the hilltop when we brought Aunt Lissy back from the greenhouse.

"Dance with me this evening," she said, as we saw her mounted and ready to ride home. "Both of you."

Max nodded abruptly and she gathered her mount and rode away.

[82]

"Come with me, now," said Max.

"What are we going to do?"

"We'll drive down to Standish's house and pick up my dog and exercise him for a while."

"I must be back at four. Your mother is expecting me for a little talk and some tea after her rest."

"We'll be back. Let's remember something."

"What."

"When we're as old as they are, let's remember how it is to be as young as we are now."

"Don't they remember?"

He shrugged hopelessly. His disarming charm settled over him again. When he was unsure of himself, he was at his best, though I envied what I thought of as his sophistication.

"You know? Richie? I really don't know. I have thought about this problem a lot. It is really quite a problem. Once or twice I have thought that the trouble is that they remember too well how it was to be young and sure of everything; and that what makes them the way they are now is that they can't bear to think of everything they have learned since. I don't know. The more everything seems less certain, the more they have to act as though it were more so."

I frowned to conceal my determination to talk that way. Would I ever go to Harvard? We changed cars, leaving the sumptuous old Packard, which looked like a galleon with its high poop, in which we had ridden down to the Crystal Palace earlier, and vaulted into the Isotta. It was well dried out since the night before. Max laughed as we drove off in a roar like a battery salute.

"Frazier told me I would do well not to leave empty whiskey bottles in my car."

"Perhaps you wanted the bottle to be seen."

[83]

He turned to face me with delighted amazement.

"Richie, that's the line! Get behind what anything says to what it might mean. It doesn't matter if you turn out to be wrong. The thing is, to shake 'em up with what you say."

Perhaps I was learning how to talk that way right now.

"Why does your dog live at Mr Standish's?"

He made a great slash at the air with his hand and said that it was all right for him to have a dog in his *rooms,* but the trouble was, to go there, it would have to go through the rest of the house, and this would create disorder, they believed, and so it had been arranged, without his taking part in the discussion, for Chief, his dog, who was a firehouse dog, or Dalmatian, to live two and a quarter miles down the road with the head gardener's family, who would take the best of care of him.

"I have visiting privileges," said Max wryly. "When I can, I go down there and take him out for a run. He loves to run alongside the road and keep up with me as I drive along. He's the most stupid animal I ever saw, and this makes you love him, you see?"

He said that he had thought a couple of years ago that he might work out a rig to bring Chief up to his window with a basket and a rope, and they had tried it out.

"Chief would get in the basket and sit down, and Frazier would back off a little holding the coil of rope one end of which was attached to the handle. Every time he began to throw the rope up to me at the window, Chief would jump out and chase the rope. When he caught it, he shook it and gruffled over it, looking up at me with one eye—he has one green and one brown eye—to see how pleased I was. We tried tying him in the basket but he thrashed about so that he always tipped the basket over and ruined the balance. We never got it to work."

We went roller-coasting along the narrow gray road, swooping with the little hills. Soon we saw the greenhouse and just beyond it the gardener's house, which I had not noticed before. The road ran on past and was lost in a high ridge. How could it be that one of the richest boys in the nation could not keep a dog with him? Max said,

"What would you do, if you were I?"

"If I were twenty-one I would say politely but firmly as I was now of age that I would have my dog with me or I would have to live somewhere else."

"Oh, no, no, I don't mean about the dog. I mean about everything."

I had not thought about "everything"—I was too full of impressions, some bewildering, some beguiling, to have an answer. Out of my confusion leaped a question in return.

"Why do you behave like that to your mother?"

His profile, with its regularly spaced notches clear against the sky, grew still and severe.

"It is a pity you didn't know her before, as she used to be," he replied coldly. It was all the answer he was going to make. Anyhow, we were drawing up to the gardener's white cottage. Waiting at the gate in the low white picket fence was the Dalmatian, who knew the sound of the Isotta. Max skidded the tires to a halt and leaped out. The tall dog, with its bright black marks in its smooth white coat, leaped up to greet him, and they clasped each other at the neck and made two or three turns in a hilarious waltz. Chief barked and Max imitated him. They both threw their heads back and bayed. Then they danced apart and Max, waving me to come along, ran down the road to a rail fence at the edge of a meadow and sailed over it. Chief followed, and then I. We played Chase the Stick, with Chief cantering between us to retrieve as we threw a stick back and forth. Sometimes we let him get it, and then we had to play hunter and prey, stalking the dog who would let us approach almost within reach before he heaved himself up to plunge farther away in the tall, pungent grass. Max gave a brilliant performance pretending to be a coach dog like Chief, and Chief, in the spirit of the game, honored the impersonation. Soon we were exhausted not from exercise but from laughter and we all three came to ground in the middle of the meadow panting and looking at the sky.

"By God, it's hot," said Max.

"Yes. Awfully."

"It's great, isn't it!"

"No. I hate it."

"Oh, no, summer is the best time."

"Yes. I believe you are a summer man."

"Is that good?"

He could never forego occasion for praise, the garland of forgiveness. He courted it mockingly, yet with a hint of pleading.

"Well, it's good for you, I suppose. It wouldn't be for me."

The answer was not satisfactory. He desired to be what everyone else could hope to be.

"Richie, God damn it, I don't know what to make of you. Sometimes I think I've got you pinned down to the mat, and then you pull a surprise maneuver, and off you go."

"Why do you care what I think?"

"I guess it is because you won't really tell me. I have to find out."

I replied to this with silence and a steady gaze. His spirits fell. He said,

"I wish I knew what was the matter with me."

Now it was my turn to seek. I had not thought about what might be the matter with him, if anything really was, which I could not believe for I did not know what to do with knowledge.

"Is something wrong, Max?"

He rolled over in the tall grass and put his face down into the cradle of his arms.

"I think just about everything," he answered in a voice muffled against the soft damp secret earth.

I waited. I had no experience out of which to make the next inquiry which would enlighten me or deliver him. Chief lay nearby, panting sociably. With his tongue hanging out and his teeth shining, he looked like a lost guest smiling at a party.

Presently Max said,

"When I'm away, I remember how badly I acted at home, and I swear when I am home the next time I will show them all that I love them. I will make them forget how offensive I have been, and I tell myself that I need not say much of anything, but only let them feel that I love them and am grateful for everything they have given me." He rolled to his side and faced me. "Do you feel that for your own family? *when you're with them?*"

"Yes."

"Then why don't I? —After I make my promises to myself that I will be the son they want, I always feel good for days. I write home and jabber about everything and anything. I think of things to make them laugh, as they read my letters. I sleep better for weeks. I even do a little work—I mean, more than just the necessary. And then."

I nodded.

"And then," he continued, "I come home, and when I see them again, and how everything is, it all starts again. I hurt them twenty times a day, I see myself doing it, I get disgusted with myself, and that makes me act all the worse toward them. They can't even take notice any more. My mother told me she had decided never to shed tears again, over me, or anything. Marietta is the only hope, and I treat her like hell sometimes."

"She's great."

"Yes, I know. She thinks you are, too. She and my mother have had a long talk about you. They think you're good for me. They wish I were like you."

I laughed. If he only knew how I longed to be a Max, handsome, brilliant, careless, cruel yet irresistible, a prince who lived in disguise most of the time.

He jumped up. Come, he motioned. He gave Chief a whack on his glossy hard rump, and we all ran to the car and were off down the road toward the curtain of hills ahead. We passed a boarded-up schoolhouse. We saw cows in one field and horses in another. The road crossed a little brook. We flew over it. Faintly through the wind of our speed I thought I heard a train whistle and looked at Max. A train seemed a most unlikely thing to find in those pastoral hills. He nodded and pointed. Along the floor of the valley close to the ridge ahead ran a track. I saw a small black engine trolling toward us under a skein of white smoke. It pulled four freight cars. Soon we could see the crossing. Max calculated the closing angle of our speed and the train's. For a quarter of a mile he navigated nicely as the collision course

[88]

he was dramatizing became more and more certain in its elements of distance, nearness, speed, time, and power. I began to feel the excited joyful horror which I always knew watching a black and white movie comedy, when the train and the Ford car full of cops ran toward each other. Max gave a shout and pressed the gas pedal. The trainmen saw us now, and began tooting violently on their three-note chord of steam and flue. Max waved to show that he saw them. They rolled the engine bell and we could hear the hot scream of iron brakes. The road lifted, it took us up to the crossing, we bumped hard on the rails, and I half stood up staring at the engine which grew and grew in my vision until everything looked black, except the engineer's eyes, which were bright blue, and his red face, which was ready to burst with fury. He opened his mouth to shout and so close were we in that closing instant that I saw a gold tooth in the flash of afternoon. With one inch and a half-second to spare we were across and as the engine rang heavily past us we could feel its wind on our necks. The engineer released his brakes and the little train took a curve at the base of the hills. The fireman was leaning out of his cab window shaking his fist at us. Max let the car coast down to an ambling speed. He was laughing and shouting.

"Next time I won't give him so much leeway!"

"You damned near got us knocked off," I said. "You God damned fool!"

"Wasn't it great?"

"I'm not so sure. —I admit it was exciting."

"He'll report me. Nobody's supposed to play with a railroad."

"Where does it go?"

"It's a little junction line. Once every morning a passenger train comes down to Olympia, and goes back up in the late afternoon. And once every afternoon that freight train goes up, and comes down between ten and eleven o'clock at night. They used to let me ride in the engine when I was young."

When he was young. As soon as he said this, I realized how old he had seemed to me. Childhood should not end suddenly, as his had ended. I think now of Byron, and the uses of scorn to cauterize early wounds.

"Where does this road go?" I asked.

"Only to the quarry." He pointed to the rise before us. The road wound out of sight in a fold of the hills. As we left the flat valley we saw a small brick house contained against the meadows by a tall hedge of laurel.

"Who is there?"

"That is where the Danas live—he is my father's librarian. You met him."

"Oh yes."

"It is a nice house. I always wanted it for myself. Maybe some day I will have it. It is the only house across the railroad tracks. There would be nobody to keep track of my coming and goings."

We drove toward the barrier of the ridge, but Max let the car slacken its speed with the effect of revealing a pause in his thought. Suddenly he asked,

"Do you like children?"

"I suppose so—like everybody."

"No, but *do you feel their lives?* They are the greatest. They cannot lie. When a child tries to lie, even the artifice of it is an honest betrayal. You know the great secret?"

"I—probably not."

"It is to keep alive the child inside, alongside the man growing up."

"I thought we were supposed to outgrow various stages of life."

"Nonsense. We must keep every one as we enter the next. —Let's go to see my children."

Before I could ask who and where they were, he was turning around and heading back toward the Dana cottage. Drawing up parallel to the laurel hedge he stopped the car and leaped out, calling to me to follow. In the rear of the house he found a gateway through the hedge, and within, he found the two children of the Dana family. They were a boy four years old and a girl two. On seeing Max, they lost their heads. They screamed for him, "Uncle Max, Uncle Max," and began running in circles like ponies in a ring, showing off in delight, their heads down, the girl imitating her brother, their hard little chests pumping. Max chased them, caught them, and took one up in each arm. They kicked and strove for freedom hoping he would not let them go. His face shone with pleasure; perhaps even with love. All at once after this initial show of energy they settled down and I was introduced as "Cousin Richard whom you must love very much," and a dialogue followed in mock gravity, during which Max gave an exhibition of how to use the child within him as he sought the children without.

He asked for their news. They had none until he particularized for them.

"How is the cat?"

"Fine."

"Where is she?"

"She is there."

"Where?"

"I don't know."

"Is she off in the field looking for fieldmice?"

"Yes."

"Will she find any?"

"I don't know."

"Do you love fieldmice?"

"Yes."

"Do we want the kitty to let them go?"

"No."

"*Yes.*"

"Yes."

"How is the goldfish in the house?"

"Fine."

"Does he swim all day long?"

"Yes."

"Would the kitty get him if he isn't careful?"

"No."

"*Yes.*"

"Yes."

"We don't want the kitty to get the goldfish, do we?"

"No."

"That's right. What does the goldfish say?"

"Nothing."

"Oh yes he does—he says *gwup-gwup-gwup*. Doesn't he?"

"Yes."

"Say it."

"*Wup-wup-wup.*"

"Ve-ry good. How are the spiders in the garden?"

"Fine. —We have one."

"You do? Have you seen him?"

"Yes."

"Can you show him to me?"

"Yes."

"Where is he?"

"There."

"Show me."

They made a small procession, going to an old rickety arbor where, sure enough, spun as if by the heat-veiled summer sunlight, a misty web was spread between the upright and a diagonal support of the arbor under an overhang of limp vine leaves. In its center was a great brown spider hung in wary stillness. In a whisper which was used to promote danger and mystery, Max said,

"If we leave him alone he will not bite."

"Not bite."

But the idea stirred the little girl. She reached for the protection of Max's arms. He hoisted her aloft to face him. She was serious. She brought her great eyes close to his and put her finger on his mouth and watched her finger and his lips and then took her finger away and with a blow of breath threw her thick little arms around his neck and kissed him passionately. At this, her brother felt the need of attention. He grasped Max about the thigh and threw his head back and hanging heavily away swung his body, so like that of a *putto,* from side to side, making a high song within his closed lips. Soon enough it was time to let go, but they would not let go. Max had to put them off and set them down on the grass. It was question time again.

"How is the little celluloid boat I brought you last time?"

"Fine."

"Do you play with it in the bath?"

"Yes."

"Do you bathe together in the tub?"

"Yes."

I felt a stir of something alien.

"Do Mummy and Daddy bathe together in the tub?"

[93]

"Yes."

"Does the kitty bathe with everybody in the tub?"

"Yes."

"*No.*"

"No."

"The kitty does not like to get wet. Now tell me—"

The mother appeared at the back door and stood inside the screen. She greeted Max and he waved, laughing, comfortable in his privileges, which included ownership of employee family secrets granted by small children. She was heavily pregnant. Her straight dark hair hung in limp hanks beside her tinted glasses which gave her owl eyes. She was so uncomfortable and unattractive in her weighted condition that she thrust it proudly at us with every air of challenge in her knowledge of herself as a woman mindlessly at the mercy of woman's utmost function. I was introduced.

"Jane, this is my Cousin Richard. He's visiting. He's already met Andy at the house."

"Hel-laow," said Mrs Dana.

"We've been having a romp," said Max.

"Yes, I knaow. I could hear in the kitchen."

Max laughed.

"Good-by, chickadees," he shouted to the children, who dragged at him and hung on him all the way to the gate. He kissed them and we left.

Resuming the road toward the ridge, he said,

"Why do they love me?"

"Because you love them and want them to love you."

"No, no. It's more than that. —They know exactly how beautiful they are and how they are made of nothing else, as yet, but love itself. It is not that they are morally pure—actually they will commit tiny crimes to achieve what they want which is love—it is that they are love in the flesh, in its unadulterated state. When I get depressed I remember that they, anyhow, will always scream and jump for me if I go to them. They will not ask me any questions which their lovely little bodies cannot answer for themselves. *My* internal child wants to be as direct and as pure as that."

"Can it?"

"How can it? Never. It is too late." He stared at the hill face of the ridge, which we were rapidly approaching, and added, "How lucky are those who never know ahead of time that everything is *always* too late."

"Why did you ask them about the parents taking baths together? Was that necessary?"

"Necessary?" He laughed. "Necessity doesn't come into it. It was an amusing notion that just came to me. It wouldn't mean anything to the children, and somehow it fascinates me to consider the Danas playing with my celluloid boat and solemnly splashing each other in their old-fashioned enameled tub.—Why? Have I offended you?"

"I don't think one need get children's thoughts going along that line. And besides, who has any right to know what the Danas, or any couple, may do at home?"

"But, Richie, who knows if what the children said was true or not? They will always say what seems to be expected in the convention of the moment. Cheer up. It meant nothing."

But though I didn't have the word for it then, what I thought was that there was something lightly satanic in his use of other lives, at any age, to amuse him. And yet when I thought of his glowing joy at the company of children, I was ashamed of my qualms, and I lapsed into silence.

[95]

⚸ ⚸ ⚸

We rose on a long shelf road along the leafy face of the ridge and at the top we doubled back sharply, went down a short slope on the other side, and into our view came the great silent hollow of the quarry.

"What is this!"

"They used to quarry limestone here. Many of our family houses came from this stone. My grandfather owned it and finally closed it down and got a zoning ordinance because he did not want any industrial plants or any organized sort of thing anywhere near the Hills. Our steel mills are the nearest, and they are fourteen miles away, near Calverton. Sometimes at night you can just see the red glow of the furnaces if you look south from Newstead."

The road became a thread of gravel and loose stone. The Isotta skidded and swayed. We went down sharply along the other side of the ridge. A sheer wall fell away from my side of the road straight down to the black water of the quarry lake. Half of the great cavity was in shadow. The walls were three hundred feet high or so, opened out in a great fan shape. Shallow ledges appeared here and there and in their cracks dust had lodged and from the dust green branches grew against the otherwise bare, palatial limestone faces. Our engine made explosive echoes. By their return to us off the opposite cliff we could gauge the size of the quarry— it must have been a quarter of a mile across at the widest point. We scratched and slid our way down the single-track road until we were almost at water level, and there I saw a narrow spit of rocky land which ran out into the lake for a hundred yards. A few bushes clustered along the waterline, and some great blocks of limestone rested like arranged ruins at the far end. We had to leave the car and walk out on the narrow stretch.

"We always called this the Peninsula," said Max. "It was our favorite picnic place. They always made us get out at the top and walk all the way down. Nobody ever has driven down the trail but me."

The day was caught in the silence of the beautifully chiseled cup of the quarry, and the silence seemed intense and sacred—almost as if it could not be broken. Though this was a work of human artisans, the limestone pit seemed to my imagination like some prehistoric natural wonder. The stone cliffs gave off cool air, the winds of the ridge were wafted across and above, and nothing stirred the polished surface of the water. When we spoke our voices took on an added ring. I wondered if there was an echo in the quarry, almost a living spirit.

"Ah, God," said Max, throwing himself down flat to gaze deep into the water at the tip of the Peninsula. Looked into deep down, the water had a midnight-blue color. "This is where I ought to live."

I squinted at him to be sure of my impression. He was like a burdened man from whom cares fell away leaving a brilliant-looking youth whose certainties would take him far.

"We used to keep canoes here when I was little. My father would bring us down here and we would spend whole afternoons on the water."

"Who came?"

"All of us—my sister, my mother, my father, myself, Marietta sometimes." He looked into the water where the past might hang upside down but clear, sweetly colored, untroubled. "We had lovely games. My father and I in one canoe, my mother and Lina in the other. Lina was good with a paddle. My father had us pretend that this was the sea and that we had rival kingdoms on opposite sides. Sometimes we would pay state visits to each other across the sea singing hymns, and other times we had naval battles and tried to tip each other over."

"But wouldn't it be dangerous for children?"

"We swam like fish. If you can believe it, my father was a wonderful swimmer. He taught us early. Lina looked like a watersprite. She could race my father and beat him. He worshipped her. When I was four, she was sixteen. You couldn't think so, but they resembled each other, except that she was blonde like my mother, and Alexander Chittenden has always had dark hair. But Lina was like wheat, silver-gold, and as slim, and as pliant, and she was as strong as wire. She could make my father do anything. He loved her but never said so, and when things went wrong for her he tried not to love her any more, but he couldn't stop. The confusion withered him inside and out."

I must have stared at him like a bumpkin. Uncle Alec? He had known hunger and beauty and joy? When? How long ago, before his time of gray and black, with grape-colored stretched lips, and unacknowledged fears which made him hollow within?—he, an exultant young father, making his children a gift of the natural world of water and sky, gaiety and love? Then—I was chastened and ashamed —there was more to see in him than a caricature, as I had seen him?

"Lina. *My sweetling,*" said Max. "He called her that, and I took it up. I used to take my nap with her, insisting that otherwise I could not sleep. I don't know what she ever knew about things, but I knew—I knew then as physically as I know now."

"I don't follow you."

"It is bad form to talk about such matters, but I am not famous for my good form. I don't know why, but I can talk to you. Marietta said the same. Anyhow. When I was supposed to be taking my nap with Lina, I lay with my eyes closed and I was like a small cat dozing with love and desire. I held her and she actually slept, but I had a lover's proof of my feeling; my desire was evident to my touch and to my own eye. I wanted her to see and touch, too, but something told me not to let her know. So I made my love to her under the guise of play and teasing. But children can't keep secrets. Maybe nobody can."

"No."

"Anyhow. One day Father somehow saw what was going on. It was the end of my afternoon loving." He paused looking backward in time, and a hard smile rippled over his lips. "I decided long later that he was jealous of me."

"Good God! Your father! Your sister!"

"Yes. Classifications and labels. But as Leonardo pointed out in his notebook, the *verga* lives an independent life, and among other things it ignores are labels and classifications." He sounded like a fallen angel; but if he did not believe in angels, as I was sure he did not, how could he fall? I shook myself away from the idea.

How many first love affairs must happen in the nursery, an Eden that smells of flannel, cocoa, paste, poster paints, and the righteous perspiration of nursemaids.

"But you know?" he said. "I never could be sure that Lina did not know. How could I be sure? They never scolded me or anything, they just separated me and Lina. I had to take naps in the nursery after that, with Nannie sitting by in a rocking chair which squeaked like a mouse. She used to say a rosary under her apron. My family never knew she was a Catholic and I never told on her. One time when I had a high fever she thought I was going to die and she baptized me secretly. When I got well I washed it off with soap, and told her so, but she only smiled mysteriously and looked up to heaven where, by her act of saving me, she felt she was sure to go, bypassing purgatory. When Lina was eighteen she was sent abroad with a maid and a governess to make a tour of Europe in the summer. My father did not want her to go."

Max would overhear discussions between the parents about it. His mother was calm and certain that everything would be all right, after all, they had friends in every city, and Uncle Alec finally consented, provided the foreign agents of his company made a cabled report every day from each city where the travelers paused.

"When she kissed me good-by, Lina cried. Her tears ran into my mouth and I felt desperate with love and lust."

"But a child!" I said, for I had never known of the revelation of the devouring mystery to a young child.

"Yes. And I have often wondered if it would ever have happened so soon with anybody but Lina. —After that, of course, it was bound to happen with someone else, and in a few years, it did."

He looked at me to discover if I knew the one to whom he referred. I was tempted to suffer by a little hot lick of grief at my heart. Was he referring to Marietta? I must not believe so. I had no right to be jealous, but I was. My face told him to keep silent, as I must be silent. I was jealous of love, and of him for having had it since childhood, and of Marietta for her freedom, and of the life they had grown up in together. I took shelter in the ambiguous, and not for the last time in those summer days with that family.

Max turned and yawned to dissipate the threat of revealed emotion.

"So Lina never came back."

"Was that when?" I asked.

"You knew?"

"Marietta told me she married an Italian and had not come home since."

He laughed.

"I have seen her, they couldn't make me not see her. But my father has never seen her since. She made a reasonably happy ending for herself out of what everybody—all my local cousins and the rest—called a scandal. It's not a long story, except that it is, because it is still going on, for her."

One night in Venice there was a great dinner to which Lina was invited. Her chaperon took her to a palace where the feast was spread and came to fetch her at midnight. She was not to be found at first. She had never been as free in her life. She had gone for a small voyage in the gondola of a youth her own age. They fell in love. He had a mistress whom he promised to give up for her. She told him it wouldn't be worth his while as she could only stay in Venice for four days, after which her governess would take her to Vienna. The tour schedule would have to be kept or her father would be distressed. Her friend said four days were an eternity, and much could be accomplished in an eternity. She agreed to let him come to lunch with her at two the next day at her hotel which faced the lagoon and where she had two balconies to choose from. He came, and for the sake of strategy, paid more attention to the chaperon than to

Lina. He was lively and amusing, and though he had no education in the Pennsylvania sense, he seemed to know much about everything that interested Lina. Like someone in a Mozart opera, no, she said long afterward with a husky laugh which suggested endless cigarettes and vats of champagne and frankly comfortable, and transient, infidelities—no, like an earlier Venetian, like Casanova himself, her suitor spirited her away from the Danieli Hotel late in the afternoon. They went to a place he knew and she became his. She stayed with him for two days while the chaperon tried to conceal the loss in order to protect herself; but finally she had to ask a Chittenden representative to come from Milan to help find her, and the lovers were found and unmasked. They were forced to marry, which was not what either of them had in mind, but they were now wildly in love, and they didn't mind marrying. Lina would have to become a Catholic, for her husband's family insisted, and as they were important, they obtained a dispensation from the Cardinal Patriarch for an immediate marriage, with instruction in the Faith to follow. The story had every accent of betrayal in it, and the Chittendens were the victims. Their daughter had broken their hearts, or rather, the once single heart of their marriage.

"That was how Lina became a Principessa," ended Max. "She is still beautiful, but she doesn't look like a gather of wheat any more, but rather like an armful of full-blown peonies with lazy bees drifting over her head. She has a little gesture, as if waving them languidly away now and then. —I met the Prince, later, myself. Lina asked me whom he looked like. I said I didn't know. She said, 'Look again.' I did, and I saw what she meant. He looked like my father as a young man. In old photographs, I mean. You never really _know,_ do you."

"Are they happy?"

"You never know, with Europeans, do you. She and her husband are still together. They're not as rich as she would have been otherwise, but people with money like to be seen with them. It is one kind of a career, anyhow."

I was suddenly annoyed by all his yawning worldliness, and I had a hot pit of anger at Marietta in my middle. I would do well not to see her again, I thought. Perhaps she was like Princess Lina, who made love freely. Perhaps Marietta had been making love with Max for who knew how long. But this was my own new love flinching at imagined outrages, and the anger soon dissolved.

"I think we'd better be going," I said. "I am to see your mother at four."

"Our sordid histories depress you," he said. "Very well. Come on."

We went to the car and I had a new grasp of what it meant to drive down the trail instead of walk.

"Where can you turn around?" I asked.

"That's just it. You can't. You have to back up all the way. It is tricky."

Bored by his satisfactions, I had an impulse to walk up the trail rather than ride as he wrangled the Isotta up the sliding gravel incline. But I then thought he would think me afraid, which was what he hoped. I got into the car and as Max took us, jerking and precarious, backwards up the trail, I looked over the deep-shadowed quiet of the man-made crater which seemed like a secret world apart where cares could be lost in memories of better times and human cross-purposes could be dissolved by gazing deep, and wondering what lay at the bottom of the quarry lake.

❦ ❦ ❦

Aunt Lissy's sitting room opened off the corridor near to the great staircase at the center of the house. Her door was open and she was waiting in the hot blurred light of four o'clock. The tall windows were ajar. Their thin curtains drifted in the humid breeze, and I saw her in silhouette with a haze of silver all about her. She was half reclining in a long chair with many cushions. Her fabricated hand rested on a small cushion at her lap. I felt its weight much more there than at the lunch table, where she had supported it with her live hand.

"Come in, Richard. I am expecting you."

She inclined her head toward a deep armchair covered in white linen. I sat down. A sober silence lay between us for a long moment, and then, not knowing what else to do, I smiled. She sparkled her eyes at this and said in a breathy voice which bespoke deep weariness,

"You smile just like Rose. I never thought I'd see her again, but now in a way I have. —Tell me, tell me all about her. Is she well? Your father? Isn't it shameful that I know so little about all of you. But now we know you, Richard, and we feel rewarded."

"I—I yes, well," I said, always confused by compliments face to face, "thank you. Well, my mother is very well, and so is my father. She asked me to remember every little thing here so I could tell her when I got home."

"Does she think of me now and then?"

"All the time."

"You make me feel so remiss—I have not written for ages, and it seemed an inspiration when we thought of asking you to our Fourth of July. Were they pleased to have you come?"

"Oh, yes. They argued and argued with me, and said I would have a wonderful time."

"Ah. You didn't want to come?"

"I am sorry," I said, hot in the face for my tactlessness, "I mean—"

She closed her eyes at me and then opened them with dancing lights set in the twilight of her sorrowful face.

"I know, I know. Some young people dislike any change, and it is all their parents live in hopes of. —But you are I hope having a pleasant time with us?"

"Oh, yes, thank you, yes."

"We all think it such a pity you must leave tomorrow."

I looked glad at the prospect, and she said,

"Will you be eager to get home?"—wistfully, as if to test the possibility that some people really loved to go home, and had a real one to go to.

"Oh, yes."

"You love them."

"Oh, yes."

"Yes, your father was such a handsome man. I was maid of honor, you know? at your parents' wedding. He was full of the most flashing blue-eyed humor that day, he was perfectly certain about everything, and your mother kept looking at him to see what she should do. She was the prettiest human being I ever knew. She was well named. Rose. But still we always called her Kitten because she had such soft brows, and gathered them so often in a look of puzzled interest and charm."

"My mother said she always tried to imitate how *you* looked whenever she wanted anyone to do something for her."

"Oh, no, it was always the other way round. We all tried to talk like Rose, and look like her, and sing like her—she had a lovely voice, you know—and all of us learned from her how to be clever with our fingers." She held my eye with a candid gaze to keep me from glancing down at her lost hand on its cushion. With effort I managed not to look at it. I said,

"She told me to ask you if you remember how dreadfully she behaved at the picnic."

"The picnic?"

"At Lilydale."

"Lilydale. —Oh, my dear. Now I do. Oh, it was priceless." She covered her eyes with her left hand and a whiff of faded laughter rode out on her memory. "It was at the end of our last year in school, we all went on a picnic to the spiritualist colony at Lilydale, near Dorchester, your father was there, and your mother said to him, 'Dan,' she said, 'if you hear me cry out, come in and get me.' —You see we were all going to have a séance with different mediums, all the women had little separate cottages, and your mother went into one of them for a séance, while your father—they were engaged then—while Dan waited behind some lilac bushes outside. Some of us waited with him. Soon we heard a mortal cry coming from the house and Dan dashed in. Your mother was lying on the floor in a dead faint. Dan picked her up and carried her outside. The lady medium followed demanding her three dollars. But your father scolded her for doing anything to make Rose faint dead away. We all cried, 'Doctor, Doctor,' and 'Water, water,' and Dan was so worried he forgot that he was supposed to expect a scream. We began to carry her away, the spiritualist lady went indoors and slammed the door to show what she thought of us, and suddenly Rose with her eyes still closed gave a little coloratura laugh, just like Tetrazzini in *The Barber of Seville,* we all said, and then she leaped out of Dan's arms and stood up and made a deep bow, as if taking a curtain call. The whole scene was staged! Dan turned white with fury. She had made a fool of him, he said, and she said, 'Oh, no, I told you to listen for my cry, I knew all along what I was going to do.' 'No,' he said, he hated to be fooled, especially in front of so many people. —We were all day getting them to make up. Can you believe it? Or do all children dislike to hear anything about their parents from the time long ago when everything was so different? Why are children ashamed of the lives that gave them life?"

To tell the truth, I was embarrassed by the story. How silly of my mother, how boyish of my father, to behave as they did; and worst of all, to keep remembering a thing like that with such self-pardoning happiness.

But Aunt Lissy, telling about it, had grown two little glowing touches of color on her wan cheekbones, and she was stirred by dwelling on a time of love long ago, and her powers seemed to return, so that for a little while she seemed less an invalid. And then she became aware of my stillness which fully expressed my abashment on behalf of my parents for their lost gaieties, and her weariness returned, brought back by my immovable commitment to the present, with all its sorrowful reminders for her. She glanced about the room. All its little pieces of a lifetime's furniture—

framed photographs, objects which were given through the years to mark stages, favorite books each of which retained the time of its first reading, water-color sketches of flowers—condemned her to a present time whose fate she had never expected. She rapidly brushed away unhappy visions with her luxuriant lashes, and said,

"You know, Richard? We have done almost nothing else since you arrived here but talk about you."

"Oh. Then, how?"

"Marietta and I are great friends. We see each other daily, and we chat by telephone also. And my son has indicated his feeling about you, and my husband wrote me a note after lunch saying how much he was taken by your great interest in his library."

I had a sense of an unseen network of information and discussion about me going on everywhere at Newstead. I was uneasy, though vaguely flattered. I had a notion that something was pending—something more than kind sentiments. Aunt Lissy wore a pleading look, as if to say that I must listen patiently, and try to see things her way. She continued in a low voice.

"Max so likes you, Richard. He has told Marietta who has told me. Since you have been here—even this little while—he has been so improved."

"Improved"? Did Max have a "condition"? I had a strike of apprehension.

"Marietta's father does feel he is so very highly strung, we should not be too harsh in our judgments of him when he says or does unkind things. Some days it is very sad and trying." She looked into the future to imagine, like an ailing queen-consort, what the fate of the kingdom must be if the heir were to succeed to it burdened with infirmities which

[108]

could only mean distress and even ruin for him and for others. Everyone should do the utmost, however awkward and embarrassing, to secure all possible help for him, while there was yet time. "It is difficult to know just how to say what we—Richard, let me be direct. We all think it would be so wonderful if Max could have his cousin with him— you do seem to understand him so well, and it has been years since we have seen him take to anyone as he has to you."

"I like him very much. We seem able to talk."

"Oh, yes."

"Perhaps I could come back sometime, or he could come to visit me."

"Yes, how delightful. But actually, I was thinking of something else—we would of course see that you were not in any way confined, and that you would have time to pursue your own interests, and in fact, though these are difficult things to discuss, a generous allowance would be arranged for you, and you would have as much time to yourself as you might want. . . ."

Could it be that Aunt Lissy was suggesting that I become a member of that household? I was ready to go home, because everything had been planned for that, but I felt a treacherous lick of excitement at the thought of remaining at Newstead—for how long nobody had said—with all its grandeur. It would be like being summoned to Court in France before the Revolution. The strangeness, constraint, and gloom which I had already seen at the heart of the domestic machine of the Chittenden family would surely not reach me, for if I had something they wanted—so ran my swift and greedy thought—they would obtain it by giving me what I wanted, which I could not yet precisely define. Was this what parents meant when they spoke of "going out into the world"? In her anxiety Aunt Lissy could not help pressing her purpose, which, even if in her excitement she thought it original and novel, was common enough; for families with "difficult" children always hope that someone their own age can be acquired to exert "a healthy influence."

"You must not think it odd that there should be such a helpful friendship between two boys such different ages. Max has always been entirely at ease with both older and younger people. And you strike us all as being really: oh very much so: really more mature than your actual age. —What is it again?"

"Seventeen."

"Yes, seventeen. Well, Max is twenty-one; you are both, really, young men. He has lacked real companionship at home for years—except for our darling Marietta, but then a man always needs at least one really good man friend. —You know what would be so splendid? —It would be for you and Max to do a course of reading together, I mean on a regular, daily, disciplined basis. He scatters himself so. He knows everything too easily. He seems to be running from something. We don't know what. Oh, Richard, how beautiful it would be if you could help find it, whatever it is, and help him to face it!"

Her eyes were full of her familiar pale tears caught in the tangle of her lashes. She was waiting for me to say something.

"Yes, it would be, wouldn't it? But he knows much more than I do."

"Perhaps—but what he knows isn't as good as what you know."

"I don't know what that is."

"How to live with what God has given you."

It was true that so far in life I had never had any problem about doing that. Ideas were passing through my mind fast and clear. What did this family hope to acquire in me, what did they hope to take for themselves of what was mine? Perhaps my still unshaken provincialism with its undisturbing values. Perhaps what they thought of as my healthy lack of involvement with tyrannical ideas or persons—since they could not know how my buried wants and wonderings tormented me. Perhaps they thought I could transfer my even temper to the household—but they had never seen me either afraid or triumphant. Did they yearn for my politeness? —How lovely it would be, perhaps they thought, to see some good manners again, and with this hope, they brushed the margins of my parents' lives which spoke through me at my best: my father's confidence in his powers of charm, intelligence, honor, belief in progress, the optimism of Dorchester, a city still innocently growing in all the energetic faith preached by the Chamber of Commerce; my mother's witty gaiety, her intuitive understanding of many umbrageous depths of life's evil underside and the mercy which always showed through her first horror, her innocent avarice for the graces which wealth must surely bring, her wistful hope that her life had been well-used if she had given me to the world (an attitude which weighed upon me), her undismayed acceptance of the years which passed by taking her youth along, and above all, that edifice in life built by my parents together, which consisted of happiness within moderate bounds of material power, sustained by their belief in the forgiveness of sin and their faith in the attainment of heaven.

"What are you thinking, Richard?"

I must have jumped a little in my chair at being brought back by Aunt Lissy's question, and I said,

"Why, I don't know just what you really want of me."

"I was afraid to state it outright to start with, without some little hint of what it would mean to us—what we hope is that you might consent to spend the rest of the summer here, until time for Max to return to Cambridge, and you to go back to school."

"Oh. I see. —I would have to ask my parents."

"Oh, surely, surely—" Her relief was plain as she saw that I did not refuse outright. "We will send a telegram to Dorchester and ask permission to keep you until the first of September. Perhaps your parents could come for a visit just then, and take you home with them. May I tell them you want to stay?"

Now that the first decision was to be made, I felt a qualm, but it seemed impolite to say I wanted to think about it, and I nodded.

"Oh, very good. —And even if they say *No, you must come home,* at least, Richard, you will be here until we have their answer—and that means you may see the night-blooming cereus open! We are all hoping for tomorrow night."

Her animation was charming, and yet there was something feverish in it which made me look away from her white face with its seeking eyes. She added,

"Max will be so pleased."

"Does he know I am being asked?"

"Marietta has mentioned it—*lightly,* I believe, in case of disappointment. —Richard, where do you think we lost him? —No, you have no idea. No. But if you ever find out, do, please, tell us?"

I nodded, glumly inadequate before all such longing manipulation of human relations. I had a somewhat wild feeling, caused no doubt by my inexperience, but now I think I was dimly wondering about the great chain of seeds by which life is perpetuated, and about how the newly grown seed claims freedom from its own source and kind. Such thoughts made my head ache.

"Come here, dear child," said Aunt Lissy, "let me thank you," and when I went, she lifted her live hand and put it to my face and traced its contours slowly and gently, in a sort of kiss by her fingertips, as if to lure forth the tiny unseen government inside my head which made my kind of life and character seem so desirable to her and to those who worked with her to keep hope alive for the future. She sighed and desisted. I turned to go. She spoke after me.

"Richard, don't get too fond of Max."

I turned to take her meaning. She said nothing further, but her face was ruefully affectionate—she was so fond of me, she hoped for so much, that she was warning me that Max would hurt me if he ever knew he could rely on my love. It was a marvel that she could make me know this without telling me in words. Perhaps she even knew how much I wanted to be like Max—even if it had been possible, to assume his bodily being, and dazzle the world with it. Only the great saints are ever free of externals. I was at an age to live by them in longing and envy.

꒫ ꒫ ꒫

Because the household had to be there early to receive, I saw the party from the first. The Crystal Palace was itself like a great firework laid out in the air, arrested to earth, and sparkling with thousands of lights and their reflections. Green depths within the long glass vaults underlay the glitter, and as night deepened, a row of searchlights laid face up at the edge of the terrace below sent a colonnade of beams straight up into the heavy air. Cars coming on all the valley roads made a web of lights converging on us. Where they came to a halt to deliver their passengers, servants took wraps, and the guests came into the Crystal Palace, across the central court where a fountain kept its plume hovering high under tall palm trees, and out to the terrace overlooking the valley. There in a sort of pavilion made of painted canvas and large flags the family stood waiting to say how do you do. Farther out on the terrace and reaching both ways along its floor were supper tables dressed in bright colors. At each place, party favors commemorating the Fourth of July were laid out—miniature hatchet with a sprig of cherry attached; eagle and shield with the red, white, and blue worked in shiny silk; a tiny trophy of drum, musket, saber, and laurel; and for everyone to wear, a black tricorn hat made of shiny thin cardboard. On a red-carpeted platform against the wall of the greenhouse an orchestra in Continental Army uniforms and white bag-wigs played popular, polite dance music. In a clear space among the tables a dance floor was waiting for the couples who gradually drifted to their places at the tables, only to leave for a few steps before supper. No cocktails were served—only wines at table. Uncle Alec did not believe in Prohibition, but he felt that serving mixed drinks before food went too far, and that a law prohibiting this practice would be justified. But no one could ask a handful of friends, as tonight, when he expected a hundred and some guests, without bringing out twenty dozen each of sherry, Pouilly Fuissé, claret, and champagne. Below me three terraces made great steps down the hill front. The second one supported a row of fountains whose basin waters spilled down to the third, which held an illuminated pool of white stone lined with peacock-blue tiling. The fourth terrace was given to grass and plants, and it was there that the fireworks crew were working at the final arrangements for the pyrotechnic concert to come later. I could see the figures of the men—Frazier and others of the staff, and a few boys from their families, in their white shirts with the sleeves rolled up so that they dramatized the style of free citizens on an outing, however much during the rest of the year they were decorously confined in the guise of servants—and I could detect in their movements the controlled excitement they felt for the occasion and the form of celebration they would presently release into the darkening summer sky.

As people arrived, I kept to shadows, for a number of reasons. I knew nobody, everybody sounded intimate with each other and spoke in loud, calm calls which seemed to me like a foreign tongue, they were all older than I, though many were of Max's age, and all were so self-assured that I believed they would look at me with blank politeness and move on, if I spoke to them. And there was another reason —they were all wearing dinner jackets to go with the evening frocks of their girls, and I was outcast by my clothes, for none of Max's had fitted me, and I ended by putting on my Dorchester blue suit, which in drying out under the iron of Max's valet had shrunk enough for me to feel it, though Max assured me after I was dressed that I looked "spiffy."

"But you," I said, when he came to my room to drive me to the party, "why aren't you dressed?"

For he too was wearing a blue suit with a long dark tie, just as I was.

"I thought we'd *both* be different, and tell them to go to hell if they didn't like it," he said, with a general smile of rebellion which made him my accomplice in bumpkinry.

"You didn't have to do that," I said.

"Don't be proud," he said. "If it suits me to do it, I do it, and vice versa. The funny thing is, they'll pretend not to notice, but they'll all mention it to each other. Let's go."

He was right, for as people came down from the receiving line, I could see them indicating Max with a glance or a wave, and laughing over him. I had a leap of belief that later when they should happen to notice me, the visiting cousin, dressed as outlandishly, they would suddenly decide that it was really quite distinguished of the two of us to set our own style.

I kept watching for Marietta to arrive with her parents. I had been feeling a strange knot of resentment and excitement about her since the afternoon; but now, alone in this loud and alien throng, I longed for her; and so my eye was on the pavilion most of the time. My cousins were now in their public character, and I could only admire it. Uncle Alec, in his old-fashioned tuxedo that was a bit more loose on him with each passing year, looked, from my distance among the tubbed trees on the terrace, whiter and more frail than before, but his smile was flashing, as he made his birdlike lifts and turns, and his glasses winked, his high handshake with his elbow up seemed like an accolade, and now and then a fragment of his welcome came to me in a sort of stylish shriek which made others turn and laugh, and say, "Alexander is really marvelous tonight," so indicating that his general incapacity was well known, but in a sense admirable, if he could work it up to such a party as this, in such idle magnificence, with such dynastic implications.

For his wife standing beside him was, if you watched from a little way away, for all to recognize the perfect consort for a reigning house. She too was pale, but the fall of light from overhead modeled her with such strong relief that her famous beauty came back upon her, and as she felt that it was being seen again by others who had almost forgotten how beautiful she had been, she was given strength to stand so beautifully erect, to offer a smile so general that was yet taken so particularly, to give her hand so fondly that nobody noticed at the time which hand it was. She wore white kid gloves that reached above her elbows. Her right arm was suspended in a sling of black lace and hung heavily at her waist; but in the lace she had twined a long chain of small diamonds—far from attempting to conceal her deformity she called attention to it by this device, and pleased everyone by putting them at ease to notice the sling and its jewels which as she moved winked like fireflies inside the cloudy lace. Her dress was white, long, and shimmering. She had obeyed her husband to the extent of celebrating the day by wearing a string of rubies, below which was a string of white pearls, which was supported by a string of sapphires. Guests could exclaim at the wit of this, and use their time with her by doing all the talking themselves, which spared her saying much herself, so saving her strength. How wonderful they are together, was what many of them said, seeing with what animation Alexander would relinquish a guest to her, and how she would thank him with a sparkle of her eyes as she accepted her charming duty, and then, how, leaning sweetly to remind Max who it was he must now welcome in his turn, she would make the word "darling," which she meant to be overheard, seem to include playful love as the open secret of motherly pride, and an adult gaiety which took the guest in for tonight as one of the family. It was hard to remember the exhausted and troubled lady whom I had been with at four o'clock that afternoon.

Max in public himself was all she could ask, as he took one after another of the guests in his turn. I was reminded of my first glimpse of him—how he leaned a little forward, his glowing face turned to seek in other faces the nature of their desires, which he would promptly meet—and in certain cases of the old and corrupt or the young and eager who came this evening he would (unspokenly) suggest desires of his own, and invite excesses in their thoughts which if they should ever be revealed he would then laugh at.

While I was observing him from an orderly thicket of tall plants, where spokes of shadow wheeled across the terrace cast by figures that moved in the crowd, a voice said near to my ear,

"I don't know how much longer he can stand it."

I turned.

"Marietta. I was watching for you."

"I came around the other way. I never go down the receiving line."

"They are all being splendid, aren't they?"

"Lissy loathes to be seen, and this means she must put herself for all to see. You know what the locals in society call the Chittendens? They call them the Imperial Family."

"You look lovely."

"A junior hag," she said.

"Oh, no."

"Oh, yes. I am exhausted. Always. Don't I look it?"

In the flickering half-light of the party, I regarded her. Her face was pale, her eyes were deep under her brows, and her face narrowed about her smiling lips which quivered in a tiny spasm now and then. Somehow this suggested wit. She looked ghostly and lovely, in spite of the remote reminders she again gave me of the look of a skull, and of consuming appetite the nature of which was ambiguous, except that the working flare of her nostrils suggested the perennial presence of desire. Unlike the other girls at the party, who wore modish knee-length frocks weighted with crystal fringes and bangles, she was dressed in a long close gown of light silk patterned in leaves and branches of several shades of green, so that her thin, eager, restless figure seemed to be entangled in a thicket of vines. Her hair fell loose on her bare shoulders. She looked small and vital, and I wanted to enfold her protectively with my arms, as if she were an exquisite child escaped from the nursery in her warm, trailing nightgown. With her knack of catching a thought and talking in refraction, she said,

"You are going to save us all. I am so glad, the telegram has been sent."

"You mean to my parents?"

"Yes."

"You know all about it."

"All."

"Does Max?"

"No—only that you were going to be asked. Are you pleased?"

"I—"

"You don't know. You rather hate the feeling that someone is buying you. But you see what is needed and you feel you might do some good. And we are all strange but interesting, and one can learn something from any situation. You half hope they will say no at home, but if they say yes, you won't be sorry. Perhaps this will be a summer you will think of as memorable. But you cannot help the notion that there is something a little unwholesome about having so many odd new friends wanting something they think you can give them." She shrugged. "Or don't you want to talk about it?"

"No, I don't."

"Oh, Richie, as Max calls you, you are priceless. I adore you when you look lofty. It means you are puzzled but refuse to admit it. Do you want to dance? Or be dragged around to meet people?"

"Let's dance."

We moved to the dance floor where she hung upon me, yet not close to me, stepping shortly in her own rhythm, and not facing me but swaying limply at right angles to me. In an elusive way, she was like a small wild creature under restraint. Friends called to her and she flickered at them with the fingers entwined in my hand. The party was suddenly complete. We saw the Imperial Family come down from their place and move slowly to their tables. It was a signal for the dancing to stop and everyone to be seated. Uncle Alec presided at one round table, Aunt Lissy at another, Max at another where places for myself and Marietta were arranged with her between us. Three other couples completed the table. I was not introduced to any of them.

"Oh," said a ripe, brunette girl in a throaty voice, "let's all

be George Washington," and put on her tricorn hat. Everyone glanced at Max. He nodded and put on his hat, at which
everyone else did so. Marietta put her fluttering hand on
Max's arm.

"I *know*," she said, "but it can't last forever. They love it.
You're being superb."

"Richie, am I?" he said, leaning across her toward me.

"If you are," I said, "I don't know what about."

Max and Marietta sighed in concert at my insensitivity.

"Isn't it all divine?" said another girl who sat at my right.
I turned. She was an enthusiastic blonde with a permanent
smile and a clear, lifted voice in which she drawled her
remarks, carelessly confident that they would be of interest
to everyone. "I mean, the Alexanders really are something,
don't you think? I mean, who else gives such divine parties.
I have never seen you here before. Who are you?"

"I am a remote cousin of this family. I have never been
here before."

"Where are you from?"

"Dorchester."

"Delaware?"

"New York."

"Oh, *there*. Good heavens above. Do you hear?" she said
generally, while others turned to hear her. "He's from
Dorchester, New York. Can you bear it? We had a girl from
Dorchester, New York, at school, for a short while. Nobody
could understand a word she said. She was a pretty little
thing, too. She had to leave us because she didn't care for
horses—or perhaps it was the other way round."

"Gwennie, you're awful," said a boy across the table.

"I know, and you love it," she replied. She turned and
pointedly looked at my suit. "Love your suit," she said.

[121]

"And Max's?" asked Marietta, suddenly appearing to her. As she stretched to speak she leaned against me and I could feel her deep quivering energy.

"Oh, and Max's, naturally," said Gwennie. Then she turned away to her partner on the other side.

"Thank you," I said to Marietta.

"She had to be sent packing. Let's us three just make social noises at each other."

Max looked at me with his head lowered. For the benefit of the party he retained his smile. But for me he had a simmering gaze which silently said what he must not say aloud.

"Absolutely *divine*," came at random over the shoulder on my right.

The party was now fully launched.

❧ ❧ ❧

Max took Marietta to dance. I kept my seat. Presently Gwennie turned to me again.

"I'm a dreadful bitch, don't you think?"

"If you think so."

"Oh, come *on*. React."

"There's not much point."

"I suppose not. What do you do, at college, I mean."

"I am in my last year of school. I plan to take a premedical course."

"My dear. I took you for a college man. *Now* won't you forgive me?"

"Why do you want me to?"

"Very well. If you won't keep it *social*, I'll tell you.

Because you are a cousin of Max's, and that means we really ought to be nice to you, because if Max ever gets mad at anyone they have an awful time making up with him, and I *like* being asked here, and my mother would snatch me *bald* if I ever did anything to make trouble for any of us with the *Alexanders*. So now you know why I took any more trouble with you, and now I suppose you will tell Max anyway, so why should I ever *not* be a bitch?"

I laughed out loud at this, and I remember thinking what a remarkable report I could take home to my friends about how children of the rich behaved at Chittenden Hills.

"No," I said, "I won't tell Max anything."

"Say, you're a real prince of a fellow," she said, burlesquing an innocent air. "—Did you know they're engaged?"

"Who."

"Then you don't. Max and Marietta. My mother—all the old people—have been told quietly this evening. No formal announcement. Just intimate family news. No wedding, of course, until after Harvard."

"I see."

"Do you like her?"

"Oh, yes."

"Yes, I can see you do. You really open up to her, don't you? I mean, it's how you look when you talk to her or she talks to you. I can tell by the back of your head."

"You ought to take it up professionally."

"Now who's a bitch."

I was beginning to like her. She thrust and invited, she was working so hard to put forward her own idea of herself, and her inverted style of offensive attention was in the end flattering, as she meant it to be.

The music was slowing to a pause between dances. Max and Marietta returned. She said,

"Gwennie, let him alone. He belongs to us."

I think now of the reflected meanings of this, none of which were consciously intended; but at the time, all I felt was a little chill of apprehensiveness at the note of possession, and I dreaded to know how my parents would reply to the telegram which asked for me. Gwennie ignored Marietta and made a kiss through the air to Max and turned back to her other dinner companion.

"Dance with her," said Max, handing Marietta to me.

"You might let him ask," said Marietta.

"No," I said, "I was going to."

As we went to the dance floor Max took his way off between the tables, turning and twisting among them and pausing as arms and smiles went out to him. He had a word for each, and a kiss here and there, and beyond, I had a shuttered impression of his mother's face, watching him fearfully between the heads and bodies whose relation to him, and to her, and to us on the dance floor, changed as he moved, and we. Aunt Lissy's head was held beautifully erect and her throat was stretched in a regal pose so that a casual glance would seem to collect an impression of a reserved but serenely confident and happy lady of great position enjoying with her devoted husband and her handsome, gifted, and adoring son a simple meeting of friends to observe Independence Day. Banking upon their long history, the Chittendens could be pardoned for making something of a proprietary reference to the Revolution, in terms beyond the appropriate privileges and material means of most others.

We danced a little while more or less on the same spot of the dance floor in obedience to Marietta's habit of ignoring the rhythm, the movement, and the idea of dancing. She said,

"It is idiotic, isn't it."

"What."

"The idea of dancing. I mean people on their hind legs going around face to face in couples to noises made by other people to keep them moving all the same way. I never do."

"I've noticed."

"Let's go and be somewhere."

Holding my hand she took me away to the end of the terrace where high stone urns held flowering bushes whose branches showered down to the terrace floor. In the shadow of one of the urns we sat on the wide balustrade looking out over the valley. Fireflies defined a low ceiling over the meadow floor with their little lost and found lights. The dance band was muffled at the small distance where we were. The dense summer night seemed to have its center in my belly. I was choked with anticipation of I knew not what. The air was heavy and sweet. Down in the valley, with the power to hurt which is part of any universal banality, the lights in Mr Standish's house looked somehow promising and dear, making me wish I had a house with windows lighted at night against the impersonal dark, while inside the house might abide my life with someone I loved.

Marietta took my hand and made her butterfly touch on my upturned wrist. I was flooded with desire and my pulse leaped in my wrist and made me shift my thighs.

"Oh, it is lovely," she said.

"Marietta."

"I mean, to have it respond that way."

I think it was in that moment that I first knew how desire reached outward as well as inward. I took her in my arms. She flinched away into nothing and turned her head away.

"Oh, Richie, let's wait. Nothing is clear."

I held her and then let go. The night was heavy on us again. She breathed in a loud whisper and shook her head and made a groan of longing under her breath.

"What's the matter," I said.

"The same thing. Always."

"Max?"

"Yes. —Richie, what can I do when things engulf him until he has to disappear for a day or a night?"

"What does he do?"

"He says he cannot help it, he does not know what causes it, he does nothing, he just sits somewhere or lies on something, and the tears run down his face. He does not even weep, I mean, with noises and things. But something inside breaks like a dam, or a heart, or something, and he cannot stand anything for a while, but all he can do is be a part of some sorrow of the whole world. And so young! Like tonight. You know? When he left us?"

"But he seemed to be having a beautiful time."

"Oh. It was nearly killing him."

"The party?"

"All of it. Everything. And especially his family."

"But they seem happy."

"Oh, Richie. It is just because you are generally happy. Everyone else seems happy to you. I hope you can always stay that way."

"I'm not any way, particularly."

"Oh, yes you are, and I adore it; but I know more about it than you."

"Can't you help Max?"

"I keep thinking so. I used to be able to, at first, but when he began to see that things were not going to be good again, nothing seemed to help him. We've tried lots of things. You're the latest."

"We?"

"Oh, yes. I keep having ideas."

"Did you tell them to keep me?"

"Yes. —D'you mind? Oh, don't, please, mind. I was so— so desperately pleased when I saw how Max took to you. If you knew. He hasn't taken up anybody new in ages. —Oh, but how can I make you see. Even this, now, with you—he is furious at me underneath because he *knows* without being told that I have tried to give you to him. He hates to be managed, he knows he needs it, and what he misses most is the joy of discovery. Perhaps I have made a dreadful mistake."

"About me?"

"Yes. Perhaps he should have been left to make you love him."

"Oh, I never heard so much talk about love."

"But, darling Richie, all this is about that, and nothing else. In fact, that's all anything is ever about, if you look far enough."

I was so much stirred by this that I must pretend not to be, and so I said,

"It doesn't sound quite decent, to me. Are there no things you won't talk about?"

She sighed and set her head against my arm, like a wishful child.

"It is talk or go mad," she said. "If I had one wish for us all here in the Hills it would be that we would never want to look past the surface of things. That is what is killing Max—feeling and knowing things under the grand outsides of the life he comes from."

"What outsides?"

"Oh: surely you know. His non-father, and his crippled mother. The loss of everything too soon. We are all going to lose everything, but most of us have a chance to get ready. He didn't. —He has such doubts. He remembers such happiness."

"I know. He told me about when he and his sister were young, and his father, and the games they played at the quarry. Uncle Alec was evidently quite a man in those days."

"Oh, yes. Even I can remember. Alexander was a darling —so handsome and such imagination and so much fun. The clever thing to say around here is that Lina murdered him. And when Alicia needed him, he was dead, and he couldn't"—shrug—"anything. And Max lost the mother he knew, and so he has to hate her for it, and of course everybody else, and himself, and everything about his life, and this party, and those Gwennies and Sonnies and Didis and Tooties and Poopsies over there dancing. —My father told me all this. I am too dumb to know it by myself. Aren't you sorry you ever came?"

"I didn't want to."

"I know. I adore the terrible candor of the provinces."

"That's not very nice."

"We don't have to be nice, do we?"

"Not if you're rich enough, I suppose."

"Oh, Richie, I have made you cross. I am sorry. My father

told me years ago to begin by saying half as much as I'd like to. And then to cut what was *left* in half, if I ever wanted to be liked."

"It's all right."

But I was made forlorn by a memory of the city which had shaped my life, Dorchester, of which my father approved so warmly and innocently; and when it was made fun of, as vaudeville comedians always did to raise a sure laugh, I was indignant. I wondered what was so funny about being born in a city in Upstate New York, at the other end of things from New York City, and I would think hotly that people in New York City and Dorchester were both people, and I would ask what could be so different about them? But tonight there were differences to be seen, and these were too new for me to know how I felt about them. That they existed was enough of a shock. I kept silent, watching the lovely net of firefly lights far below. The dance band went silent, too, and in the pause, I heard another sound—drifting under the low clouds from the fold of the hills it was the whistle, given in long phrases, of the night freight train downbound to Olympia. It had a sort of rainy sound, for the night was humid and the air pressed close.

"Oh, how beautiful," said Marietta. "I love to hear it and feel sad—it is so wonderful to have something *there,* and not *here,* to be sad about."

"Let's stop being sad," I said, happy that we had come together again.

And as if in reply to my words, just then, from the lowest terrace below us, with a hissing chord of fiery power into the sky rose a golden curtain of sparks made by the exhausts of twenty rockets which went up in a long row at the same instant. Startled, the guests all gave out a great chord of their own, crying "Oh-h-h!" in a sustained sigh of enchantment. The curtain rose to a ragged edge across the sky, there was an instant of darkness and silence, and then the rockets burst in a line, throwing firelights of green, red, yellow, and rose, which exploded to release showers of diamond white needles falling back from the apex like spray of fountains or fronds of willow trees against the dense summer night. The concert immediately cast a spell against whose dazzle of glory no one who watched could maintain, while it lasted, any visions of his own, especially those which fed on darkness or sorrow. In their act of enchantment supremely innocent, fireworks restored innocence, for the moment, to anyone who watched them.

⚹ ⚹ ⚹

How suddenly a rocket went out at the end of its glory; and how craftily Uncle Alec's crew timed the elements of the display so that there was hardly a pause between one glory and the next. The concert was to last an hour, and for the time I saw of it the heavens were never dark, and there were few outright repetitions of effects. Salutes exploding on high had their bombardment doubled by the echoing hills, and when these were topped by falling stars of red fire we thought of battles and patriots. Arbors of green arcs were woven in the sky, and in turn these were pierced by hissing comets which streaked aloft and still climbing died in wafts of golden sparks which fell slowly into nothing. Gardens of immense gold chrysanthemums were planted high over the meadow—bursts of curly light all radiating from a sun which burned the dark and then joined it. Pagodas rose crown by crown, and in the little pause before each stage took fire, we chanted "Oh-h-h-h" in chorus, and our voices rose each time a new shaft grew from the last, and we ached with delight at how the splendor was protracted, and when at last the pagoda was finished, we still held our breath, thinking another climb and burst would surely come. But before we could measure disappointment, something else went up, and took us with it.

The greatest rockets were those which on reaching the apex made a great soft sound something like a kiss, and then released their fronds of light in falling traceries which seemed to me like a picture of the very nerve tree within the human body. Having it made visible in fancy was like suddenly feeling everything everywhere at each nerve end, a sensation mercifully brief, for its intensity and wholeness must have been impossible to bear for long. Our very flesh was pierced by those threads of light, and we possessed glory and color as part of our being.

I looked about at the rapt faces and tense positions of the guests. I was struck by a notion which, I am sure, would never have come to me at home at such a moment. I thought of what pathos attended the need and fulfillment of play. Playgrounds and amusement parks, fireworks and games, all seemed pathetic monuments to human desperation. Why must our lot be made bearable by spectacle, and what must it be if the longing to be delivered from it even briefly was so constant? How much better, for the most part, people deserved in the way of relief from their human estate than what they were given, usually at considerable expense.

"Oh-h-h-h!" we said again, as the darkness was made bright by a great rise of whirling discs in every color. They filled the sky and seemed to fly away to infinity, growing smaller and yet brighter, until, mere sparks, they seemed to part an invisible curtain and enter another sky where we could not follow.

❦ ❦ ❦

We were holding hands as we watched when Max suddenly stood behind us and leaned over between us.

"Let's all get away from here," he said in an urgent whisper.

We turned. In the light of the fireworks he looked to be carved out of marble. Marietta groaned and put her hand on his face.

"What do you mean," she said.

"We've had enough."

"Yes, of course, though it is lovely. But we can't leave."

"Why not."

"It would look dreadful. It would hurt Alicia. This is supposed to be *our* party."

"Yes. I give it away freely."

"I cannot go. If you want to, go. But I must stay and handle things if people ask for you."

"Come along, Richie," he said, disdaining further discussion. Confident that I would follow, he started toward the steps leading down from the terrace away from the tables. I looked at Marietta.

"Oh, go," she said. "If it wasn't this, it might be something worse. Bring him back in an hour or so."

Feeling that my duties had already begun, I followed Max

down the steps, around the grassy hump beyond the Crystal Palace, and down the driveway until we came to his car. He drove without lights until we were headed away from the Crystal Palace along the quarry road. I was full of things to ask which Max would hate to answer. Feeling this, he drove in silence, refusing to break the wall of privacy which contained him.

The headlights were now turned on, and he drove fast. We rapidly closed on Mr Standish's cottage. I saw and was about to exclaim a warning of what Max saw in the same moment. Standing in the middle of the road, watching us bear down on him, was Chief, the Dalmatian.

"God damn them," cried Max, braking hard, "they're not supposed to let him out!"

Before we skidded to a halt, the dog was dancing alongside our right front wheel trying to bite the tire.

"Careful!" I yelled, "you'll run over him!"

"That's all I need!" exclaimed Max. He jumped from his seat and his dog rose to dance his old dance with him but Max cuffed him down, grasped his collar, and led him through the picket gate to the cottage. There he pounded angrily on the door. I saw a woman's shadow slowly and heavily move on to the frosted glass door panel, and then the door opened. I could not hear what they said, only the blur of their voices. With irritating calm the woman—it was Mrs Standish—took the dog by his collar and drew him into the house, a process which he made as awkward as possible by relaxing into a dead lump of weight. Max returned now freed into speech by his encounter with the gardener's wife.

"The silly cow. What horrors that sort of women are. She thinks it vulgar to do what she is paid to do." He started the car and we were off again. He imitated the woman's bridling whine. "It wasn't her fault. It wasn't Standish's fault. There is a hole under the fence of Chief's pen which they'd been meaning to fill up, but what with Mr Standish, she called him The Mister, being off at all hours in the greenhouse watching for that thing to bloom, and herself so busy around the house, they never—and my! aren't the fireworks just so pretty, she was watching from her bedroom window, and she thought she heard a knock, and so she came to see. —She thinks she will cease to be a lady if she ever admits she's been wrong about anything. Poor Standish. Anyway, she promised to keep Chief in the house till they get the hole filled. My poor dog, living with that sagging slut."

"Max, Max."

" 'Max, Max,' yes, yes. I know."

We came to the ridge and climbed the chattery road. At the top I said,

"We'd better walk down."

"Scared?"

"No."

He turned toward me with a calculating grin, moving his jaw slowly. By the light of the instrument panel he could see that I was not scared. He laughed and said,

"I believe you. Then we'll walk. I only drove back up once after dark and I actually did run the rear wheel off the edge. They had to come and haul me back onto the road."

He left the car on the ridge. With a flashlight he took from under the seat he showed our way down to the quarry lake. We walked out to the point of the Peninsula and climbed up on the limestone blocks which looked like architecture. From there, the air was black, the high chiseled walls blacker, and the water blacker still. It took minutes for my eyes to become adjusted to the cup of darkness where we were, and all seemed quiet. But slowly the senses reached for the world outside, and I could see, as though I were pressing upon my eyes with the lids shut, a wavering faint glow in the far sky, a wash of light cast on the low clouds by the fireworks four or five miles away. I watched hoping to see a rocket reach its dying height above the quarry walls so far above us; but never did. And too, in the quiet I began to hear the faintest reduction of the explosions from the airy salutes at Newstead, and then nearer to us I could hear the murmur of summer creatures, an occasional flap and splash of a fish, and the threading song of distant crickets. A great trembling seemed to hover above the stillness which was made of so many combined live sounds. By the contrasts slowly made manifest in sky and air, the lake seemed to be deeper and darker than ever, a pool of oblivion, a world nowhere and welcoming, to a self lost and searching.

We sat in silence for perhaps a quarter of an hour. Was I supposed to break the quiet? "How peaceful," I might say— but though I could hardly see him, my cousin beside me was held by anything but peace, for if he was silent, he seemed to be using silence as a refuge from powers which menaced him from within and without. How was I supposed to help him? How could I know what he wanted not of me so much as of his life? At last I heard him move—I could hear the small moist sound of his eyes as he rubbed them roughly. When he spoke it was with his familiar air of mockery but his voice was choked.

"When was the last time *you* shed tears?" he asked with almost a dry, professional inflection.

"I would have to remember."

"Tell me why you did, and where. How long ago?"

"It isn't very interesting."

"Never mind. Go on."

"Why, I think it was two years ago when I broke my arm tobogganing in Commodore Perry Park. The run was icy and I missed a turn and flipped over. It was when they picked me up. It hurt so that I couldn't help it, I felt the tears running down my face and I couldn't stop them for several minutes. But finally I did."

"You are right, it is not very interesting. You were not really *shedding tears* about something. Physical pain is of no importance."

"I suppose not. But you asked me."

"Yes, I asked you. And I have asked others. And nobody can tell me."

"Max?"

"Yes?"

"What is it?"

A pause. Then,

"Are you going to stay?"

"Oh. I won't know until I hear from my parents."

"Do you like them?"

"Yes, I do."

"Do you want to stay?"

"Partly yes. Partly no."

"A just reply, most potent, grave, and reverend signior. I could phrase it better, but the substance is surely proper. —Do you hate beauty?"

"Good God, of course not."

"Do you hate staying well by keeping busy?"

"God, I don't know."

"Don't be impatient. These are great questions. And so is this one: do we find true happiness only when we live **for** others without regard for self?"

Mocking the precepts played at him at home in that house of invalids, he was trying to show me something of life which unless it engulf him he must despise, and despising, fight against. He talked on in the darkness. His thoughts were not consecutive, but they were all radial to his central unhappiness, about the nature of which there were many theories but no proofs.

Doctor Osborne had used his privilege of old retainer now and then to advise Max to seek professional help for his "nerves." But Max told him that he felt intelligent enough to find his own cure for what ailed him. Doctor Osborne sighed and disagreed, knowing what he knew, but not risking any direct reference to it, and aside from keeping a keen eye on him, he let Max alone, obviously waiting for the moment when Max would no longer be able to make a show of rationalized resistance. Meanwhile, though he was willing to let Max and his daughter be the closest of companions, he withheld his approval of an official engagement—hence tonight's seepage of romantic information through the medium of matronly gossip. In due course if all went well with Max he would be happy to bless the union. But not yet. Not yet. The idea occurred to Max that Doctor Osborne was entertaining in thoughts to which he denied full daylight the idea that time and mortality would resolve Max's difficulty. When he came into his inheritance, when his parents died, when he need not hate what he loved too well in memory, Max would probably be fully one man instead of a collection of fragments from his own childhood, and from the youth of his parents, and from the bored, fastidious, languid, but brilliant Max of Harvard. People went to such lengths to "understand" him that they ended by misunderstanding him into unreality. The black water in the quarry, whose every rock and ledge and face he knew so well above the water, held depths he could only imagine. Did they only mirror what was above? How would he ever know? When did his life turn into an eternal question, while the lives of other young men seemed arrogantly and joyfully to be certain, however wrongly, only of answers?

I heard a reflection of his voice in that rocky cup. I asked, "Is there an echo here?"

"Ai, God," he said. Then in a deliberately restrained voice he said, "When we were little we talked to it all the time. We never saw it, but we knew it lived here, and we used to think of things to ask it. It always answered. If you want to hear it, I can summon it up for you. —All right." He stood up and drew a deep breath, and then in a tremendous voice, he cried out one word four times, lengthening it as far as his breath would let him:

"Howl, howl, howl, howl!" —and the great palatial rocky walls threw it back at us and then echoed their own echo, and I heard "Howl—owl—owl—wl—l . . ." and though I did not then know where his word had come from, it plumbed me with a weight of dread which pressed my heart down, down.

When the echo had returned to the silence where it lived, we said nothing for a moment, and then Max said,

"Do you want to try it?"

"No, thanks."

"No, there is little use. All you discover is that every question is finally its own answer."

It was the kind of remark which meant nothing or everything, and I was not at ease with such. Kindly accepting my silence,

"Smoke?" he asked, taking his cigarettes and a briquet from his pocket.

"No, thanks."

"You don't ever?"

"No."

He lighted his cigarette. His shapely head bent over the flame, his high color, the tawny marble of his hands carved out by the brief light, gave a picture of such fine health that I was startled, for what he had been trying to say for so long and dark an interval had made a different likeness of him— that of an invalid being drawn helplessly into the illness all around him, which he had helped to create.

"Why don't you smoke. Do you disapprove?"

"No, I don't disapprove. Years ago, my father promised me a thousand dollars when I reach twenty-one if I promised not to smoke until then. I promised."

"So now," said Max to whom a thousand dollars was not a fortune, "you don't want to lose a thousand dollars?"

"It isn't the thousand dollars, though I can't sneer at it as you can. But what I don't want to lose is my promise."

My cloddish virtue exasperated him, with its terms of innocence and honor. He said, envious of the settled simplicity of my life,

"How do you know your father will keep his? Great God, haven't you ever taken a straight look at life? Don't you know even yet that nothing is what it seems to be? When are you going to wake up?"

But under his words something else said: Richie, Richie, don't ever wake up; and I knew long later that the very thing everyone hoped to purchase of me for Max was that part of my father and mother's abiding faith which I carried in me—their faith in whatever it was which created instead of destroyed.

"If my father is alive when I reach twenty-one, he will keep his promise," I said.

"Ah, God," he said, cast down even further by what he had not credited me with—the ability to contemplate with calm, though surely never to experience without grief, such a catastrophic event as the death of the father. If Max was frantic as we escaped from the fireworks party—"festival for the peasants," he had said—now he seemed deeply depressed by his conversation with me, which was just the opposite of what was supposed to come from our healing contact. He sat and smoked in silence with his head turned away until his cigarette was gone. Then abruptly he stood up and began to haul off his clothes.

"Let's take a swim," he said.

"I'll wait for you."

"You don't want to?"

"Not specially."

"The water is cold."

"Yes. It isn't that. I'd rather just sit here and feel the night."

My flesh threw out goose pimples and my teeth made as if to chatter, but I bit my jaws together. It was a close, hot night. How could I shiver?

"Then a good night to you," he said, and dived off the great limestone cube and vanished into the black. Would he come back? I asked myself, and then I recoiled from the question, asking why anything like that should ever occur to me.

✹ ✹ ✹

The summer night pulled all the rankness of the country-
side into the heavy air. I listened for water sounds but heard
nothing. Across the quarry rim the distant lights came and
went in the sky but gave no illumination here. It was like
seeing the dying flicker of a hearth fire gone so low that its
last cast of color was not rosy but wan pale. The fall of
another coal or two, a final spark, and all would be dark. I
thought of calling out his name, but for fear of seeming
foolish if he should answer, I kept silent. I held my breath to
hear without the drumming of my pulse. Somewhere an
owl spoke—a small one, by the sound. What would they say
if I returned without him? First I must find Marietta and if
necessary put my hand over her mouth to keep her from
crying out when I told her my news. Then we would have
to find a stratagem to take Alexander and Alicia away from
the terrace party without having anyone notice anything.
Could we say that the head gardener wanted them briefly in
the Crystal Palace, perhaps because the night-blooming
cereus was showing signs of movement in its folded buds?
And then beyond the crowd of guests, we would go in a
motorcar back to the hilltop house, and there my duty
would end with the news I brought. Surely it would be wise
to ask Doctor Merriman Osborne to be with us at that
moment. Nobody would shed tears but Uncle Alec, who
would turn his narrow head aside and extending his long
neck in birdlike thrusts, would then release a series of
broken dry sounds which would sound more like illness
than grief. A few cars would presently come up the driveway with people who would want to know if anything was
wrong. What instinct would have brought them? A word

would have to be sent at once to the estate work force to go to the quarry with lights, ropes, a boat, a Pulmotor, perhaps a salute cannon to fire across the water in classical fashion to bring up by its vibrations any burden held by the deep. Such activity would be impossible to conceal. In an instant the entire throng of guests would have the news, and face each other with it in horror and excitement. How could it possibly have happened? He had been such a superb swimmer—so excellent that, because of his prep school record in the pool, he had been asked at Harvard to join the varsity squad, which he had disdained to do. Someone was sure to say that something like this could have happened all through the years, the quarry lake had long been a menace, and nobody had heeded warnings that it should be drained and dried up for good. Over Newstead and its impregnable evidences of great position the fates would seem to be gathered, as if one success in calamity after another deserved still another. How would it be possible to look into Aunt Lissy's face as she was turned and taken up the long wing-like curve of the grand staircase to her room and ultimate solitude? Before daylight the reporters and photographers would be everywhere. The efficient apparatus of disaster would come into play for the satisfaction of all who could read.

I could not be still with my racing thoughts. I clambered down from the blocks and tiptoed—why I tiptoed I did not know—feeling my way to the edge of the Peninsula as if to see and hear better. I felt like a prisoner in a palatial dungeon whose invisible chains were made of darkness itself. But where was the flashlight? I returned to the rocks and felt for it everywhere but could not find it. I did not know whether five minutes had passed or a half hour. I looked across the lake toward the opposite limestone wall. If I called out my voice would echo strongly, and surely there would be an answer from some quarter of the sheer cavity? Then I saw a long edge of most dim pale light along the top of the wall. It revealed the crest, and as I watched transfixed, it traveled with breathless slowness down the limestone face, throwing into dark relief against the stone the occasional ledges where foliage had rooted and grown in a wonderful persistence of life out of siftings of dust caught in invisible crevices. I turned, and there over the other crest was rising a hazy quarter moon which as it rose sent its light down the far quarry wall and must eventually show it all, and touch the water. How long this would take I could not calculate, but my entire will was bent to join the rising of the moon, as though I could hasten its movement, for if there was light, however remote and confusing, I would not feel buried in mystery and solitude.

"Yes," I said aloud, in an idle tone calculated to sound reassuring, "perhaps it is time to go."

I turned my head to listen for a reply. None came. My body seemed compact of a silent groan which if it could have been heard would have said, "No, no, no, please."

I went to the blocks, climbed up, and lay down on my back to watch the sky and the moon. I was trapped with them in the inexorable design of the passage of the heavenly bodies. Like the heavy air itself, my underthoughts hung under a misting atmosphere of dread into which flickers of reasonableness tried to penetrate. But like the shadows in the summer undergrowth at night, everything conscious within me merged into a single depthless form, which slowly made itself felt as a knot of suspense and desire, hunger and shame—for what, except for life itself, I could not say. Later,

I knew how any extreme of feeling—grief, rage, relief—
could find expression, however inappropriate it might seem
at the moment, in an act of sex.

I suddenly sat erect.

What sound was that—what touched the water with a
little slap?

I turned my head. I heard it again. Then I heard the long
luxurious indraught of the swimmer lazily rolling aside for
his breaths in an Australian crawl of, surely, perfect form. It
was my cousin returning. I felt a thump of relief in my
chest, immediately followed by a prickling gather of anger.
My wild concern, with its ceremonies of the imagination,
now seemed childish and idiotic. I was humiliated by it.
Before I would let it show to Max, I would perjure myself. I
lay back on the rock and rolled to my side and curled myself
in a position of sleep, and pretended to be asleep when he
climbed up dripping to the edge of the Peninsula and came
to the block where he had left his clothes. There was now
enough moon for him to see me.

"Richie?" he called.

I slept on, disgusted at having been a fool.

Max laughed gently and began to dress. In his coat he
found cigarettes and lighter and began to smoke. The little
flame, the smell of tobacco, made a distraction which I could
recognize with dignity as a reason to wake up. I awoke.

"Hello," I said sleepily, sitting up.

"Hello. What time is it?"

"I don't know how long I've been sleeping."

"Were you concerned about me?"

"Asleep?"

"I see."

"Did you have a good swim?"

"Mostly under water. I wanted to see the view from Lethe. I've always believed an underground river ran below the quarry. The upper world would look quite different from there. The quarry is my entrance to the underworld. I went to be washed of my other life."

"And were you?"

"I won't know until I return to it again."

"Then you weren't, if it is still there."

"What are you so irritable about?"

"I hate to be waked up."

"I don't think you were really sleeping."

"You don't?"

"No, and I believe you were beginning to be worried when I stayed away so long, especially before the moon came up. You couldn't find the flashlight, could you."

"I didn't look for it."

"I put it in my shoe so I would be able to find it if I ever wanted to. You wouldn't think of looking there."

Unguardedly, I said,

"No, I didn't."

"So you did look."

"What of it."

"You were concerned for me," he asserted calmly.

Was it this he had gone to find out? How many suicides have been aborted by vanity, the curiosity of the self-victim to know the effect of his act? What pleasure remains in punishing someone if you don't know what you have made them feel? It was too much to admit, and moreover, it needed no further admission. He seemed content for the first time that night. To some degree, anyhow, he knew that I thought of him, and with concern. Our bickering annoyed me further, while it gave a small lift to his spirits. Suddenly again in his attitude of command, he said energetically,

"Let's go back. It must be late."

In silence I followed him up the ragged trail on the side of the ridge. He played his flashlight about with bravado, as if its beam were a rapier. Our return was so much less spectacular than the one I had agonized over in the dark by the quarry lake that I preserved my silence as a measure of dignity and reproof. What could I say to him? I could hardly say that I was glad he had returned safely without confessing below the words that I had thought of the alternative; and no more could I reproach him for not drowning without admitting that I regretted the loss of the sensational consequences which would have followed. Max, too, said little, only remarking as we drove up toward Newstead,

"Richie, I'm beginning to think you are a very complicated individual."

Nor could I protest this without claiming to be simple, and, so, not very interesting.

As we approached the Crystal Palace we saw that its grand illuminations were turned off. A few figures moved here and there in the limited light of ordinary work. The staff were restoring order after the party. Everyone else had gone.

So we must after all have been at the quarry for a matter of hours—two or more? The moon was high above the horizon. Its washy light made the countryside insubstantial, and the mists of long after midnight muffled the night creatures in their secret lodgments.

Running on to Newstead, we saw the house dark but for the main portico and lobby. No one was there—or so we thought until we came in. Max's mother was waiting in a huge brocaded armchair near the foot of the stair. When she saw us she rose and we went to her. She had put off her red, white, and blue jewels and had folded about herself a dressing gown as plain as a linen sheet. She wore a ravaged look, and now that she saw that her son was home, whatever effort of self-supporting control she had kept up in her vigil fell away, and cradling her carved hand she seemed to diminish in her bones and sway on her feet. Max moved to steady her but she nodded him away imperiously. We stood before her. She turned to go upstairs, but paused facing me. She looked into my face—to read what? I did not know. But so intense was her look that I was aware only of her eyes— dark coals of burning spirit in the long, blank oval of her face. The anguish and energy of her wondering, all gathered in her gaze, made the powdered skin about her eyes tremble uncontrollably. Max lounged nearby, but she did not look at him. She seemed to indicate that anyone who could abandon his social duty and be rude to a hundred guests, not to mention his parents and his all but fiancée, need not detain the interest of any responsible person. But as for me: who but myself could be interrogated with justice about the matter? Who else had been asked to assume a splendid responsibility? Who else had betrayed it either through compliance or—worse—inspiration? If I was to blame, I must be made to feel blameworthy. Where had he taken me—or I him? Why? Was this what trust came to, always? I could read such notions in her regard, and I felt a spurt of anger at my bondage and the injustice which accompanied the views of the rich. I made to speak, but she closed her eyes in tragic patience, silencing me by her choice of misery. Then disentangling her closed gaze from its mesh of lashes,

[147]

she looked long into my—I think this was the word she would have me use—my conscience; then she turned and with infinite weariness made her way upstairs.

❦ ❦ ❦

When I closed my eyes in the dark of my room I still saw the eyes of my cousin Alicia trembling in formless pale light. What made her wonder so, and look so into my heart, to discover what I knew of her son? Why had we vanished during such an important family festival? What had we fled from, what had we fled to? With what faith—broken or reaffirmed—did we return? Had we seen death? Life? Love? Despair? Futility? I could only dissolve her remembered gaze by opening my eyes and when I did so, I was once again the creature of a hostile summer.

The hum of summer was like the fever in my ears and in my bones which summoned me to manhood. Awake and mighty with desire I felt the hot meadows beyond my open window. Their scent, moving heavily on the slowly stirring air, smelled of generation—sap, crushed vegetable pungency, cast seed, snowy bark, dried sea foam, the ozone of wet minerals, the salt of tears and kisses. I begged of the dark to be let go, or granted consummation. The little motors of crickets sounding away in the multitudinous summer night seemed to eat mindlessly into the edges of my conscious mind. To resist such an invasion I must summon thought, any thought, and I remembered that country where I was the ruler, which I entered whenever I took a book to read.

Our house at home (the night began to lift its pressure as I thought of this) was full of the dark red leather volumes of Everyman's Library. My father would often come home with a package of five or six of the volumes and let me unwrap them. They had intricate gold designs on the spines in the manner of the Pre-Raphaelites, vines and leaves intertwined, and it was usually I who had first claim on the new volumes. I was not permitted to take them to my room on the top floor unless I could state that my schoolwork was all done; but if it was, there was no limit to the time I could spend with Everyman's. —I now was able to shut my eyes with safety, and instead of the stinging night, or Alicia's anguished wondering, I saw the backbones of our books, and I told over all the titles I could remember. I remembered a little scene of one time when my father had brought us some new books of the series, which lay rich and unsullied on the table in the living room. My mother took up one of the volumes and with a gaiety which abandoned her to a piece of drama in the presence of her husband and her son, while my father stood smiling at her with his arm around me, she read aloud in a lovely pealing tone of intimate belief in life's good things, so that we all had the same heady feeling: "Everyman, I will go with thee, and be thy guide, In thy most need to go by thy side"—the motto printed on the flyleaf of all the volumes, of which we had so many. In this modest cultural possession, which stood for more than itself, we all felt learned and lucky, valorous and faithful.

All the next day Newstead was silent. During the morning a message was brought to me that Mr Dana, the librarian, would like to see me in the library.

"The secretary thought we should give you this, although it is addressed to Mrs Chittenden. She is resting, so is Mr Chittenden, and Max is out of the house."

He handed me a telegram. It was sent by my father, granting permission for me to remain at Newstead for as long as pleased my cousins, provided I would be home for a week before schooltime, and provided further that all arrangements to remunerate me for my presence be dropped. My mother would send by express various articles of clothing and other things I might need for an extended stay.

"Thank you," I said to Mr Dana.

"It will be nice: to have you with us," he said. "Please use the library as much as you like. Max often spends hours here."

"Is he interested in Byron?"

"Ah: yes: the collection is the only thing at Newstead which appeals to him. But he reads everything else, too. We get the new books mainly for his sake. He likes to give me lists. A game—I make my own list of the new books, and when he brings his, we check them against each other to see how well I have guessed what he would like."

"Do you make a good score?"

"Quite: he is quite a remarkable young man. We often wonder what he—" He paused with the tact of a gentleman and the discretion of an employee.

"Wonder what?"

"My wife and I are extremely fond of him, he comes to

supper with us now and then, he adores our children, and we wonder what he will really do with himself. We can see how hard it is for someone in his special sort of position to decide what really interests him, and what he will spend his life at."

"He won't go into the Chittenden business, I suppose."

"Never. The last thing. He reads a great deal of science, but the big questions, he says, are not matters of fact but of feeling. Lately he has been reading miles of poetry. One day not long ago I asked him something, and he laughed and said he had been wanting to ask me what I thought of the same thing."

"What was it?"

"I asked him why he didn't make teaching his profession—studies of literature, chiefly poetry. And he said he had already been thinking of that. I think he would make a wonderful teacher. And you know?—it is one of the only things that an impossibly rich man can have as a vocation without seeming to have bought his way, or else remain an amateur."

"What do they think at Harvard?"

"His marks have suddenly improved almost out of sight. Next year, his last, should be his most brilliant; and of course: I think he ought to go right on and take his master's and doctor's degrees without interval; and then go to teach somewhere. —What do you think?"

He looked at me rather sidelong, from behind his thick dark-rimmed glasses. He was small, neat, gently spoken, and hungry for a little touch of the world beyond Chittenden Hills, and even I, a prep school senior, could bring him something that he, as a doctor of philosophy, a recognized expert on Byron, and the father of two young children with another expected in a few weeks, could find interesting. But possibly he was asking me without words what I really thought of the prospects of any future for Maximilian. He was not sure of just the degree to which I might be considered "family" at Newstead, and so he invited my comment by hints and glances rather than by frank exposure of the clear thoughts behind his large lenses and alert black eyes. He was the same Andrew Dana who ten or twelve years later began to publish a series of successful stylishly "intellectual" novels which belonged to the end rather than to the beginning of a tradition, and so never had much influence or any imitators. But his dart of mind and charm of manner were in his pages, and reading them long afterward in their seasons I could hear his well-bred voice, and the comic accents with which he invested serious affairs, as if I, his early audience at Newstead, and the large public which rewarded him later, were all at about the same superior schoolboy level. He made up for being a man small in stature by taking cheeky risks now and then in what he might say, and at such moments he invited forgiveness in advance by the candid self-mockery of his smile, while rocking from side to side on his excellent English brogans.

He seemed always to be watching himself, and speaking for his own pleasure. There was something of all this manner in his books. The best known of these was a set of three novels which he called *Ruins by Moonlight: A Gothic Trilogy,* and its separate volumes reflected well enough what he knew about Newstead: Volume One, *The Abbey,* Volume Two, *The Heir,* and Volume Three, *The Quarry.* He published also a speculative biography called *In Search of Lord Clare,* about the friend of Byron's long-cherished youthhood passion.

"I think Max would be a fine teacher," I said. "He always seems to go direct to what interests him. Students would like that. He could make things seem simple."

"Ah. But do you think him simple?"

"Oh, no, not himself. —And he doesn't think anybody else is, either. He told me yesterday that I was complicated."

"And aren't you?"

"I never thought about it. I don't think I am."

"Do you ever have dreams?"

"Oh yes."

"And do they seem at odds with your waking world?"

"Often."

"And isn't that complicated?"

"I suppose so. —But the dreams don't really seem like me. I have no control over them."

"Ah. Ah. My dear fellow: perhaps I should not inform you: but we are everything that happens to us, including those things we cannot control. Once you know that, you cease to be simple. And knowing so is to pass a certain stage of life irreversibly and forever. It is a *kind* of loss of a *kind* of virginity—" with a gleam on the last word which must have caused any prep school class to break into rowdy laughter. I laughed.

"The Family are invisible today," he said. "Would you lunch with me here?" He was desperate to have anyone to talk to, even a sixth-former.

"Thank you."

He used the house phone on his desk and told the pantry that there would be two for luncheon in the round conservatory. Then,

"Yes," he resumed, "the trouble is: if it is a trouble: that once you are aware that everything is complicated, you never

[153]

can get away from it. Anything that you once saw as simple seems like a reproach and a mystery once you are taken beyond it. It ought to be quite the other way round. But there it is."

"But many people never even think about it."

"Or anything, of course. —But others, like Max, for example, see all aspects of everything at once, and if you do that, how do you know which one is the one that belongs truly to you? Is it luck? It may just be luck. Perhaps it all depends on how lucky—that is, how creative instead of destructive—our early dreams are. Perhaps they establish for us in our youth the principle of our choices in the world. But yes: oh heavens yes: they must be true dreams, that is, they must come to us unconsciously, and only later have some meaning. Otherwise there is real danger in what they might do to us."

"I don't think I understand."

"Ah: I am clumsy: I mean of course that if dreams cease to be unconscious, and begin to be asked for consciously, or if they come from events we have known consciously which have the power of nightmare, then: then: something about them sets us in their light forever, perhaps." He looked at me with his signal of daring, the smile which said he was going to step beyond the station to which the munificence of Alexander Chittenden had summoned him, and said (to a member of the family!), "I have wondered if Max's at times unsettling behavior might result from confusions once known face to face but long forgotten in the upper mind while they continue to propose denials and defiances in the lower."

We were called to the conservatory. On our way out of the great dusky room we came to a heavy and highly polished

Renaissance table on which a single object rested. From a pinpoint aperture in the center of a gilded rosette in the coffered ceiling high above came a narrow cone of light which cast an island of soft glow upon the center of the table; and in it rested a bronze sculpture of Leda and the Swan. Mr Dana paused and looked upon it.

"It could hardly be more explicit, do you think?" he said invitingly.

And yes, it was a bronze enactment, in the most passionate elegance, of the union of Leda and Zeus the almighty father. I remembered the story from my schoolbook of Gayley's *Classic Myths,* but I never thought to see so intimately that godly embrace enfolding the queenly body whose head lay back in wonder while her eyes gazed out of sight in ecstasy at the divine invisible. Classical rapes in art always made me thoughtful in the youthful days of my awakened but unsatisfied desire, and in museums I gave my attention less to mythology than to anatomy. Now I could not help the bent of my thought toward a perhaps unworthy but quite practical question. How did the swan actually manage what he was about? A breathing quilt of white feathers? A secret portal of pulsing smooth flesh? What possible union? But then I remembered of course that since he was a god, explanations were beside the point. The statue was perhaps fourteen inches high. I wanted to touch it but refrained.

"Jacopo Sansovino," said Mr Dana. "1486–1570. We sent photographs to Mr Berenson. We have two letters from him here. In the first he gave it firmly to Jacopo, and Mist' Chittenden was delighted. Then came the second in which B.B. said that on further study of the photographs, he would have to say 'Follower Of.' Consternation. We then had Duveen down to look at it, and he didn't hesitate. He said he would be proud to acquire it as a Sansovino for Mr Frick at twice what Mist' Chittenden paid for it, whatever that might be. Relief and joy. But of course there was no idea of letting it go. —The Metropolitan has since asked for it, too."

We were supposed to be going in to lunch, but Mr Dana was held by the Leda, though he saw it a hundred times a day. He put his hand on it and reminiscently traced the serpentine curve of the swan's neck.

"Yes," he said in daydream; and then grew brisk and professional in a librarianly way. "Yes, this: it has just come from Chatto and Windus." He held up an almost square slim volume of poetry called *Leda*. "By Huxley's grandson," he said. "Listen to this—" and he read from the poem in a voice which at first he caused to bleat artificially as if to strike me with the power of poetry as a universal classroom instrument:

"Closer he nestled, mingling with the slim
Austerity of virginal flank and limb
His curved and florid beauty, till she felt
That downy warmth strike through her flesh and melt
The bones and marrow of her strength away.
One lifted arm bent o'er her brow, she lay
With limbs relaxed, scarce breathing, deathly still,
Save when a quick, involuntary thrill
Shook her sometimes with passing shudderings,
As though some hand had plucked the aching strings
Of life itself, tense with expectancy.
And over her the swan shook slowly free
The folded glory of his wings, and made
A white-walled tent of soft and luminous shade
To be her veil and keep her from the shame
Of naked light and the sun's noonday flame."

[156]

Losing its make-believe, his voice went dry and he looked aside with a truly suffering glance at another world, and the sting of tears seemed to sound in his voice when he resumed and finished the poem:

"Hushed lay the earth and the wide, careless sky.
Then one sharp sound, that might have been a cry
Of utmost pleasure or of utmost pain,
Broke sobbing forth, and all was still again."

He softly shut the book and with bent head restored it to the rack of current publications. He blinked his eyes free of the Attic skies, and said,

"Yes, we must go to lunch," and again began to lead me from the library. But after a few rocking steps he paused and began to laugh.

"But the best part: perhaps you haven't heard the best part of our Leda story—unless Mist' Chittenden told it to you yesterday?"

I shook my head.

"Oh, really priceless," said Mr Dana. "About the new housekeeper and Leda?"

"No, really," I said.

"Well, if Mist' Chittenden does tell it to you, you must pretend not to have heard it before. It always makes him laugh to tell it."

I promised.

"Yes: well: a while ago we engaged a new housekeeper, and Miss Magruder was showing her around the place. They came in here, and the housekeeper—she was a bony old thing got up in black alpaca—ran her finger along the table looking for dust, and suddenly she saw the Leda there in the center. She stopped and gasped, and said to Miss Magruder, 'My stars! *what's that duck up to!*'"

We both laughed, and this time we really marched on to the conservatory where lunch was waiting.

"I might add that the housekeeper did not last here very long. Somehow not quite our tone, don't you know. —But I have reflected on the episode many times, in relation to the optimistic belief that great art sanctions any subject matter. You know?"

I said I did, and then as we took our places amidst the greenery which gleamed with fine drops of spray recently syringed over the tropical leaves, I asked,

"Where do you suppose Max is?"

"He didn't tell you?"

"No."

"Nor me. I don't know. His man simply said he'd gone out early leaving a note saying he wouldn't be back for lunch."

"Do you suppose he went to the quarry?"

"I don't know. —Have you been there with him?"

"Yes. Yesterday afternoon, and then again last night."

"Oh. Ah. So that's where you went last night. I rather thought as much. —He always goes there when those times overtake him."

"Times?"

"Or you might prefer to say moods. But moods is a trivial word for what comes to him. —The quarry seems to have almost a mystical fascination for him. How often I have seen him go past our little place to the ridge and up the road and over. In winter vacations when the quarry is frozen he goes there to skate, and in summer, to swim, and sometimes for a whole day he will go there with books and come back after dark."

"He said the quarry is his entrance to the underworld."

Mr Dana put down his knife and fork and gazed at me.

"Ah: yes: ah: you see? As I said? It is that sort of conscious dream I meant. Do you see? Is it—can anything be—truly a legend if one makes it deliberately?"

I shook my head. I did not understand.

I remembered later that all during lunch, whenever I handed Mr Dana something he could not reach at the table, he did not take it direct from me, but waited fastidiously until I had set it down and taken my hand away; only then would he take it up in turn.

಼ ಼ ಼

It was a day of messages. Late in the afternoon Marietta telephoned to me to say that Max was with her, they were getting things together right now, we three were going to the quarry for a picnic supper, with nobody else along. We were going to swim and drink beer (excellent Canadian beer purveyed to Max by his bootlegger) and think up things to do for the rest of the summer now that it was known that I was to remain until late August. They would come for me within the hour. Dress sloppy, Max said, and bring a large towel. We would stop for Chief and he would swim with us. Max wanted the concertina from his cluttered sitting room—would I please look for it and have it with me at the rear terrace when they called for me? He did not want to come into the house for fear of getting involved.

[159]

Presently there was another telephone call. Miss Magruder, the secretary, whom I never saw, was asked by Mrs Chittenden to say that Mr Standish had telephoned from the greenhouses with an alert about the night-blooming cereus—it was certain to open tonight, and, in his opinion, during the late evening, if the twilight were overcast. Mrs Chittenden wanted the household to gather for dinner on the terrace at the Crystal Palace so as to be readily at hand when the flower began to move. Cars would be waiting at a quarter before seven to take us down the hill. Mr Chittenden was resting and did not plan to come, but Mrs Chittenden expected everyone else, including the Danas, as Mr Dana would be "taking notes." Mr Maximilian, she hoped, would take photographs. Could Miss Magruder tell Mrs Chittenden that I would be there?

I explained about the picnic.

In that case, she would telephone to Miss Osborne at once and ask her to rearrange her picnic plans, for Mrs Chittenden of course wanted her also to be with us, as well as Mr Maximilian.

Should I wait to know what to do?

No, thought Miss Magruder, I could assume that the picnic was canceled, as Mrs Chittenden particularly wanted everyone with her at a moment which meant so much to her.

—So much to her who had so little else to excite her interest or happiness, I knew, and I knew that the event of the cereus held more than merely the tyranny of a hobby. During how many hours had my cousin Alicia thought about the slow gathering of forces within the impassive cactus plant, and wondered when it would come in flower, and whether she would be present to see it, and if anyone

[160]

else might possibly realize what it would mean to her to see it? In her helplessness she, who no longer made acts of charm and objects of beauty with her hands, had faithfully given of what she possessed—her interest, money, and time —to assure the *cereus grandiflora* the fulfillment of its cycle. Surely those who loved her and whom she loved would of their own hearts wish to be with her tonight?

But it was too much to hope for from Max. My telephone rang again and he spoke to me.

"Forget this commotion about the Crystal Palace tonight. I told my mother's secretary we would not come. She said you already told her about the picnic. The picnic still holds."

"No," said Marietta, taking the phone from him, "I told Max and I tell you we must; Richard, we must go with Aunty Lissy. Just tonight. It wouldn't matter any other time. But we are going to be with her if she wants us, and she does."

"I think we should, too," I said.

"You see?" she said to Max behind her, "you can't have a picnic alone. Let's just have ours tomorrow night, and tonight we'll—"

There was a stormy mutter off-phone, and Marietta relayed it to me.

"He says he hates to have anyone change his plans for him. Oh, yes, and so do I. But tonight is different.—What?" she asked turning her sound away from the phone and listening to Max beyond her somewhere. Then, "All right, I'll tell him," she said, facing her words toward me over the phone again. "Max says we have to have this picnic for a special reason."

"What special reason?" I asked.

[161]

She turned and repeated my question and came back with an answer.

"He says he has to get back something he gave you."

"Gave me?" I said. "He didn't give me anything."

Pause, inquiry, return, while my mind's eye watched them in their exchanges.

"Yes he did,'" she reported, "he says he did. He says it was an idea of himself that he gave you, and he says he has to get it back, and give you another."

I was exasperated by this complicated exchange, with its suggestion of negotiations through a neutral party, and yet I was also ready to laugh at it. An idea of himself? I frowned trying to remember, but could not. All I could think of was his concern of this moment, and that seemed very like him.

"What?" asked Marietta, turning to Max again. "Oh. Of course. Why not. —Richie, he says we'll go to see the damned cactus perform, if we are all being so dull about it; but he says we'll go to the quarry anyway, afterward. He says we should probably stay all night on the Peninsula, without telling anyone, the three of us. Would you like that?"

"Oh, yes."

At the suggestion, and its formless promises, a little spray of desire seemed to go throughout me, along my nerves. I laughed, and at how I sounded, Marietta laughed, too, in an involuntary betrayal of unexpected excitement, as if I had suddenly forced her breath by laying my head below her breasts and pressing it hungrily upon her soft belly. She broke the spell by turning again to Max.

"What?"

But Max had come closer and I heard his own voice.

"Tell him that there are only three creatures I love on this earth—my girl, my cousin, and my dog. Don't you ever leave me, any of you." He was, then, sure of no one. Solitude beckoned.

❧ ❧ ❧

In Max's bearing, that night as we dined on the terrace, I thought there was a hint that his perverse unkindness to his mother now represented an attitude he had established so firmly that he must sustain it for the sake of what was expected of him. It had the air almost of a protective convention—an eccentricity excused by its long-established habit, no matter where it came from. Marietta could work nervously to keep the peace between him and us all, and this would add to his importance as a trying creature to have around. It was an effect his mother enhanced by her pleading sweetness that night. In her longing desire to let nothing mar her great moment, she presented to Max and all of us a ravaged face that held a smile of forgiveness for her son's brutal rudeness, past, present, or future. The sentimental tug of this was great, and it gave her an advantage over Max which was almost intolerable. It seemed to him unfair, when so much in life was disgusting, to smile it away. If he could have defined his duty, he might have said that it was his duty to let nothing escape exposure and punishment which deserved it. If he were asked, "Under whose laws?" he would have answered, "My own."

There were places set for Mr and Mrs Dana but we sat down without them and the footmen began to serve us at once.

"I wonder what can have become of the Danas," murmured Aunt Lissy.

"I trust they had the wit to forgo this doubtful event," said Max. "Many people would not willingly squander a whole night waiting for a somniculous plant to bloom which comes in season only once in several years."

Aunt Lissy said to me, instead of replying to him,

"Jane Dana is to have a baby soon. Possibly something to do with that. They are so polite, I am sure there would be a reason for their not coming, or coming late."

"Mr Dana has learned in a hard school how to be polite," said Max. "We have a way here of collecting our dues."

"Yes, my dear," said his mother, and her fabricated hand actually made a small beginning of a loving gesture toward him, before it must halt and be restored by her other hand to a position less physically painful.

We were at a small round table in a pool of lantern light. Behind us the high glass wall of the Crystal Palace rose to its pinnacles and domes and slopes like an iceberg. The lights within, reflecting off the airy greenery under the vault, had a greenish-blue cast, and turned the air into a likeness of underwater distances.

I do not remember all that we talked about, only that Marietta, Aunt Lissy, and I kept up a semblance of conversation while Max limited himself to an occasional sardonic comment, at which Marietta would scream with comic reproof, while Aunt Lissy thanked her with luxuriant blinkings. My discomfort was great. It was not eased when at one point Aunt Lissy said to me,

"Richard, we are all so happy that you are now a member of our household. We are now *family* in the best sense, aren't we? We do so hope you will be happy with us. You

[164]

must always feel quite independent with us, for that is how we all are with each other, aren't we?"

She rayed the table with a serenely confident glance. There was no response except a small rapturous groan of appreciation from Marietta. But I felt now that I had been sealed in my position as one of the Newstead staff, and to be warned to preserve my independence by the very one who had taken it away was chilling. Before I could comment, one of the servants came and leaned over me and said softly that I was wanted outside.

I looked at Aunt Lissy to be excused, and she nodded, too gracious to show surprise. I left the table and followed the manservant through great aisles of glass lined with tropical trees and plants to the driveway entrance of the Crystal Palace. There, moving his body, but not his feet, with perturbation, was Mr Dana.

❦ ❦ ❦

Without preamble, he said in a thin voice,
"Listen: he's dead!"
"Who?"
"I killed him. —But it could not be helped!"
I felt my face taking the wild look of his own as I tried to read his message. So fast does the mind work that before he spoke again I conceived a drama in which the librarian, out of years of envy and false respect, had murdered Alexander Chittenden in a book-lined bay of the library where even now the body lay at the edge of a spill of gold lamplight.
"Who, Mr Dana? Tell me plainly."

[165]

"I can't go in there and tell them," he said, pleading to be excused like a sick man, "you must do it for me. But don't tell them until I have left."

"You aren't staying?"

"Great God no."

He moved from side to side with distress. In the spill of greenish glow from the great conservatory he was haggard. With his chick haircut, he looked like a sick child. He had a motoring cap in his hands which he wrung. I had never before seen anybody actually wringing anything with agitation. He said that he and his wife Jane had left home out on the quarry road in good time to get here for dinner, and to see the cereus—he had his notebook and pencils in his pocket to describe the blooming as Mrs Chittenden had asked him to do. They drove along the road near Mr Standish's cottage and all of a sudden, when he could least have expected it, Maximilian's dog had leaped out from the hedges and attacked his left front tire, dancing and growling. His wife had screamed, "Look out, Tony!" and he had swerved the car to the right, toward the roadside ditch, but the dog pressed his attack, having a frolicking time, and then Jane cried out again that they were going to fall into the ditch and turn over, and she had half-tried to jump out, but he had grasped her and at the same time turned the car up on the road again. Chief had not expected this, but he leaped out of the way, or rather, tried to, but the car was jumping also, and as it regained the level road it had a spurt of speed, the front wheel threw the dog back under the car, and the rear wheel passed over him, and he was dead.

"Are you sure?" I asked, horrified at last.

"Oh yes. We stopped, my wife became almost hysterical, she made me get out to go and look. I have trouble with that sort of thing, I couldn't go closer, and I said we could see he was dead, but she insisted in being sure, if the dog should need help, and I had to go and look, and while I looked he heaved once or twice and then stopped. He died. It was too dreadful. You've no idea."

He was shaking with the recollection of it.

He had gone back to the car and his wife told him she could not possibly go on to dinner. She was faint and sick, and she too was trembling at what happened. She told him to pull the dog off the road on to the grass by the roadside, and then they would have to go home and telephone their regrets, and tell what had happened.

He looked at me sorrowfully. All his dancing literacy and authority had left him. He was a man in shame and trouble. He said that he had been unable to touch the dog to pull him away decently, he could not say why. As he now thought of doing it, his stomach heaved and he went into a sweat. His wife began to cry—she was afraid for her unborn baby, for the wrath of Newstead, for the loss of a good job just when expenses were going to increase, and for everything. He had to get her home. But first he went to the Standish house to tell someone what had happened and to ask them to take charge. No one came. Then he knew of course that Mr Standish was at the greenhouse, and his wife probably off visiting somewhere. He returned to his car and took his wife home. She nearly fainted when they got there. Then he turned around and came here to explain—but he found he was unable to face Max, or his mother, and so he had sent for me.

"Is the dog still there?" I asked, for my mind was still crowded with pictures of what had happened and how.

"Oh, yes: hideous: I was almost unable to drive past it.

[167]

What am I going to do? What am I going to do? —Will you tell them for me?"

"I don't know," I said, thinking not of his misery but of the already charged evening in the family. Aunt Lissy's lovely event, great to her, however trivial it might seem to anyone else, would be marred by this wretched story. Maximilian's state of mind already seemed desperate. Surely the thing to do was wait to bring any bad news until after the flowers had come. I told Mr Dana,

"If I tell them I will wait until this is over here."

"Yes, splendid": he said, ghastly in the eagerness of an indicated reprieve. "In that way they won't hear it until after I am gone. How revolting it all is!"

"Yes. But it was an accident."

"Yes, it was, wasn't it! Yes: how criminal of those people to let their dogs run loose. What can you expect! —Oh yes, another thing, though," he said, his eyes working in search of his thoughts, "you'll have to tell them *something* right away. —Tell them my wife has suddenly been taken ill, nothing serious, but she cannot come, and I cannot leave her, and thank Mrs Chittenden for me. Here": he thrust his notebook and pencils upon me. "Tell her I asked you to make the notes instead, as I have to go."

With a sudden dry sob he felt the urgency of having to go, and turned, and ran to his little car, and drove away.

I returned to the family and told how Jane Dana could not be left this evening, and we all sounded regretful; but Marietta hunched her thin active shoulders toward each other, and told me in silence that she knew there was something beyond this to detain me for so many minutes with Mr Dana. I felt my responsibility, and I frowned slightly to warn her to let things be. It was a heavy sky over us, darkening toward night. I thought of everything in black and white, and I saw the quarry road running straight away toward the lost ridge, and in the foreground, inert in a sprawl that would have looked playful if there had been any chance of recovery from it with a leaping gaiety, lay the smooth white body with its startling black spots.

"What?" and Marietta, leaning to read my face.

"Nothing."

❦ ❦ ❦

We were lifting our coffee cups for a first sip—mine shook a little in my hand—when the butler came to lean over Mrs Chittenden to say,

"Mr Standish thinks you had better come without delay, madam."

She put her hand to her cheek like a girl and came lightly to stand.

"Oh, how beautiful," she exclaimed, as if she could already see the flower. "Max, darling, hurry, fetch your camera from the car."

"I didn't bring it."

"Ah, Max. Ah, dearest, why could you not— No matter. Let's hurry."

She took my arm. We went into the Crystal Palace and made our way to the far bay of glass where alone on its earth bench stood the wooden tub with its five uprearing stalks of prickly glazed green. Mr Standish was waiting.

"Oh, Mr Standish—"

"Yes, ma'am. You can already see just the littlest lightening of color in the nearest bud."

We crowded to the bench. Each of the thick upright stalks supported a slender stem of dove-gray about two inches long, at the end of which was a folded bud of succulent green, perhaps as large as a pecan nut. The sleeping petals were folded tight in each bud, but in the one nearest to us the first faint movement had already begun, and though we did not yet see movement, we could see how a fissure between petals was made plain by the revelation of a paler green than that of the outer shells. Mr Standish, not daring to train lights on the plant, even so had set up a movie camera on a tripod, in the hope of recording what we had all come to see. Aunt Lissy said,

"How thoughtful and kind of you, Mr Standish, to arrange for the filming. We forgot to bring our camera."

I saw Marietta press Max's arm, to prevent any relentless restatement of this.

"Oh, look, my darlings," said Aunt Lissy, leaning forward. Mr Standish released the camera trigger.

The nearest bud showed us a tiny quake as the sticky edges of its petals tried to separate from the form which had held them in obscurity for months. The pale fissure widened ever so slightly, but we could detect the difference.

"And look!"

A higher stalk behind the near one gave its hidden, fiercely defended power to its bud, and that too made a miniature tremor in the air and declared its life.

There was something awesome and painful in seeing the act of blind fulfillment so faithfully enacted even in so small a scale. How much of my feeling was induced by the emotion so tensely suspended all about us in the air I do not know. But the blind flowers reaching for light, and the longing of my Aunt Lissy to have a part in this act of life, and the brooding resentfulness of Max playing about the great purity of the event, and my own susceptibility to charged atmospheres—all made my heart beat and my mouth dry up.

Mr Standish shut down the camera.

"It will be slow," he said, explaining why he must be thrifty with his available film.

Aunt Lissy held my arm and I could feel her quivering with concentration which I mistook for fatigue. Mr Standish offered to bring her a chair. She thanked him and refused. There would be time for exhaustion later, later, but for now, she knew only a time for passion, even if it was a passion which we bestowed on the flowering which in itself, so far as we could know, had no feeling.

How unbearable a certain kind of silence could be to those who had no peace within. The minutes, the quarter hours ticked by, and we stood and watched while nothing further happened. We could hear each other's breathing, the remote rustle or creak of cloth or leather as we moved to find relief after holding one position. Now and then I thought I heard rain, or a fountain, but I could not be sure it was not the hiss of my own pulse in my ears. Some of the air vanes were open in the upper vault of the Crystal Palace and in our stillness we could hear the passage of air making a soft leathery clatter in the highest leaves of the banana palms which stood along the tallest aisle. I watched the cereus so intently that I would see movement where there was none until, after what seemed an endless and unnerving time of attention, Aunt Lissy glanced sharply at Mr Standish, who nodded, agreeing that it had begun again, and we all gazed with our various love or scorn at the awakening buds.

It was like a strange earthbound astronomy—so slowly, yet now so continuously did the flowers, all of them, begin to move. As you can measure the passage of stars best by glancing away and then returning to see them in new positions, so from now until the end we could measure the actual opening of the *cereus grandiflora* best by resting our eyes, looking away into the misty green of the aisles, and then returning to watch again; and each time as we did so we could see each flower more open to the air than when we had last looked.

For after the first struggle of each bud to free itself of the confining form of long sleep, the flowers began to declare themselves not only free of restraint but of darkness. They unfurled what seemed to be shafts of light. The flowers were going to be pure white, with petals rather like those of a ragged daisy. Their white as it was revealed with infinite slowness seemed to release radiance. To see them giving off light as they unfolded their fresh delicate fabric was to see a mystery solved at last; and to feel a sense of life's blessing.

The smallest change in the size, position, or tint of the flowers became a large event. So it was when the nearest flower reached the point of opening at which we could see that its center was a soft golden yellow, the color of bees, in the shape of a small mounded cushion.

"How adorably exquisite," exclaimed Aunt Lissy on an indrawn whisper, as if she were fearful of disturbing the continuing fulfillment with a breath or a word. Above the rich green of the stalks, with their protective sheath of fine needles outlining their fibrous living strength, at last the white flowers with their golden centers stood fully open.

[172]

"Oh, how to thank!" whispered Aunt Lissy.

She herself felt like the cereus opening, in a transference of life. The white pure light of the petals seemed to open in order to free her of sorrow and loss in her own life, and as she joined the life of the flowers, her radiance was rapt and beautiful, if painful, to behold. I saw the face my mother remembered with so much lasting youthful love. She was forgetful of all but what reached into the dense air before her.

The mystery unfolding had held us all so that we had lost awareness of each other; but now I happened to glance at my Cousin Max, and I saw him watching not the passion of the flower but his mother's. As I watched him, his face clouded over and I thought I saw in it the love which he refused her. For a moment his ambiguous eyes under their classically chiseled brows shone with tears; but the heat of his feeling dried them up, and he looked away. He puckered his lips in silent whistling, like a small boy watching the empty distance as if idly unconcerned.

The cereus, opening, existed to achieve what no one there could do—to bloom into fulfillment without let or thought, and in opening to full life, neither give nor feel pain. No wonder, I think now, that Max, so quick to see the opposite face of the obvious, could not bear it.

The flowers were so white that all near things seemed to be revealed by them. We had abandoned our scale of time and adopted that of the secret calendar of growth and delivery deep in the shafts of the plant. It was difficult to return to our own sense of time measured. How to withdraw from a sacrament?

Max felt his obligation to manage this for us. In a light, clear voice, he said,

"The event has simple material implications, too. For example, it would be amusing to know how much it has cost in money to bring this one hideous, prickly vegetable to its climax tonight."

"Max, hush, please, dear," said his mother. "Let us simply enjoy it."

"Yes, but once it is over, an orgasm—even such a stately one as this tonight—means little."

Mr Standish had stopped his camera, and now he began to fold it away. He was offended by Max's tone.

"I believe that it is all finished, ma'am," he said.

Aunt Lissy nodded wearily.

"Yes. I suppose so. But I believe I shall wait a little while and just look at the blossoms. I can see just how to paint them."

"Yes, then," said Max, "we will run along. —You will be taken home?"

"Yes, there will be a car. Good night, children?" Her inflection asked us a question of loving care—where would we go? What would we do? But no one replied.

We thanked her and guiltily began our escape. I remembered that I had meant to take notes, but had neglected to do so, but thought it didn't matter, as I would never forget anything of that evening. Aunt Lissy suddenly made a wild little cry, as if shaken by a premonition of sin or death. She called after us,

"Max, please come here a minute!"

He stopped, motioned us to go on, and returned to his mother. Marietta and I walked down the aisle and then paused to wait for him. He went to his mother, and I saw her raise her face and look long into his. She spoke to him. He stood motionless. We could not hear what she was saying, or what he answered in a moment. Marietta said to me urgently,

"What was all that at dinner? You looked so odd when you returned."

I told her.

"Oh, no, no!" she exclaimed. She crossed her arms and clutched her shoulders as if to protect herself from blows. "What are we going to do? I have had the saddest time all day with him—Richie, I am really afraid for the first time."

"Of him?"

"Yes, and more than that, for him."

"What did he do?"

"Not what he did. But oh, how he sounded. My father is worried about him. God knows what he might do. —The quarry, last night, you know?"

I nodded.

"He told me he wished he had never come back."

I remembered the thought I had tried to resist all that night at the quarry.

"Help him, Richie. I have tried. I am useless."

"Perhaps everyone is."

"We must never think that, if we love him."

"Do you love him?"

"Yes. I ought to leave him but I can't. Do you?"

"I don't know. It is soon. And he won't let me or anyone."

"He loves you."

"He doesn't show it."

"Oh, yes he does, if you read backwards everything he says and does. —He doesn't need a long time to know if he loves somebody or not."

"Why does he hate his mother so?"

"Oh, Richie, he doesn't, doesn't. I just told you:"

[175]

How young we were, and trying how hard, to bring into the common light the shadowy troubles that beset Max— and all youth, to one degree or another. We turned to see him then. His mother set her hand upon his cheek. He shook his head. He held his arms out from his sides as if to forbid them. And then, almost as slowly as the unfolding of the cereus flowers, he brought his arms to embrace her, he bent to her, and kissed her, and even from our distance, we felt the aching bewilderment of his demand and denial, and the balm of that kiss. We never knew what she said to him to bring him to her for that moment; but the sight of their peace together is what I see most plainly when I think of anything that happened that night.

"He is coming now, Richard—what shall we tell him?"

"You tell him."

"No, you!"

"No, he will take it better from you."

He joined us and we went quickly outside. He moved abruptly, with airs of command which silenced us. Strange currents of feeling were adrift in the castle, cold winds blew compellingly through the prince's thoughts, he desired his people to be silent while he asked questions of the future which could not be answered.

I felt like my younger self at the time when I read our Everyman Shakespeare—the last act of *Othello,* with troubled wonderings which seemed to call toward them in fateful answer those events which were no less powerful for being imagined.

Once outside we came to Max's car which shone with rich dim lights in the glow reflected from the Crystal Palace. There his racing thoughts seemed to slow their pace. He turned and leaned against the side of the car facing the glass walls. He smiled with unarranged sweetness. He said,

"Richie?"

"Yes."

"Come here."

He took my shoulders in his grinding grip and shook me not in anger but in longing to know what he now asked, while Marietta, excluded from the mystery, looked at us in turn, back and forth, back and forth.

"Richie, why did you pretend to be sleeping? That was the worst thing."

"You mean last night at the quarry?"

"Yes."

I was humilated at any reference to my foolish games of the imagination the night before. I replied coldly,

"Why do you care?"

It was a question I have wished I had never asked. The effect of it was to make my cousin, that imperious, self-regarding youth who ravened splendidly after life without knowing what he sought—the effect of it was to make him diminish in spirit until he was forlorn—or, better said in the language my mother spoke from her German-American girlhood, *verloren*. Lost? He? He dropped his hands from me and his lips parted ruefully. In the just sufficient glow from the Crystal Palace I saw what came to him in answer to my heartless question. He suddenly looked old and ravished, betraying his likeness to his mother and his father. If I ever loved him it was then—and too late. I saw that I had committed him to suffer—just how, I did not then know; but a surge of feeling made me want to repair what I had done. I put my hand toward him, and said,

"Max! I mean, I don't know what to say!"

[177]

"You have said it," he answered, and then he inflated his chest and assumed his public presence—solicitous, impersonal, and charming. "Let's go," he said, with all the courtesy of despair.

We entered the car.

"Max, where are we going?" asked Marietta.

"As we said. To the quarry."

"Max, something," she said in a voice made light by fear.

"Yes?"—driving with a sweep down to the quarry road.

"Do you remember when Dana came at dinnertime?"

"Of course."

"He has done something dreadful."

"I've always expected that he would."

"Richie, tell him."

"Are you both afraid to tell me?"

"Yes. —Richie, tell him."

I told him. He slowed the car as he heard but did not come to a stop. When all the details of how Chief had been killed and where he lay now were told, Max said nothing. He took up speed again. We looked at his profile in the faint light from the instrument dials. He was scowling deeply over a smile which gave a musing sweetness to his mouth. We burrowed into the dark heavy air with our headlamp beams. The shafted light bobbled above the wavery macadam road and Marietta was the first to see what it revealed in our lancing thrusts ahead. There on the road lay a white object with startling black spots marking its sprawled form. The car gained speed, and I thought that it must have done so through some independent power of its own. The sprawl grew larger directly in our path. We must turn aside, and decelerate, and stop.

"Max!" cried Marietta. "Don't you see him?"

A new thrust of speed answered her. We were aiming directly for the dead body of the dog.

"Max! Look out, you fool!"

There was a certain bulk to the volume taken up by a full-grown Dalmatian hound. Even the long, heavy frame of the Isotta-Fraschini must reflect a rubbery impact with such an object. The front wheels held but the rear wheels danced aside in a small skid, quickly recovered, reflecting the action of passing solidly, with tumbling disturbance, over the obstacle which lay in the roadway. We could feel in our own contained, moist, living flesh the trundled deformation of that inert mass on the surfaced road in the dark beneath us. One, two, and we had passed—but not before we knew what destruction in break, evisceration, crush of bone, and spurt of fluid we had done. Max drove on and we dared not look at him, but Marietta, leaning forward and crushing her hands upon her face, screamed,

"Stop, stop, I must get out!"

I was still thrown about in my bones by the abandoned form my cousin had violated. Marietta cried again,

"Make him stop!"

She pulled at me, drawing blood with her nails, and I shouted,

"Max, stop! Let her out!"

In a hundred yards or so he began to slow down, and in another hundred, the car came to rest. Marietta, holding her hand across her face, threw herself past me into the roadside and ran away into the brushy shadows to the rear. Max sat still gazing without expression into the darkness ahead.

"Good God," I said. "What did you do that for!"

There was no answer, or so I thought; but held aloft by the instrument lights his profile against the darkness had a dreamy detachment of expression which in its way was sufficient answer, when I saw it.

"Listen," I said vehemently, "one of us ought to go after her!"

"No, don't," he said. "She will come back. She always has."

I was immobilized by his unconcern, until I saw it as another aspect of the despair which had brought us to this moment. Then I was driven away by desire to disbelieve what had happened.

"I am going to her!" I shouted, and I vaulted out of the car and ran back into the darkness where Marietta had fled. The car remained still, its lights flooding ahead, its controlling intelligence captive to the dark of its own nature.

※ ※ ※

She was kneeling in the undergrowth by the side of the road. When I spoke to her she answered me with a breath and sank down lower. I bent to touch her and found her hands, which she held upon her head, drawing it down, down, into darkness darker and friendlier than the night. She was shaking helplessly. I lifted her into my arms and she lay upon my breast covering her face with her hands. Everything was still except night sounds in the meadow.

"Hush," I said to her, speaking to the outcries in her thought. She shook her head, then she shuddered away from me to look up at my face as if she could see it and she said in a caught whisper,

"He doesn't know how he is!"

It was a discovery which she had never thought to make. Through years and days it had all been a game, in which she was Max's creature, doing whatever he asked, and always thinking that so long as everyone understood that it was only a game, nothing harmful was in it. But now she knew, and the knowledge did not release her. She said,

"But now more than ever I cannot leave him."

"I don't see why not."

"No, you don't see." She took her hands from her face and put them to mine. She said, "Richie, don't leave us!" At the idea of being abandoned, she began to cry. She scolded herself for this, and presently added, "But I am sure we are all too much for you."

"We'll see."

"But you know something?" She was trying to return to the local habit of prattle about serious affairs. "One thing I can never believe: I can never believe that beauty can hold danger, or evil."

I have thought about this since, but at the time, I was put off by it, and a distraction came out of the meadow air, and I turned to listen. It was the whistle of the down-bound freight, coming along the level roadbed at the base of the ridge. It made me think of going: we could not stay in the roadside bramble all night.

"Marietta," I said, "let's go back, now, we'll get Max to take us home."

She nodded against me and we stood up. I held the low branches aside for her as we stepped out to the road. We saw the car bulked against its headlights, and as we looked, the car began to move away from us. In the grind and growl of its sudden furious acceleration, we heard nothing else, but as it took speed, we heard again the call of the freight train, and then saw its yellow spotlight moving swiftly along in the dark.

"No!" whispered Marietta, in stricken knowledge.

The two machines moved in perfect convergence. The engineer must have seen the car lights charging toward the crossing, for he began to sound his whistle again, at first in long wails, and then, as the distance closed with steady swiftness, in short hoots. He sent the engine bell rolling. His brakes began to shriek.

"Max!" cried Marietta and began to run away from the living design of the right angle which was about to meet itself at the crossing of the quarry road and the tracks of the Olympia spur line. But just as quickly she turned and ran back to me, and was with me when the lights of the car flew into the air before they went out, and when after a long minute we heard the metallic impact which was muffled by the meadow. There was then silence except for the rolling of the locomotive bell which continued to terrorize the night even after the heavy train screamed itself to a standstill.

※ ※ ※

So, late that night, all the details of excitement, publicity, and grief over Max which I had lived through the night before now came true.

After the crash I ran to Mr Standish's door to ask for a car to go to the crossing. He was home and drove us. In the distance we saw lights come on in the Dana house. At the crossing the train was halted blocking the road. We saw lanterns swinging from the hands of the trainmen, and all too soon as we approached we saw the wreckage and heard the outraged plaints of the train crew—"ran right in front of us and stopped."

"Perhaps the car engine stalled?"

"—Can't say as to that. Stopped smack on the tracks is all."

Nothing could be moved until Doctor Osborne and county police arrived. The concertina was caught in a bush.

"Where is he?" I asked the engineer.

"Over there by the bushes."

"Is he . . . ?"

"Oh, yes. Instantly."

Marietta wanted to see him. The engineer said,

"Oh, no, young lady. You don't want to."

I drew her away. Mr Standish walked on to the Dana house and made the necessary telephone calls. Doctor Osborne arrived in fifteen minutes. He sent me home in his car with Marietta and told me to wait for him there. We sat in his car in front of his house saying nothing until he arrived, driven by Mr Standish, almost an hour later. He took Marietta upstairs and I waited for him. Presently he returned and drove me to Newstead. There it would be his sad honor to tell Alicia the news before the press, alerted by the police, began to ring up for colorful background. He would not tell Uncle Alec, who had retired early under heavy sedation. We later heard how Doctor Osborne knocked at the bedroom door and entered. There was a night light burning. Softly he said, "Alicia, dear?" Instantly she replied, "It's Max!"

"How is Marietta?" I now asked him.

"She is asleep. I had to give her something. She is very

[183]

highly keyed nervously, as you may have seen. —Would you describe what happened?"

I tried to speak flatly but my own excitement made me incoherent and he had to ask questions. In the course of these it came out that Max had acted oddly at the quarry the night before.

"You mean," said Doctor Osborne, "that you speculated about his committing suicide?"

"Not in so many words, but, yes, I did think of it."

"Had he seemed depressed?"

"Well, at times, and then again, sort of wild."

"M'm." He was a tall, heavy man with a square, ruddy face in which his eyes were large, patient, and kind. His voice had the burry resonance which many medical men and priests seem to develop from years of professional enunciation of arcane formulas. "Wild: how?"

I told him about Max's playing tag with the train on my first afternoon at Newstead. He listened with searching speculation in his eyes. Then,

"I see. You gather it was not the first time he had played such a game with the engineer?"

"No, it was not the first time."

"I see. So perhaps he was doing the same thing tonight, if he was in the same 'wild' mood?"

"I suppose yes, it is possible."

"Yes, it would be quite like him. —Do you think you could make this as an assertion which would result in a statement of accidental death?"

"Why, I suppose so."

"It is a distinct possibility; and we have no firm information on which to base an assumption of suicide."

"No, sir."

[184]

"Thank you. I was not there, but you were. It will be a comfort to Mrs Chittenden, if anything can be, to hear that it was an accident."

But as we looked at each other, we saw another answer; and by this conspiracy I was mercifully distracted for a little while from my own feeling of sickness and horror at my cousin's death.

Newstead was dark except for the fingers of light thrown by the bronze lantern high in the towering main porch. As we entered the silent house where troubled sleep must now yield to waking into nightmare, Doctor Osborne asked,

"Are you all right now?"

"Yes."

"Try to get some sleep. We're all going to need you tomorrow. Try to see Marietta. This is very rough on her."

"Yes, sir."

"Good night, old man."

Nobody had ever called me that, and I had never heard it outside the theater or novels. It was just the trifle to brace me so that I could feel like a true man doing his part—for the first time—to preserve the order, justice, and mercy of the world in a time of trouble.

But as I was quieting to sleep, with an odd ringing in my ears which would not go away when I turned my head from side to side on my pillow, I became aware, with puzzled shame, that my emotion was avowing itself in a new turn. Every secret fold of the hills in the late and again silent night spoke to me of the places of desire; and with the patience of lust I invited visions and schemes; and because these had more to do with life than death, I felt false to the sorrow of that house, and could not desist but dreamed on

[185]

awake, wondering if she was also sleepless, whether in Max's name, or—so clear was my fantasy—mine.

ᨰ ᨰ ᨰ

By unspoken agreement neither Marietta nor I ever told anybody about Max and the dead dog.

ᨰ ᨰ ᨰ

Late the next morning came a note, typed by Miss Magruder and initialed by Aunt Lissy.

Richard my dear,
  forgive me if I do not see you for the present. I am sure you understand. I know what you must feel for all of us, and for yourself. Say a prayer for me and ask my dear Rose if she will do so too. I am sure you are now eager to go home, but I would be grateful if you would remain until after the services tomorrow, and it would help me very much if you would be with me then. There will be no one else but the family, including, of course, the Osbornes. My poor boy, how sorry we all are to have brought you here only to know tragedy. You must put it all out of your thoughts when you are home again. Devotedly,

                                                              A.C.

I went to the Osbornes' for dinner that evening. Marietta looked like a ghost. Whenever I caught her eyes she silently implored me to forgive her—for what, I did not know. Her mother, a weathered, gristly woman whose chief interest was breeding jumpers and showing them, was nervous at the hovering solemnity of the time, and in her inability to let us alone, she conducted a running monologue about preparations for the horse show to be held in early September. She wanted Marietta to ride Cavalier Girl.

"She jumps so beautifully," said Mrs Osborne, and we did not know whether she referred to horse or rider. "Wouldn't you come back for it?" she asked me.

"No, he wouldn't," said Marietta.

"But we'd love to have him."

"No. We must never expect him here again."

Doctor Osborne intervened.

"There was a cable from Lina this afternoon," he said.

"Oh? Did they notify her?"

"Alicia cabled her."

"Is she coming?"

"No—not now. If they need her later—"

"I see. So sensible. —How is Alexander?"

"It is sad to see him."

"I don't suppose he will be able to go tomorrow?"

"No, I have advised against it."

"It's really better, isn't it. He might really collapse, as he does."

"I am not going," said Marietta.

"Mar, my dear: you cannot mean it."

"I do."

"But Max—your own—"

"I know. But I hate funerals. And I would be false to him if I went. I know how he felt about such things, too."

"But for Alicia's sake."

"I know. I'm sorry. But she will understand."

"Then she is more clever than I. I simply don't understand how you—"

"We'll see," said Doctor Osborne mildly.

Mrs Osborne took a deep breath to proclaim her essential health in the presence of so much odd feeling. Her bony breast rose wholesomely, and on the oakleaf brown of her skin her strand of pearls showed white as good teeth.

❦ ❦ ❦

After dinner,

"Richard and I are going for a little ride in my car," said Marietta.

There were no objections, for which I was glad, because she seemed in a state of utmost urgency, and another wrangle would have been hard to endure.

She asked me to drive, saying,

"I'll tell you where to go. There's a back road by the river. I want to feel *away!*"

She sat for a few minutes with her hands over her face. She seemed to be making a brave effort to recover herself. Finally she said,

"Nobody ever told me how exhausting grief is," she said. "And yet I can't be still for a minute. I can't. —I will die of home unless I can leave it when I must, and come back when I can!"

I remember the hot density of the night, and the fireflies more wonderfully profuse than ever, and how we took a road I had not been on, and came out beyond the meadow to a small river blacker than the meadow where mist and fireflies hovered. "Turn here," she said, and we went along under overhanging trees, following the river for miles toward the city of Calverton, Delaware. "Now that way," and we could begin to see a glow above the city, and I remembered how the streets had looked on the day Max met my train there. "There, turn off here," and we entered an aisle of deep shadow in the darkest groves between the country and the city. Now we could see outskirts across open fields and towers of lights, and then suddenly, a great shuddering flare of firelight which revealed the stacks and domes, the lofts and ranked retorts of a steel mill. They were pouring molten metal from the Bessemer converters, and though we remained in the night-shaded trees, the whole sky beyond us was like a curtain lighted by flames. As we looked the sky went dark again except for an updraft of sparks which went out in their turn. Our lane narrowed, and then we had to stop. The river was beyond the grove. Some obstacle to the current made a ruffle of water and sound.

"Now we are *away*," I said.

"Oh, yes. Richie—"

"What:"

"He called you Richie from the beginning."

"Yes."

"So did I."

Her voice sounded as if it were choked with unsought tenderness—a sign of tyrannical desire, a matter of wonder in that time of grief, and yet impossible to deny. Our hearts began to beat together. In that sooty thicket, by the tarnished river, under the vast sky waverings of the distant furnaces, we escaped into each other from that summer. Much of the world's literature has been expended in search of metaphor which will recall and hold forever the instant of love's consummation. At first, then, I became the cereus, laboring to leave the long sleep of neutral preparation, and almost with suffering to approach the release of petals which would seem to give their own white light. And then I became the fountain of light itself, like one of the innocent rockets over Newstead; and when I fell through darkness in the exquisite extinction of her embrace, with her I entered into the kingdom of earth.

※ ※ ※

How was it then possible to leave our transfigured wasteland and return to Chittenden Hills?

But we must and we did, though we paused several times to be silent together, or to talk in assuaged small words which spoke of nothing great, and asked little. Max was never far from our thoughts.

"Richie," she said, "is it possible? Will we die, too?"

She did not think of when or how, only of the large question. That she asked it seemed to me another way of affirming what we had affirmed against death, in love's way.

I replied, "We will, but how lucky that we don't know when."

"He knew, but he couldn't help it," she said.

"I know."

"When did you first have any thought about it?" she asked.

"Death?"

"Yes."

I saw again, then, a vision out of my extreme childhood, and told her of it. When we had to go downtown in Dorchester long ago, we would go to the corner of our street and take the Elmwood Avenue streetcar. We often had to wait and I would gaze along the tracks in the direction from which the car would come. I first understood what was meant by "distance" as I followed the lines of the tracks converging at infinity, and when in school we had drawing exercises in perspective, I always saw the streetcar tracks instead of the plain black lines which started here, far apart, and receded, there, to the vanishing point. It was marvelous to think about a vanishing point, and how all things went away to it. But even more marvelous was the notion which struck me one day watching for the streetcar—the notion that *things might come from the vanishing point toward me.* What was it like, there, where things vanished, and where did they wait until it was time for them to follow the black lines—the car tracks—which would bring them to me? I never took my eyes off the blurred point far down the straight vista of Elmwood Avenue where the car tracks converged, for if I looked hard enough perhaps I might see some great hand setting the streetcar suddenly on the tracks and starting it off. But I never caught this happening, and it was always a surprise which I felt viscerally when I saw the object moving toward me out of the mote-trembling distance. One day watching it in its delayed approach, I saw what it looked like—it was like a yellow skull, and the idea that a skull was moving along the streetcar tracks did not seem at all strange. It was wide and bulging at the top, and it had two absolutely empty eye places, and an empty nose place, and under that, it narrowed to a jaw without a mouth but with a kindly smile showing long pieces like teeth. Under it was shadow along which it glided and rocked, with, of course, the many stops for people at street corners far up the line. It was a patient skull, not frightening, for it preserved its smile, like the one on pirate flags or poison labels. It kept this image until always at about the same place each time it assumed the familiar likeness of the streetcar seen from the front. The wires overhead began humming, we could hear the bell tone of the metal wheels on the rails, and when it stopped at the corner of Herkimer Avenue and then started again toward us, magically I saw only the yellow front of the streetcar, with its two cavernous windows, its dark headlight, and its almost perpendicular cowcatcher. But I knew what a skull was, and that it was something about death, which had nothing to do with me.

"Let's never believe it ever will have," said Marietta.

❧ ❧ ❧

The memorial services for my cousin were brief and private. In a transept of the Episcopalian Cathedral of St John the Divine in the city, I stood with Aunt Lissy and heard with bowed head the ritual of mortal consignment, read out of the Book of Common Prayer. Her strength and calm were remarkable. She seemed ageless and insubstantial.

If a bitter peacefulness now possessed her, perhaps it was because she was able to grieve for the dead instead of for the living.

When it was time to go, she walked leaning on my arm. Her pace was infinitely slow, and I felt strain in my muscles from working to keep step with her. At the door she thanked the Dean who had conducted the service, spoke briefly and gratefully to the Doctor and Mrs Osborne, and tenderly asked them to tell Marietta that she understood her absence. Then she let me help her into her car.

"Richard? Could you accompany me?" she asked in a voice whispery with fatigue.

I entered the car and sat beside her. Frazier closed the limousine door and we drove off toward Newstead. My cousin held her gaze away from me, seeing or not seeing the gray streets pass by until we reached the country. A black veil so thin that it looked like the color of smoke covered her head and shoulders, and seemed to remove her far away. I felt I must not look at her if she so clearly wanted to keep silence and privacy; yet I could not help watching her and I felt desperately that I should think of the suitable things to say at a time like that. Luckily nothing occurred to me, however hard I tried. When at last we left the post road for the country lanes leading homeward, Aunt Lissy forced herself to take strength out of nowhere by drawing two or three deep breaths, and then said,

"Richard, how strange and wonderful to have you here just now—somehow you have become the whole family. Will you help me with one more difficult matter?"

"Yes—" My word must have sounded as my eyes felt—open and awed by mystery.

"Thank you, my dear. Let me tell you."

Maximilian's body had been cremated before the memorial service in the Cathedral. His ashes were present in a small bronze urn inside a cubic box of polished ebony which rested on the front seat of the limousine next to Frazier. She could not bear the idea of a burial service, and certainly it was intolerable to think of preserving the ashes morbidly in their urn. She had no illusions about the immortality of any material thing—her faith in the spirit was enough to bring her peace in time. But now in her sorrow she searched for some gesture of freedom for Maximilian's mortal residue. If there was no way to work some act of justice to sanction the tragic waste of so young a life with its form so comely, she obeyed the old blind impulse of seeking to do for the dead what the living might have wanted. Could I help her by thinking of what to do with her son's ashes? It was extraordinary, they all decided, how well I seemed to know him in so little time.

I was made obscurely uneasy by what she said and what she sought, but it was the subject of death, really, which I shrank from. Death to me at that age was an obscenity. I did not know the reasonableness it carried with it into the thoughts of those who were within hailing distance of it. My manners helped me at the moment to recall that persons in grief often behaved oddly, and with almost hearty politeness, I said,

"I'll try to help, Aunt Lissy."

She touched my hand, expecting a further answer then and there. Behind her veil her eyes were deeply far away but their determined light shone with the extremity of her fatigue and her desire to consummate her son's life and death. I searched my thought. I saw Max in his utmost self. I said,

[194]

"Aunt Lissy? I think I know what I would do."

"Yes: yes: tell me."

𝕩 𝕩 𝕩

So it was that late that morning after Aunt Lissy had
retired to her apartment at Newstead, I was driven by
Frazier to the top of the ridge which gave the first view of
the quarry. There I left the car, carrying the ebony casket.
As I started down the ragged trail toward the lake, Frazier
said,

"Do you mind if I come along, Mr Richard?"

"No. Not at all."

He followed me. Of all those at Newstead, he had seemed
to be Max's closest friend. Hitherto I had seen only the back
of his head and neck and shoulders in Aunt Lissy's car. He
was a well-built young Englishman with shiny black hair,
strong facebones, a ball chin, and pink, scrubbed skin. Now
he carried in hand his chauffeur's cap—a gesture of respect,
for we were about to commit mortal remains, and his sense
of the occasion sought to make ceremony for it. In silence
we came to the Peninsula, and I walked out to the tip.

The lake was like dark glass under the misty noonday
heat. I looked down and could see nothing of the depths.
The stillness was pure and entranced. I handed the ebony
box to Frazier. When he had hold of it, I opened the box and
took out a small but heavy bronze urn which had a lid like a
cone. The whole vessel was elaborately ornamented with
Christian symbols. I looked for hinges but there were none,
and I found that the lid came off by twisting. The bronze

fitting turned in its grooves with velvety smoothness. Open, the urn revealed its contents—a modest double handful of gray ash with specks of hard matter which must have been fragments of bone.

I kneeled down at the water's edge and with lid in one hand and urn in the other I let both down into the water slowly and gently. When the water entered about the ashes, I let go of the bronze pieces. They sank, creating with astonishing swiftness a small eddy which swirled upward. Most of the ashes were caught in the spiral current before they sank, and showed as gray cloud, roiling in the shape of those forms so often drawn for drapery or folds of garment by William Blake. A thin residue of ash—the lightest particles —floated on the surface and created a silvery drift which held the light of day like the humid air itself. If I had thought the lake to rest in perfect stillness, I now saw by the drift of the weightless ash that it was never still, for the invisible currents which turned so slowly along the limestone shore now took the thin film of ash aside and away and out toward the center of the quarry lake where it was soon lost in the small distance.

I was oddly without thought or feeling at the moment of performing my task for my cousin. The quarry seemed eternal and all things there—dust in the rocky walls, dwarf trees growing from crevices, the cold lake water coming from springs far below and evaporating into the air which became sky far above, the silence, the last presence of my Cousin Max—seemed to enter the present tense forever.

"—For Thine is the kingdom, and the power, and the glory, forever. Amen," I heard behind me. Frazier finished his prayer audibly. I turned to look at him, admiring his unself-conscious propriety. He returned my look sturdily.

His blue eyes were intense and dark with emotion under control.

"That's raght," he said, in his Londoner's accent. "It's where he ought to be."

I nodded and we returned to the car. Frazier held open the door for me to enter the limousine cabin where I had ridden from Newstead. But I shook my head and said,

"May I ride up front with you?"

He seemed pleased, and as we returned to the house, he sought relief in chattering to me. He and Max were great friends, they were. He had come from England when Max was twelve years old with a consignment of British motorcars for Newstead and had remained ever after, first as mechanic, later as chauffeur, and best of all, as a sort of hired chum for Max. He laughed. Max it was who did most of the chumming, in the sense of teaching things not hitherto known. For just one example, Max at fifteen had taught him how to play blackjack, and had won most of his wages from him week after week, but that had to stop when the time came for Frazier and his girl—one of the upstairs maids at the house—to get married. He and the boy remained good pals, and everything had looked so bright for the coming year at Harvard, for Max had leased a house in Cambridge, and had planned to take Frazier, as houseman, and his wife, as cook, and Patrick O'Boin, the valet, back with him when the college year began again, and they had all looked forward to a lordly time of it. Now Frazier didn't know: he had not said anything to the Madam yet, it was too soon, but he had had his American citizenship for three years now, and he had talked it over with Mrs F., and he had got some idea of what this country was all about, and he rather thought he would give notice in the autumn, and go into politics—starting modestly, of course, with some job in the municipal government of Calverton, or perhaps Philadelphia. He looked at me obliquely to wonder what I thought of all this talk, and of such an ambitious prospect.

"When everything changes," he said in extenuation, "it's best, I always say, to make a clean break of it. You know, sir?"

In his way, he measured Max's absence.

I nodded seriously.

※ ※ ※

In early afternoon they said Uncle Alec wanted to see me before I left.

He was lying in an armchair in his sitting room at the opposite end of the house from my quarters. Though the day was heavy with thundery heat, he wore a dressing gown with a fur collar, and a wood fire was burning in the grate at his feet. By his side was a low round table piled with books in magnificent bindings. A huge disclike reading glass lay on opened pages. He was as pale as bone china, with a glossy luster over his skin which suggested extreme age, though as I had last seen him he merely seemed a man well past middle age, frail but durable. He was certainly thinner than he had been two nights ago. Neurotics can impersonate health as well as illness, but they must always have a stimulating pretext. I could not imagine what would ever occur to unite Uncle Alec with vital concerns again. When he spoke to me it was with a thread of voice. At first, I had regarded him as grotesque; then as a memory of a

[198]

man quite lost in time; now I saw him as a human being in extreme suffering, and I think I learned just then that I must never again content myself with an easy judgment, based on superficial evidence, of anyone else.

"Sit down, Richard, just for a moment. Such an end to our hopes. We hoped so much of you with our son. I thought it cruel when he fled our pahty, it quite sickened me. But now it is clee-ah that he was suffering from something which drove him to reckless acts until the accident which destroyed him."

He looked at me with his dimmed and dry eyes as if to discern any disagreement I might have about the terms of Max's death. I did not try to conceal anything—but my appalled and serious demeanor as I looked upon Uncle Alec in his wreckage made me seem to agree with him. Max's death must have been like the fall of a temple—the edifice of the family gods which in crashing to the ground and abolishing a future was most cruel when it failed to kill the last progenitor, the father himself.

"Yes. How difficult any farewells can be. Still, we must do our best to let you go with some kind recollection of Newstead. I believe you were fond of Maximilian. We know he instantly became devoted to you. So this."

He took up from his book table a little buckskin sac and handed it to me. With a palsied forefinger he indicated that I was to open it. I did so, and found a heavy polished gold ring which held a large dark red carnelian bearing in deep intaglio an heraldic design.

"That was Max's ring," he said. "He rarely wore it. I gave it to him on his twenty-first birthday. The seal is my family's device. Will you have it, my boy?" I hesitated out of amazement, not reluctance. He was short of energy and so spent more than he should have in impatience. "After all, we are cousins, you have a right to wear it, especially if I say so!"

Then I saw that he was in a remote way bestowing the ring on me as upon an heir, and I bowed and thanked him.

"Yes," he said. "That will do. —And this," he said, picking up an octavo book bound in blue leather with gold tooling. He riffled the pages weakly. "This was his, too. I could not bear to read more than a line or two, but my son wrote the notes and perhaps you would have it?"

He handed it to me and I glanced at the first page. A title was inscribed there. It read, "Detached Thoughts. By Charles James Maximilian Chittenden." It was a thick blank book, of fine rag paper. Only a few pages seemed to be written upon.

I thanked Uncle Alec.

"Let us have your news now and then," he said. "We shall always be interested in your progress. Do come back any time. How splendid if you should become a scholar, and have need of our books." A hot far glow appeared in his eyes, some fire of an ambition not yet taken from him, as so much had been taken. "That will endure, at least," he said with a brave effort at strong statement. "The Alexander and Alicia Chittenden Library will survive, even if none of us and nothing else ever will!"

"Yes. Thank you, Uncle Alec."

"May I see you wear the ring?"

"Oh, yes."

I put it on two fingers before I found one where it would fit, and then showed it to him. He took my hand and touched the ring.

"Thank you, dear Richard. Now you must go, or you will

be late. Everything is always too late. Come." He drew me toward him and to my embarrassed astonishment I felt his dry, scratchy lips on my cheek. It was like being kissed by straw. The tears started up in my eyes at the signs of love in one who had no one left to love.

"Good-by, Uncle Alec," I said, thickly.

"Good," he said, "you can feel. Never be ashamed to show feeling. Good-by, do go now, yes."

A mindless smile suddenly stretched his bony face, and he put up a finger to detain me after all. He worked his grapeish lips for a moment and then began to speak weakly, but with all the old social air of his delightful duty as master and expositor of the great library downstairs, where it had always been his pleasure to bring forth his best anecdotes for impressed visitors.

"One day the most peefectly killing thing happened," he said. "We had just engaged a new housekeeper, and Miss Magruder was showing her around the place. They came in here, and the housekeeper—she was a bony old thing got up in black alpaca—ran her finger along the table there looking for dust, and suddenly she saw the Leda there in the center." Uncle Alec pointed to where he saw the statue, and began to weep. "She saw the Sansovino of Leda and the Swan, and said to Miss Magruder"— Uncle Alec could hardly shape his words through the sobs which shook him like gasping coughs, and lost a few words from what he tried to say— "she said, '. . . *stars!* . . . *duck up to!*' "

He buried his face in his hands and rocked himself back and forth while his heartbroken sobs coughed through his fingers. The opposite ends of his world had suddenly met in his mind, short-circuited by grief. As he could not see me, I decided in panic that he was also invisible, and before he should reappear, I tiptoed out and ran down the corridor. I knew I would never see him again.

❦ ❦ ❦

Marietta was waiting to take me to my train.

Before we reached town I asked her to drive aside into a country lane.

"There's no use," she said, "Richie. Don't. It can't, no matter what we want."

She knew what I was hoping for. She continued on the high road.

"But it meant so much more," I protested.

"It always does, if one feels anything at all. And we did."

"Then why not?"

"No. The world would say no, and they would be right, and all we could do would be to protest, and I am tired of protesting."

"You are not that weak."

"Oh, but I am. And another thing."

She drove in silence, and I had to ask,

"What else is in our way?"

"You do surely know, dear Richie."

"No, I don't."

I reached for her and she gave me her cheek, but she kept driving.

"Then if I must: it is Max: we made love for him as much as for each other last night. You will realize that later if you don't now."

I was shocked, and exclaimed bitterly.

"No, you don't see," she insisted. "But when you think of everything that made us feel the way we did, you will see that it was not just you and me, but the whole thing, and he was at the center of it. —Don't you feel how exhausted I still am? That may really be what lifelong sorrow is."

She was not asking for pity or sympathy, but it was what I felt for her, even as I fed my sense of betrayal after what I had taken the night before as an avowal for a life. She had the knack of answering me when I said nothing.

"No, you see, you are a boy in his last year at school, and I am, in effect, a widow. Max said you understood how it had been with us ever since we were old enough. You cannot be surprised."

But I was surprised at last, and cruelly hurt. She felt this. She took my hand and kissed the inside of my wrist; her lips made her butterfly touch on my pulse.

"I am trained for life by him. You and I would never see anything the same way," she said. "You always see things standing in light and shadow, just things themselves. But he lived by opposites. Joy made him think of misery. Love of hate. All the rest. And now, it is the same with me. It would infuriate you. But there it is, and there I am. —When I am an old woman with a skin full of bones and a hectic laugh, I'll still be thinking of him, and I'll be married to a ghost."

It wasn't too long after that summer until I saw that she spoke the truth, for the ghost to whom she was married called out again and again. She looked for its likeness in life; married its approximation three times. Her husbands were all playboys, two of them foreign, all sleekly handsome, bland in their excesses, and just enough like the perturbèd spirit within her memory to mock her true quality. Forty years later she fulfilled her description of herself, though her eyes were still hungrily lovely, and the skull had never changed its fine bone.

But when we said good-by at the station I was still too close to the events and discoveries of my time there to yield them up easily; and I kissed her as if to change her mind. But she was stronger than I. We heard my train rumbling in on the platform above the street.

"Darling!" she cried, like someone wholesomely sending a boy off to school for all to hear. "Hurry, you'll miss it!"

If she had sent me away happy, I would never have noticed the manner of my going; but as it was, scrambling up the sticky iron stairs, I was painfully aware of my awkwardness, and when the porter handed me into the train, I was blushing so hotly that he shook his head at me, exhaled a comical sigh, and said richly, "It sho' do!" I wondered all the way to Philadelphia what he could have meant by that.

❧ ❧ ❧

Gradually the sound and movement of the train took away my immediate feeling. Soon I was looking for something to do, and I remembered the bound notebook which Uncle Alec had given me. I took it from my suitcase and began to read it.

The title page was lettered rather grandly in imitation of a published book:

DETACHED THOUGHTS
by
Charles James Maximilian Chittenden

and each page held a single brief entry written in his handwriting, which had a brisk, thorny look, in black ink. The entries ran for ten pages, as follows:

. . . I like him, because, like myself, he seems a friendless animal.

. . . My whole life has been at variance with propriety, not to say decency; my circumstances are become involved; my friends are dead or estranged, and my existence a dreary void.

[This] is written in an evening and morning in haste, with ill-health and worse nerves. I am so bilious, that I nearly lose my head, and so nervous that I cry for nothing; at least today I burst into tears, all alone by myself, over a cistern of goldfishes, which are not pathetic animals . . . I have been excited and agitated, and exhausted mentally and bodily all this summer, till I sometimes begin to think not only "that I shall die at the top first" [as Swift remarked of himself when he saw an elm withered in the upper branches] but that the moment is not very remote. I have no particular cause of griefs, except the usual accompaniments of all unlawful passions.

. . . [She has] been dangerously ill; but it may console you to learn that she is dangerously well again.

. . . I am not sure that long life is desirable for one of my temper and constitutional depression of spirits, which of

course I suppress in society; but which breaks out when alone, and in my writings, in spite of myself. It has been deepened, perhaps, by some long past events.

. . . I am like the Tiger: if I miss the first spring, I go growling back to my jungle again; but if I do hit, it is crushing.

. . . I am violent but not malignant; for only fresh provocations can awaken my resentments.

. . . A man and a woman make far better friendships than can exist between two of the same sex; but these with this condition, that they never have made, or are to make, love with each other. Lovers may, and, indeed, generally are enemies, but they can never be friends; because there must always be a spice of jealousy and a something of self in all their speculations. I indeed, I rather look upon love altogether as a sort of hostile transaction. . . .

[What I write] may be now and then voluptuous: I can't help that.

There he was, in fragments, in those pages. I thought his accent unmistakable, and he filled my thoughts to the fullest, until for the first time I felt a real sorrow for him, that thickened my throat and made me pretend to lean with excited interest close to the train window looking out to hide my feeling from any passenger who might be staring at me. Where before I had known horror at his death I now felt loss. How real a lost life could remain—perhaps we never lose anybody.

But it was not for a long time that I understood fully the purpose and meaning of those notebook jottings. One day in a later year I was reading the letters of Byron, and in a letter to his mother from Falmouth in June 1807, I came upon the phrase "a friendless animal," and I remembered Max's first entry. I compared the words—there, sure enough, was the exact statement with which Max began his little series of sketches in self-portraiture. With some excitement I hunted through the poet's letters and found every one of Max's entries—they were all quotations from letters to friends: Dallas, Hobhouse, Moore; to his publisher Murray; to his wife and an unnamed lady, written variously from New-stead Abbey, Bologna, Ravenna, Pisa, Albaro, ranging in date from 1807 to 1822. Moreover, I discovered that in an early Murray edition of Byron's collected works there was a section entitled "Detached Thoughts," which were auto-biographical notes written in his last days at Ravenna. The manuscript of this was given by Byron to Lord Clare, his closest companion at Harrow, who came to pay him a visit at Montenero in 1822. Clare was commissioned to carry the manuscript to Murray in London. The two schoolmates never met again. "I have a presentiment that I shall never see him more," said Byron to Teresa Guiccioli, who saw that his eyes filled with tears at the thought. My cousin, steeped in the Byronic tradition and lore of the house, had found his counterpart. I found it piercingly sad that Max had turned to someone long dead to find emotions and actions which might help to account for his own. What a prison of loneliness he must have been in. Had he been idly drawn to Byron's style only to see it come all too true in himself?

How longingly they had all tried to explain my cousin's life—and death. With theories ranging in source from common sense and intuitive love, to restless systems in Viennese psychology, they brought their poor wisdom to the task, and found it insufficient. It seemed in the end most reasonable to conclude that romantic dislocation, whatever the cause, was a disease which existed, and could be recognized. It was even possible, as we have seen, to die of it, even if no one could remember or speak of what may have started it on its hidden life. The final impression I kept of him in after years was of a spirit struggling to appear, and whether it was a good spirit or an evil, I did not know, and the older I became, the less I wanted to make the distinction, for as I left my youth, I was no longer omniscient.

I was helped to that conclusion by another odd small circumstance. It was not until years later as I was leafing through Max's notebook to identify the passages in Byron that I found further entries in the last six pages. Separated from the Byron passages by a hundred blank pages, they had never come to sight before. These last entries were in blue ink and were more hastily inscribed. Except for the final one, they were to be found nowhere in Bryon, for I searched; but in any case, whenever written, what they all said belonged only to that summer:

. . . I saw a small, four-year-old boy, on crutches, struggling forward, bringing each crutch ahead in the awkward thrust of an upright insect. Two older and healthy

children were behind him. Suddenly he falls forward—
nothing to sustain him. He falls direct to the earth—meets
it with his cheek. The others bend to save or help him.
Too late. I become that child, for a moment.

Why do I frighten him? Perhaps because of the different
degrees of our apprehension of emotion.

We all see Byron in ourselves, even my father, however
implausibly.

Only in autumn do I feel immemorial, when the year is
dying. Never in spring, which seems prodigal, wasteful, of
seed.

Autumn: when I see the death of the year transpire in
such glory, why do I hesitate? Must I await my own
autumn?

At the quarry:
>   *Though the night was made for loving,*
>   *And the day returns too soon,*
>   *Yet we'll go no more a-roving*
>   *By the light of the moon.*

At home for the rest of the summer, I felt that I was looked at with troubled but loyal recognitions. My parents had to hear every detail of what I could tell. They exclaimed repeatedly over Max's tragedy, and loved me the better because I lived. As I described what the newspapers had reported, they said, "Yes," already well-informed but eager to find *me* in all the events I told them of. It was like my mother to come rather dreamily to a loving acceptance of my new relation to Alicia and her family. My father exclaimed with impatient realism when she said,

"How nice if you could go back again. They really must have become quite fond of you. I imagine you can go back all your life, at any time."

But even if I had wanted to, any return in the long future was made impossible by further changes which no one had foreseen. The family's posterity was lost as the years broke over its memories. Who is ever prepared for change? If it is to be met without surprise, it must first be imagined. No one thought of what would at last become of Newstead. In our cousinship we came to know all the details of how Uncle Alec's and Aunt Lissy's posterity was denied to them —and to me, should I ever have wanted to return to Chittenden Hills.

Aunt Lissy died in 1927, and Uncle Alec in 1931. Lina di Gregorio was the sole heir. There was nothing to bring her back to Chittenden Hills, and everything to keep her away. She had no need to sell the place to bring her a fortune, for the rest of her inheritance made her richer than even her husband could ask. She found a satisfactory outcome to her real estate problem when she encountered in

Rome the agent of what many believed to be a providential solution.

It came about through the busy goodness of a friend of her mother's and mine. This lady, a devout and imaginative widow, with an eye to her personal salvation, decided to live out her days in Rome. Her name was Mrs Cornelia O'Shea. In the course of years she had made for herself a formidable position whose obscurity was its strength. She lived on the delights of burrowing helpfully in the tunnels of Roman ecclesiastical politics. When she was awarded the Cross of Honor "Pro Ecclesia et Pontifice" she sent a copy of her papal citation to my mother with exclamation marks dashed along the margin. "Nell O'Shea!" exclaimed my mother. "Imagine!"

Princess Lina happened to meet her at an evening party in Rome and received her condolences on the death of the last member of her immediate family. Mrs O'Shea wondered what would become of her old friend's magnificent property, which she had never visited, but which she knew well through photographs in fashion magazines. As it happened, Nell O'Shea knew the Pro-Secretary to the Abbot General of the Calixtines in Rome. It appeared that the Order had plans to establish in America a priory or monastery whose continuing mission would be the renewal of the Christian ideal of matrimony as a sacrament.

A year later the work of Nell O'Shea was done, for Princess Lina deeded the property to the Order, and within two more years of remodelings and improvements, as they said, the members of the Priory were able to enter upon their mission in surroundings which I would have found difficult to reconcile with my memories of Newstead.

Sets of postcards were sold, with other souvenirs, at the Priory tourist shop, and a caption read: "Part monastery, part church, part experimental farm, and above all, part guesthouse of unexampled magnificence, the great estate of Newstead Priory sits imperially on its hill." Another told how the house had guest accommodations for thirty couples at a time. And more: carriage house and garages were converted into administrative offices, with a new blacktop parking area behind. "Literature" told that a feature of the main floor of the mansion was what was formerly the library. It had once contained the country's most distinguished collection of materials relating to the English poet Lord Byron. The collection was disposed of at public auction, realizing a handsome return for the Priory from purchases by leading university libraries and various private collectors at home and abroad. The library became the assembly hall of the Marriage Counseling Conference, where group retreats were held, and films were shown dramatizing marital problems which were used as a basis for seminar discussions. The vast dining room was converted into a cafeteria-style refectory, equipped with Monel Metal steam serving counters, an electric deep-fat fryer, and wood-grained Formica-top tables to accommodate sixty at a sitting. A chapel was installed at the rear of the mansion, with a sweeping view of the valley.

From that point the relaxing visitors could see in the distance the towering walls of the greenhouse, which still retained specimens from the famous collection of exotic plants brought together by the late owners. These included a small grove of banana palms, citrus trees—orange, lemon, and lime—and a rare plant of the cactus family (*cereus grandiflora*), and a few varieties of rare orchids.

I remember how the newspapers of the time were full of stories of a bitter family quarrel over the disposal of Newstead. Two of the other Chittenden brothers brought suit to void the gift made by Princess Lina, claiming that certain zoning laws must prevent the establishment of any institution in Chittenden Hills. Editorials raised the issue of religious prejudice. The wrangle was carried through the courts and my father referred to the affair as "an exercise in the higher squalor," causing my mother to exclaim in admiration, "Why, Dan!" In the end, as the daughter's wish prevailed, my Newstead vanished. Nell O'Shea could never have known what ironies were consequent upon her ardent efforts along the curial galleries.

❧ ❧ ❧

As that summer waned, I felt much older, but I thought it strange that this did not draw me closer in age to my father and mother. I saw them no longer as beautiful ageless parents with a happy boy, but as an older couple whose son felt like a man.

My mother shed tears now and then for Aunt Lissy, and, I think, for my lost childhood, and she murmured about how I must feel at the death of one near my own age.

My father showed a frowning solemnity at life's hardness, but his standards were not softened to accommodate suffering. When with thoughtless satisfaction I showed Uncle Alec's ring, my father said,

"It is a very handsome ring, a nice keepsake of the summer. But I'd rather have you wear *mine* someday."

He made a fist toward himself and looked at his heavy gold seal ring where his initials were engraved with flourishes. He took my gaze with him. We were both looking at the honor of a family and its succession—the honor which waits upon death at home.

He also looked at me now and then from under one cocked eyebrow—that expression which made him so handsomely attractive to the wives of his friends; and from that time on he ceased using my boyhood nickname, for something he read in my face and in my body's gesture, and a note he heard in my voice, told him that the time had come and gone, the moment which fathers wonder about, which he could never speak of, when his burgeoning son would have broken man's common secret of the flesh. The nearest he came to referring to the matter, in his mixed emotions of secret pride, humorous speculation, chagrin, and concern for my soul, was when he said, on the first Saturday after my return, "Richard, are you going to confession?"

❈ ❈ ❈

As the first hint of autumn came off the lake on chill, misty morning winds, I began to feel zest for the season and the approach of my last year at school. I presently knew that I had been wounded, and that I was recovering; and I had moments of meditation in which, if I could have stated my thoughts clearly, I made up prayers which meant something like this: "Lord, keep me safe from powers I do not understand. Let me never destroy any living thing in the name of lost love."

But presently the fears behind these pleas went away, and I was able to remember Newstead in peace. Time mosses over even the most sorrowful events, until long afterward people speak of them in the most ordinary expressions of acceptance which do the work of moss in another way, joining experience and survival, rock and earth, together in gentled contours. If my father and mother spoke of Max, I would shake my head as they shook theirs, and in silence agree with their last word, and the world's, about my cousin; for without any reserved thought or remembered pang behind it, they all said that it was a pity he had to go, when he had everything to live for.

Book Three

THE THIN
MOUNTAIN AIR

❧

FOR MARTIN GRIFFIN

This story is concerned in part with political events as they might have occurred in New York State in the 1920s. I have chosen the period arbitrarily to serve the established time frame of the sequence of the novels. As my politics are imaginary, so are my politicians. In present-day usage, referring to American citizens of Spanish-Mexican heritage, the correct term is Mexican-American, or, as some prefer, chicano. *At the time of this story, however, they were commonly referred to, by themselves as well as by others, as Mexicans, and accordingly, they are so referred to here. The names I have invented for my characters are not to be taken to apply to any persons who by coincidence might bear the same names.*

P.H.

CHAPTER I

❧

The Niagara

"IN EVERY LIFE, RICHARD, THERE IS SOMETHING, great or small, to be ashamed of," said my father with more force than necessary, and with reference to a concern unknown to me then; for we were simply conversing in general. But the priest hidden in every Irishman was being eloquent in him, and his eyes flashed, even as he smiled with scowling charm. "Just as there is something noble. Never fail to be ashamed of the first, and never take credit for the second. You'll remember this . . ." He paused. Then, "I've tried to."

He looked at my mother for confirmation. She gave him a glance and held her embroidery hoops away to look at them with a blurred gaze, judging the effect of what she was making so deftly. In her lovely expression there was a hint of reserved wisdom which briefly brought the conversation to a halt.

"Rosie," said my father, "it's a little unnerving when you put on that look."

"Oh, really?" said my mother lightly, in a way which could have been either ominous or meaningless. My father sighed comically at the old mystery of marriage, and said to me,

"Come on, Doc, let's take a little walk to Park Lake and back before bedtime."

In my youth I was a cultural migrant. Unexpected events came my way instead of my seeking them out, in places or conditions far from my native moral climate.

When my father was acclaimed in public, I was there to witness the crashing homage; and I wondered if I contained worthiness as his son. But my undoubting mother, rosy with excitement, strenuously took my hand and cried above the clamor,

"Oh, Richard, aren't we proud of him? He has never looked so handsome— My dear, my dear!" she called suddenly, not to me but to him, across the teeming convention mob below, as if he, there on the platform which was gaudy with bunting and harsh with light, could hear her.

His first words, accepting the nomination, had set off the great crowd, so that he could not speak again for a quarter of an hour. The delegates, marching and colliding in their struggles to dramatize their joy, looked like microbes aimlessly darting about in the lighted field of a microscope. My father had to keep nodding and smiling, his arms high, his eyes roving the vast hall, searching out and recognizing his particular blocs of supporters, lighting upon an individual or two in the front rows to trade flattering public confidences with them, finally looking up to us in the balcony over the rostrum. When he saw us, his eyes seemed to go bluer and to send out light. We called to him, and though he could not hear us, he knew what we gave to him and it filled him with still more joy. A few people in the crowd saw this exchange between the nominee and his family and redoubled their acclaim. The air was full of a sense of propitious fortune.

There had been a long and exhausting struggle for my father's nomination as lieutenant-governor of New York State; and, coming after an acrimonious, even an ugly, fight to nominate Judge Pelzer for governor, the protracted business of the Democratic State Con-

[4]

vention had worn everyone out, so that when the matter was finally resolved the relief was explosive, and my father was the heroic pretext for letting go. As he stood waiting for silence in which to speak, and even as I exulted in his share of public glory, I was ashamed to feel something heavy in my breast—was it doubt of an unknown sort? Was I disconcerted to be the son of a man approaching the first step of a success which "could lead anywhere," after this, as everyone predicted?

Nothing was clear, but if my father was about to become a great man, what would I be? Why should seeing him newly that night at Niagara Falls in the early 1920s make me obscurely troubled about what I was like myself, in my second year of college, and why should I even wonder? Even as I rejoiced for him, I was ashamed of being conspicuous as part of his new prominence. He seemed to know himself so well—myself I hardly knew.

My mother pressed my arm.

"To think that we belong to him!" Her happiness in her loyalty was so great that it made me blush, with love and anger, the one for her, the other for myself that I could not be as free as she in the tumult of our feelings. My father had a gold watch with a hunting case inside of whose back lid was an engraved testimonial. (I have it still.) It reads, DAN, COMMAND OUR WHOLE CROWD, ALWAYS WITH YOU, ALWAYS FOR YOU. It was unsigned, for there were far too many names to fit within the golden disk; but they all knew who they were, and so did my father. They were those men in Dorchester—professional men, bankers, business leaders—among whom he had steadily emerged as the most articulate spokesmen in the community. Whatever in life they were confident of, they believed in it entirely, and because my father did too, but could speak for it better than any of the others, he seemed to embody that bright time, after the First World War, when victory, prosperity, and unlimited progress rose as a vision beyond the fact of that mortality to which many ideas, and all men, were subject.

But so new in college as I was, optimism had come to seem to me naïve. I would not then have said it just so; but an immemorial melancholy, something like the leaf smoke drifting out of the ashes of summer in our street in Dorchester, where yardmen in fall piled leaves to be burned along the curbstones, appeared to be inseparable from any aspect of life. The strongest thing, I would say to myself, was to face this with love for any beauty of statement about any subject, knowing that human fallibility would at last be left visible, ashen and black, like the fallen leaves in the yardmen's burned-out bonfires.

꙳

During the convention there were many hours when there was nothing to see. My father would be invisible with committees. In order to have some family privacy, we were staying in a hotel on the Canadian side of the Niagara. My mother would sit in her bay window writing letters about the excitement of the week. Left to myself, I would go across to the American brink of the falls, which always filled me with many strands of feeling. The strongest of these was a fascination terrible in its hypnotic power as I watched the constant yet ever-changing brink, and I felt a resigned fury at the impossibility of truly describing in my notebook what I saw there at Prospect Park.

What I saw was of course what the world saw—the other tourists, the traditional honeymooners, the children who seemed abashed at the power before them—but there was something more which drew me back again and again. It was the memory of my first sight of the falls, and the rumor of them even before I saw them when I was a very small boy. Dorchester was near enough to the falls and their city to be convenient for a day's "outing." My fear of the heavy power of the river as it fell persisted as much from ancestral mem-

[6]

ories as from my own sight of it, for we had family legends connected with it. One of my mother's brothers, out canoeing with a friend, had been drowned upstream in the rapids and his body had never been found. The tragedy was talked of so often in my presence that the falls, the river, the lake behind them, all began to mean more to me than simply bodies of water to be seen by anyone. My uncle's body could have vanished on only one course, and I knew enough about this on my first childhood day there to imagine its journey over the brink into the chasm below. This uncle was young, with—so everyone said, sighing—a wonderfully fine singing voice. A serious career awaited him. They used to speak of how splendid he was as he stood by the piano singing "Die Beiden Grenadiere," handsome and martial, and I saw a heroic manliness in him, for I knew his oval photograph on my mother's dressing table, and I was often thoughtful about the drowned song and the fine body sweeping by in tumult.

My grandfather used to go to the falls on every anniversary of this son's death. He would go alone in his famous Panama hat, with his gold-headed stick, and his notebook and Waterman fountain pen, and, as we were told, he would write "reflections," sitting in a grove of birch trees near the bank, making a picture which later I related to Brahms walking in summer fields, or Goethe seated meditating on a Roman ruin, or Beethoven lost to nature in a woods clearing— the stuff of romantic German culture sternly imposed by my grandfather. It turned out that his riverside "reflections" were poems in German which he later published in Munich (he had emigrated from Germany as a young man) under the title *Am Niagara*. Not all of them were elegiac, but all made reference in one or another way to the falls, and the book's embossed binding showed a stylized image of the American brink. Staring long enough at the cover, if no one was around, I could make the image seem to move, in its eternal fall.

And, too, in early years, I was pinned in imagination to the ordeal of certain men whose boat of heavy timbers was wedged into a cluster of rocks hardly a hundred yards above the falls. I heard how—three of them on a sporting expedition—they had threaded their way through the upper rapids, knowing just where to turn toward shore and safety after challenging the current with the high spirits of young fellows who knew how to manage the natural powers of life to their own advantage. But even in their certainty they miscalculated. The rapids seized them and threw them forward and sideways out of control, while people on the banks watched in horror. The men cried out, their voices thin and distant over the clamor of the water, as they staved away from rocks trying to turn their boat, while the mist and the roar of the cataract came closer with terrible speed. They could see the rainbow lights of the mist clouding upward, and they must vanish into it like my uncle, and I voyaged with them to their very fall of disaster—but in a wild turn, the boat headed for almost concealed rocks forty feet offshore and suddenly lodged among them.

Would the stay hold?

The river's driving power was at its greatest just there as it approached the falls; but as it swept by the boat, it drove the hull into the rock formation more deeply. The wedging held, though every now and then a strike of the current would make the boat shudder and slip, as if to come free and bound ahead into the tumultuous foam. Darkness fell before rescue crews could be brought, while the men wondered when the river would break the boat free again and throw them to their doom. Lanterns and bonfires, cries of encouragement from the bank now and then reached the eyes and ears of the men in danger, one of whom could be seen praying.

All night long, as the boat gave its periodic lurches, with what outcome they dreaded to think of, the men awaited their death. At daylight the boat was still there, lines were shot across to it, the men were brought ashore, and everyone in the rescue party marveled to see that the hair of one man's head had "turned white overnight"—

[8]

so it was reported to me by an aunt who used the phrase as proudly as though she had coined it.

All of this had happened before I was born, and the boat was still there on my first picnic at the falls, and it was there still all those years later, a sodden hulk, when we went to the state Democratic convention, and I gazed at it with an old respect. The rocks, the violent sameness of the current, met in a terrible nicety to preserve the evidence of the river's mighty nature and man's folly. In my boyhood I sometimes had nightmares about being on that boat and hearing the cries, and the sound of the falls, and seeing figures moving in the shoreline groves by lantern light with desperate hopes which they were unable to enact. When at about five years old I awoke from the first of these nightmares, I went to see in the mirror whether my hair had turned white. It had not, and then I slept easy.

All such information added richly to the physical fact of the falls.

On that latest visit, I found changes in the fixtures added for the convenience and safety of the visitors. There was a long, narrow platform built as close as possible to the brink, so that leaning on the barrier of three iron bars which was elbow high, you could stare almost directly down at the great curve of the water as it swept over its shelf of rocks to be lost in the clouds of mist rising from so far below. A wooden stairway, turning back and forth with many land-ings, led along the face of the chasm a little way to the right of the platform, and I went down several of its flights to recognize, if I could, the rocky face and the slippery ledge where Chateaubriand, in his early twenties, as I then was, had let himself down by twined creepers, only to lose his grip and fall. He was saved when he landed on that ledge, though he broke his arm in the act. It was a relief, reading about this a year earlier in my French class, to know that a friendly Iroquois Indian had managed to rescue him, in the story he had to tell of wild America in 1791.

[9]

But nothing man would do to the place could diminish what was to be still the open mystery of it, every time I went there free of my father's affairs in the convention; and that was the river's sudden and fearsome change of character. With the vast, calm reservoir of Lake Erie behind it, it placidly enough entered into its channel and went downstream, yet with something ominous in its glassy progress. Even so, riding, as I did once or twice in boyhood, I could bring my hired pony close to the bank, coming through the birch groves of my grandfather; and I remember bone-deep pleasure in hearing mingled the sounds of the river washing along and the steady, slow strikes of an ax biting into a live tree trunk somewhere deep in the groves. The river went levelly along and I would parallel it as closely as I could through woods and brush. And then it became agitated as it met rocks. The rapids boiled noisily; yet still the river was level with the earth—true to its gradual lowering, until out of the inscrutable distance came the first pounding upon the air by what the river was soon to do. Abruptly the stream was divided by little islands. The distance was cut off by towering clouds of mist, and suddenly the river left its level way and with mightiness all unsuspected fell tremendously, transformed, it seemed, into an entirely different phase of nature.

Yet given the hidden edge of the chasm, how could it do otherwise? I stared by the hour at the instant of transformation, which now brought all strange analogies and metaphors to my thought— for like many students I was in search of meanings of change, and the word "fall" became heavy with these the more I thought about it, when I then had nothing to attach to them beyond my groping wonder. In the presence of the vast slide of endless water beyond its lost bed, I was, like everyone, unable to reach much of any meaning except the stupendous beauty and menace of that shining emerald-green curve which below the brink turned into iridescence and vapor. How take my eye off it? For my inner eye was as fixed as my outer.

So it was that I almost always became unaware of the people around me who came to marvel, and then to go away to buy postcards. On certain days there was a strong wind over the falls when voices were driven away which otherwise if shouted might have just sounded above the booming of the endless heavy plunge. But on that last day of the convention, when I leaned my chin on my arms on the railing of the barrier and lost myself in looking, the falls thundered, but the day was calm, and I heard people a few feet behind me. Their voices were heightened to reach each other. A woman cried out shrilly in an accent I was not used to,

"Now do come, Pamela, silly girl. You'll not see the like of it again."

A little girl's voice cried out tearfully in reply,

"No, I don't want to, I don't *want* to!"

"You really are such a silly. Look, Christopher isn't afraid. —Christopher, come back here, not too close, you can see quite well from here!"

I turned to see them. They were a small boy of four or five, a little girl who was surely his twin, and a tall, bony, middle-aged woman who wore a sort of blue uniform which included an elbow-long cape and a bonnet tied with a ribbon under her chin. The girl was half hiding behind the woman's ankle-long skirt. They were an English nanny and her charges. The boy stood leaning forward with his hands on his bare knees. He wore woolen shorts, long socks, and miniature brogans. He and his sister had identical camel's hair topcoats, though the day was warm. His pale-yellow hair was topped by a small round cap with a shallow visor. Looking at the falls from his little distance, his eyes were huge, bright blue, in his healthy pink face. Both children were as freshly shining and beautiful as new apples.

Without warning, while the nanny struggled to force Pamela around to give at least one glance at the terrible falls (a matter of discipline now), Christopher bolted forward, running in glee, and struck the barrier of iron bars with a force of a projectile right next to me.

He scrambled up the fence like a wild young kitten. His cap flew off into the river and there was a glimpse of it sailing over the brink. He threw his leg over the top railing, and then, like someone using too much energy in mounting a horse, he could not keep the rest of him from going over the railing which he had meant to straddle, just above the water, which seemed to slide faster as it was about to plunge.

I flung my arms across him. The nanny screamed. For a long moment I held Christopher where he was, most of his body on the far side of the fence; and then slowly I pulled him back toward me, across the rail, and into my arms. He pinned his arms around my neck and the force of this knocked me off balance and together we fell to the wet planks of the platform. I was on my back. His small, brilliant face was close to mine. We were making the nursery game of owl eyes at each other. We were both panting. He did not yet know what to think.

The nanny shrieked,

"Come here, come here at once, you wicked boy!"

His sister burst into sobs.

I rose to my feet as the child clung to me, and with his sturdy legs dangling, he tightened his arms around me in a hug, so that I held him even more closely. It was one of those small instants of the present which seem to open into the common, unknown future. As I held him, I felt for the first time the meaning of potential fatherhood, in a rush of tenderness so great at his trusting hug that I was amazed to feel it edge over into a love which stirred in my loins— the first coupling of the idea of sexual joy with procreation. The vital stir of the little boy in my arms brought powerful intuitions of beauty and purity at the same time, as if I held the infant god Eros in my arms, and knew all his hot little life.

"Well," I said to him, "that was rather close."

"Yes, wasn't it, rather," and now that he could speak, he lost his composure. Looking ruefully over my shoulder at the falls, he turned pale.

"Come on, let's go to the others," I said.

We started toward the nanny and Pamela. Halfway to them, he began to struggle in my grasp, to avoid being delivered over, for once we were at a safe distance from the falls, the nanny darted forward and in a rage of relief began to berate Christopher. She reached across me to slap his face and pull at him, Pamela's sobs turned to shrieks at the commotion, and Christopher himself caught their fear and began to howl. His face was pressed against my ear, his grasp grew tighter than ever. No matter how furiously the nanny tugged at him, he would not let me go. What had been an adventure, a near calamity not understood by him, now became a crime for which he must suffer. He began to shiver and shake. Hysterically he cried out through his tears, "No, no, no, let me alone," and successfully kicked at Nanny until she had to retreat a little.

"Don't you know," she trumpeted, while people all around stared in curiosity at how the scene of the little death they had just missed observing must end, "you could have been drowned? Killed? Oh, wait until I tell—"

"No," he wailed, "you shan't tell my father!"

"Oh, won't I just!" she cried. Her face was naturally pale and now it was as gray as stained ivory.

"I didn't do anything! I didn't," but an image powerful in his small world returned, and he cried, "My cap, my cap!" and again he saw it sailing terribly over the brink, and he redoubled his howls, seeing himself gone with the cap.

"You nearly went over the falls, that's all, if this young gentleman had not caught you! Come!"

But he would not leave me, and as her heartbeat began to subside, she suddenly became efficient. She said,

"Would you just carry him to the car, sir, if you don't mind? I must get him back to the hotel and pop him into bed and give him something hot to drink."

With Christopher still clinging to me, I rode with them to the Royal Canadian Hotel across the river where the English family also were staying. The little boy soon enough recovered himself, though he refused the nanny's orders to leave my lap and sit properly on the jump seat of the hired limousine driven by a fresh-faced young Canadian. When we came to cross the highway bridge, Christopher craned to see far away the churning rapids below the falls. He pointed.

"Is that where I might have gone?" he asked in the offhand tone of a miniature Englishman abroad.

"I'm afraid so," I said.

"You wicked boy," said the nanny automatically.

At this, Pamela, who had almost done with her abating sobs, broke out again and the nanny had to give all her efforts to consoling her in the atmosphere of terror which was too fine to lose. Pamela's tears only made her great blue eyes more brilliant, her exquisite flower-like little face and her gleaming pale hair more appealing. Her brother leaned to pat her wet cheek. They looked so exactly alike that they seemed to be two parts of one life. Nanny pushed away his little paw and said to Pamela,

"There, my pet. —*Oh, you wicked boy.* —Now, now, Pams, *we're* all right, aren't we. —*Oh, just wait till I*—"

"You cannot see my father. You *shan't* tell him!" cried Christopher. "He is gone for the day with Mummy."

"There is always the evening," snapped the nanny grimly.

When we came to the great white wooden hotel with its shingle turrets and whipping flags, Christopher at last had to yield me up.

As he was dragged across the lobby he kept his rueful gaze on me, and just before the elevator doors closed on him, he made a good-bye, repeatedly opening and closing his extended fist to me.

❦

My father returned early from the post-convention committees. He was tired, he said. My mother put out her hand to his brow.

"Are you hectic?" she asked. "You've been overdoing."

"That is politics," replied my father. "You get nowhere under-doing a campaign."

"I hate it all," she said.

"Now, Rosie."

But there was an undercurrent such as sometimes flowed between them in my presence—something so private as to exclude me even as I was with them. At such moments I would think of them not only as father and mother but as husband and wife.

No, all he wanted now was a hot bath, and an early dinner, before a short evening meeting with Judge Pelzer, to discuss final details of the rest of the campaign. My mother and I were to go along, as the judge had asked for us to be introduced to him, since we were all going to be one great happy family. My mother shuddered comi-cally. Judge Pelzer, said my father, was in a high state of elation at his nomination for the governorship of the Empire State, and my father's designation as his running mate. "An unbeatable ticket," Judge Pelzer had said to everyone. My father made his comic face at this—George M. Cohan's lower lip stuck out—and said to us,

"We'll wait and see. *He* has something to live down, all right."

For only last year the judge had been accused of accepting a bribe from a powerful client in a civil suit involving millions of dollars, and by only a narrow margin had emerged from the scandal with safety. No proof had been produced against him, but his political opponents would be making the most of it, even so, and it was generally understood that my father, after a fierce floor fight at the convention staged by certain industrial interests, had been chosen to head the ticket with the judge in order to lend the Democratic campaign an air of honor, disinterestedness, and enlightened progress.

"Of course," my mother said with her habit of outspoken loyalty and even flattery, which my father had come to enjoy as his due, "*you* should be the governor, Dan. I cannot imagine why they don't see that."

"Oh," he replied, "I have no political base as yet. —But just wait." And he embraced her and rasped the fine line of his jaw along her temple, at which she seemed to wilt a little with what I used to regard as simple pleasure, but now saw in my emerging maturity as love and desire. But these could wait, as it was early evening, and I was there, and it was time for the hot bath and the early dinner.

I roamed about the hotel until they joined me in a little while. The Royal Canadian's porches were wide and rambling, as they echoed the white façade with its many bay windows which culminated in the turrets with the flagstaffs. Its many decks, like the rooms upstairs, held much white wicker furniture. The public rooms downstairs were paneled in mirror-dark mahogany. The main dining room was long and narrow, with a side of windows giving on the view of the Canadian Horseshoe Falls, which at night were illuminated by green floodlights. Something about the establishment had that air of shipboard—the trimly uniformed pages, waiters, and maids, the brisk service, the majesty of senior employees who took their manners from the distant example of royalty— which the British so often imparted to their civilization wherever it might be encountered. The hotel, long since demolished, was, also, a tightly knit establishment, so that any news traveled fast throughout the ranks.

We were about to finish dinner at eight o'clock when a man and a woman came toward our table with a slightly inquiring, hesitant look to them. The man was only about ten years older than I, a slender, pink-faced person with a blond mustache brushed sideways. He held himself smartly, as though in uniform, though like my father he was wearing dinner clothes, as people regularly did in those days. He had neatly carved features and a lively blue eye. His wife was almost as tall as he, very slender, and beautiful with a pink and white delicacy set off by her auburn hair and an evening dress of frost-blue lace. As they came still closer, and then paused, my father looked up in some surprise.

"Yes, excuse me, please," said the man, addressing my father by name, "I am Hugh St Brides, and this is my wife."

My father said,

"Good evening, Mr St Brides," rising, and I rose with him.

"We simply had to come," said St Brides, "to thank your son for what he did for us today."

My parents turned to me and laughingly my mother said,

"And what did you do, if you please?"

I wanted to be gone. St Brides went on,

"My wife and I have been away all day—we went to Dorchester to the Historical Society Museum, where there's a portrait of an American ancestor which I've never seen. He fought in the battle of Lake Erie. I had an American grandmother, you see. When we got back, we found out your son had saved the life of our little boy—" and the whole story was quickly told.

My mother gasped in quick sympathy, putting her hand out to the young couple, not so much for the danger which was now past, but for the anguish which they must feel as parents, even in retrospect. To me she exclaimed,

"But you never said anything!"

"No, I suppose he wouldn't," said St Brides, smiling at me with warmth. "I cannot tell you," he continued to me, "what we feel for you in thanks. There's no way, really, to say much when a thing like

[17]

this—so final, or potentially so—is the thing. Anyhow, sir, we are grateful beyond measure, and to hear Christopher talk, Niagara Falls are nothing, and you are everything."

"—Nothing," I murmured.

"No," said the lady, "not to embarrass you. But really"—her voice was lovely, the words shaped, each perfectly—"what to do?"

"How is Christopher?" I asked.

"Oh, of course he is now appallingly smug."

"And Pamela? She was really the frightened one."

"Fast asleep as we came down."

"And Nanny?"

"Shocked to the marrow, and absolutely loving it," said St Brides.

"Yes, but you see," continued the lady, "we did want to do something, and do so hope you don't mind, so my husband asked me if I would give you, for us, a little memento of today."

With that she took from her small satin bag a long, flat, gold cigarette case and held it toward me.

It was a fine object, gleaming richly, with a heraldic device engraved on it. Instinctively I put my hands behind me and said,

"Oh, no thank you, I couldn't."

My father nodded at me with approval.

"No, really," urged St Brides, "we are immeasurably indebted to you, and this is not a reward, heaven forbid, but a reminder, however trifling."

"He doesn't smoke," exclaimed my mother radiantly, as though this would settle the matter in good sense.

His wife looked at St Brides inquiringly, and he shrugged.

"I daresay he is quite right," he said. "I wish there were some other way we—" and then saw that he must give up any effort at recompense, and knowing that chance encounters must end, tried to end this one with a little further idle friendliness. "We are on our way to our ranch in Alberta, we come over every year to spend a while there. It is a working ranch, you see, we all work like fury. The children love it all, riding Western saddles, and the rest. —Perhaps during the summer you might like to have a taste of ranch life?" he said to me. "We'd be so delighted to have you . . ."

"That would be a treat," said my father, "but I have commandeered him for my campaign. —I'm running for office this year."

"Oh, yes, I know," declared St Brides. "I am in politics, back home, in a mild sort of way, and your American campaigns do fascinate me. We've been going to your convention hall for part of each evening, I heard your speech last night. It was absolutely first class. I do wish you well in the election. November, isn't it? We shall be home by then, but no doubt we'll be reading about you."

"What an extraordinary man the other man is," said his wife, referring to Judge Pelzer.

"I say, Phyllis, perhaps we should keep out of that."

My mother laughed with forgiving charm.

"Many people think him more than extraordinary," she said, clearly meaning it not as a compliment, and looked at my father as if to nominate him.

"Hush, my dear," he said, laughing. Then he looked at his watch, and said with polite regret, "You make us proud of Richard, and we are tremendously glad your little boy is safe. But we have an appointment with 'the other man' and I'm afraid we must ask to be excused. It was kind of you to come to speak to our son."

St Brides took his gold case from his wife, slipped it into his pocket, and made their goodbyes, saying,

"Well, we're off early tomorrow, but we'll never forget today and what we owe your son, and neither will the twins. Good night, and all fortune in your campaign."

After shaking hands all around, they turned toward their table.

"What a beautiful dress, Mrs St Brides," exclaimed my mother, in farewell. Then, as they receded, "What an attractive couple. What are the children like?"

"Just like them, but of course in miniature. Such clear, tiny, lovely features. Twins."

"Sometimes I wish you were twins," she said, so fondly that I knew what she meant. If one of me was good, think of two! I felt a small rise of irritation at this, which subsided at once; but outright love was then difficult for me to accept, for reasons obscure to me, except that a few years earlier I had fallen in love only to be sent away after one encounter with love in the flesh. I thought of it so much—its brief amazing joy and the denials which followed—that it seemed to me more real than actual later opportunities, and it seemed to seal me off from feeling in return for what was sometimes offered to me, even such love as my mother offered to me daily, in small, ingenious ways. But in this she reminded me too much of my childhood, for it was her nature to please, and her reward came in how she imagined others must admire her sweetness, never allowing for their self-absorption.

As we were leaving the dining room of the Royal Canadian, the headwaiter, who clearly cultivated a long-cherished resemblance to King Edward VII, bowed us out with more than his usual remote grandeur. Struck by his manner, my father assumed it was a tribute to his new political eminence.

"Thank you," he said with the cordial modesty which served him so well in his campaign. "Good night."

But the headwaiter's respect had its own origin.

"I did not know that you knew His Lordship and Lady St Brides," he said.

"Oh: is that who they are?" asked my mother. "Good heavens, I called her Mrs."

The headwaiter with an air of privilege made a subdued announcement.

"The Earl and Countess of St Brides, and their children, Viscount Covington and Lady Pamela Covington, have been our guests here for three days."

"Ah!" murmured my father. "So his mild politics are in the House of Lords. A charming pair," he added to Edward VII, who leaned slightly backward, elevating his grand front, to indicate that this was an inadequate American estimate. As we left the heavily

[20]

draped archway of the dining room, my father turned and waved to the St Brides', confident that they were watching us go, and they waved back.

"What a pity we won't ever see them again," said my mother; but early next morning as I was out to watch the first sunrays through the rising cloud of the Canadian Falls, I saw Christopher running toward me. When he could be heard, he asked, with his precise air of tiny adulthood,

"Are you going to take care of me from now on?"

I laughingly shook hands with him and answered,

"No, Christopher, I'm afraid now we go our ways. But what a spectacular time we had meeting!"

"Oh! ever so spectacular," he cried. "Goodbye, then. We have all spoken most gratefully of you."

He sounded like his parents. They were calling to him from the steps of the hotel—"Come, darling—" and he turned and ran to them. They all waved to me from there. Some invisible fiber joined us all. I thought with regret how I would never see any of them again. Some vague, new knowledge of myself remained with me as they went. What if Christopher were my little son?

❧

Judge Pelzer received us in his hotel suite on the American side. His wife was with him in their bird's-eye maple sitting room. I had seen him only at a distance and only now realized how tall a man he was. Distance gave him, because of his large features and frame, a heroic, almost noble aspect, so that facing a crowd he made a sculpturesque impression. Near to, his proportions seemed coarse, and the smile which carried like a shaft of light over space now looked up close like an arrested guffaw. He leaped out of his armchair with heavy, bony energy when we came in. With a sharp U-shaped smile he greeted my father loudly, pounding him on the shoulder in a sort of public fellowship which I had seen in summer camp meetings upstate, where in my pre-college days I used to go to examine what I defined as "religion in the interior of America."

"Well, Dan," he intoned from deep in his cavernous chest, "we're off and running!"

"Yes," replied my father, "and here are my magic charms—" introducing my mother and me.

The judge took my hand and held on to it with a huge, moist grasp, never looking at me, but keeping his eye on my mother as he spoke—the old political trick of detaining one constituent while addressing another.

"This is a fine boy. Just like his sire. He will go far. Far"—still holding me but gaining my mother's "vote" with flattery. "Miz Pelzer and I would give a 'pretty' to have a son like this, wouldn't we, Mo?" and he turned to her, still holding my hand, and said, "Thiz my wife, Mo, the long-suffering cushion of my doubts and the inspiration of my days."

Mrs Pelzer nodded vigorously at this portrait of herself. She was short and so enormous with flesh that she did not seem fat but molded immensely of hard substance from without. She gave a hearty little burst of laughter, twisting her head aside in monstrous coquetry. Her hair was graying white, pulled so tight in a topknot against her skull that it drew the skin of her brow and cheeks taut, until, for all her smiles, she appeared to have a chronic headache. Her arms were bare and as large as thighs. At that age I saw matters romantically as well as in caricature, and I thought that beside her tall, lean husband, she made a farce out of marriage. He gazed down at her with his fixed scowl—for his eyebrows were thick as mustaches, and as coarse as iron shavings, and their outer ends were trained to curl up and outward to give a satyresque look to his face, in which his dark eyes held a piercing yet unfathomable stare. His merest glance from the bench when he was trying a case was said to make all defendants and witnesses give up hope. Despite all this he had a sort of egoistic appeal whose vitality drew many people to him. The lower part of his face, with perpetual smile creases, and the velvety trumpet sound of his voice on which he seemed to breathe forth his words through his great black nostrils, gave his remarks a confidential sound which flattered many a listener, and made him a plausible candidate, despite the public damage done by his earlier indictment for bribery, and his escape from it. But he was evidently well separated from that now, though his support for the present campaign came from huge sums of money invested in it by some of the state's greatest corporations, including the coal and steel interests which ran fleets of the splendid ore and grain boats on the Great Lakes. His air of genial, almost fierce, confidence, was in fact awesome.

"My, Judge," declared his wife with tremors of agreeability animating her vast surface, "such a dear little family"—making anyone of ordinary proportions sound underfed. "We must get t'be just such good friends! After all, we're going t'be seeing such a lot of each other, en't we?"

She could never have been a girl, I thought, but the unnerving thing about her was that she still behaved like her idea of one. Everyone knew sooner or later that she had been a schoolteacher in Binghamton, where Henry Sabin Pelzer as a young law-school graduate had first practiced law. His inclinations drew him toward corporation law; he prospered, some thought too rapidly to be explained; his wife Emmeline Moberly (hence "Mo") Pelzer gave herself conspicuously to public good works and the more arcane works of the Order of the Orient Sands, of which she became Grand Orphic Sibyl; and both husband and wife presently outgrew Binghamton. The judgeship at Albany followed, thanks to Pelzer's personal formula of how to mix politics with expedient prosperity. His later recovery from almost certain ruin was so astonishing that in an odd result it drew a certain admiration to him.

Now, with practiced but clumsy amenities out of the way, he took my father to chairs in the bay window to talk of campaign plans and personalities, while his wife and my mother set out to charm each other while taking each other's measure. My mother was over-polite, leaning forward like a lady to show interest in the cottage affairs of someone less fortunate, and Mrs Pelzer countered with aggressive heartiness, asking how many jars of plums her visitor expected to put up this year, while in her small pale eye a needle of light betrayed her resentment of my mother's beauty and kindly prattle. I sat apart, watching them all, wishing I were on the way to Alberta.

The conference did not last long—the two nominees would meet in New York in ten days, and in the meantime would return to their homes to dispose of personal affairs before spending the rest of the summer on the hustings. I was an unpaid aide to my father "for the duration," as he put it. When we said good night, Judge Pelzer put his great gray hands on my shoulders, looked down at me with his hairy glare, and said,

"When we *get in,* we must keep this young man in mind for something rewarding!"

"But he's still in college," explained my mother.

"College doesn't last forever," said the judge, blinking both eyes at me like a welcome conspirator, again with his U-shaped smile, which resembled the habitual expression of a mature male goat. When he let me go, he turned to my father and gave him an important afterthought.

"And, oh yes, Dan: we could do with a little less of Woodrow Wilson in your speeches. You quote him quite a lot, and of course he was our great party leader for a while, but what brought him down? Idealism, that's what." He blinked his eyes again persuasively. "Let's stay with the practical interests of the voters. They want to know who gets what. Am I right?"

Mo gave her vigorous supportive nod, but my father turned his face a little sideways and, with his jaw forward, replied in his most quizzical Irish manner,

"Well, Judge, the strength of our ticket lies in its variety. You stick to your line and I'll stick to mine. In that way we'll catch everybody."

Pelzer could only give his loud hollow laugh at this, and clap my father on the shoulder as if he were a "card," and send us off with false pastoral geniality.

Once back safely in our rooms across the river, my father would have preferred to say nothing about the encounter, but my mother would not leave it at that.

"*Was* there anything to that old accusation?" she asked.

My father sighed fondly, as if to say that she would never learn to leave well enough alone.

"We Democrats never talk about it," he said. "The Republicans would yell 'foul' and score off us."

Outside of marriage—their kind of marriage—this would have been a snub; but I marveled at the true meaning of their intimacy, which could agree or disagree, attack or defend, give and receive endearments, with the same abiding love, and, if overshadowed for a moment by a mood, would soon again make itself known by some small attention unrelated to the passing withdrawal. I looked at them now with a stir of reassurance in their beauty together, in contrast to the Pelzers.

My mother really looked like her name, which was Rose—a rose whose petals, pink, edging toward gold, were just fully opened. She had light-brown hair, which she wore loosely dressed. Her face was a classic oval, her eyes a deep blue, her mouth slightly open to her ardent breath. All this was relieved of vapid sweetness by her energetic spirits, her shrewd if uncomplicated mind, and some impression she gave of laughing stubbornness under her outgoing manner. She knew how to dress to bestow both elegance and modesty on her trim figure. She was never idle. Her fingers were always busy—writing notes at her desk in her sunlit upstairs window where so often I saw her edged with light; embroidering, knitting, making gifts (many of my early toys were her handiwork); sewing to improve her various dresses; assembling packages for orphans at Father Raker's famous orphanage across town, where, if I were a bad child, I was always threatened with exile, so that I hated the very sound of Monsignor Raker's name and I thought of his children's home as a set of dungeons under the huge dome and twin towers of his baroque basilica.

All my life my mother had gone to any length to please me, in the way of effort; for priding herself on proper economies she dealt mostly with unextravagant trifles. Her particular grace was to put herself out—exhaust herself, really—to do something for someone else. The result of this was now and then a day or two of "sick headaches" and silent darkened rooms. Her weakness used to frighten me when I was small, as by a sense of strength withdrawn; and I would sigh with restored confidence when Dr Breuer, departing from a visit to the silent front bedroom with his black bag, which he sometimes let me open for a glimpse of instruments and rows of beautiful little phials of colored liquids and pills, and shut with a click which sounded professional, even when I caused it, would say under his large sandy mustache, "A day or two . . ." meaning that all would come well. Because I so admired his powers, to which I assigned no limit, I early decided to study medicine, and at five I was known as Doc to my father, who fixed my ambition more firmly for himself than I did for myself.

When a momentary irritation in either parent, from a cause which might have nothing to do with them, put a distance between the two, she always ended it with a little "surprise" which required thanks; thanks brought forgiveness; and forgiveness secured my world again for me. Why, I would wonder in these youthful years, was I so often put off by my mother's great love for me? What would give me again my freedom to return it in the feeling I actually had but disdained to show?

My father could dominate her, and as they both knew this, he rarely tried to do so. Sometimes he mocked this power by quirking one eyebrow at her, which made her laugh and say his name with a scoff. He was tall and finely, sparely, built, holding his head high, and his chest too. He was something of a dandy, which meant that he was glad of his distinction of body and face, and he loved occasions to wear formal clothes, which he knew showed himself at his best. It was an innocent enough vanity, for he had risen, as they used to say, from a poor boyhood as the son of Irish immigrants, was self-educated, read valuable books late every night, and had the Irish knack for quickly assimilating the best taste and style as he found prosperity. People always thought him a very rich man, which he was not; but he had the easy air of one. Something about him made rich people feel less rich near him. Among his deep simplicities was a strong religious spirit. He often went to weekday Mass and Communion but never referred to it. Our pastor, Monsignor Tremaine, could never understand why, with all his devotion, my father continually refused to join parish organizations and committees and the Knights of Columbus. With a kindly nod he would tell the old priest, "We'll leave all that to the others," indicating that lesser worthies could do all that the parish required. As he could not be faulted in faith, and was a friend of the bishop, he was never disciplined for his fastidious exclusiveness. He had a way of showing that he meant what he said. This was a way of smiling with his mouth and eyes, and at the same time scowling with his brows, which gave a striking intensity to his presence. He used it on me either playfully or sternly, as game or reproof might suggest, and now, in politics, it became a powerful trait suggesting his public integrity. Blue-eyed, like the rest of us, he often used his quizzing look on people. It was an expression which seemed to say, not "What are you hiding?" but "What makes you so interesting?" Most people responded quickly to his unarranged charm. Until I was old enough to know why, I would wonder that some of my mother's women friends would gaze at him, half closing their lids speculatively.

My mother was not through with the Pelzers.

"Well," she said as we sat in our white wicker chairs for a bed-time chat, "if we are elected, I know one thing."

"Yes?"—my father.

"We are not going to move to Albany and have to see those people day in and day out. —We can go for the assembly months, and stay at the Ten Eyck Hotel, and you can preside over the senate; but we won't close our house in Dorchester."

"Are they that bad?"

"Dan!"—*you know they are.*

"He has an excellent mind, despite everything else."

"That may be mechanically true. But I think he will do anything for money. —And she would do anything, poor thing, for a flirtation. The difference is that he will receive offers. She never will."

"God knows, you can take people apart," he said, laughing at her. "God help them when you do."

She leaned forward and stamped her foot in imitation of the tyrannical fury of the outraged Gibson Girl type which had been the model of her youth, but she, too, laughed, and added,

"Then I hope the excellent mind will manage with decent means for the sake of the public. Have you any influence with him, Dan?"

"No. And he has none over me—though he thinks he has—as he'll discover when I get to work in the senate. He's the kind of very stupid man who got high grades in college. With all his famous shrewdness, he sees only himself in people."

She regarded him for a long moment, then asked,

"Why did you take it, dear?"

"Not for Pelzer, I assure you. But the fellows all kept after me."

"Civic leaders," I said, " 'Our Crowd,' " and though I meant it ironically, it sounded more disagreeably superior than I had intended. My father gave me a straight look which made me feel small for mocking his values.

(Something which happened a few weeks later in Utica during the campaign falls into place here. I was with my father at a conference held in the Fort Schuyler Club. Pelzer was also there, and at one moment he converged with us during a break in the meeting. He said to me,

"Dick"—which no elder ever called me—"you just wait outside here. There's something quite confidential I have to take up with the lieutenant-governor."

He took my father into a nearby card room and closed the door. I waited in the hall. Ten minutes later my father came out alone. His eyes were burning like blue fire under coals. His face was brick red. I never saw him before or since in such a fury. Whatever Pelzer had discussed with him must have violated my father's every principle. In response to my open-faced stare of inquiry, he shook his head, roughly turned me around, and walked me out of the club. For a long time he did not reveal what had happened, but as we rushed by cab to the railroad to leave for a speech in Buffalo, he said, *"Never trust a man who trains his eyebrows!"* and he campaigned for the rest of the summer as far from Pelzer as he could be, though necessarily they met on a few scheduled public occasions.)

From Niagara Falls, after the convention, we made a leisurely return to Dorchester in our old high-decked Packard, which rocked as though on long waves. I was permitted to drive in the country. It was an open car. My mother wore a broad motoring hat with veils. We lunched in Batavia at a favorite family tearoom inevitably called The Copper Kettle. My father was asked to autograph the menu. I was generally silent. At one moment my mother leaned over and felt my brow for fever, found none, but kept her hand there a trifle longer for love, while she made an impatient little breath at the ways of youth. I wished I were ten years older, with a wife and two children, preferably twins, and well beyond the uncertainties and contradictions, the broken ease, of my age; and I deeply luxuriated in the romantic pessimism which, like my friends, I regarded as proof of high intelligence. At the same time, I longed to be back in college, where this philosophy, though generally esteemed, did not preclude driving physical activity.

[29]

CHAPTER II

✼

The Fire Ship

THEY CALLED ME OFF THE SOCCER FIELD during a varsity practice game.
I was not a natural player, but I was determined to play, though I
was lighter than my mates, and my scrawny obsession impressed the
coaches enough to land me on the varsity back-up squad. There was
a great matter at stake. We were training for a college match in
England to which we had been invited for play during Easter vacation. Six days at sea, each way, on the *Aquitania,* three days in
England. A high prospect. Perhaps—in fantasy—I would meet the
St Brides' again. I was working hard to be among those chosen for
the trip, and the head coach kept encouraging me to try, at the same
time making it clear to me that he considered me not only rather
light for hard scrimmage but generally under par in other ways—
"run-down," as he put it. "Do you study too hard?" he asked. "Get
enough sleep? Let yourself alone in bed?" There was no way to
answer him with dignity and yet not force him to put on his tough,
anti-academic face, and write me off as "a nut," which would hurt
my chances for the *Aquitania* and the British adventure. I kept
"trying" harder than ever.

It was a cold, violet-gray day in early March. We played harder
and faster for the sharp air off the river beyond the town below the

university. I played, too, for more than the game. All things merged in a great oneness which was like a disembodied well-being, even though its medium was physical—breaths of spring under the wintry airs, silvery streaks of light in the long, gray New England clouds, bite of cold on our bare legs, running pattern of our bodies edged in light like golden liquid along our flanks, back and forth in sudden shifts and turns like those of birds over the rye-green field, joyous insult of the impact when with all our impersonal might we collided with each other, ball sailing fast and straight and taking us after it, freedom from everything but the fierce intention of the game, on whose outcome nothing depended but a finally unserious victory: in sum, thoughtless joy of our own making. That, we were sure, was what all life ahead must be made of.

During a scrimmage I heard the coach's whistle and my name being hooted from the sidelines. I turned my head as I ran, and a flying elbow struck me near my right eye. A classmate at the edge of the field was jumping up and down and waving both arms at me. His urgency, the fact of his interrupting play, were serious. The game stopped, and with a signal, the coach summoned me to run to the sidelines.

An emergency message at the dean's office, I was told. "They want you right away."

※

So it was that I was on a train that night bound for Dorchester. My father was seriously ill, at home, though I had heard nothing of his having left Albany, where since January he had been presiding over the first session of the new senate. My mother had been un-available to talk to me when I tried to reach her by phone from the dean's office, but my father's legislative assistant, a young law graduate named Samuel Dickinson, had gone home with my parents, and he gave me the message tersely and without many details.

As most of the night I pondered it in the sleeping car which would let me off at Dorchester at six-thirty in the morning, I reviewed incidents of the campaign and after. Some of these, though not alarming, had seemed too odd and frequent for comfort. My father's nature had always led him to "overdo." He spent his energy with such focus and drive that this habit was what had brought idler men, men perhaps less surely ambitious, to create a following around him: Our Crowd, who in a kind of instinctive aggregate lodged their undefined goals in him, with such large visions for him that he was finally persuaded to step out in front for them—and for himself. He went at life as we went at soccer.

In late summer, as the campaign drew toward its close, he had tired more rapidly with each day, and he made some people impatient by leaving them early after the speeches and the little local caucuses were done with. He said he had his homework to do—and with a flattering hand on a shoulder, a glimmer of his blue eye, which confidentially made an accomplice in intelligence of his listener, a general wave of the hand which told them all that he would never forget any one of them individually, creating the emotion which always reaches forth from great actors, he would leave for his night's lodging. Not to study, not to write, but to sleep. Behind his fine smile, his dark gaze, which at will he could make sparkle with interest in the light under his quizzically furrowed brow, I sometimes saw a wincing sort of fatigue; and sometimes his voice became as hollow as straw, though when necessary he managed with main force to make it reach through all the municipal halls and hotel ballrooms where we made our nightly stands in town after town. From any distance, he always looked vital, powerful, and charming, standing below the great banners which bore the two huge oval portraits.

Midway in the summer he would ask to be left alone for half an hour before having to give an evening speech. He said he had to

collect his wits. Only I was allowed to break in, and then only if
something important required his notice. One evening in Glens
Falls, I knocked and then went into his hotel bedroom. He was
sitting in an armchair facing out into the high summer twilight.
The room was shadowy. He was looking at nothing. I spoke his
name. Without turning, he said almost under his breath, "Violets."

"What?" I said.

"Ah. It's you. —Nothing. What've you got?"

I handed him my copy of his speech, which I'd typewritten from
his beautiful handwriting, with its strong down-curves and its classical spacing—he used his flexible Waterman fountain pen as an
instrument of visual artistry. In some assumed animation, to convince me that his odd lone utterance had been without meaning, as
it then was for me in any case, he asked.

"How does it read?"

"Great, I think. I like the line from Wilson."

"That'll show the old goat," and suddenly with his vigor and
charming mischief he was on his feet ready to go to the rally as if
impatient to put something behind him.

Was there anything? What could it be? I was depressed, even
somewhat cross, at what seemed to me an undertone of abstracted
melancholy in him, as though he might be sorrowing for something.
I had theories. Did he think himself unworthy, after all, in what he
was doing? Was he thinking his ticket might lose? Did the thought
of internecine battles with Judge Pelzer exhaust him? Was he sorry
he had taken on the nomination? And then I would feel disloyal for
holding such unsympathetic thoughts at a time when he, or any
man, must be tested to the limits of his natural strength by elation,
real to start with but more and more simulated as the work went on
at dreary banquets, endless reception lines, eager interviews, the
result of which for the most part was honest misrepresentation of
what he actually had said, and the shameless egotism to be maintained in full view of the public if they were to believe as he must
about himself, and the image he made stronger by the day in the

[33]

huge state over which we campaigned. With him I came to know possessively the Mohawk Valley, the Hudson Valley, the Batavia flats, the Adirondacks, Lake Champlain and Lake George, and the shores of Lake Erie and Lake Ontario; from farms, to wooded mounds, to granite mountains, to the placid canal way, to the Finger Lakes and their classical towns; and rocky gorges and chasms. Such variety was exciting, and I would think my father as stimulated as I by it.

But again my qualms would seem justified when at home on weekends I would think I saw concern in my mother. One Sunday evening she said,

"Dan, where are you?"

He looked sharply at her, almost apprehensively, but he said with comic patience,

"Right here, in the bosom of my family. Why?"

"Oh—sometimes you seem so far away. Of course, there *are* days of that, literally. But I don't mean just the campaign"—for she had declined to travel most of the time along the election trail—"and of course I hate all of it."

He shrugged.

"I suppose I'm rather tired."

"Poor darling. Yes. But sometimes I wonder if you're running *for* something, or *away* from something."

"There we go, Doc," he said to me, not unkindly, but with mockery and a blue fire of suppressed anger in his eye, "a laboratory specimen of woman's intuition." Then he turned to her and added, "I don't know what you're fretting about, Rosie. Running away! Not from you, not from you, you may be sure. Come here."

She went to him.

One night at Binghamton, he was feverish, and we called a doctor, who ordered him to rest for a whole day and night. When the next rally was canceled, an irate phone call from Pelzer ordered him to be up and about their furious business; for the campaign was running uncomfortably more close than anyone had expected and

[34]

the judge was beginning to fear his defeat as the old charges against him were, after all, shouted by the opposition. Wearily my father obeyed him and reconvened the canceled appearance, and from some mysterious source called forth enough strength to make one of the best speeches of his life. Again he commanded all his Irish ingenuity of rhetoric and every device of the magnetic appeal he could assert even against the cleverest of hecklers, whom he either won over with laughter in which they could honorably join, or failing that, genially made fools of, so that everyone laughed at them, and with him.

But the cost was considerable, and luckily a weekend followed in which he could rest. He slept off and on for thirty hours during the next two days. My mother said to me with a shrugging sigh,

"Richard, is it worth it?"

She asked me with her eyes whether we were losing him, had perhaps already lost him; and I had at moments the notion that she was with difficulty holding some knowledge away from me. But then she would dismiss her underthoughts, wafting with the backs of her hands the loosely caught waves of hair at her temples as if to brush away doubts which would only trouble if left in possession, and I would swallow questions which I could not ask because they had no final form.

On the Monday after that weekend, he went forth like his old self. I was astonished that day to notice for the first time little feathers of whitish hair at his temples. They must have been coming gradually (not overnight—where was his night of terror in the rapids?).

During the mid-year holidays, with the election safely behind him—Pelzer and he and their whole ticket won by a comfortable majority after all; my father was editorially credited with the victory; Our Crowd told him, and each other, with words and souvenir gifts, that they knew he would bring it off—my mother had plans for a celebration at our house in Dorchester for the closest family friends, and some of my friends from college, who were expected to stay for the best of the holiday dances at the big houses and the clubs of the city. But two days before the party, my father suddenly woke up with a high fever, the party was off, the guests were sent telephone and telegraph messages of regrets, and the papers were notified that the lieutenant-governor-elect was confined to his home with an attack of influenza—an ailment dangerously prevalent throughout the country. The inauguration was not long away: the press asked daily whether the lieutenant-governor would recover in time to attend the inaugural ball and the swearing-in ceremonies of the day after. They were continually obliged to report that the attendant physicians gave them every assurance that he would be present.

My mother was indignant when Mo Pelzer telephoned her from New York to ask her what color dress she would wear at the ball. On being told that it was American Beauty satin—a pun on her own name which my mother and father had arrived at with measured merriment safe enough for the sickroom—Mo Pelzer did not ask her, but ordered her, to change to something else, as that was the color and material she herself had chosen, it had always been her color, she had worn it at her installation as Grand Orphic Sibyl years ago, the new dress was already finished, and after all, she was the First Lady of the state, she should have been consulted in advance about the issue, and in her position she felt she should have her way. My mother made a high, cool reply without committing herself and flew to my father's dark bedroom about the matter. He laughed so hard that he coughed, which hurt him badly, but he managed to say,

"Rosie, if you wore a flour sack for her sake, nobody would look at her anyway."

She took this to mean that she was to keep her American Beauty plans, which gave her satisfaction, and telling me about the affair, she said,

"Do you know that thousands of people voted against Pelzer because of her? 'Imagine that "washtub" in the Governor's Mansion!' they kept saying—I heard it everywhere all summer!"

We all went to Albany, escorted by a great delegation of my father's associates and supporters—Our Crowd, which now had many new recruits in honor of achieved success. By their possessive admiration, they made him their creature, and he responded to their comradely love with a show of health. They could never follow a weakling. His energy returned—perhaps in too great measure, and his cheeks were heightened by high color under the eyes. His brilliance seemed to burn as he entered into all the convivialities of the train ride to the capital; and there, afterward, into all the incidental meetings and the big parties at which he and my mother were obliged to make appearances. The Pelzers were always present. There was no denying the magnetism of the governor when he was observed across a room or from greater distance. All his features, his size, were larger than life, and carried conviction deep into crowds; but while talking to him, you felt all was exaggerated and assumed, and were uneasy with him.

There was a small incident at the ball of which my mother was the heroine, showing an unsuspected gift for political adroitness. Photographers asked for a picture of her and the governor's wife together. When they were brought to stand side by side, resembling a slender vase beside a tub, a reporter spoke of the similarity in their ball gowns, both of satin, weren't they? in American Beauty crimson? Was this an accident?

As Mo Pelzer turned dark red herself, my mother quickly said,

"Oh, no, not at all. The First Lady and I intended to show a spirit of the new harmony we have all brought to Albany. We thought if we wore the same color, this would be evident!"

And she put her arm through Mrs Pelzer's with a lighthearted smile. Mo nodded her strange topknot in agreement, though a shiver of fat woman's rage went all over her under her skin, and she gave forth her deep, rapid, fellowship laugh from her great sloping bosom, and the press had its picture.

Later, leading the grand march to open the ball with the governor, she made an impressive show of dignity, which was enlarged by her bulk. Like many heavy people, she was light on her feet, and when she danced the first dance with her husband (a slow, stately waltz), she even conveyed the romantic satisfaction which the usually envious girl within her felt on an occasion so splendid. My parents, following their lead, were less visible on the ballroom floor; but I saw them—slim, elegant, and beautiful. With my grim analytical mood upon me, I watched it all, examining all the details of the event, which, with a posture of ironic disdain and embarrassment, I classified as a folk ritual of fixed recurrence. A persistent image was that of Mo Pelzer, vastly gleaming in her red satin, dancing with the new secretary of state—a man so small that when the waltz turned them with Mo's back to me, he was totally eclipsed, and she seemed to be treading a mysterious measure alone; then slowly veering, she gradually revealed her small partner again.

On the following day my mother and I sat in the guest rows of the outdoor tribune to witness the inauguration. It was a clear winter day. The men sat in heavy topcoats but uncovered, the ladies in furs and every variety of enormous hat garnished with dead birds, sprays of feathers, cloth flowers. At the head of the steep front flight of capitol steps, the platform stood against the Renaissance doorways and fenestration of the ornate gray stone façade, all of which sprang oddly from a ground-story base of heavy Romanesque arches. Even as he rose to take the oath of office, my father turned to us a swift glance proclaiming our own unity—rays of blue light, conveying an almost liturgical power of style and spirit to us, and to those who saw him do it. My mother, with that ageless and formless foreboding which women harbor for those they love, said in a half voice,

"Oh, I hope he's all right . . ."

I thought his mere unspoken appearance was more eloquent than Governor Pelzer's in the inaugural address which horned forth in that strange tone of his and seemed to resonate from caverns of nasal cartilage. Pelzer trumpeted a fearless call, supported by oddly uncoordinated gestures of hand and arm, proposing that the great commonwealth of New York should stand as a model for the federal government at Washington. He promised that with his first budget message on February 15 he would astound the people, through their legislative branch, with certain innovations, economies, guarantees of integrity never before offered to them by their highest elected state official. Glaring deeply at his audience, his eyes took accent from the long, twisted, black hairs of his eyebrows with their upswept Mephistophelian ends, as he called his hearers to righteous battle. I said to myself that he knew all the same tricks as those of the itinerant evangelists whom I had sardonically studied in the summer-heated towns and valleys when the teeming nights combined with practiced eloquence to turn the listeners' hearts at first toward God and later, secretly, in the heavy-shadowed, rank bushes of rose of Sharon and lilac and rhododendron, toward sweaty, hungry love. Could high feeling, I began to wonder, turn from one expression to another without losing its energy? Of Pelzer, I believed, and it turned out to be true, that it would not be long until a struggle would begin below the surface of the administration between him and my father: between the governor's office and the state senate: between differences of visible style and invisible character.

After I returned to the university I would see newspaper stories and editorials—*The Albany Times-Union, The Dorchester Chronicle*—marking these emerging differences in terms of specific issues, and occasionally my father would send me a clipping with a hasty penciled note on one of his memorandum forms with some such comment as, "Keep your eye on this one—there is a very interesting principle involved. We'll see. Government is an iceberg, and the part that shows is labeled Good Faith, but the part below! etc. Sometimes I wish I were a sea lion and could dive deep enough for a real look. Tear this up. Liked all your grades but chemistry—should be better for incipient M.D. Love, D."

All night long the train to Dorchester kept company to my thoughts, for I slept almost not at all, reviewing the previous months, and the puzzling alteration in my father's health, and even state of mind—or heart. Of little help to me all night long in the wakeful secrecy of my green-curtained Pullman berth was that personality which in common with my intimate fellow students I cultivated under the fashion of the times. It was a personality of grinning hardness which we expressed in all possible ways. We dramatized our youth and health in violent exercise. We closed our minds against all persons and ideas which our fraternities did not represent in membership. Fanatical about bodily hygiene, our vanity was saved from effeminacy by our rough tweed suits, our expensive, colorless cravats, our short haircuts, even our shoes, which were heavy brogans with extra-thick soles and solid, hard leather heels which made our steps, crossing the bare parquet floors of clubs, sound loudly like those of a race of young giants who trod the earth heedless of anyone who was not a young giant. If our frivolities were alcoholic, they were always unsentimentally so. If we had talents of an unusual sort, the thing to do was mock or conceal them. Hard men had no talents. They had powers. My hardness was counterfeit, but I gave a fair impersonation of it when not alone. But alone, now, in the train as it passed through hushed towns where few lights showed, and the crossing bells rang a rapidly descending scale as we raced by, and the occasional boarding or leaving passengers made dreamlike sounds as we stopped at stations where steam rose in comforting hisses alongside the car, I was filled with weakening qualms, wondering what awaited me at home. How fared my father—the thoughtlessly accepted tower of our family strength—in the illness which Sam Dickinson had described on the long-distance call to the dean's office as serious—serious enough to call me home? I turned my face into my pillows and felt like crying—for the first time since finding love and losing it three summers ago. But I was afraid that someone else might be awake, and might hear me if I wept. Instead, I began to say a prayer for us all, which summoned up images of the past, even from my earliest childhood, in the company of saints, sacraments, and guardian angels; the banks of lighted candles at Mass far away where the figures at the altar moved in all their gold and color representing powers which had nothing to do with hardness, but with hope, and a way to hope. Yes, I said, yes, God's will be done—but it was my will I was praying about.

The nearer we came to the Great Lakes and Dorchester, the more heavily a snowstorm developed; and when at six-thirty I descended from the train, snow was everywhere, showing through the darkness under the clouded lights of the train shed. Faithless, I had slept after all, and had awakened only in time to dress and, unshaven, hastily combed without a mirror, to be greeted by Sam Dickinson.

"Awfully early—thank you, Sam," I said.

"Your mother wanted me to tell you how things are before we get home."

We moved out into the grand Roman hall of the station waiting room, where the early-morning electric light was golden and melancholy. Sam laughed, looking at me, and said,

"You've got quite a shiner there."

I put my hand to my eye, wondering about a vague ache I felt.

"The other one," he said. "Brawling again?"—which was lightly sarcastic, and possibly rather hopeful, as the idea was so foreign to my nature. I suddenly remembered the elbow in my eye on the field.

"Soccer," I said.

He nodded gravely at an honorable wound. Sam was a small man between twenty-five and thirty, neatly made, with a clever face full of charm. His small black eyes, like cloves, behind large-lensed spectacles, gave him a look of amused awareness which he was too well-bred to assert. In an odd way, the glasses made good looks out of his neat, regular features. He was one of those people born to look clean all their lives in any circumstances. He had a law degree from Harvard, his father was president of a small, distinguished New England college, and Sam, too, was destined for an unemphatic career of distinction and public usefulness—an ordained supporter, not an innovator. He was devoted to my father, and brought to him a dimension of witty and intelligent advice which in their blind fealty Our Crowd could not equal.

Outside the station, Sam took the driver's seat of our car and we started home in the snow-muted dawn. If he had ominously been sent to meet me, I was afraid to hear what he had to tell. As we left the station, I caught a glimpse of the frozen harbor with its grain elevators, moored lake steamers, and the ice-covered breakwater far beyond. A faint peach-colored light drifted up from the lake horizon. On Iroquois Avenue the great houses were still asleep, the street lamps still alight but paling. We came into the park, where the little lake was under ice and snow. The shoreline pavilions looked like black brush strokes against the white, and in the falling snow the white marble museums of the Historical Society and the art gallery were made visible only by their shadowed sides and classically shaded porticoes. Sam was silent but for trivialities until we had passed Yates Circle with its great fountain and basin, where I had played for so many childhood hours with little boats which, in the way known only to children, I inhabited even as I pulled them along the pond by strings. Finally,

"Your mother wanted you to be pretty much ready for how things are with your father."

"Why did you say emergency?"

"Because that's what it is. —He has been home ten days, though this is not publicly known. I was with him in Albany when—"

They were alone, the two of them, working late one night in my father's inner office in the capitol, when about midnight my father seemed to choke, and when he coughed into his handkerchief, the white linen was heavy with blood. Sam at first thought this was caused by a nosebleed; but my father shook his head and put his hand on his chest. Sam made him lie down on a black leather settee while he ran for a glass of cold water, thinking to cool the blood and stop its flow. It was a hemorrhage. It seemed to come from below the throat—from the lungs. The flow stopped, and after he had rested for half an hour, during which my father and his aide said almost nothing, but, said Sam, told each other serious conclusions with their eyes, both thinking of what might be happening, Sam carefully, carefully raised him up, took him by freight elevator down to the car, unseen by anyone, and home. My mother was waiting, as she always did unless my father advised her not to. When she saw how pale he was, how frightened, she automatically did all those things which an experienced wife and mother did for sickness in the family; and only when my father was quietly in bed did she hear from Sam what had happened in the office. Her cheeks seemed to go hollow at the information—she said she had been dreading something for many months, but not this, after all the little warnings of the campaign and since. And so had I, without knowing quite what. If I had felt that extra, unknown drain on his resources, had she not also? She telephoned old Dr Breuer, who had taken care of us all my life. He said the matter was surely grave, but nothing sudden could be expected before morning, when he would come with Dr Morton Frawley, a chest specialist, to make a first examination. After several days in the hospital for X rays and other tests, pulmonary tuberculosis was firmly diagnosed. My father was returned home. Bulletins were issued saying that he had suffered a relapse of the influenza and was threatened with pneumonia. Meantime, the temporary president of the senate presided in his absence, and Governor Pelzer reigned alone in Albany.

"What is the emergency now?" I asked. "Is he worse? Is he going to die?"

"No," said Sam. "He is not going to die—if he does what Frawley and the rest of the doctors say is flatly necessary. But your mother needs you because of all that."

"What do they want?"

"They want him to be moved as soon as possible to a high, dry climate, take a leave of absence from his office, and have nothing on his mind but getting well. They say that last prescription is the most difficult *and* important. Evidently tuberculosis has a high relation to emotional states. I never knew this."

"You mean leave Dorchester?"

"Probably for quite a while. Nobody can say how long. Every case is unique; but all seem to share a general course."

"But where will they send him?"

"They think New Mexico. They think Albuquerque. There are specialists there, sanatoriums, altitude a mile high, sunshine. —Frawley (you must meet him, he's quite a specimen of the fashionable medico) says the disease is the leading industry of the city."

"But what will he do? He is so active."

"Too active. We all saw it in the campaign. We should have arranged matters better for him. Anyhow, he will do nothing for some time; then he will get back to things a little at a time, until— until he is well again."

"Sam, have you talked to the doctors yourself?"

"Yes," he replied, without expression, and his restraint told me much.

"How is he now?"

"You'll find him changed. He has lost weight. He is fighting to remain cheerful and be a good patient. Your mother is frightened, tries not to show it, but it shows, and it upsets him, for he is frightened too, and trying to hide it. One day I came upon her weeping in her upstairs sitting room. She has a thousand things to talk over with you."

We reached the house and went up the long driveway at the side. There was a rich mantle of snow on the fan-shaped glass canopy above the door, and on all the shrubbery, the roofs, the trees, rounded beautifully at the edges. Hating through fear to know what was within, I had a flash of thought about my father, seeing him as he raised his glass in a toast during the inaugural party. He was alight with gaiety and power. His evening clothes fitted so well that his raised arm did not disturb the elegance of their line. His smile of the moment seemed like an unending statement of what life was really like, and it persuaded me, I thought, forever. His high color, his shining brushed hair, the rays from his eyes, the light, far-reaching pitch of his voice, and his words of victory, joyful in tone and magnanimous in style, seemed to stand for something which could never die, though I could not define it, sure as I was of it.

❦

My mother was watching for us and opened the door as we came up the outside steps. Light poured upon us from the vestibule. She was ravaged by fatigue, which strangely gave some new loveliness to her face. We embraced. Blinking her eyes and shaking her head quickly to hold back the tears which started up, she said with lightness meant to postpone what we must speak of,

"Why, look at you, darling. You have a paint-box eye"—using the phrase out of my childhood which used to greet me when I would come home from play or fight with an eye all yellow and purple—a phrase meant to diminish self-pity and suffering. It was like her to summon strength from the trivial, if harder trials had to be faced.

Smiling, she took me to have breakfast at a little table set up in the sun porch, which was filled with green plants against the winter. Sam did not join us—went up "to see the Governor," as he always called my father. Our cook, Marie, embraced me with old privilege out of the nursery, saying little, and then brought breakfast. Until we were alone, my mother spoke of the sudden return of winter, the effect of this on the lilacs in the deep garden behind the house, the way the house had "deteriorated" while we were away in Albany, so much to be done, and what to do about my eye? Was soccer worth it? Yes: of course: battle wound: she supposed I had had no raw beefsteak to hold to it all night on the train to "draw out" the inflammation. And wasn't I rather thin? Had I been working too hard? I must keep my weight up, get more sleep—

The association of this struck suddenly at her withheld concern. Unable any longer to hold back, she suddenly put her hands over her face and began to weep. It was some minutes before she could speak above incoherent murmurs.

So sudden. The change was hardly to be believed. A lifetime built together so gradually, so surely, advancing so steadily on course, was now like a ship dead in the water. They had the best care, nurses day and night. Morton Frawley was not discouraged, but was fearfully firm about his orders. The sooner the better.

"Richard, we need your help so much! Oh! Plans? Plans? What to do with everything? How can we? What is that desert going to be like? But what does it matter, if only it will make him well again!"

"How long?"

"Nobody knows. —We don't know a soul out there, though people here have written to friends who have gone there before us for the same reason; they say it's odd how the place casts a spell after a while, you know. But how can I manage it all . . ."

She meant *alone*. She looked at me so longingly that I knew what she could not bring herself to ask me. I thought of college, and all my ties there, the game waiting to be played in England, which at once, and newly, became all-important to me. She gazed away from me, out into the falling snow, and at last I said,

"Do you think I should go with you?"

Knowing what this would demand of me, which unkindly I had

not concealed in my hesitation, she again gave way to tears, and silently nodded.

"Does Father?"

She nodded again, and said in a broken voice,

"But he was not sure we should ask you to leave school this way."

I put my arms around her. She grasped my hand and kissed it, and postponing her urgent hope for fear of a disappointing answer, she said,

"I think you can go up now. The nurse probably has him ready."

—Has him ready: my father: a great child.

Uneasy, reluctant, dreading the encounter, I said,

"Should I shave and bathe first?"

She shook her head. She touched my black eye and said, "Oh! Will you ever get over getting yourself beaten up!" and sent me away.

※

My father lay against a low bank of pillows. A bed light was dimmed by a large manila envelope pinned to its shade. He was in shadow. How thin he was; colorless; how lighted his eyes. When he put his hand to my sleeve I felt his fever. His hand rested there in smooth, bony beauty, like a carving. He ground his jaws together in the old smile he used to have for me, and said,

"Well, Doc, here's a fine pickle of fish," and I replied, in our game of "mixed-up sayings," "Or a pretty kettle, hey?"—for we were all hungry for even the idlest reference to more confident days.

He suddenly began to cough, a rapid, liquid sound, as shallow, it seemed, as he could keep it, in order not to strain the fiber of his lungs. His mouth filled with who knew what particle of his flesh.

Taking up the utensil called a sputum cup, which had a light aluminum frame, handle, and lid enclosing a disposable paper container, he discharged the disturbed mucus into it and with a sigh set it back on the bed table.

"Excuse how I look," I said, explaining about the eye and my generally disordered appearance.

He nodded.

"Heavy practice? A heavy schedule coming up?"

"Pretty heavy." Should I tell him? I told him. "We have an invitation match in England next month."

"England! Have they picked you to go?"

"Not yet. But I'm on the squad."

"Well. That's—that's really great."

Despite his smile, and the forced sparkle in his eyes, I saw why this bothered him. I was sorry to have told him. I did not know which emotion should stay on top.

"Yes," he said, "well, you'd better get bathed and changed and shaved. And put something on that eye. You look like a dog with one black spot. Can you twist your head sideways and let one ear flop and the other stand up? Cute? Go on. I have to rest now, but when you're ready, Sam will let me know, and if Miss Cleary"—the first nurse of the day—"will let me, I must talk things over with you. Your mother has been *suburb* but she can't go on alone much longer."

In our exchanged look we both knew what he was talking about. He added huskily,

"We're going to lick this thing after we get away. That'll be the worst part for us all. Leaving."

With a slight movement of his jaw, and a drift of his gaze, he made me see the whole fabric of our life where we had lived it and all that had gone to make us. For the first time, I felt not my emotional need of him but his of me. I felt my childhood tugging at me. I knew it must be cut away. My middle was hollow, hearing him, seeing, remembering him, and I said,

[48]

"I'm going with you, of course."

With relief so great that it weakened him, he closed his eyes and pressed his lips together until they were pale. Unwilling to show me further feeling, he nodded against his pillows, and faintly motioned to me to go.

When I found my mother downstairs, and told her what I had just said, she put her hands on my shoulders and remarked so endearingly that I felt unworthy and therefore cross,

"You do look more and more like your father . . ."

I scowled.

"What's the matter? Don't you *want* to?"

I scowled, not because I didn't want to look like my father, but because I didn't believe it, and wished it were true. If it were true, I could be more at ease with my new manhood.

❦

Knowing I must leave it against my will, I fell awarely in love with my city then, even though its furious lake-blown winters and exhausting hot summers must have contributed to my father's susceptibility under strain to the tubercle bacillus. I had many duties at home in helping my mother and Sam. My father's office secretary, Lillian O'Rourke, came daily to work at packing, and at lamentation, at which she was expert, and to cheer my mother with bright, pious words and swimming eyes. Miss O'Rourke had the image for me since childhood of a plump parrot which could say more than a few words. Once, during my mimicry phase as a boy, I twisted my neck and rolled my eye out of sight, and pronounced her name, "O'Rour-r-ke," in a grainy squawk imitating a parrot, for her name sounded like a parrot's natural utterance. This made my parents scold, telling me it was wrong and unkind to make fun of so good a soul as Lillian. They sent me into exile upstairs; but as I lingered on the mid-stair landing, I could hear them laughing after all. My father said, "He's a scandal," and my mother, "Yes, but it was just like her." I felt righteous, then, even in my caricature of a person we all thought so good, so self-sacrificing, so devoted to my father and to the Sacred Heart of Jesus. We often spoke of her as "poor soul."

Still, she did have a parrot's beak in the form of her nose, which rose between her pouched little pale eyes and curved out and downward above her small mouth, which it almost concealed. Her chin receded toward her heavy throat in tremulous folds. When I was little she would clasp me to her hungry, rolling breasts, for she was a spinster, filled to overflowing with love to give, but unable in her catechetical chastity to bestow it upon any man and, therefore, upon children of her own. She believed in God the Father, God the Son, God the Holy Ghost, and—my father—God the Unattainable. In this she was happy. Her body was numbed, I concluded, to the idea of sex, and I was sure she met it only in dreams, which she confessed to the priest as mortal sins. Meantime, she became almost part of the family. Her worship went on daily in my father's local office in the Iroquois Building, where she ruled with intolerant exactitude over the office staff. At daily Mass she renewed her blessèd state in thanksgiving. She was to go West with us as companion to my mother, and to deal with my father's forwarded business mail. Oddly, she was openly jealous of Sam Dickinson and his confidential access to my father. Though she was unaware of this, Sam understood it, and took every occasion to give her precedence in the sickroom, which filled her with suppressed fury so that she would thank him with her idea of queenly dignity for favors which were not his to extend.

My own preparations for leaving were simply managed. I telephoned my roommate to pack up my clothes and books and express them to me. The dean granted permission to drop out for the rest of the semester, with the privilege of returning for the fall semester. The head soccer coach said this was a fine time to tell him, when he had his squad all picked out, including me, after all; and with the athlete's single-mindedness dismissed me with a word about how loyalty ought to work both ways.

Now that we were about to abandon it for nobody knew how long, I grew more acutely sensitive to our house. The cook, Marie, and her husband would live in it until we should return. They had been with us since the death of our old servant Anna, whose melancholy and innocent realism had played a great part in my early education. I was sensible of the individuality of the house—any family's house, and how much what was often unnoticed gave character to its atmosphere. I had always taken for granted the comforts and the mild beauties which my mother had arranged; a sense of how the rooms downstairs glowed with light, silvery through wide windows in the daytime, golden in the evenings, with curtains drawn and exactly convenient lamplight playing over soft colors of pale rose and ocher and gray, and firelight, gleaming wood, pictures and mirrors, walls of books, and prevailing little tyrannies of order in the events of meals, parties, and quiet times alone. What contrasting moods, too, left their lingering tones in the atmosphere of memory. Intimacies. Health and illness in their seasons. The odors of the body—our bodies—in the common humanities of physiology; the density of bedroom air after the night; the coffee-in-the-morning kisses; petty estrangements and patient misunderstandings, and occasional ruefulness drifting in the shadows of the house, to be dissipated by the fresh winds of joyful moments scenting the drafts of air all the way from the open cellar door to the living room, and up the stairs to the upper halls, and into the attic itself, from which the mystery of the unused was never quite dispelled. The times of my wickedness and punishment, the festivals of birthdays and holidays; the gaze-widening, bowel-changing, greedy ecstasy of Christmas in childhood gradually giving way to the calmer satisfactions of "thoughtfulness" in useful gifts of later years. Above all, a house as a garment habitually worn but consciously owned as the most protective and precious of all possessions. To keep busy now seemed my mother's source of strength, even as she mourned each object she must leave behind, and with it a fragment of our lives.

※

Aimless with waiting, I began in a sort of anticipated nostalgia to revisit places which I had always valued, once idly, now with purpose.

When in good conscience I could leave the house and its living questions, I went to the white marble palace of the Historical Society. There, years before, I used to go idling along the exhibits where mementos of Dorchester and upstate New York and the Great Lakes were displayed. I knew the battle of Lake Erie in terms of its uniforms, its cutlasses, its (model) frigates, including the *Niagara,* which was Commodore Oliver Perry's flagship, a little ship barely a hundred feet long carrying twenty-two guns. I had belonged in its longboats, manned by sailors in ribboned caps and striped jerseys. The *Niagara's* fiery broadsides matched exactly the color of the orange pan in my watercolor paint box, which had less exact colors for the great pearls of battle smoke above varnished green waves.

Again, for hours, in an aggregate of many visits, I would linger a few feet away from the catafalque on which the coffin of President Lincoln had been laid in state during his funeral train's pause at Dorchester in 1865 on its way home to Springfield, Illinois. The cloth which covered the catafalque was black and musty, faded (like a coachman's coat) to dusty green in places. Unseen moths had done their work. The bier slanted upward toward the head. I made my eyes see the coffin and within the coffin the famous face as it looked in my school book, only with the eyes closed instead of looking at me with printed sorrow, which was expressed throughout the whole figure—how long it was! judging by the bier—in its loose-hanging frock coat and rumpled trousers. Here he had been. I wondered many times whether I might touch the catafalque; and one day, when I was sure nobody was watching, I did so, and shivered, implicated in death and history. Now, with thoughts of my father, I touched it again in an obscure filial rite.

To be exorcised of ultimate thoughts, I sought out the narrow gallery where portraits of local heroes were hung. I was looking for a certain one. I must have seen it many times without particular attention. Now I wanted to see Hugh St Brides's American naval ancestor. I found Commodore Perry easily, and then three portraits down the line I stopped before a young ensign in blue and gold, beardless but for silky sideburns, bare-headed, pink-faced, with the lake wind blowing his pale-yellow hair forward above his brow. His eyes were as blue as the sky above the gold-lighted clouds behind his head. They looked directly at me, and I said, "Christopher," for the young officer was the child grown up, and once again the present was the child of the past. I leaned to read the gold label on the frame, to document my recognition. It read only, *Portrait of a Young Naval Officer, Battle of Lake Erie,"* by Thomas Sully, 1783–1872. But I knew what I knew, and was satisfied, for I was searching for the mortal upon the mortal which eventually reached the present, and gave mortality its quietus. In their continued life, I said goodbye again to the St Brides . Pointing heroically with arm outstretched toward a painted battle on the lake where fire and smoke from twelve-pounders, and burning shrouds, and fallen spars, celebrated both victory and defeat, the young ensign was like an anonymous prophet. Through the truth of the past, I was consoled by a sense of the actual immanence of a future. No story existed only in its single moment of the present. I was surrounded by the history of my birthplace, whose great men and events were kept in honor. Surely one day the portrait of my father, some of his possessions, the marvel of his once having lived, and worked, and been lifted up by his fellows, would rest here with the ensign, and the dead President who had passed by, and the men who had created buildings, parks, streets, and colleges?

※

Even though I was virtually alone in the museum, I felt too exposed to feeling which might be observed. The truth was, I didn't know what to do with my emotion. It would be no help to those at home if I let them see my fears and discontents. To be unknown—to see what I loved without knowing I must lose it as if it had never been mine, I went from the history of Dorchester and the lake and the *Niagara* to the inactive docks of Dorchester harbor under ice. I spent the rest of the afternoon walking by the piers to look out into the basin within the breakwater. Here and there I found a shed which when I sat in its shadow protected me from the wind. The great ore and grain freight ships were winter-locked. Against the gray sky and the pale ice their immensely long, black hulls—empty now and riding high above the ice—their white castles at the stern with their dead funnels, their delicately etched masts, their helpless imprisonment in the very element which in the warm summer months they could command in majestic, leisurely progress, had some heroic quality of endurance obscurely comforting to me. I went there to think over my problems, but actually was trying to escape them, as I soon discovered at the frozen harbor.

In the inner harbor the lake excursion boats were also tied up for the winter, with their decks and their stacked deck chairs covered by lashed tarpaulins. One ship, the old wooden *Inland Queen*, was the largest, most famous, of the summer steamers. The lake ports, Canadian or American, all the way from Dorchester to Toronto to

Cleveland, were proud of her when cloud-white against lake blue she steamed into view bearing passengers whose idea of joy was to sail with her on an "outing." There she lay, now, at her dock, with her stilled walking beam, her two tall, black, cable-braced funnels, her semicircular wheelhouse. I could hear her faintly creaking when the icy wind blew my way. Moping against a pier shed that afternoon, I saw a young man and his girl come across the dock to the gangway, unlock it, and climb to the first deck and disappear behind an overlapping fold of lashed canvas.

Did they live on board?

That first glimpse of them was like a jolt of freedom to me. I did not define it at the time, but my strongest desire was to find a way to evade the responsibility of a witness to suffering, and the duty owed to the family godhead. I was greedy to enter the lives of others, any others, to any degree.

The winter evening fell early, and I saw a light begin to show in a forward porthole of the *Inland Queen*. There the young pair must live. The black water lapped and sucked below cracks in the ice. Built for gaiety, the old ship faintly moved with the life of some under-ice current; and the round glow of light inside her, and the thought of the two people of my own age, secure and alone together, aroused in me my latent treason. I wanted to be in that weathering old steamer, snugly removed from our troubles of the time. I wanted to belong to another life: an unseen partner of those two whom I invested with beauty until my thought became hot with lust. I wanted to embrace them, even at the risk of denial and shame—for in my settling adulthood the body was ordinarily turned away in constraint from chance persons, strangers, while in childhood, in a life of close-ups, it had been given freely and in innocence.

How did they live in the forward cabin? Or did they come only occasionally, to love each other, to leave the ship, and to disappear into the city where others knew them? Perhaps he was a watchman? If so, he had not seen me, loitering by my shed. On certain days perhaps she came alone—why I could not think. But I was hot with desire to belong to them, he a comrade, she a lover, both needing me as I needed them. The emotion of home in which I felt so helpless was turning over in my breast into another which had nothing to do with good sense; only with power which drove me toward new wants—for protection, assuagement, removal; and the key to these seemed in imagination the life of those two in that secret space beyond the round lighted porthole of the excursion steamer, vessel of seasonal gaiety, now locked by ice and privacy.

I watched to see if they would return to the world; but soon, mysteriously, the porthole light went out. They were there to stay. The knowledge pierced me, and so, suddenly, did the cold, the dark, as evening fell; and so, like shock, sanity fell again upon me, and I was shivering, not only with winter, but with realization of my foolish desires, which had the aftermath of sin committed. I turned from the docks and walked uptown. Snow was beginning to fall again in flakes so huge they seemed to descend slowly, each in a spiral, which, multiplied infinitely, dazzled my vision against the blooming street lamps.

Going against the storm with turned and lowered face, I began to know the full meaning of my private betrayal; and secure because I was alone, I was not diffident about looking for forgiveness and strength when in my homeward walk I saw looming through the lamplighted snow the white marble Cathedral of the Holy Angels— the scene of my rescues from earlier visions and betrayals. Prayer stirred in me without words, but with an urgency loftier than what I had felt in childhood whenever I asked God for a particular toy after which I imperiously lusted. What had I just done but ask the impossible of chance?

The immense bronze doors of the cathedral were still unlocked. I let myself in, making an echo far away and above as I stamped off the snow which clung to my galoshes. I went up the long central aisle and knelt down before the deserted but not empty chamber of the sanctuary. From its high shadowed arch came the lofty gold chains which suspended the crimson glass of the eucharistic lamp, whose tiny flame burned without a flicker in the stillness. I brought clear to mind my contrition for my thoughts of folly and treachery; vowed not to entertain them again, to put away forever the life of the young man and woman of the *Inland Queen* and all they called me to. Again I was grateful to be alone, now because I was afraid of being seen at prayer, especially by someone of my own age.

But the next afternoon, going by my watch with the anxiety of one who is committed to a crucial appointment, I was at the dock again. The snowstorm was over, the sky was overcast with gray color which matched that of the lake, and I waited to see if they came back at the same time.

They came, entered the ship; their light slowly became visible, making me think they must use a kerosene lamp whose wick caught flame slowly, and I felt both chagrin and hot comfort at this regularity. There was that world again. I was that young fellow whom I longed to be: a working man, with my scarred black lunch box, which I would carry by its frayed leather handle. There was my girl, whose job observed the same hours as his, so they could come and go together. The shipping line must pay them for living on board, guarding the ship. It was now clear that it was their daily habit to return to the ship toward evening. It was their home. A new thought struck me. What if they were married? Why had I not thought of this before? With a rush of feeling, I hoped they were not married, for if they were, how might I expect to enter their lives? The idea was tormenting. How foolish of me to have come back, after my deeply meant vow of the night before. A sense of urgency came alive in me. We were, the family, to leave in a very few days. Until I knew more of the lives I hungered for, how could I leave? Waiting and watching to see their light go out, I made another vow—one I knew I would keep.

Tomorrow I would return. I would be waiting for them. When

they approached the gangway and were about to disappear into their privacy with all its imagined joys, I would come out of the shadow of my shed and intercept them. I would have ready a few apologetic general questions about the ship, the harbor; and with diffidence, which made my heart beat even in thinking of the scene, I would ask if they might let me see the ship's interior. Did they live on board? How lucky they were. Lucky? they would ask in honest puzzlement. Yes, I would say, to have such a life to themselves, away from the usual habits of the city. How I wished I were as lucky. They would look at each other, silently asking whether this stranger was to be taken seriously, or dismissed as a nuisance, possibly as someone dangerous to their matter-of-fact comfort. But my sincerity would win them. They must not see my hunger just yet. They must remain as uncomplicated as I must seem. If they were not people of many words, they might just shrug and make small smiles, and let me come on board, and after a brief tour of the shrouded decks, when they would be ready to have me go, I would ask where they lived—they would pause to consider again, and then won by my earnest liking for them, they would tell me where, and lead me there, and light their lamp, and out of common decency would have to ask me to sit down for a moment, perhaps to have a cup of coffee, warmed over from their pre-dawn breakfast. Soon we would have more to talk about than we could use, for we were all young, and wanting to stay beyond time, I knew I would soon have to leave the city, and when they heard this, they would become fonder of me than ever, and as if to defeat time, we would exchange news of our separate lives, an act which would give us to each other . . . I would not leave them until it was clear that I would be welcome to return; and with that, and a disarmingly worried look at my watch, which made clear that I was late for an urgent event elsewhere, I could go. They would walk the deck with me to the gangway and close the canvas after me and padlock it through the brass grommets for its lashings and I would say, "Until tomorrow!"

I felt there was now another dimension to my life. It gave me energy. Early the next morning I was up and about, out to the snow to rescue the morning paper before it was dampened through. I went to the kitchen to brew coffee for myself and, while the water heated, opened the paper and glanced at—

But what I saw was hardly a news event to me; it was a private calamity. In the middle of the front page a four-column photograph showed the *Inland Queen* burning by night. Against the wild blaze of her flames, the huddled figures of firemen were silhouetted. Their hoses sent great arcs of white water over the ship, but to no avail. She burned like any wooden house. Through smoke, sparks, dazzle, I could see parts of the ship as if they were broken and hanging in air—the forward wheelhouse, the funnels, the walking beam, masts, lifeboats dangling at crazy angles, great sheets of fallen canvas like curtains open on a theater scene.

"Fire of unknown origin," said the news story. Officials of the navigation company which owned the ship declared when interviewed that a young man—they gave his name—was employed as a watchman who stayed on board at night, after his daytime hours as a student (senior) at Dorchester City University. He was working his way through college and was regarded as a thoroughly reliable young man. So far as could be determined at press time, he had been on board when the fire broke out. Efforts to find him, or his body, were prevented by the intense heat and rapid spread of the flames. Further photographs would be found on a later page. I turned the pages until I found them. The ship from several angles; the fire chief calling commands to his men through a white megaphone; and a photograph of Jay William Drew, Jr., taken from his high school yearbook. He was posed leaning slightly forward. The photographer told him how to cock his head, and to smile, which he did evidently with some unwillingness, and to look right into the camera. His hair was brushed glossy and flat, dark in color. His eyes looked very dark under thin black brows which met just above the bridge of his nose. He had large ears and square bony jaws. I had never seen his face, but I had seen him moving. There was no mention of anyone else on the ship. The fire had broken out at about 2 a.m., and was first seen as glow in the sky by the motorman of a streetcar making its last run of the night two blocks away. He turned in the alarm. His name was Herman August Winckelmann, of 233 Rohr Street.

By the time my father called for the morning paper, I was composed enough—inscrutable, I believed—to take it to him. But when I handed it to him, he asked,

"Are you all right, Doc?"

"Oh, yes. —I didn't sleep very well. I read till very late."

"You must get your sleep. It's important for later"—he was thinking of resources against tubercular breakdown.

As soon as I could I went to the harbor to see the ruin. Was his body found now that the char had frozen under the hose water? A small crowd stood on the dock gazing, mostly in silence. I heard someone answer my silent question, telling someone else in the crowd.

"They never found him, but the fire evidently started in the cabin he lived in. Nothing was left there but the kerosene stove. The chief had it taken out an hour ago."

The *Inland Queen* lay half sunken and at a sharp list away from the dock. She was like a burned-out house, with icicles bright against her blackened superstructure. She would never again sail the Great Lakes to Toledo, Toronto, and Cleveland. Down, now, in the slow current under the ice, she shifted now and then ever so slightly —or was this my imagination, as I stared at her so intently that I made her move? My loins shrank, at a general loss of love. A part of my secret life was over in tragedy; and I was ashamed that for a while I mourned this more keenly than I did the threat suspended over the lives of my father and the rest of us.

When I reached home later in the day, my mother said,

"Everything is settled. I cannot believe it. We go on Saturday. Sam says so. The train and all."

Her wondering look was replaced now by a brave lift of her neat, small head, as if to say the worst was over.

"Yes," I said, delivered in my way from the obsession which had taken me for those few days from the emotion proper to a member of any family; and in my way I asked that from our trials we would emerge as safely, under that disembodied mercy forever addressed by mankind.

❦

Departures and arrivals were occasions I disliked because they required visible emotions and ardent, often false, demonstrations. We were at the railroad station early, because of the special arrangements needed for bringing my father into the train. He did not want to be seen by other passengers as they boarded. His ambulance was allowed to drive along the wide concourse at track end long before the passenger gates were opened. At the farthest track, standing alone and clouded with steam from temporary connections, was the combined gesture of fealty by Our Crowd; for to make my father's three-day journey to New Mexico as comfortable as possible, they had, without telling him until a day ago, "chipped in" to charter a private railroad car to take him all the way West. It was called the "James Buchanan." In the dusky, cold train shed, the yellow-shaded lights within the car looked inviting and reassuring. Polished wood paneling showed within, and a round-vaulted ceiling painted a soft green. Horace, the steward of the car, stood waiting on the rear platform with its shined brass railings and deep, overhanging canopy.

As my mother and Lillian O'Rourke, Sam, and I stood watching, the ambulance attendants brought my father on a specially narrow stretcher and lifted him across the brass railing, through the rear door of the car, and to the first stateroom down the corridor. It was then that I fully understood how ill he was—that he was not allowed to take even one step. My father remained silent, guarding himself, but he nodded and gazed keenly at each stage of the arrangements. Dr Morton Frawley arrived and made rapid bedside tests, said all was stable, and departed without further words, but glancing at each of us as he left the car to note what we thought of him, on his way to more urgent matters. My father's favorite of the nurses from the house was going with us—Mrs DeLancy. In no time she had the intimate Pullman stateroom established as an efficient hospital room: lights, window shades, pillows, blankets, racks of medicine, bedside table, placed pillows, just so. My father sighed in the contentment of the moment, which was the best, now, that he dared do with respect to time and the future. The door of the room was left open as the rest of us found our quarters. The car had six staterooms, a dining room, a galley, and, occupying the last third of its length, a sitting room with sofas, easy chairs, magazine racks, and little tables.

I was looking at our departure time on my watch when we felt a gentle jar. A switch engine had coupled itself to the "James Buchanan" and now pulled us to the end position on another track, and there by particular permission (since limited trains were not supposed to pull private cars) the famous flyer called The Wolverine slowly backed into position until with jets and screams of steam, and metal clinchings, train and car were attached.

Ten minutes before the station gates were to open for the public, a sizable crowd of men came to the train from another entry—Our Crowd, who had to see my father off, as they said, and also inspect the private car which at great expense they had provided for him. They filed through the car from the rear platform, each pausing a second at my father's open doorway to say a word to him, while he

[62]

waved back in silence. I was moved and therefore irritated at the open show of emotion which so many made—I saw more than one man trying to pretend he was not in tears.

My mother was equal to the event. She stood on the platform outside at the rear steps by which Our Crowd came down from the car. She shook hands with them all, and from a few of the closest friends she accepted a kiss on the cheek. Over the cavernous, contained noises of the high train shed, heightened words of encouragement were said, bright promises of early return and gleeful reunion, offers to do anything possible in the way of help back home while we were so far away.

"Yes, thank you, oh, we do thank you, yes, you are a dear," my mother would say, holding her fur collar to her cheeks against the cold air scraping on a long draft through the shed. "Of course we will write, yes, postcards, do keep in touch. Dan is so grateful. We are going to be perfectly fine."

But underlying much of their good cheer, Our Crowd felt uncertainty and disappointment. They had relied on so great a return for their belief in my father that they could not help wondering if all might not now be endangered. They had persuaded him to run for office when he had at times shown a strange, almost angry reluctance, they had helped powerfully to elect him, they knew that in politics he would be as brilliant and reliable as in business; and to the extent of his success they would be entitled to feel success in themselves. As they left the car, they gathered by my father's stateroom window at the offside of the car, hidden from the platform along which passengers were at last hurrying to their numbered Pullman sleepers. There followed one of those pauses when it was time to go, but when nothing yet happened, and Our Crowd were obliged to stamp their feet against the cold, and in pantomime send messages and sentiments through the steamy window, whose shade Mrs DeLancy had agreed to raise, and one or two clowned a bit.

Two interruptions took place toward the end. The first was the arrival of a florist's delivery boy bringing a huge basket of American Beauty roses from the Governor and Mrs Pelzer, with a silk ribbon saying in gold letters, GET WELL QUICK FROM JUDGE AND MO. The bouquet was so large that it attracted attention, and created the second interruption. The reporter from *The Dorchester Chronicle* regularly assigned to the daily departure of The Wolverine followed the basket of roses, discovered to whom it was going, who had sent it, and asked for clarification.

Sam Dickinson met him on the platform before he could board the car and gave the desired statement: *The lieutenant-governor had been ordered by his physicians to take a vacation of a few weeks in the warm Southwest, where the sunshine and the dry, high altitude would help to dispose of the influenza and the mild pneumonia which had plagued the lieutenant-governor earlier in the year. It was not possible to see him as he had gone straight to bed on boarding the train. No, the private car was not chartered at public expense. Yes, the lieutenant-governor would continue to keep abreast of affairs at Albany, and in fact, to make that official routine possible, he, Samuel Dickinson, the permanent legislative assistant, was accompanying the lieutenant-governor, who was taking along also his personal private secretary. Yes, there were others in the party—the lieutenant-governor's wife and son, and a registered nurse. No, it was not at this time advisable to release the party's destination, since publicity would result in activity which would make demands on the lieutenant-governor and impede his rapid convalescence. No, regrettably, a photograph was not possible—*and just at that moment, the conductor gave the long cry of "All aboard." The engine bell began to toll in its arch. Deafening gusts of steam came forth from the great pistons far ahead, and The Wolverine began to draw slowly out with all doors clanged shut, as Our Crowd, led by one of their members, broke into a chorus which rose almost unheard into the high steel girders overhead, "For he's a jolly good fel-low." From the observation platform at the rear I watched the train shed recede.

It was a scene in black and white, with smoked girders, and drifts of steam, dark empty engines and cars, and lines of frozen snow tracing the perspective of the tracks which so steadily narrowed. Our Crowd were now soundless but still singing and waving, and like a child gravely obedient to custom, I waved back.

CHAPTER III

❦

Laughter in the Desert

ON THE THIRD DAY we came to Albuquerque in a state of general blindness whenever we looked out of the windows of our car. For hours the land had been obscured by a vast dust storm which threw desert earth, almost gravel in size, against the "James Buchanan." Eager to see the new country, as if seeing it would give us the power to foresee our life there, we were denied sight of those features which such great names stood for—the Rio Grande, the Sandia Mountains, the mesa at Albuquerque, the volcanoes on the horizon west of the river valley. Though we kept all windows tightly shut, the dust penetrated the car. Mrs DeLancy laid wet towels along the windowsills in my father's stateroom to keep him from breathing the choking air.

"Whiii!" cried my mother, brushing the air away from her face. With a finger she traced patterns in the dust on the glossy furniture of the car, as later she would do so often when the dust blew into our house in the Rio Grande valley; and for her the dust (the stuff, I wrote in my notebook with gloomy literary relish, of our promised mortality) remained ever afterward my mother's main image of the new land.

But to me it showed something else—the very energy and scale of the storm spoke of vast spaces and movement. Now and then when the storm thinned for a moment, the sun, a great pale-blue disk, showed like an omen and then vanished before it could be read. At Albuquerque the "James Buchanan" was shunted off from the California Limited of the Santa Fe line to which we had been transferred in Chicago.

We waited, so it seemed, for over an hour on our side track, expecting a visit from the doctor to whom Frawley had sent us. My father was apprehensive until the doctor finally arrived; and then he found extra energy, assumed a mask of confidence and all his old charm in an imposture of health. The doctor went into the stateroom, retained Mrs DeLancy, and closed the door, while the rest of us waited in the rear sitting room.

"What do you suppose is taking him so long?" asked my mother after a few minutes.

"God have mercy," murmured Lillian.

"It's rather early for that," declared Sam, with an excusing grin, and just then the doctor in long, swooping strides came along the corridor and into the room with us.

"Well and good," he stated generally, and shook hands with us all. "My first, cursory observation tells me that the patient must remain here in the car until the air clears. We're in our third day of it. Probably the last day. Then we'll have an ambulance ride to Saint Anthony's Sanatorium. Have you time? Let me sit down with you for a few minutes," sweeping us all with a glaring smile.

Dr M. Jamison Birch was fiercely amiable in order to deny his own precarious health. He was himself tubercular—an arrested case, as they said in that colony of consumptives. He had been a classmate at Cornell of Dr Morton Frawley and ironically had become, in laboratories and sickrooms, a victim of the very disease in which he had chosen to specialize. Tall, stooped, skeletally thin, he had a skull-like face which constantly wore its fierce bony smile, as if without his volition. His head was small for his long frame, and across its dome a few black hairs were brushed flat, though several at the rear stuck out like feathers. His eyes were sunken in their sockets and his

[67]

nose resembled a hawk's beak between them. He had a way of standing with his bony hands loosely furled together before his concave chest. His coat hung on him as on a hanger.

"How is my old friend Frawley?" he asked in a thin, throaty voice. "We used to call him T.L.P., which stood for This Little Pig, he was so round and pink, you know, as a student, and he was so sure of where he was going, you know. —How is he?"

"Oh, splendid," replied my mother, astonished that we would not immediately discuss my father's condition. "He was—most professional."

"Haa. You didn't like him."

"Oh, no, no. —I simply meant *brisk*."

"Yes. But he knew what he was doing."

Dr Birch was attempting to establish a kindly social atmosphere for us all, and succeeded then, and even further, in the days following, until he became a friend who rejoiced whenever he could escape in conversation from the morbid ingredients of which his professional life was made.

"I have not seen T.L.P. for years," he went on. "He remains quite perversely healthy. I think this is because he feels it more fashionable to be well than ill." He laughed hollowly. "However, we speak frequently by telephone, and lately, quite often about your husband."

At last my mother's anxious concern was recognized openly.

"Yes—how do you find him, Dr Birch?"

"I shall be making detailed examinations during the week. I'll know more then. I expect we will be able to move him tomorrow."

He suddenly turned his eyes on me—they gleamed remotely but hotly, I thought, like anthracite coals, as in a long silence he seemed to penetrate my being, almost in a trance. But he was concentrating so fiercely that he made me feel like a specimen, which, I was to learn, was just how he saw me. Then abruptly he became social again, smiling with winning charm. He leaned toward my mother and said,

"You are quite naturally worried. But let me say this: the more you worry, the less you can help your husband. Your own health will be the best medicine he can have, once we establish him in a proper regimen."

My mother could not help asking,

"Oh, *is* he going to be all right?"

"Madam, I am an eternal optimist. Look at *me*. I was sent out here twenty-one years ago to die, as it was believed more seemly for me to die in a beneficial climate than that of New York. And now the tubercle bacillus gives a faint shriek of alarm every time it sees me."

I laughed, and so did Sam. Lillian shook her head at such a marvel. The doctor turned again to me.

"That's *better*," he remarked genially, and the emphasis set him to coughing—the liquid, shallow, self-sparing cough of the tubercular. Covering his mouth, he shook his head to discourage alarm. In a moment, "Please come to see me in my office tomorrow at the sanatorium. Four o'clock. We will know more to talk about then. Meantime, don't pay attention to the dust. It is merely an irritant. Above all," he added, again piercing me, now accurately, "do not take it as a metaphor."

With a lanky bow, he left the "James Buchanan." Watching him go, Sam said,

"We are going to like that man."

"If only he can help," said my mother, as though he was now the controller of our lives, which to a degree he was.

※

"They're all so cheerful," remarked my mother after a week's acquaintance with the staff and some of the patients at Saint Anthony's Sanatorium. Even my father's spirits seemed to rise now that

[69]

he was settled in his hospital room, facing the mountains a dozen miles away across the mesa. A sliding glass door opened on to a little balcony where in discreet doses, to begin with, he could be moved into fresh air and sunshine.

Mrs DeLancy had gone home on the same train which took away the empty "James Buchanan," and the sanatorium nurses now managed my father's needs.

They were Sisters of Charity, whose order had come to New Mexico in the nineteenth century to establish hospitals and orphanages. They were now assisted by registered lay nurses whom I thought of as civilians, as against the nuns. There was at first the kind of little flutter of extra interest, at which the nuns were innocently expert when their lives were heightened by anything at all unusual, when they identified my father as a public man; for the newspapers by now had the full story of who he was and why he was there, the news of which had been released over the wire services by Governor Pelzer at Albany. "We hope he will soon be back with us," the governor was quoted as saying. "His leave of absence is expected to be reasonably brief"—but Sam had private reports of maneuvers and speculations about what shift of power in the state senate might follow upon my father's absence, and whether the governor would now gather all control for himself. My father smiled sardonically and said,

"Well, Sam, Pelzer seems to have the luck of the Devil himself."

"He doesn't look like that for nothing," replied Sam. "We can watch him fairly closely from here. I've got the office all set up to telegraph us daily."

But as yet he was not supposed to show my father any reports which would require extended concentration. Rest, rest, was the order of the day. Time itself had to be the dosage which if properly used would cure my father. Even certain kinds of thoughts were prohibited by Dr Birch. No dwelling on the past, or on what had to be relinquished for the time being, or particularly on what opportu-

[70]

nities for a brilliant future might be endangered now. Live for each day; for each breath.

"Sam," said my father, "I don't know what I'd do—any of us would do—without you. How can I thank you for what you've left in order to be with us?"

For Sam was engaged to marry the daughter of a dean at Harvard, and it had been his habit to go to Cambridge from Albany. They had not set a date for their wedding, but the assumption was that it would come in either June or October. Now no date could be set until certain conditions became clear at Albuquerque. Joanna was unwillingly patient; thought she would spend the summer in Europe and see how she felt about things on her return. Even though there was no question of a permanent breach, she could not resist this hint of a threat. Sam was more worried than he admitted, and spent a great part of his salary on long-distance calls to Cambridge, from which he took enough reassurance to keep his gleaming good nature visibly intact. He suffered no impairment to that one trait which most pleased my father. This was a smiling irony well this side of cynicism which used the skeptical to dramatize the actual. It made him politically valuable and a fine companion responding to the daily shape of life.

"Governor," he said, "it is rare enough to be able to serve principle as embodied in a member of *Homo sapiens*. I should be thanking you."

It was never spoken between them, but their bond lay in Sam's belief in my father's great public potential, for which almost anything—Joanna, even? I wondered—could be sacrificed, and in my father's thankful acceptance of the loyalty of this young patrician whose quick mind, selfless charm, and good manners were so effortless and reliable.

The sanatorium was a long, three-story, red brick building which looked as if it had been bent from the straight into a shallow angle at the center. It had white pillars at its central entrance, and a grand curved driveway which gave a manorial calm to the front, while at the rear, a stark cement deck and wide folding doors served the emergency entrance. At the north end the manorial air was displaced by a small, added Gothic wing whose two-story windows of stained glass, tented slate roof, and slender gold-leafed steeple announced the hospital chapel, where my mother spent a supplicant hour every day. The main lobby, and all its corridors, had floors of brown linoleum which were polished daily to a high gloss, giving off a pungent smell of faintly sour wax, which came to seem, for me, like the very odor of illness; but when I mentioned this to others, they had not noticed it, and said I was too morbid, especially for someone who was to become a medical doctor—for this vocation was still tacitly agreed upon in my family, having been established in my childhood by my first toy doctor's bag with candy medicines in little phials out of which I cured the greedy illnesses of my playmates until the brightly colored pills were all gone.

The rear of the building had a long sun porch. There the ambulant patients went to drink the air and sunlight. Waiting there sometimes for my father to be made "ready" for the day and visitors, I saw the patients in their long deck chairs and made the acquaintance of a few, and saw enough of others to recognize what they had in common—an acute awareness of their physical states at every moment, and their almost furtive but zealous care of the moment's evidence: taking their own pulses, counting their respirations, inhaling with deliberate measure, exhaling with luxurious caution. They held their hands forward to see if the color beneath their fingernails showed a trifle more pink today, indicating new red corpuscles.

When they changed position they used slow gliding motions so as not to disturb tissues in tender suspension between healing and hemorrhage. They observed a programmed gladness in their greetings of each other, since any admission of their constant concern would express pessimism, which Dr Birch had said was an enervating state of mind.

Cheerful under eternity, the nursing sisters of Saint Anthony's, with death postulated all about them, established an early intimacy with us all; and when we came daily to see my father, we were recognized and welcomed as if we belonged to their family, as in their professional eyes and actual faith we did.

Among the rather large circle of the staff which seemed to take form about my father as they felt his interest in them despite his own state, one nun in particular became a family intimate. This was Sister Mary Vincent, a nursing sister, who supervised the floor where my father lived. On duty, she was a stony-faced tyrant with a restrained and awesome temper; but when she was free for a moment from professional pressures, she was an amusing woman who loved harmless gossip (the hospital was full of all kinds of gossip) and had to be the first to know and tell it. Her countenance was bright pink, plump, naturally full of gleams, which were doubled by the flash of her enormous rimless eyeglasses. These reflected light in streaks as she swiftly turned her head to catch every facet of any possible interest in the life about her.

My mother, who had always had a feeling for nuns, in early times would now and then infuriate my father with an idle speculation about why she had abandoned her girlhood dream of becoming a nun herself, and whether after all she had done the right thing to change her mind. "You simply grew up," my father would say, scowling, and add, "Do you think it altogether kind to the rest of us to bring that up *now?*" And she would be flooded with comic remorse, as all along it was just this response from him which she had been playing for. Observing this, my father would be more cross than ever, so that my mother was forced into the delicious duty of winning him over again, and calming my fright at imagining the loss of her.

Now, at Saint Anthony's, my mother could not resist claiming affinity with the nuns on behalf of gaining their special attention to my father's needs. One day she confessed her schoolgirl vocation to Sister Mary Vincent, who replied,

"I had a feeling you understood us; but you obviously did what God wanted you to do, and now: your lovely family. You must not complicate matters by having any regrets."

"Oh, I don't, I don't! —How do you think he is? You have seen so many—"

Sister Mary Vincent folded her scrubbed, capable hands within her bloused sleeves and pledged with her eyes that my father's case would have her special attention.

She was particularly interested, too, in knowing everything about me, which led to my unexpected involvement in the hospital life. As I could never give an account of myself, my mother did this for me, usually forcing me to leave the room when my attainments were recited. Now,

"Exactly the one," declared Mary Vincent, as we soon began to speak of her, and then address her. "We need someone for the volunteer library, and since he is idle"—it being too late in the year for me to enroll in the university on the mesa beyond Saint Anthony's—"we shall put him to work."

She made a wagging command and promise with her forefinger; and within a few days, I was spending three hours a day as librarian at the desk in the indoor solarium, where ranks of donated books ran along the shelves facing the opposite glass wall. My working hours were in the morning, since the patients had to rest all afternoon.

On my first day two patients became individuals to me.

One of these was a young man of about my own age. He idled along the shelves, glancing my way when he thought I might not notice. When he saw me smile dutifully at him, a library patron, he took heart and came to my desk, holding a book which he asked about. It was a battered blue volume called *Memories of an Ambassador's Wife,* by Mary King Wallington. I had never heard of it.

"It has things about life at the Imperial Russian Court," he said in a light voice, cadenced with italics and deliberate refinement, and carrying an emphasis on the sibilants. "I think I would like to read it."

I took down the title and author, and asked his name.

"Carlton Gracey?"—as though I might recognize it.

I recorded him as the borrower.

"Have you just come here?" he asked. "Have you chased the cure very long?"

"Oh: I am not the patient in our family. It is my father." I told him the name.

"Oh: the New York governor. *Oh my!*" impressed.

I explained my father's actual status.

"*Still,*" said Carlton, needing to hold on to any distinction when he met it. I was somewhat startled that by my appearance he had assumed me to be a tubercular like himself. Surely I had none of his visible symptoms? He was skeletally thin. His face was pointed and narrow, with flushed cheekbones, and eyes, sunken under blond brows, with something of a bird's look about them. Under his carefully neat, pale clothes his body seemed to be working to remain upright. He moved with conscious grace. When he coughed he closed his lips to contain politely a rude sound which might offend others. When he spoke he tossed his head faintly as though demonstrating pathetic courage in the face of a hard world. "*Thank* you," he said, and with elegant steps made his way out of the library, holding his book curled into his shallow chest with one hand, and balancing his steps with the other in a restrained sway.

If he made me want to smile at his airs of excessive refinement, he also touched me with his desire to show himself as a superior person. In repeated visits, he began to feel my uncritical friendliness, and I was soon given his history. He grew up in Rolla, Missouri, conducting a longing search there for *the finer things of life,* without much success. In Rolla, there was no accounting for him, and he was made to feel this. His high school years were *torture,* for his difference from all the rowdy students. When he could, he escaped to Chicago with a small inheritance from his maternal grandmother, who died just as he was graduated from high school. He went to the Chicago Business College, training for secretarial work. Chicago was the great lodestone for those of the Middle West who starved for the cultural life. Carlton was so happy there he thought at first he could hardly *stand* it. I nodded. The Art Institute; the magnificent mansions of Lake Shore Drive; the Chicago Symphony Orchestra; most wonderful of all, after all the years of reading and wanting, the great Chicago Opera. He knew the names of all the artists, and suddenly released from his cultural loneliness at Saint Anthony's, he would spend as much time as we both had in describing them, their roles, and their world, which, from his top balcony seat when he could afford it, he entered like one coming home. The music, yes, but above all, it was the *ballet* which entranced him, and of the ballet, it was one dancer who became his *idol.* She was not the female star, but even so, for him, in her second leads, she outshone everyone on that vast distant stage. He watched the playbills for her name, and saved his ticket money for her nights onstage. Her name—he pronounced it with a sound which seemed Russian to him—was Stasia Rambova.

He looked about. If nobody was in sight, he would show me how Stasia Rambova stood alone in a spotlight as the curtains parted. He asked me to notice how the line of the left leg was continued in the upraised right arm, and was countered by the sharp turn of head. Glancing down, he would call attention to the perfect placement of her feet—the heel of one set into the instep of the other, both turned wide at a stylized angle. Best of all—

He was about to show it, when another patient came from nowhere into the library. Carlton's world collapsed. Coldly, he took up some books and walked out with his left shoulder raised.

"Getting a free show?" asked the intruder.

This was Lyle Pryor, who read two or three books a day. He too spent time talking to me in the solarium. In his way, he too was hungry for a world denied him by the disease. He was a New York journalist who lived at Saint Anthony's, but his case was close enough to a cure to permit him to come and go, as though from a hotel. "General activity in moderation," as Dr Birch had said. Tall as a heron, and built rather like one, he had a bony pink face, pale eyes, huge eyeglasses, and a high braying voice in which he rapidly spoke comic insults under the privilege of genial cynic—a role he had created for himself. As soon as my father was permitted visitors for a few minutes at a time, he made habitual calls on him, asking rapid-fire questions like an interviewer, and offering opinions which were deliberately provocative. He would tire my father with his energy, and then, with a scratchy laugh, he would go away. Under the pseudonym of T. B. Crabb he contributed gratis a weekly column to the local morning paper in which under the guise of humor he made biting comments on local and national affairs. One day he remarked to my father,

"Politics, eh? Albany, Chicago, Albuquerque, Santa Fe—there's no difference, y'know? A vocation for poltroons"—H. L. Mencken was his model—"and here, locally, for small-time crooks. You're lucky, Governor, you come from the land of big-time crooks. I'm glad to see you have overcome the temptations of the gaudy life."

This was too much for Sam, who was with my father, sifting the morning mail.

"The Governor," he said with smiling mouth and angry eyes, "has already done more than any other man to begin cleaning up the leading state in the Union!"

"And they got him for it, didn't they?" cackled Pryor, beyond logic. "Look where he is now, out here with the rest of us lungers and social parasites!"

My father, weary of this fevered irony, simply shut his eyes, and Lyle Pryor had to go.

But Carlton Gracey had no one to guard him against Pryor, who stared after his scornful departure with a snicker that day in the solarium.

"No, not a show," I said, "he was explaining things about ballet."

"Stasia Rambova, eh?—I got it all a long time ago, when he first got here. The poor little bastard."

"You don't really sound very sorry for him."

"Oh, hell, I feel sorry for him, and for everyone, what's more, but there's no use moaning over it, is there? One day when he was raving to me about his Stasia Rambova, trained in the Imperial Russian Ballet School, who escaped just in time from the Bolsheviks, I said, Oh hell, kid, she was probably just Bella Feinblum of East Side Chicago. He turned white and said he for one was not to be addressed as 'kid,' and that I was never to address him again."

"You're pretty rough on him."

"What else can you do with a Missouri Exquisite? —They tell me you want to be a doctor, eh?"

"Who says so?"

"Oh, Mary Vincent, for one."

"The two of you are the town criers here, aren't you?"

"We trade items. —But you're always writing in some notebook or other. What about?"

"Not medicine."

"Clams up, don't he." He laughed. On principle, he liked an adversary. He drifted away.

The next time Carlton came about books, he said,

"If you ever see *that creature* coming while I'm here, I'll be *grateful* if you will give me a word of warning."

I promised.

"Look," he said, "here is her picture. I cut it out of a program. She does look Russian, really, don't you think?"—for something of his belief in his fantasy about the Imperial Russian Ballet School had been damaged in spite of loyalty by Pryor's grinning skepticism.

"Oh, yes. Black hair and Tartar eyes. She is beautiful."

"Thank you," he said soberly, as though he could take credit for the opinion. "I *was* going to show you her most wonderful gesture: her curtain call."

With that, once sure nobody else was watching, he drew himself up nobly, lifting one arm with his hand upward and its fingers curled open to receive the world, the other arm cradling an imaginary spray of roses, then turning his head slowly from side to side to sweep the great balconies, the boxes, the orchestra, as though inhaling the ozone of glory; and when he had surveyed the whole house, he slowly sank with bowed head to one knee in grace and humility. The illusion he created was startling. When he returned to himself,

"Wonderful," I said.

"You *see* why I love her?"

"Oh, yes."

He sighed.

"The late spring season opens very soon. Perhaps I'll be there."

Was this the optimism of the tubercular?

Actually, it was the very opposite.

Soon afterward Lyle Pryor said to me,

"We're losing the Missouri Exquisite."

"How do you mean? Is he worse?"—for I had not seen him for some days.

"No. He's leaving."

"Good Lord, why? He's not all that well."

"No. Mary Vincent told me. His money is all gone. He can't afford to stay any longer."

"Oh, no. Can't anyone help with funds?"

"It wouldn't make much difference. Matter of fact, I offered a little something on the sly to the san. But Birch says he might as well be let go." The first note of sympathy came into Lyle's voice. "Incurable."

"Do they really think so?"

"Listen, kid. I'll tell you something about this disease. Physically, the poor little idiot is far gone. But he's dying of more than t.b. Can't you see that? Some people, when they're denied what they most want, die of the denial. That's what's happening to the Missouri Exquisite."

"You mean, he's actually dying of love for Stasia Rambova?"

"Not quite as you mean it. He wishes he could *be* Stasia Rambova. He can't. He's dying of it, with t.b. to help it along. We'll never see him again. Nobody will, for long."

The revelation was so startling to me that at the time I saw nothing beyond it. As Lyle left me, I felt, though, that I had judged him too simply.

The next day Carlton Gracey came to say goodbye.

"This is quite sudden," he said, with simulated high spirits, establishing his version of his news, "but I simply decided I *can't* miss the spring season at the ballet. I'm leaving this afternoon. I'll be on *tenterhooks* till I have my reservation."

"For the train?"

"No, Richard. For the *opera house*. Oh! To see her again!"

I put an enthusiastic face over what I knew now.

"You lucky dog!"

"Yes, thank you, aren't I?"

He straightened himself up in rickety vitality. Pallid, sand-colored in various shades, skin, hair, neatly pressed suit, he held himself gallantly until the effort made him cough; then he slumped protectively until the spasm passed. When he could, he said,

"You've been very kind. I *really* oughtn't tell you something, but for some reason I want to. You know that *dreadful* thing that *dreadful* creature said about Stasia changing her name? Yes. Well, of course she didn't. But actually"—he leaned confidentially closer— "*I* changed *mine*. My real name is Homer Morper and I couldn't stand it after I left Rolla. I thought and thought on the train all the way to Chicago the first time, and by the time I got there, why, I was *Carlton Gracey*. Don't you think I was right?"

I reassured him energetically. I wished I could tell him what Lyle had tried to do for him. Everything was impossible. We shook hands. His hand was moist and trembling, holding on to what he must, for as long as he could, which had nothing to do with me. I was sorry and relieved when someone else entered the solarium to return books. With a face suddenly real and woeful, Carlton Gracey silently took leave of me with all his mortal information secretly intact—so he thought, in his final bravery.

❦

From the first, Dr Birch had said that as soon as it seemed prudent he wanted my father to be moved to a domestic atmosphere. He would let my mother know when to start looking for a house. In the meantime, she and the rest of us stayed at the Fred Harvey hotel beside the railroad tracks which bisected the city.

At that time, the hotel, called the Alvarado after a Spanish captain of the early explorations out of Mexico in the sixteenth century, was the social center of the town. It was a long, low, stucco structure in what was called the "Mission Style," imitated from the California foundations of the Franciscan monks of the eighteenth century. There was a patio with a fountain, there were arcades with low arches and tiled floors, the lobby was amber-lit, the main dining room with its arched windows was furnished in heavy dark woods amid which the starched white linen and the shining glass and silver promised excellent service, and the best—the only good—public food in town. For us it was a temporary home, much as a resort hotel might have been. We had our fixed table in the dining room, and always the same waitress—a hearty girl named Della, who seemed to enjoy her work. Now and then she would lean against my back, serving my dishes, and I would think that she might have an even more enjoyable life after working time. She had loose, bright-orange hair and she put rouge high up under her eyes on her ivory-white skin. Lillian disapproved of her on the basis of her appearance. My mother said,

"Oh, Lillian, nobody is always what they look like. —Say a prayer for her and be done with it."

But her smile excused any hint of offhand impiety, and Lillian, summoned to charity, lowered her eyes. When next Della came round the table, my mother favored her with a specially bright smile of thanks.

Sam asked one evening,

"Are all these people going to be a problem, or a welcome distraction?"

"It depends," said my mother, "whether they play a good hand of contract."

For letters from home were beginning to bring callers—people who like us had migrated from the East and now lived in Albuquerque. Some of them were already easy members of the local population, others kept their faraway origins visibly present in manners and styles. All of them shared a fraternal sense of victory—they had survived the bacillus, and had decided to live where they had won. All had begun their local life at the sanatorium, which, like Lyle Pryor, they called Saint Tony's, in his same spirit of deliberate lightness. The first new friend to call on my mother, introducing herself, said,

"First the traders, then the railroaders, and now the lungers," after which she gave a loud, husky laugh, which spoke more of cigarettes and whiskey than of tuberculosis. She was Eleanor Saxby, a large, white-haired widow whose lung disease had long been considered arrested; and she remained in the Southwest because, simply, she had nowhere else to go. She had money, she needed no interests beyond evening bridge games and afternoon movies and her skillful gathering of local gossip. She knew before anyone when a celebrity came to town—a curiously large number of these drifted in and out of town every year—and she was often at the railroad platform beside the hotel as the California Limited paused, going east or west in those great days of transcontinental railroading when a dozen trains by day and night went by with their huge Mallet locomotives. Early movie stars were often to be seen striding the platform during the stopovers while the limited trains were being serviced and Pueblo Indian vendors sat in the sunlight with their pottery and turquoise set out for sale on native blankets. Mrs Saxby never hesitated to introduce herself to any one of the travelers whom she recognized, and always brought away anecdotes, reproducing every word of the dialogues she enjoyed with the lustrous film stars. Under her white hair and black eyebrows she had eyes as brown as chestnuts, a short nose with widely cavernous nostrils, a thick-lipped mouth heavily painted, and a heavy throat, where she fingered her pearls for comfort and attention. In her coarseness she was the opposite of my mother, and I would wonder why they rapidly became such friends; but her robust curiosity, her heavy voicings of her comic view of the world, had such vitality that I think my mother found her reassuring as a lesson in how well one could recover from an often fatal disease. "My Gahn!" Mrs Saxby would cry when animated by joyful shock or true dismay.

She spoke her credentials from friends in Dorchester, and also introduced the man who came with her the first time—and every time afterward. This was a slim, dark, hollow-cheeked Spaniard who was spoken of as Count. The convention was that he was truly a Spanish nobleman named Jaime d'Alvarez y Cuesta, Count of Alarcante. But in the circle of friends who grew up around us, his title was always used as though it were a nickname. He did not mind, so long as it was used. His narrow brown face was thinned further by his glossy black hair, brushed straight back close to his skull. He wore pince-nez and trim suits. I remember his bending forward constantly to ingratiate himself, uttering extravagant compliments, which he would affirm excessively by saying, "No, *really!*" in his correct but oddly stressed English. This gentility did not conceal the fact that he was mercilessly clever at bridge. Eleanor Saxby was heard to say that he made his living out of his winnings, even at a tenth of a cent. When she won a hand, or a round of Mah-Jongg, she regarded it as a personal victory over him, and expertly snapping her cards or loudly rattling her tiles, she would cry charitably, "My Gahn, Count, I never thought I'd see the day when I took a trick from *you!*" He would take her thick hand and kiss it, gazing at her four or five heavy diamond rings. They were invited as a couple to the bridge or Mah-Jongg evenings in our hotel rooms, though nobody thought of them as lovers.

As it took more than those two for the table games, since neither Sam nor Lillian played, and I was present as little as possible, another pair, and Lyle Pryor, whom everybody knew, became habitual guests in various combinations. Lyle brought a couple whom he introduced with his rapid bray as "high-toned, if you go in for high tone"—a gibe which they themselves passed over with concealed satisfaction at being properly recognized.

They were Percy and Serena Sage, who came from a then fashionable part of Long Island, where the Sage family money had been gathering itself for several generations. "Sage Paints for the Wise" was a slogan known nationally. As one sometimes did over maddeningly trivial matters, I speculated whether the second word was a noun or a verb, and when I asked Percy Sage, he smiled stylishly and said, "Both," with an air of achievement. He was deeply tanned and bony, easily elegant in tweeds. His bronzed, sharply chiseled face in profile was almost a medallion of a purebred Mohawk Indian. Speaking of others, he often adverted to the general idea of being "well-bred," and Mrs Saxby would adjust her deep bosom, which she comically called "my bust," and say she was content enough to be "well fed." Percy was full of the idea of being a Founder in the colonial American sense, for if his fortune went back only three generations, his remote ancestors had taken part in the Revolution of 1776—some even on the King's side, as he would admit with falsely modest amusement in his confident gravelly voice.

His wife, Serena, often wore suiting materials matching his. She had a plain, lumpy, droll face and an air of dowdiness somehow beyond and better than fashion. She had brought her own great fortune to her marriage. She and her husband kept their Eastern seaboard accents, spoken in lifted, clear sounds, through excellent teeth, and an effect of almost clenched jaws. Lyle would often pretend not to understand what they said.

"Y'know, I'm just a hayseed, I don't always get your lingo. —What did you say?"

"You know peefectly well," Percy would reply with a little laugh which ignored any false appeal.

The fevered irony which, spoken or unspoken, seemed to filter its way into the group personality of the ex-invalids was accepted by them all. All having had a glimpse of fatality, they suffered each other, locked in a knowing, and outspoken, comradeship. I wondered how, when he was well enough to join us all, my father would respond to the general manner of my mother's evening circle.

After one occasion of provocative mockery, Lyle Pryor said,

"Oh, think nothing of it—it's just laughter in the desert. Y'know? All those bleached bones out there among the mirages. Silent laughter, in the end, of course, kid, y'know? because a skull hasn't anything to laugh out loud with any more: only a few teeth. Y'know?"

And they would all think of themselves, and perhaps a small silence would fall, except for the snapping cards, or the clatter of the pretty Mah-Jongg tiles with their ivory faces and carved, painted characters.

One day, when my mother, Lillian, and I were all spending an

hour with my father on his balcony at Saint Tony's, he asked for
more information about the established circle of the "Inevitables," as
Lyle had dubbed the finally winnowed group of the Alvarado
evenings.

"Oh, in their various ways, they are a comfort," said my mother.

"But what do they *talk* about?" asked my father. He disliked
table games, thought them inane, and had no interest in the mental
ingenuities they required.

"Mostly about how that last trick should have been played," I
said.

"But after all, we don't gather to *talk*," murmured my mother.

"Why else?" asked my father irritably. "They sound rather silly,
all of them, except Lyle, who drops in on me here rather often. —At
least, he thinks some of the time."

"Yes, they're silly, mostly," agreed my mother. "Richard mimics
them."

"Do me somebody," ordered my father.

I pretended then a rapid entrance from the bedroom on to the
balcony, eagerly bending forward to ingratiate, a swift glance
around through pince-nez, which I sketched in the air by removing
and replacing them with my fingernails, and I kissed my mother's
hand in a flattering crouch, making her laugh, and say, "It *is*
Count!"

But I did not enact all I knew about him. One evening when I
went to fetch ice from the pantry of the apartment for the depleted
drinks of bootleg liquor at the table, he followed me and, with
careful, rapid looks over his shoulder, asked me in a hurried whisper, dried by an excitement which I half understood and disliked,
whether I would go with him the following weekend to Juárez, at
the Mexican border three hundred miles to the south, where he
went every six weeks "for sexing." Nobody else knew of this, but
after all: a man had his needs: if I went with him people would
think it just for the "sightsees," and in a way it would be, for he

knew every place there was to see in Juárez, where "a bery good time" was to be had in any way one might enjoy. His rising inflection was like an ambiguous inquiry about my own tastes. Taking up my ice bucket, I thanked him and said I was too busy. He felt my disdain and drew himself up with a flare of pride, as if it had been I who had made an unseemly proposal. But I wondered if corruption was everywhere, and if it was a characteristic of the disease all about me.

My mother, lightly drawing conclusions from my performance as Count, said,

"What a little snob you are. Of *course* he is not a count, we have all decided that, but if he wants to be, what's the harm? Even Eleanor Saxby won't gossip about him. —Besides, he *looks* like one."

Sam joined us with the daily papers.

"Are you playing the animal game?" he asked.

"No, but let them do it," said my father. "I'm trying to get a view of the gambling den operated by my wife."

"All right," I said, "I am a cow who has been first to the beauty parlor, and then to Tiffany's. Who am I?"

"Mrs Saxby!" cried Sam.

"Correct. —Your turn."

"I am a tailored monkey who leans forward all the time to prove that he never committed mischief. Who am I?"

"Count!" exclaimed my father, confirming my dramatic art.

"You're all dreadful," said Lillian, "talking about your guests that way."

"I am an elegant bird," announced my mother, "and I turn my head this way and that because my brain is a little small for my hat."

"Dr Birch," answered Lillian brightly.

"No, no, someone else."

"Percy Sage," I said.

"I see," said my father. "Sam?"

"I am a little pony wearing a heather-colored cardigan and pearls."

"Too easy," said my mother. "Serena Sage."

"That's darling," said Lillian, touched by the word "little." Then she darkened ominously, like a prophetess, and said, "But they're troublemakers. I know their kind."

"Who?" asked my mother. "For heaven's sake."

"Those Sages. They always do the *wrong* thing. They never think anybody else knows the *right* thing."

"Why, Lillian. Whatever put those ideas into your head!"

Lillian, in her great soft bulk, gave a momentary impression of stern hardness, and said,

"They don't believe in God. Besides, they're rich, and they don't work."

"Now, Lillian," said my father, "we're never serious when we play the animal game. —I can finish this round. Here's one": and he gave us Lyle Pryor as "a plucked, hyperthyroid crane wearing large spectacles."

"Yes," said Lillian, "but how do I know you don't say things about *me* when *my* back is turned?"

And we all had to work for a few minutes to convince her that she was our treasure, our indispensable Lillian, who kept everything together for us.

"Oh, I don't know," she said with a heavy squirm, but so pleased that her eyes welled, which relieved my mother, for she now counted on Lillian's usefulness and good temper.

My mother amazed me with the strength with which she covered her fears. I had always considered her, if not frail, so delicate that she must be given every protection which my father and I could offer. But now I began to see that the prettily wondering, slightly abstracted air we had always known in her was a contrivance meant to make my father, and me as I grew older, feel bigger and stronger than we were, as guardians. Now she was the stronger one, and her playfulness, once like that of a kitten of many moods, was a form of power by which she kept our spirits up. Now, in any situation, she "reasoned" like my father of the old days, while he listlessly acceded. The power of decision had passed to her.

❦

Privately instructed by the doctor, my mother was looking for a house to rent "for a year" where we could all live when my father would be allowed to leave Saint Anthony's. For fear of arousing hopes which might have to be deferred, she was not to speak of it yet. But in his daily visits to my father, Dr Birch, often nursing one eye with a curled forefinger to ease what seemed to be a chronic pain there, used the other eye to pierce my father's moods; and sometimes to stare at me as though to make a case out of me, too, which made me uneasily feel like one.

But he had just the mixture of sardonic humor and professional realism to distract my father from his periods of lengthy regrets, uncertainties. For someone who had been so affirmative as my father, these were new traits. Dr Birch dismissed them as integral parts of the disease itself.

"I am like the recovered drunkard who can help another to sober up: I've been there," he said in various ways and times. "This room won't be your world forever."

My father gave him back a Birch-like glare of ironic comedy, indicating that the room would cease to be his world when he was carried from it to the grave.

"No," said the doctor, "given a prolongation of what is now going on, which will depend on several factors, of which the psychological is highly important, you will make a more fortunate escape."

"How do you telescope time?" asked my father.

[89]

"Time is *not* being wasted, even though many patients think so. It is working for you. It is literally medicinal."

"Why do I feel—"

"Some mornings you wake feeling like cracked ice in sunlight; brilliant and cooling. Other days you can hardly open your eyes. Some mornings you feel like the cleverest man alive. Others, you wonder at your vacant head." My father smiled at having his feelings so exactly understood. "Sometimes in the afternoon, late, after your nap, you feel hot and angry, but it is only a rise in temperature. Some evenings you feel almost well enough to dress and go down to the Alvarado and meet people in the lobby and go outside and watch for the trains to go by. Often when you wake up at night, you feel you contain all the sorrows in the world, and nobly, perhaps, you decide to assume them for the relief of all suffering humanity. You are Christ on the cross, until, as soon as this notion becomes explicit, you have to laugh at yourself, and turn over cautiously, and define the act of falling asleep again as the ultimate pleasure and goal of all life."

My father stirred and laughed like a child in its bed. He nodded, nodded.

"Then I am not unique," he said.

"Not in all that. But don't forget the ways in which you *are* unique. There is a terrible democracy about a disease common to much of humanity. If you let it, it can slowly edge out of mind everything but itself. What you should now do—for you are recovering steadily if slowly—is begin to think about developing some sort of continuing interest in something productive, if still physically restricted. I think you might now consider what this is going to be, and you should be ready to take it up when I release you from the sanatorium. That day will come."

He turned to me.

"What are you doing these days, Richard?"

I said something about the patients' library, and the errands I did for my family.

"More."

"Well, I like to go rambling out to the river. It is still wild along most of its banks."

"Good. I think you should use this climate, too."

My father made an inquiring sound. The doctor said,

"He's rather run-down, I'd say. —What *are* you interested in?" he asked me. "You seem to spend much time alone."

My father answered for me.

"We think he's going into medicine. —Besides, he writes."

The doctor nodded ominously at me.

"I understand. I've heard it before. *Medicine is a splendid way to examine human nature, which is the writer's stock-in-trade.* Hey?"

There was a note of harsh sarcasm in this. It extended my silence. My father said with spirit,

"He knows what I wish for him. If he must choose otherwise, and if I am here to know it, he will have my confidence."

Dr Birch shrugged, lifting his great bony arms and settling them again, like an old eagle on a rock from which—the foot of my father's bed—he rose and declared,

"Yes, you see, one sees one's youth so often in others." This was mollifying, and he turned to me and added, "One of these days I want you to come round to see me. I want to look you over."

"Yes, sir."

"Why?" asked my father with anxiety. "Do you think there's something—"

"Nothing serious. Simply a generally good idea, in his case." He turned back to me. "Meantime, stay with your river as much as you can," and left.

"Odd," said my father. "I always thought him so direct, and now he turns out to be a laminated character. —I suppose there is no such thing as a tubercular without his finally accepted disappointments. Not," he added, grinding his jaws in his familiar amiable mockery, "that I have accepted any, just yet."

[91]

We had bought a Ford touring car, black, like all the Fords, in which Sam or I or Lillian (who learned to drive with the same reckless competence with which she attacked the typewriter) drove my mother on her errands and visits. For myself, they had given me a new bicycle, an Indian Flier, which gave me independence in my explorations of the city, the great empty plain of the mesa between town and mountain, and the Rio Grande. Lillian bought me a klaxon horn for my handlebars "for safety" and I demonstrated the sound for her—"oo-ah, oo-ah."

There were three parts to the town. The central part was built in a grid about the Santa Fe tracks, and in fact, the main street was called Central Avenue, which cut across the tracks at right angles. In its middle section, for several blocks, the main commerce of the town went on in shops, movie theaters, offices. Above, to the east, rose the residential town into the sand hills which led to the mesa, at whose edge the university marked the city limits. Ten miles away, in a grand arched profile, lay the Sandia Mountains, pale rocky brown by day, with blue clefts and inky cloud shadows over their many faces. To their south, another range, the Manzanos, dwindled away in fading blue ridges. At evening, the mountains were washed by a deep rose glow, and at night, during the full moons, they abided in a sort of silvery dark wall against the pale moonlit sky. The other end of town to the west reached from the twentieth century into the eighteenth, when Central Avenue arrived at the original settlement beside the Rio Grande.

There, the oldest houses were still made of the dried earthen bricks—adobes—which the Pueblo Indians and the Spanish-Mexican settlers both used for building. The streets were unpaved in Old Town. The original plaza still stood, with its church and convent at one corner, and old adobe houses with deep *portales* along their fronts casting cool shadows out of the great glaring light of the sky. Closer to the river, and reaching north and south along its banks, were small farms along the dirt road which paralleled the river course. Between the fields and the river were thick groves of cotton-wood trees and willows into which straggling paths led here and there to reach the riverbank.

I rode everywhere to see the town and to watch the people. As everyone discovered, there were three distinct orders of people—the Indians who came into town from their pueblos to sell their pottery and weavings; the Latin descendants of the first conquerors; and the Anglo-Americans, like us, who represented the third occupation of the land, and now dominated it, in all material ways.

Abstractly, I found myself apologetic for this domination, not on behalf of the Indians, who lived self-sufficiently in their unchanged ancient ways; but to the Mexicans, as everyone called those Americans whose ancestry was derived from the Latin Americas. Some Anglos used the term with condescension. Consequently, the Mexicans resented it, though they used it themselves, thinking of it in terms of their heritage instead of their position. The fact was, their position under the moneyed energy of the Anglos was subordinate in their own land, and in many cases, close to menial. They were laborers, servants, lesser employees in business and public service. Most of them spoke English with a lilting misplacement of accents, in their trials at joining the society of their employers.

"But," said Lyle when we were talking about the laminated society one evening, "it will be a long time before they will be allowed to join it."

"But why?" I asked. "They were here before us. They even have the very look of the land."

"True, true, kid, but it's all a matter of who has the power, meaning the money and the know-how. You know who. You, your father, me, the Anglo bankers, railroaders, doctors. And like all colonists, we bring our style of life with us, and we make it prevail over the old life we find here, and the two don't yet mix, or if they do at all, they mix on *our* terms."

"Sam says they resent us—he has read all he could get about the Southwest, and he says it goes way back to the Mexican War and the American conquest."

"Don't you feel it?"

"No, the Mexicans I run into are polite."

"Spoken like a true colonist. The natives know their place: how convenient: and they damn well better, y'know? —Isn't that the usual attitude?"

"I suppose it is."

"Well, let me suggest that you avoid getting caught alone in Old Town, or up in the sand hills, if there's a gang of Mexican kids around. You and your nice shiny red Indian Flier bike. —They like bikes, too."

"They won't bother me."

"Don't give them the chance."

"I don't feel hostile. Why should they?"

"You don't have any reason to. They do."

"But why?"

"Have you ever been an underdog in your own back yard? —See how you'd like it."

I heard newcomers talk of how outlandish the place seemed to them, with its grinding dust storms, its distance from everything that mattered elsewhere, its searing sunlight, the bad roads, the Spanish/Mexican language and its speakers; and I would be reminded of our first impressions of the desert where fate had brought us as a family.

But as the months went by, I felt a spell coming over me; and, in my mind, I claimed possession, like an explorer, of a whole empire where I spent all the free time I could. This was the east bank of the Rio Grande for a stretch of two or three miles where nobody lived and nothing was cultivated. Instead, a wonderful wilderness of cottonwood and willow groves cut me off from everything but the wide, shallow, brown stream. By bicycle, I went as far as I could along a certain broken path in the groves, and when the footway almost disappeared, I dismounted and chained my bike to a young cottonwood trunk and put the elastic cord with my key around my neck and went on toward the river on foot, thrusting away branches and changing the daylight branch by branch. For a hundred yards or so I was closed in by my woods; and then I came into a small clearing, like a green room, whose trees had been washed out by flood, so that only seedlings grew up against the older thickets. The fourth side of the room was open upon the river. The water flowed past only a foot or two below the cut sandy bank. The flow was hardly three feet deep, and it reached out into the riverbed for only fifteen feet or so. Then came a long, dry spit of pale, fine-grained silt. Beyond that was another, narrower trickle, and still farther, another long, dry island where a few willows clung by precarious roots. Where the water was not shaded, it reflected the sky in a cool bronze blue. The opposite bank of the river rose away in gravelly slopes which eventually reached a wide mesa, stretching away westward for miles until a black facing of centuries-dead lava rose abruptly. Far away beyond that cliff, the profiles of three extinct volcanoes rose and fell like a melody against the sky. Their old cold craters were edged with burned-out fire color above their tawny sides.

In my glade I was alone and lord of that immense sweep of light, heat, water, and vision. To the north in the searing heat of the desert afternoons, impossible continents of cloud towered—by a rude triangulation I made in the dry sand with a stick—to a height of seventy thousand feet. Against the intense blue sky they shone with white radiance broken by every imaginable sculpturesque form. Every dimension there was lordly; and when I threw off my clothes to idle in the warm, clinging, brown water—swimming as such was difficult in so shallow a stream—I felt I must possess the land by its river with my whole skin. There were hot muddy shallows in which to roll sensually, from which to rise and fall again into the river flow to be cleansed. There were hours to lie on the bleached dry islands and embrace the sky through the empty air, made sweet by the hot scent released from the cottonwoods—a scent which mingling with the rich rankness of the river mud brought a drowsiness under eternity filled with the faraway drone of insects and the tiny, crackling commerce of unseen woods creatures and birds. I heard and saw beavers, herons, high-sailing hawks with tawny undersides; and now and then, as far away as memory, came the occasional sound of a railroad engine's steam whistle, or when the wind was right, the musical chord of the sawmill's whistle, which brought to inner sight its tall stack and the white banner of smoke which it released against the blue mountain screen at the ends of the earth.

When done with the water and the sand for the afternoon, I would return to my encircling green and lie drying, while reading slowly the book which had been assigned in one of my classes in preparation for the following year. This was P. D. Ouspensky's *Tertium Organum*—a book much talked of at that time in the intellectual mode. Often I fell asleep over it in luxurious indifference.

❦

"We have a house, my dear!" exclaimed my mother on an important morning at Saint Anthony's.

My father scowled.

"I know nothing of this," he said.

"No—the doctor wanted to be sure."

"So I did," said Dr Birch, appearing like a stage figure at that moment in the doorway. "You are pleased with it?" he asked my mother.

"Oh—it is so charming. So right for *here*." (But later when people praised the house, she would say, "Yes, but it's not *my own*.")

She described it. It was on the Rio Grande road a little north of town. A hacienda, really, set in wide fields of alfalfa belonging to neighboring farmers. It was an old house, one story high, made of adobe, with a front patio flanked by a living room and dining room and kitchen, and a rear patio enclosed by half a dozen bedrooms and a glassed-in sun porch which was like a long gallery, with tables, chairs, and bookcases. There was a little fountain in the second patio. The mechanical fittings were modern, but the original flavor of the Mexican style was carefully maintained. The interior walls were lime-washed with painted dadoes. Dr Birch nodded. Some floors were tiled in a terra-cotta from Mexico. The ceilings were held up by beams—*vigas*—each a single tree trunk left in its natural color stripped of bark. Navajo rugs and wall hangings were scattered here and there. Paintings by Taos and Santa Fe artists of immense thunderheads at sunset, vistas of mountains in the always mystical blue, adobe huts enlivened with strings of red chili peppers, Indian drummers—the art slang of the time—were on the living-room walls. From the road a hundred feet away you could not see much of the long, rambling house, but it was proclaimed by a wonderful grove of very old cottonwood trees towering almost a hundred feet, like a great bouquet, shedding faint bittersweet fragrance and bounteous shade like blessings over the house. Behind the house were thickets on an old dried course of the Rio Grande, and farther yet was the live river itself. No other houses were visible, though others were scattered farther along in the riverside groves.

"It is like a piece of the past!" exclaimed my mother, hoping with enthusiasm to stir my father's pleasure.

"But precisely that is what it is," said the doctor. "I know the place," and told what he knew.

It had been built in the mid-nineteenth century by an early Santa Fe Trail merchant importer of goods from the East and Europe. It had remained in his family for two generations, and then had been sold to later comers, and sold again. The latest owners, who now rented it out, had restored it to its original quality. The founder's family had many descendants, some of whom were Dr Birch's patients. Their name was Wenzel. Very well-off Mexicans.

"But that sounds German," muttered my father.

"Yes, but the first Wenzel married a Mexican lady. The *raza* absorbed the Teuton."

"Oh, you will love it, Dan," said my mother, taking his hand. "From the back patio, you can see the mountains through a lovely opening in the big trees. A lovely place to read, and rest, and get well!"

"When do I go?" asked my father.

"Whenever your new place is ready," said the doctor. "A few days, I gather. —Now, let's have a look at you," he added, politely nodding to my mother that she could leave the room now, and with a jerk of his head indicating that I should stay and observe examination techniques, for he soberly pursued the convention that, as I was to be a physician, the more I saw of practice the better.

The philosophy behind the move from Saint Anthony's to domestic surroundings was clear. The hospital atmosphere, necessarily suggestive of illness and reminders that death was never far away, would henceforth work against my father's cure, now that various clinical mileposts had been safely passed. He must no longer be confined by sanitary white walls and gleaming aluminum and enameled vessels and regimented hope. Freedom in his thoughts must come to prevail. The vague sounds from far down the spotless echoing halls and the nearer and more explicit sounds of suffering need no longer raise speculations in his mind. The signals of death when rapid steps went past his door accompanying the little creak of wheeled stretchers must no longer let him place his imagination at the center of these events.

But as the doctor went over him with the stethoscope, my father plainly had qualms.

"What is it?" asked the doctor.

My father wondered—intent as he was on swift recovery—whether his progress might be slower "at home," where professional care day-long would be missing.

"You will rapidly adjust to freedom," replied Dr Birch with his cavernous, sardonic grin. "You will now follow on your own the regimen I will prescribe for you in detail. I will see you there as often as necessary."

Still oddly reluctant to yield up the enclosing reassurances of Sister Mary Vincent and her shifts of nurses, my father said,

"But my shots?"

For he had to have a daily hypodermic injection of a clear fluid whose name I never learned.

Where he now sat on the foot of the bed, Dr Birch swung his crossed leg, which was so thin it looked like something whittled out of wooden slats hinged at the knee.

"Anyone can give them to you at home."

"I don't want to ask my wife—she has enough to bear."

"There are others."

"Not Miss O'Rourke. She is so modest she would faint if she had to pinch my bare flank and jab it."

"Others."

"That is not what Sam is for. He is already giving up much to be with me, without making a male nurse out of him."

The doctor looked at me.

"Why not Richard? I'll show him how."

I flinched visibly. My father scowled. Would I not do so little a thing for him?

"I'd bungle it every time," I said.

"Nonsense. Come here," said the doctor, for it was time for the daily shot. He signaled my father to turn on his side. He then took the hypodermic needle from its nest of sterile cotton and found the ampule in its white japanned box, filled the needle to the proper level, expelling air bubbles, and then said,

"Observe closely."

He took a thick pinch of flesh at my father's bared hip and with a darting throw set the needle in, and with slow, steady pressure emptied the contents into the pinched flesh. Whipping the bed-clothes back over my father, he asked,

"Did that hurt?"

My father shook his head.

"Very well. You see? The first time you do it, I'll be there to help and watch."

My father reached for my hand. He knew what troubled me. I could not bear the idea of giving him physical pain.

"Never mind, Doc. I promise you it won't hurt."

So it came to be that every day before lunch at the river house I gave him the injection; but I could never do it quite the same way every time. I never knew when I was going to hurt him—for I hurt him often, and try as he might, he could not always suppress a wince when the needle went in wrong. One day he said irritably,

"Don't try to be careful. That's what makes it hurt. And if it hurts, don't be upset. The point is, you are helping me, and I love you for it."

But I never became easy about this life-making duty, and I would sometimes see a grin on my father's face when after I had done my worst he would say, mocking his hope for my entire future,

"Thank you, Doctor."

※

The owners had named the house "Casa del Rio" and we kept the name. Newcomers took to the Latin style as joyfully as they did to gift shops full of Mexican importations. Once we were settled, the game evenings were resumed at Casa del Rio. Lyle said, "Here come the Inevitables," and once again on two evenings a week, when my father now watched until his bedtime, even occasionally taking a hand at poker, which was his only game, the snap of expertly dealt cards or the rattle of tiles and chips simulated merriment at the duty of killing time, as I priggishly thought.

The Sages sometimes came to dine. Their own house was farther down the river. Percy had built it when his cure indicated that he should remain in New Mexico, taking only a few brief trips to the East every year for his directors' meetings and Serena's shopping. They were amiable and detached, and though as Republican as they were Episcopalian, they had a sort of connoisseurship about my father, the Democratic Catholic politician from Upstate; and they seemed to share a never-spoken secret about how "second-rate"—one of Percy's words—the other guests were who gathered for the evenings. It was a secret which my father recognized and repudiated with humorous attentions to Eleanor and the others. Serena Sage would watch these with her plain, contented face, and in her wide smile, and her expensive dowdiness, made kindly excuses for him. Every time Mrs Saxby shouted, "Oh, my Gahn!" Serena would wince slightly, and look about for some object to point out as "pretteh."

When my father would leave those evenings early, there would be protests, but he always said he had "work to do." It was a fine joke, and they nodded, knowing that the point of it was rest, rest, this side of eternity.

But they were wrong. He always had a certain amount of reading he must do before going to sleep. The household knew that his work was pursuit of the health-bringing preoccupation which Dr Birch had advised my father to develop. During hours alone at Saint Anthony's, he had long thoughts about what this might be. He was happy when he decided that he must write a book on *Woodrow Wilson's Theory of Government*. He believed that no man since Jefferson had brought so rich an intellect to the idea of government as his hero, though he admired others for their human intuitions and—Lincoln—a sense of individual compassion for the anonymous citizen which in Lincoln's acts seemed to see the whole nation as one man, to be understood and honored in all degrees of need, suffering, and dignity.

Accordingly, during most mornings, while Sam was going over bulletins from Albany with my father, which was now permitted by Dr Birch, I went to the edge of the mesa where the university was, and spent hours in the library taking notes on Wilson from books and periodical files. These would later be copied on her typewriter by Lillian O'Rourke with a rattling virtuosity which made the profusion of cheap rings she wore dance with light. She had fine tremors of fulfillment in reflecting on my father's gifts—"Such a mind, all this information, he is a marvel."

Sam obtained books and other material from the state library at Albany and himself made the first rough references and classifications which my father would leaf through while his book slowly took form in his thought. He kept a color reproduction of Sir William Orpen's portrait of Wilson in a standing frame on his bedroom desk. The white margin on the picture showed a facsimile of President Wilson's signature, and I quickly learned to make a fair forgery of this, and took to signing my library notes with it, or with "Okeh, W.W."—the pedantic rationalization of "O.K." which Wilson had once given, declaring that it was an early American Indian locution (Choctaw) and thus a correct American usage. It was a proper undertaking, this book, since it forecast a long future for its realization; and a future was most of all what my father needed to believe in. He believed it would not be long before he would be ready to begin dictation of a first draft with, but only with, the approval of Dr Birch.

So the Wilson portfolio grew, and after going over the regular reports from Albany every morning with my father, Sam would bring out the material for the book and they would discuss the pattern which began to show. In the afternoon, after his nap, my father saw Lillian, dictated short replies to personal or private mail, and then spent the long twilight in the back patio, reading Joseph P. Tumulty, Colonel House, Champ Clark, Admiral Grayson, H. H. Kohlsaat, Walter Hines Page, Herbert Croly, Elihu Root, and others whose public life and personal contacts with President Wilson at various periods fed my father's imagination. He would mark the margins, Sam would evaluate the markings for extracts, and Lillian would transfer those approved to working cards.

The systematic procedure soon became a vital factor in my father's pursuit of his health, as the doctor had expected. When it was interrupted for any reason my father fretted: a few days of unusual fatigue, requiring total rest; or a diversion on Sam's part when his fiancée, Joanna Winthrop, came for a brief visit to see with her own eyes what so fascinated Sam in the outlandish Southwest that he chose it above attendance upon her at home; or—most disturbing—a series of bulletins from Sam's "spies" at Albany which made my father scowl over his enforced absence from his duties in the state senate.

※

For Sam received, first, hints of suspicion, then, confidential statements of fact that Governor Pelzer was running all too true to form. Certain metal and coal-mining interests, along with Great Lakes shipping lines, were building up a large secret fund for the governor's personal fortune, in return for his sponsorship of legislation which would show leniency to those businesses in regard to taxes, franchises, and raised transportation rates. The information about all this was not yet public, and Pelzer's advisers were working hard to keep it from ever coming out. Some, in fact, had urged him to return the money (by now in the hundreds of thousands of dollars) before the legislature would be acting on new bills already introduced to gain the favored ends. There had been veiled hints in the *Albany Times-Union* which meant something to those who knew how to read them.

What could the lieutenant-governor do, so far away, so unwell, so devoted to nothing but recovery until he could return in full strength to Albany, and there, in person, carry on the struggle for integrity?

He and Sam spent hours discussing alternative actions, and in the end, Dr Birch had to be invited into the matter. How far should my father try to enter into the affair to save the New York State administration from scandal, and the people of the state from being legally robbed?

The doctor wasted no time.

"The answer is simple," he said on that morning in the patio, "if you intend to recover completely, you must not interrupt your present regimen. You must concern yourself with nothing but what is right here." He gestured to the half-shaded patio, the house, the desert, the mountains beyond, the world of light above.

"But this matter is gathering force all the time, like an infection," protested my father.

"So will yours, if you provoke it."

"But *when,* then, do you think I might count on—"

Going back to stay: it was a question which no one had yet asked. Birch was silent for several long thoughts while my father, Sam, and I all watched that saturnine hawk's face for a hint of a reply. Finally,

"Has any limit been fixed to your leave of absence?"

"No. It is left to me, so far. I am on leave—without pay, at my request. *But I am still in office.* One feels responsible, you see."

Another long silence. Then,

"Nobody can predict with accuracy. One always considers the possibility that wisdom might require the patient to spend the rest of his life in some such place as this."

"Is that the case with me?"

"No certainty. One watches the course of a given case and finally one comes to a decision."

"Then I must be thinking along the lines that possibly I may have to decide on permanent exile?"

"You should, without despair, consider it a possibility. Not a foregone conclusion."

"Percy Sage," declared my father in a bitter voice, while an image of that agreeable idler roved between us all.

"There are others," remarked Dr Birch dryly, "who have led useful lives in this most beautiful of landscapes."

"Oh, yes, yes, forgive me," said my father hastily. "I meant nothing personal!"

"This is, quite understandably, a disease more self-centered than most," said Dr Birch with an ironic note of forgiveness.

"I've been wondering," said my father. "Is it possible that there exists a predisposition to it which can be detected early and might help prevent it?"

"There are certain typical physiologies and temperaments, yes, which suggest a vulnerability."

Without looking at me, my father said,

"He seems healthy enough, but I know you've suggested giving my son a check-up. Is that what you had in mind?"

"I can hardly say so. But I share your concern for every possible precaution." He turned to me. "Come to my office at the hospital tomorrow at three, if you are not otherwise engaged?"

My father nodded at me.

"Very well, sir," I said, so angry that I left them.

❧

For the next few days, we were like a household of strangers, polite to each other, but unsuccessful in concealing our separate

[105]

miseries. My father saw himself as if under life sentence, my mother was almost at the end of her good nature at the prevailing gloom, I was withdrawn into reproachful dignity at having had to endure Dr Birch's physical examination, whose results would be reported when the tests were all analyzed. Most trying of all, Sam was torn between his duty and concern for my father and his longing attempts at mollifying his fiancée. Joanna Winthrop was staying with us, and Sam had to spend more time with her than suited my father, though he granted the reason its emotional purpose.

Joanna did her best to show interest in all that went on, but this amounted to little more than a display of overeager good manners. She disapproved of us all, and therefore was overly pleasant in her use of the charm in which she had been drilled at the Mayhill School in Virginia and Wellesley College in Massachusetts. She would write little cheering notes to my father and send them to him by me in the mornings. Her writing looked like little square boxes all leaning to the left—a hand much favored by Mayhill girls, several of whom I had taken to dances at home.

"Dear Guv," she would write, "Golly-day, I am having the most *superb* time since I don't know when. How lucky you all are in this divine house and this absolutely *adorable* little town! I'll simply *loathe* leaving when I have to. I have a *frightfully* funny story for you at dinner tonight. Be well! Joanna."

Sam was in love with her even as he resented her patronizing and mannerly indulgence of the household. She was slender, tall, handsome rather than beautiful, very good with horses like all Mayhillies, and she spoke in a stylized drawl which put to shame the one we had always heard from Serena Sage. When she spoke, her head and neck moved in small not quite involuntary shifts, from side to side, from short to tall, like a bird with a long, exquisite, and expressive neck. She was taller than Sam. It was clear that she adored him, but so possessively that even in company, when speaking to someone else, she looked mostly at him, as though to keep their intimacy

inviolate and privileged, shutting out those others present. His sparkling intelligence, his perfectly neat, symmetrical, strong, small
body, his unassumed good manners coupled with his lighthearted
but direct ironies, all fascinated her. She saw herself as the perfect
career wife whose cool good sense included a willingness to snub
unsuitable or useless beings, while bestowing favor for Sam's advantage where appropriate. How she longed to wrest him away from
this house of the sick, this land of dust—for during her visit another
great dust storm blew for three days, obscuring all vistas like dry
fog, stinging the face if one ventured out of doors, and reducing my
mother, a proud housekeeper, to misery at the hopeless task of
keeping the dust out.

"Why don't you go home with Joanna when she goes?" I asked
Sam one day in a low temper affected by the abrasive storm.

"Two reasons," he said without his usual excusing smile, which
beguiled men and women alike. "She will wait. Secondly, I think
your father worth anything anyone can do for him—assuming I am
doing anything for him."

In this he was both real and ideal. My selfishness was pinned like
a specimen to my self-image.

҉

"So it's off to the ranch, eh, kid?"

This was Lyle Pryor as he noisily shuffled the Chinese tiles between games. During the patio supper earlier when he sat beside my
mother he learned that during the afternoon Dr M. Jamison Birch
had reported on my examination and had made firm recommenda-
tions regarding me. The tests showed an old tubercular scar healed
from my time of infancy, which signified nothing, as probably 90
percent of the population showed similar evidence of completely

[107]

healed lesions. But I was looking "run-down." I was too thin for my age and height. Despite being tanned by the desert sunlight, I showed something about the eyes Dr Birch did not like the look of. I needed to be "built up." Physical labor was wanted, somewhere, away from this atmosphere of illness and fretful concern. Dr Birch told my mother he thought he had an ideal solution.

There was a prominent ranching family who had great land, and sheep and cattle holdings, in the western part of the state. He had seen to some of their medical problems for many years, and in fact had made ranching investments on the advice of the head of the family, Don Elizario Wenzel, who lived here in town. He would ask Don Eli (as he was often called, pronounced in the Spanish way) whether I might be given a few weeks' summer job at one of the Wenzel ranches. No favors asked. I was to be worked as hard as anyone else. It would build me up. I was too introspective. It would be infinitely good for my later life if I could base my interest, which was likely to be that of the study rather than that of the strenuous world, on a strong physique. Dr Birch spoke now both as a friend and a physician. He would, if my parents agreed, promptly speak to Don Eli about me and report the response.

Much of this dismayed my mother. Should she start to worry about me? She had been so attentive to my father that she hardly saw others around her except in a smilingly absent fashion. But a ranch. Did that mean cowboys and steers, dangerous creatures both, surely, for someone so young (I was over twenty) to live with?

No, at this season, it would most likely be a sheep ranch. Sheep were mild enough, in fact, safely stupid at worst. As for ranch hands, some were rough and some were gentle; and that was how the world ran, and it was not too early for me to discover this. Don Elizario Wenzel himself was an old man, shrewd, generous; too old for his age, thanks to certain earlier prodigalities, but still actively working on the ranch during such times as that coming soon—the season for dipping the sheep, which was hard work for everyone.

Dipping the sheep?

Yes, every season before time for shearing, the flocks had to be driven together and brought to the ranch headquarters to be disinfected of ticks and other parasites. Ranchers often took on extra help at such a time. Don Eli might well be able to use someone like me. It was a rough job, but a newcomer could learn his part of it soon enough. Every young American ought to have a taste of ranch life. It had played a great part in our history, our economy, and the health of those who had the privilege, don't you see. Look at Theodore Roosevelt. It made a man out of a weakling. And thus and so.

"I would miss him so," said my mother.

"Yes. Properly. But you have Mr Dickinson and Miss O'Rourke to help out. Richard won't be gone for more than a few weeks. He wants toughening. I saw it as soon as he arrived here."

"Yes," mused my mother, my father had often said as much to her.

"A man can be strong and sensitive, both," said Dr Birch.

At that moment of their talk, so I was told, I came home, and my mother said,

"Richard, darling, Dr Birch has something wildly interesting to tell you."

I then heard the whole proposal. In glum intuition I had been expecting some sort of doom, because of the conspiratorial emphasis on my medical examination, but not precisely what I now heard. Before I could make any comment, Dr Birch looked at his thick, heavily chained watch and said,

"I have only a few minutes. Let us discuss it with Daniel."

My father listened without interruption, but, in his familiar little gesture of rumination, set his jaw slightly sideways; then turned to me.

"Would you like to go?"

"Not really." I disliked having plans made for me. I reached for an excuse which would involve my father. "How am I to drop all the work on W.W.?"

It swiftly appeared that Sam could manage all that would be

[109]

wanted by the book project while I was away. What persuaded my father in his concern that I must be physically fortified against his own disease was the doctor's insistence on the benefits of toughening hard work in the open country. He said,

"Yes, please, go ahead and ask your friend Mr Wenzel. I am sure Richard will see the wisdom of this in the end."

Later, then, at supper, my mother, who always thought that in order to keep conversation going almost anything should be talked of, gave Lyle Pryor next to her an animated account of the family plans for me.

"Make a man of you, buster," resumed Lyle with his whinnying laugh. But he looked at me with an odd waft of sympathy across his face, and despite my dislike of his slanging ways, I saw that he was no fool, and that he covered both his thoughts and his feelings with abrasive mannerisms—the only way he had of defying the mortality approaching him on the evidence of X rays and other clinical tests.

The evening party adopted my topical importance. The Sages were alert at once to the excellence of landed labor.

"Some of our best months," declared Serena, "have been spent on one of the ranches—Percy's fathay was clever enough years ago to buy those places in Montana, Wyoming, and northern Mexico. When we're there, at any one of them, I become such a clever housewife, cooking, baking, *all,* you see."

"Serena adores being Marie Antoinette," remarked her husband with a stylized arching of his slim black eyebrows. "She even wears an apron when she gives her orders to the head ranch cook."

Count was interested in something else.

"Wenzel," he mused. "I have met them. First I met him, then I met her, after he married her." He gleamed through his thick pince-nez, which reduced his pupils to a tiny focus, giving a signal that scandal was to be had. Eleanor Saxby was greedily alerted by this and cried,

"Tell us about them, you wicked thing, my Gahn, is there *any*-thing you don't know about *any*body?"

Count shrank into himself with the effect of bowing to a compliment. Then, recovering, he told us all he knew about the Wenzels. In a small city—Albuquerque at that time had fifteen thousand people—there was no difficulty in learning anything you wanted to know, if you asked enough searching questions of barbers, waiters, barmen in speakeasies, newspaper people. Elizario Wenzel he described as a "rich peasant"—a statement which reassured some as to Count's own title.

"I will tell you something remarkable," he said. "This very house was built by Don Elizario's grandfather. Your house, where we are playing Mah-Chongg."

"Our house?" exclaimed my mother. "Of course: I thought I had heard the name before—Dr Birch mentioned it when we found the house."

My father, who had to keep early hours, indicated that he would let the last round of the game go by if Count would go on with his history.

※

Old Heinrich Wenzel—the ancestor—was the German merchant trader who had come to the Southwest over the Santa Fe Trail in the 1850s, like others of his countrymen. Some had settled at Santa Fe, others at Las Vegas, he at Albuquerque. In time, he prospered, bought great reaches of river bottom land from Mexican families, and built his hacienda. Originally it was about half its present size, but when he married a local Mexican girl—one of the Apodoca family—his household grew as children were born and rooms and servants were needed, and he then added the rear section with its patio. His youngest son, Elfego Wenzel—for as the whole tribe assumed the Mexican style, the German flavor of the founder disappeared except for the surname—married a Margarita Montoya, whose father was a sheep rancher with big properties in the west toward Arizona, where great peril from Apache raiders continued for decades. Their oldest son was our man, Don Elizario Wenzel. When his time came, he married a daughter of one of the Basque sheep-ranching families near Vrain, New Mexico, and so more sheep-raising country was added to the already considerable Wenzel holdings. The wife of Elizario, Rosario Ybarra, bore him two sons, Lorenzo and José, and two others who died in infancy. Two still lived. Each operated one of the ranches, while Old Don Elizario managed the whole empire—a holding of some hundreds of thousands of acres. When he was fifty-eight years old, his wife Rosario died. Count was already in town at the time, and he would see the lonely old man, heavy in the middle, who walked like a cinnamon bear in the mountains, looking for something he could not name. He would drift into the Elks Club at Sixth and Gold Streets to drink an illegal bottle of corn whiskey with anyone who would talk to him. People paid him respect because he was well-known, and rich, and politically influential. But when his back was turned, the Anglos made fun of him—so simple, so old, and a Mexican, with all that money.

"He spends money like a peasant," said Count, "throwing it around to show that he was always some*body*," and Percy Sage nodded in recognition of his truth that some people simply ought not to be rich.

And then, last year, said Count, the old fool astonished everyone by marrying again, at sixty-five.

"You see?" trumpeted Eleanor Saxby at having her general view confirmed—that sex would have its way regardless. She rolled her wide-open brown eyes and flared her nostrils, which always looked as though they took more breath than she could use in her great chest cavity. "Who was the bride?"

"Ah." Count now had his moment. He removed his pince-nez, polished them with maddening delay, and smiled provocatively.

Then in a wide arc of gesture replacing them on this thin nose, he said,

"She is the, but *the* most beautiful girl—"

"Girl! But he was sixty-five!"

"—girl in the world. She is eighteen years old, and now she is Señora Elizario Wenzel and has all *that* money and fifty milliard sheep, and sousands of *square* miles, and an old man, and that's all."

"But why haven't we ever met her? Or him? Or seen anything of them?"

"I'll tell you," said Lyle Pryor harshly. "Because she is a spic, and he is an old Mexican with a German name who goes around without a collar on his shirt and his collar button showing, and a sad look on his old face, with a walrus mustache, and all the money in the world wouldn't do them any good at getting in with people like you, y'know? and the rest like you, because they're Mexicans, and we're Americans, y'know?"

"Oh, Lyle, how unpleasantlay you put it," murmured Serena.

"But it's the fact, and you know it. Here's their land, and we came and took it, and made second-class citizens out of them. They hurt every day because of it, and we take it for granted that we are simply superior."

"But we *are*," said Percy Sage. "After all, education, and wherewithal, and a certain sophistication, and manners really ought to go together, don't you think?"

They were both touching on facts, though one was sourly sympathetic and the other frivolously snobbish.

"How do you know so much about them?" Eleanor asked Count.

"*Sí, sí,* I have *a* lot of ways," replied Count archly, and I said to myself, "Here? as well as in Juárez?"

My father sat listening and turning from one to the other, like a judge weighing evidence.

"Why do you suppose she ever mahrried him?" wondered Serena.

[113]

"I know why," said Count.

"Yes?"

"She was from poor people, she wanted position more than anything, she knew she deserved to be with all the other girls in society,
she thought the money would make the difference. —The wedding
present he gave her was that house on Copper Avenue, you know?
the one with the tiled tower, and the conservatory, the slate roof,
three stories high, the biggest house in town that was the house of
the old mining engineer millionaire Macdonald, who came here
before 1900? *The* grand house. Concha was going to be *the* grand
lady. Everybody was going to come to call on her and leave cards,
and invitations, for Mrs Wenzel, eh? Nobody came."

"But what does she *do?*" demanded Mrs Saxby.

"But nothing. She rides around all day in the big Cadillac he gave
her."

Now I knew. I had seen her. Count was right—her beauty, at
eighteen, was something you could see from far away. In her bright-
yellow touring car, with the top down, she was one of the familiar
sights of town. She was usually alone, or if anyone sat beside her as
she drove, it was likely to be one of her small nieces or nephews.
Nobody ever saw her parents. They were poor, and though Don
Elizario had bought them a new brick house far away from their
old adobe riverside hut, with its animal yard, and the wrecked
tonneau of a Model T Ford out front, and half-dressed grandchil-
dren and loose chickens and somnolent dogs and foraging cats obscurely aimless below the cottonwoods, they could not take up their
daughter's new life. They stayed home in a sort of exile in their
small modern house on the uplands, where Concha went to see
them daily during her ceaseless roving by motor. All she could have
of the new life she had thought so desirable was the ability to move
around and see from the outside what was going on everywhere in
town. She was caught halfway between the ancestral ways and the
newly imposed ways of the invader. She seemed never to know that

by her constant visibility in her lumbering yellow car, which she drove sulkily, she had made of herself a kind of personage—exclusive and virtuous—in that small, intimate, isolated city, which, with its Indian, Spanish, Mexican, and American traditions, was only a stopping place on the great transcontinental railroad where passengers were fed in the Harvey House and the mighty Mallet 2-4-2 engines were refueled and watered, and the Pullman car windows were sponged clear of their desert dust.

Her face was a perfect oval. Black with blue highlights, her hair was pulled smoothly back and fixed by combs. Her eyebrows were black, and almost met above her exquisite small nose, and her lips had the curves of perfectly carved scrolls. It was her eyes which brought all these features together in a splendor of loveliness which was visible at a distance as though in a theater. Her eyes were darkly and luxuriantly lashed, around their pupils of lilac gray. It was the unexpected contrast between her palish eyes and her dark coloring of hair and her dark creamy skin which made her beauty so startling. She had what I later thought of as a theater of the eyes—there were shadows and brilliances, hazy starings, and sudden flares of interest and excitement which revived old desires out of their earlier lives in those who saw her for the first time. When I was younger I had been taken to see great actresses who in their world glory would come to Dorchester on tour; and in their artifices of personality enhanced by every theatrical aid, they conveyed across hushed dark spaces the inner life of the characters they assumed, while retaining boldly their own surface beauty as almost a thing apart. Like everyone, I was their self-forgetful subject. I thought that if Concha only had talent, instead of the puzzled innocence which I soon came to know, she might become a great actress herself. The spirit within her was unquiet, questing after something she could not define.

Meanwhile, her theater was the town, or whichever of the ranches she went to with her old husband when seasonal work called him. But wherever she was, she was the most lonely person I ever saw.

[115]

She lived only on glimpses of the complacent life which was denied her by the local immigrants and no man could come near her for the watchfulness and the jealousy of Don Elizario.

"Of course," said Percy Sage, "now I remember. I have seen them both—I have seen him at the Sandia State Bank, they say he owns almost half of the shares; and I have seen her out in her car, but I never knew who she was. How would I? But she even drives down our river road now and then. I wonder if she knows this was her grandfather-in-law's house?"

"She wouldn't like it, y'know?" said Lyle. "It is the most beautiful house in this valley, but she wants brick, and stained glass, and that tile turret and that cement carriage block that says 'Macdonald,' y'know? with the cast-iron little nigger groom and his iron ring for the reins? Yes: she ought to have a victoria carriage in Mexico City, and a coachman on the box, and she ought to be riding around the Alameda there every afternoon, with *caballeros* beside her on their horses, scowling bloody murder at each other, because of her, so beautiful, and so disdainful, eh?"

"What she needs," declared Eleanor Saxby, "is a good, hearty love affair, *all the way,* in spite of that old man." She rolled her large brown eyes. Lyle called her the Wife of Bath. She went right on. "I tell you something: she's going to have it, too, sooner than anyone thinks."

Saying this, she smiled conspiratorially at Sam and Joanna, as if to nudge them with her understanding—mistaken as it was—that, unknown to everybody but herself, they were lovers.

Joanna with her bird-like stretchings became erect at this, and with fastidious lifts and turns of her tall, lovely neck, said to my mother,

"I hate to leave all this fascinating information, but something has given me a blinding headache, and if you don't mind—" She stood up.

Mrs Saxby answered for my mother.

"Sure enough. It's the altitude, of course—they blame everything out here on the altitude and the freight rates."

At this everyone laughed in reassured recognition. It was comfortable to have access to any local mythology, so long as enough people believed in it.

Sam took Joanna to the far wing of the house, where her bedroom was. I followed to say good night, and before they were aware of me, I heard Joanna say,

"What perfectly terrible people. —Oh, Richard. Hell-a-o. *Good night.*"

❧

Two days afterward, obedient to a telephone call from Dr Birch, I went to meet Don Elizario Wenzel and his wife at their house on Copper Avenue to arrange my job at the sheep ranch beyond Magdalena in western New Mexico.

The front door was set into a corner of the house under an overhang which rose to a pointed turret of oxidized copper and blue tile. The upper half of the door consisted of a heavy mosaic of cut and faceted glass of many colors, depicting a peacock with its feathers all spread.

I was admitted by a housemaid in black with white cap and apron—a young Anglo girl who held out a silver salver and asked for my card. I had none, and told her my name. She said, "Please wait," and disappeared down a long, dim hall heavily laid with Oriental rugs. Nobody else in town carried on with such airs. I saw a little silver dish on the hall table which held several calling cards. I glanced at them. Of varying size, they bore only the names of the Wenzels. They were bait for other cards, which they had never attracted. In a moment the maid returned and brought me to the living room, which opened into a large glass conservatory filled with heavy green plants.

Old Don Elizario, in a black coat, with a necktie, and loose gray trousers, came forward to meet me. His courtesy was instinctive. He had a stubble of beard, his white hair was awry, his hands were horned with the color and roughness of hard work. His drooping gray mustache hid his mouth, but his cheeks rose in a smile and his dark eyes smiled amid their heavy wrinkles as he said, in a Mexican accent,

"Come in, come in, welcome, you are the friend of my friend the doctor."

We shook hands.

He led me to a sofa draped with Spanish shawls, in the center of which sat his wife, Concha. She raised her hand languidly, but her state of mind, with no change of expression, betrayed itself through her eyes. They seemed to ray with light. In a plain silk dress, she was being grand for my benefit and, without speaking, waved me to a heavy, square armchair of bright-blue cut plush. As I sat down, the maid came with a tea tray and set it before Concha on a low brass table inlaid with bits of ivory and colored glass. Her husband watched her with pride as she poured tea into china cups, each of which was nestled into a sort of gold filigree cage with a handle. The maid handed around the cups and passed a dish of macaroons and then at a nod from her mistress withdrew.

Silence fell. Don Eli wrinkled his eyes almost shut, the better to see me. He inspected me thoroughly and frankly. Concha drank her tea with delicate movements, but when I saw her saucer tremble slightly, it was plain that she was undergoing a private ordeal. I looked about me at vases of peacock feathers, stands of cattails—*tules*—from the river, paintings bought for their frames. The silence had to be broken. I said,

"What a fine place you have."

Don Elizario waved his hand dismissively as if to say, "Why not?", but Concha came alive for the first time, and with a smile asked,

"You like it?"

"Oh, yes."

"She did it all herself," said her husband, transferring his heavy gaze from me to her.

Having made our first sounds, now we could talk. Concha ceased her trembling. Don Elizario was not discouraged by what he saw of me. The work at the Magdalena ranch, which was called the WZL after the brand which for two generations had marked the ranch animals with letters of the family name, would begin in about ten days' time. He would have a month's work for me. I must go by train to Socorro on a certain day, and there change to the freight train with one coach which went west to Magdalena. There I was to wait to be picked up by the ranch foreman, who would be coming to town for supplies and mail. Someone else employed for temporary work would also be waiting. We would be driven forty-two miles farther west to the ranch headquarters and the work would begin the next day, when the sheep would all be gathered from the pastures and from the Wenzel ranch farther to the south. Had I ever been on a ranch? I would not need much in the way of clothing. Did I read? I should bring a book, as there were none at the WZL ranch. There was a small bunkhouse where I would sleep. Another young hand would probably have the other bunk in it. Most of the ranch hands were older men, some from Mexico for temporary work, others from the distant Wenzel ranches. They would live in the larger bunkhouse near the corral. The main house was occupied by Mrs Wenzel and himself.

"It is a good life. A good life," he said, in his clouded old voice, and through him spoke the oldest of man's work. He had dignity and the dormant power of confidence in his wealth, his position, and his heritage. I thought he liked me on sight, but found me a somewhat comic creature, in my youth, my alien style; and that, without avowing it, he would if necessary keep a protective eye on me if I should meet with any trouble at the WZL.

"It is hard work, hard work," he remarked with satisfaction. "Have you got the muscle?"

He lunged heavily out of his chair and came to feel my biceps. With a slow, subdued laugh, "Not much now, eh, but more after!"

"Oh, Don Eli," exclaimed Concha in reproof of such intimacy, preening herself to show detachment from it. Her voice had a low flute-like tone which made me think of how nuns sounded—obedient to decorum and deprecatory of the body.

Somewhere in the ornate, stifling house a telephone bell rang. The maid came to say that Mr Wenzel was wanted. He excused himself, and as he went, he pulled off his black coat and the necktie he must have been instructed to wear for the social occasion, and he disappeared. Concha let him go in silence while she eyed me to see what I thought of him; of her; of their marriage; of their race. I looked at her with clear admiration.

"This is your first time in New Mexico?" she finally asked. "Will you take more tea?"

"Yes. No, thank you. I'll tell you something I think about it."

"Yes"—with a hint of suspicious alarm.

"I hated it to begin with. Now I am in love with it."

"I am glad. Will you like the ranch, though?"

"Why not?"

"Oh, you're so different."

"Yes, I will like it." I gave her a flattering look, at which she scowled and raised her head. "It is very kind of your husband to take me on faith."

Did I mean it? She lowered her head, keeping her eyes on me.

"Such an important rancher," I continued. "He can't take risks with ignorant strangers."

"You know he is important?"

"Certainly. Everybody has told me. He is one of the great men of the whole state. They all say that."

"They do? —Yes, he is, I know it." She added sharply, "He is a very kind man," as if to justify her marriage.

"I can see that. I feel very lucky."

It was a long telephone call. We could hear Don Eli's voice but not his words, shouting far away as though to make his voice carry across the implausible wire. Concha asked,

"How is your father?"

Dr Birch had given them our history, then.

"We think he is better."

"He is a governor?" —*Was this a governor's son who sat in her parlor?*

"No—not quite." I explained. She did not seem unduly disappointed.

Suddenly a strange sound came from somewhere in the green undersea light of the conservatory, whose glass doors were open into the room. It began with a low, ominous ruffle, and then, in a series of shrieks leaping wildly free of the proper pitch, but unmistakable in what it meant to declare, a voice sang, amidst the ferns and the vines of *copa de oro,* "O-h-h-h-h, the sun shines BRIGHT on my-old-Kentucky HOME!"

At my astonishment, Concha burst into laughter, putting her hands to her mouth like a child in an effort at polite concealment which failed.

"What in the world—" I said.

Suddenly she was a girl instead of a stiff impersonation of her idea of a grand lady. Still laughing, she rose, took my hand, and pulled me to the glass doors and pointed. There in its polished hoop was a great green parrot, hanging upside down by one claw, and giving us one eye which blinked lightning fast its granulated lid as though to invite an opinion of its performance.

From that moment Concha Wenzel and I were friends, at ease with each other in our years, and without pretense.

[121]

I soon made a move to go, but she detained me.

"You will say goodbye to my husband?"

I sat down again and we talked of her yellow motorcar; the heat which was already on us in early summer; the mountains which I would see west of the WZL ranch; how the nuns treated us while we were attached to the hospital.

"My friends are nuns," she said, and looked around idly as if to see what was detaining her husband, for the remote yelling had ended, but he did not return. She was afraid I would leave. She was lonely. She felt obliged to entertain. Her eye caught a pile of albums on a wicker table in the bay window which was cloudy with two layers of heavy lace. She could now entertain me.

"Let me show you."

She brought the albums to the sofa and seated me beside her. She was drenched with a strong perfume.

"What are these?"

They were mementos of her days as a pupil in the local convent academy of Saint Vincent, which she had attended for three years. It was conducted by the Sisters of Loretto, who had taught her how to be a lady of polite accomplishments.

"They know everything," she said.

She demonstrated. How to pour tea, had I noticed? How to sit down like a lady, first leaning forward, then placing one foot slightly to the rear, the other a little advanced, the hands upon the front of the skirt to hold it modestly in place, and then with a graceful and slow bending of both knees held together, to settle upon her cushions without suddenness or a rush of air. More: in addition to reading, writing, arithmetic, cooking, manners, and piety, they had instructed her in embroidery, piano, working designs with colored yarn on heavy paper, "Italian" painting (madonnas with distant landscapes), walking properly, and, best of all, living pictures.

"What are living pictures?"

She patted the albums.

"I can show you."

Every year at commencement, the academy exercises included "living pictures" directed by the sisters and enacted by the elect of the year's graduates. Concha opened the first of the albums, and there she was, in tinted photographs, portraying some of the nuns' favorite subjects. She was heavily made up as if for theater, which masked her own beauty. In the first picture she appeared in nun's robes, with a full-sized harp leaning upon her shoulder. Her hands were daintily spread upon the strings and her eyes were cast aloft to heaven. To see what I thought, she looked sideways at me, leaning close so that a strand or two of her shining black hair tingled against my ear.

"Saint Cecilia," she explained. "Patron saint of music."

"Beautiful."

She turned the stiff cardboard pages. There were many pictures from different angles of each pose. Now she was Queen Isabella of Spain, in a pearl crown, with a high-standing lace collar, in full robe edged with cotton ermine. She held an exposed Rand McNally map of the United States in one hand, and with the other she extended a sword toward an imaginary Columbus kneeling at her feet. A great queen, her head was held haughtily high, even as her imperious gaze was cast down toward him whom she commanded to find the New World. The gallery continued.

"Spanish Dancer," she announced, and showed herself in high comb and mantilla, with one arm high in front, the other low behind, her hands clutching castanets, her red bodice high and tight, her flaring yellow skirt, her little feet set together in purple slippers, an expression of defiant provocation on her face.

There followed "The Shepherd Girl," "The Madonna and Child (a female doll whose golden ringlets were not quite concealed by a pale-blue baby blanket), and finally, "The Bride of Christ," all in white lace, with white prayer book, rosary, gloves, and veil and with downcast eyes whose dark eyelashes on her dusky cheek

called for kisses, all depicting the image of a novice about to take the
nun's lifetime vows.

"I almost became a nun," she said. "The sisters said I had a real
vocation."

"Why didn't you?"

Shrug.

"He did not want me to."

"Who?"

She made a silent, very Mexican, gesture, of her chin across her
shoulder, indicating the far part of the house where Don Elizario
must still be.

"Oh. —Did they ask him?"

"Yes. So did I. They understood."

"Understood?"

Well: it seemed that when she was thirteen years old, Don Elizario, recently widowed, saw her one day when he came to hire her
father for some small spell of work. He was struck by the already
special beauty of the child, and seeing her again on any pretext, he
proposed to her father that she be placed in Saint Vincent's Academy
to receive a proper education. Don Eli would pay the tuition. The
family were doubtful, but Don Eli was a powerful man. He prevailed. He saw her through her years at the convent. She became an
interest greater to him than his absorbing affairs with sheep and
cattle and banks. He made two conditions with Concha's father—
one was that she was to be told that the nuns had offered the family
a scholarship for her with no mention of where the money came
from; the other was that when she was graduated she would be
given to Don Eli in marriage. She was doubtful when the time
came for the second condition to be met. All of this I later heard
or deduced for myself. I could reconstruct the reasons, and also the
persuasions which overcame her. He was a kind old man, but oh,
that tobacco-stained mustache, that heavy belly, that old black coat
smelling of sour tobacco. She and her father had a fierce quarrel,

during which the secret of the first condition was betrayed. She owed all her years of learning to him, then? He was rich enough for that? Her father told her how much richer. She would be as rich as any of those Americanos in town. Her eyes were opened to opportunity. In the academy she had been condescended to by the Anglo pupils. For years she had seen their world and been denied it. Only the nuns were continually kind to her. If she married the old man, she would be in a position to buy that other world. She went to the altar with him in the old Jesuit church of San Felipe de Neri in Old Town, acquired her splendid house, and settled down to await her social success, which never came.

She remained a perfectly proper convent girl, still longing for what everyone else believed in aside from God. She said, in a mixture of ruefulness and anger,

"I told my husband, I said, 'I'm go'g to have that house, then they'll come.' "

It was time for me to leave, having nothing to say to comfort her. Feeling me move in advance, she reached for more albums—"my wedding pictures"—but she did not take them up, for her husband returned, walking heavily but softly on the thick rugs. He looked severely under drooping brows at me, as I stood up and away from Concha on the couch. Why had I been so close to her? With weary dignity she waved her hand at the albums in explanation. He nodded and slowly lost his suspicion. But he had seen enough of me, and so, he thought, had she. He put out his hand to shake mine in dismissal. His handshake, like that of most Mexicans, was soft and loose. He saw me to the peacock door, which from the inside was dazzling. As I walked off, I glanced back, and now Concha stood with her husband watching me go. In a remarkable illusion, the tiny space of air about her eyes sent forth a hazy light which conveyed the sense of her deep and confused emotions, reaching to me like a message from a theater stage. "Such puzzled virtue," I thought. "Such longing beauty."

When next the evening crowd of the Inevitables came for their game, Eleanor Saxby set herself to inhale whatever information she could force from me, saying,

"They tell me you have been to the Wenzels'?"

"You h'have been in that house?" asked the Count of Alarcante, with a face stricken open as though I had unbelievably beaten him in a race.

"I am sure it must be entirely Grand Rapids throughout," murmured Serena Sage. "My deal, I think, dawling."

Her husband gave over the cards, saying,

"Nao, more probably pure Juárez."

Count cringed in suspicion at this.

"You h'have been to Juárez?" he said, wondering if anyone but myself knew about his disappearances there for sexing.

"Once. It was enough for a lifetime."

"No, but tell me," demanded Mrs Saxby. "You haven't told me!"

I heard myself defensively describing the Wenzels.

"Well, first of all, it is what they want and what they think is beautiful, and as far as they are concerned, that is enough. It does not concern anybody else."

"Are you a young prig, dawling?" asked Serena.

"Better than a young snob," I replied.

"Then you *are,*" she said in an amused drawl and leaned to pat my cheek.

"Oh! you're impossible," exclaimed Mrs Saxby. "What we want to hear is what it looks like, and how they are together—that child, and that scruffy old man."

"She is the most beautiful girl I have ever seen," I stated without emphasis.

"Yaa," jeered Lyle, "you'd better watch youself, buster."

The knowingness all around me seemed like prurience. I said, now with feeling,

"He is formal, she is respectful. They belong to a world of manners we know nothing about. I do not speculate."

"No, but tell me," persisted Eleanor Saxby, "what *do* you think? Do you think they really—? I mean, they *are* man and wife, after all. But can you imagine—?"

I was outraged. But that was decades ago; and until very late in this chronicle I wondered about such matters, never without a qualm of chagrin mixed with an ironic admission that so the world ran, in its curiosities and conclusions about private lives—probably more often untrue than true. That very evening, they all looked at me (except my mother, who disliked intrusions behind the face of things) and they hoped to read the Wenzel history behind my face. There was something to tell—the ardent unhappiness of Concha, the possessive and suspicious pride of Don Elizario; but I did not tell of it, even by significant evasions.

"Of course I have seen her now and then at the movies," sighed Eleanor, having to fall back only on what she herself knew. "She always sits as far down front as she can, just as if she wished she could jump up on the screen, actually, my dear. Sometimes after I have seen the whole feature, and she has too, and I am leaving, my Gahn, she doesn't get up to go. She wants to see it all again."

There were two motion picture theaters on Central Avenue, a couple of blocks apart. They were shaped like large shoe boxes, with nothing of the gilded and draperied opulence of the great picture theaters in the big cities—those palaces of the people where popular dreams were enacted for them amidst every elaboration of plaster splendor. We had no huge Wurlitzer organs which rose on electric platforms into amber spotlights, or symphonic orchestras in the pit with glamorously advertised conductors who led grand overtures before the film and accompanied parts of it until the organist would take over. On Central Avenue, our movie accompanist to the silent films was a single operator who presided at an upright player piano which went automatically through its paper rolls of music selected for general suitability to the theme of the picture—love, or horror, or fast-riding adventure. The operator augmented the automatic music by working a wonderful set of percussive effects—drum and cymbal, rattles and bells, gun shots and train whistles, each set going by a pull on a rope with a wooden handle for which the player would reach when the screen action called for it. These added some old excitement to the mechanical pictures—live human play of the saltimbanque reaching as far back as the history of the theater. When I went to the picture shows, I was as much fascinated by the percussionist at the player piano and the rack above from which dangled the pull cords as I was by the aching and overrapid motions of the chalk-white and stark black figures filling the grainy screen with their stock gestures—not to forget the worded subtitles which gave us dialogue or pressed home meaning. It was a transporting experience; and when Eleanor Saxby saw Concha coming out of the movie matinees now and then, I could imagine the drained look on the girl's longing, beautiful face, and how painful it must be for her to stagger back to life after hours in the fulfilling if untouchable dreams in the humble darkness beyond dimension. Who was she, of those whom she had been with for that hour or so in the dark— Louise Glaum? Clara Kimball Young? Mary Miles Minter? Bessie Barriscale? selves all too quickly banished by the pitiless reality of the New Mexico sunlight and the hot sidewalks of Central Avenue.

Count asked peeringly,

"Did she wamp you?"

(For vamp was then both noun and verb born of the movies: the fatal woman with rings of black around her eyes who destroyed men in the act of maddening them.)

"Well, I know one thing," remarked Eleanor, "the old fool would be a fool to leave those two alone together. —*Did* he leave you alone together?"

I pretended absorption in my cards and she gave a rasping laugh which ended in a coughing spell. Count mistook my diffidence.

"*¿Usted es virgen?*" he asked with his head tilted at what he thought a beguiling angle.

"Oh, come on, Count, leave the kid alone," said Lyle roughly. His intervention was a surprise.

Mrs Saxby leaned to give me a probing look, and, satisfied, settled back in her chair and declared,

"No, I don't think he is."

Count shrugged in guilt, as though to ask me for absolution, which must be in my power to give, as, perhaps, it was, considering his emotional addiction, and my youth and remoteness. Something in his plea—monkey-like in its self-absorbed appeal—gave me compunction; and I smiled at him on general principles. At once he took this for encouragement; raised his eyebrows at me; breathed happily and became arch, cringing toward me in bodily flattery; and then, in haste, added Eleanor and Serena, as women, to his homage.

My father glanced at the clock, and stood up.

"Bedtime," he announced. "You can cash in my chips."

Percy Sage flushed darkly under the unnatural health of his heavy tan.

"I've barely begun to reap my just rewards," he said irritably, looking at his depleted pile of chips. Like many rich men he was mindful of the pennies. "Don't you think you might give me just another half hour?"

"Good night," said my father genially, as though Percy had said nothing, and made his way to his bedroom. Bad feeling, gathering all evening, openly fell upon the rest as they prepared to leave. How sensitive those half-people were to each other. What a maimed society it was. Their disease had forced them back to the self-regard of children. Every frustration, however trivial, was magnified. I would soon be going away. My departure for the first time looked to me like deliverance and I exulted privately like a young pharisee, for I was not as they; and I remember thinking how this was treason, and how pleased, a spiritual criminal, I was with it.

❦

"Here," said my father, handing me an open book, "read me the paragraph I have marked."

We were working in the patio on the Woodrow Wilson material. I began to read while my father listened with his eyes closed under the shadow of his visored cap.

Here muster, not the forces of party, but the forces of humanity. Men's hearts wait upon us; men's lives hang in the balance; men's hopes call upon us to say what we will do. Who shall live up to the great trust? Who dares fail to try? I summon all honest men, all patriotic, all forward-looking men, to my side. . . .

It was a message from Wilson's first inaugural address. By the look on his face, my father was living these words for himself. He could hear his voice speaking them. His thought was animated by them. One day, again a well man, strong and resonant before the great crowds whom he had learned how to reach, he would be saying words like these.

"I remember," he said, awakening to me and the patio, "exactly where I was and what I was doing when he died. It was February 3—almost six months ago. I was in the office at Albany. The ticker was sounding out in the big room. I was at my desk, working on new wording for a bill that was coming up—it had to do with taxes on some upstate counties for farm roads. Suddenly Sam came in. His face was white. He said, 'Boss, you'd better come out and read the ticker.' I got up, went out to the big room. The secretaries were crying. 'What is it?' I asked, and went over to the ticker, where the tape was clicking out from the glass dome. I read: *Former President Woodrow Wilson died quietly a few minutes ago at 11:15 this morning, in his home on S Street, in the nation's capital.* It is odd how we react to tremendous emotion. Right then I had resentful and uncharitable thoughts about Mr Harding." (My father was never heard to refer to him as President Harding.) "Also, in that moment, I felt so numb that almost as if to prove I was alive I did a most prosaic thing. I took out my watch to see what time it was, though the office clock was right on the wall facing me. —Do you remember what you were doing then?"

"I was in class. Someone came in and told the prof, and the class was let out. They had a concert that night by the Boston Symphony Orchestra on tour. Before the regular program, they played *Siegfried's Rhine Journey* in memory of the President, and the orchestra and the audience all stood during it except the little man who played the glockenspiel. People cried. The next morning the university had a memorial service in the chapel—he once taught there, you know, as a young professor."

"No! He did? I didn't know. —Did you go?"

"No."

"What did you do?"

"We—we had a little soccer scrimmage, just a few of us. It was snowing a little."

He sighed.

"No, I suppose the world never stops, no matter what. —Read me some of the other places where I have put slips."

We can have no sympathy with those who seek to seize the power of government to advance their own personal interests or ambition.

I knew whom he was thinking of.

"Go on."

I know that you will appreciate the scruple upon which I act.

"There: that's the word: *scruple*. This is from a letter he wrote denying his support of a certain bill sponsored by a good friend in the Senate. —Did you know Wilson was the first man to go personally before Congress since John Adams? He said he would do anything in his power to free business from control by monopoly and special privilege. That is what I preached all through our campaign."

"I remember."

"He called his program the New Freedom," said my father, and fell silent. I thought he was brooding upon the idea of freedom in his own case, longing for escape from the captivity of his disease. Presently he said,

"Take a little note for the book: title for a chapter heading: 'Progress with Honor.'"

I thought he was seeing his own future in the phrase.

It was late in the morning. There was a slow breeze off the river half a mile beyond our house, bringing the sweet scent of warm cottonwood boughs and pollen, and the lazily inciting odor of the riverbank mud, where decay mixed with fresh growth, and the rank earth was released into the air by the slow-flowing brown stream. Our very house made of earth gave off a breath of ancient life and renewal, and the great shadow of our huge tree fell and stirred over us like a benediction. All of it made me feel lazy, drowsy, aware of the power of sexual desire. It was heady to breathe deeply of such clear, thin air. Through the wrought-iron patio gate showed the blue of the far mountains—pale where the sun was direct, inky where the cloud shadows drifted over the immense rocky faces of the distant heights. It was country which cast a spell like no other, as I had already discovered. How could our vast peace ever be disturbed?

We knew soon enough.

Sam arrived with the morning mail. As usual, he had read all of it which was in any way official, and was ready with summaries for my father. At such times, in case confidential matters might arise, I usually withdrew. Today, Sam, with a brisk nod, indicated that I should stay. He was unsmiling—an unfamiliar state.

"News?" asked my father.

"Three things," said Sam, in demonstration of his mental ordering of matters.

First: there was now clear evidence that the earlier charges against Governor Pelzer would undoubtedly be reopened and brought to light along with new suspicions as yet unexposed.

Second: there was a letter this morning from Governor Pelzer, the gist of which was that constant questions were being asked about the lieutenant-governor's absence from his duties. It was becoming most awkward to respond to such questions with sympathetic evasions. The governor felt obliged to ask for some definite indication of a date when the office of lieutenant-governor could again be actively filled by the official duly elected to it. If it were impossible to fix such a date, then, however painful it must be to consider, the alternative of resignation would have to be seriously weighed. Signed, "Yours ever admiringly, Judge."

Third: behind this, of course, lay a real and brutal desire to eliminate the lieutenant-governor and his "scruples" from the scene. Sam had discerned earlier that there was a new partisanship beginning to form in Albany around my father, even in his absence. Pelzer could see this only as a threat. If he was to meet the growing danger of alignments against him in the accusations of corruption which were impending not only in rumor but in new evidence, then he could not afford to have forces organized against him within the administration.

Sam's exposition was clear and without emphasis; but its burden was charged with emotion. My father listened impassively until Sam finished. All implications went through my father's mind as he looked from one to the other of us. He knew what Dr Birch would say if consulted. He knew by now that we had taken the Casa del Rio on a year's lease. Above all, he knew the state of his own health.

He was at a crossroads. At last, in a husky whisper, he said musingly, "Resignation?"

The question hung in the air. But we all knew the answer—we had known it, actually, for some time before Governor Pelzer's letter arrived that morning. My father reached for his watch in the little breast pocket of his sweater-coat. He did not look at the face of it, but at the engraved message on the back. What would Our Crowd think? He smiled with a tough, youthful expression, and said,

"Sam, prepare a draft of the resignation letter. I will go over it with you this afternoon. —No: no need to say anything at all to me now. We all know how we feel."

He wanted to be left alone. I picked up my W.W. materials and retreated with Sam. When we were out of earshot, Sam, with almost a catch in his voice, said,

"He's probably seeing a parallel between his breakdown and the President's—great things thwarted by the body giving out."

"But he must get well!"

"He must get well. There's still plenty for him to do when he can."

In a few days, then, Sam left for Albany to gather my father's personal possessions in the capitol office. Joanna left with him, visibly suppressing an air of victory. In a coolly sympathetic voice, she had pointed out that now, since there was nothing "official" for Sam to do for my father once he had cleared the office, they were free to set a date for their wedding. If Sam returned to us, it would be only for a brief interlude to report, to help outline plans for the future of my father's intention to return to public office—two years? four years?—and to say goodbye for the meantime. The wedding would take place in Cambridge.

As I finished giving my father his daily injection, he took a few breaths to subdue the pain I had caused him, and then regarded me quizzically.

"Doc, will you do something for me? I've been thinking about it for some time, but now that you'll be going off to the country pretty soon, I want to speak of it. —Find my key ring in the top drawer there. Go to the storage room behind the garage and open the big blue steamer trunk. In the second tray on the right, you will see several large black leather envelopes. They have brass locks in their flaps. Bring me the one which has my initials on it in gold and the words *Personal and Private*."

When it was in his hands, he turned the envelope over several times, as if musing whether to open it. He seemed to be looking through it at another time and place. Finally, taking the smallest key in the ring, he unlocked the portfolio and took out a sheaf of letters fastened with a broad rubber band. These, too, he regarded with some uncertainty—would he release them from the retaining band and read the letters, or hand them to me to read? But no. Without disturbing the packet, he replaced it in the leather case, which he locked. He then removed the small key from the ring and gave me both envelope and key.

"Go to the Sandia State Bank. Ask for Mr Ramsey, introduce yourself, and tell him you want to rent a safety-deposit box, *in your name*. He knows who I am. Have him charge the box rental to my bank account. When you have the box, put the portfolio in it. After that, I want you to keep the two keys—the box key, and the little key—yourself. I don't want anybody else to know about this. Not even your mother. It is a private matter and I am ready to trust you with it. If the time comes to do something about the safe deposit, I will tell you what to do. If anything should happen to me before

then"—I found the hackneyed euphemism brave and touching—
"destroy the contents of the box, envelope and all. Is this all clear?"

"Yes, Father."

"Off with you."

He sank back against his pillows with a long breath of relief,
closed his eyes, and nodded me, and whatever concerned him, away.

The business was done within the hour, after which I retreated to
the riverbank and my willow glade with my notebook, from which,
and many others like it, much of this chronicle has been assembled.
I was puzzled but proud that my father had given the confidential
task to me instead of to Sam. I lay in the leafy play of light, and
wondered what I was now custodian of.

※

The Wenzels had gone ahead to the ranch some days ago. My
train would leave Albuquerque at ten o'clock at night and arrive at
Socorro about midnight. There I was to change trains—to a freight
train with one passenger coach attached—for Magdalena, arriving
during the forenoon. One of the cars from the ranch would come to
pick me up. The other newly hired hand was to be there also,
coming from El Paso. I had no idea of the country where I was
going. I thought of some ancient map with unexplored blank spaces
where a legend was hand-lettered in brown ink: *Terra Incognita
Hic Sunt Leones.*

"Will Sam stay a while when he comes back?" I asked.

"I doubt it. Have you seen this?"

My father handed me a letter from Governor Pelzer acknowledg-
ing my father's resignation personally, and enclosing two official
things. One was the formal acceptance of the resignation from the
little Secretary of State of New York; the other was a file of news-

paper clippings announcing the resignation, which included several editorials. *The New York Times* deplored the loss of a new public servant whose great promise had scarcely been tested. "It is to be hoped that his health, fully restored, will soon permit his return to political life, perhaps in a greater capacity than that which ill fortune obliged him to vacate." There with febrile determination my father saw his future.

"Ah," he said suddenly, "I almost forgot. Here is a present which Lyle left for you this afternoon." It was *Prejudices, Fourth Series,* by H. L. Mencken. "He is reviewing it for the *Journal.* He says it will keep you from going native out on the ranch."

"Does he like it?"

"Mencken is his God. Lyle thinks you need disillusioning. He means it kindly. Fact is, he himself is afraid of *not* being disillusioned. It explains much about him—and t.b. or any chancy disease. You must write and thank him."

It was odd to think that Lyle, in his abrasive, grinning mistrust of sentiment, should have thought of me. On the flyleaf he had written, "See essay on 'The Husbandman,' if you get romantic about your bucolic role. L.P."

When I said goodbye to my mother, I saw the signs of her endurance which I had not really noticed before—the suffering which she had concealed, which I had been too self-absorbed to see. Her delicate, wistful, mischievous prettiness—so much of it lingered from her girlhood when she had been called "The Kitty" by her brothers and sisters—was marked by changes. When she smiled, it was to mask the weariness in which her face was set. Permanent shadows were under her eyes, giving them an intensity which was not impulsive, as before, but constant. Lines faintly showed between her eyebrows. Her cheekbones were more prominent, her cheeks a little hollow. Slightly parted, her lips seemed to permit the silent escape of words framing the worry which she must not let be heard. None of what lay behind these changes would she acknowledge openly. She was as active, ingenious, and original as ever in making the house-hold one of grace and comfort. It was her courage which made tears come to my eyes when I said goodbye to her. In her selflessness, she misread them, and said, in a family idiom as though I were still a small boy,

"Richard, my darling, it will only be three shakes of a lamb's tail until you are with us again."

Then in a gesture out of my childhood she made a tiny sign of the cross on my forehead.

My father, who was now taking daily walks with caution and humorous pride, went out to the car in which Lillian would drive me to the train for Socorro.

"You see?" he said, indicating his feat of strength.

As we drove away, Lillian, with her voice as always misted with worship, declared,

"He is a marvel."

When I was leaving her, about to shake hands, she threw her heavy arms around me and hauled me into her deep-cushioned bosom and kissed me, and, through me, my father.

So I went away blessed by many loves whose images of me I thought it would be impossible ever to betray: my father, my mother, the gods of my river glade. Who has ever managed to express enough love in saying goodbye?

CHAPTER IV

✴

The Animal Creation

THE SILENCE: only an immeasurable emptiness, a prehistoric solitude, could have held such quiet. What sound came was an occasional animal call, remote and pathetic in its meaningless statement. A sheep, "Nbla-a-a," far away. A sighing mutter from a dozing sheep dog. Now and then a creak or a singing waft on the night stir of air from the windmill cutting the silence with its canted sails, which looked like the petals of a single great flower against the sky. The very silence, against which the broken night sounds carried, seemed foreboding. I was removed from every aspect of my supporting world, and for much of my first night at the ranch I traveled again in wakeful dreams the journey to this other country.

At Socorro I had waited from one in the morning until about six, when a freight train hauling empty coal cars departed for Magdalena. I rode in the caboose. The exciting smell of coal smoke blew back from the stubby, toiling engine far ahead. It was a run of about twenty-seven miles, which took two more hours, during which I dozed, for I had sat awake in the wooden station at Socorro watching for the other new hired hand to appear from El Paso; but he was not on the early-morning train which went north.

I was again dozing in the Magdalena station—a shack by the

black water tower—when someone roughly shook my shoulder and asked my name.

"Yes?—yes," I said, coming awake in a lunge, to see a tall, bony, weathered man more than twice my age.

"Come own. You're comin with me out to the Wenzels'. My name's Tom Agee. I'm the foreman."

We shook hands and sleepily I followed him out to a Ford touring car in the dust outside. "We'll get us a cup of cowffee and I'll pick up a few things Miz Wenzel wants from the general merchandise before we get goin."

He drove through the earth streets raising veils of dust which the hot south wind blew forward upon us in the open car. There were few streets, and at the end of each one was the immediate country. Rolling, abrupt, bare hillsides rose at the west side of the town. Tailings added to the hills all about the timbered entrances to old mines, where little activity showed. Wilted trees—cottonwood, tamarisk, mulberry—sparsely edged the streets. Most of the houses were wooden, some unpainted, with here and there one made of brick or stucco. None was over one story high. The morning light gilded the sunward faces of all things, and promised a beating heat as the day advanced. We came to the Marigold Hotel, which stood a few blocks from the station.

The hotel was a long, two-story, red brick building with a white-railed balcony along its whole front and far end. It was a fading remnant of the years when the little town had first been a thriving center for silver and coal mines. In its size, the Marigold spoke of old aspiration, when men had come to grow rich, and to bring every expensive comfort alive when the gold should begin to pour in. Now, even from the outside, it was evident that the hotel was mostly empty. One or two cars and a wagon with two mules were drawn up to the entrance porch, at one end of which a window showed the word CAFE in an arc of gold leaf.

There we went for breakfast. A cup of coffee turned out to be three cups, with ham, gravy, eggs, biscuits, lick (a heavy molasses-like syrup), and a piece of pie made from canned peaches. We sat at a long counter, and were served by a waitress whom Tom called Larraine. She was about my age. So plump that her dress was pulled into streaked creases about the armpits, breasts, and waist, she was sober-faced and almost solemn in her bearing. She waited on us with a quick economy of movement which told of long experience, young as she was. As she leaned across the counter I could hear her breath expelled. It was intimately physical. About her there was a sort of misty warmth—not quite sweat but redolent of it—suggesting ardor, which she seemed to deny out of melancholy propriety. She wouldn't look directly at me. Tom—if he had ever been young he left it to others to remember this—preserved an oblivious courtesy toward her which made her in effect invisible to him. But I saw how in her round face deep dimples appeared when she smiled in response to Tom's short greeting. When she walked to the cook's window behind the counter, her knees were close together, and her body swayed to a rhythm which made the rolling flesh of her buttocks rise and fall in a two-part pumping motion at each side like thrusts of a soft little machine. Her eyes were a bluish gray, her eyebrows were golden brown. She wore a little curl in front of each ear, and piled the rest of her heavy bounty of pale-red hair in a high spiral which resembled a cone of cotton candy. Under her eyes were pale-brown hollows which seemed older than the rest of her fleshy face. Her hands were small, and her wrists had bracelets of creases where her plump hands met her rounded forearms. Pedantically, "Rubens," I said to myself, trying to fix the quality which made her a personage in her own anonymous right in that long narrow café where window shades were torn and the scarred floor and specked walls reflected lost hope. As we ate, she stood away from us, affecting indifference, though I thought she was making an examination of me, the newcomer. Presently she came dutifully to us again with her coffee pot. Her high full breasts jellied at every step.

"More cowffee?" she asked. I smiled at her but she ignored this. Her voice was rich and throaty, low in pitch, the one beautiful detail of her whole being, and reflected a curious, dainty, unspoken pride. I wondered if she was unhappy. She seemed tired. Perhaps she had been at work since five o'clock, when Magdalena began to stir in the morning. How long every day must she work? It was a lost life, so I thought.

"Well, sir," said Tom, suddenly rising. "Time t'go. —Put it all in the book, Miss Larraine," he said with a plainsman's courtesy. She nodded, reaching for her charge-account ledger, and we went out to the Ford. Tom, with a gesture, told me to crank the car while he sat at the wheel working the gas and spark levers.

We drove to the old stone store, which seemed a block long, with its sign *General Merchandise* painted on the irregular surface above narrow windows. As we went, he asked without looking at me,

"What for you so interested in that girl?"

I was startled at having been watched, and I said vaguely,

"Well, there's something about her."

"You look out."

"What do you mean?"

He shrugged and said nothing, but with a sideways jerk of his head told me to get out and go with him, while he shopped for items on Concha's list.

She was at the WZL headquarters with her husband, had little to do, wanted some yards of stuff for embroidery, and if they had colored yarns she was going to make a set of small rugs, and she had seen a set of madonna-blue drinking glasses from Mexico which she wanted: he shopped for the whole list which took three quarters of an hour, until he could say, "Well, that's about everythin but the blue glasses, which went and got sold yest'day"—for there were just enough families left in Magdalena to make a town with an occasional want for touches of life from elsewhere to lend grace in a land of hard terms and gritty substance.

By half past nine we were heading west on a gravel and dirt road with deep ruts dried after hard, infrequent rain. The ruts often turned the steering wheel within Tom Agee's grasp. In the country-man's certainty of his own need of others, and of their need of him in all he could give, Tom talked without pause. His pace was so unhurried that you could see the end of his sentence long before he spoke it, and you silently begged him to hurry up. His gestures were crabbed but eloquent, and his subject was his life up to the present moment. He seemed like a creature of the desert and mountain wilderness singing the song of its life in response to the beating sunlight.

"Well, I get tired of it. Who don't get tired of theirself and their life now and then?"

He stared at me in challenge. I nodded satisfactorily and he re-sumed the road. His face was like a piece of miniature landscape such as we were bumping over, with its gullies, buttes, ragged brush, pittings, sunned to a brick color. Every slow word from his dust-whitened lips was matched by his slow gestures. Every word, however simple, became weighty because of his authority of experi-ence in matters however trivial. His pale eyes were folded over at the corners by slants of flesh after a lifetime against the sun. Until he'd made his point, his humor was stone-faced; then it broke open, and you knew you must laugh. Life with animals and their mute contrariness had hardened his sinews; the work of survival in the ungiving land had sharpened his values. He was marginally literate except in referring to the Bible, and then he expertly echoed its style. Talk was his medium. In this he had dignity, which came from the belief that his days and his world were of as much interest to everyone as to himself. He must have been handsome in his youth, like a crag seen from a distance. Now in his years he was impressive as an earth feature seen close to. A curious childlike sweetness lay about his light eyes in the form of heavy dark lashes. His hands were like roots of an old tree, and to make a point he would elevate them with spread fingers, and a sideways jerk at the air, where invisibly his ideas seemed to loom for him.

"For as the Lord telleth, then must man abide by the telling and bow his head unto the orders of the Lord," he remarked, with his right hand hanging up between us.

He said he knew the whole country from the Mississippi west to the copper camps of Arizona and from the Rio Grande to those nests of hell's eagles in the shack towns of the Colorado Rocky mines. Oh, and he knew the cities, where corruption burned like sulphur at every corner. How did he know? He knew because the real work of his life, now behind him, was that of a revival preacher. If he did say it, nobody in the whole West could bang the Good Book down on the lectern harder than himself. There was that time when he had three singers traveling with him, and a trombonist, and two young men drawn to God who managed the collections, and the transportation of the tent, and the folding chairs, and the Coleman lanterns, and who loaded the melodeon onto the flatbed wagon he owned to carry the freight. Them was the days of the Lord. How he loved it when he saw the next town slowly come into his gaze far ahead as his party of wagons and his flatbed drawn by mules went along the dusty roads which often paralleled the single tracks of the railroad, where the telegraph wires sang and picked up the sunlight against the sky like threads of silver. Ho, yes. He would see low clumps of trees and a water tower shining high, and a steeple or two, and mebbe a courthouse dome; and he knew people was there a-waitin, and here he went, a-comin, and Lordy! they was all gon meet the next evenin. It was blessed work just to get the tent set up and the chairs in rows in the orange-colored shade by day, and by night the lanterns hung a-hissin on the tent poles, and some outside, usually from big trees, cottonwoods mostly, throwing their light around in bright circles so men, women, and children could see their way down to the Lord's bench in front.

Well, he always stayed at least one week, sometimes two, mebbe three, if the harvest of souls was plentiful enough; and you wouldn't know it now, from his husky old voice, but he would hoot and cry night after night, and pray with his eyes shut, and his arms up, so clear and strong so's't they could hear him blocks away, even as far as the courthouse square, from his revival lot which he set up mostly on the edge of town after getting permission from the town clerk or mebbe the mayor himself.

The people. His people and the Lord's. How they listened, first, and then spoke back to him, like lambs all a-cryin at once, Praise the Lord, praise Jesus, oh, Lord, I know, I know. And when the Spir't came down on them, the Holy Spir't, so's't they were out of their-self, all callin and cryin to be saved, and their tears flowin like unto Jordan itself, and the singers' voices and the trombone risin, and the fine young men bendin over the sinners feelin of their flesh and urgin them to go down to meet Jesus, and him liftin his voice over them all like the Patriarch over his flock, why, then he sometimes felt so powerful he believed he could work mir'cles, and sometimes, too, he felt like the great breed bull, for the power to breed was in him, but it was for the good, not the bad, but the flesh rose up like a tower in the strength it had, and he gave the strength to all, for all was purified.

"And I tell you, young man, there was the Lord's work bein done, and I done it s'long as He called me to do it until it happened."

There was a silence of a rough mile or two. I felt I should not ask what happened, for I knew he would tell me, and soon he said that one year he heard his voice growing feeble, and he thought he must have strained it for the Lord, for he had never spared it, and it was that power which brought thousands down to the bench to find salvation; and it soon came about by the Lord's will that he had no more voice than I heard this minute, and his days of travelin and shoutin the glory of God was over. Oh, he repined bitterly at times, for he was but a weak vessel of flesh, but there was nothin to do but go on the best way he could. He had been before the public for nigh on twenty years. He knew what he just might do then.

As I listened for mile upon mile, hearing the voice of the land I was gazing at, I saw mountains to the west ghostly in the blanching sunlight. There were foothills like crouching old lions. On the horizon—how far away? it seemed like infinity—were strange pyramids of perfect shape, and even farther, green-blue mountains under opalescent veils of light and distance. In the universal light, clouds floated in flocks and cast their shadows over the rise and fall of the earth, and made new shapes of what they traveled over. Never had I felt so dislocated in place or time, or even in my own character, as on that ride across that unknown country, and even in what came later. I heard the voice of the land with its rude poetry, its animal nature, and its blind acceptance. My father, my mother, the friends I knew at college, seemed lost forever to me as we advanced through the dust and the light into the hard, alien country, which yet had its own little easements, for I saw wild white poppies by the road, and purple, white, and yellow verbena.

Midway in Tom's soliloquy we came to a view of land which made me exclaim. He waved a hand at it and identified it as the Plains of San Agustín. It was like a lake of light, reaching endlessly away to the south. Faint, far mountains seemed only to emphasize its isolation and superb vacancy. It was like a mirror of an empty sky. What lived there? What *could* live there? Was there courage enough in the human world to know that land? An odd exaltation possessed me. I resolved that man was equal to anything—and the corollary to this, that man was capable of anything, was to come to me later.

The sight of the plains made me impatient to ask Tom Agee about the Wenzel ranch, but his steady, slow emission of what must be told any stranger kept me silent.

"So I said—this was in West Texas, where I was at the time, asking the Lord what to do now that I could not but bow my head under the silence He had put upon me—so I said to myself, Tom Agee, I said, you're goin to run for county judge and bring the justice of the Lord to people under the law."

[146]

The fissure of his mouth closed in stern triumph for a second, and then its irregular seam opened and the stream went on. There was a fall election. He ran, but was defeated by the evil forces of Six-sixty-six. It was the Mark of the Beast itself, he said, and the Devil had managed the whole thing. Tom had sold his revival equipment to the handsome young men of his troupe and they went and made a shady business out of it, reaping money, not souls, and, so he heard, they also took their fill of women whom they first drove blind with holy emotion. Did I know one thing? They had learned their trade under him, and then they *per*-verted it. Oh, Job. Job's suffering remained his example and con-*so*-lation. His wife died, his sons were growed up and gone, he was alone. He worked his way across New Mexico till he got a job as a ranch hand, and after a few years, dad-burned if he waddn't the ranch foreman for old man Wenzel at the WZL; and there he was to this day.

"What is it like at the ranch?"

He sketched a random design in the air with his cracked spread old hand as if to show me the picture he had in his head. Then he said it was real pretty. Old lady Wenzel—he meant Don Elizario's first wife—loved flowers and trees. She planted and tended them all day long. There was two long brakes of salt cedar, nigh unto twenty feet high by now, and over the house was a mighty stand of cottonwoods. The old man had rigged up running ditches to the flowers and trees from the windmill tank out back beyond the salt cedars, and he, Tom, had never seen so many roses when the season was ripe. But that was before.

"Before?"

"This new Miz Wenzel let the roses go to rack and ruin, for she said they was nobody out there to come and see them." The house? It was one-story, made of stone, and it had a new part out back built for the young wife, and it had wooden porches front and back covered with trumpet vines. Inside, it was sure enough beautiful. Old man Wenzel was never one to spare money givin his wimmin what they wanted. It was a sorry time when his first wife died. Before then everything seemed so happy. He paused and nodded grimly ahead at the alkali dust of the road. Times changed. He made me think of how recently I had come to this conclusion for myself.

"I met them in Albuquerque," I said. "I mean Don Elizario and his new wife."

"I know. I know. We're supposed to work you so hard you'll get some tough meat on you. Time I was your age I could rope and throw a bull caif and sit own him in nine and a half seconds. —I was raised up own a ranch, though, and you wasn't."

"She's a beautiful girl. What does she find to do out there all alone?"

"All alone." He mused quietly for a moment. Then, "I sure feel sorry for that child. He treats her nice, but she sure is lonesome. Fact is, she don't do anythin, all day long. He won't let her talk to any of the men. She means no harm. I'll tell you what." He turned and looked squarely at me. "She's plain hungry."

"Hungry?"

"Now don't you go to askin me questions, for I ain't sayin ary another word about it. If you don't know what I mean, then keep your own counsel."

He frowned as though I had offended him. To change the subject, I asked,

"What is going on now at the ranch?"

Well. They's just about done shearing the sheep, and the wool was being bagged for shipment to Magdalena and Socorro and Chicago in the empty railroad cars that came up during the night. Then they would start in a few days with the dipping.

—How was that?

—Didn't know what sheep dipping was?

—No, sir.

Well. They taken and get the sheep in one corral, and they's a

runway that slopes sharp downward and the sheep are driven down
it into a long cement trough filled with the dip, and they have to
swim to pass through it, for the trough is deeper than they could
stand up in, and more than three feet wide, with straight walls so
they can't take and scramble out, so they have to swim mebbe seventy-
five feet to get out of the trough at the other end, where they's
another corral they finally jump up a ramp to get to. As the sheep
swim along, yelling like Beelzebub, the men on each side of the dip
along the way push them under, head and all, and they come up
shakin their heads and crying and blowin, but they have to be got
under to be sure all the ticks and scabs and burrs is killed or
loosened.

"Ticks."

Ticks that got buried under the wool and bored in the skin, and if
they waddn't killed and sores and scabs treated, the next coat of
wool would be poorly because of patches of dead hide underneath.
They had to do it for every crop of wool. Hot work. Hard work.
The smell was enough to stink a dog off a gut wagon. But to see it
done right, old man Wenzel was there, and so was Tom Agee.
They always took on a few extra hands, some from Mexico, some
from the sheep camps south of the ranch, and that was why I was
comin, and why that sorry no-good stranger from El Paso was
hired, who had answered an ad in the El Paso *Herald Post,* and that
was all they knew about him. The good Lord only knew what had
become of him and where they'd get another this late.

"*Breach of contract,*" pronounced Tom, and added, "Sometimes
people still call me *Judge* though I never did fill that office."

"I see. —Where do the fellows live?"

There were two bunkhouses, one big one, where Tom Agee had a
separate room at one end. The other, smaller one had room for two.
That was where I would be put, along with the other new man if he
should ever appear.

"It's a right nice layout, the whole place. —You a college boy?" he suddenly asked with a ferocity half-curious, half-scornful. I said, "Yes." He nodded silently, and then putting his jaw forward grimly, he said, "Well, we'll take care of that."

"Well, Mr Agee, don't let it prey on your mind. I just did what the good Lord in His wisdom set me to do."

"You mockin me, young man?" But he suppressed a twitching smile that betrayed satisfaction at my cheeky answer, and waving jerkily off to the far northwest ahead of us, he said, "That's the Gallina Mountains. We'll be turnin off right soon. And don't you go to calling me Mister. My name's Tom."

I began to notice that the country to the north of us—we were traveling due west—slowly changed in character. Scrub piñon and other pine trees dotted the hills and darkened the distant land. To our south, the Plains of San Agustín faded into the distance as low rises of land began also to show scattered vegetation. It was those plains, now behind us, which gave me my image of how far I was, how alienated, from any world I knew; and lying awake on that first night, it was the plains which shone so brightly behind my closed eyelids in the dark. When we left them behind I felt we had crossed a boundary. I wished I was already at the ranch, familiar with it, and without qualms and questions.

"What is Don Elizario really like?" I asked Tom. "I know Concha—I had a long talk with her in Albuquerque. He went off to talk on the phone."

"You call her Concha?" asked Tom sharply.

"No, no, I don't call her anything. But that's how everybody refers to her."

"They do, eh? Who's everybody?"

"Everybody talks about her in Albuquerque."

"They do, eh? Well, just you be careful what you call her. She's Miz Wenzel and don't you forget it. And don't go near the house. Nobody gets there."

"Why?"

"Why! Why, because they're all men, that's why."

"I see. But I think she would like to have parties."

"Heh. Now about him. He's different."

—Different this year from last. He was older. He seemed more careful. What about? About everything. He was hard-working and he worked everybody hard, and he was fair, but he stood for no nonsense from anybody, and he liked to come out after supper and sit around the cowffee fire with the men for a while, but he seemed tired. That is, tired inside. He made like he finally give up to something. Mebbe it was just bein old. But you wouldn't think he was old during the day, workin. Didn't know.

"I don't know. If I was still before the public doin the Lord's work, I'd get him down on his knees, Cathlick or no, and pray with him and find out what's holdin down his soul. I b'lieve I know but I can't say 'thout I am certain and *then* I wouldn't say. I did always respect him. But now I feel a little bit sorry for him. He'd have my hide if he knew that. But some way, I got the feelin I want to comfort him. —Now you stay away from that house, hear?"

"I was just going to call and pay my respects."

"Just don't you do it. He'll know right off that you're there and why. As for her, she's none of your business. —There's the gate. Get out."

He waved to a turnoff leading toward a barbed-wire fence in which a gate of wire strands was rigged between two posts and held at one end by loops of wire which could be lifted and lowered. Tom expected me to open the gate. I went to the post with the wire loops and tried to lift off the top one. It did not give. The tension of the wire was so great that I could not free the moveable gate post from its top loop and the other one at the bottom in which it was footed. I looked at Tom. He showed no interest. I struggled with the gate again. He let me, but at last he ambled out of the car, pushed me aside, wrapped his left arm around the moveable gate post, threw his weight toward the fixed post, the other one yielded, the top loop came free, and then the bottom one. With scornful silence more searing than profanity, he threw the whole gate aside so the car could pass through. He drove through and stopped the car to wait for me. I ran to get in. He blew a sigh like a bull and declared,

"Don't you know *innythin? Close* the gate. In this country, you never open a gate 'thout you close it. Git."

My initiation had begun. I went to the gate and, after many tries at imitating Tom's method of using arm, shoulder, and body against the stretching of the wires, got the gate in place again.

We rode silently and slowly along a road worse than the one we had left. We were heading north over earth which showed pale brick red now, and far off the Gallina Mountains had turned dark under cloud shadow. Here and there a red gully lay, dry, ravaged by past cloudbursts. In the bushes of pine which we passed the song of cicadas rose like the scream of machine metal. Presently Tom spoke again, shouting to be heard. Though I did not hear all he said, I was relieved that no trace remained of the scorn he had shown me at the gate. I heard scattered phrases.

"But it's a good life—hard—the old man—let him make the move —I remember him—then mighty handsome—prize bull—people had ought to think before they—"

He interrupted his broken monologue and pointed ahead with a finger like a big dried twisted carrot. The ranch headquarters slowly came into view.

First we saw the windmill. It was not turning, but its vanes were so set that they caught the full white midday sun and they blazed like a source of the sun itself. The galvanized-iron roof of the house also gave back the sky in a hot white glare over two of the long rooms. The house had several angles, indicating rooms facing differently. A huge cluster of old cottonwoods stood behind the house and by afternoon would shade it. On each side but somewhat removed stood the breathless brakes of salt cedar. The old wife, Rosario

Wenzel, had planted them as protection from the winds of dust in their season. There was a faint brown blur of outbuildings and penciled lines of corral fences, and lesser structures of obscure purpose, in one of which I would probably live. The ground rose slightly and the track of our path ahead wavered crazily, according to the ruts, in a long and diminishing scratch of pale-orange dust.

"Nigh there," observed Tom.

❧

Sooner than I had expected we had come through another barbed-wire gate. I heard the subdued bleat of sheep, which sounded to me like the onset of collective nausea.

Tom brought me to the upper corral, above the house to the north, where men were shearing. Beyond a glance or a lifted chin gesture, nobody acknowledged me as Tom handed me a long-tined rake and pantomimed how I was to collect the shorn wool falling from the heavy clippers. As a sheep was worked on, it was held down by the shearers, who bent over their job in their big hats, which shaded their faces from me. The dust rose breast high and hung there. The heat was under the skin. Tom disappeared. I swept wool with my rake. As the piles grew higher, a middle-aged Mexican hauled them away into lesser piles to be bagged. Sweat ran from us all and dust made a little skin plaster with it. The sheep exuded a smell of dried feces mixed with dust, and the rankness of desert grass, and sour decay of stuff caught in the wool which once wet by rain or urine dried rancidly. Raking away, and breathing as shallowly as I could to avoid taking into my lungs all the foulness suspended in the air, I felt blisters spring up on my hands as they gripped and slid on the rake when it dragged the filth-heavied wool.

After time which I did not measure, the work was suddenly interrupted when a clanging summons came from the chuck wagon, which stood among the outbuildings. It was the cook calling us to the evening meal at a little past five o'clock. The men straightened up and stretched. Some—there were about seven or eight in all— looked at me with hard curiosity as we all started toward the chuck wagon, which stood at an angle to the cookhouse. Tom reappeared and, vaguely waving first at me and then the rest, spoke my name in introduction.

By his supper fire built in a U-shaped brick fire hole in the open, the cook, a small thin man wearing an apron, and beating a huge spoon against a tin plate, kept up a wordless cry with his face turned upward like a coyote in a performance which he seemed to enjoy for its own sake. It was his ritual invitation to us to eat. He had gray whiskers standing out like the face fur of a lynx and—to me an incongruity—he wore a pair of tin spectacles at a crazy angle far down on his nose.

We lined up to take plates and load them from the small vats and trays where his food was to be spooned out—beans, beef in hunks and stew, biscuits like lumpy fists, and at the end, a bushel basket full of bruised apples and a huge enameled coffee pot much battered and surrounded by tin cups. The sun was still hot, still a while from setting, and we all drifted to the shade of a few cottonwoods, which brought us within fifty yards of the house. We settled down on the ground in silence.

Nobody spoke when Don Elizario came out of the house and ambled toward us. He seemed not so tall as I remembered him in his elaborate house in town. He walked with a slight lurch to the left at every other step. Hatless, he showed his white hair, which was mussed forward over his brow like a boy's. His gray-yellow mustaches were slightly raised in a friendly smile, and as he came closer he said a few words—"*Amigos—qué colór, qué no?*"—and nodding around the scattered group, some of whom lifted a chin to him, he came over to me and put out his hand, squatted down beside me with a blown breath of effort before I could stand up in respect.

"Welcome," he said with a husky little laugh, which referred to the conditions of this meeting so different from our last. "You will have to work twice as much now that the other *hombre* never showed up."

I was too tired to do more than smile back at him. He gave me a grave, long look, then, as though to read my whole nature and make a judgment. Uneasily I looked back into his narrowed stare, which revealed only a little drop of light in each of his eyes. The others watched this inspection silently, and then one or two nodded, as if they knew what it was about. Abruptly Don Elizario rose and waved his hand around over the other men, a patriarchal gesture, then slowly returned to the house.

The sun went behind some horizon clouds as it fell. The cook whacked his tin dish again to signal for the return of utensils to be rinsed in a common tub of hot water. Tom came beside me and asked if I wanted to see where I was going to live. After I rinsed my plate, cup, and big spoon, he led me off to the little bunkhouse, which stood thirty or forty feet from the big one. He kicked open the door and nodded at the interior. It had one small window at the far end. He said the door was left open all night for ventilation, and that bein the case, it was a right good idea to keep an eye out every morning for critters such as scorpions, tarantulas, and rattlers, which had been known to settle in on some ole night or other. The room had a bunk along each wall. Between them was a space five or six feet wide. Two nails for clothes were fixed opposite each other on the raw walls. There was a table with one chair under the window. On the table was a coal oil lamp.

"Which bunk?" he asked.

I pointed to the one on the left as we faced it. He said I could take my suitcase from the car and settle it under my bunk, which made that territory mine,

"You can wash outside with your basin"—he pointed to it on a shelf above my bunk—"or you can get yourself over to the windmill tank. There's a pipe where you can stand for a bath if you're willin to wait long enough, or you can bring a can of water over here. You'll find the outdoor privy for yourself. Anythin else?"

I shook my head. I did not say that I had expected the Wenzels to ask me into their house on my first evening.

"Sometimes the hands set round the fire after supper and sometimes somebody sings a song, or tells a story, and you can have a cup of cowffee till bedtime."

He left me. I was ready to drop into bed. But tired as I was, it was almost morning before I slept with all that behind my eyes.

꽃

At half past five Tom woke me by kicking the bottom of my open door. He set a tin bucket of water on the floor and said, "I won't be bringin this every morning," and added that breakfast would be there to be taken in ten minutes and work would start at six o'clock. He watched me to be sure I was awake and upright, then went off to get the other men to the chuck wagon.

Stepping outside, I splashed myself and dressed, aching. The morning at that hour was like balm. Above the Magdalena mountains the sun was coming up and its golden sky merged overhead with the palest blue. Shadows were long toward the west. A cool little wind passed over us but stirred no dust. Our grove of trees was like some enameled marvel, sparkling with freshness. It was a morning new under creation, so delicate and precisely formed were all objects, so perfectly lighted and shadowed by the rising sun.

But an hour later, again in the corral, we already felt the heat of the day, and it seemed to me that our humanity disappeared, merged, into the character of the creatures we worked upon. Once during a brief rest we heard a distant sound over the flat, short-grassed land. It was the combined bleatings of another herd of sheep being driven from the other Wenzel ranch far to our south. They were being brought for shearing and dipping. Their herders walked beside the sheep, whose course was kept in line by two black-and-tan sheep dogs who ran back and forth, barking at the edges of the little dusty procession. The sheep, with their knock-kneed walk, their sharp little hooves, their white eyelashes and half-dropped lids, their Assyrian noses and self-satisfied mouths, took on an anthropomorphic character for me; and I reflected that like much of humanity, having no idea of what was in store for them, they came on their way with crowded and witless good nature. They were soon driven through the corral gate in struggling eagerness, making their vomit-like noise, and in turn came to us where we worked.

My right hand was swollen and burning from burst blisters. I tied a handkerchief around my hand. Nobody offered to trade jobs. I could see why, for the shearing took practice and skill, and when now and then the shearing blades nicked the skin of a sheep and drew blood, the man who had let it happen was jeered amiably by the others. It would be easy to injure the animals—they struggled at being held down. My heaps of sheared wool grew bigger and bigger, and it was clear that we needed another man to haul them away to be bagged. The missing ranch hand made his absence felt.

At noon Ira—the cook—set up his clamor for chow, or grub: words which the men used naturally but which because they carried for me the professional cant of cowboy fiction I thought false. Once again Don Elizario came to join us, this time to eat. He sat on the ground with us, asked questions about the work, talking mostly to Tom, though he spoke also, in Spanish, to the Mexicans in the crew. When he was done with his plate, he stood, sighed a belch of repleteness, and came over to me.

"This evening, eh?" he said. "You come and have supper at the house? Six o'clock, eh?"

I thanked him, he nodded, and then, with droll sweeping motions, sent us back to work.

❦

It was mid-afternoon when one of the Mexicans cried, "¡MIRA!" and pointed. We quit work and turned to see.

Up the rutted dusty road just beyond the eastern clump of salt cedar came a figure. He had a canvas bag slung over one shoulder. He walked with a swinging gait, as though his single smallness were equal to the whole land. Tom Agee sat back on his heels to watch him approach. It was a young man, perhaps twenty-two years old. Coming to us, he smiled in full confidence of a good reception. He pulled off his hat, which was sweat-stained and trough-shaped at its brim by the clutch of his hand. He was covered with dust and spotted with sweat. His clothes—a red-checkered shirt, trousers of dark striped material, and Western boots all scuffed at the feet and brightly stitched in fancy designs at the sides—were shabby. At the corral rails, he threw down his bag, which looked heavy, and leaned on the middle rail, smiling genially. Tom was not disposed to smile back.

"Just who might you be?" he asked while everyone listened.

"I'm the new hand."

"You was supposed to be the new hand yesterday."

"I know. I got delayed by unforeseen circumstances."

"Never mind talkin fancy. How'd you get here?"

"I got the Springerville stage out of Magdalena this morning, and got him to drop me off at your gate on the highway. Then I walked. Pleased to meet you-all."

Tom hesitated. He was offended by this cheerful composure, and for a moment seemed to consider turning him away; but we needed help, and at last, he said,

[158]

"Just what do you think you can do?"

"Well"—looking at the work interrupted—"I can shear."

"Well, oh, Lord, I guess—well, get on in here and get to shearin over there with that set in the corner."

"I'm sort of hongry, you know. It was a long walk and the stage had no place to stop for dinner."

"Get on it or get on your way," said Tom, and nodded to us to resume work.

The newcomer climbed the rails and went to work in the far corner of the corral. As he passed me, he said, "Hi," and gave a short laugh, as if to say that he saw at once how different he and I were from the rest. I had the irrational superiority of the predecessor, even if by only one day, and I merely nodded back at him. But I watched him get down to work and saw, as everyone did, that he was expert at the job; and the air was alive with combined respect, speculation, and dislike for him.

Dislike: for in that company of work-graven men, older, resigned, scornful of ways not their own, he was by his looks alone an offense. Despite sweat and dust he looked clean. After his long walk he radiated energy. In the midst of hard, clamorous work he shed good will with smiling indifference. Most offensive of all, he was like an allegory of all-knowing innocence in the midst of ignorant experience. He bore himself as if he could turn his hand equally well to any task, and as if any task were hardly worth doing. His confidence came from his good looks. He had no right, when the rest of us were runneled with distorting wet dirt, to look not only comfortable but handsome. He was not tall, but the proportions of his body, the harmony of its parts, shone right out. He had the look, and the quickness of reflex with sharp, continual turns of the head, wary and keen and interested, of a lion cub; his lean frame covered with the finest pelt—golden tan; light hair. His face was younger than his body, and as unmarked as a child's, with small features so regular and color so high that somebody, in disguised envy and resentment, yelled at him,

[159]

"How you doin, Babyface?"

To this nickname, which was commonly used from then on, he merrily made an obscene gesture, and got on with his work.

When I went at suppertime to wash off the day's fetid residue, I saw him tearing at his food like a dog. There was more than hunger to it; there was the power of all appetite. He paused long enough to call out, "See you later," for he had been told he was to share the small bunkhouse with me, and now he viewed me with a conspiratorial attitude: two young men of superior style amidst that small simple mob of sheep shearers, herdsmen, and ranch hands. With a short nod I rejected his assumption and made ready to dine with Don Elizario and Concha. As I changed into cleaner clothes I resented having to share my quarters. How could I read my Mencken and the other voguish book I had brought—the *Tertium Organum?* I moved the table and the coal oil lamp closer to my bed to establish from the first that by right of prior claim they were more mine than any newcomer's. I doubted complacently that he had any such thing as a book in his bag. I decided to endure him merely as a specimen to observe for my notebook entries.

❧

The ranch house of gray stucco was half hidden by heavy trumpet vines and the tamarisk brake which separated the bunkhouses from it. The front door had two panels of frosted glass etched with a design of flowers through which someone within could have a slim glimpse of anyone outside. All that could be seen from the porch was a vague, still presence, as though someone inside were deciding whether or not to open the door in response to my knock. Then suddenly it opened.

"Yes, come in," said Don Elizario, standing aside ceremoniously for me. He brought me into a parlor which was left as his first wife had furnished it with pieces from Mexico—stiff chairs covered in prickly red plush, and a center table draped to the floor with an embroidered Spanish shawl heavily fringed. The house was stifling, though the air outside had begun to cool with the lowering sun. On the walls were oval portraits of earlier Wenzels covered with convex glass. In faded sepias the fathers and grandfathers looked out above stiff high collars and high-buttoned, thick black coats and sweeping mustaches and heavy-looped gold watch chains, while mothers and grandmothers stood behind their men with timid hands wristed with ruffles resting on broadcloth shoulders. The women wore high pompadours and frozen expressions of chaste calm. Their faces were supported by boned net collars and their bosoms looked as if carved out of shining wood with no hint of fleshly shapes beneath. Propriety denied passion, even simple feeling, in all the portraits; and sitting with me, Don Elizario, as the issue of such ancestry, was an image of the same impassive convention.

"My wife is getting our supper," he said. He sat with his knees apart, leaning a little forward in the faded refinement of the parlor. He was in shirt sleeves, without collar. A collar button gleamed on his neckband. "You are satisfied here?" His Mexican accent sounded in all he said.

"I hardly know yet—the work is hard, but I can get used to it."

"We are not what you are used to," he said, meaning not the place, or the work, but the men.

I did not know how to speak to this without sounding superior or rude. I replied,

"It is good of you to let me spend some time here."

"If I were younger—" He sighed, and the inarticulate love of the hard life reached through the plushy dusk. The rank animal male society, the animals themselves, their natural smells, ways, perversities, and innocence, their brute powers to be overcome, their instinctive cautions and fears to be outwitted—these were the burdens of life in which he was most at home.

In the depths of the house we could hear kitchen sounds. He

turned toward them and then to me proudly, as if in them he saw Concha.

"She is a good cook," he said.

"She is very beautiful, sir. You are a fortunate man."

To my surprise, he frowned, leaning a little nearer to me with a strange appraising squint.

"You have seen her again?"

"No—only that day at your house, and then, too, far away when she drove by several times when I was out on my bicycle."

He leaned back.

Was it possible that this reassured him? I could not imagine—and then I could: he was jealous of how any other man saw her, and with anguish he imagined them as a pair. This notion went sharper for me when he asked, almost pleading below controlled calm,

"You are Catholic?"

"Yes."

"Yes. —A good one? You go to Mass?"

"Yes."

He was not yet satisfied.

"You go to Communion?"

"Yes," I said a little stiffly.

"Every Sunday?" he insisted.

I nodded, preferring not to speak further about a private matter. If I was impolite, he did not notice.

He was eased. My conscience, then, would be his ally, if I should be drawn to his beautiful girl. I was uneasy at the pathetic bareness of his concern. Burdens seemed to fall away from him. With his knuckles he wiped his eyes, where ready feeling—relief, in this case—brought a start of moisture.

"You write to your *madre?*"

"Yes. —I don't know how often I can, from here."

He waved his hand. I need not worry. I must write to my *madre* often, and my mail would be taken to Magdalena by the ranch car, which went to town every few days for supplies. I could count on my letters coming and going. In fact, sometimes, if I wanted to, and if they could spare me at the corrals, I could take the car myself. All I had to do was ask. Don Elizario was more than jovial—he became merry.

"One moment."

He went to the next room and returned with a bottle of José Cuervo tequila and two small glasses, and poured drinks which with a silent toast to each other we took in one toss and swallow. In answer to a question I had not spoken, he said.

"She does not drink."

In a moment, Concha appeared in the parlor doorway. In the dim room her vividness was subdued, and so was her temperament, but her gray eyes gave light. She greeted me silently, letting me press her inert hand, and then with bowed head she led us to the dining room which her husband had built for her. Between the old parlor and the new dining room was a narrow unlighted hallway. On its wall was a telephone in an oaken box with a small hand crank and a cradled receiver on its side. The mouthpiece stood out from the rest at the end of a long brass bracket. As we moved past it to supper, Don Elizario indicated the phone with complacency:

"We are *moderno* out here at the ranch, also."

"Unless," ventured Concha, "there is thunder and lightning"—she shuddered—"and then we cannot hear anything."

"Yes, yes, the wire. There is a wire connecting us with the line from Magdalena to Datil. Sometimes we can see the *electricidad* on it."

He laughed gently at belonging to such a proud trick of science and nature.

In the dining room, suddenly all was bright, garish. In her own part of the house, Concha had had her way. Excess and expense were everywhere visible—the heaviest silver, the most profuse cut glass, the brightest curtains and rug and wallpaper. Above the table

[163]

hung a cluster of electric lights twined about with glass grapes and vine leaves. The electricity came unsteadily from a dynamo run by the windmill. As we sat down, Don Elizario said to me, as if testing my credentials and good faith,

"You will say grace, eh?"

I recited the common Catholic grace, ending with *"Per Dominum Jesum Christum in vitam aeternam, Amen,"* to give a priestly turn for his reassurance. He gave a wan little laugh of appreciation.

It was a heavy meal, almost unseasoned except for a paste of *guacamole,* which was fiery with red chili powder and seeds. There was almost no conversation. Concha kept her eyes lowered as though still in her convent school. Her husband ate with great sweeps of a big spoon which he used instead of a fork. His napkin was tucked in above the collar button. Once he paused to ask me,

"¿Más tequila?"

"No, thank you."

"Es muy bueno para la digestión."

"No, thank you. I don't really drink."

He sighed with comfort.

"This is delicious," I said to Concha.

"Thank you," she replied without looking at me. She was enacting her husband's view of her role.

Concha took away the dishes and in the kitchen readied our dessert—a bowl of mangos awash with juice. Before she returned, Don Elizario asked me how I liked "the big city" of Magdalena—a joke.

I should have seen it, he declared, years ago, when the mines were working full time, and the hotel was filled day and night, and the railroad siding was crowded with the private cars of Eastern capitalists. Many a time he had dined on board one or the other of these, talking investments with those New York bankers. They listened to him. He knew what he was talking about. He was not as rich as they were, but he was rich enough for their respect, and before the mines began to give out, and the town to fade with them, he got enough money buying and selling shares—more, in some cases, than the bankers themselves. What times they used to have at the Marigold Hotel! One time the secretary of President Díaz of Mexico came to talk investment, and Don Elizario himself was the host, and when the secretary went back with useful information, the President sent a letter and a medal. Between the words, Don Eli was telling me what a great man he used to be.

"In those days, they used to call me Mr Magdalena. I knew everything that went on there. Even right now, there is someone who tells me everything that goes on there."

He wheezed a little contented laugh.

After supper he sighed with contentment, and said he had to go out to see how the men were doing, as he did every night. He left me with Concha.

She led me to the new sitting room which her husband had built for her. It was like a movie set of the vamp period—satin draperies, two floor lamps with pagoda-like shades hung with long silk tassels, a fur rug on a deep sofa, pierced brass lanterns shedding a patterned soft light, many cushions on furniture and floor, and on a velvet ottoman an almost life-sized toy of a leopard with green glass eyes.

Here she became animated. She now felt it her duty to entertain, and like a child, the only way she knew how to do this was to bring out things to show.

"Now I can show you my wedding pictures. I brought them along from town."

We sat side by side, though not dangerously near, as she opened her albums of white imitation leather. She photographed superbly. In only one or two pictures her diffidence at being a bride showed through all the lace, tulle, the waxen tuberoses of her wreath, the enormous bouquet of lilies she held. For the rest, she posed expertly, even in the joint pictures with Don Elizario, who was resplendent in stiff evening dress as they stood in full sunlight outside the church of San Felipe de Neri in Old Town, Albuquerque. She looked up at him with lustrous gaze. Her freshness in years was lovely, and to it she added the statuesque allure which she had learned from afternoon hours in the dreaming darkness of the Central Avenue movie houses at home. After half an hour of slowly turning the pictures, where I saw also her impassive parents and relatives, her four flower girls, her train bearer (a little male cousin) and her ring bearer (another), and the parish priest in his jubilee vestments, I said,

"The camera suits you, Concha."

"Don't let my husband hear you call me that, Richard."

"Mrs Wenzel."

By her use of my first name, though, she put us in some sort of league. Starving for any connection with anyone, she abandoned her impersonation of a grown-up, submissive, but important wife. She said, hopelessly,

"Movie star."

"You could have been."

The past tense made her gaze at me with a dispirited sigh. But it was true. In the silent films, conventionally directed, she might have captured audiences with her beauty alone, while her actions and lips went through the accepted signals of movie passion. A little tuck in her smooth brow reflected her resignation now. She looked around at the terms of her luxury, which represented a prison she had entered almost without thinking.

"He is very good to you. He worships you."

She nodded impatiently as if to dismiss an irrelevancy.

"I worry about him, you know," she said.

This, coupled with her misery, touched me. I asked why.

"You know—you should not tell this to anyone, he does not want them to know—you know, he is not well."

"No? He looks like a robust old man."

"Old man, yes. —Yes, he has something wrong here." She gracefully indicated her heart. "Pecta-something."

"Angina pectoris?"

"Yes. That." She shivered. "Sometimes at night I am afraid, will I wake up next to him and he will be dead? Or—"

Or herself in his dead arms? occurred to me as she halted her thought.

I had not before seen in mind so vividly the image of them together in bed, like any man and wife.

"And then," she continued, "I am even more afraid when I wake up at night and he is gone."

"Gone?"

"Yes, late at night he often gets up and goes outside. He says he looks at the stars, and listens for the cows, if they are all right, and there he stands, looking and listening, I don't know what for, until he gets cold, in his old nightgown, and then he comes in again, to me—"

—To get warm of her lovely body, after being alone and silent in the starry darkness, taking stock of his world, and perhaps wondering how much longer he would be able to see it?

If I had felt sympathy for her, now I had pity for him. His fears were now doubly poignant when I saw them in light of hers. For a moment, an even further notion of what their marriage might lack lighted and then went out in my mind. I must spare them (who in their ways so mutely asked for reassurances) any speculation. They must be allowed the dignity of what they chose to show the world.

Setting her albums aside, she said,

"Your hands. They are all raw."

"Yes. That rake."

"You see?" she said, commenting on the expert management she immediately decided upon. She went and fetched a bottle of liniment and some bits of cotton. Sitting beside me again, she began to bathe my blisters with the soaked cotton, holding my hands in turn. I was watching her face so intently, and she my hands, that we did not hear or see Don Elizario come in. He must have stood for a long moment; and then, scraping his steps, went back to the hallway and returned at once with a pair of old cracked leather work gloves. Concha was by then across the room from me, holding her liniment bottle to her breasts as though in self-protection. Don Elizario ignored her. To me, giving me the gloves, he said,

"These will help you. So, good night. Come to see us whenever you like." His voice hardened a little. "My wife gets lonely."

At this she put her hand over her mouth, wondering at him. What did he mean? But I thought that his bestowing sanction upon my welcome in her name robbed her of a last independent pleasure in imagined variations of her days.

※

The light in the small bunkhouse was still burning and I was sorry if it meant that Babyface was still awake. But he was asleep, so exhausted that even facing the lamp did not bother him. If he had been waiting for me, he had been unable to keep his eyes open. He was bare to the waist, with his blanket thrown across his legs. He looked more than ever like a large child. He had been too tired to wash before throwing himself down on his bunk. The dust of the day paled his skin and darkened his cap of light hair, which was like thick short fur. His head was on his doubled-up right arm and his left arm hung straight off the bunk almost to the floor. Around his neck rested a thin tarnished brass chain which vanished into the shadow of his pillowing arm.

Resenting the loss of privacy, I undressed as quietly as I could, hoping I would not awaken him. As the lamp was still lighted, I decided that I must establish my prior right to read as late as I liked, and that it was my habit to read every night before sleeping. I opened my volume of Mencken, which Lyle had given me, and turned to the essay on "The Husbandman," which made such hilarious if extravagant fun of the farmer—"the lonely companion of

Bos Taurus" who renounced "Babylon to guard the horned cattle of the hills," but than whom "no more grasping, selfish and dishonest mammal, indeed, is known to students of the Anthropoidea," the living reason for "saddling the rest of us with oppressive and idiotic laws, all hatched on the farm. There, where the cows low through the still night, and the jug of Peruna stands behind the stove, and bathing begins, as at Biarritz, with the vernal equinox, there is the reservoir of all the nonsensical legislation which now makes the United States a buffoon among the great nations. . . ." I was suppressing impulses to laugh out loud at such passages when in turning a page I saw that my bunkhouse mate was watching me.

He was grinning. The lamplight showed me his face closely for the first time. It seemed open and guileless, but it was difficult to see into his eyes; for in the right eye there was a curious disfigurement. It was a wedge of light in the circle of the iris which gave his stare an elusive direction, though I knew he was looking straight at me. It was something not visible at a little distance. Close to, it seemed to put him into a different dimension of space from anyone he looked at. Evidently he had no loss of vision. The effect was strangely powerful, for while it made you hesitate to look directly at him, it forced you to do so.

He said genially,

"I don't have any of that c-r-u-u-d."

"That what?"

"The book, and that."

It was my introduction to his habit of talk. He was more foul-mouthed than anybody I ever heard, even in my army years later in the Hitler war.

"I read before going to sleep every night."

"Oh, I can read, sure enough. I just am not interested. I have enough to fill my days. And my nights."

He gave a comradely laugh at this reference to his prowess at night. He was now wide awake and in a mood to talk.

"My name is J. Buswell Rennison, but everybody calls me Buz—

have ever since I was a crawlin baby in south Texas by the Rio Grande."

I told him my name.

"Where're you from, Richie?"

"Albuquerque"—thinking any of my history further back need not concern him.

"Come on. They tell me your daddy's governor of New York."

I was then forced to say a little more to correct the news about me which probably beginning with Don Elizario had been enlarged throughout the sheep camp.

He took this as an invitation to sit up and listen with sociable interest. As he did so, his neck chain swung around upon his tight-muscled chest and I saw a metal disk hanging from it. It was the size of a half dollar. He saw me looking at it and pulled the chain over his head and handed it to me.

It was colored with bright cheap enamel. Around the rim it read ATLANTIC CITY BATHING BEAUTY. In the center was a bossed figure of a young woman in a striped bathing suit. Her head was tilted in flirtation, and across her middle she held a lettered ribbon which said, A LUCKY PIECE. Her left knee was laid provocatively against her right thigh.

"My lucky *piece*," he said as I handed it back to him. "I got it in a hock shop in Mexico. I call it my ice breaker. I let it slide out of my shirt, and I can tell by the way they look at it the first time what it will or won't do for me." He fondled the amulet and chain and added, "It's a mighty handy little thing to have around. Not that I've needed it too often—my personality generally does the work."

He was amiably settled for a ramble though autobiography, which he undertook with pleasure in himself. For a few minutes I held my book open to suggest that I meant to return to it; but I finally gave up, closed it, put it on the table, and let him go on. His voice was light, his mood candid, and he laced almost every sentence with smiling obscenities. (I exactly quote only a few which carried meaning in moments of high feeling.) He was so certain of the interest of his life, because it was his, and he someone of well-confirmed excellence in all he undertook, that I was soon far beyond my pose as a collector of specimens.

As he talked, sitting up and gesturing freely, I never knew exactly where his flawed gaze rested whenever he turned toward me; but with genial power, he made me see with almost a familiar eye much of what he talked about. Presuming a universal lack of reticence in others, he invaded my attention with exuberant candor as though he had known me from boyhood. His experience was limited to the physical; and yet he had acquired a sharpness of mind and an ease of expression, however crude, such as I had not heard equaled among even the best of my fellow students of that time. On that night, as well as on many later occasions, he spoke of his life. Here I have assembled in one place the gist of many notes recorded at odd times. By the rift of light in his eye, and the working of his mind behind it, I wondered how much of what he told was true and how much fantasy; but what he invented—if invent he did—told as much about him, I thought, as what might be fact. He said he remembered everything that had ever happened to him, and it flowed out of him like a stream.

His family were fruit growers on the lower Rio Grande in Texas. He had worked in the orange groves ever since he could remember. How a water moccasin had actually chased him in the river when he was nothing but a tiny boy, pecker-high on a pickaninny. How he used to shuck himself buck-naked with the other boys and spend all day Sunday swimming and messing around—"you know how kids do each other"—in the shallow brown river. How they used to take their BB guns and hide in the grass in the banker's orchard where his horses grazed and shoot them in the rump to see them jump and hear them holler. What they did to a naked sissy boy one time in the school basement with a bottle of Dynashine shoe polish and then when he went and snitched on them, what they did to him after that with lighted cigarettes. The way it felt when the young wife of a fruit trucker showed him and the boys everything and let them in all the way. He was the leader of the gang because he already knew about that, and he was leader for three years, until he had to run away at fifteen for getting the daughter of the leading chiropractor in Harlingen, Texas, pregnant. That was the best thing he ever did—running away, not the other thing, there was nothing that special about her, but he always had his mind on bettering himself and how could you do that at home? He had never been back since, but he never had trouble finding jobs, on ranches or in towns, and someday when he and I were off on a long trip together, hitching rides on freight trains or autos, he would tell me about some of them. He learned more about human nature by the time he was eighteen than any old man he ever saw. Did I know what the best rule was? It was not to give a flying frig about anybody else's feelings, for you could never know what those were anyway, and all that mattered was what you felt yourself, and you know that what you felt the most was right down there, where he was pointing. He got East as far as Chicago, and Northwest as far Vancouver, and then he gradually came down the coast to San Francisco. There as a bellhop he made more money on the side (he particularized at doing what for old widows and married women after hours) than he ever saw until he got to Los Angeles. That was where the rainbow began and ended, with him in the middle, as someone told him. One day they took one look at him and said he belonged in pictures, if only he would get dressed up to be somebody else, like a cowboy, or a tango dancer, or an international prince in disguise who was on his way to claiming his rightful kingdom. It sounded mighty inviting to him. A number of people had the same idea about him, but it seemed a long time before he got anywhere nearer a movie camera than somebody's bed. Not but what he didn't enjoy it, with the stuff they gave him, that he could sell, or when he couldn't stand the others for a while, that he could give away in turn to someone young when he wanted them for his own personal enjoyment. They did not care, out there, what they did. It was wild and mighty nice, and he had to admit that he still enjoyed being the leader of the gang by natural right, and if they thought they had done it all, they had another think coming at the things he showed them. One of them—he spoke a famous name—tried to kill theirself when he told her he wouldn't be back. But that about being a movie star—he finally insisted, one day, and they got him to have a screen test, and that did it. It was all over. That thing in his right eye made him look blind on the screen. He saw it himself, and they said they couldn't have a movie star who showed only his left side all the time. He could see the sense in this, and they had him back where he was before, in and out of their big cars and swimming pools and fancy bedrooms, until one night he was having such a good time with several people that somebody got hurt sure enough, she had to have the ambulance, and he lit out for Mexico. He stayed there for a year and he never heard if she died or not, though he certainly hoped she didn't, but he thought he should not go back to Hollywood, even when his money gave out and he had to sell all the little gold things they had given him back then. The next thing he knew, he had a full beard. It was blond, like his head, and he got a job as night clerk in the hotel at Avanzada, Mexico, where tourists who talked English kept coming down from Arizona. He was known there as the former assistant manager of the Palace Hotel in San Francisco. Messican women certainly went for blond-bearded gringos. It was a fine job, but the hotel burned down one night when a bunch of bandits rode into town and had a battle with the local army garrison. So everything he had in the world including his hidden wallet of new savings that he meant to better himself with burned also. He headed for Agua Prieta, across the border from Douglas, Arizona, but there wasn't any work in either place, and he got on over to El Paso. He thought the beard wasn't needed any longer. He shaved it off and slept several nights at the Salvation Army. Then he saw an ad in the paper for a job. He answered it, and made a date to be in Magdalena, New Mexico, to get a ride to the ranch and [here his affability became almost boisterous] what did he do but miss the date.

"But I'm not sorry," he added. "I had me a time in Magdalena."

He arrived there a day before he was supposed to and went to have a cup of coffee in the café of the hotel. That did it. There was that girl, the waitress, and he knew before he said anything about a "lucky piece" that she was one.

"Larraine?" I said—that downcast, tired, plump young woman?

"That's her."

They went upstairs to her room at the far end of the corridor of the Marigold Hotel in the afternoon. She had been given a bottle of bootleg corn by a friend. They got drunk—he ve-ry drunk, and except for when she had to go downstairs to work at suppertime, they stayed up there, because she couldn't get enough of what he had to give. She swore she had never known anything like it. Maybe she was just saying it to make him feel good. Anyway.

"That doesn't sound like her," I protested, I suppose in a haze of chivalry. "I saw her the next day when I had breakfast. She was not like that at all. She was quiet, hardly looked at anyone. You must have been with somebody else."

"Not at all. She was just hung over."

So was he—so badly that he had to stay upstairs to sleep it off, which was how he happened to miss Tom Agee and me for the drive out to the ranch the next morning. In the afternoon, when he felt a little better, she took him around to see some friends of hers, a girl and her young man who were going to be married. They were making plans. Larraine was asked to the wedding. She asked whether she might bring Buz, if he could get back to town for it. They agreed.

"Look, let's you and me go together," he said with animation. "You'd sure like Larraine. We'd have us a high ol time."

Everybody always got horny at a wedding, he declared. He knew he could fix me up. He sounded like a boy aching with possessive happiness over a new jitney—innocent and jubilant. My silence seemed like assent to him. He was sure we could manage to get to town somehow on the wedding day, which was a Saturday. If nothing else, we could walk the eleven miles to the highway and flag the Magdalena-Springerville stage. Or maybe we could just appropriate the ranch Ford and be gone before anybody would know it. I then made a mistake.

"The boss says I can borrow it if I want to go to town to mail my letters."

"Then it's all settled," he cried, rocking back and forth with physical satisfaction in how things fell right for him. "You and I are going to hit it off, Richie. I can always tell."

Why had I listened to him so attentively, after all? He had the invaluable knack of holding your interest, whether by his sheer vitality, self-loving confidence, exotic information, I didn't know. But I had never known anyone like him who showed such encompassing good will coupled with a startling lack of moral sense, and I was fascinated by the smooth mix of those opposites. Perhaps I felt envy at his unrestrained life, even as I wondered how much of what he told might be only romances and lies in which to see himself. But in these as well as in truth lay much of his essential self.

I was now sleepier than he was. He would have talked all night if I had not been overwhelmed by engulfing yawns. He laughed forgivingly and huddled himself down into his blanket. The night was turning cool, we had to be up at half past five for the first day of dipping the sheep.

"Douse it," said Buz, his voice thick with comfort. I turned out the oil lamp. In a few minutes I could see the stars through the open door. "A high ol time," he murmured. "It's no fun havin it alone."

How much he took for granted. The frontier American must have been like him—his sociableness so confident that he could not imagine reticence in others. Always on the move, he had no roots. Always encountering and leaving strangers, he had to make the

[175]

most of whatever contact he had with them. His assumption that every life was like his made it only friendly to trade lives as soon and as fully as possible. Sophisticated travelers on the early frontier were always amazed by the garrulity and curiosity of the plainsman, and also by the appeal of the individual man who felt himself equal to the joys and hazards of a whole wilderness.

※

I see my own work of that summer of a half century ago as though the years were a deep physical distance away. Everything stands in miniature though distinct detail lighted by halations of memory, watched from a height looking down at the swarming creatures, men and animals, at their hard tasks; and somewhere in the midst of it all at my various jobs is my young self.

The figures are tiny, seen from so long ago, but brightly lighted. I have the feeling of an illicit observer, an eavesdropper, for they do not know I am looking and listening. Years and distance away, they seem to create a harmony now out of the confusions of that far time. Even as I remember those, I taste the foulness of the task they are doing. Their colors are brilliant, they throw shadows like spilled ink, for the sun is furious. This little group seems to stand as all humanity at timeless purpose and act, and they forge again a link in the human chain reaching from antiquity, so that their commonness becomes a marvel of discovery about man's enduring habitude. A dimly remembered passage from the third of Vergil's *Georgics* in Dryden's translation tells me again of the persistence of human ways in the parallels between the Roman shepherd's husbandry and mine, as a youth:

> *Good shepherds, after shearing, drench their sheep.*
> *And their flock's father (forced from high to leap)*

Swims down the stream, and plunges in the deep.
They oint their naked limbs with mothered oil;
Or, from the founts where living sulphurs boil,
They mix a Med'cine to foment their limbs,
With scum that on the molten silver swims:
Fat pitch, and black bitumen, add to these,
Beside the waxen labor of the bees,
And hellebore, and squills deep-rooted in the seas . . .

I hear the mixed noises of the job—the shouted orders of the men, the sound of hammering huge nails repairing timber work, the chorus of cries from the sheep, and I know again the stenches rising from the various acts of work, cooked to a sickening intensity by the blaze of the heat from the sun and the fires.

For there, between the corrals, they are hauling logs and building fires to heat a mixture in two huge tanks of galvanized iron with open tops. These are supported on iron trestles, braced with timbers, and the fires are set beneath. Men are driving burros to bring kegs of water from the windmill tank. They lift and pour the water into the iron vats, where it is mixed with gallon upon gallon of a dark-gray, lumpy mass consisting mostly of a powerful disinfectant called Black Leaf 40. This gives off a stench like vomit mixed with creosote, released into the air through a bubbling scum. Many of the men wear kerchiefs tied around their faces under broad shadowing hats.

On platforms by the vats, one man at each keeps stirring the mixture as more water and disinfectant are added. The fires are constantly fed. In the day's heat the fires have become almost unbearable, and the men who have to come to them, shielding their faces, and in their faded colors and crouching haste, resemble details taken from vast old paintings of catastrophe. Other men are driving sheep in the upper corral toward one corner of it, where a cleated incline awaits them. At their head is the emperor ram who going first will have all the others blindly follow. At the end of the incline is a solid wooden gate like that of a sluice which can be raised in grooves; and when the time comes, the shorn sheep will be driven up the incline and through the gate, and down a slippery slide into the cement trough which has been filled by feeder pipes from the high vats with the thick, hot, stinking mix.

Their cries are wild as they slide into the trough, which is four feet wide. They must swim to live, all seventy-five feet of its length. They cannot scramble out of the dip over the sides, which are sheer, and eight feet deep. Struggling to keep their heads above the surface of the foul dip, the sheep make a continuous bleat. Their shorn legs lash, they survive by sheer terror and instinct. But not an inch of their skins is spared the treatment of the dip, for men with long poles which end in Y-shaped prongs are stationed at intervals on each side of the dip, and with their prongs, the men push every animal under the surface as it passes them. The sheep struggle against each other, tightly packed, choking and crying, lashing the dip mixture to spray which scatters upon the men. At the end of the long trough, its floor rises with cleats. The sheep scramble up it, and a timber alley fences them in and directs them in all their foul crowding into the lower corral, where they shake themselves, and cry and cry at the terror they have been through. A sluice carries their drippings back to the trough. Overhead, low and circling, a network of buzzards cast their exact shadows over the creatures of the ground.

The old hands are ready for the job to be done every summer, but a newcomer can hardly work at first for nausea at the sight, sound, and smell of the dip. The old man is at hand throughout much of every day until all the sheep have been treated for ticks, lice, and other parasites. He does not handle a pronged pole, but his eye is everywhere, governing the timing of the sheep in their approach, their slide, their passage through the hot slime, their emergence at the other end; the feeding of the log fires under the vats; the replenishment of the tanks; the rhythm of the men at their work of submerging the sheep and the skill with which they time it so that as few sheep as possible may drown—though now and then one does, and its body must be probed for and hauled out and burned, adding a new stench to the air.

If a wind comes up, and dust stirs, the sounds and smells of the work drift everywhere, even to the ranch house, where invisible and alone the old man's young wife is awake and dreaming of affairs far away from the brute world at her doorstep. Other creatures do their duty at the work: running up and down the corral barriers and the length of the dip are the sheep dogs, barking with excitement and concern. Now and then they turn aside for a quick rough caress from a worker, and feeling their duty approved they seem to smile with their tongues hanging out; and wagging their handsome tails, they return to their charges. The shorn wool already bagged is on a flatbed, horse-drawn dray which leaves for the highway and Magdalena, where the wool will be loaded in the railroad cars and taken to the rail junction at Socorro, and be on its way to the markets of Kansas City and Chicago. The hard work hidden by the unmarked distance is brought into the organized commerce of the cities and the world. Never under the summer sun has work seemed harder, and men closer in their anonymous part of it to the very nature of the animals they tend. The marvel is that with means so primitive, and with relatively so few men, and with animals so frantically self-protective, a degree of efficiency is reached, a job done in its annual cycle for a space of days; and at the end of work, an exhausted and at moments even a rude lyrical humanity returns in the evening to those who have borne the burden of the day.

※

At the end of the first day of dipping, Don Elizario came from the house after supper as we were all sitting or lying around the coals of the fire where the cook's big enameled coffee pot kept his brew steaming for our tin cups. The sky was washed with the last rosy light of the west. Our aching bodies sought ease and cool. It was time for sociability.

Don Elizario made a point in such evenings of joining his men, to give them his comradeship as unspoken gratitude for their work. If we were to have entertainment, we must make it for ourselves; and he must do his share. Anyone who could sing a song, or tell a story, or dance a jig, was called on to do so. We left a little clearing between us and the campfire for anyone who would perform by the faint glow, like stage light cast upward. Don Eli sat on an upturned bucket, as his legs were too stiff to let him get down to the ground and up with comfort.

On our first evening festival, Ira the cook—the men called him Irene for their view of him as female in his role as cook, and because of a way he had of shrilling and shooing like a woman when anyone tried to steal anything from his stores of food—usually began the show as someone cried for his fiddle and his dance.

Irene ran to his wagon. He slept there rather than in the bunkhouse and guarded all his possessions in neatness. In a moment he returned with his violin. Making a great act of tuning it, listening critically with the box close to his ear among his wild but sparse tufts of hair, he created anticipation as by an overture to a play. Finally, satisfied, he pushed his crooked spectacles up on his nose, slapped the ground twice with his right foot to announce rhythm, and began to play with a scratchy thin tone a repetitious piece like a tune from a square dance. After one stanza played standing still, he began with the next one to shuffle and stamp and turn to his own music. Turning one way, he was the man, crazily gallant and stiff; the other, he was the woman responding, mincing in exaggerated gentility. Soon we were all clapping hands and whistling encouragement to his music. At this, he would flare his eyes at his audience like a flirt, and then toss his head at our impertinence and beat away at the dusty ground while his mosquito noise kept up with perfect, insane regularity. It was growing dark. Someone threw wood on the fire and light blazed up, throwing the footlight glow over Irene in his greasy rags. He scorned, dominated, and wooed his audience like a great star. Finishing his performance, he slowed it down, and, at the very end, made a deep, rickety, but splendid bow, holding his fiddle and his stick of horsehair widely apart. He created the illusion of a large theater, transforming our enthusiastic but sparse applause into an ovation.

There was a moment of satisfied quiet. Don Elizario nodded his approval of the show, which he had seen many times. His presence among us was so at home and so easy, yet so sure of its authority, that we were all sure of it too. Nobody was immediately moved to follow the cook with an act, and so, clearing his throat, making rusty little sounds, Don Elizario grandly brushed his profuse mustaches upward with the knuckles of both hands and said,

"I will tell you a little story."

Nodding and smiling faintly, he slowly told in his mild old voice a story about a certain Saint Jerónimo—not the famous Saint Jerónimo, but another less well-known but a saint just the same.

"Did you ever hear of the Devil himself making a saint out of anybody?"

Well, that was exactly what happened in the case of Saint Jerónimo. It seemed that Jerónimo was a ver' handsome young man who had his way with all the fine young beautiful girls in his town (this was somewhere in Spain a long time ago). There wasn't a girl who didn't lie down with him the minute he asked her to. When he made pusha-pusha, they cried out in joy, "Jerónimo, Jerónimo." All the other young men said he had the ver' Devil in him. He had to fight many duels, but he never lost one, and turned up fresh as ever to pick out a new girl.

The Devil got him all those girls, everyone said there were two thousand five hundred and nine of them—Don Elizario with a wheezy little laugh gave the signal for a general stir of carnal laughter, in which all joined—and when it came to number two thousand

[181]

five hundred and *ten*, the Devil made a saint out of young Jerónimo; for when Jerónimo tried to make pusha-pusha with her, the
Devil prevented his *verga* from rising, just exactly at the moment
when it was needed. The young lady, who was the daughter of a
king, and ver' used to having her own way, slapped Don Jerónimo
in the face, saying, "You are good for nothing but being a monk,"
and went home to the king's palace.

And Don Jerónimo saw the Devil sitting over there on a tree
stump with his own *verga* pointed like a carrot and jumping around
like a goat's. The Devil was laughing and laughing. Don Jerónimo
said, "Ver' well, I will become a monk." And so he became a monk,
and lived a long life of good works, and his *verga* never tempted
him again, and after he died, he performed many miracles and
became a saint.

Everyone stirred. The subject had been raised which was most on
their minds, far away from women, tired enough to believe or
dream anything, and hungry for any expression of their desire
which it was impossible to fulfill; and, too, the possibility of sanctity
in any human predicament crossed their minds, however faintly,
since everybody believed in goodness as well as evil.

Someone cried out,

"Hey, Irene, tell us about the last time you tried to get you a
sheep, and what the ol ram did to you for it!"

The cook, in shadow beyond the firelight, tossed his head and
waggled his tongue at the question. Everybody laughed at both the
questioner and the questioned, and at the inevitable folk joke about
those who work with sheep year in and year out. A sort of anonymous comradeship descended upon us all. Sanction, so mildly introduced by Don Elizario, was now rudely confirmed.

Just at that moment, out of the darkness between us and the
house in its dome of cottonwoods silhouetted against the stars,
Concha came toward the firelight and entered its long rays, which
stretched away on the ground between the shadows of the men.

Her husband stood up and said sharply,

"What are you doin here? You get back to the house!"

"There is a telephone call," she said. "The Datil operator is trying to get you—"

She turned to go, gathering herself in fear. As she turned, she saw Buz for an instant. He was staring at her with his mouth open. The firelight was on both their faces. The exchange of a look between them was like a bolt of feeling, as if a door had been thrown open and closed on a revelation. Everyone saw this—Don Elizario saw it. He lunged toward Concha and struck her on the buttocks to drive her to the house. They diminished away into the darkness.

"Jesus Christ!" exclaimed Buz softly. "Did you see that?" He asked me, "Who is that? His granddaughter?"

"His wife."

He exclaimed,

"Wife!" making the word obscene. He spat scornfully.

The others were all long aware of Don Elizario's marriage, and by now were indifferent to it. They saw no reason for the evening to come to a sudden end. Someone called out,

"All right, there, Babyface, now you just give us a song or a story."

This was said in a tone slightly menacing, and the others added their voices. In the air was a threat of hazing the latecomer if he should refuse. Buz shrugged and asked,

"Well, is there anybody got a *guit*ar here?"

One of the Mexican herders handed him one. Buz tuned it even more elaborately than Irene with his fiddle. As he strummed for his own satisfaction, he said,

"I'll sing you a song I made up myself."

Stolid silence met this. Finally, in an expert imitation of the show-business singers who broke their voices sentimentally on stressed words, he sang:

> *Oh, my darlin Bonnie Mae,*
> *I said goodbye to you today,*

And I wonder if I'll ever see you more.
With your hair so golden bright
And your eyes so full of light,
Oh, my darlin, wait for me I do implore!

Oh, no gal was ever sweeter,
If so, I'd like to meet her,
But my darlin Bonnie Mae need have no fear.
As long as stars are in the sky
Then my love will never die,
And my blue-eyed Bonnie Mae will be my dear.

Bonnie Mae so sweet and slender,
All her words so true and tender,
I will carry in my heart until the end.
Hand in hand we'll walk through life,
Oh, my darlin little wife,
And nothing from each other shall us rend.

Slow final chords. Silence. Then,

"She somebody real?" asked a voice longing to believe.

"Hell, yes," replied Buz. "Only her name was different."

"Did you marry her?"

"Hell, no. The sorry little bitch ran off with a horny circuit preacher. Them shoutin sons of bitches get all worked up with their Bible whackin, and then can't keep their pants buttoned."

Tom Agee half rose and hoarsely cried out in his weak voice,

"Now look here, you little squirt, you just keep some respect in your mouth for the good men who harvest for the Lord!"

"He was a preacher," I told Buz.

"Well, Reverend, no offense," said Buz. "They's all kinds."

But he grinned like a rosy satyr at those nearest him. There might have been a reply, but from the house dimly away came two sharp little screams. We looked at each other and most probably saw the

[184]

same picture. Don Elizario, done with his phone call to Datil, which would connect his line with Socorro and Magdalena, had turned to Concha and beaten her to teach her a lesson, and, I thought, to chastise himself for what his jealousy had to remind him of.

There was an animal look on Buz's clear little face. If she had made a powerful impact on him, in their lightning-quick meeting of eyes, his excitement, and its nature, were now doubled by the idea of her being hurt physically on his account until she had had to cry out. Someone went to the coffee pot on the coals, which breathed now bright now dim on the light night wind. The pot was empty. It was clear that Don Elizario was not coming back. Tom stood up to signal the end of the campfire hour. Everyone drifted off to bed.

When we were alone in the bunkhouse, Buz asked,

"Did you mean what you said about him and her?"

I nodded.

He groaned.

"She's too beautiful to live—especially with *that*. If I could only—"

"You'd better not. He's crazy when it comes to her."

He locked his hands behind his head on the hard uncovered pillow and stared up at the rough beams of the ceiling.

"All my life I said I only wanted to get me a rich woman and settle her down and keep her pregnant and then, whoo! I'd be free to do for myself with anybody I wanted to. But when I see someone like that—what's her name?"

"Concha."

"Concha. I don't know. Did you see her lookin at me? —Oh me, oh my. I just bet she'd welcome the change . . . One more look, and it'd be all over."

I remembered Tom Agee's advice to me about Concha; but I did not repeat it now.

Buz had a new idea.

"They tell me you are the only one here who goes over to the house."

"I don't know. I *have* been there."

"You goin back?"

"Maybe."

"Yes, Richie. Take me with you! That way, I—"

"I couldn't."

"Sure you could. You could just say you brought your friend to play a game of Crazy Eights, or talk about the weather, it wouldn't matter what, just so I—"

"No. The old man wouldn't have it."

"Well, so how come you get to go there and not me?"

I explained how I happened to be at the WZL.

"Well, I don't have any society doctor to get me in where I belong, but I thought I had a *friend.*"

"You do. I just know how things are over there. You wait till the old man asks you. Then I'll take you."

"You sure are the prize gutless wonder!"

I picked up my book and began to read. It was like closing another door in his face. He could not endure being excluded. If he lost me, he lost everyone here. After a while he said,

"Where will you go after this job is done? We've got only a little while more."

"I'm staying on till September some time."

"What are you suppose to do here all that time?"

"Oh, odd jobs after the cattle come back and the range men come in, I suppose."

"I bet they aren't paying you anythin. I bet you are just a dude on vacation. *I* have to work for *my* living."

"No, they aren't paying me anything. They are doing me a favor, so they say."

"And you work your balls off for nothing?"

"Listen, I'm trying to read."

He most of all dreaded separateness. He went on,

"I get paid off at the end of the dipping. I don't know where I'll

[186]

go." Expertly, he put pathos into his voice. "Listen, Richie. Why don't you go with me? We'll figger some place to go. Nobody ever turned ol Buz down yet, at anythin. With your brains and my guts—*you* know—why not?"

I remember the power of his confidence in himself, and the appeal this allowed him to exert. His energy was compelling. His color was high, his eyes sparkled, and the flaw in one of them seemed to evoke a vision of a world in which he was all-powerful. His light voice softened with the excitement of conspiracy.

"We'll show the sons a bitches," he said urgently, meaning the world at large.

I had to shake my head.

"But why? Why?"

Saying why took much time and wrangling; at the end of which he was deeply aggrieved, and I was sorry for him, angry with myself, and wondering how I could find a way to be his friend, in spite of everything.

❧

The next evening, Don Elizario was back with us as gently merry as though nothing too real in its revelation had happened the night before. He was ready again for imagined romance, and the rituals of comradely obscenity invoked by men isolated together. Don Elizario cleared his throat.

"I have a song tonight," he said as though to make us forget the night before. We became quiet. In a moment he began to sing. The sound was remote and clouded, in a quavering husk of a voice. I thought of the slowed song of some shelled desert creature—a cicada—created to celebrate the hot and empowering desert light, but now making its last salute to life and creation. That it came from a

man full of present regret, and still lively longing, made it, instead
of lusty and funny, as touching as shame for that which could not
be controlled. He sang:

> Darling, I am growing old,
> Silver threads among the gold
> Shine down there on me today;
> Life is fading fast away.
>
> Let me feel you everywhere,
> Where I'll find your golden hair.
> Let us mingle though I'm old
> Silver threads among the gold.

Applause for the boss man was lively; but even before it died
down, Buz, gleaming with hard high spirits, took the audience with
a song which sounded like a direct reply to Don Elizario's gentle old
obscenity. Whacking the box of Pancho's guitar for attention, Buz
cried out like a comedian over a boisterous crowd, pressing the
unspoken rivalry he dared to feel against Don Elizario:

> H-o-o-oo,
> Will you love me when my batteries need re-chargin?
> Will you love me when my carburetor's dry?
> When my inner tubes have lost their self-respect?
> Will you be satisfied just to bill and coo?
> Or will you sit around all day and cry?
> H-o-o-o-,
> I'll drive that ol tin lizzie till I die!

He sang it through again, to clapped hands. Don Elizario stood up.
When the stanza ended, he said sharply,
  "*Mañana, mucho trabajo, amigos.* So now break it up, break it
up."

The circle began to drift away. Don Eli called out,
"Bebbyface, you come here."

Buz paused, and then, with a mock-humble skip, went over to the
old man, who held out a hand, slightly trembling, with forefinger
pointed at Buz.

"You stay 'way from my wife, you hear?"

"Yessir. Me? I don't even *know* your wife, Mr Wenzel. Sure, sir.
Anything you say."

But his smile contradicted his respectful promise. Don Elizario
waved him off and turned homeward. Buz watched him go, then
turned to me, expecting approval. But he saw in my face, apparently, that he had ended forever any chance of his being invited at
last to come with me to the house on some fine evening.

"What the hell!" he said defiantly. "There's more'n one way to
skin a cat—if you know that I mean."

⁂

Like most young people, I was not then fastidious—inclined more
to endure what was about me. Through no choice of mine, Buz
Rennison was a fixture of my days. In his deceptively slight, neat,
clean body, there was something of the confident child, and if self-
love and innocence were not the same thing, he made them seem so.
He had the intuitive sense of a cat when it came to feeling the mood
of another, and like the cat, if he felt himself momentarily rejected,
he set out to win fond attention.

"Richie, I've been watching you and thinkin about you. I figger
you can help me to find out how to better myself. I said to myself,
How does a man get ahead? He don't get all the way there, where
he wants to be, just by using his physical culture. I said to myself,
No, I said, they have to use their brains. You use your brains all the

[189]

time, even when you're alone, don't you? You're always readin in a book, or puttin things down in those little pocket books of yours."

"Yes."

"Well, I never went to college, hell, I never finished high school, even, but I've done a lot of livin, and I'm not so dumb. But I figger I've got a lot more to me than I know how to use."

"Everybody has."

"Don't turn me off like that. I want to make a *contribution*."

He mixed pleading modesty with worthy ambition and I had no idea how much he meant any of it; but uncomfortable as I was under the implied flattery and envy of my state of life, I was touched by the other self he showed me, and I was depressed at not knowing how to guide him into ways he sought. It was impossible to tell anyone to begin at the beginning, all over again, and make a new life.

"Will you help me?" he asked.

"I'll have to think about how I can do it."

"Well, for now, that's good enough for me. I knew you would never let me down."

This made me more uncomfortable than ever. If I suffered his worst simply as features of a specimen, I found it more difficult to come to terms with his creature best. I was sure of only one thing about him—never had I seen anyone whose fullest expression was physical, the center of which was blatantly sexual. In act and response, even self-unaware, he revealed this. You'd never see in him any of the humble proprieties of "simple" people. He rarely modified his behavior but enacted his impulses directly. His physical life was intense—even to the way he slept, breathing heartily. Sometimes he kept me awake with this.

One night I had enough of it. Stealthily I got up and pulled on my blue jeans and went out into the cool calm darkness.

The night yielded a waft of wind which slowly turned the windmill, whose gong-like sound drifted over the ranch. The ground was pebbly, prickly, and I was without boots. I walked with wincing care toward the salt cedar grove between me and the house. There was joy in being alone. The waning moon was still so bright that the stars were paled. The day's ungrateful ground became the night's pale velvet. Over the house the cottonwoods were modeled like sculpture—clusters of soft light in relief against caverns of deep shadow. I savored the natural world so fully that a youthful kind of ecstasy lifted me out of myself, until the great mosaic of the stars, and the moon in its decline, united for me the urgency of man's concerns with the vast impersonal glory of the abiding universe. Despite promises and longings, I did not know where I was meant to go in life. And yet there I stood, myself in the center of the visible world, possessed in my own thought and feeling which united all; I the vessel of dimensions I could never measure. It was one of those moments of mystery—or was it revelation?—which came to the young in terms sublimely dislocating, all the more marvelous because it was beyond the asking.

It was therefore jarring suddenly to see a figure emerging from the moonshade of the salt cedars into the moonlight, and to hear a voice come huskily calling,

"*¿Quién es?*—who's there?"

I was not used to night vision, but he was: it was Don Elizario. I replied softly,

"Richard."

I could hear him come toward me, and in a low murmur of relief, he said, "Ah, ah." When we came to stand near each other, he said,

"You are night owl, like me?"

"No, I was just awake. I felt like going out to look at the night."

"Yes," he replied, "yes, I too." He laughed gently. "And I always come outside by myself to make my water on the ground, you know? I grew up doing it. There is something about it, I don't know what."

He invoked antiquity in his natural act and pleasure. We stood looking at the sky. I could see him well now. He wore an old-fashioned nightshirt with his feet in shapeless masses which I took to be carpet slippers. With his fingers spread like elongated paw pads, he pointed in a lurching gesture at the sky and said,

"You know? I come out at night and I wonder why all that goes on"—the firmament—"and we pass away. If I can see it, and you can see it, we have it inside us. Why don't we last like the stars?" A pause. "Well, we are good, and we are bad, but the stars are nothing, they are just faithful and they are just beautiful, eh? There is no reason for them to die."

"Well, but they do, sir, you know? After billions and billions of years, some stars do die."

Again his wheezy mild laugh.

"It might just as well be forever, then, eh? —How old are you, *chico?*"

I told him.

"Aa-ha. When I was your age—" He stopped, muted by his memories, and so was I, whatever they might be. Presently, "I was married a year younger than you are now. I was a ver' handsome man. Many girls. All I knew was the land, from my *papá.* He told me once, *The land will either kill you or you will make it serve you.* I have made it mine." He waved at the horizon, and the south, where his other ranch lay so far away out of sight. "My sons. There were four. Two are living. They are like me. They live for the work. We are rich and we still work hard. I come out and look up there, and I say I have done all a man is made for." He faced toward me. The immense night had induced in him an impersonal intimacy. "When you have done all you can do—" His voice fell away. The wind stroked the slow turning blades of the windmill. A sheep dog barked once, remotely, loyally. The softest stir went through the salt cedar shadows. His world was speaking to us. His silence was melancholy, but seemed also to carry the content of acceptance. He shivered. He crossed his arms as if to seek warmth. He asked,

[192]

"You are happy here?"

"Yes, sir."

"Here is where I belong," he said as though to set happiness aside for himself as irrelevant, if he was where he belonged. "Go to bed, *joven,* much work tomorrow. Good night, good night—" He was moving away and his voice faded with him. *"Buenas noches."* My heart came into my throat, why I could not say, as I watched him taken into the shadows of the brake.

※

It was a measure of how lost and tired I was in my new world of hard work and rude life that I thought so little about my own world of parents and home. It was doubly shocking to be reminded of all I had left when Tom came back from a turn-around trip to Magdalena bringing a parcel for Concha and mail for me.

Her parcel was what the p'ione call had been about on that earlier evening: it contained a bright-red silk dress which Don Elizario had ordered for her from Daniels and Fisher in Denver as a second-anniversary surprise. The postmaster at Magdalena had been watching for it, and when it came, he had placed that phone call with the news by way of the Datil exchange. I saw the dress on its first evening when the Wenzels again asked me to supper to celebrate the wedding anniversary. Tom Agee was there also. At the proper moment he rose and made a courtly toast with his water glass. We answered with our glasses of champagne, which the host had ordered from Juárez. Concha wore her dress with joy, showing it off with seductive passes of her hands along her beautifully posed body. Her husband watched her with pride, and looked at Tom and me for the approval which we could both give without alarming him.

"It is my favorite color," said Concha. She kissed her husband on

[193]

the cheek and he put his heavy arms around her for a moment and then dropped them and turned away.

At the end of supper, he said,

"Aah, I almost forgot. Tom brought some letters for you. The Socorro paper, too, if you want it."

He gave these to me as I left. The men were at the campfire. I went alone to my bunk and by the light of my oil lamp opened my mail. The newspaper lay on the table, and before I read the letters my eye caught a headline over a brief item in a lower corner of the *Socorro Defender* which read: IMPEACHMENT PROCEEDINGS, NEW YORK GOVERNOR CHARGED. There were only a few wire service lines. I read them at once. A motion to impeach Governor Pelzer had been made on the floor of the assembly. Evidence of improper influence and financial peculation was reported to a committee appointed by the assembly to investigate, and the assembly had now voted overwhelmingly to send a bill of impeachment to the state senate.

My mother's letter, which I read next, said,

"—and you can imagine the effect this has had on your father. His fever went up, I had Dr Birch in, who told him he must positively stop fretting, but all Daddy would say over and over was, *To think, at such a time, I have to be out of the picture.* But the doctor told him that he would be able to come back into the picture all the sooner if he now put the whole affair out of his mind. But of course he can't and I know how he suffers. Sam arrived here two days ago with the news before it broke out in public. He brought Daddy all the documents, and all the talk behind the scenes. Oh, how shall I ever stand it, to see him tormented in mind as well as body"—and then she went on with questions about my welfare, my work, and added, "Don't get into any trouble with those cowboys, and don't worry about us, I'll let you know if we should ever need you in a hurry." This was like her—the imprecisely ominous references which went with her kind of motherhood. I smiled at this, but my heart was beating fast for the turn of events, and my disquiet was increased by a letter from Sam.

He had no doubt that the senate would find Pelzer guilty. The trial there would be ugly and protracted. Sam was bitter at the irony inherent in my father's absence at exactly the moment which might make him governor; and once governor, who knew how far my father would go later? Sam had every belief that Washington would follow in some form or other after, say, two terms in the governor's mansion. His own plans had been always predicated on my father's running for the United States Senate, with himself as chief legislative secretary. Sam, in his loyal conviction, believed that would be only another beginning, though he never actually dared name any office higher still. And now, having resigned as lieutenant-governor, my father was not eligible to succeed Pelzer, even if his health should permit this.

"What I believe," wrote Sam, "is that the greatest medicine your father could have had would have been actually to become governor when Albany is at last through with Judge (and Mo). I have done some reading about t.b. and I gather the mental element is at least as powerful and in some cases more so than the physical. I think your father would almost literally take up his bed and walk, and then throw it away, if he had the chance to go on to what should rightfully be his. It is a staggering irony that honor, ability, and opportunity should all be at hand, and yet all now be powerless. I won't conceal from you that your father is much depressed. I knew he would be; and that is why I came right back out here the minute I saw how affairs are sure to end. The Eastern papers have all taken notice of the fact that only a matter of weeks ago the lieutenant-governor resigned for health reasons, and they all deplore it more than ever. The clippings (your father insisted on seeing them all) make bitter reading for him. I have tried to set him going again with the W.W. material (he has actually written two chapters, lovely stuff) but he is too real to settle for a deliberate distraction, and he is also working hard to obey Dr Birch and keep the Albany affair out of mind, which only makes it more incessantly obsessive. As you may gather, I am myself in a howling rage at this maddening convergence of events. I'm afraid I'm not much help to your parents since I'm no good ever at concealing my state of mind and opinion. But I am staying on, for a little while, anyhow (though Joanna, having refused to come with me, now threatens to come and fetch me home). I suppose I can be useful in a few little things, such as protecting your father from reporters (the *Journal* here asked for an interview following a query from the AP), and taking him for afternoon drives, when the country shows its greatest splendor, but even this makes him rueful, with things as they are. And I am certainly useful in reminding Lillian not to heave her great sighs, keening over what might have been, etc. etc. She is a devoted fool, but a fool nevertheless, though her mere presence is of some comfort to your mother in managing the household and your father in handling office matters relayed from Dorchester, and who can be ungrateful for loyalty, anyhow? Are you a rancher by now? Lyle Pryor was cackling over the indignities you must be putting up with. I hope you have learned to say *Go to hell* with passion—it was all that saved me in the army among my physical superiors, bantam-weight that I am, before I became a lieutenant. I'll keep you informed."

I was scarcely done with my news from home when Buz returned from the campfire. Giving up on my hope of being alone, I spoke to him. He did not answer. Turned away from me, he threw off his clothes, and in every line of his figure I could read a sense of self-righteous anger. I said something again to him, and again he ignored me. But it was I who had wanted to do the ignoring, and now in a perverse turnabout, I disliked being snubbed by him. We lived too closely together to indulge a continuing animosity. I knew what was bothering him—I had gone again, and without him, to supper at the house where Concha was to be seen. Nothing I could say would convince him that I could never have managed to get him into that house. He was unreasonable. This angered me in my turn. Pulling the lamp closer, I consigned him to hell, and settled down to write letters to my parents and to Sam. Perhaps Lyle was right: what was I enduring among the people around me? But as I wrote, my description of the life at the WZL was full of praise for everyone and everything.

※

The weekend halted our work at Saturday noon. I went to Don Elizario.

"I have to send some letters home, very important, about things that have happened there. Do you think I could borrow the Ford to go to Magdalena to mail them?"

"No bad news, eh?"

"Not good."

"Eh, eh. Yes, then, take the Ford this afternoon, but be sure you get back by Sunday evening."

"Yes, sir. Rennison wants to go with me, to attend a wedding in town. Would that be all right?"

He smiled and spat.

"You take him as far as you can and lose him, as far as I am concerned. —No, bring him back, too, we have to finish up next week."

"Thank you, sir."

"You know? Nobody else regularly calls me *sir*."

He laughed breathily and, like the head of a family, waved me on my way with the effect of a blessing.

Buz was lying on his bunk staring at nothing, still disdaining my presence. I was sure he was bored with his self-imposed loneliness, but he knew of no way to break out of it with dignity. I said, rather stiffly,

"I'll be driving to town this afternoon in the Ford, if you'd like to come along."

He sprang to his feet like a cat. He swung a hard blow at my upper arm in exuberance, and said,

"Boy, you are somethin. I knew we would be partners. Let's go! We'll make that weddin after all."

He said he would let me drive out of the ranch gate, and then when we reached the highway, he would take the wheel, as he had covered the whole West in a Ford in his time, and if you could ride a horse, you could drive a Ford on those rutted roads, with their chuckholes and juts of gypsum. All he hoped for was that it wouldn't rain, for when a car got stuck in that red and white dirt, all you could do was wait and dry out.

"Why are you goin to town?" he asked.

"To mail some letters home."

"I never write any letters. I never get any, either." Not entirely with humor, he added, "Nobody knows I'm alive except just where I am."

But the prospect awaiting him in town—and me, he generously made clear—had raised his spirits until, driving the car sitting partly sideways, and hiking up exaggeratedly with the bumps as if riding an animal, he let out an exultant yell on general principles.

He had plans all made. First we would run by the post box near the tracks and get rid of my letters, as he put it, dismissing my whole life at home; then we would go to the Marigold Hotel and get up to Larraine's room and wash up. There was a rusty old leaky shower down the hall. Then when Larraine got off work, she was to get herself prettied up, and then we all three were goin to the weddin of her friends. She would be surprised to see us, especially me, as she knew nothin about me, but she'd do innythang he told her to. I would see later on how true that was. And we would help make that weddin somethin *they* wouldn't forget in a hurry.

He spent a few miles in repeating his repertory of bride-and-groom jokes. His mood was so merry and his anticipated enjoyment so frankly indecent that my initial squeamishness gave way to his vitality, and I saw him as a phenomenon instead of as an alien in my world of manners. I paid him the honor of speculating whether modesty was a matter of shame, or an attitude protective of what was so precious to the making of human life itself. I was much concerned just then with life, and death, its complement; and the more Buz rattled on with his obscenities delivered in his light voice and his features illuminated by a boy's glee, the more I began to welcome a sense of deliverance from troubles at home about which I was powerless to do anything. I began to feel anonymous through his presence, and the immense land we were riding through raising a long plume of dust added to this feeling. The plains sweeping away in every direction toward scattered mountains far away, the short parched grasses, the scrubby trees and bushes widely apart dotting the land made a country where you could be lost, perhaps forever, perhaps until accidentally found. Dimly, out of the very sympathies I felt so keenly, and yet could not act upon, I wanted to be someone else; to be myself lost.

Magdalena began to show in the distance—a low straggle. The only two-story building was the brick Marigold Hotel. As we came among the dusty streets and unpainted houses, all looked deserted, but here and there a tended yard, a watered tree, a window with curtains, a yard of chickens, and a dog or a cat spoke of the remote and essential life which still clung together to make a town.

We posted my letters in a box at the one-room railroad station by its black wooden water tank where the stubby locomotives of the branch line took on water. Then we returned to the main street, and Buz, lounging over his wheel, made a speeding run of four blocks to the corner where we must turn to the Marigold. The Ford rattled along and flapped its exhaust pipe. It was a sporting passage through town and a few people came to their store fronts to watch in amazement. I expected a local constable to stop us; but we scraped to a halt by the café end of the Marigold. Buz threw himself out the door of the car and, knowing I would follow, crashed his way into the restaurant to confront Larraine.

She remembered me. Her eyes asked Buz what I was doing there. "He's goin to the weddin with us and afterward we're goin to have us a time, all three."

I spoke to her. She smiled with her face lowered, but with her eyes meeting mine. She looked prettier than I remembered. My new knowledge of her may have shown in my face, for she suddenly blushed and turned away down her counter at some improvised work. Buz gave me a jab in the side and whispered loudly,

"She likes you. They always do that when they like somebody and don't want to admit it to theirself. Come on."

He called to her that we were going up to her room to get ready. When would she follow?

"I get off work at four o'clock. You better be out of there before then," she said. "The wedding's at four-thirty."

"We've got our car," he replied. "You just show us the church and we'll all go and c-r-r-y our eyes out."

She blurted a laugh as though unwilling to belong to him in any way, but also with a hint of an admission that he had made her his when with his boisterous lust he had entered into her lonely life earlier that summer.

※

"Two blocks over and one up" from the Marigold, as Larraine directed, the First Pentecostal Church of Christ Kingdom Come stood on a gravelly corner. It was a plain box of pebbly stucco with a squat, slatted tower covered in black tar paper and surmounted by a short wooden spike. The interior was stained in yellow calcimine, and a raised platform at the far end supported a box-like lectern.

Friends of the bride had decorated the bleak stage with gallon cans covered by white paper and filled with already wilted wildflowers. The afternoon was stifling hot. The packed benches sent up a steamy atmosphere composed of excitement and sweat. The minister—a rangy man in a black suit with a white necktie—sat on his chair at one side of the platform waiting for the wedding party. Small noises, dimmed for the sake of propriety, came out of a room opening out of the—so I thought of it—sacristy.

There was no place to sit when we arrived. We stood against the rear wall. Out in front only a few cars were parked at random. Most people had walked, though evidently a handful had ridden, for five saddled horses were tethered to a weathered telephone pole at the corner. Expectancy and a sense of what was fitting kept the little throng in the church in a fixed stillness. Their daily selves were stricken with a sense of serious occasion. Now and then someone could not help turning to discover whether anything could be seen at the door. But all knew that the signal would be given when the schoolteacher who sat at the abused piano which stood under the right front window would sound the first note of "Here Comes the Bride."

At last it came. To jangled chords the bridegroom stepped out of the sacristy and across the platform to await his bride. He was a tall, thickly built young man of the country whose face was pale under his sun- and windburn. He was trembling a little. He licked his white lips. Under dark brows, his eyes were glazed and fixed. He was soberly dressed, and so was his best man, who came to stand beside him. This one was a smaller, gleeful fellow, who peered with mischief at friends in the congregation, making silent references to what his friend, ol Cecil, was about to experience, now, and especially, afterward. Cecil saw nobody. He was the one person in the event who showed a detached solemnity. When the pianist with soulful restraint went on with the march, he did not turn to watch his girl come up the aisle.

She was small. She trembled even more than he. Her head was

topped by a veil which was crowned with a spray of artificial lilies of the valley. They shook with her emotion. She carried a bunch of white carnations which everybody later said had been brought on ice from Socorro. Her dress was white with a long train—the product of weeks of work by local housewives who told each other afterward at the reception that they had never seen a finer. Set off by her wiry gold hair, which stood away in curls from her thin little face, her cheeks were rosy. In her feeling, suppressed for the sake of the sacred vows which all had gathered to witness, she brought a pang to many an observer, as to me. However mean the surroundings, and meagerly pretentious the preparations, an ancient debt was being paid to itself by life: ceremony given as due to the means by which life would be renewed.

The minister rose and came forward to receive the bride at the platform, the music stopped, the young rancher took his bride's hand, and they stood, he stalwart and suddenly at ease, she with her head raised in pride, both staring straight ahead. The minister said,

"Now here we stand in the presence of the Holy Spert, to join this man and this wumman together in the holy bonds of wed-*lock* which is ordained by the Lard that no man nor wumman shall put asunder, so help them God."

By his loud, hooting voice, and his hands spread above the bride and groom, and by his head thrown back with his eyes closed, he invoked the invisible powers of which he was the spokesman. An almost palpable shiver of communion went through the congregation. How often was there occasion in that lost little town, and among the prisoners of that immense land, for a lofting of feeling which would deliver them from their common lot? Their emotion was contagious, and as the ceremony proceeded with homily, vows, and an interminable blessing with the minister's hands spread wider, he invoked the whole world's sanction upon this man and this wumman as they did now enter solemnly into the holy wedded state. There was an inarticulate beauty in what all believed in at that moment. In a silent prayer I added my blessing to that shared one beating in the hearts of those gathered there. I heard a small sound beside me and glanced down. Larraine was weeping in subdued gusts which raised and lowered her shoulders convulsively. She saw a self which could never be reached, I thought. Beyond her, Buz made a slight thumbing motion at her and above her head winked at me, sharing his comic scorn for all which everyone else took solemnly, and which he knew could not last.

It was true that when the end came, and the teacher began to pound away at her recessional with ecstatic inaccuracy, the assembled mood changed as if a cloud had gone off the sun. With bent heads the young couple ran down the aisle, everyone laughed and applauded, and on his planks the minister trumpeted out repeatedly, "Ho, yo, yo, glory be!" in a laughing roar which sounded above all else, and all left for the wedding reception, which would be held at the home of the bride's father, who was the rich cattle-feed merchant of the town.

Smiling through her tears, Larraine took a moment to powder her face. Then with a radiance which had something wanton in it, she said, "Here we go, boys," and Buz drove us, bucking the car, around the corner and down the dirt street for four blocks to a gray cement one-storied house with a deep porch whose short stone pillars were covered with sweet pea vine. Behind the house rose olive-gray foothills, in one of which an abandoned mine entrance with fallen timbers spoke of the prosperous past. Guests crowded after us. Cecil and his bride, Allie Sue, received them in the front room to shake hands. The parents of both stood with them. Decorum prevailed in the front room; but out in back of the house, as Buz discovered immediately, several young men were drinking bootleg corn whiskey while they carried out a rite as old as the wedding itself. They were imposing lewd mockery on the greatest joy of the animal creation in its human form.

Cecil's own Ford touring car was waiting at the back door for the moment when the newlyweds would run out to it under a shower of rice and catcalls, to drive away for their honeymoon in El Paso. Cecil's friends were at work. A pair of them at the back of the car were tying tin cans to the rear axle with long strands of baling wire. Two others, one to each side of the car, in rutting hilarity, were painting words on the car body. Buz joined them, drinking of the jug which was passed around. The young men were drunk on whiskey and prurience. They slapped with their brushes:

GRAND OPENING TONIGHT

CHERRY, CHERRY, WHO GETS THE CHERRY

SHE GOT HIM TODAY HE'LL GET HER TONIGHT

Buz seized a brush from one of the young satyrs and across the rear of the car, he painted:

WHAT WAS THAT, SHE HOLLERD

which brought a roaring cheer from the others.

A flushed young man began to festoon the car with toilet-paper streamers. There was intensity to all their work. They got drunker and drunker, and so did Buz, and so did I. The final touch was given the car when the best man put a jug of whiskey behind the driver's seat. It was labeled *Love Tonic*.

Now everyone went into the house to join the crowd. Decorum had begun to break down there, too, though no liquor was being served. But wives were remembering, and husbands were speculating enviously and full of laughing pity for what ol Cecil had got hisself into. Erotic feeling was running through the guests, as earlier

[204]

in church all had been taken by the holiness of the ceremonial sanction.

Buz came to me at a lace-curtained bay window. He was drunker than anyone, yet his ready talk was not blurred. In his strange slit of light his eye contained something wild. He half turned his head and gave me his well-rehearsed smile, which had done so much for him around the world. He took hold of my heavy belt buckle and tugged at it to pull my attention and tell his power. Working it up and down, he put his other hand behind my neck and jerked at me there. With great confidence, in a burry voice thick with appeal, he said, while his eyelids drooped and opened with the sleepiness of drunken affection,

"You son of a bitch, you know what I'm goin to do from now on with you?"

"No. Let go of me."

He did not let go, but went on, earnestly close to my face,

"I'm goin to be just like you. I'm goin to read a book every time I can get me one. I'm goin to look at everybody the way you do and make them wonder what I think of them. I'm goin to fix it so's I know anythin they ask me. I'm goin to better myself and make you proud of me. We're goin to be a real team. You son of a bitch."

"You're drunk."

"So're you. So let's get drunk. Ol Richie and Buz."

Just then Allie Sue came out of the back room dressed for travel. A shout went up. Cecil took her arm. They struggled through the crowded rooms to the back door. Running down the back steps with lowered heads, they tried to enter the car as though unseen. But Cecil saw some of the poor jokes on his car. His neck turned an angry red. He made two or three swipes at the drying white paint with his fine new Stetson hat, and even brushed at the car with his shiny new sleeve. He knew the folk custom which mixed obscenity with marriage. But something he now knew in a new way was being demeaned. Allie Sue tugged at him. In her face turned to him there was radiant satisfaction at how every single element of a proper wedding—even to these painted words—had come to them. *Everybody did everything just like they always did:* the joy of this was in her face. Her husband's outrage seemed to her ungrateful. He finally thrust her into the car, ran around to the driver's seat, and jumped into the car, which his best man cranked for him after several young guests tried to prevent it, and scowling like a cloud shadow, Cecil drove off, spurning gravel and dust while all cheered. Allie Sue's mother stood in the back door, waving and weeping. No matter what the terms, she saw the universal in her child's ordeals, past, present, and to come.

❦

Larraine had to return to work at the Marigold café until after nine o'clock.

"We'll meet you upstairs at ten, hon," said Buz, "and then! *zowie!* if you know what I mean!"

She knew. In her familiar gesture, she lowered her face, but her breath caught in her throat, and her bounteous breasts rose and fell with a gust of excitement. Looking like a modest high school girl, with her delicate hands, shadowed eyes, and sweetly plump cheeks, she wore shyness over a nature whose ardor Buz was able to arouse by the simplest suggestion.

We followed a couple of the young men from the wedding to houses where they knew a drink was to be had, and a good story. Though he grew drunker as ten o'clock approached, Buz never lost his power to dominate and cozen with his talk, but only became more confidentially eloquent. More susceptible to liquor than he, I heard only part of what went on as we ranged the town.

In one house we sat with a middle-aged couple who had three

children—all small boys. The father was as sun-cured as saddle leather. His face was creased like old mine tailings gullied by rain. Hard work and joylessness marked him. His wife was made up for the wedding like a burlesque show girl. Under all her blue and red and white color, and her fiery dyed hair, she looked used-up to exhaustion, and her weariness was caught in the hard edge to her voice. They both put on company manners for us at first, until we drank with them. It did not matter that we were strangers. They had just had a taste of conviviality outside their crowded shack, and they hated to let go of it. Soon the father sighed with comfort and pulled off his boots. When the three little boys, a year apart in age, with the oldest about seven, looked around the door jamb like curious small cats, I was almost sobered by the contrast between the inquiring wary sweetness of these cubs and their worn, life-tried parents. The children had caps of burnished gold hair. Their big eyes were light sapphire blue with thick dark lashes which shadowed their tawny cheeks. They held their chiseled, delicate mouths open, the better to hear what was going on where we sat in the kitchen. Their little pointed chins and short noses and small nostrils looked as though carved by the most innocent of sculptors. Children! I wished they were mine and I wished for my own. Would life do to those children what it had done to the rasping woman and the disgusted man who had given them life? With drunken lucidity I had thoughts about the stages of life which I had never thought before. The idea of purposeless purity as it gazed at us in timid hunger from the doorway made me half rise from my chair to go to the children, as though they were mine.

This was a mistake, for the father, who had not seen them, followed my look, sat up, took one of his sweat-and-mud-roughened boots, and threw it at the children, roaring,

"Get the fuck out of here, you sneaking little sons of bitches!"

They ducked swiftly out of sight while their mother shrieked after them,

"And see that you get to sleep, or I'll whup the shit outen you!"

"So, as I was sayin'," remarked Buz, as though the family tumult had never happened, going on with a story to which I did not listen, but which our hosts found arresting, for they watched his lips and feasted on his energetic presence, which brought them a world away.

Later, out on the gravelly walk, I said,

"What will ever become of those little boys!"

"Whoof. What do you care? They'll just grow up. All kids do. Look at me."

"What about you?"

"My daddy beat the livin tar out of me day in day out because my mother liked me more'n she did him. He worked in the lumber yard sometimes and he had a great collection of boards to slap me with." He laughed as though his boyhood was now a good joke. "But I had me enough and I just ran off and I never been back or had a word since."

"But what about the doctor's daughter?"

"Sh't! Anybody of us did it to her all the time. She used to meet us for it."

He mused genially over his history, and after a few steps, he said,

" 'V'you ever played around with more'n one at the same time?"

It took me a while to read his meaning, but he flung his arm around my neck to press his question and free my memory, and I said,

"No."

"Son, ain't livin."

Larraine knew what was comin—he had told her, and she let on she didn't believe him. But she knew, for he had told her the time he first met her about the things they used to do out on the coast, and she got all excited about it, and asked him to tell her more. Tell her? Buddy boy, tonight we were not goin to tell her, we were goin to show her. How about it?

My head throbbed in the bright overcast light of a dusty sky as we left the Marigold Hotel on Sunday morning.

Slumped at an angle in the driver's seat, Buz drove with his wrist hanging over the wheel. After several miles, he asked,

"What the hell's the matter 'th *you*?"

I shrugged silently and looked aside at the blurred hills. He persisted.

"Why'd you leave us?"

"I'd had enough—" in meanings lost on him.

For those hours in the pit of night, Buz by his elated example worked to make me over in his own likeness, to the joy of Larraine. He cheered me on like a trainer taking credit for his player. He was happiest when he shared his pleasures. I went after my own, in my turn, drunkenly intent and persistent. At one moment Larraine shed a few tears, saying she was a lonely person, and was glad of us. But as the loveless night began to fade, along with my fill of bootleg corn, I began to see not only Buz and Larraine but myself.

As my father said, in every life there was something, great or small, to be ashamed of. Where would last night ever fit into the comforts and graces of our life at home?

"You were pretty rough with her, you know," I said.

"So that's it," he replied. "Well, they all love it. You better learn."

I now faced two ways—one, toward the inner self where my father still reigned; the other, toward a world of knowing which, good or evil, I must see for myself, and judge and use.

Buz felt no concern. Envying him, I dwelt on mine.

To exhaust memory, I worked harder every day of the following week. The dipping would be ended by Friday and the flocks driven southward. Whenever he could, Buz tried to talk about our night with Larraine, as though endlessly reviving it in words would make it more exciting than the event itself. He still expected to excite me with this, as he excited himself, and he was honestly injured when I evaded the subject.

"You sure are sore about somethin, after the good times I set up for you," he would say in a baffled sulk. I had no answer for him. Facing his simple zest, I was ashamed of my shame.

There was another consequence more puzzling. Concha sent word by Irene that I was to come for supper to tell her every detail about the wedding. Within an hour of this invitation, Don Eli ordered me aside and said,

"No supper. You will stay away from my house from now on." He stared without expression, and after he spoke his jaw was set jutting forward under his whiskers like that of an old lion. When I made a bewildered gesture, he went on, "Never mind, I know about you and that girl and Bebbyface, that *cabrón*. I have people in Magdalena who tell me everything. I did not think that you—" Turning away, he motioned me back to work at the dip. Here was a judgment against me, on top of my own. I wanted to blame Buz. But could I?

I watched him now and then with Don Elizario in the working background. Between them continued a truce, baleful on one side, cheerfully wary on the other. When I caught one glancing at the other, I wondered whether the silent game between them would have further moves.

I knew for certain on a late afternoon when the declining sun was changing color from white to pale gold, and the coming evening seemed as perfect and fragile as an eggshell.

※

Foul from work at the dip, I went to my bunkhouse for a shirt which I had washed and hung out in the morning. After a shower I would put it on before supper—"dressing for dinner," I said sourly to myself. Buz was not in the bunkhouse. I found my shirt, a towel, and some lava soap to use with the hard alkaline water pumped slowly forth into the windmill tank. A pipe with a valve provided the shower bath. To the valve a rope was attached, and when with one hand you pulled the rope, the pipe let forth a cold thin stream, while you soaped and rinsed with the other hand. The work at the nauseous dip made you blench at your own smell; but of all the workers only Buz and I regularly used the shower at the end of the day. Whenever he stood under the cold stream, he made a great show of shock, yelling and capering. His presence there, even unseen, could be known by his howls, which sometimes turned into song.

To reach the windmill I had to go toward the ranch house until I came to the westernmost brake of salt cedars; and there I would take a path which put the brake between me and the house. The windmill stood beyond. Its eight-foot galvanized-metal tank was hidden from the house if you looked from the porch, but the salt cedars, though tall and fully plumed at the top, grew more sparsely at the stems. If you stood near to them, you could see through their cluster to the mill, the tank, the shower, and the long waver of the plains beyond.

I passed the large bunkhouse and saw Don Elizario conferring with Tom Agee. They were resting on their haunches close to the earth. Tom was evidently working out with his boss some plan for work. He would take up a little clod of earth and place it nicely, pointing to it as if to say that this represented one thing; then with another he would establish a different thing; and finally, with a twig, draw a line making a conclusion with the two, while Don Elizario gravely watched and nodded in agreement. Their conference was absorbing and leisurely. Neither glanced up as I passed a few yards away. It was a companionable hour. From the chuck wagon came petulant noises and a scrap of wailing song where Irene was getting supper. The stillness otherwise was broken only by the drifting rankle of chains and the airy chime of the windmill slowly turning. All was at peace and nothing called for my attention until I came around the end of the brake, from which I could see both mill and house. But then my eye was struck by color as though I saw the streak of a cardinal bird which would be gone if I looked directly.

I turned to look and stood stock still. At the mill, after bathing, Buz was dressing—pulling on his boots, tucking in his shirt. His pale hair was plastered down on his neat skull. In a moment he shook it off his brow and out of his eyes, and in doing so, he saw what else I saw, the flash of scarlet behind the brake.

There stood Concha watching him through a little gap in the salt cedars. How long had she watched—a young Susanna reversing the whole scene of the desirous elders? She was wearing her red dress, the anniversary silk dress, and her body was fixed in a stillness of desire which took Buz with her whole being.

When he saw the red dress, he looked quickly around, saw nobody else, and in a few running bounds he was at the brake, through its barrier, and had her in his arms. She thrust him away, she tried to keep her dress from getting wet from his dripping hair, but he held her fast, devouring her mouth and face as though she were Larraine. In a moment, laughing, he let her go free. His face was gleeful and he knew she would reach for him. She did. He took her again, but now she was terrified less of his assault than of her longing; and she pushed him off balance. He grasped her red silk at the shoulder. It tore, a visible betrayal. She felt for her bare shoulder, and in terror, she began to run to the house with one hand over her mouth, while with the other she crossed herself three times. Her heavy black hair fell like a veil over her face. She reached the porch and safely disappeared within. Laughing silently, Buz let himself with caution back through the brake and returned to take up his towel at the shower.

I went forward. He said,

"You sure missed some fun."

"I saw."

He looked startled.

"Did anyone else—*you* know?"

"No. I left him talking to Tom. But you're a damned fool to take a chance like that."

"No, no, son. *She* was. He can't do *me* anythin, but he can *her*. —And what was she doin there in the first place?"

He capered in delight, presenting the self which drew Concha toward what she desired most, and most disastrously.

"Don't you *ever* think of what *might* happen?" I asked.

"I do, and I did, and *it did,* and it will again! It's just a matter of time. Oh me, oh my."

"I don't mean that—I mean the trouble you could cause?"

"Oh. That. —No, because it may never come, and you can lose a lot of things if you go to thinkin that way. I hate to think of everythin you've missed all your life till the other night. —Here. You take the water now."

He slowly ran off like an athlete in a long training exercise, down the path, and around to the chuck wagon, where he enjoyed deviling Irene.

When in my turn I left the tank, I looked toward the ranch house and saw Concha on the porch steps, framed by the blowsy trumpet vines. She was safe in a different dress—white—leaning against a porch post. Anyone would think she was at peace, taking in the immense evening as the day's great event. The eastern horizon was softening with what looked like a rise of pale smoke, and the first stars were beginning to show. But what a tempest must bewilder her mind and heart, I thought; and how commonly, wonderfully strange that none of this showed in her lovely form. She might seem only weary and content. What can ever be really known, I thought with a sort of desolating fellow feeling, of what really troubled, pleased, or concerned anyone; and, with that unknown, how was it possible for one human being ever to judge another? Even one most alien? Even J. Buswell Rennison?

※

His excitement of the afternoon lasted into the night. He would not let me sleep. He did not know exactly when, but he knew for sure now, that he would have her. He had known all along that she wanted him. It was something he could tell with any wumman. He wadn't even surprised this afternoon when he happened to turn and see her through the stalks of the hedge. She must have been there all the time he was havin his shower. Well, then, she had an eyeful. It wadn't that far away—ten, fifteen feet—but what she could get a real good look at him. He was satisfied with what she saw, and he bet she was too. Like to drive her crazy. Plenty of others had been— and so he was off on detailed accounts of adventures, real or mythical, which I had not yet heard. He was so vain about his body that he sometimes seemed to be talking about that of somebody else, both aggressive and narcissistic in an admiring way. But by his elaborate confidences he was inviting mine; for if he could not be enacting his joys, the next best thing was to be talking about them, and those of anyone else who would respond in kind. I had nothing I wanted to tell him. My earliest love was the briefest of initiations, and if I told him of it, he would make remarks about it whose happy foulness would lead to violence between us. Finally, he would have been puzzled at the complications of purity, desire, and the single-mindedness of an idealized love.

"Oh, ah," he mused, lying back luxuriously with one hand behind his head and the other briefly answering to his loins, "I needed only a few more minutes there today. You know what? You don't know what I know, and that is, they all have got it on their mind just as much as I have, and once you know that, there's no stoppin anythin, with any of them."

He gave me an oblique smile, and that odd transfiguring chip of light in his right eye seemed to give out a shaft of energy, even while it seemed to avoid seeing me directly. He had a habit of hugging himself in self-pleasure, and he did it now—the very image of a healthy child physically happy, with blooming cheeks and no need of life at the moment but the plumbing sense of well-being.

"All I know is," he said at last, when I reached to turn down and out the wick of the coal oil lamp, "I'll go crazy if I don't get her."

"You never will," I said in the darkness.

I could hear him rise up on his elbow to face me.

"What's to prevent?"

"The old man. Her fear."

"What's she afraid of?"

"Well, apart from him, she's afraid of committing a sin. She's very religious. There is such a thing, you know, as all that."

"Oh me, oh my, Richie, what you don't *know*. Religion always comes *afterward,* don't you know that? I found that out long time ago from lots of *them*."

"All right: you know why she ran away from you this afternoon? —She crossed herself three times while she was running away. I saw it, you didn't."

"But just's I say: *afterward*."

He made a soft breathy laugh and fell back to his hard pillow and the sleep of the justified.

❧

In midweek under the searing August sky we were nearing the end of our Vergilian job of dipping the sheep. There was little enough classic lyricism about it. The hot winds blew the breath of the vat fires toward us. The sheep raised a fearful din as they were driven after their rams into the slide, which then threw them into the deep and stinking trough of the thick dip with its thickening film of scabs off the sheep and the excrement of their panic and the rubbery clots of creosote and Black Leaf 40 which had not dissolved. We stood, four or five on each side of the trough, with our long poles, which had the curved iron Y's at the end with which we pushed each animal under the surface, holding it just long enough to be sure the drench had reached its every part, and just short of drowning it. When we let it up, the sheep struggled to the surface and frantically swam in the only direction possible—ahead, bumping against the thickly packed flock fighting to reach the far end of the trough, go free, and live. Finally, choking and yelling on a sustained bleat, the sheep hoofed its way up the cleated incline, shaking and coughing, to join the roiling massed circle of its flock mates in the corral from which the return to the far pastures would be made.

It was too hot to leave off our shirts—for all but one of us. Buz worked bare from the waist up, taking pride in his dark biscuit tan, against which his lucky piece swung and winked in the sun. We all wore work gloves which were caked and stiff with dried dip. Don Elizario wandered along one side of the trough from end to end, watching, advising, nodding at the importance and efficiency of the job which he had performed hundreds of times. He knew how in itself it was nasty work, but he knew it had to be done, and how to demand of his men that it be done properly. Tom Agee matched him by overseeing the opposite side of the trough.

By mid-morning, we had been at the job for nearly five hours. The strangling clamor of the sheep, their endless choking and coughing and crying as they rose from their submersions, came to seem like part of the natural day, in its blazing monotony. In the white sky, the great hawks with their undersides reflecting the sandy color of the plains flew low above us, and above them, slowly spiraling, the black buzzards kept watch for carnal prey and cast their slow shadows over us far below as they sailed.

I was opposite Buz at the trough. Tom Agee was next to him.

At a moment, I happened to glance over at Buz, and saw a look of tight-jawed delight in his face. Then I saw that as his next sheep came along, he pushed it under the opaque slime, as we all did with ours; but he did not release it as soon as he should. At first, nobody saw that he was trying to drown the animal. His body was bent like a tensed bow. His face was lighted by excitement. When the sheep fought to come up, he pressed it down again as though running a spear into a victim. I waved to him to let go. He did not see me. But Tom Agee, following my gesture, turned to Buz next to him and saw what he was doing.

"Let it go!" bellowed Tom in as loud a voice as he could use.

Buz faced him with a mischievous grin and then turned back to press the rod against the drowning sheep.

"I said—" shouted Tom, and then, with no more time for words, swung his huge hand and heavy arm at Buz, knocking him down. Buz's sheep prod flew into the air. The sheep came to the surface and began to sink again until two of the men held it with their poles against the densely packed bodies of the other sheep. Weakly it strove for breath and began to find it. It was not dead after all, however zestfully Buz had tried to kill it.

He sprang up from the ground and swung to hit Tom, who held him off with his long, bony arms. Buz shouted at Tom with words that snapped like bullets from his mouth fixed in a hard muzzle.

"Aw, you God damn ol Bible-whackin, pants-pissin, chickenshit, son of a bitch!"

Rage in another can cause fear and nervous laughter. We all started laughing when Tom, with his face whitened in shock, knocked him down again as if with a length of two-by-four. Leaving him on the ground, Tom went toward Don Elizario at the other end of the trough. But the old man had heard the commotion and was already treading across a plank at the end of the trough to see the trouble.

"He tried to drownd a sheep!" yelled Tom hoarsely, pointing at Buz with a trembling hand.

"I never!" shouted Buz.

"I saw him," Tom continued, "and so did everybody else—?" He turned to inquire with a look at the other men if he were not right. Several nodded. "Don Eli, you got to fire the no-good runt."

Don Elizario seemed not to hear him. Keeping his eyes on Buz, he motioned to the rest of us not to slow down the work, for the sheep kept coming. Then he said to Tom,

"No, we need him till we're done. But a little lesson, *qué no?*"

With that, in a suddenly revived surge of virile power, he astonished Buz and the rest of us. He picked him up bodily and threw him with a mighty heave into the struggling stream of the tightly packed sheep as they went past in the slime. Don Elizario then stood with his hands on his hips and looked impassively at each of us in turn, and the world, having shown what a man can do when he must.

Buz clambered against the sheep. He did not sink into the trough, but like the bodies which flailed all about him, he was soaked with the hot dip. Stinking like one of them, he hauled himself out of the trough and took a few steps toward Don Elizario and shouted,

"I quit!"

"No," said Don Elizario in the mild voice of a man who has shown his strength. *"Oiga, cabrón,* you pologize to Tom *muy pronto!* Then you get back to work."

There was an irresolute pause.

But power lay with the old man, and need with the young.

"Well, then," muttered Buz with his head down, "I take it back."

We looked at Tom. He decided this was enough of repentance. He picked up Buz's pole, threw it to him, and Buz went back to work like the rest of us. The whole matter took a very few minutes; but it had been so charged with feeling that we were all subdued. Three passions had been so powerfully exposed against each other that, instead of jeering and hazing the loser, none of us felt like looking at him, or at each other. As the wet muck on his clothes quickly dried into a crust, his humiliation was complete, and a current of sympathy could be felt among the dipping crew.

When it was time for Irene's noon dinner, Buz did not come near the chuck wagon. He went to his bunk and found a change of clothes in his vagrant's bag. While we ate more or less in silence, he was at the tank, trying to wash off the filth and stench of the trough. When he was done, he brought his fouled clothes to the vat fire and threw them into the coals.

That night, as though in answer to my strong but unspoken question about why he did not quit after all, he said, with fatalistic simplicity,

"I need the pay."

Now I understood how the other men, poor in their rough, all-enclosing world, must have felt pity and fellow feeling for him, which they could not openly show, even if they might condemn his cruelty. The power if not the right lay always where the money came from; and after all, what was a sheep? Only an animal, worth so much a pound for its wool and its mutton. Anyhow, many a sheep died out on the pastures from weather or distemper, and what did it matter?

"Richie?"

"What now?"

"When this is all over, let's you and me really team up. How about it? You never answered me about this."

I tried to dodge again, saying,

"Well, where are you going from here?"

"I don't know. Do you?"

"Yes."

[219]

"Well, how about it?"

"No, you see, thanks, but I have to get back."

"Well, go to hell! You're just like the rest of them. The ol bastard thinks he can do anythin he likes to Buz Rennison. Well, he'll find out. Th'ain't anybody livin can do what he did to me and get off like nothin ever happened!"

I did not answer. His anger, like that of a hurt child, soon gave way to ruefulness. He sighed.

"No, you've been a real friend. I don't have any other real friends. Nobody stays my friend for very long. I keep wonderin why."

"Oh, nonsense. People will always admire you, no matter what"— but if I sounded bored, he did not notice it.

"You think so?"

"I do."

"Well, I've done all right so far, seein that I have never wanted to settle down."

There was relief in his voice; some note which meant that he thought he might have lost me, and was now glad that he could think this wasn't so.

The next morning (it was the last of the long days of dipping) work was taken up again as though nothing out of the ordinary had happened the day before.

※

All day Friday we saw nothing of Don Elizario. Several times Tom Agee went to the house and returned. He said the old man was resting: seemed like he might have strained something yesterday when he threw that foul-talkin Babyface into the dip. Innyhow—and Tom as foreman went about finishing the work of the past days. The men would be paid off at the end of the day. Early the next morning before the day's heat began to grow the flocks would be set on the trail for the lower ranch. Irene and his cook's wagon would go with them. One man would be picked by Don Elizario to stay behind to help Tom and me empty and scour the vat, skim and bail out the trough. The Wenzels might remain at the ranch for a little while to see things closed up, and then return to Albuquerque in their big car.

Throughout Friday Buz worked with zeal at his last day of dipping. There was anxiety in his labor. He worked hard to re-establish himself sociably among his fellows and with Tom. Tom ignored this. But by evening, when the job at the dip was done, Buz had everyone else restored to him in comradeship; and when we came to the firelight with our tin cups, there were calls for him to entertain us. He responded with winning modesty.

He had an instinctive sense of what an audience would like. On this final evening, the mood was sentimental. These men were sorry to separate from each other now, for they had known a bond in their work, and now that the work was over, if there was nothing else to keep them together, simple habit ruled their feelings. Each had his own vision of sentiment, and Buz touched it with songs he sang that night.

He played the guitar with tenderness instead of the slapping bravado of his earlier shows. He sang what the men thought of as songs of the range, the rude poetry of their hard lives. Their horses were loved and mourned as their best friends. The sheep and cattle they tended were given loving nicknames. The comradeship of the ranges and the pastures was celebrated as something they would never forget, even as in turn they would ride up the Last Trail, which led to Glory Up Yonder. It was a quiet little crowd that listened. Buz's voice was light and true. He seemed like someone incapable of a low thought or an evil act. With the purity of his playing and singing, he told us that if no man was either all good or all bad, every one of us no matter what his faults believed most in the good. Few fellows got what they deserved in this life; but every one of us could be sure of one thing—no matter where our work might take us, we would always know there was someone to come home to; and he sang his song of Bonnie Mae again, to state this comforting illusion, and this time, he let her remain real for us, a vision of purity and constancy we all believed in as we believed in our right to carouse when the spert moved us. Just now, we were as ready to be wise and virtuous men as at another time we might let ourselves go to hell-raisin. When Buz fell silent, bending his head like a juvenile innocent, I was as glad as the rest when someone called out,

"Just one more!"

He remained quiet with a showman's instinct until the listeners wondered. Then with a few gentle chords he began the song, "I Dream of Jeanie with the Light Brown Hair"; and under the pleading sweetness of his true young voice, that lone little society thought of itself at its best, in the chaste celebration of absent love.

The fire was low when he finished singing. The men were unwilling to rise and go to their bunks. They talked now in easy comfort about what they would do next—who would stay on the lower ranch, who would move on to other itinerant jobs, who had families to go home to, who would go back across the Rio Grande to Mexico, where they lived.

During this murmur of farewells, Don Elizario slowly came out of the shadows into the dying firelight to be with his men once more. Despite his inescapable power as the man who paid them, they revered him for what he was. They hoped to come back next summer when the time came. He took his due as patriarch so simply that when a few half rose to greet him, he absently put them down with his thick old hand, and with aching difficulty let himself down to be with them on the ground. He had little to say at first. He traveled the circle with his gaze, nodding his thanks and his good wishes to them all, even Buz, who ducked his head as though humbly before the old man's steady look.

Silence, full of companionship and respect, waited on Don Elizario. We could all see him as our eyes got used to the loss of the firelight, for the moon was nearly full—would be full tomorrow night. In that lucent silver pour he seemed almost a monumental figure. His great head was bare and his white hair shone in the moonlight. The heavy locks of his brow, lying as if roughly fingered there, made his head seem boyish in silhouette. Heavily his body breathed at rest. He seemed now to believe in his old age, for he was tired. When at last he said a few words, his voice was thin and husky. Where was the strong old man of the days of work who had been equal to most tasks that had to be done? At home, my father's illness had always made the daily present seem precarious, and we had always veiled our own uncertain future in hope. But something in Don Elizario's presence that night gave me my first intimations of how precarious, also, was any future.

"Well," said Don Elizario, "we have done good work. *Muchas gracias a todos*. Every year. Every year, we must do the same thing at the same time. There is something good in this. Eh? You are all younger than I am, some of you much younger. Do you know? If you have to go on a long walk with the flocks over the range, you watch for landmarks. You know where you have been and next time how far to go. Now I look at my life that way. You will some day." He sighed with acceptance. *"Bendito sea Diós*. Yes. *Sí, cantamos,"* and then in a quavering tone he sang the line from the favorite Mexican hymn which used the same words—"Blessed be God." Some of the Mexican men picked up the tune and the text and sang with him.

> *Bendito, bendito,*
> *Bendito sea Diós,*
> *Los ángeles cantan*
> *Y alaban a Diós,*
> *Los ángeles cantan*
> *Y alaban a Diós.*

At the end of this impromptu act of familiar piety, we all felt blessed. Without any further words of benediction and farewell, Don Elizario came painfully to stand and, waving his heavy old hand at us, turned to go.

Buz stepped after him and said,

"Sir? Mr Wenzel?"

The old man paused. Their figures were edged with moonlight.

"*¿Qué tal?*"

"Sir, I sure am sorry about yesterday, and I'm wonderin if I could just stay on to do the extra work after the others have gone? I need the pay and I don't know where I'm goin next. I sure would appreciate it."

There was a little pulse of urgency in his voice. The last thing I had come to expect was compunction of any sort. The cock of the walk now acted forlorn.

"Well, well," said Don Elizario in a soft marveling voice. "Bebby-face is sorry. So. *Pues,* all right, you can stay, work with Richard, but you will have to work on Sunday, and you will have to be done as soon as you can. *El Tom* will pay you. My wife and I are going to Albuquerque. You can stay with Richard. Tom knows the work that is to do. —Irene"—he raised his voice for the cook—"leave food for these two. They will have to feed their own selves."

With nothing further to say, he went off to his house, where no light showed, and to his wife, who waited in darkness.

The gathering began to break up. Irene produced a Jew's harp from his pocket and gave a tuneless buzzing twang to which he took exaggerated steps away to his wagon, two at a time, pausing to strike an attitude of disdainful elegance; and then again he advanced and paused, over and over, making a stylized exit from the company, the place, and the occupations of the past days.

When we saw a light come on inside the canvas wall of his wagon, Buz and I went to him to draw our rations. He received us with a social air, and then shrewdly calculated the least amount of food on which we could live for four more days.

"Four days will do for *you*," he said, sassing us with word and gesture. "I'm not going to empty *my* shelves for two no-good gold-brickers."

He stuffed a burlap sack with our supplies. When Buz reached for a box of potato chips, Irene slapped him on the hand with petulant grace and cried,

"No, sir! Not in a *million years! Those* are for myself. You think I'd serve delicacies to common ranch hands? Not on your life. *Stealing.* The idea. In the *Marines* we'd know how to handle an uppity pup like you"—for he always claimed that he had served as a Marine in the recent Great War.

"Oh, Miss Irene," said Buz with mock humility, "I'm just so sorry, dear!"

"And I'll have you know my name is *Ira*," snapped the cook, handing me the sack and slapping the air to drive us out of the wagon.

"Yes, Irene," answered Buz as we left, and we heard the cook exclaim to the indifferent world,

"Oh, why was I ever—!"

Later, Buz took a long time to go to sleep. He tossed and grunted until I called out to him,

"Why don't you settle down, over there? You're keeping me awake. There's a lot to do tomorrow."

He exhaled noisily.

"Boy, I sure have got it bad tonight. —It isn't fair."

"What?"

"They're leavin and I haven't seen her again."

"I think they're going to see a doctor about the old man. He has you to thank for that. It took a lot out of him to handle you that way."

"So it's my fault? The old fool. He'd better not get in my way again!"

"In your way! You got what was coming to you. He's been good to you, letting you stay on."

"Come on, Richie. If he'd done *that* to you, you wouldn't forget it in a hurry. *I* never will!"

"You said you were sorry."

"Sorry? I've never been sorry or ashamed for anythin I ever did in my whole life. But now I don't care if I stay or go."

"I thought you needed the pay."

"I could use it. But there's more to life than pay. You notice he's taking her away early and that's why he's lettin me stay on. I don't owe him any thanks." His voice grew edgy. "Just the opposite, if you ask me."

His temper was rising. He was ready to enlarge his grievance. I blew a yawn, turned over, and went to sleep.

The next thing I heard was the rankle of gear and the disturbed bleating of the flocks, and the distant voices of the men, before sunrise, as the southward drive began over the range to the lower ranch.

꙳

We worked all day with Tom. There was no sign of life at the house. In the silence of the ranch the noises we made seemed even greater than they were, after the days of yelling sheep, shouted orders.

First we dug a trench leading from the far end of the trough down a low slope which led to the arroyo. Into the trench we would bail the settled brew of the dip, using five-gallon buckets. Eventually, the stuff, with all its scabs and clots and stench, would slowly edge down the incline and into the arroyo, where we would cover it with loose dirt. We would then go to the vat and scour it with iron scrapers and coarse steel wool until, said Tom with stern satisfaction, our hands, even in their cracked gloves, would turn raw. We would haul leftover firewood back to the piles beyond the corral from which it had been taken.

As the hours passed on Saturday at our work, Buz began to appreciate the irony behind Don Elizario's kindness in letting him stay. I saw Tom Agee read Buz's face with righteous pleasure as the demands of the job in time and effort came clear. Tom was used to the work. He worked steadily, in a long-sustained rhythm, and as the day went by, Buz and I saw that this was both more effective and less racking than our fits and starts. We seemed to make little progress. The trough seemed almost as full at quitting time as when we began.

When evening came, with it came the rise of the full moon over the Magdalena mountains. It was at first a deep orange-rose as it lifted into the earth's haze; and then as the sky darkened above, the moon color changed into an unearthly yellow. Tom observed it. Speaking generally in order to avoid addressing Buz, he said,

"Now you look at that. Now you look backward over your shoulder to the west. They's some weather workin up." Over the Datil mountains hung a long straight bank of clouds. The mountains were an almost gemlike blue, but somber as well as clear. Between clouds and mountains there was a long, even gap of open sky. Its color was ominous—a strange deep yellow. "That kind of a sky means change. I believe we goin to see some rain mebbe tomorrow. If that rain had o' come before we was all done with the dippin, why, we'd a been days more gettin done. Fires out, sheep ornery, dip all thinned out. I tell you. When it comes, it sure does come. I've been marooned here days at a time in these August rains. This red clay."

I felt a weight in the pit of my stomach. Would I be marooned here? When would I get home? What was happening there? What would they say when they saw me? Did I look any different? Would they see me inside out? I had made sport of the virtue of my father and mother. What was I going to do with myself? They needed me. How could I save anybody?

⚜

After the heaviest day's work I had yet known, I fell asleep before the moon, now so clear and white that no stars could show near it, reached its height, and I did not stir all night. With the habit of dawn, I awoke but for a last moment of luxury kept my eyes shut. It was Sunday, but the job had to go on, and if I'd known any way to manage it, I would have risen and gone to Magdalena, Socorro, and home.

But without hope of that, I opened my eyes and turned to wake Buz. He was not in his bunk. He must be outside getting breakfast. I dressed and went out into the morning twilight. At first I did not see anyone, and then I saw him, between the house and the campfire place. He was bent over, swinging his foot across the sharp grass, closely searching the ground for something. I called out to him. He straightened up sharply as though to deny that he was looking for anything; and then he trotted waggishly over to me and said we ought to get ourself busy over a fire and a coffee pot and a frying pan.

"You're out early," I said.

"You cert'n'y were sleepin."

We built a little fire. Its smoke drifted toward the main bunkhouse and brought Tom out for the day. He joined us for breakfast, which we made out of Irene's rations—coffee, stale cold biscuits to warm over, fried eggs and bacon. The early sun was now hidden by a general overcast. Tom looked up.

"I told you, didn't I?"

"It ain't rainin yet," declared Buz.

"I did'n say it was," replied Tom, to me.

We had the rest of the meal in silence. At the end, Tom, slapping his gaunt thighs, got up and said,

"Let's get to it before that sky opens up on us."

We went to the trough. Tom handed each of us a long-tined rake from the edge of the trough.

"We'll get it all out quicker if we scrape off the top of the slime," he said. "Yesterday, the buckets didn't get ver' much."

So we were right—we had not made much progress, so far.

"Why didn't you think of this yesterday, dad?" asked Buz.

"Fer your information, buster, I spent half the night tryin to locate these rakes. Somebody put them away after the shearin and I didn't find them till nigh midnight, out back of the feed house. Then I threw them down here. Now pick up your rakes and you get on it."

We all three dragged the rakes across the thick wet crust of the dip, pulling the hardest and largest lumps out over the edge along the length of the trough.

After an hour or so Buz went to Tom. There was a strenuous air of new respect about him.

"Mr Agee, sir," he said, "I got some urgent business in Magdalena. And I just wish I could borrow the Ford and run into town and tend to it, and then come right back?"

Tom leaned on his rake and scowled as if to destroy him with God's lightning, of which His minister was the wielder.

"I know your kind of business in Magdalena, Master Rennison, and I don't like the nature of it. The answer is no. Now you get on back to your rakin."

Buz turned white. In a pleading voice I had never heard him use before, he went on.

"No, sure enough, sir, this is mighty important and it ain't what you may be thinkin it is. I wouldn't ask you if it wadn't. I just beg you, Mr Agee."

"You haven't earned any favors around here, young man. You get back there now, right quick!"

Tom made himself larger in wrath. He could whip Buz with one hand and both knew it. Buz turned away and looked at me with the breaking face of a boy almost ready to cry. Then, wiping his eyes on the back of his hand, he went slackly along the trough to his rake and his station near the far end. As if harvesting a new crop, Tom returned to his long, slow, rhythmic sweep with his rake, and where I worked between him and Buz, I imitated him.

It must have been almost at once that Tom cried out in a cracked hoot,

"Oh, my gret God Ammighty! Richard! You come right quick!"

There was such horror in his voice that I ran to him. Bending all his weight on his rake handle against the trough edge, he was holding up something half revealed from the dip. He nodded for me to see it. "Gret God Ammighty!" he said again, now in a hush.

On the wet end of his rake he was supporting in much strain the body of Don Elizario. The face and shoulders and one arm were visible, glistening in a coat of the gray clotted dip.

"Quick," cried Tom, "we must get him out! Go get your rake and he'p me lift him out! Hurry now!"

His first shock gave way to urgent efficiency. I ran to my rake, and as I ran I saw Buz staring at me.

"Buz! Come and help! Something terrible—"

I didn't wait for him to answer, but took up my rake and ran back to Tom. I set it under the lower part of the body and together we drew it to the edge of the trough, and when Tom said, "Now!" we knelt quickly and grasped Don Elizario and brought him out to lie on the ground. The creosote and Black Leaf 40 flowed slowly from his face. One arm was twisted above his head with fist clenched. The other lay beside him. In the gray muck which was upon him he looked like a wet statue of himself in a posture of torment, molded in his clotted nightgown.

I felt a shadow over me and turned to see Buz, leaning over us to look at what we had found.

"Oh my, oh my," grieved Tom, "isn't this the worst pitiful thing ever you did see!"

The sorrow in his voice had a hard lifetime behind it. He shook his head heavily, looking back and forth over the whole length of the old man.

Then abruptly, noticing something barely visible in the clenched fist, he said, "What's this?" and leaned to find out. He picked the rigid fingers apart and released the slide of a thin brass chain, and when the whole hand was opened, there all plain was Buz's lucky piece, with its "Atlantic City Bathing Beauty." Tom held it up, and when he saw its face revealed as the wet dripped off it, he shouted,

"Where did this damnation thing come from?"

Then he remembered where he had seen it almost daily at work with Buz and the rest of us. He heaved to stand and reached for Buz. Buz wildly looked about for somewhere to go. There was nowhere to go on the endless land under the sky darkening with its bated storm. He looked to the house. His body tightened with the same bolt of energy I had seen when he caught his first sight of Concha. In a second he twisted just out of Tom's reach and ran to the house and up to the porch and began to beat at the door. He threw himself against it and beat and beat. The door was locked. There was no answer. His face was turned so his cheek was pressed with the rest of his body against the old white wood panels. His eyes were shut, his mouth working silently open.

Tom ran after him, whipping off his belt as he went. Taking the porch in one jump, he pulled Buz away, threw him down, and tied his hands behind him with the belt. He walked him roughly and fast past me to the main bunkhouse. As they went by, Tom said to me,

"You get on in to Miz Wenzel and you tell her the best way you can. You tell her to wait inside a while."

I went to the house and knocked gently, and waited. Silence. I called her name. No reply. Dread, and the memory of Don Eli's law, kept me from trying the door. The curtains were all closed. I tapped at a window. The house was silent.

I went back to the porch steps and sat down to listen for any sounds from within. I crossed my arms on my knees and put my face down on them to hide from that morning.

☙

In a little while Tom returned alone.

"You tell her?"

I shook my head and explained why.

"I'll go own in," he said. "I have to get to the telephone operator and get to the law at Socorro. She must be sleepin mighty deep."

He went up on the porch just as raindrops as heavy as spent bullets began slowly to fall on the tin roof, making sounds that rang separately. In another moment the sky opened and a cloudburst was upon us. I ran on to the porch and then I looked back at where Don Elizario lay where we had left him in his befoulment, and I made as though to go to protect his body from the downpour. Tom detained me.

"It's a mercy," he declared. "He must be washed clean before she gets to see him. —In all my years—"

The deluge suddenly increasing drowned out his words. He unlocked the door and went inside. I stood behind the screen of vines on which the rain beat as if to destroy what it would end by slaking.

☙

The storm, said Tom, interfered mightily with the telephone lines. Thunder and lightning came with the deluge, and the connection to Socorro by way of Datil was blanked out time and again. Tom said—and I thought of suppressing this detail for fear of playing too close to allegory—the tremendous crashes after the lightning which tore the sky were the wrath of gret God Ammighty at the foulest crime there could be.

He finally saw Concha. With her husband somewhere out in the day, she had locked the front door and gone to her bath deep in the house. When the thunder broke, she came to hide in the middle passageway of the house, where there were no windows. She remembered how dangerous it was to be in water during thunder and lightning. No, she had heard no one knocking.

"Did you tell her?"

He did. She crossed herself and backed away from him at his news. Then fell to her knees and, wailing in a passion of grief, said it was her fault, and began to pray aloud in Spanish. How was it her fault? Tom asked, and she replied that she should never have let her husband wander around outdoors alone at night that way. He couldn't see very well at night, he had been feeling faint in the last day or two. It would be so easy to fall into the dip and drown. She wept into her hands and kept saying, Oh, God, oh, God, in Spanish.

"No," said Tom, "that boy had something to do with it."

She screamed and hid her face in her arm. The harm of the world was now human instead of abstract in the will of God.

Tom told her then we would all have to go to town as soon as things could be arranged. I would help him. Please, she would please go to her room and stay there until we called her. She ran away and shut the bedroom door. Tom let her be.

I helped him bring Don Elizario to the house, where we did what we could with tubs full of water to clean away what the storm had not. We cut away his nightgown and sponged his body. He seemed diminished out of life, and a noble strangeness lay across his face. As we worked, I was "much possessed by death," and there were moments when I thought I could not continue; but Tom Agee's angry, sorrowful strength put something in me which let me go on, even when, using our sponges, we cleaned away from the old man's body the last film of the dip and saw what lay revealed. Tom looked up at me and silently pointed to the bruised, torn marks on Don Elizario's heavy old breast. Spaced precisely, they were cuts, violently made, by the tines of a rake, such as we had used at the trough.

Tom sat back on his heels and held his silence as though he could not speak to anyone of what he now knew for certain. But after a while he looked at me and said,

"I *thought* he was lyin. Now I know it."

He had taken Buz to the bunkhouse and had tied him to a stanchion of one of the double-decker beds. He showed Buz the amulet and asked formally if it was his. Buz, after a panting silence, admitted that it was.

"That was what I saw him looking for in the grass early this morning," I said.

Then Tom asked him, you did it? No, not exactly, Buz answered. He had never meant to. The old man was wandering around and Buz was restless—he did not say for what—and when he saw Don Eli he went toward him just to be sociable, but the old man swore at him and demanded to know what he was doing out, like that, near the house, and ordered him back to bed. Buz said he had no cause to talk to him like that, and refused to turn and go. The old man took a step toward him and hit him—oh, not very hard—on the side of the head. Buz pushed him back. The old man lost his balance and grabbed at him. Buz pushed him off. To recover himself, the old man leaned toward Buz again with his arms whirling around. He reached for Buz again and caught Buz's neck chain. Buz stepped away, the little chain broke, the old man staggered backward, lost his balance again, and fell into the sheep dip.

Tom asked him what he did then.

"Do you know what that ornery little devil said?" Tom asked me with awed disgust. "He said he just walked off and left the old man in the dip. He said, 'He threw me in, didn't he? *I* got out, didn't I?'"

Tom said to him,

"You pushed him."

"I never."

"Did you push him under?"

"No. I never."

Then what did he do? asked Tom.

Buz said he just walked away.

And him an old man? exclaimed Tom, and Buz replied that that wasn't *his* fault.

Tom said to me,

"To the shame of my hand and my faith, I hauled off and smote him as hard as I could across the face, and I left him. I was ashamed because he was tied up and he was scared and saying the first thing that come to mind. But now I see those rake wounds, I'm not ashamed any more."

❦

The law, at the county seat, Socorro, when all was finally understood over the storm-troubled telephone line, told Tom to head out toward Magdalena with the body, the prisoner, and whoever else might be there at the ranch. Two deputies would start out from Magdalena to meet him, soon's they could get going.

The ranch would be deserted when we left. Tom locked what could be locked. Our procession formed shortly after noon on that Sunday. We laid Don Elizario wrapped within blankets which concealed him entirely on the back seat of Concha's big yellow car, which Tom would drive. Buz, with his hands tightly tied behind his back, sat next to Tom in the front seat. I drove Concha in the Ford.

We started out in the downpour. Tom sent me ahead, in case I got stuck in the red clay of the road which by now was deep mud. His orders were to go as slowly as I could, and drive on the tufted grass between the ruts and on the roadside, where my wheels would have better traction.

The early afternoon was like deep twilight. I leaned forward over my wheel to peer through the rain. I would turn my lights on and then at once turn them off, for their beams only made the huge individual streams of rain more dazzling, and further hid the immediate distance. I remember how my heart was beating—not actually fast, but in heavy blows. In our two cars we made a procession of sorrow, with the killer and the dead following me and the widowed girl through the downpour. Now and then I felt my nerve begin to falter in a sudden, weakening tingle throughout my flesh; and I managed to hold on by forcing my will to fight the mud sucking at my wheels. If I glanced now and then at Concha, it was only to be sure she was in control of herself. She was silent. Her face was gray-white, her eyes were circled by hollows the color of dark ash, her lips were pressed tight as if to suppress shock and sickness. In her lap her fingers ceaselessly climbed in and out of a tense pattern. She was not even praying now. She was oddly removed from all that had happened. She was somewhere else in her mind, far away, where she would rather be, now and hereafter. We did not speak.

It took us until mid-afternoon to pass the few miles to the highway gate. I opened it and stood in the rain until Tom had brought the large car through. As it passed me, Buz lifted his chin at me and smiled in a comradely greeting—old friends, weren't we?—and he winked as though to promise something we could share when "all this" was over and done with. He was desperate in his refusal to believe what was real to other people.

The land began to slope gently toward the east as we edged our way along the dirt highway now. Here the rain ran off more swiftly. Where there were lifts and then falls of the contours, the red water collected in wide pools obscuring the track we were following. When we came to the western edge of the Plains of San Agustín, the road was like a slow river, flowing eastward. Under the opaque red surface, the ruts held their shape, and suddenly my wheels slid into them, the power was wrenched from my hands, and the Ford sank into the grip of the mud and came to a halt.

Tom was fifty feet behind me. He saw me try to rock the Ford back and forth to come free. Spinning the wheels only threw up mud and dug the car in deeper. When I could not move the car, Tom halted his at a safe distance behind me and ran to me.

"Here," he yelled against the rain, "you get back there! I'll get this car out. Go on, quick, he's alone! You guard him!"

He handed me his rifle, pushed me toward the big car, and took my place at the wheel of the Ford. I heard him race the engine as I ran through the water to the yellow Cadillac. My mind was not on the prisoner—in heavy dread it was on the blanket-wrapped figure in the back seat.

Soaked through, I reached the big car and ducked behind the wheel and slammed the door. My teeth were chattering. The rain was cold, like my vitals.

"Boy," said Buz genially, "you look a sight."

Catching my breath, I did not answer him. The air suddenly lightened as the curtain of rain opened briefly. The Plains of San Agustín showed. I saw the sky-colored vacancy, and then the curtain closed again and we were as if nowhere.

"Lissen," said Buz in a hissing whisper. He glanced over his shoulder in case the still form of Don Elizario might hear. "Richie! Now's my chance! He'p me get these ropes off!"

I scowled at him, completely puzzled.

"I mean, *listen,* Richie, you can let me go free, ol Tom is busy up there, he won't see or hear, give me the gun, and I'll just hop out and get lost over there in the plains. Nobody'd ever find me there! I'll get me on down to Messico. Richie!"

I held the gun away from him. I stared at him. I felt like someone else. If I let him go free, could he make his way from bush to bush, gully to gully, in the Plains of San Agustín, and in that lake of light, day after day, could he disappear? If he could use the land like an animal, might he come to the border far to the south, cross the Rio Grande, and be free? Or would he only be a prisoner, not of men, but of the country itself?

"God damn it, Richie, hurry up!" He had no doubt at all of my willing complicity. "There iddn't all that much time. Come on, my buddy—" with all the sentiment of his sweetest songs.

"Buz, you know I can't. Now cut it out!"

He rubbed his chin on my shoulder like a cat and said, "These ropes sure do hurt."

"I said, cut it out, Buz! This is no fooling, you know." I lifted the rifle an inch or two. "After what you did!"

*"He p'voked me! —*I'm not foolin. Don't you remember the good times we had?"

He called up a whole imaginary history of us together. Even though his hands were tied behind him, he tried to draw his shoulders forward in his old gesture of cuddling himself to remind the world of his appeal, which had always got him what he wanted, and must always do so, because he believed in it.

I was scared by his unreality. At the same time, I was sickened by the power of any human being over another; captivity: restraint as upon an animal: any measure of indignity performed upon any individual by any body of people, for any reason. Though he was in custody for the worst of crimes, I was even so pulled by a sense of our common humanity and its general sorrows. At once, this sentiment angered me for its softness. He was a gross criminal. He deserved all he would get. But I was even angrier at the thought that if I were in his place, I too would look irrationally to anyone for help. I could give no help. I felt a perverse share in his guilt because I was so free of his trouble. How long ago, really, had it begun? Staring at him I had a view of him so impersonal that for a moment it seemed to suggest man's common lot—the newborn infant drawn with wet head and blind wrinkled shocked face from his mother's womb; the child growing with who knew what hopes and blessings over him, or what maltreatments, by those who had given him life; the boy learning how much? how little? beyond animal ways; the youth making the self which brought the young man to this; the man shackled by fellow men and helplessly subject to them.

"You hurry now, boy, hear?"

I shook my head but my mind was hot and senseless. I said, holding my sympathy where it had to be,

"But he's dead."

"That's right, so nothin can he'p him. But you can he'p me, Richie. Let me go. This is ol Buz, you ol son of a bitch"—his voice mellowed—"you can't forget that night at the Marigold, can you? Richie, come on, come on, just the plains, there, and I'll get me down to Messico."

What to do with a maimed creature but let it go?—as I could not.

Something in my face must have changed, looked to him like promise, freedom, Mexico.

"That's ol Richie! Quick now!"

He turned to give me his back and the shackled arms.

But just then Tom came walking heavily like a giant through water. I saw now that he had coaxed the Ford free, and that it stood a little higher.

At my failure to act, Buz turned, saw Tom, and knew then that the Plains of San Agustín were forever beyond him. He half rose in rage from his seat and fell back again, shouting,

"A-a-h, you're all shittin sons a bitches!"

Tom looked keenly first at me and then at Buz. What had he

prevented?—this notion went across his face; but he had no time for imaginings, and roughly he gestured to me to get out, go to the other car, and start forward again, while he took the rifle and climbed in beside Buz and put the big car in gear.

"Keep your front wheels turned a mite to the left, till we get out of this here little lake," he said. "Go own, now. It's gettin darker."

I went to the Ford.

A few miles and a long while later, Concha said,

"Are you sure he did it?"

I could not speak of the proof clutched to the death in Don Elizario's hand, and the rake slashes on his breast.

"Yes, even though he says he did not mean to do it."

She fell silent, though she shivered, almost with the effect of clattering, as if she were at last coming awake to knowledge that had numbed her.

Passing the whole stretch of the Plains of San Agustín, I shook my head over the notion that any sort of freedom could ever lie that way, or any other, for Buz. Escape, but not freedom.

Shortly before evening the rain thinned.

Soon I thought I saw lights through the rain; then I was sure. The lights of two other cars were showing, coming to meet us, as the Magdalena mountains began to clear and fade and loom again way ahead through the varying rain.

❧

We reached Magdalena at nightfall with the rain still falling. There we were to be detained until the sheriff of Socorro County arrived. Tom took us to the Marigold Hotel, where he found rooms for us all. Concha wanted nothing but sleep, sleep. Tom and I went downstairs late in the evening to drink coffee and eat what we could. I wondered what to say to Larraine if she should ask me about Buz; but she was gone. Another waitress said Larraine had left, talking about a job in Lamesa, Texas, which she had heard of.

"She said she don't stay long in any one place. —Would you wish the regular dinner?"

The next morning, the sheriff was waiting for us in the lobby. He swore Tom in as a deputy to form part of the escort when we went by train to Socorro, where Buz was put in jail and all of us were questioned in turn. Tom and I knew what we knew and told it.

The whole town had the story by noon and the press by evening. It made a great sensation. Don Elizario belonged to the whole region as its great man. A mob gathered outside the Socorro County jail at the end of the street, south of the plaza. They were ready to lynch the murderer. Armed deputies stood them off until time for the evening train, when under an order issued by the county judge, the prisoner was bound over under a change of venue to Santa Fe County, there to await trial.

Again we were all together—Concha, Tom, Buz, myself, and Don Elizario—northbound by the same train to Albuquerque. From there Tom and another deputy took Buz to Santa Fe. Concha went home to her family and I to mine.

CHAPTER V

Prayers for the Dying

"LET ME LOOK AT YOU, my darling! What you have been through! Hideous nightmare, from all that we've read. Murder! Oh, and"— my mother shifted gaily into one of her little irrelevancies—"so much about *you* in the papers, your picture on the front page, a horrid picture, all full of mud, and those clothes, but we *did* recognize you. To think of it all!"

I felt her shudder and also her loving satisfaction at my brief notoriety as she held my shoulders and looked into my face, searching for the child she knew so well in the man who with every year was becoming someone else. But never much inclined to pursue the "shadow side" of human nature—so I thought—my mother went on,

"But how well you look, how brown. Did they work you so hard? You look like a sailor, all ropy muscles after a voyage. Tell me, what was the food like?"

She was being busy and merry to make a great event of my return; but she seemed older. Her formerly occasional habit of winking both eyes against distraction or emotion was now incessant. Her life had turned inward to one purpose—my father's hourly need of reassurance.

"And oh!" she exclaimed, "I know now what you went through giving those hypos to Daddy—I've been doing it every day, and when I make him bite his lips, I could die. I'm so glad you'll be doing it again, won't you?"

It seems to me now that I came home readier to deal with pain than before. I came home from a land which gave space to my vision, and loss to my youthful conviction that virtue controlled all. Now I knew that virtue had to be salvaged as best it could out of every human situation. The sacred and the profane had previously been separated for me. Now they had blurred edges where they met. Even so, I was home again in my native moral climate.

"It was crude and monotonous, but after a while, we never cared," I said. Then, to justify myself in a matter about which she would never know, I added sharply, "Distraction of any sort was welcome for the moment."

"I suppose so. Well, it agreed with you. Come, your father is waiting to see you and hear all you have to tell."

He said, when I found him in the patio,

"You've had quite a finale to your own fresh-air cure, Doc."

He was expert in the hectic humor of the tubercular. There were pink spots at his cheeks, whose bones threw a deeper shadow now. Under his scowl, his eyes were brilliant and carried a strong mixture—peculiar to the Irish, I suppose—of strong sympathy and self-protective gaiety. He was lying in the sunshine, wearing a cap, with a steamer rug over his long frame. His hands looked sculptured, with an unearthly pallid cleanliness about them. In his voice there was a strong, new grain, and his movements were abrupt and vigorous. He meant to show the world—and me—that he was not being consumed with corrosive thoughts about his condition, and the loss of what at any moment now might have been his proper office as governor of the state of New York.

But once our greetings and idle solicitudes were done with, it was the one topic he could not stay away from.

"Sam tells me not to keep going on about it," said my father drolly, "but it's the only interesting thing I know at the moment."

"Where is Sam?"

"Down at the telegraph office picking up telegrams. We get several a day with all the play-by-play news—the senate trial is in process."

"And the Pelzers?"

"You know, the strangest thing"—his eyes took on the fire of malice—"Mo Pelzer actually telegraphed asking for a deposition from me as a *character witness* for the defense. I was stricken with admiration for the boundless nerve of that family. There *are* people who never see themselves at all, don't you think?"

Indeed I do, I said to myself, and there are others who see too much of themselves. I said,

"How did you handle that?"

"Superbly. I had Sam wire back to say that my attending physicians—we made it plural—advised against any emotional concerns at this time."

He laughed, laughing made him cough, his eyes brimmed with merriment, he waved his white hands at me to express what his breath would not permit, and then I had to laugh at his high spirits. As his cough subsided, he put up one finger to hold the conversation until he could speak, and then he said,

"Do you remember that day during the campaign when we were at the Fort Schuyler Club in Utica when Judge took me aside for a brief conference?"

"Yes."

"I never told you what it was about. Well. Now. This: would I agree to lead the action in the senate to get the lenient tax laws passed in favor of the Chippewa Shipping and Steel people? If I would do so, behind the scenes of course, would I be satisfied with a payoff: he called it a donation to my campaign chest, if you please: of a hundred and fifty thousand dollars? When I stood numbed by amazement, not greed, he misread me and hastened to add that he thought he could get them to go to two hundred thousand. His share, he admitted with an air of honest good fellowship, would be considerably more, but he was sure I would agree that that was only proper, as he was the designer of the whole progressive concept, as he called it; and also, he stood to lose more than anyone else if anything should go wrong. *Should go wrong!*"

"Is that why you were so furious when you came out to me?"

"Of course."

"What did you tell him?"

"To go to hell, naturally, and moreover, I told him that if I was ever asked under oath, I would quote the whole interview verbatim. You should have seen his face. He looked like a vulture in shock. He could have killed me with his beak."

"Have they asked you for the story?"

"Not yet. Sam is sure they will."

"Will you have to go to Albany?"

"Ask my attending physicians. —No, probably not, but I am beginning to believe I could do it. A deposition will answer, I suppose."

"Bombshell?"

"Bombshell, with patriotic flares. —Are you all right, Doc?"

"Yes. Why?"

"Oh, I don't know. You look sort of:"

He shrugged.

❦

At five minutes before ten the next morning, the bells in the two towers of San Felipe de Neri in Old Town began to toll for the Requiem High Mass of Don Elizario Wenzel. My strongest wish was to stay away. But I also wanted to join in the general absolution over him in the Mass. The old church, with its paper flowers and

[245]

pink-washed walls, baroque white and gold wooden altar, leaning dim old sacred paintings, was crowded breathless.

In the middle aisle, before the sanctuary, lay the purple-draped coffin of the old man, flanked by three towering candelabra on each side. I stood in the rear of the church, where many Mexican men were also standing. I saw local officials—the mayor, the police chief, leading businessmen, both Anglo and Mexican, and reporters, including Lyle Pryor, who would write a serious column in place of his usual cranky little paragraphs about "lungers," local politics, and Congress. The city, the whole state, were angrily moved at the circumstances of the murder. In ranching country, most people knew what sheep dip was like.

There was a long wait in stifling propriety before Concha arrived with her old father and mother and a long string of family connections. She was all veiled, but her face was dimly beautiful in its pallor and stupefied by endurance. They went into black-festooned pews at the front of the church. Soon afterward, another group arrived, two men in black suits, with their women, who wore black shawls over their heads. The men were middle-aged, heavy, frowning likenesses of Don Elizario—his two surviving sons by his earlier marriage. They sat across the aisle from Concha and her people. They stared straight ahead, ignoring her. An almost palpable enmity was in the air between the two families. People nudged each other to call attention to this, and so crowded was the church that finally I felt the nudge as it traveled back along the pews, accompanied by little murmurs. Everybody knew that there was a matter here of a fortune which must be divided by death as once before it had been divided by marriage portions. When speculative stir subsided, as if a swarm of bees had collected itself and droned away, the celebrants of the Mass, three Jesuit priests in black and silver vestments, entered from the sacristy, and the last act of Don Elizario's history began.

The tension was extreme. I felt it in my vitals. For those more openly susceptible, it soon became too great to bear without response. A muffled shriek came from the front pew—Concha. Her tiny mother, who looked as though grief and endurance were woman's natural state, bent to comfort her; but the outcry was a signal for others of the family to honor the occasion, and a chorus of wailing women paid tribute to the young widow. Why can't they shut up, I said to myself, but the truth was that my decorum was not so much offended as that my nerves were caught up in a contagion of feeling. Something in me longed to let itself go free in some sort of expression. I felt the gathered emotion grow in the whole church. It seized me, tempting me, until I began to feel like someone else. The heavy air, hot with August and thick with incense and hysteria, seemed unbreathable. But it was more than that hour in San Felipe which was working in me. It was the focused effect of the weeks beyond Magdalena, and their culmination; and roughly, hardly knowing myself, I pushed my way to the door, through the thick crowd of standing men, away from the presence of God and general guilt, and across the street to the plaza. There I fell down, shaking, upon a bench near the weathered bandstand in the center of the park. From there I could dimly hear the chanting and the dutiful screams through the open door of the church, about which children clustered, peering and climbing against each other like a litter of puppies, trying to be part of what was happening within. After I had subdued my shakes, I went to my river glade, fell down on the fine sand, and with my arm covering my eyes against the light, the troubles of days past and of that morning, and others which I saw but did not want to see in days ahead, I sought sleep.

❧

The others left the dinner table to move into the long, glass-enclosed gallery at one side of the patio where the card tables were set up. Sam and I stayed behind with coffee and brandy. He had a little habit of looking keenly at me and then dropping his gaze and then looking keenly again. He did not ask me directly, only with his eyes, about my weeks away. He was closest to me in age of anyone in the house and I longed to lighten my thoughts by telling him every detail of the summer. But his strong intelligence was lodged in a rectitude which, while it would make no judgments in the case of a friend, would still hold to a fastidiousness which I could not put to a strain.

"It must be an extraordinary matter, to be close to a murder. And such a one!" he said, with an air of disposing of the painful topic for me.

I refused his tact.

"Is there strong feeling here about the case?" I asked, to bypass my own feeling.

"Oh, yes, terribly. They tell me no case has made as much outcry since the territorial days, when the frontier was still pretty close."

"You know law. What will happen to Rennison?"

"I think even if he changes his plea to not guilty, he will be convicted. Everyone I have talked to is sure he will be executed."

"You know, he will be killed for what he *is*, as much as for what he did."

The lowered and raised look again.

"You knew him very well?"

"Very well."

"Did you get along with him?"

"He always thought so, I thought so only at times. There is something appealing about him, but he is a fool. He doesn't see things like anyone else. He is unable to help it."

"You saw it coming?"

"Not exactly. But neither was I entirely astonished, though appalled, of course."

"I suppose you will have to testify."

"I suppose so. I don't like the idea."

[248]

"You have a certain sympathy for him?"

"I suppose I have, in the abstract. No—even personally."

"Why?"

"I suppose— I think probably because I have never known so clearly how events, combined with somebody's big inner world, can so entirely overwhelm any one creature, however much he may deserve what may follow."

"Yes, it is even more ironic and final when the events are of the creature's making, isn't it?"

"You mean, one really ought to imagine all possible consequences before taking action at any time?"

"Yes, but without becoming paralyzed. There are choices, after all."

"Yes, I know," I said, meaning more than I would ever tell him. He felt my reservations and quickly moved on to a topic we could equally share. He said,

"Governor Pelzer, for example."

He went on to tell of the senate trial in process at Albany. They were still hearing witnesses. Damaging evidence was being forced out of hiding day by day. The press was given a running digest of the proceedings. By direct telegram and by ravenous consumption of the newspapers, both local and imported—*The New York Times, The Albany Times-Union*—my father followed the trial, seeing himself as he might have been but for his removal and resignation.

"Do you think," I asked Sam, "that Pelzer made my father resign because he saw this coming? What good would it do him to have my father officially out of the way, if he was already exiled across the continent?"

"Thieves' honor, I suppose. Pelzer wanted to prove to the Chippewa people that he was doing everything possible to keep his commitments. Three more reasons. One: because he can't match your father's mind, style, and above all, decency, he hates and fears him, out of vanity. Two: with your father firmly out of the way, the tax swindle might squeak through the legislature. Three: if worse came

[249]

to worst—as it has—then he could feel justified in asking the Chippewa people to get him off by strategic 'contributions,' *videlicet* bribes, to susceptible legislators, which would not be possible if your father had any position left."

"It sounds fatally unrealistic."

"A definition of most politics. Things of the sort have been pulled off at every level of our government—town, county, state, federal."

"Will it work now?"

"I think not, not with all the publicity so far. It's been incredible. But even so, a strong partisan fight is developing which will delay matters some. The party is being idiotic."

"How is Father taking it?"

Sam made a little circle in the air with his brandy glass.

"Some days it seems to get up his Irish, so that he wants to fight; and on other days, he knows he hasn't got the physical fight in him yet, and he goes into absolutely abstract Gaelic gloom, when we almost tiptoe around the house and want to be cross with each other. Lillian, the poor dolt, weeps so much that she powders her eyes before coming to the table, and you want to laugh because her moon face looks like a clown's, where the brimming eyes wash away the powder, and then you want to pat her arm and say 'There, there,' which is what your mother usually does. And then Lillian *really* lets go, rivers run over her cheeks through the talcum." He sighed. "I'm only glad Joanna didn't come out with me, after all. She'd say unlucky things in this atmosphere."

"Are you—?"

"No date set yet, but we think October."

"Good. I think you've had enough of us and our goings-on."

"Rubbidge"—a word of my father's—"we're not done yet, you know."

He looked grim, an expression which made you forget that he was a small man. In his fine neatness, his chiseled look of breeding, and his keen wits under polite control, Sam gave me heart. Abruptly he stood up and said we should go in to see what the others were up to—"as if we didn't know." It was one of those game evenings. In the early days of my return, I welcomed their wasteful distractions.

❧

They had just finished a round, and when they saw Sam and me, they gave up to gossip. Eleanor Saxby, Count, Lyle, and Serena Sage were at the bridge table. At another, Percy Sage and my mother were playing Russian bank. My father had gone to bed. As we came in, Lyle in his bawling nasal voice cried out at me,

"Well, kid, it did the trick, eh? Look how he's changed. My God, youth snaps back and forth, don't it? We sent him lily-white and drooping, and here he is, bronzed and tough. How do you like the real world?"

"Don't talk nonsense."

"You're right. *All things* belong to the real world. But finding out more of them is what I'm talking about. I expect murder is rather maturing, eh?"

"Oh, Lyle," said my mother, "it is nothing to make fun of. You can't make fun of *everything.*"

"What else do you suppose keeps me alive?"

"No, he's right," said Percy with a lift of his left shoulder—an expression of disdain too mild to be offensive. "He has no real *center* to his life."

"Bingo," answered Lyle. "You've said it. You're luckier. You have your money."

"What a peefectly extraordinary remark," said Serena, who thought noticing money was vulgar if you didn't have it, but not if you did have it.

"Yes, money, you know," said Count eagerly. "Do you know about the Wenzel money?"

"The Wenzel—" cried Eleanor Saxby, gathering her full breasts together like possessions to be cherished by her gemmed fingers.

"But let me tell you!" exclaimed Count. "I have the, but *the* whole story!"

First of all, nobody knew where Concha was for several days in her early widowhood, but Count had found out from one of his downtown sources that she had gone to the Loretto nuns at her old school, Saint Vincent's Academy. They had taken her in. In those few days, much had been done.

"You can be sure of that," interrupted Eleanor. "I know what they—"

But Count quelled her with a fierce glance and went on. The two Wenzel sons, so much older than their young stepmother, Concha, and hating her so much, had arranged to buy, after the probate court action should be concluded, the Magdalena ranch and animals from her for a great sum: about half a million: and thus gain control of all of Don Elizario's real property, never to deal with Concha again. But his will, in addition to leaving the ranch to her, had left her all the remainder of his estate in stocks and cash, and she was now "*en*-hormously," said Count, "but *en*-hormously rich, *millones y millones. ¿Cuánto? Creo que,* I think, t'ree, four, millions dollars."

"Really!" exclaimed Percy with new respect.

"But she won't have the faintest idea of what to do with it all, will she," observed Serena.

"Well, *I* know," said Eleanor with her most worldly confidence. "Those nuns got hold of her and they will get the money too. I used to be a Catholic, and my brother is a priest in Milwaukee, and there isn't anything I don't know about how those people get their money and what they do with it."

"What *do* they do with it?" asked Percy. "Aside from running industrial schools where they teach indigent youths how to make crutches to be thrown away at shrines."

Varying degrees of laughter met this, but Eleanor was not to be robbed of her initiative.

"Well," she said, "half of it goes for all those well-stocked rectories, and the other half goes to Rome. The Vatican owns the six largest banks in Europe. Did you know the Pope is a Jew?" she added as both heretic and anti-Semite.

"Eleanor!" exclaimed my mother chidingly, on both counts.

"No, really. It is the best-kept secret in the world, but a cardinal told my brother in Rome once, and then put him under automatic excommunication if he ever told a soul. Well, when he got home, he told me, and then went to Confession. —Why do I make up such nonsense?" She laughed, self-forgivingly.

"I know," said Lyle.

"Why?"

"Because it is in your nature to do so, madam."

"Oh," said my mother, "I keep thinking of that poor girl. She is probably trying to think out her own life, after what she's been through."

"I might go through it for four million dollars," wheezed Eleanor. She turned to me. "Wouldn't you like to marry a rich widow?"

Sam saved me from replying, for he saw that I would be rude.

"Do you mean yourself, Mrs Saxby, or Mrs Wenzel?"

She laughed, tacitly admitting that she had been talking nonsense, and that what she most enjoyed was the sound of her voice, heavy with cigarettes, experience of sex in happier days, scarred lungs, bourbon whiskey, and genial malice.

At the time, I saw and heard all this with confused dislike. What arc could ever connect the world of these people with the life of the earth and its labor, the blind needs of the animal creation, the sorrow of evil and savage death which I had come home from? Moreover, I had briefly become a snob of the bucolic. Now I see them all without scorn or laughter, but only with memory of their various postponements of the fatality which held them in thrall, to their full and anxious awareness.

They were ready to resume their games. Sam went to the library at the other end of the house where on my father's worktable lay the folders of notes for the next chapter—it was still only chapter 3—of *Woodrow Wilson's Theory of Government,* to which Sam, in offhand tact, hoped daily to return my father. On my way to bed, I paused at my father's door. No light showed under it; but he heard me, and he called huskily,

"Come in, Doc."

I opened the door. The hall lamp made a triangular plane of light across the room and reflected dimly on the bed, revealing my father. I stood beside the bed.

"What do you think you should do this fall?" he asked—for we were near to the end of August and we had never made plans for the coming academic year.

"It depends on several things."

"Yes. For one thing, it now seems likely that we won't be returning to Dorchester this year." He seemed healthier for having accepted the idea. "We'll still be pretty far away, won't we?"—and he meant from each other, if I returned to Aldersgate University in New England.

"No," I said, "as long as you stay here, I am going to stay too, and I will apply at the university here, if you approve, and then we can all go home together when the time comes. And that will be fine. Sam has careful plans about things for you there when you're well again."

"He has?"—but he knew it.

"Yes. And I believe him."

"We'll see," he replied, with an impersonation of a judicious attitude; but I heard through his measured words that same energetic belief and joy in public position coupled with honorable ambition which had brought him so swiftly to prominence in the city and the state where he had spent himself so prodigally. "Thank you, Doc, and good night." I started to go. He added, "I want you to be a happy man. I have been. I hope you discover how to be, for yourself, while you are still young."

We said good night. He always made me feel more than he said. Did I now seem unhappy to him? How did parents know things never mentioned?

❧

"Who is calling, please?" I heard Lillian ask in the blithe office voice she used on the telephone. In a moment she came rapidly and heavily to me and whispered as though the telephone could hear, "It is Sister Mary Aquinas, the superior of Saint Vincent's Academy! She wants *you*, Richard!"

"Hello?"

"This is Sister Aquinas at Saint Vincent's. Will you please to come here this afternoon at three o'clock?"

Her voice was cool, commanding, polite, with sibilants exaggerated by the telephone.

I agreed.

"Thank you," she replied. "It seems rather important—" with a hint of suppressed and impatient skepticism, but mannerly.

"Yes, Sister."

I was prompt. The academy sat on a corner lot on the north side of town. It was a pale-red brick building out of the nineteenth century, with windows rounded at the top, half shuttered within, and surrounded by a little procession of thin evergreen trees. I was shown by a novice all in white with downcast eyes into a corner parlor where the daylight scarcely entered through heavy lace curtains above the lower half of closed indoor shutters. On the wall was an enlarged, thinly tinted photograph of old Archbishop Lamy, in whose time the school had been founded by the Loretto sisters, who came originally from Kentucky.

Sister Aquinas did not keep me waiting. She came through the door and closed it, all in a single gesture, while gazing at me with an analytical smile which never left her firm, pallid face.

"Please to sit down." She made an ample but delicate sweep of her long, strong hands, and then chose a chair close to me at right angles. For a silent moment, leaning rigidly forward, she continued her probing inspection of me; and then, for discretion, she cast a habitual glance to right and left, which required her to turn her whole body because of her deep, starched hood, and said,

"There is someone here who desires to see you. I wanted to see you first. She does not yet know that you are here in the house. You know of whom I speak."

"Yes. I think so. —How is she?"

Sister Aquinas glanced upward, leaning slightly back, and shut her eyes up to heaven for a second. Then, recovered,

"You will see. But I have consented to send for you on condition that nothing is said or done to upset her further."

"Upset? I don't wonder."

"I believe you were present at the time of the tragedy?"

"I was."

"And you have not seen her since?"

"Not to talk to. I saw her at the funeral."

"You will keep this visit confidential entirely?"

"Yes, since you ask it."

"There is excellent reason. You will not see her again."

"She is going away?"

"I have not said so."

"No. I see. I will of course never speak of today at all."

"To give scandal is a grave sin. I believe you are to be trusted." In the habit of command, she put her white hand on my sleeve and squeezed my arm with remarkable strength, as if sacredly binding me in duty. "Wait here, Richard. Thank you for coming. Our Blessed Mother will reward you for it so long as you do not betray Her."

She rose. Her full folds and heavy cincture and long rosary swung regally about as she turned and left me, again shutting the door.

In the door were two frosted glass panels. About ten minutes later I saw a blur on their other side and then the door opened slowly and Concha came in. Full of feeling, I called her name and started toward her. She put up her hand to halt me. She was thin and colorless. Her gray eyes were paler for the dark hollows below them. They had found clothes for her which made her look like a grown-up convent girl—a middy blouse, blue serge skirt, black stockings, and buttoned slippers. She seemed years older, yet years more beautiful despite her spiritless bearing. She took the chair of Sister Aquinas and I resumed mine, leaning toward her to let her read my feeling.

There was a long pause. We could hear the academy clock ticking slowly outside in the narrow hall, where it hung on the wall high above the black and gray tessellated slate floor. Finally, we both started to say something at the same time. I fell silent, to hear her.

"—ever seen him since?"

I shook my head.

"Have you prayed for him?"

"No." It had never occurred to me.

"Will you promise me to?"

"After what he—?"

She nodded and two huge tears came and went in her eyes. Repeatedly she played her fingers together and apart as she had done in that rain-blurred ride from the ranch to Magdalena. Having now made a resolve, she took a deep breath and faced squarely toward me. She told me what could hardly be told and—I now knew why—was never to be repeated.

"That night? You know? After it happened to my husband? He

[257]

came to the house. The door was unlocked. I thought it was my husband. I was in bed, I woke up, in the dark. I said, *Are you all right?* but there was no answer and then, and then, he was-he was at me."

With the fewest words she made me know what had been done to her in her terror, and against her will. In my knowledge left over from the Marigold Hotel I remembered how that must have been.

She fought. He almost smothered her to death with her pillow. She screamed unheard. Forcing his way, he hurt her. It was like storm raging upon her. If only she could be dead, then. She was almost dead and at the same time alive, as though out of her head.

"When he discovered how I was— That-that I was a—"

She could not say the word, but when he found that she was a virgin,

"He went wild."

She put her fingers to her eyes as though to keep me from seeing her.

Nobody knew now but the sisters and me.

Her emotional artlessness in wanting to tell me moved me as much as the facts themselves. The usual murmurs of sympathy would have said little. I took her hand. She let it lie in mine limply. It was damp and cold, half alive. She was incapable of physical response of any sort. After a while, staring toward the old archbishop's portrait but not seeing it, or anything else, she said,

"The sisters have places to send people like me. They still like me just like before. They know it wasn't my fault. Nothing like-like it has ever happened to them, but they seem to understand all about it better than I do. They know how to take care of me, and when the baby comes"—she looked away. I tightened my hold on her hand but there was no response. "They know how to take care of it and they have a place to keep it to grow up and all like that. Two of the sisters are going away with me tomorrow. One was my old dramatics teacher." Now she looked at me again. "Sister Superior said I could see you after she met you if she thought it was all right then."

She withdrew her hand and put it across her mouth to muffle a sob. She said,

"I just had to say goodbye to *someone*."

"Concha!"

"Thank you for coming. You—"

There was a blur of a figure at the ground glass, and a discreet sound at the door—the turn of the knob, but no opening of the door, to mark the proper end of the interview. With propriety, she stood up.

"Goodbye, Richard. You were the only one to treat me like a lady."

She approached the door, which opened silently before her. She passed through it to join the one who waited outside. Steps retreated up the slate hallway, turned a corner, and were gone. Concha receded uncritically into whatever her life must be. I was left alone with the open door, and the slow, walking tick-tock of the academy clock. After waiting a moment for someone to come and tell me to go, and no one coming, I let myself out.

What I had heard needed an outburst, in act or thought. What came to me was a mental tirade against Eleanor Saxby. I said to her, "Well, you're right, they've got her, and thank God; and yes, people like you are sometimes right; but for the wrong reasons."

※

Sam woke me up with the news that Governor Pelzer had just been found guilty in the New York state senate trial for his impeachment. Before the day was over he would be out of office, and indictments for perjury, violation of election laws, malfeasance in office, and bribery were waiting for him. In the absence of the lieutenant-governor, the senate would vote within twenty-four hours on a successor who would serve for three months while a special election would be readied to bring a new governor to Albany for the balance of the vacated term—a period of some fifteen months.

"The pressure is on," said Sam.

"For what?"

A spokesman had telephoned the news that if my father would consent, he would be nominated by the Democratic Party to run for governor in the special interim election.

"But don't they understand?"

Oh, they listened, but they were blinded by enthusiasm. Sam had reported faithfully my father's health. Even so, a delegation, chosen from the legislature and my father's original supporters in Dorchester, were talking of coming West immediately to see my father, consult with his physician, and urge the great purgation of the disgrace laid upon the party and the Commonwealth of New York State.

"What does my father say?"

"You'll be amazed. He seemed to lose years of age and all preoccupation with illness when I talked to him half an hour ago. He hedges the issue round with every possible objection, but you can see by the light in his eye that he asks to be overruled, and that he has been given a remarkable second chance."

"But Dr Birch?"

We knew what the answer would be to that question. Later in the day he came to the house and listened to the whole exciting story. He then made a general examination of my father, and ended by saying dryly,

"Not *quite* yet."

My father assured him buoyantly that he felt ever so much better since the news had come. Imagine what this could mean to him: you see, he would accept the call only if he were not forced to endure the rigors of campaigning. He would make it a condition that he would respond only to a genuine draft. Then, once elected (for there was no doubt that he would be elected, even if Mr Coolidge's people should try to intervene from Washington) he would continue to rest for a greater portion of every day. Why, he knew exactly which men in the legislature would carry on most of the work for him . . .

"Delusion," remarked Dr Birch. "As for the decision, I recognize of course that as yours alone."

He departed without saying goodbye. My father looked at Sam. Sam said,

"Another opinion?"

It was a straw. My father clutched at it; and as messages flew back and forth between Albany, Dorchester, and the Rio Grande road, the plan for the visiting delegation grew rapidly, now to include, at enormous expense underwritten by an anonymous backer, sending Dr Morton Frawley with members of Our Crowd from Dorchester. He would consult with Dr Birch, hoping to establish a contrary medical opinion. The delegation would come by the California Limited, stay at the Alvarado, and hold political and medical consultations at the Casa del Rio.

The household seemed to glow with new purpose and optimism. My father was like a boy after a great prize, eager to do more than was asked of him in good behavior. He rested for longer hours each day, slept more every night, took his own pulse and temperature less often than usual to prove that these could tell little of interest, and even wondered if my daily hypodermic injections were really necessary (though he continued to receive them stoically). He delighted us all with his high spirits.

"But not a word," said Sam, warning us all, "to anyone of what is going on. We need the value of one stunning surprise announcement. Nobody should know about our visitors until they have left, when we'll make the news release."

But as Lillian O'Rourke heard these instructions, her proprietary pride in my father and his golden future—for once elected, nobody doubted that he would be re-elected to the full term—betrayed her. Before the delegation arrived, she encountered Serena Sage one day in a shop and under vows of holy secrecy told her what was impending.

❦

My mother, though compliant, was restrained in her view of all the hurried optimistic plans at home. No prize of ambition or obligation to public service meant more to her than her husband's health. Such as she had seen of political life seemed to her more farcical than rational, and founded on a system of expedient treason. How could we be sure—my father, Sam, even myself—that the mighty powers which had supported Pelzer might not throw overwhelming opposition against my father if he consented to run? And how could anyone expect to limit himself in any performance of public duties? She remembered well enough the dreadful campaign summer under which my father had broken down. She had to agree that my father seemed noticeably improved in his condition, but the local lore of what Lyle called the lungers was full of cases of those who had gone home too soon, believing themselves cured, only to collapse again in their return to active life.

"I'll show them how much better I am," my father would protest. "How? Nothing is worth it if there is any risk at all!"

❦

Unwittingly, out of their social sense, Serena and Percy Sage provided an opportunity for my father to prove himself to the delegation.

They came one day to propose that they entertain our visitors.

"Visitors! What visitors?" asked Sam vehemently.

"Ah," said Serena archly, "a little beed told me."

"What little bird?"

Sam guessed soon enough. But the point was, the Sages would give a superb picnic for our guests. They knew a peefectly heavenly spot for a picnic which would give the Easterners a maavelous taste of Western life. It was a little canyon made of ancient lava at the foot of the volcanoes on the horizon west of town across the Rio Grande. We would go in motorcars through the dunes until the sand was too soft and heavy, and then we would walk the rest of the way, perhaps a quarter of a mile, while their "couple" would bring all the hampers, ice buckets, drinks, cushions, and steamer rugs for the picnic lunch. The Sages needed to know only how many guests to expect. How few chances there were "out here" for any fresh events! Always the same faces, the same gossip, the same hectic hopes! And how amusing it would be to start, right here, way out in New Mexico, the campaign for the next governor of New York!

Percy, though a North Shore Republican, said he was *"intrigué"* to be, as it were, sponsoring a Democrat. Back home, politics to him had always been a matter of appearing occasionally at outings with shirt sleeves rolled up, a hot dog in one hand, a handshake in the other, a candidate's name on the hatband of his straw boater, and a general air of having descended from the great house of the neighborhood to exhibit three timely virtues: democracy in action at the lowest level, virility, and highly bred good nature. Even resorting to the chewing of gum, he was the patrician accepting this revolting duty every two years. If his endorsement weighed less with voters than he believed, giving it vested him with a fine eighteenth-century sense of doing a squire's duty—really, he said, a constitutional *privilege* which made him a citizen simple as any other. As for Serena, she was *enchantée* by the idea of the picnic.

To our amazement, my father agreed to it.

My mother shook her head and gave in. But not Lillian. She

advised against the whole venture. Her familiar mood of sustained "gladness" at anything we did gave way to one of her rare stubborn fits. It was possible that she felt remorse for having gossiped to Serena Sage about the political visitation, thus setting off the plans leading up to the picnic. She thought my mother agreed with her about the hazards for my father in any unusual exertion. When my mother sided with him, Lillian felt snubbed and retired into a wounded gloom which was as Irish as her other mood of teary, smiling worship. Her very appearance changed. Despite her heavy flesh, she managed to look haglike, curling her lip in silent foreboding, glaring sideways at the contrary world.

"Oh, Lillian," exclaimed my mother, "for heaven's sake, let the clouds lift."

"Insult me all you please," replied Lillian. "I will stay home and pray. *Some*body has to."

Despite her use of piety to punish others, no plans were changed to mollify her.

"Nobody is to mention this whole thing to Birch," decreed my father.

"No, we know what he would say," said my mother. "I insist upon one thing. Morton Frawley is to come with us to the picnic."

"Naturally. He is a guest, like the others."

※

Dr Frawley was one of those people who are always referred to by their full names. Both tribute and intimacy were established by this for those who liked attachment to eminence, and who enjoyed both names together, provided they were euphonious. Personality added weight to the tradition. Morton Frawley, M.D., was a rather short man whom I had hardly glimpsed in Dorchester. He was trimly built except for a slight thickening about the waist which admirable tailoring almost concealed. His dark hair was thin but brushed so well that it revealed only a brilliant shine instead of a glimpse of pink scalp. He wore thick, rimless glasses which greatly enlarged his eyes to liquid brilliance above his excellent, short, straight nose. He removed his glasses to read. His dark mustache was trimmed to accent his full, ruddy lips. All his patients swore by him, which sometimes meant that they liked him not so much for his skill as for his reassuring charm, which lit up his round face, gave brightness to his cheeks, and made his glance merry. He looked to me like an idealized man of medicine wearing a white coat in an advertisement while holding a test tube up to the light.

With the delegation, he arrived one afternoon on the California Limited. The usual local crowd was gathered nearby to see the great train make its half-hour pause. Who on board for California might take a constitutional along the brick walk by the tracks? Any movie stars? There was sure to be a wheelchair or two for arriving invalids. Worlds away came, paused, and departed with the train.

When the delegation alighted, the Albuquerqueans observed a group of obviously substantial newcomers; and when they saw my father go forward to greet them, a few knew who he was and waved on general principles. He leaned on my arm until he was within a dozen feet of the visitors; then he straightened up, and with his high good nature as evident as ever, his "public" animation at its best, he gave hearty handshakes all around. In the style of his great days, he was dressed in his cutaway coat and all its accoutrements, including a high silk hat, even though they might be out of place in the desert. He knew how well all this became him, for if he had a single visible vanity, it was for dressing up to the nines. Clearly, he made a brilliant impression on his visitors, who had no idea of how much of an invalid to expect.

Dr Frawley was fully indoctrinated about his mission. My father's friends from Dorchester and two from the Albany legislature—one from the senate, one from the assembly—had assured Morton Frawley that provided his medical findings were favorable he would be professionally occupied with the Next Governor of the Empire State. Under expressed concern for my father's welfare, this carried a lively hint of professional prestige by which Morton Frawley (such was his reputation) might be moved. He knew my father's case— had sent him West in the first place, an invalid on a stretcher. Straightway, he would see his old friend and classmate Dr Birch, study X rays, discuss the prognosis exhaustively, and then himself examine the patient. As a professional man, after all, he refused to promise anything before having all evidence before him. Meanwhile, he promised that he would enjoy his first journey to the West, where he had sent so many patients from the icy or steaming, frozen or boiling, climate of Dorchester.

The Albany legislators were substantial men, given to appraising glances, and heavy with paunches, watch chains, and clouds of cigar smoke. My father's friends from Dorchester—the two representatives of Our Crowd—were keen in another way. They had known me since my childhood, and I was supposed to call one of them "Uncle" as a courtesy. They were leaders of their city, they believed what they had sworn to on the watch they had given my father, and they had adopted his reform policies so righteously that their indignation at the Albany scandals concealed any self-interest they might have retained. Though I did not question their real affection for my father, their present anxiety and hope were too visible to be met with comfort. I let Sam play host. They all knew him from the earlier campaign days.

When the two doctors held their conference, nobody else was present. After it was over, Frawley came to the house and spent half a day alone with my father. Escaping the event, I only heard my mother say, "Dan, here is Morton Frawley to see you," and my father reply heartily, and then Frawley exclaim, "Well, you're looking like a very different man from when I saw you last," and then doors closed.

"Iffy."

Morton Frawley was quoted as having given this judgment to the delegation after considering my father's case and the wisdom of going after the election. But he went on to say that, under well-understood and agreed-upon restrictions, the whole notion of a return to politics at present was, actually, not *altogether,* in his opinion, out of the question. His qualified statements were given with what Sam called moist charm. We were told that Our Crowd and the lawgivers were jubilant at this ruling. Everything moved cheerfully toward the day of the picnic at the volcanoes.

❧

The whole land lay a mile high, and to this altitude was added the further grand upsweeps of the mountains at every point of the compass. The mountain air was over all, and at times, taken with a deep breath, it was so light and pure that it made you feel giddy for a moment, in a pang of conscious well-being.

Through miles of diamond-clear light the volcanoes to the west rising from a long, half-buried crust of black lava lay against the far horizon like those man-made deities of Egypt which seemed to become natural earth forms. The volcanoes had been dormant for centuries. Lyle, who fancied local history, said their active time must have been coincident with the prehistoric general volcanic upheaval in northern and central New Mexico, which was remembered with awe in the spoken lore of the Pueblo Indians.

Percy and Serena had found their picturesque picnic spot during Percy's third year at Albuquerque, when he was declared an arrested case for whom it was safe to go exploring the country all about. Not many people went across the river to the entirely vacant sand shelf which stretched far north and south in the foreground of the volcanoes. It was for just this reason that the Sages liked the place. Once, having driven too far into the dunes, their car had been stuck in the scarcely marked sandy road. Now they knew just where to leave the car and walk to the black lava wall where the sand ended, and where a little canyon opened which could not be seen from a distance.

When I said I did not want to go to the picnic, I was overruled: I would be needed to drive one of the cars, and to help fetch and carry picnic supplies—rugs, hampers, ice buckets, along with large, festive standing umbrellas to be opened against the beating heat of the sun. Too, Percy's portable phonograph with its hand crank and his case of records—jazz, which he had lately discovered and was "simply dippy" about, and so should we be, he promised, when we heard Paul Whiteman or Bessie Smith, who was "peefectly killing."

It was a large party, for it included not only our household, the visitors, and the hosts but also Mrs Saxby, Count, and Lyle Pryor (who gave his word not to report the event even confidentially to his newspaper).

With poor grace, I took part in the day, for since returning home, I did not want to see much of anybody.

We drove out in three cars, crossing the wooden bridge over the Rio Grande at Barelas. In my car were Eleanor Saxby, Lyle, Sam, a member of Our Crowd, and Dr Frawley. As we crossed the sandy riverbed, the doctor exclaimed,

"But where is the water? I thought the Rio Grande was an enormous river!"

"Look how wide it is," replied Lyle.

"But it's two thirds dry sandy bottom!"

"So it is. But its flow and depth are not to be seen here," said Lyle irritably. Like many new residents, he had become proprietary about the Southwest.

"Then where?"

"In history. The river itself has never been as deep as its name."

"What on earth are you two palavering about?" exclaimed Mrs Saxby, who had other plans for herself and Dr Frawley which had nothing to do with local history. At her most confident, if overblown, femininity, she appropriated her new friend Morton Frawley with an opening move in the game of important mutual friends, and in five minutes, she had brought him to acknowledge four persons, all of whom, carefully chosen for mention, were prominent in one or another way, but chiefly through wealth. Of these, her triumph, acknowledged by Dr Frawley with a frank new appraisal of her, was her establishment of intimacy with the Ramson family of Dorchester ("steel") on whose Great Lakes steam yacht, the *Marianna,* she had been a guest.

"Oh, yes, Teddy and Marianna Ramson are great friends of mine," said Dr Frawley, comfortably continuing the game.

The caravan was led by Percy and Serena in their seven-passenger touring car. Percy drove with the top down for the sake of the bronze sunburn which gave him his cosmetic health. Heading toward the sands, his car carried his wife, my father and mother, the other member of Our Crowd, and the New York state legislators. The last car of the column contained the picnic ingredients and the Sage servants—the only "couple" in domestic service in Albuquerque—and Count, who carried an oddly shaped leather case.

High spirits animated the expedition, which Percy called an "outing." We drove for about fourteen miles, and then, at a signal with lifted arm from Percy in the leading car, we halted in the heavy sand of the road, which faded into the dunes.

"Everybody out!" he called gaily. "It's shanks' mare from here on!"

I glanced at Dr Frawley.

"How far?" he asked, thinking, as I was, of my father—could he safely walk under the blazing zenith through sand which would drag at every step we took?

"Percy Sage says no one can drive all the way. Cars get stuck in the sand," I said, "but he says his little picnic place is much less than half a mile farther."

Frawley frowned.

"You and I," said Mrs Saxby, flaring her nostrils like a fine thoroughbred mare retired from the track, "will walk with Dan and take care of him."

"You'd make a gorgeous nurse," replied the doctor, flirting on the sort of reflex which had gained him the reputation of being a *dashing bachelor* and *fast*. The compliment did not entirely please Eleanor for the social level it assigned to her.

※

When I was a very small boy I used to imagine the nearest and most common of conditions or events as tremendous. A certain thicket of rose bushes in our garden I was able to transform, thanks to fairy tales, into a dense forest filled with hidden rewards and thorned menace. The little lake in the park faced by the museums near which we lived became the Atlantic Ocean, where I could rehearse odysseys already traced with a finger on the globe which stood in its tripod by my father's library desk. The Alps on occasion were no greater than the sierras of not yet muddy snow piled up along the streets of Dorchester by snowplows the day after one of our Great Lakes blizzards.

Now, in my state of mind, the walk through the dunes on that early September day became for me a crossing of a desert. Time was suspended, distance was measureless. With all the others I toiled, conscious of every step through the sand. My breath came shorter because of exertion in that altitude. The sand dragged heavily at our feet, but how heavily I did not know until ahead of me my father

[270]

faltered for a moment and put his hand to his side. Eleanor and Frawley leaned sharply toward him. I heard the doctor say, "Perhaps a few minutes' rest?" but my father shook his head and ground his jaw forward and immediately resumed his trudging against the sand. The others were all ahead of us. No one else saw the incident. The official future was intact. I saw our file as little moving dots on a horizonless tableland of an undiscovered continent.

At last, and suddenly, over the crest of a dune, we came to the pitted sloping face of the old lava flow, and there before us was a narrow cleft leading into deep shade, which we gratefully entered. The little canyon opened out as we went farther. One wall was in shadow, the other in sunlight. The canyon floor was sandy and irregular, and Percy halted us at a spot where separate hunks of lava lay about, close to each other like furniture placed at regular intervals.

"I call this place Stonehenge or the Henge for short," he cried, as though it was his creation. "Isn't it scrumptious?"

The couple began disposing steamer rugs over the rocks and on the sandy floor, and Percy himself set up a long folding table of aluminum, which was soon covered with a pink linen cloth. Rows of food and drink began to appear there. The organization was flawless. The mood of the laborious walk was transformed into a festive air. My father, glistening with sweat from the walk, was animated and outgoing, as he always used to be when surrounded by people for whose comfort and pleasure he assumed responsibility whenever they had assembled for his sake.

"Isn't it remarkable!" exclaimed my mother when I came to her with an iced drink. "He really can *do anything,* can't he, when he thinks others depend on him!" But this was as much a plea for reassurance as an admission of a marvel.

The party settled down.

"How do you like my Henge?" demanded Percy.

"You buy it," said Lyle, "and build a grand hotel *and* a paved road, and a fine restaurant and a bootleg bar, and I'll manage it for you."

But he was still panting and pale from the walk.

"I could never," replied Percy, opening a hamper of deviled eggs and caviar, "have anything to do with a business which catered to people's *appetites* in any way." He shuddered. "People become *beasts* if anything goes wrong when they order drink or food or beds."

Mrs Saxby gave one of her coughing laughs and spoke through cigarette smoke.

"You're so right, Percy. There's only one appetite that can give satisfaction just about every time." She wheeled her prominent gaze on Morton Frawley and added, "That is best managed by ladies of the profession, one at a time."

"You tell 'em, kid," said Lyle. He was breathing easier. "Have you ever tried it?"

Mrs Saxby took this as so preposterous as to amount to a racy compliment. She turned the sexual reference into a full-bosomed blandishment, once again in the direction of Dr Frawley, who gave her a ribald gleam which made her blush.

"My God, I'm blushing," she declaimed hoarsely. It was her policy to draw attention openly, even at her own expense.

Percy waved the company to serve themselves at the picnic table.

Nobody hurried to move, but Frawley, after an inquiring look about at everyone lounging on cushions and rugs, said, "I am famished, it must be the altitude," and under polite control, he went to the table, took up his plate, and, leaning forward over the delicious array, he inspected the dishes from one end to the other. His lips worked as he rehearsed the flavor of each dish before him. He moved his sleek head in pleasure as he looked closely from one to another platter or bowl or slicing board. His whole body was tensed with appetite. He seemed to postpone the delight of choice as he let his fork hover above now this, now that, enticing dish. He swallowed once or twice as the juices of taste began to run in his mouth. He made me think of a fastidious buyer shopping for exactly the article he had come to find. At last, darting his fork at a succession of dishes, he became the brilliant surgeon who knew his work so well that he never wasted a movement. When his plate was full, he turned and saw that we were all watching him. Sweeping his fork over us all, he inquired in well-managed surprise, "Am I the first?" and without further delay sat on a rock and began to eat. Percy ordered the champagne opened. Frawley had bestowed well-being upon everyone by his frank and jolly response to the food. The picnic was already a success, and was given democratic sanction when Percy unbuttoned his starkly plain gold cuff links and rolled up his shirt sleeves. My father and his visitors drew aside by unspoken agreement and ate their lunch as a separate little group, talking politics. Sam was with them. The rest of us subsided into the usual banter. My mother almost never took her eyes off my father, at the same time helping to keep alive the gaiety required by the event. I berated myself for not being able to add to it.

"Cheer up, kid," said Lyle, "nothing lasts forever."

※

While the political conference went on in deep shadow several rocks away, Count brought out the odd oblong leather case which he had carried to the picnic. It showed many scars in spite of much polishing. From it he produced a narrow, flat, stringed instrument—a really old vihuela, the ancestor of the more familiar guitar.

"To entertain," he said, watching himself with coy modesty as he began tuning his pegs. "I will sing for you." Another minstrel of that summer.

"Why, Count!" exclaimed Eleanor. "You never told us. You are talented!"

The rest of us reclined in the hot shadow of the little canyon wall. Lighted as in a theater by the upward reflected glare from the sand where Count now stood in full sunlight, we made a random pattern of shape and color as we waited in stillness. Count struck an elegant, sloping attitude. In his straw boater, his old striped blazer, his yellowed white flannels, he impersonated a juvenile leading actor. I could imagine theatrical make-up on his narrow face, with his eyebrows darkened and raised to give an expression of sad innocence.

With his ancient, sparsely strung bow, he scratched a few long chords; and then in an astonishing tenor voice with a rapid bleating pulse to it, he sang an elaborately ornamented melody after the flamenco style:

> *Sierras de Gra-na———da,*
> *Montes de Ara———gón,*
> *Campos de mi pa———tria,*
> *Para siempre adiós, adiós,*
> *Para siempre adiós . . .*

The vihuela despite his scratchings had a mellow sound. He contrived a throbbing emotion with the unlikeliest means—his middle-aged imitation of a fine, youthful singer, his intense but unmusical voice, his swaying posture. Lost in what he sang, he was a Count we had never seen. Far from entertaining us, he was rapt in lament as old as the history of his province in Spain.

"How curious," murmured Serena.

"He makes me nervous, what's he saying?" whispered Eleanor to me, refusing to allow real feeling to reach her.

"He is saying goodbye to the mountains and plains of his homeland," I whispered back. "It is a song by Enrique Granados."

"I don't care who it's by, have him stop!" and she put her hands over her ears.

Luckily, Count was so carried away that he heard and saw none of the embarrassment which his performance put upon us all. As music, it was so excruciating, as feeling, it was so powerfully forlorn, that we all knew we were in the presence of the real creature behind the daily gloss of a desire to ingratiate with his elegance of manner. The light bore upon us upward from the brilliant sand. The desert stretched away, the distant mountains and the day's far-gathering thunderheads made us all small in the wilderness, and Count smallest of all, yet the only one of us at the moment to assert his ultimate solitariness openly, like a lone locust energized by the boundless heat of space.

❀

By four o'clock we were back home at the Rio Grande house, where my father retired to rest. The visitors would return for dinner—all but Morton Frawley, who had been captured by Eleanor Saxby for the evening. She had access to a raffish speakeasy at the mouth of Tijeras Canyon in the mountains twelve miles east of the city. She promised him a glimpse there of what was left of the frontier spirit in Albuquerque. She would call for him at the Alvarado Hotel in her *tin lizzie,* and they would set out on an evening and—who knew?—perhaps a night of adventure.

"She is a masterpiece of self-protective ambiguity," said Sam to me, for we both heard these arrangements being made. "She leaves it to Frawley to turn the adventure either way for the night. I promise you, he will be safely tucked away in his hotel room by ten o'clock. I would venture that the overpowering Eleanor is not his type."

"What happened at the picnic conference?" I asked him.

"Well: first of all, it was a reunion—it gave them all honest pleasure to be with the Governor again. A little small talk, and a few glances exchanged over the problem of how to get to the point. But your father dug them out of their diffidence by saying they must be quite certain that they had no other candidate in mind. No, no, they said, there was now less than three months' time until the

[275]

special election—under the state constitution, you know—and there was not time to build up another candidate, and in any case, they didn't want anyone else. Your father's campaign for lieutenant-governor was recent enough so that every voter knew who he was, and why he was elected with such a wide margin on the Democratic ticket."

"Was there any health talk?"

"Of course. But they insisted that such a short time was to his advantage, for the reason that it would not tax him with a long, drawn-out campaign. Furthermore, they would even so make certain that he was spared every possible exertion."

"So?"

"He gave them each his steady, blue, keen look with his head slightly lowered, you know the look, and then he said briskly, Very well, he would run, provided—and here he had a moment's fun, for he held them up with a finger until they got uneasy—provided he could name his own lieutenant-governor. Oh, if that was all, they said; certainly; and did he have anyone in mind? Yes, he said, he had, but he would not say who just yet. They nodded modestly. None of them presumed to guess *he* might be the one, but you could absolutely see the thought cross some of the faces. It was a clever move, and then it wasn't long before we began to think of names for the usual committees. The Dorchester crowd said they knew where they could get plenty of clean money. The Albany types said they could speak with authority for overwhelming support in the State House. I put in my oar by saying that we would have 90 percent of the press with us. We all got agreeably carried away and saw a landslide as inevitable."

"Are you for it?"

How orderly Sam looked when he was direct and serious—his dark gleam of gaze through his spectacles, which oddly made him look handsomer than he was. Intelligence was visible in every feature of his finely carved face.

"Well, you know," he replied. "I'd rather see the Governor *write*

[276]

that book, just to be absolutely safe about the physical thing, and then try the political thing next time round. But he has decided to 'go,' and I'll work my hide off for him. He knows I'd gladly make a career out of serving him all the way, and I don't think there's any limit to how far he can go. Some people are born to play second lead with distinction. I'm one. —You've had a good life with him, haven't you?"

"With both of them"—my parents. "I think I've been selfish and clumsy, never to let them know how much I feel for them."

"Do you want to help them now?"

"Of course. Why?"

"Well, if you don't mind, I'll risk a word of avuncular advice." He made a comic gleam through his glasses.

"Go ahead. You're all of eight years older than I."

"Thank you. You've been pretty depressed lately. Whatever happened during the summer, do try to shake yourself free and get back to your old outgoing self. You probably never saw it, but I've seen it many times, the look on your father's or mother's face when they used to see you coming back to them any old time. It made them happy simply to look at you if you were happy. I'd like to see that look on their faces again. —D'you mind?"

He was in no way asking for confidences. He was posing a case for civilized behavior, and the power of love. He struck home in a way which released me from the self-absorbing ache left over from the events of the summer.

"I know," continued Sam, "that nobody can be happy on command. But for the sake of others, you can impersonate it. And habit, you know, has its own power. —I know something about this, or I wouldn't harangue you about it."

Without adding a word, then, he alluded to his coming marriage, and the deliberate concessions it required of him in order to give Joanna the possessive certainty she sought. He knew when to desist now. I needed no more advice.

"I've got some wires to send about today's conference," he added.

"There will be interesting speculative stories from a confidential source in tomorrow's *New York Times*. See you at dinner. There will be a windup conference afterward in the library."

For the first time since I had come home I was able to take a full, deep breath.

❧

After dinner I sat alone with my mother in the patio, while deep in the house the political visitors, Sam, and my father worked on the text of an official announcement to be released in Albany on the following Monday.

"I will allow them five more minutes," said my mother. "He is much more tired than he admits."

There was a little while of thoughtful silence. Then she said, roaming aloud in her thought,

"I keep thinking of poor Mo Pelzer. Isn't it dreadful to climb up over someone else's disgrace!"

"I thought you didn't like the Past Grand Orphic Sibyl."

"I don't. But I feel sorry for her—and for Governor Pelzer, I suppose, though that strains Christian charity."

"But he's a crook, and she's an overdressed pineapple."

My mother laughed in spite of herself.

"You're dreadful."

"We've always known that," and then, under my new policy, I said, "But what a fine day we had."

"Yes, in some ways."

She reached for my hand and held it. Presently she said, with some odd mixture of sadness and love,

"Do you really know the man he is?"

"Oh, yes."

"You will know it even more when you are married yourself, and know what it is to make one life out of two."

"Of three."

"Yes, three. It has been three, hasn't it, darling?"

She let my hand go and reached her arms toward the amazing stars and the idea of heaven. My feeling rushed up in me so fully that I was afraid to show it. I stood up.

"I think I'll turn in, Mother."

"Sleep well, dear."

I started to go. She suddenly called, strangely urgent,

"But I wonder . . ."

"Yes?"

A sigh, then,

"Nothing, *nichts*. Good night, dear heart."

I lingered a moment, for when something troubled her, she often refused it to us at first, only to change her mind and speak out. But she kept silent now, and I left her alone.

❊

How strange, when I felt before I heard great disturbance of the night in the far end of the long house. When I heard my mother cry out, I sat up wondering. There were doors, and there were steps running. Then came knocking on my door, and before I reached it Sam, calm and desperate, threw it open, saying,

"Hurry, Richard, quickly as you can, get to the car and drive like hell and bring Frawley here. He's much nearer than Birch. Hurry, for God's sake. The Governor is hemorrhaging. I have called an ambulance. Frawley must ride to the san with him and do what he can. I've talked to him, he cannot get a taxi this late. Your mother is holding on. Please, now, Richard."

He ran back to the other end of the house. By now I was enough dressed. I ran out to the car and wild in my gut drove to the hotel where they told me Frawley's room number, not detaining me because I looked as I did. I ran up the tiled stairway to the second floor. He was waiting with his door open. He had thrown a light topcoat over his pajamas and he wore his bedroom slippers. He ran to the car with me while the night clerk stared at us. At the curb a Mexican motorcycle policeman was standing by my car with its lights on and its engine running as I'd left it. When he began to ask questions, I shouted "Emergency," and, pointing to Frawley, "Doctor!" and at the policeman himself, "Help! Run ahead of us, please, we have to go fast, the old Wenzel place out on the Rio Grande road!" We raced through the city. It was empty and faintly lighted. A few forlorn night figures stood still to watch us tear by. As we came to the river road we threw up dust and gravel and at last reached the house, where all the lights were on. Lillian in her blue flannel bathrobe stood in the open front door waiting for us with her hands clasped to her breast like the Madonna, her dun-yellow hair falling around her shoulders. Her silent terror made her impressive for the first time. We raced past her into the house and down the corridor to the far bedroom, where in my mother's arms my father was leaning half upward while the blood of his life was choked forth on the towel she held to his lips. In his stare we read everything he knew now to be true. My mother ever so gently gave way to Frawley and came to stand with me, trembling within my arm. Her face was white as this paper, her eyes pouring with light amidst the sunken shadows of her cheeks. When Frawley said over his shoulder, "A bowl of ice," it was she who freed herself from my grasp and went to fetch it. Frawley made a pack with the ice in a towel and placed it about my father's neck and over his chest and slowly eased him to lie flat, keeping his hand on my father's forehead for reassurance. My mother held my father's right hand from the other side of the bed. Lillian came in and knelt at the foot of the bed, praying her rosary into her thumbs, her eyes blind with tears. I felt myself growing cold, seeing everything as happening to strangers while every feeling went dead within me; for I was saving myself by noting specifically every detail of the scene with a recording eye and ear, so that when the ambulance came, making noise on the gravel of the driveway, and Sam went to show the orderlies in with their stretcher, I could not make a move to help in any way but watched them take up my father and lay him on the pallet and carry him out to the ambulance. Frawley followed to ride with them to Saint Anthony's. He beckoned my mother to come with him, at the same time conveying to the rest of us to follow in our car. Sam telephoned the hospital once more to say we were now coming and they were to have a room prepared and people waiting in the emergency entrance where the nurse and intern on duty remembered my father and acted rapidly to do everything needed. So it was done by the time Sam and Lillian and I arrived and were told which room on which floor. We went up in the grindingly slow elevator to step into the long corridor, which was sibilant with distant hollow sounds and terrible with pale-yellow electric light making watery reflections in the polished brown linoleum of the hospital floor which led us to the door of the emergency operating room, where nurses came and went. From inside the wide door held ajar came obscure sounds, and the mystery of them brought me a stifling return of feeling so great that I said to myself, "My father," and "Oh, my God, I am heartily sorry for all my sins," as if by a crisscross of facts I were guilty of bringing my father to die that night in Saint Anthony's. But he did not die. By the earliest daylight limning the mountains he was still with us. My mother came from his side into the corridor, reaching quietly for us like an old woman for whom there is nothing more to know, and said,

"Morton Frawley says we must get some rest. There is no immediate danger now. Richard, will you take me home?"

My father, as I knew him, never left Saint Anthony's again.

Their farewells were in every detail correct, but it was plain that the delegation departed in rueful bitterness. Their hopes fell disastrously with my father's. The lesson was all too plain. Dr. Frawley had more address than the others, and took a little time, holding my mother's hand, to explain what his clinical practice had taught him.

"Yes, you see, there is an odd correlation—I have seen it so often before—between tuberculosis and optimism. I am afraid that it sometimes marks an approaching downturn for the patient; but meantime he feels almost visionary. Undue euphoria, you know. In your husband's case, it took the form of a revival of his ambition and the belief that he would again be equal to its pursuit."

My mother was less theoretical.

"Oh!" she cried, roughly fingering the tears which came to her eyes, "I could kill Percy Sage for making him walk all that way in all that sand . . ."

"Yes, that concerned me gravely," said Dr Frawley. "I myself was conscious of temporary fatigue when we finished crossing the dunes."

"But why did you let him do it?"

He gently touched her arm and replied,

"Ah, but there were many other factors. T.b. is full of surprises. It was a combination of events. I am afraid we have to look chiefly to your husband's hopes to explain his setback."

"Setback! Dr Birch thinks he is very gravely ill!"

"I have seen Jamie Birch this morning. We agree. But I am hopeful that lost ground can be regained."

"You mean that Dr Birch does not think so?"

"I do not speak for him."

Morton Frawley said this with a slight wryness, for evidently Birch had quarreled with him over his leniency in the case, and they had parted with coolness, in spite of which Frawley had prevailed on Birch to continue in charge of my father's cure. Dr Frawley smiled winningly. His hair, glasses, and bright cheeks shone together.

"You must bear with Jamie Birch. At Cornell Medical we all used to call him Jamie Grouch."

"Well, I wish we had borne with him day before yesterday," said my mother, rising to end the farewell interview. I was allowed to take Frawley to the door, where Mrs Saxby was waiting to drive him to the station. There, until the eastbound California Limited arrived, she could fill his every social cavity with impacted messages for the Ramsons and "all that crowd."

As they drove away, a delivery car arrived with a huge box of flowers for my mother. Lillian brought it to her in the patio gallery, where we were waiting for the time of our daily visit to Saint Anthony's.

"Do open it for me, Lillian dear," said my mother.

Lillian tore away the wrappings and found a card which she held up and read aloud:

Dreadfully sorry to hear the unfortunate news, and sure all will be well, much love, Percy and Serena.

Lillian gasped.

"*Dreadfully sorry!*" she repeated. "They'd better be—*and so should you!*" she added in a shriek to my mother.

"*Lillian!*"

"Don't *Lillian* me!" She threw the enormous flower box to the floor and trampled it. Her face went white and red in patches. Tears seemed not to be dropped but flung from her eyes into the air. Her huge throat quaked in spasms as she tried to make the words which her grief kept choking off. What she was trying to say was that my mother was guilty of criminal neglect: that poor darling of a man: to be dragged out of bed to go off on a crazy spree like that: what was she thinking of: nobody who really loved him would ever have—

"Shut up, Lillian!" I shouted.

"Lillian, *dear*," said my mother, going to her.

Lillian backed away, throwing her arms about.

"Don't touch me! Nobody knows what I've been through all these years, and now to see him—"

My mother gave me a look. *How she loves him!* it said, after "all these years" when we had made a comfortable joke about Lillian's slavish and satisfying service to my father.

My mother could always prevail. She held her arms out to Lillian and said mildly,

"I know it is mostly my fault, and may God forgive me, Lillian, and he needs you now more than ever, and so do I, so do I!"

With that, Lillian went hugely soft and collapsed against my mother, weeping now in remorse upon the shoulder of the wife of the man she adored and mourned. Her ugliness in grief hardened my heart; but not my mother's.

"I know, I know," she said, leading Lillian off down the gallery at the patio side. I picked up the box of flowers and took them to a garbage can on the back porch. Half an hour later, when I happened through the house again, I saw remnants of the flowers arranged in two huge vases, one at each end of the library table.

❧

It seemed almost like his decision—my father's swift descent to inert invalidism. Daily his resources, visible and invisible, diminished. When we went to see him at Saint Anthony's, either together, my mother and I and Lillian, or any of us alone, we sat for the most part in silence to spare his replying. We had our separate styles of encouragement.

My mother, using her little habit of rapidly blinking both eyes at once as she smiled against any mournful aspect, always prepared herself with a few bits of news, and even, when desperate, made some up. Then she would read to him until he signaled that she might rest for a while. Now and then he would use a single word to ask for a report—"University?" and she would tell him how matters went with me in my enrollment and classes at the university on the mesa. I went there now to give a semblance of a future to our time in New Mexico. He nodded on his pillow at the good manners, if not the good sense, of this. My mother never played nurse—pulling at pillows or window shades or asking if he wanted any special delicacies to interest his appetite. She was real with him, never implying anything but the truth about his condition, but never, either, relinquishing the future for them together, which she refused to give up. He hungered for her every time she had to obey hours and leave him. I thought I could see a whole vision of their past in his eyes. He held her hand with his, which now consisted of veins and bones; and the beauty in his face with all its new hollows and shadows was something to enrage me for what it could not enact. And then, almost within a step or two of the door closed behind us, my mother would let her courage falter, and she would show her terror and her love, almost feverishly. Sometimes we would encounter Dr Birch in the corridors alone; and he would show her a sort of deathly tenderness.

Lillian, on the other hand, when she was with my father, thought it proper to make her full face long, subdue her voice, tiptoe, and cause her soft, occupying presence to totter a little as she strove to force her sympathy into polite acceptance of disaster. Her Celtic taste for broken hearts and the infinite mercy of God gave us a delicate problem, for it became necessary to invent reasons why she should not come as often, or stay as long, as she wanted to, since her presence depressed my father until all he could do was pretend to fall asleep when she came; and then he had to listen to her massive tiptoeing and clever rearranging of objects in the hospital room as she worked at leaving little surprises for him when she should be gone and he should awaken.

On the morning after he had been hurried to Saint Anthony's she began a series of novenas to Saint Jude in the Church of the Immaculate Conception on Sixth Street, where Father Agostini, the old Italian Jesuit who had come as a youth under Archbishop Lamy fifty years before, gave her communion, and crossly tried to conceal his awareness of her tears, which were like those in plaster relief on the face of the Madonna-at-the-Foot-of-the-Cross to whom she prayed so barrenly.

There was no office work for her to do now, for all matters were being handled by the manager of the Dorchester office; and Sam— Sam, at my father's insistence, had left us to go East to Joanna. We soon received engraved cards (made by Shreve, Crump and Low) announcing their imminent marriage. At almost the same time came a letter from Sam announcing his appointment as dean of James Monroe College, the century-old institution with its special style in northern New York State which would suit him like an inconspicuously good garment. It also had a certain social cachet which would bring pleasant opportunities to Joanna. Since my father was done with politics, so was Samuel Dickinson.

And I: I watched the man born for great affairs see them recede from him, until he seemed to hear of them as in a dream. When his strength allowed, he would ask me in his husky whisper what the news was, and I assumed Sam's role of keeping him informed of how matters went at home, until the special election was over, and the Speaker of the Assembly had been elected to fill out the unexpired term which had held so much power over our family affairs. After that matter was done with, my father's interest waned, though now and then, when a flicker of his old humor and scorn managed to rise through the melancholy which had him gazing at nothing by the hour, he would ask me for news of "Mr Coolidge," and he would speak of him as "heir to our national Pelzer." I hardly ever heard him swear or resort to ugly language (my education in this art reached new heights under J. Buswell Rennison), but one day when I had to inform him that Judge Pelzer had been taken to Ossining, my father murmured, "Poor bastard." The sincerity of this effort, with all its crowding reminders of failure, sent him off to sleep. His head rolled slightly to one side, so that the light caught it in a slanting caress, making the bony structure both brighter and more deeply shadowed.

As the afternoon light failed, I sat for a long time looking at him, both through memory and a desire to find some analogy of experience ample enough to contain a sense of his life in a dimension of the heroic. In this I was looking also for an image of human life at large, and, I suppose, I was combining both visions as a response to youth's search for metaphors, in the absence of reasons.

The vast lake with its oceanic and common waters obeyed the wonderful physical law which caused it to seek always a lower level toward the all-accepting sea. So, as it narrowed at one end, and the altitude of the land gradually fell, the lake was channeled into a river. Out of the nowhere of the great lake came a new form, contained and defined by banks. Flowing placidly but with vigor, it was beautiful between its groves. For as far as you could see, the river's course was unimpeded, consistent, purposeful. It could even be governed by those who knew how. But presently, in its long serene progress, the river flow encountered obstacles. Rocks below the surface revealed changes in its bed. Hazardous rapids made ruffles of white water and sudden sweeps of emerald sheen as the current swept around rocky sluices. And then far ahead the air was increasingly filled with a roar of tumbling waters and clouds of mist flying upward. Almost before warning, the level flow, pressed by the volume of the lake far behind, and the confining riverbanks, lost the supporting bed of the land, and then, beyond suddenness, the waters fell fearsomely and gorgeously downward, so that anyone watching was lost in the hypnotic pull of that vast fateful tumble. I remembered myself throughout my childhood and after, in the groves, on the banks, and at the brink of the Niagara, where I had obeyed the need to keep life; and there, too, loomed my father and his whole course, from the illimitable reservoir of past humanity to his narrow lifetime, and his fall.

[287]

One day I brought him the mail. One of the envelopes held a little
weighty bulk, and he looked at it for a long moment before opening
it. I had noticed that it came from one of the most intimate members of Our Crowd. Ever since the time of the picnic, my father had
now and then shown a depressed concern over his failure to justify
the eager hopes they had all had of him. He had "let them down."
They must think pretty poorly of him now. It was a sorry thing to
lose lifelong friends. I had heard enough of this to assume that such
thought was running in his mind now, for he was wearing the
deliberately empty face which he assumed when his deepest emotion
was at work. This all changed when he opened the envelope and out
fell a little packet wrapped in tissue paper which yielded up a gold
watch chain with a round gold pendant. On the pendant was an
engraved message. He leaned toward the light with it and his face
broke into the first full smile since he had re-entered Saint Anthony's. Too moved to speak, he silently handed the gold chain and
medallion to me. I read the inscription: *Representing the chain of
our friendship you have wrought so well.*

He had not let them down. If a man could wear a watch he still
had time to live. This is what his friends were telling him. He was
grateful. But he was also responsible and real in his knowledge. He
said to me, trying to let some extra resonance into his breathy voice,

"Richard, will you do something for me now?"

"Of course, Father."

"Do you remember the key?"

"The key?"

He showed a sad impatience by shaking his head on the pillow.

"Yes, yes, the bank key I gave you and told you to keep for
me!"

"Oh, yes. I have it in my room—the key I used to put that
portfolio into the safety deposit."

He rested his breath for a moment, then said,

"Go to the bank and take out the leather envelope. You will find two sets of letters inside."

His excitement was rising. Trying to save him effort by anticipating him, I said,

"I see. You want me to bring them to you?"

"No, no"—irritably—"I want you to burn them all."

"Oh."

He thought for a moment; then,

"One is a set of letters written by me. I think I want you to read those. The other set I want you to burn without reading them. Is that clear?"

"Yes."

"You may be shocked, but if you think less of me afterward, you are not yet the man I expect you to be."

"I see."

"No, you don't. But you will. —When you have the letters, the box will be empty. Pay off the rent and return the key to the bank. We have no more use for it."

"Do you want me to do this right away?"

"Now. Today. I want to know it has been done, while I have time to know."

I made a gesture to deny his meaning, but he rejected my loving fakery, and said,

"We all know what we know. —What time is it?"

I told him.

"The bank is still open. Go now, Richard, and thank you, boysie" —using a nursery name I had not heard for almost twenty years.

I hurried to the bank, made my transaction, and then went to my river glade. The afternoon was coming in rays through the broken vaultings of my trees. A few feet away the little river sounds gave life to the stillness. I unlocked the leather envelope. I recognized my father's handwriting on a bundle of perhaps three dozen letters. But I recognized also the hand, in violet ink, on the top envelope of the other bundle, which was tied with a little ribbon of the violet velvet

[289]

with which florists used to tie Parma violets in a little bunch, such as my mother, and her friends, in the fashion of their time, would pin to their waists indoors, or, if festively going out into the deep white winters of Dorchester, to their furs.

※

The letters in violet ink were written by the woman who was the first passionate love of my life—that person of grace, realism, and unhappiness who was the closest friend of our household. At the edge of my adolescence I called her Aunt Bunch, though we were not related. She was in her middle thirties, I was twelve or thirteen, but with playful charm she erased the distance between our ages and let me live seriously in my love for her, while she returned my feeling tenderly and with lovely absence of mockery, ignoring the amused condescension with which all others watched our affair. She was married to a much older man, dry, rich, finicky, who had never given her a child. She saw me, I knew later, as her child as well as her chaste lover. Perhaps all women so see their truly loved men. Her eyes were violet-blue, her hair was heavy and pale golden. She wore it rather loosely gathered about her softly modeled face, whose complexion made me think of white and pink peonies. I called her Aunt Bunch from childhood because she habitually wore or carried a bunch of Parma violets, which went so wonderfully with her eyes, as I once heard my father tell her, and I recognized the truth of this, which I had not seen for myself. It was a discovery of the harmony of color and style as they expressed an innate nature. I loved her awake and dreaming, with only the remotest stirrings of sex, until the day came when at a certain age I unintentionally saw her making love with my father's business partner, a young officer just before he was to go overseas with the army in the 1914 war. My world crashed, and so perhaps did hers. But our worlds were mended for us both before too long—I began growing up, and she helped me by denying nothing of her unfaithfulness. Her beauty and her indulgence of my fantasy about her had made me think of her as virtue itself. Years later, as I read the letters which were to be burned while my father still lived, to be sure they were destroyed, I saw her as she was, exalted by making the gift of her love. She gave it to my father, who found it too precious to refuse. They were lovers.

His letters told me this and more. He suffered for betrayal. Weak before his secret desire, he was anguished in his love for my mother, which did not lessen, as his letters made clear. How could this be? Yet it was. The lovers had hopes which called from afar, impossibilities which could only be held away by brief fulfillments with no promises for the future. When her husband died, it seems that Aunt Bunch wondered if perhaps—but no, no, there could be no thought of my father's ever leaving us for her. He loved my mother, he loved me, and yet passionately he told Aunt Bunch she must never leave him.

What prodigies of skill they summoned to keep their affair secret. What private delights in their very secrecy. Qualms of hypocrisy came now and then to them both. My mother was her best friend— how could she do this to her? And yet she did, and could be forgiven only in his arms. When he expressed his own feelings of untrustworthiness, he, a leading figure in the blameless life of the community leader, the husband brilliant in his happy marriage, what velvety reassurance she gave him with her love, for apparently she promised that she would die before ever endangering his position either in his family or before the public.

I read on, page after page, seeing my father turning and turning in a new light; and between little surges of anger on my mother's behalf, and even of irrational jealousy on my own, I felt a mingling of exaltation and pity for this buried life shared by two people whom I loved so greatly.

My father's letters spared me nothing. How could it have been otherwise, with a man so handsome, so full of blue fire in the eye, piercing charm in the character, excellence of the body, who followed so hotly upon life?

Like little shutters opening upon memory, moments came back to me. I thought of the time when I overheard my father say to her at our house that she had never looked so beautiful in her life and that—he laughed delightedly—he supposed she couldn't help it. I saw, but could not then read, the look she returned to him—one so wishful and yet so hopeless that if I had been older I might have known what must one day follow.

I wanted to take down passages of the letters, for the lovers were so eloquent—my father explicitly so in his, Aunt Bunch by what he reflected and responded to in hers—so direct in their frankness, unable to resist rehearsing their most recent time together, that they must live it over again in words. But my mission was to erase all record of that love; and only a few phrases remain in my general memory of how they wrote to each other. "Oh, my darling, my marvel," he wrote, "whenever was there such an hour as yesterday? I scarcely knew myself." After their encounters he would move around as though in a dream: he felt he came and went about the world like a great Cheshire cat, a disembodied smile of delight. He found himself looking at every female with something that made her shrink a little, accusingly, as if he meant to rape her. He did not mean to be crude—he was only trying to express what was still with him every time he left her. There was evidently to be a time to meet in New York. "Oh, God, forgive me, when I think of my hands lost in your heavy gold hair and your eyes open like violets."

There were calendars of where and how to meet and for how long, and records of gifts exchanged, and vows of joy in the clandestine masquerade which could never be resolved in their open union short of calamities which neither of them wanted to visit upon anyone else. They had no idea of what would either save them or destroy them. When it finally came, their love was fired up more greatly than ever, for they both saw what must happen, though Aunt Bunch saw it before he did.

When he was first approached with demands that he run for public office, she told him he must do it, but evidently she also said that it must be the end for them. He had wondered in previous letters what could ever be the outcome of their union; but neither had expected what actually came.

What her simple realism cost her I could read in his anguished protests, and what he quoted of her words. They had managed very well so far, he was sure they need not part if they were especially clever about their continued plans. She said he must not be naïve— the political opposition would watch him day and night, hoping for private flaws to make public. She told him that a man's life was not the same as a woman's. He must have more than love to meet his full worth. She loved him so well that she would let him go to that full worth. Here were all his letters to her. He must destroy them, and all her letters to him. In his last letter he acknowledged their return; and in it I thought I read a note of the most delicate relief that the most dangerous passage of his life was about to end. At the same time he protested with loving fury her decision to "travel abroad" for an indefinite period, as she had the means, and she could always say she needed a change from Dorchester. Wasn't it ridiculous? She had always seen herself living in Paris, anyway. An invisible fabric had held two lives together. The letters gave me the sensation of hearing the fabric ripped apart.

He tied their letters in separate bundles. Where had the violet ribbon come from? Perhaps on some snowy afternoon he took her a bunch of violets tied with it, and then kept it because its scent reminded him of her. Or—more prosaically—perhaps he retrieved it from a wastebasket at home when nobody was looking, and in doing so, made an uneasy link in his thought between my mother and his mistress. He kept the bundles at some peril, always no doubt planning to dispose of them, yet unwilling to; until he made me his guardian and confidant when he was too ill to destroy the evidence himself.

The sun was falling lower beyond the willow and cottonwood leaves. I gathered dry twigs and leaves and made a bonfire. One by one I fed the letters into the little flames, holding back only one envelope with the violet writing. I took the ashes and let them sift through my fingers into the brown current of the river. My father and my love and my fear for him sifted through my thoughts. He had entrusted me with his whole life, now, in the evidence of his fallible and powerful humanity, with its pathos and the flawed beauty of its secret fulfillment. I was proud of his confidence; and I felt that unknowingly he had given me a measure of absolution for the folly and squalor of the Petronian night in Magdalena, and for the shame I had felt ever since. Not that I compared my drunken excesses with the grace of the love which had possessed my father and Aunt Bunch beyond their power to resist. But there were degrees of betrayal to be known, and perhaps judged, in both cases; and if my upright father could sin, then, however sordidly, so might his son. Knowing his secret now, I could forget mine.

In my notebook I copied the return address from the last envelope. The day would come when I would want to use it.

As I went home in the long, brilliant twilight, I brought to mind other matters which the letters revealed to me. I knew now what had given so much reckless energy to my father's campaign. How we raced together back and forth across the state for his rallies and speeches. How he would fall suddenly exhausted and unapproachable for hours at a time. How he was, then, throwing himself into a new life as much to escape the loss of his love as to purify the state of New York and gratify his supporters. Giving her up, running away, making love to a whole public took more strength than his emotions left to him. Lyle Pryor's cruel realism about what would soon kill Carlton Gracey returned to me now. Life's denials and

ambitions, more or less equally mixed, played a great part in tuberculosis. It was possible now to recognize despairing alternatives in
the histories of both Carlton Gracey and my father.

The next day, in my visit alone to Saint Anthony's, I answered the
inquiry in my father's eyes by showing him a pinch of ashes I had
saved. I said,

"This is all that is left."

With his eyes he asked what I thought.

"I read them."

"All of them?"

"Yes. That is, only yours. Thank you, Father."

He closed his eyes and pressed his lips together to contain his
feeling of relief on several counts. Peace came into his face. In a
moment he added,

"Your mother must not know."

"Oh, never! Nor anyone else."

He sighed. It was a comment of wonder at how he could have
done what would have hurt my mother to know. He lay quiet. He
was gathering strength to say something further to me. His closed
eyelids quivered a little with his thought, and then opening them, he
seemed to come fully awake in his mind. He began to speak in the
rapid, uninflected way he used now to consume as little strength as
possible. I leaned closer to hear him clearly.

He said there was something else on his mind.

"Yes?"

He hoped I could promise him something without having to go
against my own wish.

"Yes. Surely. What is it?"

He said he knew what I eventually wanted—to write books—but
he asked me to promise to finish medical school no matter what.

Then he waited, and so did I, for a moment.

I did what had to be done. I put my hand over his as it lay white
on the white sheet, and said,

"Yes, I promise, Father. I will go ahead."

"God bless you, then, Doc," and he smiled at the nickname which would turn real.

❦

In the echoing corridor where we all waited, Dr Birch came out of the room and softly shut the door after him.

"I think, now, yes," he said to my mother.

"You mean to send for Father Agostini?"—the parish priest who served also as hospital chaplain.

She nodded to Lillian to hurry to the telephone.

"Is he awake?"

"I'd say, he is aware. Just."

"Should we go in?"

"The nurse will call you. Sister Mary Vincent is also with him."

"We'll wait here."

"Yes. —I'll return soon."

Lillian hurried back to us, trying for my mother's sake not to cry. She sat down next to my mother on the leather couch against the wall and took my mother's hand. They held to each other.

In a quarter of an hour we heard the hard rustle of his cassock before we saw Father Agostini come around a corner at the end of the hall. He walked, leaning a trifle backward and to one side, as if his great weight were unevenly distributed. He was old and rheumatic, abrupt, and impassive. Putting a narrow purple silk stole about his neck, he bowed to my mother but did not pause before entering my father's room.

Sister Mary Vincent and the nurse came out, leaving the priest alone with my father.

In a little while he emerged and the women returned to the bedside. Now, without haste, he came to us and sat down beside my mother.

[296]

"All is well," he said in his burry Italian accent, and he meant, not for now, but forever. He had to leave us. We stayed all evening, and far into the night before the door opened and Mary Vincent put out both her hands to us in silence, and with a consoling smile drew us in to know my father and be known by him in his hour.

※

All too soon, then, our duties became plain. I went to the county courthouse at Albuquerque to explain my difficulty. I was listened to with the contained face which the law assumed in weighty matters; but it was presently arranged that I would be allowed to go to Sante Fe immediately to make a deposition in the district court there instead of waiting to testify at the Rennison trial, "by reason of the death of the witness's father, and family obligations in connection therewith, necessitating immediate travel to New York State for funeral services and interment of the deceased"—but I must return if called as a witness. (The call never came.)

※

Other disposals, large and small, filled the hours before we left. Lyle Pryor saw to all the travel arrangements for us—reservations, tickets, a car to meet us in Chicago. Lillian managed the flood of telegrams and long-distance calls. Eleanor Saxby's best-loved view of herself was that of the "good scout," and with reassuring good sense, she relieved us of all decisions about closing the house, shipping home what belonged to us, dealing with the real-estate agency, and selling our little car. She filled our house with her confident, well-argued proposals, coughing explosively through her cigarette smoke, and holding her whiskey glass against her shoulder between sips. She was happy to have something worthwhile to do, and in unspoken ways kept reminding my mother what it was to be a widow,

[297]

since she herself was one. We could count on her to keep us informed back home when she had anything to report. When she said, more than once, "Just leave everything to me, my dear," my mother would say, "Eleanor is such a dear, she is being wonderful." When it was time to be taken to the eastbound Limited, Percy and Serena had their big car waiting for us with their chauffeur. As they were sure we would rather be alone, they would not come to the station with us, but would be thinking of us, and meantime hoped this little hamper of nibbles would help to make the train journey more bearable. "They are so thoughtful," said my mother, in that state of contained grief—the very condition which let her accept on their own terms all expressions of sympathy.

My last act in the Rio Grande house was to send, without a note, a clipping from the local paper about my father's death to the address in Paris I had copied at my riverside bonfire. My envelope carried no return address or name.

※

Escorting my father's coffin home to Dorchester, we, as a family, were traveling in our own history through a moment which would last all our lives. I thought of Lincoln's funeral train, and the catafalque in the historical museum at home which I had often visited in awe as a boy.

On the night before the California Limited drew into Chicago, where we must change trains, I had dinner with my mother in her compartment. I wanted to be alone with her. Lillian and I each had a lower berth in another part of the car.

We dined well on trains in those days, and I persuaded my mother to drink some fine Liebfraumilch which Lyle Pryor had brought us wrapped in a newspaper as we said goodbye at the Albuquerque station. Handing it to me, Lyle said,

"I hope we meet again. If we do, I'll never again call you 'kid.' "

We never met again.

Under other circumstances, the soft-shaded Pullman lights, and the privacy, and the wine would have made the event seem like a little celebration. Now we were silent for a long time, until, looking out through the dark at the lights of isolated houses and little towns made innocent by distance, my mother said, against her palm, with her forehead resting against the cool window of the compartment,

"My poor dear."

The words settled some sort of resolve for her; for she turned to me and said,

"There is something I keep thinking of, about him, among all the other things. But I shouldn't, now."

"Not now?"

She shook her head and for the first time began to cry. I came around the table between us and sat next to her to put my arm around her. She wept against my shoulder, unable to speak just yet against the memory which engulfed her.

"What is it, Mother?"

"No, no," she replied, coming slowly to the calm of speech. "I don't know if I should ever tell you. Oh: I am so ashamed."

"Ashamed?"

"Yes. I did something I should not have done, but I could not help myself, though I believed it would make me miserable."

And she told me her story.

One day a batch of forwarded mail arrived at the Rio Grande house from the office in Dorchester. Lillian went through it, picked out the letters she thought my father ought to see, and gave them to my mother, who would take them along the next time she went to the hospital. Among them was a letter from Paris, addressed in violet handwriting which my mother knew well. She singled it out and put it in her bureau drawer. It was from Aunt Bunch. But why was it addressed only to my father, and sent to his Dorchester office, instead of directly to the house, either at Dorchester or Albuquerque? My mother was torn by qualms of heart and conscience. For years she had had thoughts which she had tried to dismiss as unworthy about my father and her best friend—there were inadvertent signals between them which she could not help noticing, and moods in my father which she had thought it wise not to comment upon.

"But I knew."

"Knew what?"—but I understood.

"Yes. I knew in my heart, but I had no proof; and anyhow, anyhow—"

She pressed her fingers against her tears. In muffled words she made me know that no matter what was going on to make my father happy, she felt it ought not to be turned into something ugly, whatever it might cost her to keep the secret. There was anguish in her tenderness as she spoke of this.

"You've no idea of the depth and power of his feeling for her, really turmoil, and for the longest time I thought it was all for me, all for me, and sometimes I scolded myself for thinking anything else."

The letter: she knew she ought to take it immediately to Saint Anthony's without comment; but for a day she held it back, wondering what to do. At the same time, she knew that if she did not deliver it immediately, she would never do so without reading it. Two more days went by while she was tormented by a need to know for certain, and by shame at what she was doing. Finally, after another day, she did what she had often smiled at in novels. She steamed open the envelope. The thin French glue responded easily. She read the letter. It told her all she had tried not to believe. It was a second farewell in which Aunt Bunch agonized over the impossibility of coming to help my father return to health. She raged at the obstacles between them, and she even said that the worst was this—that they both loved my mother so much that the thought of hurting her was unbearable. No longer deceived, with life and death now filling her days and nights, my mother felt a devouring rise of pity for the man whom she had loved singly and dearly for so many years.

With rueful self-knowledge, she now said to me,

"If he had not been so sick, I might not have been so unselfish."

She resealed the envelope, and when the next letters came from home, she shuffled it among them and with light indifference gave the packet to Lillian to take to my father. He would never know that the letter had been seen by anyone else.

"I suppose he could not help it. Perhaps I failed him in some way. Don't think harshly of him."

Knowing even more than she knew, I touched her hand in reassurance. She continued,

"So much happens to people. Mostly they remain the same people. If you love them—you know? To believe the world through each other? He was such a beautiful man. Nobody knew this as I did. I saw him hurt and downcast as well as happy and strong and *head*strong—then: then: the way he would turn to me: trust: need—"

She let silence say in weariness that if you loved anyone, nothing much else could matter. She saw tears appear and recede in my eyes, and she added,

"No, no. Richard, Richard, he was dear, and he was good. You must never think anything else."

But I could not tell her that I had a few days ago made peace with the idea of seeing my father whole, as a fallible man. I thought of what that final letter might have meant to him. He must have managed to destroy it by himself.

"Do you know?" mused my mother, "when she left him to live abroad, I sometimes wondered if he drove himself so all that summer in the campaign in order to make himself put it all away for good. He used to come home so tired he could hardly speak. But you know—the harder you try to forget something sometimes, the harder it is. If he was fighting two things at the same time—no wonder he broke down."

"Do you think Father ever suspected that you knew, then?"

"Sometimes I thought so. He said once or twice, 'Rose, what are you looking like that for!' I would just shrug and change the subject. —What power it must have had for him!"

"Do you hate Aunt Bunch?"

"No. I do not hate her. But I hope I shall never have to see her again."

"What a fool Lillian is!" I said angrily. "Why couldn't she just take the mail directly to him? All of it? She is such a fool."

"Yes," said my mother, now placidly, "she is. But like the rest of us, she must be taken as she is. Anyhow," she added, with a hint of her sweetly defiant energy, which showed when she defended herself in any matter, "I did what I did, and I'm sorry I did it, and perhaps I should never have told you anything."

"No, I'm grateful."

"You had to grow up, anyway, didn't you? This summer must have seen to that."

❧

Whenever I think of the weeks which followed, it is to remember the white marble Cathedral of the Holy Angels, where my father's solemn Requiem High Mass was held. As I watched with carefully reserved feeling the black and silver figures of the bishop of Dorchester and his deacons at the altar, behind which lay the marble sarcophagi of earlier bishops, I knew myself again as the small boy who had hidden for a whole night in the cathedral hoping for a miraculous visitation from the Enfant de Prague. The glories and fears of that night were part of my secret sensations now, and they made me smile in a sort of desperate protection against present emotion.

Lillian and the Dickinsons were with my mother and me. Lillian kept turning to see the immense throng which filled the cathedral. With tears flowing down her swollen face, she wore a look of bridling satisfaction at the honors paid to my father by his city; for as she said so often later, "Everyone was there," including Our Crowd, some of whose members served as pallbearers. The mercy of impersonality had descended upon my mother. She bore herself too proudly to show feeling—"Like a queen," as Lillian remarked to everyone so often that finally no one listened, "I said, *like a queen."*

Snow was falling, whiter than the white of the cathedral stone. Sounds in snow are different from those heard in clear weather. The passing bell began to toll as we left the church. Its sound, coming through the marble louvers so high above the scene in which everything was black and white, seemed to fall and settle upon us like the snow itself.

※

In those days of finality, Sam was once again our salvation. After examining all our material affairs, including my father's will, he set about doing what was needed. He found a buyer for our house, leased a modest, pleasant apartment for my mother in the Lenox Hotel, where she would not need her own cook or housemaid, set up a fund just ample enough to see me through college and medical school, and finally negotiated a scheme by which my father's business partner bought out the controlling interest in their joint affairs, which provided lifetime incomes for my mother and Lillian. Lillian would go into retirement, as the partner could not be expected to endure years of her reminders that things at the office were done differently in my father's day.

The Dickinsons stayed with us until my mother left our house. Sam advised me to telephone my dean at Aldersgate University to ask for readmission at the start of the mid-year semester. This was granted, I wrote my roommate that I would be back; and with a little thread of happiness weaving itself into settling emotions, I looked ahead to entering again into the student world where there

[303]

would be—as yet—no lifelong tragedies for anyone. I would return in a stage of maturity far ahead of that of my classmates. I would be already a new Richard, a "harder" Richard, among those friends who were still in the process of learning how to be "hard"—the ideal of that generation. My mother urged me to go. I was not to think of her, living alone. She had many friends. Her favorite household possessions went to surround her in her new apartment. Now displaced, they would never mean together what they once had meant. I would be with her for my college vacations. I was not to worry about her. She was already "taking an interest." In this she was aided by Joanna Dickinson, who, safe now in her own marriage, and newly filled with assurance as the wife of a college dean, was at ease, and able to reveal a lightly comic view of life which was useful to us all. We actually missed her when, happy in the seemly belongings of her world, including Sam, she went home with him to their own lives.

❀

As for the more recent past, Eleanor Saxby wrote a running account of J. Buswell Rennison's trial at Santa Fe, which she attended with zest. When he was found guilty and sentenced to die, she sent, without comment, a clipping from the *Albuquerque Journal*, giving the facts, including a reference to the electric chair.

The day I read that, I went to walk along the edge of Dorchester harbor and out to the end of the reaching breakwater. Already shielded against the new winter was a great fleet of the long ore and wheat freight boats, which again made a still colony of black idleness against the pale-gray sky. I took it all to myself to match my mood, and stared at the horizonless lake way out past the breakwater toward invisible Canada. Under the ice, Lake Erie sent its ever-renewed vastness toward the river and the sea. I felt the necessary detachment of the survivor.

EPILOGUE

❧

The Logic of Wishes

WHEN MANY YEARS LATER the Hitler war came, the sense of life for those in uniform was one entirely of chance and coincidence. There were dangers both to one's secret self and to adequate performance of duties in thinking in any other way.

❧

At the headquarters in Grosvenor Square, the young English orderly announced,

"Your driver is waiting, name of Lance Corporal Cromleigh, sir."

"Thank you. I'll be right down."

I took up the sealed portfolio which I had brought to London from Washington, signed out, and went down to the street. It was a cold autumn day with a pewter-colored sky. In the air I still noticed what had struck me the day before on coming from Hendon air-field—the smell of dead fire exhaled by burned-out ruins left by Nazi bombs.

Standing by the jeep waiting for me was a trim, smartly uniformed English girl.

"Lance Corporal Cromleigh, sir. I have your trip ticket to Fair-ford Air Force Base."

"Thank you. How long will it take us to get there?"

"If we don't strike fog, we should be there in under two hours."

"Good. My business should not take long, though one never knows. In any case, I must be back this evening for a morning flight to Prestwick and back to Washington."

She drove expertly out of London by the Cromwell Road and to the west. We spoke little, but when she answered my occasional question, her voice was light, clear, and beautifully cultivated. She held her small head high. The profile line from her brow to her short nose, purely chiseled lips, chin, and slender throat was almost laughably beautiful seen in the context of her rough British army cloth. Her color was high; pink cheeks against severely brushed gold hair. In impersonal military habit she did not look at me when she spoke, but I could see that her eyes were blue. There was some air about her which made me want to bridge the officer gap. I said,

"Excuse me, but I have to review my notes as we go."

"Of course, sir."

I took out my pocket notebook and looked at my obscure scratches—not precisely a code, but a set of references which meant something only to me, in preparation for the staff meeting I was to attend at Fairford.

※

There was a representative of each service in the Allied Command at the meeting in the base commander's office. My Pentagon port-folio was broken open by the general in command at Fairford and the discussion began. It had seemed to me that a half hour's work would be enough to produce the requisite initials and release me for my return to London; but it was late afternoon before the matter was resolved, the portfolio resealed, and handshakes and salutes exchanged. As I came out of the office whose windows were permanently blacked out with plywood, it was to find a late day blind with fog. Lance Corporal Cromleigh and her jeep were invisible until I came to within a dozen feet. She started the engine as soon as she was able to recognize me in the thick air. I climbed in and said,

"This will be slow going, won't it?"

"If any," she replied lightly.

"I suppose we ought to try, though."

"Yes, Hendon, Prestwick, Washington, of course." But she was leaning forward tensely and moving the car very slowly. We were feeling the narrow road from the base back to the village of Fairford, and, if possible, beyond.

"Lights?" I asked.

"Worse with, sir."

The earth-held cloud was coming at us in slow, thickening billows, and night was falling upon us with them. As we came to what seemed a tunnel of dirty fleece, the lance corporal declared this to be a street of the town, and driving even as slowly as she was, she saw a thick figure directly before us only in time to swerve and halt. An old angry voice demanded to know why we did not watch where we were going. This made the lance corporal laugh. Swept by the dense air, she turned toward me and said,

"I wish we knew!"

"No," I said, "this won't do. —Perhaps it will lift presently?"

"May or may not."

"Well, is there any place where we might wait it out a while?"

"There is a nice old inn, the Bull, if we can find it."

"We'll try. —Were you given any lunch, waiting? We can have some tea now, anyhow."

"If you think it suitable, sir," she said with an allusion to our difference in rank which was a brilliant mixture of military respect and mockery of it.

☙

We were given tea in the parlor of the Bull, where I received a dimly lit impression of a room lined with sooty lace and old carpet. In a little grate burned two lumps of cannel coal. Lance Corporal Cromleigh took off her stiffly visored cap and shook her hair free. We were served by the stout, wheezing old landlady herself, who explained that all three of her housemaids were off in war work. We exchanged gloomy sentiments about the fog and she left us. The tea was comforting.

Suddenly Lance Corporal Cromleigh sat up listening with her face turned. She heard before I did the growing thunder of many hundred bombers overhead. She looked at the ceiling as though to see them.

"They are trying to feel their way home to the base from a mission," she said. "Oh, God, the poor darlings. In this."

She put her hands to cover her ears. She said,

"One never gets used to it, that tremendous sound in the sky. It always makes me think of something quite mad, when I was very small—the roaring of the Niagara Falls when you are close to them."

"You've been there?"

"Oh, yes. I hated it. We were all going out to Alberta and stopped to see the falls and my darling little twin brother—we must have been five or six years old—nearly jumped over the barrier into the falls out of sheer excitement, but a young man there caught him just in time. I was screaming like a banshee and the nanny didn't help matters much. —Odd what idiocies one does remember, from the worst times. I had on a little pair of new brogans I was proud of, and the spray was getting them all wet, and I shrieked and shrieked that I didn't want to go any closer to the river, but I couldn't manage to tell them why."

⚹

Pamela. She looked into the coals. By their reflection I saw Christopher in her face. The situation was as unlikely as it was true. I had a powerful impulse to keep the secret of my part in that day by the cataract long ago. A silence continued upon us, so long that she finally turned toward me with inquiry unsaid. In her face was the light of amused and yet longing memory. I finally said,
"How is Christopher?"
"But you know his name!"
"You will not believe this, but I was the young man who held him back from the brink."
"Dear God."

⚹

If it is the logic of wishes that they come true in unexpected ways, that one of mine which I had thought of now and then through the years was granted—what had ever become of the St Brides family?
Marveling can go on only so long. We soon had enough of it, though, to let us come into the feeling of a lifelong friendship. Pamela put her hand on my sleeve for a moment and said,
"Oh, we thought of it so often!" She spoke with fond humor and

[309]

an undertone of sadness. "My brother went on for years with his heroic story. You were his hero. He kept a postcard of Niagara Falls to show everybody until we shrieked at him not to be such a bore." She looked at me drolly. "I was sure if I ever saw you again I must recognize you from Christopher's grand description of his savior. —Sorry to say, I did not."

"No. —But I can see you now, after all, as I did the first time."

"What a little wretch I was."

"Oh, no."

"Oh, yes. —But Christopher? You asked? Navy. He was lost in the Saint Nazaire commando raid. Bravely, we were told. He held back for a wounded man and then had no time to join the boat before it pulled away and the shots came. They always say it about twins, but I was absolutely cut in two, I was really half a life, for so long, afterward, even though I was already married."

The old landlady came into our almost dark parlor and asked if we might not want a nice bite of supper, "such as it was."

We followed her upstairs to the dining room. A few old people and children were already at small tables. Going there was a lucky, small distraction. I had no moment to speak what Pamela must have known in my thought—my picture of her exuberant brother in his golden childhood, and a distant turn of pain for his end.

It was a time of everybody's story of loss. She had come to terms with hers and could tell it simply and briefly. Her father had been in the War Office, on non-combat duty after a wound in France. The loss of his heir really, she thought, killed him, though he did not die until pneumonia seized him some months later. His nephew, a don at Oxford before the war, succeeded. Pamela and her mother left St Brides's Abbey, though urged to think of it as theirs, which was in any case pointless just now, as it was soon lent to the government for a convalescent hospital. She made me see the place because of how lovingly she spoke of it—a large house in two styles, one wing Elizabethan with a ruined Gothic arch, the other Georgian, with a moat on which two black swans and two white lived, all set in a vast lawn bounded by a woods on three sides. When you took a walk along the grassy edge of the moat, the swans, with an effect of taking the air with you, sailed slowly beside you on their still water. Pamela's mother had a job on Charles Street with the English-Speaking Union by day, and by night was a fire warden in Eaton Square. Major Adrian Cromleigh—an archaeologist whose name I knew—was in Africa with Alexander. He promised to bring Pamela back there after the war. They had no children, but hoped to have a large family, oh, yes, a *large* family, as Adrian said, "to restore the earth" after this wretched affair was over.

Ah, well. Enough about her. What about me?

Soon enough told—a graduate in medicine, a writer of books, married, with a son nine years old. I was diffident about adding, but I did add,

"Baptized Christopher."

"For him?"

"Yes, partly."

"How sweet."

She turned away to hide what she felt. I rose from the table. I said,

"I'd better have a look at the weather," and went downstairs and out into the street. The fog was heavier than ever.

"No, sir, you'll be going nowhere tonight," said the landlady at her high counter in the musty old hall. Yes, she had a room each for the young lady and me, and she agreed to set a clock to wake herself and let us out at five in the morning as we must leave in plenty of time to get to London on official matters. To be sure we were awake she would knock on our doors. Lance Corporal Cromleigh agreed that there was nothing else to do. In due course, we said good night and went to our damp, icy rooms.

᪥

All correctly, Lance Corporal Cromleigh returned me to London in the clearing daylight next morning. By nightfall I was far out over the Atlantic bound for Santa Maria in the Azores, Stephenville in Newfoundland, and Washington. There were many hours for some long thoughts. Failings, wishes, willed and unwilled circumstance. I remembered how, until she died, I would go to visit my mother and become her hero of occasions; and how one time, when with a familiar sense of guilt I had to return to my small, happy family and leave her to her loneliness, she said,

"Wouldn't it be wonderful not to have to make the best of things?"

᪥   ᪥

᪥

Afterword

GETTING A HOLD ON PAUL HORGAN, even one piece of him, is a daunting task. For one thing, he is a man of letters, that rarest of birds in this age of specialties when a writer is usually content to be known as a minimalist novelist, a New Formalist poet, a deconstructionist critic, a revisionist historian.

For another he is too good at too many and diverse things. I read him first in *Lamy of Santa Fe*, the superb biography of the same archbishop whom Willa Cather novelized in *Death Comes for the Archbishop*. Next I read him in the first of the "Richard" novels, *Things As They Are*, read it with that special pleasure which comes from the poetic yet precise affirmation of those things which are too close to us to be seen as they are.

Yet not once, in reading these two books, was there ever the sense that they were written by the same man as one finds, say, in reading Henry James's *The Spoils of Poynton* and *Essays in London*.

Then there is the geographer and historian of the thousand-page *Great River*, as vast as the Rio Grande itself but which, vast as it is, never sprawls because it is as carefully orchestrated as a symphony (it has been compared to Beethoven's Ninth).

Then there is the culture critic, both loving and severe, who delights with his high pessimism: "The public taste in the United States is frequently so offensive (Muzak, commercial architecture, comic strips-

and-books, rock 'music,' movies, all pop-pornography, and the rest) that it is enough to raise serious doubts about the stylistic trustworthiness of democracy. . . ."

Then one comes across the journalist who writes about his friend Stravinsky's visit to Houston, who notices everything, fetches paregoric for the maestro's diarrhea, yet analyzes his conducting style as expertly as a musicologist.

I have neither the competence nor the space here to address more than one department of this large literary subject. But in so doing I can take pleasure in countering the expected gibe from the cynical "journeyman specialist" as Horgan would call him: being good at a lot of things usually means you're not good enough at the one thing. I can only speak to the matter at hand, these three novels, and say straightaway that Paul Horgan knows exactly what he is doing and is first-class at doing it.

People like to speculate about the Richard of these novels. How much of him is Horgan and how autobiographical are the novels? I don't know and don't care. As every writer knows and as Horgan himself has said, it doesn't matter. One creates both oneself and other "real" people in every novel. One uses reality to escape it, not into unreality but into a higher reality, a vision which is one's own, but which, as Horgan says, must contain "that outline of the recognizable which will make the reader exclaim, 'Yes, that is what it is like!' "

What is at once recognizable in *Things As They Are* is that absolute and implacable selfishness of childhood and those most secret times, kept secret even from oneself, when the child does "bad" things, so bad as to seem to him unspeakable. If he is lucky, if he has a loving parent (or in the old South a loving black cook), he discovers that what he does is bad enough but speakable. Later he discovers that other people do even worse things. The action of this novel reverses the usual loss-of-innocence theme of most such novels. What is lost here is not the innocence but the solitary guilt of childhood. Horgan's gift is for showing both the beauty and ugliness of the world, both the unique ugliness of oneself, as one sees it, and of others, and that special grace of growing out of it and into a common humanity. It is the humanity of terribly beautiful and terribly flawed creatures, whether it be the unthinking cruelty of the child Richard or the calculating malevolence of the molester who tries to seduce him.

If *Things As They Are* is about both the fall from the suspect innocence and the utter selfishness of childhood, *Everything to Live For* celebrates another rite of passage, Richard's encounter with sexual love and high tragedy. A memorable encounter it is. Horgan has a way with the very rich. His liveried American footmen announcing guests with their calling cards are as believable as Henry James's. His rich Yankees are as badly flawed as James's Europeans yet manage to be quite as "aristocratic" though only one generation removed from the robber barons, what with their splendid libraries and their star-crossed sons. More than once indeed does Horgan in his high style remind one of Henry James. Most particularly it is Horgan's sharp eye when a character comes on stage and his ear for just that overtone which, nuanced as it is, nevertheless presages disaster.

Then it is as if James had headed west instead of east and had encountered not George Santayana but Willa Cather.

For here is Richard in *The Thin Mountain Air*, on the Rio Grande in New Mexico.

> *There was a slow breeze off the river half a mile beyond our house, bringing the sweet scent of warm cottonwood boughs and pollen, and the lazily inciting odor of the riverbank mud, where decay mixed with fresh growth and the rank earth was released into the air by the slow-flowing brown stream.*

His American "aristocrats" are a cosmos apart from Faulkner's Compsons. The virtues and flaws of both are utterly different and as utterly American. Rectitude in the North is different from rectitude in the South. So is decadence and impotence. For better or worse the Horgan character typically moves west and out of himself. The Faulkner character stays south and sinks into himself.

The novels move against a larger backdrop of great wars and great migrations west and returns east, but move they do. These three Richard novels are episodic, each treating a crisis in Richard's life, quite separate and self-contained dramas, each with its own distinctive narrative reach. In each we identify with Richard and turn the page.

But it is with the third novel, *The Thin Mountain Air*, that the trilogy becomes whole and of a piece. The parallel narratives, Richard's adventure in New Mexico and his father's decline are complementary and serve as effective correlatives of Richard's coming of age.

Then at the end of it and all at once there occurs to one an inkling of what Horgan is up to in his entire work, variegated as it is. There may be a common thread after all. In the novels, biographies, histories, essays (and for all I know, the paintings) there is the latent but inevitable movement from the populous and cultivated East to the great open West, from eastern oppressiveness, sickness and failure to western wholeness, recovery, health and freedom, the last allowing finally, in Horgan's case, the Return as a man whole and entire. The only way one can stand the East is to have headed west. The West is to Horgan what the North is to southern writers. You have to leave home in order to come home.

And quite as suddenly, one fancies one sees the reason for, not a fault, but a curious lacuna in Horgan's work. As pan-American as he is, his gaze is almost exclusively from East to West and back. For him, "South" means southwest, West Texas and New Mexico. The only "southern" influence I can think of here is Richard's father who is a noble Jeffersonian in politics. In all his writings I recall very few southerners except the Confederate Texans who straggled into Santa Fe after the battle at Glorieta. And fewer blacks, northern or southern.

It is as if Horgan had managed to by-pass the great American tragedy of slavery and the Civil War and the great American sin of race, settling instead for Yankee rapacity in the ravaging of the West, its lands and peoples, and preferring the sunnier Catholic reconciliation in the West to the everlasting Protestant preoccupation with Mississippi and Harlem. And perhaps one sees why. The old South, from Richmond to New Orleans, must only appear to Horgan as our European enclave with all the sadness of the old world and tragedies of caste and class, and what did he need with that? But we can't complain. After Jefferson and the great Virginians, who needs the decline and fall of the old Roman South? The epic American thrust West is surely enough for any one writer.

But lest the reader begin to imagine that Horgan the artist must use too vast a canvas and too broad a brush for a novelist, what with the great wars and migrations which overtake his characters, let him be disabused. As Horgan wrote in one of his literary aphorisms: "Those who would dismiss the story as a useful element of the novel are victims of cultural 'chic' which turns up every ten years only to disappear. There is hardly a person alive who does not wish to know 'what happened next.'"

We do, too, and particularly in reading Richard's adventures, we very much want to know what happens next. Nor need we be put off by the powerful moral imagination which informs the world of this splendid Yankee. He is, Lord help us, a chaste writer. And it is no accident that the sexual encounters in his fiction are far more exciting than Henry Miller's.

And so we turn the page.

WALKER PERCY

Paul Horgan is the author of more than twoscore books including seventeen novels, four volumes of short stories, and twenty books of history and other nonfiction. Two of his books are juveniles. His first novel, *The Fault of Angels*, published in 1933, was a Harper Prize novel. The Pulitzer Prize for History has been awarded to him twice, in 1955 for *Great River: The Rio Grande in North American History*, which also received the Bancroft Prize, and in 1975 for *Lamy of Santa Fe*. His most recent books are a novel, *Mexico Bay*; *The Clerihews of Paul Horgan* (Wesleyan, 1985); *A Writer's Eye: Field Notes and Watercolors*; *A Certain Climate: Essays in History, Arts, and Letters* (Wesleyan, 1988); *Approaches to Writing* (Wesleyan, 1988); and *Encounters with Stravinsky* (Wesleyan, 1989).

Born in Buffalo, New York, in 1903, Paul Horgan moved west with his family at twelve years of age to Albuquerque, New Mexico; the history of the Southwest thereafter became a central subject for his writing. He attended the Eastman School of Music and worked in the Eastman Theater in Rochester, New York, and in 1926 became librarian of New Mexico Military Institute, which he had attended as a boy. He served in the U.S. Army, from 1942 to 1946, as chief of the Army Information Branch in the Information and Education Division, for which he received the Legion of Merit. He had the rank of lieutenant colonel at war's end. From 1962 to 1967 he was director of the Center for Advanced Studies at Wesleyan University, where he has been adjunct professor of English; he is now professor emeritus and author-in-residence. He lives in Middletown, Connecticut.